The Knight and Sancho as Shepherds

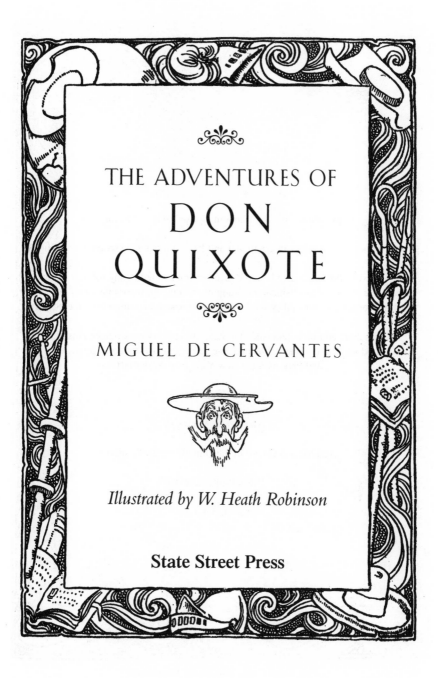

THE ADVENTURES OF
DON
QUIXOTE

MIGUEL DE CERVANTES

Illustrated by W. Heath Robinson

State Street Press

This 2002 edition is published by State Street Press by arrangements with Random House Value Publishing, Inc., a division of Random House, Inc., 280 Park Avenue, New York, New York 10017.

State Street Press

Ann Arbor, Michigan

Printed and Bound in the United States of America

ISBN 0-681-45390-7

9 8 7 6 5 4 3 2

CONTENTS

CONTENTS

CONTENTS

ILLUSTRATIONS

THE ADVENTURES OF
DON
QUIXOTE

The Adventures of Don Quixote of La Mancha

CHAPTER I

THE QUALITY AND MANNER OF LIFE OF THE RENOWNED HERO

Down in a village of La Mancha,* the name of which I have no desire to recollect, there lived, not long ago, one of those gentlemen who usually keep a lance upon a rack, an old buckler, a lean stallion, and a coursing greyhound. Soup, composed of somewhat more mutton than beef, the fragments served up cold on most nights, lentils on Fridays, eggs and collops on Saturdays, and a pigeon, by way of addition, on Sundays, consumed three-fourths of his income ; the remainder of it supplied him with a cloak of fine cloth, velvet breeches, with slippers of the same for holidays, and a suit of the best homespun, in which he adorned himself on week-days. His family consisted of a housekeeper above forty, a niece not quite twenty, and a lad who served him both in the field and at home, who could saddle the horse or handle the pruning-hook. The age of our gentleman bordered upon fifty years ; he was of a strong constitution, spare-bodied, of a meagre visage, a very early riser, and a lover of the chase.

Now this worthy gentleman, in his leisure moments, which composed the greater part of the year, gave himself up with so

* Partly in the kingdom of Arragon, and partly in Castile.

much ardour to the perusal of books of chivalry, that he almost wholly neglected the exercise of the chase, and even the regulation of his domestic affairs; indeed, so extravagant was his zeal in this pursuit, that he sold many acres of arable land to purchase books of knight-errantry; collecting as many as he could possibly obtain. Among them all, none pleased him so much as those written by the famous Feliciano de Silva, whose brilliant prose and intricate style were, in his opinion, infinitely precious; especially those amorous speeches and challenges in which they so abound. These rhapsodies distracted the poor gentleman, for he laboured to comprehend and unravel their meaning, which was more than Aristotle himself could do, were he to rise from the dead expressly for that purpose. He was not quite satisfied as to the wounds which Don Belianis gave and received; for he could not help thinking that, however skilful the surgeons were who healed them, his face and whole body must have been covered with seams and scars.

He often debated with the curate of the village, a man of learning, and a graduate of Siguenza, which of the two was the best knight, Palmerin of England, or Amadis de Gaul; but Master Nicholas, barber of the same place, declared that none ever came up to the Knight of the Sun; if, indeed, any one could be compared to him, it was Don Galaor, brother of Amadis de Gaul, for he had a genius suited to everything; he was no effeminate knight, no whimperer, like his brother; and in point of courage, he was by no means his inferior. In short, he became so infatuated with this kind of study, that he passed whole days and nights over these books; and thus, with little sleeping and much reading, his brains were dried up, and his intellects deranged. His imagination was full of all that he had read;—of enchantments, contests, battles, challenges, wounds, courtships, amours, tortures, and impossible absurdities; and so firmly was he persuaded of the truth of the whole tissue of visionary fiction that, in his mind, no history in the world was more authentic. The Cid Ruy Diaz, he asserted, was a very good knight, but not to be compared with the Knight of the Flaming Sword, who, with a single back-stroke, cleft asunder two fierce and monstrous giants. He was better pleased with Bernardo del Carpio, because, at Roncesvalles, be slew Roland the enchanted, by availing himself of the stratagem employed by Hercules upon Anteus, whom he squeezed to death within his arms. He spoke very favourably of the giant Morganti, for, although of that monstrous brood who are always proud and insolent, he alone was courteous and well-bred. Above all, he admired Rinaldo de Montalvan, particularly when he saw him sallying forth from his castle to plunder all he encountered; and when, moreover, he seized upon that image of Mahomet which, according to history, was of massive gold. But he would have given his housekeeper, and even his niece into the bargain, for a fair opportunity of kicking the traitor Galalon.

In fine, his judgment being completely obscured, he was seized with one of the strangest fancies that ever entered the head of any madman: this was, a belief that it behoved him, as well for the advancement of his glory as the service of his country, to become a knight-errant, and traverse the world, armed and mounted, in quest of adventures, and to practise all that had been performed by knights-errant, of whom he had read; redressing every species of grievance, and exposing himself to dangers which, being surmounted, might secure to him eternal glory and renown. The poor gentleman imagined himself at least crowned emperor of Trebisond, by the valour of his arm; and thus wrapped up in these agreeable delusions, and borne away by the extraordinary pleasure he found in them, he hastened to put his designs into execution.

The first thing he did was to scour up some rusty armour, which had been his great grandfather's, and had lain many years neglected in a corner. This he cleaned and adjusted as well as he could, but he found one grand defect; the helmet was incomplete, having only the morion: this deficiency, however, he ingeniously supplied, by making a kind of vizor of pasteboard, which, being fixed to the morion, gave the appearance of an entire helmet. It is true indeed that, in order to prove its strength, he drew his sword, and gave it two strokes, the first of which instantly demolished the labour of a week; but not altogether approving of the facility with which it was destroyed, and in order to secure himself against a similar misfortune, he made another vizor, which, having fenced in the inside with small bars of iron, he felt assured of its strength, and, without making any more experiments, held it to be a most excellent helmet.

In the next place he visited his steed; and although this animal had more blemishes than the horse of Gonela, which "tùm pellis et ossa fuit" (all skin and bone), yet, in his eyes, neither the Bucephalus of Alexander, nor the Cid's Babieca, could be compared with him. Four days was he deliberating upon what name he should give him; for, as he said to himself, it would be very improper that a horse so excellent, appertaining to a knight so famous, should be without an appropriate name; he therefore endeavoured to find one that should express what he had been before he belonged to a knight-errant, and also what he now was: nothing could, indeed, be more reasonable than that, when the master changed his state, the horse should likewise change his name, and assume one, pompous and high-sounding, as became the new order he now professed. So after having devised, altered, lengthened, curtailed, rejected, and again framed in his imagination a variety of names, he finally determined upon Rozinante,* a name, in his opinion, lofty, sonorous, and full of meaning; importing that he had been only a *rozin*, a drudge-horse, *before* his present condition, and that now he was *before* all the *rozins* in the world.

Having given his horse a name so much to his satisfaction, he resolved to fix upon one for himself. This consideration employed him eight more days, when at length he determined to call himself Don Quixote. Then recollecting that the valorous Amadis, not content with the simple appellation of Amadis, added thereto the name of his kingdom and native country, in order to render it famous, styling himself Amadis de Gaul; so he, like a good knight, also added the name of his province, and called himself Don Quixote de la Mancha; whereby, in his opinion, he fully proclaimed his lineage and country, which, at the same time, he honoured by taking its name.

His armour being now furbished, his helmet made perfect, his horse and himself provided with names, he found nothing wanting but a lady to be in love with; for a knight-errant without the tender passion was a tree without leaves and fruit—a body without a soul.

* From *Rosin*, a common drudge-horse, and *ante*, before; as Alexander's horse was called Bucephalus, from his bull-head; and the Knight of the Sun's, Cornerio, from a horn in the forehead.

"If," said he, "for my sins, or rather, through my good fortune, I encounter some giant—an ordinary occurrence to knights-errant—and overthrow him at the first onset, or cleave him in twain, or, in short, vanquish him and force him to surrender, must I not have some lady, to whom I may send him as a present? that when he enters into the presence of my charming mistress, he may throw himself upon his knees before her, and in a submissive, humble voice, say, 'Madam, in me you behold the giant Caraculiambro, lord of the island Malendrania, who, being vanquished in single combat by the never-enough-to-be-praised Don Quixote de la Mancha, am by him commanded to present myself before you to be disposed of according to the will and pleasure of your highness.'"

How happy was our good knight after this harangue! How much more so when he found a mistress! It is said that, in a neighbouring village, a good-looking peasant girl resided, called Aldonza Lorenzo, of whom he had formerly been enamoured, although it does not appear that she ever knew or cared about it; and this was the lady whom he chose to nominate mistress of his heart. He then sought a name for her, which, without entirely departing from her own, should approach towards that of a princess or great lady, and determined upon Dulcinea del Toboso (for she was a native of that village), a name, he thought, harmonious, and expressive—like all the others which he had adopted.

CHAPTER II

WHICH TREATS OF THE FIRST SALLY THAT DON QUIXOTE MADE FROM HIS NATIVE VILLAGE

As soon as these arrangements were made, he no longer deferred the execution of his project, which he hastened from a consideration of what the world suffered by his delay; so many were the grievances he intended to redress, the wrongs to rectify, and abuses to reform. Therefore, without communicating his intentions to anybody, and wholly unobserved, one morning before day, being one of the most sultry in the month of July, he armed himself cap-à-pie, mounted Rozinante, placed the helmet on his head, braced on his target, took his lance, and, through the private gate of his back-yard, issued forth into the open plain, in a transport of joy to think he had met with no obstacles to the commencement of his honourable enterprise. But scarce had he found himself on the plain, when he was assailed by a recollection so terrible as almost to make him abandon the undertaking: for it just then occurred to him that he was not yet dubbed a knight; therefore, in conformity to the laws of chivalry, he neither could nor ought to enter the lists against any of that order; and, if he had been actually dubbed, he should, as a new knight, have worn white armour, without any device on his shield, until he had gained one by force of arms. These considerations made him irresolute whether to proceed; but frenzy prevailing over reason, he determined to get himself made a knight by the first one he should meet, like many others, of whom he had read. As to white armour, he resolved, when he had an opportunity, to scour his own, so that it should be whiter than ermine. Having now composed his mind, he proceeded, taking whatever road his horse pleased: for therein, he believed, consisted the true spirit of adventure.

Our new adventurer, while pursuing his way, conversed with himself, imitating the style of his books as nearly as he could, and proceeding slowly on, while the sun arose with such intense heat that it was enough to dissolve his brains, if any had been left. He travelled almost the whole of that day without encountering anything worthy of recital, which caused him much vexation, for he was impatient for an opportunity to prove the valour of his powerful arm.

Some authors say his first adventure was that of the Pass of Lapice; others affirm it to have been that of the windmills; but, from what I have been able to ascertain of this matter, and have found written in the annals of La Mancha, the fact is that he travelled all that day, and as night approached, both he and his horse were wearied and dying with hunger; and in this state, as he looked around him, in hopes of discovering some castle, or shepherd's cot, where he might repose and find refreshment, he descried, not far from the road, an inn, which to him was a star conducting him to the portals, if not the palace of his redemption. He made all the haste he could, and reached it at nightfall. There chanced to stand at the door two young women, on their journey to Seville. Now as everything that our adventurer saw and conceived was, by his imagination, moulded to what he had read, so in his eyes the inn appeared to be a castle, with its four turrets, and pinnacles of shining silver, together with its draw-bridge, deep moat, and all the appurtenances with which such castles are usually described. When he had advanced within a short distance of it, he checked Rozinante, expecting some dwarf would mount the battlements, to announce, by sound of trumpet, the arrival of a knight-errant at the castle; but finding them tardy, and Rozinante impatient for the stable, he approached the inn-door, and there saw the two strolling girls, who to him appeared to be beautiful damsels or lovely dames enjoying themselves before the gate of their castle.

It happened that just at this time a swineherd collecting his hogs from an adjoining stubble-field, blew the horn which assembles them together, and instantly Don Quixote was satisfied, for he imagined it was a dwarf who had given the signal of his arrival. With extraordinary satisfaction, therefore, he went up to the inn; upon which the ladies, being startled at the sight of a man armed in that manner, with lance and buckler, were retreating into the house; but Don Quixote, perceiving their alarm, raised his paste-board vizor, thereby partly discovering his meagre, dusty visage, and with gentle demeanour and placid voice, thus addressed them:

"Fly not, ladies, nor fear any discourtesy, for it would be wholly inconsistent with the order of knighthood which I profess, to offer insult to any person, much less of that exalted rank which your appearance indicates." The girls stared at him, and endeavouring to find out his face, which was almost concealed by the sorry vizor, could not forbear laughing; consequently he grew indignant, and would have proceeded to chastise them, but for the timely appearance of the innkeeper, a very corpulent, and therefore a very pacific man, who, upon seeing so ludicrous an object, armed, and with accoutrements so ill-assorted as were the bridle, lance, buckler, and corslet, felt disposed to join the damsels in demonstrations of mirth; but, in truth, apprehending some

danger from a form thus strongly fortified, he resolved to behave
with civility, and therefore said :

"If, Sir Knight, you are seeking for a lodging, you will here
find, excepting a bed (for there are none at present available in this
inn), everything in abundance." Don Quixote, perceiving the
humility of the governor of the fortress, for such to him appeared
the innkeeper, answered :

"For me, Señor Castellano, anything will suffice : since arms
are my ornaments, warfare my repose." The host thought he
called him Castellano because he took him for a sound Castilian,
whereas he was an Andalusian, of the coast of St Lucar, as great
a thief as Cacus, and as full of mischief as a collegian or a page :
and he replied :

"If so, your worship's beds must be hard rocks, and your sleep
continual watching ; and that being the case, you may dismount
with a certainty of finding here sufficient cause for being kept
awake the whole year, much less a single night." So saying, he
laid hold of Don Quixote's stirrup, who alighted with much
difficulty and pain, for he had fasted the whole of the day. He
then desired the host to take especial care of his steed, for it was
the finest creature ever fed ; the innkeeper examined him, but
thought him not so good by half as his master had represented
him. Having led the horse to the stable, he returned to receive
the orders of his guest, whom the damsels, being now reconciled
to him, were disarming ; they had taken off the back and breast
plates, but endeavoured in vain to disengage the gorget, or take
off the counterfeit beaver, which he had fastened with green
ribbons in such a manner that they could not be untied, and he
would upon no account allow them to be cut ; therefore he remained all that night with his helmet on, the strangest and most
ridiculous figure imaginable.

While these girls, whom he still conceived to be persons of
quality, and ladies of the castle, were disarming him, he said to
them, with infinite grace, "Never before was knight so honoured
by ladies as Don Quixote, after his departure from his native
village ! damsels attended on him ; princesses took charge of his
steed ! O Rozinante,—for that, ladies, is the name of my horse,
and Don Quixote de la Mancha my own ; the time shall come
when your ladyships may command, and I obey ; when the

"Mine arms are mine ornaments".

valour of my arm shall make manifest the desire I have to serve you." The girls, unaccustomed to such rhetorical flourishes, made no reply, but asked whether he would please to eat anything.

"I shall willingly take some food," answered Don Quixote, "for I apprehend it would be of much service to me." That day happened to be Friday, and there was nothing in the house but some fish.

"Be that as it may," replied Don Quixote, "let it come immediately, for the toil and weight of arms cannot be sustained by the body unless the interior be supplied with aliments."

For the benefit of the cool air, they placed the table at the door of the inn, and the landlord produced some of his ill-soaked and worse-cooked bacallao, with bread as foul and black as the knight's armour. It was a laughable spectacle to see him eat; for his hands being engaged in holding his helmet on, and raising the beaver, he could not feed himself, therefore one of the ladies performed this office for him. But to drink would have been utterly impossible, had not the innkeeper bored a reed, and, placing one end into his mouth, at the other poured in the wine. All this he patiently endured rather than cut the lacings of his helmet.

In the meantime there came to the inn a sow-doctor, who, as soon as he arrived, blew his pipe of reeds four or five times, which finally convinced Don Quixote that he was now in some famous castle, where he was regaled with music; that the poor jack was trout, the bread of the purest white, the country girls ladies of distinction, and the innkeeper governor of the castle; consequently he remained satisfied with his enterprise and first sally, though it troubled him to reflect that he was not yet a knight, feeling persuaded that he could not lawfully engage in any adventure until he had been invested with the order of knighthood.

CHAPTER III

IN WHICH IS RELATED THE PLEASANT METHOD DON QUIXOTE TOOK TO BE DUBBED KNIGHT

AGITATED by this idea, he abruptly finished his scanty supper, called the innkeeper, and, shutting himself up with him in the stable, he fell on his knees before him, and said :

"Never will I arise from this place, valorous knight, until your courtesy shall grant a boon which it is my intention to request : a boon that will redound to your glory, and to the benefit of all mankind." The innkeeper, seeing his guest at his feet, and hearing his language, stood confounded, without knowing what to do or say ; he entreated him to rise, but in vain, until he had promised to grant the boon he requested.

"I expected no less, Señor, from your great magnificence," replied Don Quixote ; "know, therefore, that the boon I have demanded, and which your liberality has conceded, is that, on the morrow, you will confer upon me the honour of knighthood. This night I will watch my arms in the chapel of your castle, in order that, in the morning, my earnest desire may be fulfilled, and I may with propriety traverse the four quarters of the world, in quest of adventures for the relief of the distressed ; conformable to the duties of chivalry and of knights-errant."

The host, who, as we have said, was a shrewd fellow, and had already entertained some doubts respecting the wits of his guest, was now confirmed in his suspicions. To make sport for the night, he determined to follow his humour. He told him therefore that his desire was very reasonable, and that such pursuits were natural and suitable to knights so illustrious as he appeared to be, and as his gallant demeanour fully testified ; that he had himself in the days of his youth followed that honourable profession, and travelled over various parts of the world in search of adventures ; and that finally he had retired to this castle, where he lived upon his revenue ; entertaining therein all knights-errant of every quality and degree, solely for the great affection he bore them, and that they might share their fortune with him, in return for his good will. He further told him that in his castle there was no chapel wherein he could watch his armour, for it had been pulled down, in order to be rebuilt; but that, in cases of necessity, he knew it might be done wherever he pleased; therefore he might watch it that night in a court of the castle, and the following morning, if it pleased God, the requisite ceremonies should be performed, and he should be dubbed so effectually, that the world would not be able to produce a more perfect knight. He then inquired if he had any money about him? Don Quixote told him he had none: having never read in their histories that knights-errant provided themselves with money. The innkeeper assured him he was mistaken, for, admitting that it was not mentioned in their history, the authors deeming it unnecessary to specify things so obviously requisite as money and clean shirts, yet was it not, therefore, to be inferred that they had none; but, on the contrary, he might consider it as an established fact that all knights-errant, of whose histories so many volumes are filled, carried their purses well provided against accidents: that they were also supplied with shirts, and a small casket of ointments to heal the wounds they might receive. He therefore advised, though, as his godson (which he was soon to be), he might command him, never henceforth to travel without money and the aforesaid provisions; and he would find them serviceable when he least expected it.

Don Quixote promised to follow his advice with punctuality; and an order was now given for performing the watch of the armour, in a large yard adjoining the inn. Don Quixote, having collected it together, placed it on a cistern which was close to a well; then, bracing on his target and grasping his lance, with graceful demeanour, he paced to and fro, before the pile, beginning his parade as soon as it was dark.

The innkeeper informed all who were in the inn of the frenzy of his guest, the watching of his armour, and of the intended knighting. They were surprised at so singular a kind of madness, and went out to observe him at a distance. They perceived him sometimes quietly pacing along, and sometimes leaning upon his lance with his eyes fixed upon his armour, for a considerable time. It was now night, but the moon shone with a splendour which might vie even with that whence it was borrowed; so that every motion of our knight-elect might be distinctly seen.

At this time, it happened that one of the carriers wanted to give his mules some water; for which purpose it was necessary to remove Don Quixote's armour from the cistern; who seeing him advance, exclaimed with a loud voice:

"O thou rash knight! whosoever thou art, who approachest the armour of the most valiant adventurer that ever girded sword, beware of what thou dost, and touch it not, unless thou wouldst yield thy life as the forfeit of thy temerity." The carrier heeded not this admonition (though better would it have been for him if he had), but, seizing hold of the straps, he threw the armour some distance from him; which Don Quixote perceiving, he raised his eyes to heaven, and addressing his thoughts, apparently, to his lady Dulcinea, said:

"Assist me, O lady, to avenge this first insult offered to your vassal's breast; nor let your favour and protection fail me in this first perilous encounter."

Having uttered these and similar ejaculations, he let slip his target, and raising his lance with both hands, he gave the carrier such a stroke upon the head that he fell to the ground in so grievous a plight that, had the stroke been repeated, there would have been no need of a surgeon. This done he replaced his armour, and continued his parade with the same tranquillity as before.

Soon after, another carrier, not knowing what had passed, for the first yet lay stunned, came out with the same intention of watering his mules; and, as he approached to take away the armour from the cistern, Don Quixote, without saying a word or imploring any protection, again let slip his target, raised his lance, and, with no less effect than before, smote the head of the second carrier. The noise brought out all the people in the inn, and the landlord among the rest; upon which Don Quixote braced on his target, and laying his hand upon his sword, said:

"O lady of beauty! strength and vigour of my enfeebled heart! Now is the time for thee to turn thy illustrious eyes upon this thy captive knight, whom so mighty an encounter awaits!" This address had, he conceived, animated him with so much courage that, were all the carriers in the world to have assailed him, he would not have retreated one step.

The comrades of the wounded, upon discovering the situation

of their friends, began at a distance to discharge a shower of stones upon Don Quixote, who sheltered himself as well as he could with his target, without daring to quit the cistern, because he would not abandon his armour. The innkeeper called aloud to them, begging they would desist, for he had already told them he was insane, and that, as a madman, he would be acquitted, though he were to kill them all. Don Quixote, in a voice still louder, called them infamous traitors, and the lord of the castle a cowardly, base-born knight, for allowing knights-errant to be treated in that manner; declaring that, had he received the order of knighthood, he would have made him sensible of his perfidy.

"But as for you, ye vile and worthless rabble, I utterly despise ye! Advance! Come on, molest me as far as ye are able, for quickly shall ye receive the reward of your folly and insolence!" This he uttered with so much spirit and intrepidity that the assailants were struck with terror; which, in addition to the landlord's persuasions, made them cease their attack; he then permitted the wounded to be carried off, and, with the same gravity and composure, resumed the watch of his armour.

The host, not relishing these pranks of his guest, determined to put an end to them, before any further mischief ensued, by immediately investing him with the luckless order of chivalry: approaching him, therefore, he disclaimed any concurrence, on his part, in the insolent conduct of those low people, who were, he observed, well chastised for their presumption. He repeated to him that there was no chapel in the castle, nor was it by any means necessary for what remained to be done; that the stroke of knighting consisted in blows on the neck and shoulders, according to the ceremonial of the order, which might be effectually performed in the middle of a field; that the duty of watching his armour he had now completely fulfilled, for he had watched more than four hours, though only two were required. All this Don Quixote believed, and said that he was there ready to obey him, requesting him, at the same time, to perform the deed as soon as possible; because, should he be assaulted again when he found himself knighted, he was resolved not to leave one person alive in the castle, excepting those whom, out of respect to him, and at his particular request, he might be induced to spare.

The host, thus warned and alarmed, immediately brought

forth a book in which he kept his account of the straw and oats he furnished to the carriers, and, attended by a boy, who carried an end of candle, and the two damsels before mentioned, went towards Don Quixote, whom he commanded to kneel down. He then began reading in his manual, as if it were some devout prayer, in the course of which he raised his hand and gave him a good blow on the neck, and, after that, a handsome stroke over the shoulders, with his own sword, still muttering between his teeth, as if in prayer. This being done, he commanded one of the ladies to gird on his sword, an office she performed with much alacrity, as well as discretion, no small portion of which was necessary to avoid bursting with laughter at every part of the ceremony; but indeed the prowess they had seen displayed by the new knight kept their mirth within bounds. At girding on the sword, the good lady said:

"God grant you may be a fortunate knight and successful in battle."

Don Quixote inquired her name, that he might thenceforward know to whom he was indebted for the favour received, as it was his intention to bestow upon her some share of the honour he should acquire by the valour of his arm. She replied, with much humility, that her name was Tolosa, and that she was the daughter of a cobbler at Toledo, who lived at the stalls of Sancho-bienaya; and that, wherever she was, she would serve and honour him as her lord. Don Quixote, in reply, requested her, for his sake, to do him the favour henceforth to add to her name the title of donna, and call herself Donna Tolosa, which she promised to do. The other girl now buckled on his spur, and with her he held nearly the same conference as with the lady of the sword; having inquired her name, she told him it was Molinera, and that she was daughter to an honest miller of Antiquera: he then requested her likewise to assume the donna and style herself Donna Molinera, renewing his proffers of service and thanks.

These never-till-then-seen ceremonies being thus speedily performed, Don Quixote was impatient to find himself on horseback, in quest of adventures. He therefore instantly saddled Rozinante, mounted him, and, embracing his host, made his acknowledgments for the favour he had conferred by knighting him, in terms so extraordinary, that it would be in vain to attempt to repeat them. The host, in order to get rid of him the sooner, replied, with no less flourish, but more brevity; and, without making any demand for his lodging, wished him a good journey.

CHAPTER IV

OF WHAT BEFEL OUR KNIGHT AFTER HE HAD SALLIED FROM THE INN

LIGHT of heart, Don Quixote issued forth from the inn about break of day, so satisfied and so pleased to see himself knighted, that the joy thereof almost burst his horse's girths. But recollecting the advice of his host concerning the necessary provisions for his undertaking, especially the articles of money and clean shirts, he resolved to return home, and furnish himself accordingly, and also provide himself with a Squire, purposing to take into his service a certain country fellow of the neighbourhood, who was poor, and had children, yet was very fit for the squirely office of chivalry.

With this determination he turned Rozinante towards his village; and the steed, as if aware of his master's intention, began to push on with so much alacrity that he hardly seemed to set his feet to the ground. He had not, however, gone far, when, on his right hand, from a thicket hard by, he fancied he heard feeble cries, as from some person complaining. And scarcely had he heard it when he said, "I thank Heaven for the favour it does me, by offering me so early an opportunity of complying with the duty of my profession, and of reaping the fruit of my honourable desires. These are, doubtless, the cries of some distressed person, who stands in need of my protection and assistance." Then, turning the reins, he guided Rozinante towards the place whence he thought the cries proceeded, and he had entered but a few paces into the wood, when he saw a mare tied to an oak, and to another, a lad about fifteen years of age, naked from the waist upwards, who was the person that cried out; and not without cause, for a lusty country fellow was laying on him very severely with a belt, and accompanied every lash with a reprimand and a word of advice; for, said he, "The tongue slow and the eyes quick."

The boy answered, "I will do so no more, dear sir; by the passion of God, I will never do so again; and I promise for the future to take more care of the flock."

Don Quixote, observing what passed, now called out in an angry tone:

"Discourteous knight, it ill becomes thee to deal thus with one who is not able to defend himself. Get upon thy horse, and take thy lance" (for he had also a lance leaning against the oak, to which the mare was fastened), "and I will make thee sensible of thy dastardly conduct." The countryman, seeing such a figure coming towards him, armed from head to foot, and brandishing his lance at his face, gave himself up for a dead man, and therefore humbly answered:

"Señor cavalier, this lad I am chastising is a servant of mine, whom I employ to tend a flock of sheep which I have hereabouts; but he is so careless that I lose one every day; and because I correct him for his negligence, or roguery, he says I do it out of covetousness, and for an excuse not to pay him his wages; but before God, and on my conscience, he lies."

"Dar'st thou say so in my presence, vile rustic?" said Don Quixote. "By the sun that shines upon us, I have a good mind to run thee through with this lance! Pay him immediately, without further reply; if not, by the God that rules us, I will despatch thee in a moment! Unbind him instantly!"

The countryman hung down his head, and, without reply, untied his boy. Don Quixote then asked the lad how much his master owed him, and he answered nine months wages, at seven reals a month. Don Quixote, on calculation, found that it amounted to sixty-three reals, and desired the countryman instantly to disburse them, unless he meant to pay it with his life.

"The mischief is, Señor cavalier," quoth the countryman in a fright, "that I have no money about me; but let Andres go home with me, and I will pay him all, real by real, and *perfumed* into the bargain."

"For the perfuming, I thank thee," said Don Quixote:

" give him the reals, and I shall be satisfied : and see that thou failest not; or else by the same oath, I swear to return and chastise thee ; for know that I am the valorous Don Quixote de la Mancha, the redresser of wrongs and abuses ; so farewell, and do not forget what thou hast promised and sworn, on pain of the penalty I have denounced." So saying, he clapped spurs to Rosinante, and was soon far off.

Thus did the valorous Don Quixote redress this wrong ; and, elated at so fortunate and glorious a beginning to his knight-errantry, he went on toward his village, entirely satisfied with himself.

He now came to the road, which branched out in four different directions ; when immediately those crossways presented themselves to his imagination where knights-errant usually stop to consider which of the roads they shall take. Here, then, following their example, he paused awhile, and, after mature consideration, let go the reins ; submitting his own will to that of his horse, who, following his first motion, took the direct road towards his stable. Having proceeded about two miles, Don Quixote discovered a company of people, who, as it afterwards appeared, were merchants of Toledo, going to buy silks in Murcia. There were six of them in number ; they carried umbrellas, and were attended by four servants on horseback, and three muleteers on foot. Scarcely had Don Quixote espied them, when he imagined it must be some new adventure : and, to imitate as nearly as possible what he had read in his books, as he fancied this to be cut out on purpose for him to achieve, with a graceful deportment and intrepid air, he settled himself firmly in his stirrups, grasped his lance, covered his breast with his target, and, posting himself in the midst of the highway, awaited the approach of those whom he already judged to be knights-errant ; and when they were come so near as to be seen and heard, he raised his voice, and, with an arrogant tone, cried out :

"Hold ! let no one hope to pass that does not confess that there is not in the whole world a damsel more beautiful than the empress of La Mancha, the peerless Dulcinea del Toboso !" The merchants stopped at the sound of these words, and also to behold the strange figure of him who pronounced them ; and, both by the one and the other, they perceived the madness of the

Posting himself in the midst of the highway.

speaker, but they were disposed to stay and see what this confession meant which he required ; and therefore one of them, who was somewhat of a wag, but withal very discreet, said to him :

"Señor cavalier, we do not know who this good lady you mention may be : let us but see her, and if she be really so beautiful as you intimate, we will, with all our hearts, and without any constraint, make the confession you demand of us."

"Should I show her to you," replied Don Quixote, "where would be the merit of confessing a truth so manifest? It is essential that, without seeing her, you believe, confess, affirm, swear, and maintain it ; and, if not, I challenge you all to battle."

"Señor cavalier," replied the merchant, "I beseech your worship to show us some picture of this lady, though no bigger than a barleycorn, and, I verily believe we are so far inclined to your side that, although her picture should represent her squinting with one eye, and distilling vermilion and brimstone from the other, to oblige you, we will say whatever you please in her favour."

"There distils not, base scoundrels," answered Don Quixote, burning with rage, "there distils not from her what you say, but rather ambergris and civet among cotton ; neither doth she squint, nor is she hunchbacked, but as straight as a spindle of Guadarrama : * but you shall pay for the horrid blasphemy you have uttered against so transcendent a beauty !" So saying, with his lance couched, he ran at him who had spoken with so much fury and rage that, if good fortune had not so ordered that Rozinante stumbled and fell in the midst of his career, it had gone hard with the rash merchant. Rozinante fell, and his master lay rolling about the field for some time, endeavouring to rise, but in vain ; so encumbered was he with his lance, target, spurs and helmet, added to the weight of his antiquated armour. And while he was thus struggling to get up, he continued calling out :

"Fly not, ye dastardly rabble ; stay, ye race of slaves, for it is through my horse's fault, and not my own, that I lie here extended."

---

* A small town nine leagues from Madrid, situated at the foot of a mountain, the rocks of which are so perpendicular that they are called "the Spindles." Near it stands the Escurial.—*Jarvis.*

A muleteer of the company, not over good-natured, hearing the arrogant language of the poor fallen gentleman, could not bear it without returning him an answer on his ribs; and coming to him, he took the lance, which having broken to pieces, he applied one of the splinters with so much agility upon Don Quixote, that, in spite of his armour, he was threshed like wheat though his masters called out, desiring him to forbear.

At length the fellow was tired, and the merchants departed, sufficiently furnished with matter of discourse concerning the poor belaboured knight, who, when he found himself alone, again endeavoured to rise: but, if he could not do it when sound and well, how should he in so bruised and battered a condition? Yet he was consoled in looking upon this as a misfortune peculiar to knights-errant; and imputing the blame to his horse: although to raise himself up was impossible, his whole body was so horribly bruised.

CHAPTER V

WHEREIN IS CONTINUED THE NARRATION OF OUR KNIGHT'S MISFORTUNE

VERY full of pain, yet soon as he was able to stir, Don Quixote had recourse to his usual remedy, which was to recollect some incident in his books, and his frenzy instantly suggested to him that of Valdovinos and the Marquis of Mantua, when Carlotto left him wounded on the mountain: a story familiar to children, not unknown to youth, commended and even credited by old men; yet no more true than the miracles of Mahomet. Now this seemed to him exactly suited to his case; therefore he began to roll himself on the ground, and to repeat, in a faint voice, what they affirm was said by the wounded knight of the wood:—

> "Where art thou, mistress of my heart,
> Unconscious of thy lover's smart?
> Ah me! thou know'st not my distress,
> Or thou art false and pitiless."

In this manner he went on with the romance, until he came
B

to those verses where it is said :—"O noble marquis of Mantua, my uncle and lord by blood!"—just at that instant it so happened that a peasant of his own village, a near neighbour, who had been carrying a load of wheat to the mill, passed by ; and, seeing a man lying stretched on the earth, he came up, and asked him who he was, and what was the cause of his doleful lamentations ?

Don Quixote, firmly believing him to be the marquis of Mantua, his uncle, returned him no answer, but proceeded with the romance, giving an account of his misfortune, and of the amours of the emperor's son with his spouse, just as it is there recounted.

The peasant was astonished at this extravagant discourse ; and taking off the vizor, now battered all to pieces, he wiped the dust from the fallen knight's face; upon which he recognised him, and exclaimed :

"Ah, Señor Quixada" (for so he was called before he had lost his senses, and was transformed from a sober gentleman to a knight-errant), "how came your worship in this condition?" But still he answered out of his romance to whatever question he was asked.

The good man, seeing this, contrived to take off the back and breastpiece of his armour, to examine if he had any wound ; but he saw no blood nor sign of any hurt. He then endeavoured to raise him from the ground, and with no little trouble placed him upon his ass, as being the beast of easier carriage. He gathered together all the arms, not excepting the broken pieces of lance, and tied them upon Rozinante ; then taking him by the bridle, and his ass by the halter, he went on towards his village, full of concern at the wild language of Don Quixote.

No less thoughtful was the knight, who was so cruelly beaten and bruised that he could scarcely keep himself upon the ass, and ever and anon he sent forth groans that seemed to pierce the skies, insomuch that the peasant was again forced to inquire what ailed him. And surely the Evil One alone could have furnished his memory with stories so applicable to what had befallen him ; for at that instant, forgetting Valdovinos, he recollected the Moor Abindarraez, at the time when the governor of Antequera, Roderigo of Narvaez, had taken him prisoner, and conveyed him to his castle; so that when the peasant asked him again how he was, and what he felt, he answered him in the very same terms that were used by Abindarraez to Roderigo of Narvaez, when the latter carried him away prisoner to his castle (as he had read in the *Diana* of George of Montemayor), applying it so aptly to his own case, that the peasant went on cursing himself to the devil, to hear such a monstrous heap of nonsense, which convinced him that his neighbour had run mad, and he therefore made what haste he could to reach the village, and thereby escape the plague of Don Quixote's long speeches; who, still continuing, said:

"Be it known to your worship, Senor Don Roderigo de Narvaez, that this beauteous Xarifa, whom I mentioned, is now the fair Dulcinea del Toboso, for whom I have done, do, and will do, the most famous exploits of chivalry, that have been, are, or shall be, seen in the world." To this the peasant answered:

"Look you, Sir, as I am a sinner, I am not Don Roderigo de Narvaez, nor the marquis of Mantua, but Pedro Alonzo your neighbour: neither is your worship Valdovinos, nor Abindarraez, but the worthy gentleman Senor Quixada."

"I know who I am," answered Don Quixote; "and I know, too, that I am not only capable of being those I have mentioned, but all the twelve peers of France, yea, and the nine worthies, since my exploits will far exceed all that they have jointly or separately achieved."

With this and similar conversation, they reached the village about sunset: but the peasant waited until the night was a little advanced, that the poor battered gentleman might not be seen so scurvily mounted. When he thought it the proper time he entered the village, and arrived at Don Quixote's house, which he found all in confusion. The priest, or, as he was familiarly called, "the curate," and the barber of the place, who were Don Quixote's particular friends, happened to be there: and the housekeeper was saying to them aloud:

"What do you think, Señor Licentiate Pero Perez" (for that was the priest's name), "of my master's misfortune? for neither he, nor his horse, nor the target, nor the lance, nor the armour, have been seen these six days past. Woe is me! I am verily persuaded, and it is certainly true as I was born to die, that these accursed books of knight-errantry, which he is often reading, have turned his brain ; and, now I think of it, I have often heard him say, talking to himself, that he would turn knight-errant, and go about the world in quest of adventures." The niece joined with her, adding, " Ah, Master Nicholas " (for that was the barber's name), "I take the blame of all this to myself, for not informing you, gentlemen, of my dear uncle's extravagancies, that they might have been cured before they had gone so far, by burning all those cursed books, which as justly deserve to be committed to the flames as if they were heretical." "I say the same," quoth the curate ; "and, in faith, to-morrow shall nor pass without holding a public inquisition upon them, and condemning them to the fire, that they may not occasion others to act as I fear my good friend has done."

All this was overheard by Don Quixote and the peasant ; and, as it confirmed the latter in the belief of his neighbour's infirmity, he began to cry aloud, "Open the doors, gentlemen, to Senor Valdovinos, and the marquis of Mantua, who comes dangerously wounded, and to Señor Abindarraez the Moor, whom the valorous Roderigo de Narvaez, governor of Antequera, brings as his prisoner." Hearing this, they all came out ; and, immediately recognising their friend, they ran to embrace him, although he had not yet alighted from the ass ; for indeed it was not in his power. "Forbear, all of you," he cried, "for I am sorely wounded, through my horse's fault : carry me to my bed ; and, if it be possible, send for the sage Urganda, to search and heal my wounds." "Look ye," said the housekeeper immediately, "if my heart did not tell me truly on which leg my master halted. Get upstairs in God's name ; for, without the help of that same Urganda, we shall find a way to cure you ourselves. Cursed, say I again, and a hundred times cursed, be those books of knight-errantry, that have brought your worship to this pass !" They carried him directly to his chamber, where, on searching for his wounds, they could discover none. He then told them "he was only bruised by a great fall he got with his horse Rozinante, as he was fighting with ten of the most prodigious and audacious giants on the face of the earth." "Ho, ho !" says the priest, "what, there are giants too in the dance ! by my faith, I shall set fire to them all before to-morrow night." They asked Don Quixote a thousand questions, to which he would return no

"Let them all be thrown into the court-yard."

answer; he only desired that they would give him some food, and allow him to sleep, that being what he most required. Having done this, the priest inquired particularly of the countryman in what condition Don Quixote had been found. The countryman gave him an account of the whole, with the extravagancies he had uttered, both at the time of finding him, and during their journey home; which made the Licentiate impatient to carry into execution what he had determined to do the following day, when, for that purpose, calling upon his friend Master Nicholas the barber, they proceeded together to Don Quixote's house.

CHAPTER VI

OF THE GRAND AND DIVERTING SCRUTINY MADE BY THE PRIEST AND THE BARBER, IN THE LIBRARY OF OUR INGENIOUS GENTLEMAN

Long and heavy was the sleep of Don Quixote; meanwhile the curate having asked the niece for the key of the chamber containing the books, those authors of the mischief, which she delivered with a very good will, they entered, attended by the housekeeper, and found above a hundred large volumes well bound, besides a great number of smaller size. No sooner did the housekeeper see them than she ran out of the room in great haste, and immediately returned with a pot of holy water and a bunch of hyssop, saying: "Signor Licentiate, take this, and sprinkle the room, lest some enchanter of the many these books abound with, should enchant us, as a punishment for our intention to banish them out of the world." The curate smiled at the housekeeper's simplicity, and ordered the barber to reach him the books, one by one, that they might see what they treated of; as they might perhaps find some that deserved not to be chastised by fire. "No," said the niece, "there is no reason why any of them should be spared, for they have all been mischief-makers: so let them all be thrown into the court-yard; and, having made a pile of them, set fire to it; or else make a bonfire of them in the back-yard, where the smoke will offend nobody." The housekeeper said the same; so eagerly did they both thirst for the death of those innocents.   But the priest would not consent to it without first reading the titles at least.

That same night, however, the housekeeper set fire to, and burnt, all the books that were in the yard, and in the house. Some must have perished that deserved to be treasured up in perpetual archives : but their destiny, or the indolence of the scrutineer, forbade it ; and in them was fulfilled the saying that "the just sometimes suffer for the unjust."   One of the remedies which the priest and the barber prescribed at that time, for their friend's malady, was to wall up the chamber which had contained his books, hoping that, when the cause was removed, the effect might cease ; and that they should pretend that an enchanter had carried room and all away.   This was speedily executed ; and, two days after, when Don Quixote left his bed, the first thing that occurred to him was to visit his books ; and not finding the room, he went up and down looking for it ; when, coming to the former situation of the door, he felt with his hands, and stared about on all sides without speaking a word for some time ; at length he asked the housekeeper where the chamber was in which he kept his books.   She, who was already well tutored what to answer, said to him :

"What room, or what nothing, does your worship look for ? there is neither room, nor books, in this house; for the devil himself has carried all away.

"It was not the devil," said the niece, "but an enchanter, who came one night upon a cloud, after the day of your departure, and, alighting from a serpent on which he rode, entered the room : what he did there, I know not, but, after some little time, out he came flying through the roof, and left the house full of smoke ; and when we went to see what he had been doing, we saw neither books nor room ; only we very well remember, both I and mistress housekeeper here, that when the wicked old thief went away, he said with a loud voice, that from a secret enmity he bore to the owner of those books and of the room, he had done a mischief in this house which would soon be manifest : he told us also, that he was called the sage Munniaton."   "Freston he meant to say," quoth Don Quixote.   "I know not," answered the housekeeper, "whether his name be Freston, or Friton ; all

I know is, that it ended in ton."—"It doth so," replied Don Quixote. "He is a sage enchanter, a great enemy of mine, and bears me malice, because by his skill and learning he knows, that in process of time, I shall engage in single combat with a knight whom he favours, and shall vanquish him, in spite of his protection. On this account he endeavours, as much as he can, to molest me : but let him know, from me, that he cannot withstand or avoid what is decreed by heaven."—"Who doubts of that ?" said the niece; "but, dear uncle, what have you to do with these broils? Would it not be better to stay quietly at home and not ramble about the world seeking for better bread than wheaten ; without considering that many go out for wool and return shorn ?"—"O niece," answered Don Quixote, "how little dost thou know of the matter ! Before they shall shear me, I will pluck and tear off the beards of all those who dare think of touching the tip of a single hair of mine." Neither of them would make any further reply; for they saw his choler begin to rise. Fifteen days he remained at home, very tranquil, discovering no symptom of an inclination to repeat his late frolics; during which time much pleasant conversation passed between him and his two neighbours, the priest and the barber : he always affirming that the world stood in need of nothing so much as knights-errant, and the revival of chivalry. The priest sometimes contradicted him, and at other times acquiesced; for, had he not been thus cautious, there would have been no means left to bring him to reason.

In the mean time Don Quixote tampered with a labourer, a neighbour of his, and an honest man, but shallow-brained ; in short he said so much, used so many arguments, and made so many promises, that the poor fellow resolved to sally out with him and serve him in the capacity of a squire. Among other things, Don Quixote told him that he ought to be very glad to accompany him, for such an adventure might some time or the other occur, that by one stroke an island might be won, where he might leave him governor. With this and other promises, Sancho Panza (for that was the labourer's name) left his wife and children, and engaged himself as squire to his neighbour. Don Quixote now set about raising money ; and, by selling one thing, pawning another, and losing by all, he collected a tolerable sum.

He fitted himself likewise with a buckler, which he borrowed of a friend, and, patching up his broken helmet in the best manner he could, he acquainted his squire Sancho of the day and hour he intended to set out, that he might provide himself with what he thought would be most needful. Above all, he charged him not to forget a wallet; which Sancho assured him he would not neglect; he said also that he thought of taking an ass with him, as he had a very good one, and he was not used to travel much on foot. With regard to the ass, Don Quixote paused a little: endeavouring to recollect whether any knight-errant had ever carried a squire mounted on ass-back: but no instance of the kind occurred to his memory. However, he consented that he should take his ass, resolving to accommodate him more honourably, at the earliest opportunity, by dismounting the first discourteous knight he should meet. He provided himself also with shirts, and other things, conformably to the advice given him by the innkeeper.

All this being accomplished, Don Quixote and Sancho Panza, without taking leave, the one of his wife and children, or the other of his housekeeper and niece, one night sallied out of the village unperceived; and they travelled so hard that by break of day they believed themselves secure, even if search were made after them. Sancho Panza proceeded upon his ass, like a patriarch, with his wallet and leathern bottle, and with a vehement desire to find himself governor of the island which his master had promised him. Don Quixote happened to take the same route as on his first expedition, over the plain of Montiel, which he passed with less inconvenience than before; for it was early in the morning, and the rays of the sun, darting on them horizontally, did not annoy them. Sancho Panza now said to his master:

"I beseech your worship, good sir knight-errant, not to forget your promise concerning that same island; for I shall know how to govern it, be it ever so large."

To which Don Quixote answered:

"Thou must know, friend Sancho Panza, that it was a custom much in use among the knights-errant of old to make their squires governors of the islands or kingdoms they conquered; and I am determined that so laudable a custom shall not be lost through my neglect; on the contrary, if you live, and I live, before six days have passed I may probably win such a kingdom as may have others depending on it, just fit for thee to be crowned king of one of them. And do not think this any extraordinary matter ; for things fall out to knights by such unforeseen and unexpected ways, that I may easily give thee more than I promise."

"So then," answered Sancho Panza, "if I were a king, by some of those miracles your worship mentions, Juan Gutierrez, my wife, would come to be a queen, and my children infantas !"

"Who doubts it ? " answered Don Quixote.

"I doubt it," replied Sancho Panza ; "for I am verily persuaded that, if God were to rain down kingdoms upon the earth, none of them would sit well upon the head of Mary Gutierrez ; for you must know, sir, she is not worth two farthings for a queen. The title of countess would sit better upon her, with the help of Heaven and good friends."

"Recommend her to God, Sancho," answered Don Quixote, "and He will do what is best for her : but do thou have a care not to debase thy mind so low as to content thyself with being less than a viceroy."

"Sir, I will not," answered Sancho ; "especially having so great a man for my master as your worship, who will know how to give me whatever is most fitting for me, and what I am best able to bear."

CHAPTER VII

DON QUIXOTE'S SECOND SALLY : THE ADVENTURE OF THE WINDMILLS

ENGAGED in this discourse, they came in sight of thirty or forty windmills, which are in that plain ; and, as soon as Don Quixote espied them, he said to his squire :

"Fortune disposes our affairs better than we ourselves could have desired : look yonder, friend Sancho Panza, where thou mayest discover somewhat more than thirty monstrous giants, whom I intend to encounter and slay, and with their spoils we will begin to enrich ourselves ; for it is lawful war, and doing God good service to remove so wicked a generation from off the face of the earth."

"What giants?" said Sancho Panza.

"Those thou seest yonder," answered his master, "with their long arms; for some are wont to have them almost of the length of two leagues."

"Look, sir," answered Sancho, "those which appear yonder are not giants, but windmills; and what seem to be arms are the sails, which, whirled about by the wind, make the mill-stone go."

"It is very evident," answered Don Quixote, "that thou art not versed in the business of adventures: they are giants: and, if thou art afraid, get thee aside and pray, whilst I engage with them in fierce and unequal combat."

So saying, he clapped spurs to his steed, notwithstanding the cries his squire sent after him, assuring him that they were certainly windmills, and not giants. But he was so fully possessed that they were giants, that he neither heard the outcries of his squire Sancho, nor yet discerned what they were, though he was very near them, but went on crying out aloud:

"Fly not, ye cowards and vile caitiffs; for it is a single knight who assaults you."

The wind now rising a little, the great sails began to move more rapidly; upon which Don Quixote called out:

"Although ye should have more arms than the giant Briareus, ye shall pay for it."

He recommended himself devoutly to his lady Dulcinea, beseeching her to succour him in the present danger, covering himself with his buckler, and setting his lance in the rest, he rushed on as fast as Rozinante could gallop, and attacked the first mill before him. Having run his lance into the sail, the wind whirled the latter about with so much violence that it broke the lance to shivers, dragging horse and rider after it, and tumbling them over and over on the plain, in very evil plight. Sancho Panza hastened to his assistance, as fast as the ass could carry him; and when he came up to his master, he found him unable to stir, so violent was the blow which he and Rozinante had received in their fall.

"God save me!" quoth Sancho, "did not I warn you to have a care of what you did, for that they were nothing but windmills? And nobody could mistake them, but one that had the like in his head."

"Peace, friend Sancho," answered Don Quixote: "for

He attacked the first mill before him.

matters of war are, of all others, most subject to continual change. Now I verily believe, and it is most certainly the fact, that the sage Freston, who stole away my chamber and books, has metamorphosed these giants into windmills, on purpose to deprive me of the glory of vanquishing them, so great is the enmity he bears me ! But his wicked arts will finally avail but little against the goodness of my sword."

"God grant it !" answered Sancho Panza ; then helping him to rise, he mounted him again upon his steed, which was almost disjointed.

Conversing upon the late adventure, they followed the road that led to the Pass of Lapice ; because there, Don Quixote said, they could not fail to meet with many and various adventures, as it was much frequented. He was, however, concerned at the loss of his lance, and never rested until he had fitted on to the lance-head a new shaft, in the shape of a withered branch which he snapped off from a tree.

Sancho put him in mind that it was time to dine. His master answered that at present he had no need of food, but that Sancho might eat whenever he thought proper. With this license, the latter adjusted himself as well as he could upon his beast ; and, taking out the contents of his wallet, he jogged on behind his master, very leisurely, eating, and ever and anon raising the bottle to his mouth with so much relish, that the best-fed victualler of Malaga might have envied him. And whilst he went on in this manner, repeating his draughts, he thought no more of the promises his master had made him ; nor did he think it any toil, but rather a recreation, to go in quest of adventures, however perilous they might be. In fine, they passed that night under the shelter of some trees. All that night Don Quixote slept not, but ruminated on his lady Dulcinea, conformably to the practice of knights-errant. Not so did Sancho spend the night ; for, his stomach being full, and not of succory-water, he made but one sleep of it ; and, had not his master roused him, neither the beams of the sun, that darted full in his face, nor the melody of the birds which, in great numbers, cheerfully saluted the approach of the new day, could have awaked him. At his uprising he applied again to his bottle, and found it much lighter than the evening before ; which grieved him to the heart, for he did not think they were in the way soon to remedy that defect. Don Quixote would not yet break his fast, resolving, as we have said, still to subsist upon savoury remembrances.

They now turned again into the road they had entered upon the day before, leading to the Pass of Lapice, which they discovered about three in the afternoon.

"Here, friend Sancho," said Don Quixote, upon seeing it, "we may plunge our arms up to the elbows in what are termed adventures. But attend to this caution, that even shouldst thou see me in the greatest peril in the world, thou must not lay hand to thy sword to defend me, unless thou perceivest that my assailants are vulgar and low people; in that case thou mayest assist me: but should they be knights, it is in nowise agreeable to the laws of chivalry that thou shouldst interfere, until thou art thyself dubbed a knight."

"I hear your worship," answered Sancho; "and I will observe this precept as religiously as the Lord's day."

As they were thus discoursing, there appeared on the road two monks of the order of St Benedict, mounted upon dromedaries; for the mules whereon they rode were not much less. They wore travelling masks, and carried umbrellas. Behind them came a coach, accompanied by four or five men on horseback and two muleteers on foot. Within the coach, as it afterwards appeared, was a Biscayan lady on her way to join her husband at Seville, who was there waiting to embark for India, where he was appointed to a very honourable post. The monks were not in her company, but were only travelling the same road. Scarcely had Don Quixote espied them, when he said to his squire:

"Either I am deceived, or this will prove the most famous adventure that ever happened; for those black figures that appear yonder must undoubtedly be enchanters, who are carrying off in that coach some princess whom they have stolen; which wrong I am bound to use my utmost endeavours to redress."

"This may prove a worse business than the windmills," said Sancho; "pray, sir, take notice that those are Benedictine monks, and the coach must belong to some travellers. Hearken to my advice, sir; have a care what you do, and let not the devil deceive you."

"I have already told thee, Sancho," answered Don Quixote, "that thou knowest little concerning adventures: what I say is true, as thou wilt presently see."

So saying, he advanced forward, and planted himself in the midst of the highway, by which the monks were to pass; and when they were so near that he supposed they could hear what he said, he cried out with a loud voice:

"Diabolical and monstrous race! Either instantly release the high-born princesses whom ye are carrying away perforce in that coach, or prepare for instant death, as the just chastisement of your wicked deeds."

The monks stopped their mules, and stood amazed, as much at the figure of Don Quixote as at his expressions: to which they answered:

"Signor cavalier, we are neither diabolical nor monstrous, but monks of the Benedictine order, travelling on our own business, and entirely ignorant whether any princesses are carried away in that coach by force, or not."

"No fair speeches to me, for I know ye, treacherous scoundrels!" and without waiting for a reply, he clapped spurs to Rozinante, and, with his lance couched, ran at the foremost monk with such fury and resolution that, if he had not slid down from his mule, he would certainly have been thrown to the ground, and wounded too, if not killed outright. The second monk, on observing how his comrade was treated, clapped spurs to the sides of his good mule, and began to scour along the plain, lighter than the wind itself.

Sancho Panza, seeing the monk on the ground, leaped nimbly from his ass, and running up to him, began to disrobe him. While he was thus employed, the two lacqueys came up, and asked him why he was stripping their master. Sancho told them that they were his lawful perquisites, being the spoils of the battle which his lord, Don Quixote, had just won. The lacqueys, who did not understand the jest, nor what was meant by spoils or battles, seeing that Don Quixote was at a distance, speaking with those in the coach, fell upon Sancho, threw him down, and, besides leaving him not a hair in his beard, gave him a hearty kicking, and left him stretched on the ground, deprived of sense and motion. Without losing a moment, the monk now got upon his mule again, trembling, terrified, and pale as death ; and was no sooner mounted than he spurred after his companion, who stood at some distance to observe the issue of this strange encounter ; but, being unwilling to wait, they pursued their way, crossing themselves oftener than if the devil had been at their heels. In the mean time Don Quixote, as it hath been already mentioned, addressing the lady in the coach, "Your beauteous ladyship may now," said he, "dispose of your person as pleaseth you best ; for the pride of your ravishers lies humbled in the dust, overthrown by my invincible arm ; and, that you may be at no trouble to learn the name of your deliverer, know that I am called Don Quixote de la Mancha, knight-errant and adventurer, and captive to the peerless and beauteous Dulcinea del Toboso ; and in requital of the benefit you have received at my hands, all I desire is, that you would return to Toboso, and, in my name, present yourselves before that lady, and tell her what I have done to obtain your liberty."

All that Don Quixote said was overheard by a certain squire who accompanied the coach, a Biscayan, who, finding he would not let it proceed, but talked of their immediately returning to Toboso, flew at Don Quixote, and taking hold of his lance, addressed him, in bad Castilian and worse Biscayan, after this manner :

"Cavalier, begone ! and the devil go with thee ! I swear, by the power that made me, if thou dost not quit the coach, thou forfeitest thy life, as I am a Biscayan."

Don Quixote understood him very well, and with great calmness answered :

"If thou wert a gentleman, as thou art not, I would before now have chastised thy folly and presumption, thou pitiful slave."

"I no gentleman !" said the Biscayan ; "I swear by the great God, thou liest, as I am a Christian ; if thou wilt throw away thy lance, and draw thy sword, thou shalt see how soon the cat will get into the water : * Biscayan by land, gentleman by sea, gentleman for the devil, and thou liest ! Now what hast thou to say ? "

---

* "To carry the cat to the water " is a saying applied to one who is victorious in any contest ; and it is taken from a game in which two cats are tied together by the tail, then carried near a pit or well (having the water between them), and the cat which first pulls the other in is declared conqueror.

"Thou shalt see that presently, as said Agrages," answered Don Quixote; then, throwing down his lance, he drew his sword, grasped his buckler, and set upon the Biscayan with a resolution to take his life. The Biscayan, seeing him come on in that manner, would fain have alighted, knowing that his mule, a wretched hackney, was not to be trusted, but he had only time to draw his sword. Fortunately for him, he was so near the coach as to be able to snatch from it a cushion, that served him for a shield: whereupon, they immediately fell to, as if they had been mortal enemies. The rest of the company would have made peace between them, but it was impossible; for the Biscayan swore, in his jargon, that if they would not let him finish the combat, he would murder his mistress, or whoever attempted to prevent him. The lady of the coach, amazed and affrighted at what she saw, ordered the coachman to remove a little out of the way, and sat at a distance, beholding the fierce conflict; in the progress of which the Biscayan gave Don Quixote so mighty a stroke on one of his shoulders, and above his buckler, that, had it not been for his armour, he had cleft him down to the girdle. Don Quixote feeling the weight of that blow, cried out aloud, saying:

"O lady of my soul! Dulcinea, flower of all beauty! succour this thy knight, who, to satisfy thy great goodness, exposes himself to this perilous extremity!" This invocation, the drawing of his sword, the covering himself well with his buckler, and the rushing with fury on the Biscayan, were the work of an instant. He resolved to venture all on the fortune of a single blow. The Biscayan perceiving his determination, resolved to do the same, and therefore waited for him, covering himself well with his cushion; but he was unable to turn his mule either to the right or the left, for, being already jaded, and unaccustomed to such sport, the creature would not move a step. All the bystanders were in fearful suspense as to the event of those prodigious blows with which they threatened each other; and the lady of the coach and her attendants were making a thousand vows and promises of offerings, to all the images and places of devotion in Spain, that God might deliver them and their squire from this great peril.

The choleric Biscayan was the first who discharged his blow, which fell with such force and fury that, if the edge of his sword had not turned aslant by the way, that single blow had been enough to have put an end to this cruel conflict, and to all the adventures of our knight. But good fortune preserving him for greater things, so turned his adversary's sword, that, though it alighted on the left shoulder, it did him no other hurt than to disarm that side, carrying off, by the way, a great part of his helmet, with half an ear; all which with hideous ruin fell to the ground, leaving him in a piteous plight.

Good Heaven! who is he that can worthily describe the rage that entered into the breast of our Manchegan at seeing himself thus treated! Let it suffice, that it was such that, raising himself afresh in his stirrups, and grasping his sword faster in both hands, he discharged it with such fury upon the Biscayan, directly over the cushion, and upon his head, which was unprotected, that, as if a mountain had fallen upon him, the blood began to gush out of his nostrils, his mouth, and his ears; and he seemed as if he was just falling from his mule, which doubtless he must have done, had not he laid fast hold of her neck : but, notwithstanding that, he lost his stirrups, and then let go his hold; while the mule, frightened at the terrible stroke, began to run about the field, and at two or three plunges laid her master flat on the ground. Don Quixote stood looking on with great calmness, and seeing him fall, he leaped from his horse with much agility, ran up to him, and clapping the point of his sword to his eyes, bid him yield, or he would cut off his head. The Biscayan was so stunned that he could not answer a word ; and it would have gone hard with him (so blinded with rage was Don Quixote) had not the ladies of the coach, who, till now, had been witnessing the combat in great dismay, approached him, and earnestly entreated that he would do them the great kindness and favour to spare the life of their squire. Don Quixote answered, with much solemnity and gravity :

"Assuredly, fair ladies, I am most willing to grant you your request, but it must be upon a certain condition and compact ; which is, that this knight shall promise to repair to the town of Toboso, and present himself, from me, before the peerless Donna Dulcinea, that she may dispose of him according to her pleasure."

The terrified and disconsolate lady, without considering what Don Quixote required or inquiring who Dulcinea was, promised him that her squire should perform whatever he commanded.

"Then, on the faith of that promise," said Don Quixote, "I shall do him no further hurt, though he well deserves it at my hands."

CHAPTER VIII

OF THE PLEASANT DISCOURSE WHICH DON QUIXOTE HAD WITH HIS GOOD SQUIRE SANCHO PANZA

BEFORE this time, Sancho Panza had got upon his legs, somewhat roughly handled by the servants of the monk, and stood an attentive spectator during the combat of his master, Don Quixote; beseeching God, in his heart, that he would be pleased to give him the victory, and that the knight might thereby win some island, of which he might make him governor, according to his promise.

Now, seeing the conflict at an end, and that his master was ready to mount again upon Rozinante, he came up to hold his stirrup. But before Don Quixote had mounted, Sancho fell upon his knees before him, then, taking hold of his hand, and kissing it, said to him:

"Be pleased, my lord Don Quixote, to bestow upon me the government of that island which you have won in this dreadful battle; for, be it ever so big, I feel in myself ability sufficient to govern it as well as the best that ever governed island in the world." To which Don Quixote answered:

"Brother Sancho, this adventure, and others of this nature, are not adventures of islands, but of cross-ways, in which nothing is to be gained but a broken head, or the loss of an ear. Have patience; for adventures will offer, whereby I may not only make thee a governor, but something yet greater." Sancho returned him abundance of thanks, and, kissing his hand again, and the skirt of his armour, he helped him to get upon Rozinante; then, mounting his ass, he followed his master, who, going off at a round pace, without taking his leave, or speaking to those in the coach, immediately entered into an adjoining wood.

The squire now brought out what provisions he had, and they ate together in a very peaceable and friendly manner. But, being desirous to seek out some place wherein to rest that night, they soon finished their poor and dry meal, and then made what haste they could to reach some village before night; but both the sun and their hopes failed them near the huts of some goatherds. They determined, therefore, to take up their lodging with them; but if Sancho was grieved that they could not reach a village, his master was as much rejoiced to lie in the open air, conceiving that, every time this befel him, he was performing an act which confirmed his title to chivalry.

No one could be more kindly received than was Don Quixote by the goatherds; and Sancho having accommodated Rozinante and his ass in the best manner he was able, pursued the odour emitted by certain pieces of goat's flesh that were boiling in a kettle on a fire; and, though he would willingly, at that instant, have tried whether they were ready to be transferred from the kettle to the stomach, he forebore doing so, as the goatherds themselves took them off the fire, and, spreading some sheepskins on the ground, very speedily served up their rural mess, and, with much cordiality, invited them both to partake of it. Six of them that belonged to the fold seated themselves round the skins, having first, with rustic compliments, requested Don Quixote to seat himself upon a trough with the bottom upwards, placed on purpose for him. Don Quixote sat down, and Sancho remained standing to serve the cup, which was made of horn. His master, seeing him standing, said to him:

"Be seated here by my side, in company with these good people, and become one with me, who am thy master, for the same may be said of knight-errantry which is said of love, that it makes all things equal."

"I give you a great many thanks, sir," said Sancho: "but let me tell your worship that, provided I have victuals enough, I can eat as well, or better standing, and alone, than if I were seated close by an emperor."

"Notwithstanding this," said Don Quixote, "thou shalt sit down; for whosoever humbleth himself, God doth exalt;"

and, pulling him by the arm, he forced him to sit down next him.

The goatherds did not understand this jargon of squires and knights-errant, and therefore only ate, held their peace, and stared at their guests, who, with much satisfaction and appetite, swallowed down pieces as large as their fists. The service of flesh being finished, the goatherds spread upon the skins a great quantity of acorns, together with half a cheese, harder than if it had been made of mortar. The horn in the mean time stood not idle; for it went round so often, now full, now empty, like the bucket of a well, that they presently emptied one of the two wine-bags that hung in view. After Don Quixote had satisfied his hunger, he took up a handful of acorns, and, looking on them attentively, made a long harangue, in which he gave utterance to expressions like these :—

"Happy times, and happy ages, were those which the ancients termed the Golden Age! not because gold, so prized in this our iron age, was to be obtained, in that fortunate period, without toil; but because they who then lived were ignorant of those two words, Mine and Thine. In that blessed age all things were in common, and all was peace and amity. But as times became worse, and wickedness increased, to defend maidens, to protect widows, and to relieve orphans and persons distressed, the order of knight-errantry was instituted. Of this order am I, brother goatherds, whom I thank for the good cheer and kind reception ye have given me and my squire; for though, by the law of nature, every one living is bound to favour knights-errant, yet as ye have received and regaled me without being aware of this obligation, it is but reasonable that I should return you my warmest acknowledgments."

Our knight made this harangue because the acorns put before him reminded him of the Golden Age, and led him to make that discourse to the goatherds; who, in astonishment, listened to him, without saying a word. Sancho also was silent, devouring the acorns, and making frequent visits to the second wine-bag, which was hanging upon a cork-tree, in order to keep the wine cool.

Don Quixote spent more time in talking than in eating, and supper being over, one of the goatherds said, "That your worship,

They stopped . . . near a pleasant and refreshing brook.

Señor knight-errant, may the more truly say that we entertain you with a ready good-will, one of our comrades, who will soon be here, shall sing for your pleasure." Scarcely had he spoken when a youth appeared, who sang several songs excellently and played on the rebeck with great skill.

But Sancho Panza was more disposed to sleep than to hear ballads; he therefore said to his master:

"Sir, you had better consider where you are to rest to-night; for the labour which these honest men undergo all day will not suffer them to pass the night in singing."

"I understand thee, Sancho," answered Don Quixote; "for it is very evident that visits to the wine-bag require to be paid rather with sleep than music."

"It relished well with us all, blessed be God," answered Sancho.

"I do not deny it," replied Don Quixote; "lay thyself down where thou wilt, but it is more becoming for those of my profession to watch than to sleep. However, it would not be amiss, Sancho, if thou wouldst dress this ear again; for it pains me more than it ought."

Sancho was about to do as he was desired; but one of the goatherds seeing the wound, bade him not be concerned about it, for he would apply such a remedy as should quickly heal it; then taking some rosemary leaves, which abounded in that place, he chewed them and mixed with them a little salt, and, laying them to the sore, bound them on very fast, assuring him that no other salve would be necessary, which indeed proved to be true.

CHAPTER IX

WHEREIN IS RELATED THE ADVENTURE WHICH BEFEL DON QUIXOTE, IN MEETING WITH CERTAIN UNMERCIFUL YANGUESIANS *

AFTER leaving the goatherds Don Quixote and his squire journeyed onward. At last they stopped in a meadow full of fresh grass, near which ran a pleasant and refreshing brook;

* Carriers of Galicia and inhabitants of the district of Yanguas in the Rioja.

insomuch that it invited and compelled them to pass there the
sultry hours of mid-day, which now became very oppressive.
Don Quixote and Sancho alighted, and, leaving the ass and
Rozinante at large to feed upon the abundant grass, they
ransacked the wallet ; and, without any ceremony, in friendly
and social wise, master and man shared what it contained.
Sancho had taken no care to fetter Rozinante. Fortune so
ordered it that there were grazing in the same valley a
number of Galician mares, belonging to certain Yanguesian
carriers, whose custom it is to pass the noon, with their drove,
in places where there is grass and water. That where Don
Quixote then reposed suited their purpose. Now it so happened
that Rozinante conceived a wish to pay his respects to the
drove, and departed at a brisk trot to interview them. But
they received him with their heels and their teeth in such a
manner that in a little time his girths broke, and he lost his
saddle. But what must have affected him more sensibly was,
that the carriers, having witnessed his intrusion, set upon him
with their pack-staves, and so belaboured him that they laid him
along on the ground in a wretched plight.

By this time the knight and squire, having seen the
drubbing of Rozinante, came up in great haste ; and Don
Quixote said :

"By what I see, friend Sancho, these are no knights, but
low people of a scoundrel race. I tell thee this, because thou
art on that account justified in assisting me to take ample
revenge for the outrage they have done to Rozinante before
our eyes."

"What kind of revenge can we take," answered Sancho,
"since they are above twenty, and we no more than two, and
perhaps but one and a half ?"

"I am equal to a hundred !" replied Don Quixote ; and,
without saying more, he laid his hands on his sword, and flew
at the Yanguesians ; and Sancho did the same, incited by the
example of his master. At the first blow, Don Quixote gave
one of them a terrible wound on the shoulder, through a
leathern doublet. The Yanguesians, seeing themselves assaulted
in this manner by two men only, seized their staves, and,
surrounding them, began to dispense their blows with great

vehemence and animosity; and true it is that at the second blow they brought Sancho to the ground. The same fate befel Don Quixote—his courage and dexterity availing him nothing; and, he just fell at Rozinante's feet, who had not yet been able to rise. The Yanguesians, perceiving the mischief they had done, loaded their beasts with all speed, and pursued their journey, leaving the two adventurers in evil plight.

The first who came to his senses was Sancho Panza, who, finding himself close to his master, with a feeble and plaintive voice cried :

"Señor Don Quixote ! ah, Señor Don Quixote ! "

"What wouldst thou, brother Sancho ? " answered the knight, in the same feeble and lamentable tone.

"I could wish, if it were possible," said Sancho Panza, "your worship would give me two draughts of that drink of Feo Blass, if you have it here at hand. Perhaps it may do as well for broken bones as it does for wounds."

"The Balsam of Fierabras, you mean. Unhappy I, that we have it not ! " answered Don Quixote. "But I swear to thee, Sancho Panza, on the faith of a knight-errant, that, before two days pass (if fortune decree not otherwise), I will have it in my possession, or my hands shall fail me much."

"But in how many days," said the squire, "does your worship think we shall recover the use of our feet ? "

"For my part," answered the battered knight, "I cannot ascertain the precise term : but I alone am to blame, for having laid hand on my sword against men who are not knights like myself."

Sancho, sending forth thirty "alases," and sixty sighs, and a hundred and twenty curses on those who had brought him into that situation, endeavoured to raise himself, but stopped half way, bent like a Turkish bow, being wholly unable to stand upright : notwithstanding this, he managed to saddle his ass, who had also taken advantage of that day's excessive liberty, to go a little astray. He then heaved up Rozinante, who, had he a tongue wherewithal to complain, most certainly would not have been outdone either by Sancho or his master. Sancho at length settled Don Quixote upon the ass, to whose tail he then tied Rozinante, and, taking hold of the halter of Dapple, he led them,

now faster, now slower, towards the place where he thought
the high-road might lie; and had scarcely gone a short league,
when fortune, that was conducting his affairs from good to better,
discovered to him the road, where he also espied an inn; which,
to his sorrow, and Don Quixote's joy, must needs be a castle.
Sancho positively maintained it was an inn, and his master that it
was a castle; and the dispute lasted so long that they arrived
there before it was determined: and Sancho, without further
expostulation, entered it, with his string of cattle.

CHAPTER X

OF WHAT HAPPENED TO DON QUIXOTE IN THE INN WHICH HE IMAGINED TO BE A CASTLE

LOOKING at Don Quixote laid across the ass, the innkeeper inquired of Sancho what ailed him? Sancho answered him that it
was nothing but a fall from the rock, by which his ribs were
somewhat bruised. The innkeeper had a wife of a disposition
uncommon among those of the like occupation; for she was
naturally charitable, and felt for the misfortunes of her neighbours; so that she immediately prepared to relieve Don Quixote,
and made her daughter, a very comely young maiden, assist in the
cure of her guest. There was also a servant at the inn, a broad-
faced Asturian wench, named Maritornes. This agreeable lass
now assisted the damsel to prepare for Don Quixote a very sorry
bed in a garret, which gave evident tokens of having formerly
served many years as a hay-loft. In this room lodged also a
carrier, whose bed was at a little distance from that of our knight;
and though it was composed of pannels, and other trappings of his
mules, it had much the advantage over that of Don Quixote,
which consisted of four not very smooth boards, upon two unequal trestles, and a mattress no thicker than a quilt, and full of
knobs, which from their hardness might have been taken for
pebbles, had not the wool appeared through some fractures; with
two sheets like the leather of an old target, and a rug, the threads
of which you might count if you chose, without losing one of the
number.

In this wretched bed was Don Quixote laid ; after which the hostess and her daughter plaistered him from head to foot ; Maritornes contributing her share to the aggregate benefit by holding the light. As the hostess was thus employed, perceiving Don Quixote to be mauled in every part, she said that his bruises seemed the effect rather of a hard drubbing than of a fall.

"Not of a drubbing," said Sancho ; "but the knobs and sharp points of the rock, every one of which has left its mark : and, now I think of it," added he, "pray, contrive to spare a morsel of that ointment, as somebody may find it useful—indeed, I suspect that my sides would be glad of a little of it."

"What, you have had a fall too, have you?" said the hostess.

"No," replied Sancho, "not a fall, but a fright, on seeing my master tumble, which so affected my whole body that I feel as if I had received a thousand blows myself."

"That may very well be," said the damsel ; "for I have often dreamed that I was falling down from some high tower, and could never come to the ground ; and, when I awoke, I have found myself as much bruised and battered as if I had really fallen."

"But here is the point, mistress," answered Sancho Panza, "that I, without dreaming at all, and more awake than I am now, find myself with almost as many bruises as my master Don Quixote."

"What do you say is the name of this gentleman?" quoth the Asturian.

"Don Quixote de la Mancha," answered Sancho Panza : "he is a knight-errant, and one of the best and most valiant that has been seen in the world for this long time."

"What is a knight-errant?" said the wench.

"Are you such a novice as not to know that?" answered Sancho Panza. "You must know, then, that a knight-errant is a thing that, in two words, is cudgelled and made an emperor ; to-day he is the most unfortunate wretch in the world : and to-morrow will have two or three crowns of kingdoms to give to his squire."

"How comes it then to pass that you, being squire to this

"—I WILL KEEP ETERNALLY WRITTEN IN MY MEMORY THE SERVICE YOU HAVE DONE UNTO ME,—"

worthy gentleman," said the hostess, " have not yet, as it seems, got so much as an earldom ? "

"It is early days yet," answered Sancho, "for it is but a month since we set out in quest of adventures, and hitherto we have met with none that deserve the name. And sometimes we look for one thing, and find another. But the truth is, if my master Don Quixote recovers of this wound or fall, and I am not disabled thereby, I would not truck my hopes for the best title in Spain."

To all this conversation Don Quixote had listened very attentively ; and now, raising himself up in the bed as well as he could, and taking the hand of his hostess, he said to her : "Believe me, beauteous lady, you may esteem yourself fortunate in having entertained me in this your castle. My squire will inform you who I am. I only say that I shall retain the service you have done me eternally engraven on my memory, and be grateful to you as long as my life shall endure. And, had it pleased the high heavens that Love had not held me so enthralled and subject to his laws, and to the eyes of that beautiful ingrate whose name I silently pronounce, those of this lovely virgin had become enslavers of my liberty."

The hostess, her daughter, and the good Maritornes, stood confounded at this harangue of our knight-errant, which they understood just as much as if he had spoken Greek, although they guessed that it all tended to compliments and offers of service ; but not being accustomed to such kind of language, they gazed at him with surprise, and thought him another sort of man than those now in fashion ; and, after thanking him, in their inn-like phrase, for his offers, they left him. The Asturian Maritornes however doctored Sancho, who stood in no less need of plaisters than his master.

Don Quixote's hard, scanty, beggarly, crazy bed, stood first in the middle of the cock-loft ; and close by it Sancho had placed his own, which consisted only of a rush mat, and a rug that seemed to be rather of beaten hemp than of wool. Next to the squire stood that of the carrier, made up, as hath been said, of pannels, and the whole furniture of two of his best mules.

I say, then, that, after the carrier had visited his mules, and given them their second " feed," he laid himself down upon his pannels. Sancho was already plaistered, and in bed ; and, though he endeavoured to sleep, the pain of his ribs would not allow him ; and Don Quixote, from the same cause, kept his eyes as wide open as those of a hare. The whole inn was in profound silence, and contained no other light than what proceeded from a lamp which hung in the middle of the entry. This marvellous stillness, and the thoughts of our knight, which incessantly recurred to those adventures so common in the annals of chivalry, brought to his imagination one of the strangest whims that can well be conceived : for he imagined that he was now in some famous castle, and that the daughter of its lord, captivated by his fine appearance, had become enamoured of him. He began to feel some alarm, reflecting on the dangerous trial to which his fidelity was on the point of being exposed ; but resolved in his heart not to suffer disloyal thoughts against his Lady Dulcinea del Toboso to gain ascendency, though Queen Ginebra herself, with the lady Quintaniana, should present themselves before him.

Whilst his thoughts were occupied by these extravagances, it chanced that Maritornes had forgotten to execute some of her master's orders, viz., to fetch from the larder-loft some articles which were needed for the next day's use. Just when she was about to go to bed she remembered the commission, and thinking everyone would be asleep stole up to execute it. With silent and cautious step she advanced towards the larder. But scarcely had she passed the threshold of the door when Don Quixote heard her ; and, sitting up in bed, in spite of plaisters and the pain of his ribs, he stretched out his arms towards the damsel, who, crouching, and holding her breath as she went, with hands extended feeling her way, encountered the arms of Don Quixote. He caught hold of her by the wrist, and drawing her towards him, in a low and amorous voice he said to her : "O ! that I were in a state, beautiful and exalted lady, to return so vast a favour as this you confer upon me, by your charming presence ! but the plighted faith I have sworn to the peerless Dulcinea del Toboso, sole mistress of my most recondite thoughts, must keep me true to her."

Maritornes was in the utmost vexation at being thus confined by Don Quixote ; and, not hearing or attending to what he said, she struggled, without speaking a word, to release herself. The carrier, who had a fondness for the damsel, had heard her from the first moment she entered the room. He listened attentively to all that Don Quixote said. He then advanced to Don Quixote's bed and stood still, in order to discover the tendency of his discourse, which, however, he could not understand; but, seeing that the wench struggled to get from him, and that Don Quixote laboured to hold her, and not liking the jest, he lifted up his arm, and discharged so terrible a blow on the lanthorn jaws of the knight, that his mouth was bathed in blood; then, not content with this, he mounted upon his ribs, and paced them somewhat above a trot from one end to the other. The bed, which was crazy, and its foundations none of the strongest, being unable to bear the additional weight of the carrier, came down to the ground with such a crash that the innkeeper awoke; and, having called aloud to Maritornes without receiving an answer, he immediately conjectured it was some serious affair. The wench, seeing her master coming, and knowing his furious disposition, retreated in terror to Sancho Panza's bed, who was now asleep; and there rolled herself into a ball. The innkeeper entered, calling out, "Where are you, girl? what mischief is on now?" Sancho was now disturbed, and feeling such a mass upon him, fancied he had got the nightmare, and began to lay about him on every side; and not a few of his blows reached Maritornes, who, provoked by the smart, cast aside all decorum, and made Sancho such a return in kind that she effectually roused him from sleep, in spite of his drowsiness. The carrier, perceiving, by the light of the host's candle, how it fared with the lady of his heart, quitted Don Quixote, and ran to her assistance. The landlord followed him, but with a different intention; for it was to chastise the wench. Therefore the carrier belaboured Sancho, Sancho the wench, the wench Sancho, and the innkeeper the wench, until amidst all, the landlord's candle went out.

It happened that there lodged that night at the inn, an officer belonging to the holy brotherhood of Toledo *; who, hearing the noise of the scuffle, seized his wand, and entered the room in the dark, calling out, "Forbear, in the name of justice; forbear, in the name of the holy brotherhood." The first he encountered was the battered Don Quixote, who, stretched upon

* Corresponding in some measure to our police.

his back, lay senseless on his demolished bed. Laying hold of the knight's beard as he was groping about, the officer cried out repeatedly, "I charge you to aid and assist me." Finding that the person whom he held was motionless, he concluded that he was dead, and that the people in the room were his murderers. Upon which he raised his voice still louder, crying, "Shut the inn door, and let none escape ; for here is a man murdered !" These words startled them all, and the conflict instantly ceased. The landlord withdrew to his chamber, the carrier to his pannels, and the girl to her bed : the unfortunate Don Quixote and Sancho alone were incapable of moving. The officer now let go the beard of Don Quixote, and, in order to search after and secure the delinquents, he went out for a light, but could find none ; for the innkeeper had purposely extinguished the lamp, when he retired to his chamber ; and therefore he was obliged to have recourse to the chimney, where, after much time and trouble, he lighted another lamp.

CHAPTER XI

THE INNUMERABLE DISASTERS THAT BEFEL DON QUIXOTE AND SANCHO PANZA IN THE INN WHICH THE KNIGHT MISTOOK FOR A CASTLE

DON QUIXOTE by this time had come to himself, and, in the same dolorous tone in which the day before he had called to his squire, when he lay extended in the valley of pack-staves, he now again called to him, saying :

"Sancho, friend, art thou asleep ? art thou asleep, friend Sancho ?"

"How should I sleep ? woe is me !" answered Sancho, full of trouble and vexation ; "for I think all the fiends from the pit have been with me to-night."

"Well mayst thou believe so," answered Don Quixote ; "for either I know nothing, or this castle is enchanted, for an invisible hand, affixed to the arm of some monstrous giant, gave me so violent a blow that my mouth was bathed in blood, and afterwards so bruised me that I am now in a worse state than that wherein the carriers left me yesterday. Whence I conjecture

C

that the damsel of this castle is guarded by some enchanted Moor, and therefore not to be approached by me."

"Nor by me neither," answered Sancho; "for more than four hundred Moors have buffeted me in such a manner that the basting of the pack-staves was tarts and cheese-cakes to it. Woe is me! for I am no knight-errant, nor ever mean to be one; yet, of all our mishaps, the greater part still falls to my share."

"What, hast thou likewise been beaten?" said Don Quixote.

"Have not I told you so? Evil befall my lineage!" quoth Sancho.

"Console thyself, friend," said Don Quixote; "for I will now make that precious balsam which will cure us in the twinkling of an eye." At this moment the officer, having lighted his lamp, entered to examine the person whom he conceived to have been murdered; and Sancho, seeing him enter in his shirt, with a nightcap on his head, a lamp in his hand, and a countenance far from well-favoured, asked his master if it was the enchanted Moor coming to finish the correction he had bestowed upon them.

"It cannot be the Moor," answered Don Quixote; "for the enchanted suffer not themselves to be visible."

"If they do not choose to be seen, they will be felt," said Sancho: "witness my shoulders."

"Mine might speak, too," answered Don Quixote. "But this is not sufficient evidence to convince us that he whom we see is the enchanted Moor."

The officer, finding them communing in so calm a manner, stood in astonishment: although it is true that Don Quixote still lay flat on his back, unable to stir, from bruises and plaisters. The officer approached him, and said, "Well, my good fellow, how are you?"

"I would speak more respectfully," answered Don Quixote, "were I in your place. Is it the fashion of this country, blockhead, thus to address knights-errant?"

The officer, not disposed to bear this language from one of so scurvy an aspect, lifted up his lamp, and dashed it, with all its contents, at the head of Don Quixote, and then made his retreat in the dark.

"Surely," quoth Sancho Panza, "this must be the enchanted

Moor ; and he reserves the treasure for others, and for us only fisticuffs and lampshots." *

" It is even so," answered Don Quixote ; " and it is to no purpose to regard those affairs of enchantments, or to be out of humour or angry with them ; for, being invisible, and mere phantoms, all endeavours to seek revenge would be fruitless. Rise, Sancho, if thou canst, and call the governor of this fortress, and procure me some oil, wine, salt and rosemary, to make the healing balsam of Fierabras ; for in truth I want it much at this time, as the wound this phantom has given me bleeds very fast."

Sancho got up with aching bones ; and, as he was proceeding in the dark towards the landlord's chamber, he met the officer, who was watching the movements of his enemy, and said to him :

" Sir, whoever you are, do us the favour and kindness to help us to a little rosemary, oil, salt, and wine ; for they are wanted to cure one of the best knights-errant in the world, who lies there, sorely wounded by the hands of the enchanted Moor who is in this inn."

The officer, hearing this, took him for a maniac ; and, as the day now began to dawn, he opened the inn door, and calling the host, told him what Sancho wanted. The innkeeper furnished him with what he desired, and Sancho carried them to Don Quixote, who lay with his hands on his head, complaining of the pain caused by the lamp, which, however, had done him no other hurt than raising a couple of tolerably large tumours ; what he took for blood being only moisture, occasioned by the pelting of the storm which had just blown over. In fine, he took his simples, and made a compound of them, mixing them together, and boiling them some time, until he thought the mixture had arrived at the exact point. He then asked for a vial to hold it ; but, as there was no such thing in the inn, he resolved to put it in a cruse, or tin oil-flask, of which the host made him a present. This being done, he pronounced over the cruse above four-score Paternosters, and as many Ave-Marias, Salves, and Credos, accompanying every word with a cross, by way of benediction ; all which was performed in the presence of Sancho, the innkeeper,

* In the original, *Candilazos* is a new-coined word.

and the officer.   As for the carrier, he had gone soberly about the business of tending his mules.   Having completed the operation, Don Quixote resolved to make trial immediately of the virtue of that precious balsam; and therefore drank about a pint and a half of what remained in the pot wherein it was boiled, after the cruse was filled; and scarcely had he swallowed the potion when it was rejected and followed by so violent a retching that nothing was left on his stomach.   To the pain and exertion of this, a copious perspiration succeeding, he desired to be covered up warm, and left alone.   They did so, and he continued asleep above three hours, when he awoke and found himself greatly relieved in his body, and his battered and bruised members so much restored that he considered himself as perfectly recovered, and was thoroughly persuaded that he was in possession of the true balsam of Fierabras.

Sancho Panza, who likewise took his master's amendment for a miracle, desired he would give him what remained in the pot, which was no small quantity.   This request being granted, he took it in both hands, and, with good faith and better will, swallowed down very little less than his master had done.   Now the case was, that poor Sancho's stomach was not so delicate as that of his master;   and, therefore, before he could reject it, he endured such pangs and loathings, with such cold sweats and faintings, that he verily thought his last hour was come;   and finding himself so afflicted and tormented, he cursed the balsam, and the thief that had given it him.   Don Quixote, seeing him in that condition, said:

"I believe, Sancho, that all this mischief hath befallen thee because thou art not dubbed a knight: for I am of opinion this liquor can do good only to those who are of that order."

"If your worship knew that," replied Sancho,—"evil betide me and all my generation!—why did you suffer me to drink it?" By this time the beverage commenced its operation, and the poor squire was relieved.   He sweated and sweated again, with such faintings and shivering-fits, that not only himself, but all present thought he was expiring.   This hurricane lasted near two hours; and left him, not sound, like his master, but so exhausted and shattered that he was unable to stand.

Don Quixote, feeling, as we said before, quite renovated, was moved to take his departure immediately in quest of adventures, thinking that by every moment's delay he was depriving the world of his aid and protection; and more especially as he felt secure and confident in the virtues of his balsam. Thus stimulated, he saddled Rozinante with his own hands, and pannelled the ass of his squire, whom he also helped to dress, and afterwards to mount. He then mounted himself, and, having observed a pike in a corner of the inn-yard, he took possession of it to serve him for a lance.

Being now both mounted, and at the door of the inn, he called to the host, and, in a grave and solemn tone of voice, he took farewell of him, and asked if he could serve him in any way by taking vengeance on his enemies. The host answered with the same gravity:

"Sir knight, I have no need of your worship's avenging any wrong for me; all I desire of your worship is to pay me for what you have had in the inn, as well for the straw and barley for your two beasts, as for your supper and lodging."

"What! is this an inn?" exclaimed Don Quixote.

"Ay, and a very creditable one," answered the host.

"Hitherto, then, I have been in an error," answered Don Quixote; "for in truth I took it for a castle; but since it is indeed no castle, but an inn, all that you have now to do is to excuse the payment; for I cannot act contrary to the law of knights-errant."

"I see little to my purpose in all this," answered the host: "pay me what is my due, and let me have none of your stories and knight-errantries; all I want is to get my own."

"Thou art a blockhead, and a pitiful innkeeper," answered Don Quixote; so clapping spurs to Rozinante, and brandishing his lance, he sallied out of the inn without opposition, and never turning to see whether his squire followed him, was soon a good way off. The host, seeing him go without paying, ran to seize Sancho Panza, who said that, since his master would not pay, neither would he pay.

Poor Sancho's ill-luck would have it that among the people in the inn, there were four cloth-workers of Segovia, three needle-makers from the fountain of Cordova, and two neighbours from the market-place of Seville: all merry, good-humoured, frolicksome fellows ; who came up to Sancho, and having dismounted him, one of them produced a blanket from the landlord's bed, into which Sancho was immediately thrown ; but, perceiving that the ceiling was too low, they determined to execute their purpose in the yard. Thither Sancho was carried ; and, being placed in the middle of the blanket, they began to toss him aloft, and divert themselves with him, as with a dog at Shrovetide.

The cries which the poor blanketed squire sent forth were so many and so loud, that they reached his master's ears ; who, stopping to listen attentively, believed that some new adventure was at hand, until he plainly recognised the voice of the squire. Turning the reins, he galloped back to the inn-door, and finding it closed, he rode round in search of some other entrance. He had no sooner reached the yard-wall, which was not very high, than he perceived the wicked sport they were making with his squire. He saw him ascend and descend through the air with so much grace and agility that, if his indignation would have suffered him, he certainly would have laughed outright. He made an effort to get from his horse upon the pales, but was so maimed and bruised that he was unable to alight. Therefore, remaining on horseback, he proceeded to vent his rage, by uttering so many reproaches and invectives against those who were tossing Sancho, that it is impossible to commit them to writing. But they suspended neither their laughter nor their labour ; nor did the flying Sancho cease to pour forth lamentations, mingled now with threats, now with entreaties ; yet all were of no avail, and they desisted at last only from pure fatigue. They then brought him his ass, and, wrapping him in his cloak, mounted him thereon. Sancho clapped heels to his ass, and, the inn-gate being thrown wide open, out he went, satisfied that he had paid nothing, and carried his point, though at the expense of his usual pledge, namely, his back. The landlord, it is true, retained his wallets in payment of what was due to him ; but Sancho never missed them in the hurry of his departure.

They began to toss him aloft.

CHAPTER XII

THE ADVENTURE OF THE FLOCKS OF SHEEP

SANCHO came up to his master so faint and dispirited, that he was not able to urge his ass forward. Don Quixote, perceiving him in that condition, said :

" Honest Sancho, that castle, or inn, I am now convinced, is enchanted ; for they who so cruelly sported with thee, what could they be but phantoms and inhabitants of another world ? and I am the more persuaded of this because, when I stood at the pales of that yard, I could not get over them."

" And I too," quoth Sancho, " would have revenged myself if I had been able, knight or no knight, but I could not ; though, in my opinion, they who diverted themselves at my expense were no hobgoblins, but men of flesh and bones, as we are. In my poor opinion, the better and surer way for us would now be to return to our village, now that it is reaping-time, and look after our business ; nor go rambling from Ceca to Mecca, and out of the frying-pan into the fire."

"How little dost thou know, Sancho," answered Don Quixote, " of what appertains to chivalry ! Peace, and have patience, for the day will come when thine eyes shall witness how honourable a thing it is to follow this profession."

The knight and his squire went on conferring thus together, when Don Quixote perceived in the road on which they were travelling a great and thick cloud of dust coming towards them ; upon which he turned to Sancho, and said :

" This is the day, O Sancho, that shall manifest the good that fortune hath in store for me. This is the day, I say, on which shall be proved, as at all times, the valour of my arm ; and on which I shall perform exploits that will be recorded and written in the book of fame, and there remain to all succeeding ages. Seest thou that cloud of dust, Sancho ? It is raised by a prodigious army of divers and innumerable nations, who are on the march this way."

" If so, there must be two armies," said Sancho ; " for here, on this side, arises just such another cloud of dust."

Don Quixote turned, and seeing that it really was so, he rejoiced exceedingly, taking it for granted they were two armies coming to engage in the midst of that spacious plain, for at all hours and moments his imagination was full of the battles, enchantments, adventures, extravagancies, amours, and challenges detailed in his favourite books; and in every thought, word, and action he reverted to them. Now the cloud of dust he saw was raised by two great flocks of sheep going the same road from different parts, and, as the dust concealed them until they came near, and Don Quixote affirmed so positively that they were armies, Sancho began to believe it, and said:

"Sir, what then must we do?"

"What?" replied Don Quixote—"favour and assist the weaker side! Thou must know, Sancho, that the army which marches towards us in front is led and commanded by the mighty emperor Alifanfaron, lord of the great island of Taprobana: this other, which marches behind us, is that of his enemy, the king of the Garamantes, Pentapolin of the naked arm—for he always enters into battle with his right arm bare."

"But why do these two princes bear one another so much ill-will?" demanded Sancho.

"They hate one another," answered Don Quixote, "because this Alifanfaron is a furious pagan, in love with Pentapolin's daughter, who is a most beautiful and superlatively graceful lady, and also a Christian; but her father will not give her in marriage to the pagan king, unless he will first renounce the religion of his false prophet Mahomet, and turn Christian."

"By my beard," said Sancho, "Pentapolin is in the right; and I am resolved to assist him to the utmost of my power."

"Therein thou wilt do thy duty, Sancho," said Don Quixote: "for in order to engage in such contests it is not necessary to be dubbed a knight. But listen with attention whilst I give thee an account of the principal knights in the two approaching armies; and, that thou mayest observe them the better, let us retire to that rising ground, whence both armies may be distinctly seen." They did so, and placed themselves for that purpose on a hillock, from which the two flocks which Don Quixote mistook for armies might easily have been discerned, had not the view been obstructed by the clouds of dust. Seeing, however, in his imagination what did not exist, he began with a loud voice, naming sundry knights of each squadron, as his fancy dictated, and giving to each their arms, colours, devices, and mottoes.

Good heaven, how many provinces did he name! how many nations did he enumerate! giving to each, with wonderful readiness, its peculiar attributes. Sancho Panza stood confounded at his discourse, without speaking a word; and now and then he turned his head about, to see whether he could discover the knights and giants his master named. But seeing none, he said, "Sir, the deuce a man, or giant, or knight, of all you have named, can I see anywhere; perhaps all may be enchantment, like last night's goblins."

"How sayest thou, Sancho?" answered Don Quixote. "Hearest thou not the neighing of the steeds, the sound of the trumpets, and the rattling of the drums?"

"The devil a thing I can hear," answered Sancho, "but the bleating of sheep and lambs:" and so it was; for now the two flocks were come very near them.

"Thy fears, Sancho," said Don Quixote, "prevent thee from hearing or seeing aright; for one effect of fear is to disturb the senses, if thou art so much afraid, retire and leave me alone; for with my single arm I shall insure victory to that side which I favour with my assistance:" then clapping spurs to Rozinante, and setting his lance in rest, he darted down the hillock like lightning.

Sancho cried out to him, "Hold, Señor Don Quixote, come back! As God shall save me, they are lambs and sheep you are going to encounter! Pray come back. Woe to the father that begot me! What madness is this? Look; there is neither giant nor knight, nor cats, nor arms, nor shields quartered nor entire, nor true azures nor bedevilled; sinner that I am! what are you doing?"

Notwithstanding all this, Don Quixote turned not again, but still went on, crying aloud, "Ho! knights, you that follow and fight under the banner of the valiant Emperor Pentapolin of the Naked Arm, follow me all, and you shall see with how much ease I revenge him on his enemy Alifanfaron of Taprobana."

With these words, he rushed into the midst of the squadron of sheep, and began to attack them with his lance as courageously

"Where art thou, proud Alifamfaron?
where art thou?"

W.H.Robinson

and intrepidly as if in good earnest he was engaging his mortal enemies. The shepherds and herdsmen who came with the flocks called out to him to desist: but, seeing it was to no purpose, they unbuckled their slings, and began to salute his ears with a shower of stones. Don Quixote cared not for the stones; but, galloping about on all sides, cried out, "Where art thou, proud Alifanfaron? Present thyself before me: I am a single knight, desirous to prove thy valour hand to hand, and to punish thee with the loss of life, for the wrong thou dost to the valiant, Pentapolin Garamanta."

At that instant a large stone struck him with such violence on the side, that it buried a couple of ribs in his body; insomuch that he believed himself either slain or sorely wounded; and therefore, remembering his balsam, he pulled out the cruse, and applying it to his mouth, began to swallow some of the liquor; but before he could take what he thought sufficient, another stone hit him full on the hand, and dashed the cruse to pieces: carrying off three or four of his teeth by the way, and grievously bruising two of his fingers. Such was the first blow, and such the second, that the poor knight fell from his horse to the ground. The shepherds ran to him, and verily believed they had killed him: whereupon in all haste they collected their flock, took up their dead, which were about seven, and marched off without farther inquiry.

All this while Sancho stood upon the hillock, beholding his master's extravagancies; tearing his beard, and cursing the unfortunate hour and moment that ever he knew him. But seeing him fallen to the ground, and the shepherds gone off, he descended from the hillock, and, running to him, found him in a very ill plight, though not quite bereaved of sense: and said to him:

"Did I not beg you, Señor Don Quixote, to come back; for those you went to attack were a flock of sheep, and not an army of men?"

"How easily," replied Don Quixote, "can that thief of an enchanter, my enemy, transform things or make them invisible! Thou must know, Sancho, that it is a very easy matter for such men to give things what semblance they please; and this malignant persecutor of mine, envious of the glory that he saw I should acquire in this battle, has transformed the hostile squadrons into flocks of sheep. However, do one thing, Sancho, for my sake, to undeceive thyself and see the truth of what I tell thee: follow them a little way and you will see they will become men, proper and tall as I described them at first. But do not go now; for I want thy assistance; and come and see how many of my teeth are deficient; for it seems to me that I have not one left in my head." Sancho ran to his ass, to take something out of his wallets for his master; but not finding them, he was very near running distracted. He cursed himself again and again, and resolved in his mind to leave his master, and return home, although he should lose his wages for the time past, and his hopes of the promised island.

Don Quixote now raised himself up, and, placing his left hand on his mouth, to prevent the remainder of his teeth from falling out, with the other he laid hold on Rozinante's bridle, who had not stirred from his master's side, such was his fidelity, and went towards his squire, who stood leaning with his breast upon the ass, and his cheek reclining upon his hand, in the posture of a man overwhelmed with thought. Don Quixote seeing him thus, and to all appearance so melancholy, said to him:

"Know, Sancho, that all these storms that we have encountered are signs that the weather will soon clear up, and things will go smoothly. It is impossible that either evil or good should be durable; and hence it follows that, the evil having lasted long, the good cannot be far off. So do not afflict thyself for the mischances that befall me, since thou hast no share in them."

"How no share in them?" answered Sancho: "peradventure he they tossed in a blanket yesterday was not my father's son; and the wallets I have lost to-day, with all my moveables, belong to somebody else?"

"What, are the wallets lost?" quoth Don Quixote.

"Yes, they are," answered Sancho.

"Then we have nothing to eat to-day," replied Don Quixote.

"It would be so," answered Sancho, "if those fields did not produce those herbs which your worship says you know, and with which unlucky knights-errant like your worship are used to supply such wants."

"Nevertheless," said Don Quixote, "at this time I would rather have a slice of bread and a couple of heads of salt pilchards than all the herbs described by Dioscorides, though commented upon by Doctor Laguna * himself. But, good Sancho, get upon thy ass, and follow me ; for God, who provides for all, will not desert us ; more especially, being engaged, as we are, in His service."

Sancho did so, and proceeded in a direction in which he thought it probable they might find a lodging, without going out of the high-road, which in that part was much frequented. As they slowly pursued their way, for the pain of Don Quixote's jaws gave him no ease, nor inclination to make haste, Sancho, wishing to amuse and divert him, began to converse.

CHAPTER XIII

THE ADVENTURES OF THE DEAD BODY

WHILE Sancho and his master were discoursing, night overtook them. They were still in the high-road, without having found any place of reception ; and the worst of it was they were famished with hunger, for with their wallets they had lost their whole larder of provisions. To complete their misfortunes an adventure now befell them which was to have important consequences. The night came on rather dark ; notwithstanding which they proceeded : as Sancho hoped that, being on the king's highway, they might very probably find an inn within a league or two. Thus situated, the night dark, the squire hungry, and the master well disposed to eat, they saw, advancing towards them, on the same road, a great number of lights, resembling so many moving stars. Sancho stood aghast at the sight of them, nor was Don Quixote unmoved. The one checked his ass and the other his horse, and both stood looking before them with eager attention. They perceived that the lights were advancing

* Andres de Laguna, born at Segovia, and physician to Pope Julio III.

towards them, and that as they approached nearer they appeared larger. Sancho trembled like quicksilver at the sight, and Don Quixote's hair bristled upon his head : but, somewhat recovering himself, he exclaimed :

"Sancho, this must be a most perilous adventure, wherein it will be necessary for me to exert my whole might and valour."

"Woe is me !" answered Sancho ; "should this prove to be an adventure of goblins, as indeed it seems to be, where shall I find ribs to endure ?"

"Whatsoever phantoms they may be," said Don Quixote, " I will not suffer them to touch a thread of thy garment : for if they sported with thee before, it was because I could not get over the wall : but we are now upon even ground, where I can brandish my sword at pleasure."

"But, if they should enchant and benumb you, as they did then," quoth Sancho, "what matters it whether we are in the open field or not ?"

"Notwithstanding that," replied Don Quixote, "I beseech thee, Sancho, to be of good courage ; for experience shall give thee sufficient proof of mine."

"I will, if it please God," answered Sancho ; and, retiring a little on one side of the road, and again endeavouring to discover what those walking lights might be, they soon after perceived a great many persons clothed in white. This dreadful spectacle completely annihilated the courage of Sancho, whose teeth began to chatter, as if seized with a quartan ague ; and his trembling and chattering increased as more of it appeared in view : for now they discovered about twenty persons in white robes, all on horseback, with lighted torches in their hands ; behind them came a litter covered with black, which was followed by six persons in deep mourning ; the mules on which they were mounted being covered likewise with black down to their heels ; for that they were mules, and not horses, was evident by the slowness of their pace. Those robed in white were muttering to themselves in a low and plaintive tone.

This strange vision, at such an hour, and in a place so unin-habited might well strike terror into Sancho's heart, and even into that of his master ; and so it would have done had he been any other than Don Quixote. As for Sancho, his whole stock of courage was now exhausted. But it was otherwise with his master, whose lively imagination instantly suggested to him that this must be truly a chivalrous adventure. He conceived that the litter was a bier, whereon was carried some knight sorely wounded, or slain, whose revenge was reserved for him alone: he, therefore, without delay couched his spear, seated himself firm in his saddle, and with grace and spirit advanced into the middle of the road by which the procession must pass ; and, when they were near, he raised his voice, and said :

"Ho ! knights, whoever ye are, halt, and give me an account to whom ye belong ; whence ye come, whither ye are going, and what it is ye carry upon that bier ; for in all appearance either ye have done some injury to others, or others to you ; and it is necessary that I be informed of it, either to chastise ye for the evil ye have done, or to revenge ye of wrongs sustained."

"We are in haste," answered one in the procession ; "the inn is a great way off ; and we cannot stay to give so long an account as you require :" then, spurring his mule, he passed forward. Don Quixote highly resenting this answer, laid hold of his bridle, and said :

"Stand, and with more civility give me the account I demand ; otherwise I challenge ye all to battle." The mule was timid, and started so much, upon his touching the bridle, that, rising on her hind legs, she threw her rider over the crupper to the ground. A lacquey that came on foot, seeing the man in white fall, began to revile Don Quixote, whose choler being now raised, he couched his spear, and, immediately attacking one of the mourners, laid him on the ground grievously wounded ; then turning about to the rest, it was worth seeing with what agility he attacked and defeated them ; and it seemed as if wings at that instant had sprung on Rozinante—so lightly and swiftly he moved ! All the white-robed people, being timorous and unarmed, soon quitted the skirmish, and ran over the plain with their lighted torches, looking like so many masqueraders on a carnival or festival night. The mourners were so wrapped up and muffled in their long robes, that they could make no exertion : so that Don Quixote, with entire safety, assailed them all, and, sorely against their will, obliged them to quit the field ; for they thought him no man, but the devil from hell broke loose upon them to seize the dead body they were conveying in the litter.

All this Sancho beheld with admiration at his master's intrepidity, and said to himself, "This master of mine is certainly as valiant and magnanimous as he pretends to be." A burning torch lay upon the ground, near the first whom the mule had overthrown, by the light of which Don Quixote espied him, and going up to him, placed the point of his spear to his throat, commanding him to surrender, on pain of death. To which the fallen man answered:

"I am surrendered enough already, since I cannot stir; for one of my legs is broken. I beseech you, sir, if you are a Christian gentleman, do not kill me: you would commit a great sacrilege; for I am a licentiate, and have taken the lesser orders."

"What the mischief, then," said Don Quixote, "brought you hither, being an ecclesiastic?"

"What, sir," replied the fallen man, "but my evil fortune?"

"All things," answered Don Quixote, "do not fall out the same way: the mischief, master bachelor, was occasioned by your coming, as you did, by night, arrayed in those surplices, with lighted torches, chanting, and clad in doleful weeds, so that you really resembled something evil and of the other world. I was therefore bound to perform my duty as a knight-errant, by attacking you: which I certainly should have done although you had really been, as I imagined, devils from hell."

"Since my fate ordained it so," said the bachelor, "I beseech you, Señor Knight-errant, who have done me such arrant mischief, to help me to get from under this mule, for my leg is held fast between the stirrup and the saddle."

"I might have continued talking until to-morrow," said Don Quixote; "why did you delay acquainting me with your embarrassment?" He then called out to Sancho Panza to assist: but he did not choose to obey, being employed in ransacking a sumpter-mule, which those pious men had brought with them, well stored with eatables. Sancho made a bag of his cloak, and having crammed into it as much as it would hold, he loaded his beast; after which he attended to his master's call, and helped to disengage the bachelor from the oppression of his mule; and, having mounted him and given him the torch, Don Quixote bade him follow the track of his companions, and beg their pardon, in his name, for the injury which he could not avoid doing them; Sancho likewise said:

"If perchance those gentlemen would know who is the champion that routed them, it is the famous Don Quixote de la Mancha, otherwise called 'the Knight of the Sorrowful Figure.'"

The bachelor being gone, Don Quixote asked Sancho what induced him to call him "the Knight of the Sorrowful Figure," at that time more than at any other.

"I will tell you," answered Sancho: "it is because I have been viewing you by the light of the torch, which that unfortunate man carried; and, in truth, your worship at present very nearly makes the most woeful figure I have ever seen; which must be owing, I suppose, either to the fatigue of this combat, or the want of your teeth."

The bachelor having departed, as hath been said, Don Quixote wished to examine whether the corpse in the hearse consisted only of bones or not; but Sancho would not consent, saying, "Sir, your worship has finished this perilous adventure at less expense than any I have seen; and though these folks are conquered and defeated, they may chance to reflect that they were beaten by one man, and, being ashamed thereat, may recover themselves, and return in quest of us, and then we may have enough to do. The ass is properly furnished; the mountain is near; hunger presses, and we have nothing to do but decently to march off; and, as the saying is, 'To the grave with the dead, and the living to the bread;'" and, driving on his ass before him, he intreated his master to follow; who, thinking Sancho in the right, followed without replying. They had not gone far between two hills, when they found themselves in a retired and spacious valley, where they alighted. Sancho disburdened his beast; and, extended on the green grass, with hunger for sauce, they despatched their breakfast, dinner, afternoon's luncheon, and supper, all at once: regaling their palates with more than one cold mess, which the ecclesiastics who attended the deceased (such gentlemen seldom failing in a provident attention to themselves) had brought with them on the sumpter-mule. But there was another misfortune, which Sancho accounted the worst of all; namely, they had no wine, nor even water, to drink ; and were, moreover, parched with thirst. Sancho, however, perceiving the meadow they were in to be covered with green and fresh grass, said :

CHAPTER XIV

THE ADVENTURE OF THE FULLING MILLS

" It is impossible, sir, but there must be some fountain or brook near, to make these herbs so fresh, and therefore, if we go a little farther on, we may meet with something to quench the terrible thirst that afflicts us, and which is more painful than hunger itself." Don Quixote approved the counsel, and, taking Rozinante by the bridle, and Sancho his ass by the halter (after he had placed upon him the relics of the supper), they began to march forward through the meadow, feeling their way ; for the night was so dark, they could see nothing.

But they had not gone two hundred paces when a great noise of water reached their ears, like that of some mighty cascade pouring down from a vast and steep rock. The sound rejoiced them exceedingly, and, stopping to listen whence it came, they heard on a sudden another dreadful noise, which abated the pleasure occasioned by that of the water ; especially in Sancho, who was naturally faint-hearted. I say they heard a dreadful din of irons or rattling chains, accompanied with mighty strokes repeated in regular time and measure ; which, together with the furious noise of the water, would have struck terror into any other heart but that of Don Quixote. The night, as we have before said, was dark ; and they chanced to enter a grove of tall trees, whose leaves, agitated by the breeze, caused a kind of rustling noise, not loud, though fearful ; so that the solitude, the situation, the darkness, and the sound of rushing water, with the agitated leaves, all concurred to produce surprise and horror, especially when they found that neither the blows ceased, nor the wind slept, nor the morning approached ; and in addition to all this was their total ignorance of the place where they were in. But Don Quixote, supported by his intrepid heart, leaped upon Rozinante, and bracing on his buckler, brandished his spear, and said:

"Friend Sancho, know that, by the will of Heaven, I was born in this Age of Iron to revive in it that of Gold, or, as it is usually termed, 'the Golden Age.' I am he for whom dangers, great exploits, valorous achievements, are reserved: I am he, I say again, who am destined to revive the order of the Round Table; that of the "Twelve Peers of France" and the "Nine Worthies." My heart already bounds within my breast with eager desire to encounter this adventure, however difficult it may appear. Therefore tighten Rozinante's girth, and God be with thee! Stay for me here three days, and no more: if I return not in that time, thou mayest go back to our village; and thence, to oblige me, repair to Toboso, and inform my incomparable lady Dulcinea that her enthralled knight died in attempting things that might have made him worthy to be styled hers."

When Sancho heard these words of his master, he dissolved into tears, and said:

"Sir, I cannot think why your worship should encounter this fearful adventure. It is now night, and nobody sees us. We may easily turn aside, and get out of danger, though we should not drink these three days; and, being unseen, we cannot be taxed with cowardice. Besides, sir, think of me. I left my country, and forsook my wife and children, to follow and serve your worship, believing I should be the better and not the worse for it: but, as covetousness burst the bag, so hath it rent my hopes; for when they were most alive, and I was just expecting to obtain that cursed and unlucky island, which you have so often promised me, I find myself, in lieu thereof, ready to be abandoned by your worship in a place remote from everything human. For Heaven's sake, dear sir, do not be so cruel to me: and if your worship will not wholly give up this enterprise, at least defer it till daybreak, which, by what I learned when a shepherd, cannot be above three hours; for the muzzle of the north-bear * is at the top of the head, and makes midnight in the line of the left arm."

"How canst thou, Sancho," said Don Quixote, "see where

* Literally, "the mouth of the hunting horn, or cornet." So the "Ursa Minor" is called from a fancied configuration of the stars of that constellation.

this line is made, or where this muzzle or top of the head may be, since the night is so dark, that not a star appears in the whole sky?"

"True," said Sancho; "but fear has many eyes, and sees things beneath the earth, much more above the sky; it does not want much of daybreak."

"Want what it may," answered Don Quixote, "it shall never be said of me, now nor at any time, that tears or entreaties could dissuade me from performing the duty of a knight! All thou hast to do is to girth Rozinante well, and remain here: for I will quickly return alive or dead."

Sancho, now seeing his master's final resolution, and how little his tears, prayers, and counsel availed, determined to have recourse to stratagem, and compel him, if possible, to wait until day; therefore, while he was tightening the horse's girths, softly and unperceived, with his halter he tied Rozinante's hinder feet together, so that when Don Quixote would fain have departed, the horse could move only by jumps. Sancho, perceiving the success of his contrivance, said:

"Ah, sir! behold how Heaven, moved by my tears and prayers, has ordained that Rozinante should be unable to stir; and if you will obstinately persist to spur him, you will but provoke fortune, and, as they say, 'kick against the pricks.'"

This made Don Quixote quite desperate, but the more he spurred his horse, the less he could move him; he therefore thought it best to be quiet, and wait until day appeared, or until Rozinante could proceed, never suspecting the artifice of Sancho, whom he thus addressed, "Since so it is, Sancho, that Rozinante cannot move, I consent to wait until the dawn smiles, although I weep in the interval."

"You need not weep," answered Sancho, "for I will entertain you until day by telling you stories, if you had not rather alight and compose yourself to sleep a little upon the green grass, as knights-errant are wont to do, so that you may be less weary when the day and hour comes for engaging in that terrible adventure you wait for."

"To whom dost thou talk of alighting or sleeping?" said Don Quixote: "am I one of those knights who take repose in time of danger? Sleep thou, who wert born to sleep, or do what thou wilt: I shall act as becomes my profession."

" Pray, good sir, be not angry," answered Sancho, " I did not mean to offend you : " and, coming close to him, he laid hold of the saddle before and behind, and thus stood embracing his master's left thigh, without daring to stir from him a finger's breadth, so much was he afraid of the blows which still continued to sound in regular succession.

In this position they passed the night ; and when Sancho perceived the dawn of morning, with much caution he unbound Rozinante, who, on being set at liberty, though naturally not over mettlesome, seemed to feel himself alive, and began to paw the ground ; but as for curveting (begging his pardon) he knew nothing about it. Don Quixote, perceiving that Rozinante began to be active, took it for a good omen, and a signal that he should forthwith attempt the tremendous adventure. The dawn now making the surrounding objects visible, Don Quixote perceived he was beneath some tall chestnut-trees, which afforded a gloomy shade : but the cause of that striking, which yet continued, he was unable to discover : therefore, without further delay, he made Rozinante feel the spur, and again taking leave of Sancho, commanded him to wait there three days at the farthest, as he had said before, and that if he returned not by that time, he might conclude that it was God's will that he should end his days in that perilous adventure. He again also repeated the message Sancho was to carry to the lady Dulcinea ; and as to what concerned the reward of his service, he told him that he need be under no concern, since, before his departure from his village, he had made his will, wherein he would find himself satisfied regarding his wages, in proportion to the time he had served ; but, if God should bring him off safe and sound from the impending danger, he might reckon himself infallibly secure of the promised island. Don Quixote advanced towards the place whence the noise of the water and of the strokes seemed to proceed.

Sancho followed him on foot, leading his ass—that constant companion of his fortunes, good or bad. And having proceeded some distance among those shady chestnut-trees, they came to a little green meadow, bounded by some steep rocks, down which a mighty torrent precipitated itself. At the foot of these rocks were several wretched huts, that seemed more like ruins than habitable dwellings; and it was from them, they now discovered, that the fearful din proceeded. Rozinante was startled at the noise, but Don Quixote, after quieting him, went slowly on towards the huts, recommending himself devoutly to Heaven and to his lady, beseeching them to favour him in so terrific an enterprise as this now appeared to be. Sancho kept close to his side, stretching out his neck, and looking between Rozinante's legs, to see if he could discover the cause of his terrors.

In this manner they advanced about a hundred yards farther, when, on doubling a point, the true and undoubted cause of that horrible noise which had held them all night in such suspense, appeared plain and exposed to view. It was (kind reader, take it not in dudgeon!) six fulling-hammers, whose alternate strokes produced that hideous sound. Don Quixote, on beholding them, was struck dumb, and was in the utmost confusion. Sancho looked at him, and saw he hung down his head upon his breast, with manifest indications of being abashed. Don Quixote looked also at Sancho, and seeing his cheeks swollen, and his mouth betraying evident signs of being ready to explode, notwithstanding his vexation, he could not forbear laughing himself at the sight of his squire, who, thus encouraged by his master, broke forth in so violent a manner that he was forced to apply both hands to his sides, to secure himself from bursting. Four times he ceased, and four times the fit returned, with the same impetuosity as at first.

Upon which, Don Quixote now wished him at the devil, especially when he heard him say, ironically, "Thou must know, friend Sancho, that I was born, by the will of Heaven, in this our Age of Iron, to revive in it the Golden, or that of Gold. I am he for whom are reserved dangers, great exploits, and valorous achievements!" And so he went on, repeating many of the expressions which Don Quixote used upon first hearing those dreadful sounds. Don Quixote, perceiving that Sancho made a jest of him, was so enraged that he lifted up his lance, and discharged two such blows on him that, had he received them on his head, instead of his shoulders, the knight would have acquitted himself of the payment of his wages, unless it were to his heirs.

Sancho, finding he paid so dearly for his jokes, and fearing lest his master should proceed farther, with much humility said : " Pray, sir, be pacified ; as heaven is my hope, I did but jest."

" Though thou mayest jest, I do not," answered Don Quixote. "Come hither, merry sir, what thinkest thou ? Suppose these mill-hammers had really been some perilous adventure, have I not given proof of the courage requisite to undertake and achieve it ? But that thou mayest abstain from talking too much with me henceforth, I apprise thee of one thing, that in all the books of chivalry I ever read, numerous as they are, I recollect no example of a squire who conversed so much with his master as thou dost with thine. And really I account it a great fault both in thee and in myself : in thee, because thou payest me so little respect ; in me, that I do not make myself respected more. The favours and benefits I promised thee will come in due time ; and if they do not come, the wages, at least, thou wilt not lose."

CHAPTER XV

THE GRAND ADVENTURE AND RICH PRIZE OF MAMBRINO'S HELMET

ABOUT this time it began to rain a little, and Sancho proposed entering the fulling-mill ; but Don Quixote had conceived such an abhorrence of them for the late jest, that he would by no means go in : turning, therefore, to the right hand, they struck into another road, like that they had travelled through the day before. Soon after, Don Quixote discovered a man on horseback, who had on his head something which glittered as if it had been of gold ; and scarcely had he seen it than, turning to Sancho, he said :

" I am of opinion, Sancho, there is no proverb but what is true, because they are all sentences drawn from experience itself, the mother of all the sciences ; especially that which says, 'Where one door is shut another is opened.' This I say because, if I mistake not, there comes one towards us who carries on his head Mambrino's helmet, concerning which thou mayest remember I swore the oath."

"Take care, sir, what you say, and more what you do," said Sancho; "for I would not wish for other fulling-mills, to finish the milling and mashing of our senses."

"The devil take thee!" replied Don Quixote: "what has a helmet to do with fulling-mills?"

"I know not," answered Sancho; "but in faith, if I might talk as much as I used to do, perhaps I could give such reasons that your worship would see you are mistaken in what you say."

"How can I be mistaken in what I say, scrupulous traitor?" said Don Quixote. "Tell me, seest thou not yon knight coming towards us on a dapple-grey steed, with a helmet of gold on his head?"

"What I see and perceive," answered Sancho, "is only a man on a grey ass like mine, with something on his head that glitters."

"Why, that is Mambrino's helmet," said Don Quixote; "retire, and leave me alone to deal with him, and thou shalt see how, in order to save time, I shall conclude this adventure without speaking a word, and the helmet I have so much desired will remain my own."

"I shall take care to get out of the way," replied Sancho; "but Heaven grant, I say again, it may not prove another fulling-mill adventure."

"I have already told thee, Sancho, not to mention those fulling-mills, nor even think of them," said Don Quixote: "if thou dost—I say no more, but I vow to mill thy soul for thee!" Sancho held his peace, fearing lest his master should perform his vow, which had struck him all of a heap.

Now the truth of the matter, concerning the helmet, the steed, and the knight which Don Quixote saw, was this. There were two villages in that neighbourhood, one of them so small that it had neither shop nor barber, but the other adjoining to it had both; therefore the barber of the larger served also the less, wherein one customer now wanted to be let blood, and another to be shaved. To perform these offices the barber was now on his way, carrying with him his brass basin. It so happened that while he was on the road it began to rain, and to save his hat, which was a new one, he clapped the basin on his head, which being lately scoured was seen glittering at the distance of half a league; moreover, he rode on a grey ass, as Sancho had affirmed. Thus Don Quixote took the barber for a knight, his ass for a dapple-grey steed, and his basin for a golden helmet; for whatever he saw was quickly adapted to his extravagancies. When the poor knight drew near, without staying to reason the case with him, he couched his lance, intending to run him through and through without more ado : but, when close upon him, without checking the fury of his career, he cried out :

"Defend thyself, caitiff ! or instantly surrender what is justly my due." The barber, so unexpectedly seeing this phantom advancing upon him, had no other way to avoid the thrust of the lance than to slip down from the ass : and no sooner had he touched the ground than, leaping up nimbler than a roebuck, he scampered over the plain with such speed that the wind could not overtake him. The basin he left on the ground; with which Don Quixote was satisfied, observing that the pagan had acted discreetly, and in imitation of the beaver, which, when closely pursued by the hunters, tears off with his teeth its tail, which it knows by instinct to be the object of pursuit. He ordered Sancho to take up the helmet; who, holding it in his hand, said :

"Before Heaven, the basin is a special one, and is well worth a piece of eight, if it is worth a farthing." He then gave it to his master, who immediately placed it on his head, turning it round in search of the vizor ; but not finding it, he said :

"Doubtless the pagan for whom this famous helmet was originally forged must have had a prodigious head—the worst of it is that one half the helmet is wanting." When Sancho heard the basin called a helmet, he could not forbear laughing ; which, however, he instantly checked on recollecting his master's late choler.

"What dost thou laugh at, Sancho ?" said Don Quixote.

"I am laughing," answered he, "to think what a huge head the pagan had who owned that helmet, which is for all the world just like a barber's basin."

"Knowest thou, Sancho, what I conceive to be the case ?

" He scampered over the plain with such speed."

This famous piece, this enchanted helmet, by some strange accident must have fallen into the possession of one who, ignorant of its true value as a helmet, and seeing it to be of the purest gold, hath inconsiderately melted down the one-half for lucre's sake, and of the other half made this, which, as thou sayest, doth indeed look like a barber's basin : but to me, who know what it really is, its transformation is of no importance, for I will have it so repaired in the first town where there is a smith, that it shall not be surpassed nor even equalled by that which the god of smiths himself made and forged for the god of battles. In the mean time I will wear it as I best can, for something is better than nothing; and it will be sufficient to defend me from stones."

"It will so," said Sancho, "if they do not throw them with slings, as they did in the battle of the two armies, when they crossed your worship's chaps, and broke the cruse of that most blessed liquor which made me vomit up my inside."

"The loss of that balsam gives me no concern," said Don Quixote; "for knowest thou, Sancho, I have the recipe by heart."

"So have I, too," answered Sancho; "but if ever I make or try it again while I live, may I be fixed and rooted to this place. Besides, I do not intend to put myself in the way of requiring it; for I mean to keep myself, with all my five senses, from being wounded, or from wounding anybody. As to being tossed again in a blanket, I say nothing; for it is difficult to prevent such mishaps; and if they do come, there is nothing to be done but wink, hold one's breath, and submit to go whither fortune and the blanket shall please. But tell me, sir, what shall we do with this dapple-grey steed which looks so much like a grey ass, and which that caitiff whom your worship overthrew has left behind here, to shift for itself? for, by his scouring off so hastily, he does not think of ever returning for him; and, by my beard, the beast is a special one."

"It is not my custom," said Don Quixote, "to plunder those whom I overcome, nor is it the usage of chivalry to take from the vanquished their horses, and leave them on foot, unless the victor had lost his own in the conflict; in such a case it is lawful to take that of the enemy, as fairly won in battle. Therefore,

Sancho, leave this horse, or ass, or whatever thou wilt have it to be; for when we are gone, his owner will return for him."

"God knows whether it were best for me to take him," replied Sancho, "or at least to exchange him for mine, which, methinks, is not so good. Verily, the laws of chivalry are very strict if they do not even allow the swopping of one ass for another; but I would fain know whether I might exchange furniture, if I were so inclined."

"I am not very clear as to that point," answered Don Quixote; "and, being a doubtful case, until better information can be had, I think thou mayest make the exchange, if thou art in extreme want of them."

"So extreme," replied Sancho, "that I could not want them more if they were for my own proper person." Thus authorized, he proceeded to an exchange of caparisons, and made his own beast three parts in four the better for his new furniture.

This done, they breakfasted on the remains of the plunder from the sumpter-mule, and drank of the water belonging to the fulling-mills, but without turning their faces towards them—such was the abhorrence in which they were held, because of the effect they had produced. Being thus refreshed and comforted, both in body and mind, they mounted; and, without determining upon what road to follow, according to the custom of knights-errant, they went on as Rozinante's will directed, which was a guide to his master and also to Dapple, who always followed, in love and good-fellowship, wherever he led the way. They soon, however, turned into the great road, which they followed at a venture, without forming any plan.

CHAPTER XVI

THE ADVENTURE OF THE GALLEY-SLAVES

As our travellers were slowly pushing on, Don Quixote raised his eyes, and saw approaching in the same road about a dozen men on foot, strung like beads, by the necks, in a great iron chain, and all handcuffed. There came also with them two men on horseback, and two on foot; those on horseback were armed with firelocks, and those on foot with pikes and swords. As soon as Sancho Panza saw them, he said, "This is a chain of galley-slaves, persons forced by the king to serve in the galleys."

"How! forced, do you say?" quoth Don Quixote: "is it possible the king should force anybody?"

"I said not so," answered Sancho; "but that they were persons who for their crimes are condemned by law to the galleys, where they are forced to serve the king."

"In truth, then," replied Don Quixote, "these people are conveyed by force, and not voluntarily? Here the execution of my office as a knight-errant begins, which is to defeat violence, and to succour and relieve the wretched."

"Consider, sir," quoth Sancho, "that justice—which is the king himself—does no violence to such persons: he only punishes them for their crimes."

By this time the chain of galley-slaves had reached them, and Don Quixote in most courteous terms desired the guard to be pleased to inform him of the cause or causes for which they conducted those persons in that manner. One of the guards on horseback answered, "Draw near, sir, and make your inquiry of themselves; they may inform you, if they please; and no doubt they will, for they are such as take a pleasure in acting and relating rogueries." With this leave, which Don Quixote would have taken, had it not been given, he went up to them, and demanded of the first for what offence he marched in such evil plight? He answered that it was for being in love.

"For that alone?" replied Don Quixote; "if people are sent to the galleys for being in love, I might long since have been rowing in them myself."

"It was not such love as your worship imagines," said the galley-slave. "Mine was a strong affection for a basket of fine linen, which I embraced so closely, that, if justice had not taken it from me by force, I should not have parted with it by my own good-will even to this present day. I was taken in the fact, so there was no necessity for the torture. The process was short; they accommodated my shoulders with a hundred lashes, and as a further kindness, have sent me for three years to the Gurapas (or the galleys) and there is an end of it."

Don Quixote put the same question to the second, who returned no answer, he was so melancholy and dejected; but the first answered for him, and said :

"This gentleman goes for being a canary-bird—I mean, for being a musician and a singer."

"How so ?" replied Don Quixote; "are men sent to the galleys for being musicians and singers ?"

"Yes, sir," replied the slave; "for there is nothing worse than to sing in an agony."

"Nay," said Don Quixote, "I have heard say, 'Who sings in grief, procures relief.'"

"This is the very reverse," said the slave; "for here, he who sings once, weeps all his life after."

"I do not understand that," said Don Quixote.

One of the guards said to him, "Señor cavalier, to sing in an agony means, in the cant of these rogues, to confess upon the rack. This offender was put to the torture, and confessed his crime, which was that of being a Quatrero, that is, a stealer of cattle; and because he confessed, he is sentenced for six years to the galleys, besides two hundred lashes he has already received on the shoulders. He is always pensive and sad, because all the other rogues abuse, vilify, flout, and despise him for confessing."

"And rightly so, I think," answered Don Quixote : who, passing on to the third, interrogated him as he had done the others. He answered very readily, and with much indifference.

"I am also going to their ladyships the Gurapas for five years, merely for want of ten ducats."

"I will give twenty with all my heart," said Don Quixote, "to redeem you from this misery."

"That," said the convict, "is like having money at sea, where, though dying with hunger, nothing can be bought with it. I say this, because if I had been possessed in time of those twenty ducats you now offer me, I would have so greased the clerk's pen and sharpened my advocate's wit, that I would have been this day upon the market-place of Zocodover, in Toledo, and not upon this road."

Don Quixote, having interrogated an old man who had been a

conjurer, and a student who had been a coiner, came at last to a man about thirty years of age, of a goodly aspect, only that his eyes had a bad squint. He was bound somewhat differently from the rest, for he had a chain to his leg, so long that it was fastened round his middle, and two collars about his neck, one of which was fastened to the chain, and the other, called a "keep-friend," or friend's foot, had two straight irons which came down from it to his waist, at the ends of which were fixed two manacles, wherein his hands were secured with a huge padlock; insomuch that he could neither lift his hands to his mouth, nor bend down his head to his hands. Don Quixote asked why this man was fettered so much more than the rest. The guard answered, because he alone had committed more crimes than all the rest together; and that he was so bold and desperate a villain that, although shackled in that manner, they were not secure of him, but were still afraid he would make his escape.

"What kind of villanies has he committed," said Don Quixote, "that have deserved no greater punishment than being sent to the galleys?"

"He goes for ten years," said the guard, "which is a kind of civil death. You need only to be told that this honest gentle-man is the famous Gines de Passamonte, *alias* Ginesillo de Parapilla."

"Fair and softly, Señor Commissary," interrupted the slave: "let us not now be spinning out names and surnames. Gines is my name, and not Ginesillo; and Passamonte is the name of my family, and not Parapilla, as you say. Let every one turn himself round, and look at home, and he will find enough to do."

"You seem to be an ingenious fellow," said Don Quixote.

"And an unfortunate one," answered Gines: "but mis-fortunes always persecute genius."

"Persecute villany," said the commissary.

"I have already desired you, Señor Commissary," answered Passamonte, "to go fair and softly; for your superiors did not give you that staff to misuse us poor wretches here, but to conduct us whither his Majesty commands. Now by the life of —— I say no more; but the spots which were contracted in the inn may perhaps one day come out in the bucking; and let every one hold his tongue, live well, and speak better. Now let us march on, for we have had enough of this."

The commissary lifted up his staff to strike Passamonte, in return for his threats; but Don Quixote interposed, and desired that he would not ill-treat him, since it was but fair that he who had his hands so tied up should have his tongue a little at liberty. Then turning about to the guard, he said, "Gentlemen guards, these poor men have committed no offence against you: let every one answer for his sins in the other world: there is a God in heaven who fails not to chastise the wicked, and to reward the good; neither doth it become honourable men to be the executioners of others, when they have no interest in the matter. I request this of you in a calm and gentle manner, that you would let them go, that I may have cause to thank you for your compliance; but, if you do it not willingly, this lance and this sword, with the vigour of my arm, shall compel you to it."

"This is pleasant fooling," answered the commissary. "An admirable conceit he has hit upon at last! He would have us let the king's prisoners go—as if we had authority to set them free, or he to command us to do it! Go on your way, Señor, and adjust the basin on your noddle, and do not go feeling about for three legs to a cat."

"You are a cat, and a rat, and a rascal to boot!" answered Don Quixote: and thereupon, with a word and a blow, he attacked him so suddenly, that, before the commissary could stand upon his defence, he threw him to the ground, much wounded with a thrust of the lance; and it happened, luckily for Don Quixote, that this was one of the two who carried firelocks. The rest of the guards were astonished and confounded at the unexpected encounter; but, recovering themselves, he on horseback drew his sword, and those on foot took their javelins, and advanced upon Don Quixote, who waited for them with much calmness; and doubtless it had gone ill with him if the galley-slaves had not seized the opportunity now offered to them of recovering their liberty, by breaking the chain by which they were linked together. The confusion was such that the guards, now endeavouring to prevent the slaves from getting loose, and now engaging with Don Quixote, did nothing to any purpose. Sancho, for his part, assisted in releasing Gines de Passamonte,

D

who was the first that leaped free and unfettered upon the plain ; and, attacking the fallen commissary, he took away his sword and his gun, which, by levelling first at one and then at another, without discharging it, he cleared the field of all the guards, who fled no less from Passamonte's gun than from the shower of stones which the slaves, now at liberty, poured upon them.

Sancho was much grieved at what had happened, from an apprehension that the fugitives would give notice of the fact to the Holy Brotherhood, who, upon ring of bell, would sally out in quest of the delinquents. These fears he communicated to his master, and begged of him to be gone immediately, and take shelter among the trees and rocks of the neighbouring mountain.

"It is well," said Don Quixote ; " but I know what is the first expedient to be done." Then, having called all the slaves together, who were in disorder, after having stripped the commissary to his buff, they gathered around him to know his pleasure ; when he thus addressed them : " To be grateful for benefits received is natural to persons well born ; and one of the sins which most offendeth God is ingratitude. This I say, gentlemen, because you already know, by manifest experience, the benefit you have received at my hands ; in return for which, it is my desire that, bearing with you this chain, which I have taken from your necks, you immediately go to the city of Toboso, and there present yourselves before the Lady Dulcinea del Toboso, and tell her that her Knight of the Sorrowful Figure sends you to present his service to her ; and recount to her every circumstance of this memorable adventure, to the point of restoring you to your wished-for liberty : this done, you may go wherever good fortune may lead you."

Gines de Passamonte answered for them all, and said, " What your worship commands us, noble sir, and our deliverer, is of all impossibilities the most impossible to be complied with : for we dare not be seen together on the road, but must go separate, each man by himself, and endeavour to hide ourselves in the very bowels of the earth from the Holy Brotherhood, who will doubtless be out in quest of us. What your worship may and ought to do is to change this service and duty to the Lady

Dulcinea del Toboso into a certain number of Ave Marias and Credos, which we will say for your worship's success; and this is what we may do, by day or by night, flying or reposing, in peace or in war; but to think that we will now return to our chains, and put ourselves on our way to Toboso, is to imagine it already night, whereas it is not yet ten o'clock in the morning: and to expect this from us is to expect pears from an elm-tree."

"I vow, then!" quoth Don Quixote, in a rage, "Don Ginesillo de Parapilla, or whatever you call yourself, that you alone shall go with your tail between your legs, and the whole chain upon your back!"

Passamonte, who was not over passive, seeing himself thus treated, and being aware that Don Quixote, from what he had just done, was not in his right senses, gave a signal to his comrades, upon which they all retired a few paces, and then began to rain such a shower of stones upon Don Quixote, that he could not contrive to cover himself with his buckler; and poor Rozinante cared no more for the spur than if he had been made of brass. Sancho got behind his ass, and thereby sheltered himself from the hailstorm that poured upon them both. Don Quixote could not screen himself sufficiently to avoid I know not how many stones that came against him with such force that they brought him to the ground; when the student instantly fell upon him, and, taking the basin from off his head, gave him three or four blows with it over the shoulders, and then struck it as often against the ground, whereby he almost broke it to pieces; they stripped him of a jacket he wore over his armour, and would have taken his trousers too, if the greaves had not hindered them. They took Sancho's cloak, leaving him stripped; and after dividing the spoils of the battle, they made the best of their way off, each taking a different course: more solicitous to escape the Holy Brotherhood, than to drag their chain to Toboso, and present themselves before the Lady Dulcinea.

The ass and Rozinante, Sancho and Don Quixote, remained by themselves: the ass hanging his head, and pensive, and now and then shaking his ears, thinking that the storm of stones was not yet over, and still whizzing about his head; Rozinante having been brought to the ground, lay stretched by his master's side; Sancho stripped, and troubled with apprehensions of the

Holy Brotherhood; and Don Quixote much chagrined at being so maltreated by those on whom he had conferred so great a benefit.

CHAPTER XVII

THE ADVENTURES WHICH BEFELL THE RENOWNED DON QUIXOTE IN THE SIERRA MORENA *

Don Quixote, finding himself thus ill-requited, said to his squire:

"Sancho, I have always heard it said that to do good to the vulgar is to throw water into the sea. Had I believed what you said to me, I might have prevented this trouble; but it is done— I must have patience, and henceforth take warning."

"Your worship will as much take warning," answered Sancho, "as I am a Turk: but since you say that, if you had believed me, the mischief would have been prevented, believe me now, and you will avoid what is still worse; for, let me tell you, there is no putting off the Holy Brotherhood with chivalries; they do not care two farthings for all the knights-errant in the world; and I fancy already that I hear their arrows whizzing about my ears."

"Thou art naturally a coward, Sancho," said Don Quixote: "but, that thou mayest not say that I am obstinate, and that I never do what thou advisest, I will for once take thy counsel, though thou must never say I ran away."

"Sir," answered Sancho, "retreating is not running away, nor is staying wisdom when the danger overbalances the hope; but get upon Rozinante if you can, if not I will assist you, and follow me; for my noddle tells me that for the present we have more need of heels than hands." Don Quixote mounted without replying a word more; and, Sancho leading the way upon his ass, they entered on one side of the Sierra Morena, which was near; and it was Sancho's intention to pass through it, and get out at Viso or Almodovar del Campo, and there hide themselves for some days among those craggy rocks in case the Holy Brother-

* A mountain or rather chain of mountains, dividing the kingdom of Castile from the province of Andalusia.

hood should come in search of them. He was encouraged to this, by finding that the provisions carried by his ass had escaped safe from the skirmish with the galley-slaves, which he looked upon as a miracle, considering what the slaves took away, and how narrowly they searched.

That night they got into the heart of the Sierra Morena, where Sancho thought it would be well to pass the remainder of the night, if not some days ; or at least as long as their provisions lasted. Accordingly there they took up their lodging, under the shelter of rocks overgrown with cork-trees. But destiny, which, according to the opinion of those who have not the light of the true faith, guides and disposes all things its own way, so ordered it that Gines de Passamonte, being justly afraid of the Holy Brotherhood, took it into his head to hide himself among those very mountains ; and in the very place where, by the same impulse, Don Quixote and Sancho Panza had taken refuge ; arriving just in time to distinguish who they were, although they had fallen asleep. Now, as the wicked are always ungrateful, and present convenience overbalances every consideration of the future, Gines, who had neither gratitude nor good-nature, resolved to steal Sancho Panza's ass ; not caring for Rozinante, as a thing neither pawnable nor saleable. Sancho Panza slept ; the varlet stole his ass ; and before dawn of day was too far off to be recovered.

Aurora issued forth, giving joy to the earth, but grief to Sancho Panza, who, when he missed his Dapple, began to utter the most doleful lamentations ! Don Quixote, on learning the cause of these lamentations, comforted Sancho in the best manner he could, and desired him to have patience, promising to give him a bill of exchange for three asses out of five which he had left at home. Sancho, comforted by this promise, wiped away his tears, moderated his sighs, and thanked his master for the kindness he showed him.

Don Quixote's heart gladdened upon entering among the mountains, being the kind of situation he thought likely to furnish those adventures he was in quest of. They recalled to his memory the marvellous events which had befallen knights-errant in such solitudes and deserts. He went on meditating on these things, and his mind was so absorbed in them that he thought of nothing else. Nor had Sancho any other concern, now that he thought himself out of danger, than to appease his hunger with what remained of the clerical spoils; and thus on he trudged after his master, appeasing his hunger while emptying the bag; and while so employed he would not have given two maravedis for the rarest adventure that could have happened.

While thus engaged, he raised his eyes, and observed that his master, who had stopped, was endeavouring with the point of his lance to raise something that lay upon the ground: upon which he hastened to assist him, if necessary, and came up to him just as he had turned over with his lance a saddle-cushion and a portmanteau fastened to it, half, or rather quite, rotten and torn, but so heavy that Sancho was scarcely able to lift it. His master ordered him to examine it. Sancho very readily obeyed, and although the portmanteau was secured with its chain and padlock, he could see through the chasms what it contained; which was, four fine holland shirts, and other linen, no less curious than clean; and, in a handkerchief, he found a quantity of gold crowns, which he no sooner spied than he exclaimed:

"Blessed be Heaven, which has presented us with one profitable adventure!" And, searching further, he found a little pocket-book, richly bound; which Don Quixote desired to have, bidding him take the money and keep it for himself. Sancho kissed his hands for the favour; and taking the linen out of the portmanteau, he put it in the provender-bag. All this was perceived by Don Quixote, who said:

"I am of opinion, Sancho (nor can it possibly be otherwise), that some traveller must have lost his way in these mountains, and fallen into the hands of robbers, who have killed him, and brought him to this remote part to bury him."

"It cannot be so," answered Sancho; "for had they been robbers, they would not have left this money here."

"Thou art in the right," said Don Quixote, "and I cannot conjecture what it should be: but stay, let us see whether this pocket-book has anything written in it that may lead to a discovery." He opened it, and the first thing he found was a rough copy of certain verses, which, being legible, he read aloud, that Sancho might hear.

Then, turning over other parts of the book, he found verses

and letters, some of which were legible, and some not; but the
purport was the same in all—their sole contents being reproaches,
lamentations, suspicions, desires, dislikings, favours and slights,
interspersed with rapturous praises and mournful complaints.
While Don Quixote was examining the book, Sancho examined
the portmanteau, without leaving a corner either in that or in
the saddle-cushion which he did not examine, scrutinise, and look
into, nor seam which he did not rip, nor lock of wool which he
did not pick—that nothing might be lost from want of diligence,
or through carelessness—such was the cupidity excited in him by
the discovery of this golden treasure, consisting of more than a
hundred crowns! And, although he could find no more, he
thought himself abundantly rewarded by those already in his
possession for the tossings in the blanket, the sickness caused by
the balsam, the benedictions of the pack-staves, the cuffs of the
carrier, the loss of the wallet, and the theft of his cloak; together
with all the hunger, thirst, and fatigue he had suffered in his
good master's service.

The Knight of the Sorrowful Figure was extremely desirous
to know who was the owner of the portmanteau; for he concluded, from the sonnet and the letter, by the money in gold,
and by the fineness of the linen, that it must doubtless belong to
some lover of condition, whom the disdain and ill-treatment of
his mistress had reduced to despair. But as no information could
be expected in that rugged and uninhabitable place, he had only
to proceed forward, taking whatever road Rozinante pleased (who
invariably gave preference to that which he found the most pass-
able), and still thinking that amongst the rocks he should
certainly meet with some strange adventure.

As he went onwards impressed with this idea, he espied, on
the top of a rising ground not far from him, a man springing from
rock to rock with extraordinary agility. He seemed to be almost
naked, his beard black and bushy, his hair long and tangled, his
legs and feet bare; he had on breeches of sad-coloured velvet, but
so ragged as scarcely to cover him: all which particulars, though
he passed swiftly by, were observed by the knight. He endeavoured, but in vain, to follow him; for it was not given to
Rozinante's feebleness to make way over those craggy places,
especially as he was naturally slow-footed and phlegmatic. Don

Quixote immediately conceived that this must be the owner of the saddle-cushion and portmanteau, and resolved therefore to go in search of him, even though it should prove a twelvemonth's labour, in that wild region. He immediately commanded Sancho to cut short over one side of the mountain, while he skirted the other; as they might possibly by this expedition find the man who had so suddenly vanished from their sight.

"I cannot do it," answered Sancho; "for the moment I offer to stir from your worship fear is upon me, assaulting me with a thousand kinds of terrors and apparitions; and let this serve to advertise you that henceforward I depart not a finger's breadth from your presence."

"Be it so," said he of the Sorrowful Figure; "and I am well pleased that thou shouldst rely upon my courage." Then he pricked Rozinante on, and Sancho followed; when, having gone round part of the mountain, they found a dead mule lying in a brook, saddled and bridled, and half-devoured by dogs and crows; which confirmed them in the opinion that he who fled from them was owner both of the mule and the bundle.

While they stood looking at the mule, they heard a whistle like that of a shepherd tending his flock; and presently, on their left appeared a number of goats, and behind them, higher up on the mountain, an old man, being the goatherd that kept them. Don Quixote called to him aloud, and beckoned him to come down to them. He as loudly answered, inquiring what had brought them to that desolate place, seldom or never trodden unless by the feet of goats, wolves, or other beasts that frequented those mountains? Sancho promised, in reply, that if he would come down, they would satisfy him in everything. The goatherd descended, and coming to the place where Don Quixote stood, he said:

"I suppose, gentlemen, you are looking at the dead mule? In truth, it has now lain there these six months. Pray tell me, have you met with his master hereabouts?"

"We have met with nothing," answered Don Quixote, "but a saddle-cushion and a small portmanteau, which we found not far hence."

"I found it, too," answered the goatherd, "but would by no means take it up, nor come near it, for fear of some mischief, and

"He came out to us with much gentleness,"

of being charged with theft: for the devil is subtle, and lays stumbling-blocks in our way, over which we fall without knowing how."

"So say I," answered Sancho; "for I also found it, and would not go within a stone's throw of it: there I left it, and there it may lie for me: for I will not have a dog with a bell."

"Tell me, honest man," said Don Quixote, "do you know who is the owner of these goods?"

"What I know," said the goatherd, "is that six months ago, more or less, there came to a shepherd's hut, about three leagues from this place, a genteel and comely youth, mounted on the very mule which lies dead there, and with the same saddle-cushion and portmanteau that you say you found and touched not. He inquired of us which part of these mountains was the most rude and unfrequented. We told him it was here where we now are. The youth then, I say, hearing our answer, turned about his mule and made towards the part we pointed out, leaving us all pleased with his goodly appearance, and wondering at his question and the haste he made to reach the mountain. From that time we saw him not again until some days after, when he issued out upon one of our shepherds, and, without saying a word, struck him and immediately fell upon our sumpter-ass, which he plundered of our bread and cheese, and then fled again to the rocks with wonderful swiftness.

"Some of us goatherds after this, sought for him nearly two days through the most intricate part of these mountains, and at last found him lying in the hollow of a large cork-tree. He came out to us with much gentleness, his garments torn, and his face so disfigured and scorched by the sun, that we should scarcely have known him, but that his clothes, ragged as they were, convinced us he was the person we were in search after. He saluted us courteously, and in few but civil words bade us not be surprised to see him in that condition, which was necessary in order to perform a certain penance enjoined him for his manifold sins. We entreated him to tell us who he was, but could get no more from him. We also desired him to inform us where he might be found: because when he stood in the need of food, without which he could not subsist, we would willingly bring some to him; and, if this did not please him, we begged that at least

he would come and ask for it, and not take it away from the
shepherds by force. He thanked us for our offers, begged pardon
for his past violence, and promised thenceforth to ask it for God's
sake, without molesting anybody. As to the place of his abode,
he said he had no other than that which chance presented him
wherever the night overtook him; and he ended his discourse
with so many tears, that we who heard him must have been very
stones not to have wept with him, considering what he was when
we first saw him, and what he now appeared : for, as I before
said, he was a very comely and graceful youth, and by his
courteous behaviour showed himself to be well-born ; which was
evident even to country-people like us.

"Suddenly he was silent, and, fixing his eyes on the ground he
remained in that posture for a long time, whilst we stood still in
suspense, waiting to see what would be the end of his trance : for
by his motionless position, and the furious look of his eyes, frown-
ing and biting his lips, we judged that his mad fit was coming
on ; and indeed our suspicions were quickly confirmed, for he
suddenly darted forward, and fell with great fury upon one that
stood next him, whom he bit and struck with so much violence
that, if we had not released him, he would have taken away his
life. In the midst of his rage he frequently called out, 'Ah,
traitor Fernando ! now shalt thou pay for the wrong thou hast
done me ; these hands shall tear out that heart, the dark dwelling
of deceit and villany !'

"We disengaged our companion from him at last, with no
small difficulty ; upon which he suddenly left us, and plunged
into a thicket so entangled with bushes and briars that it was impossible to follow him. By this we guessed that his madness
returned by fits, and that some person whose name is Fernando
must have done him some injury of so grievous a nature as to
reduce him to the wretched condition in which he appeared.
And in that we have since been confirmed, as he has frequently
come out into the road, sometimes begging food of the shepherds,
and at other times taking it from them by force : for when the
mad fit is upon him, though the shepherds offer it freely, he will
not take it without coming to blows ; but, when he is in his
senses, he asks it with courtesy and receives it with thanks, and
even with tears.

"This, gentlemen, is all I can tell you, in answer to your inquiry; by which you may understand that the owner of the goods you found is the same wretched person who passed you so quickly"—for Don Quixote had told him that he had seen a man leaping about the rocks.

Don Quixote was surprised at what he heard from the goatherd; and, being now still more desirous of knowing who the unfortunate madman was, he renewed his determination to search every part of the mountain, leaving neither corner nor cave unexplored until he should find him. But fortune managed better for him than he expected; for at that very instant the same youth appeared descending towards them, and muttering to himself something which was not intelligible. The rags he wore were such as have been described: but as he drew near, Don Quixote perceived that his buff doublet, though torn to pieces, still retained the perfume of amber, whence he concluded that he could not possibly be of low condition. When the young man came up to them, he saluted them in a harsh and untuned voice, but with a civil air. Don Quixote politely returned the salute, and alighting from Rozinante, with graceful demeanour and address, advanced to embrace him, and held him a considerable time clasped within his arms, as if they had been long acquainted. The other, whom we may truly call the Tattered Knight of the Woeful Figure, as Don Quixote was of the Sorrowful Figure, having suffered himself to be embraced, drew back a little, and laying his hands on Don Quixote's shoulder, stood contemplating him, as if to ascertain whether he knew him; and perhaps no less surprised at the aspect, demeanour, and habiliments of the knight than was Don Quixote at the sight of him.

CHAPTER XVIII

CARDENIO AND DON QUIXOTE MEET

"Assuredly, Señor," said the tattered stranger to Don Quixote, "whoever you are, for I do not know you, I am obliged to you for the courtesy you have manifested towards me; and I wish it were in my power to serve you with more than my goodwill, which is all that my fate allows me to offer in return for your civility." "So great is my desire to do you service," answered Don Quixote, "that I had determined not to quit these mountains until I found you and learned from yourself whether your affliction, which is evidenced by the strange life you lead, may admit of any remedy, and, if so, I had resolved to make every possible exertion to procure it. And I swear," added Don Quixote, "by the order of knighthood I have received, if you gratify me in this, to serve you with all the energy which it is my duty to exert, either in remedying your misfortune if it admit of remedy, or in assisting you to bewail it, as I have already promised." The "Knight of the Mountain," hearing him of "the Sorrowful Figure" talk thus, could only gaze upon him, viewing him from head to foot; and, after surveying him again and again, he said to him, "If you have anything to give me to eat, for Heaven's sake let me have it; and when I have eaten I will do all you desire, in return for the good wishes you have expressed towards me.'

Sancho immediately took from his wallet, and the goatherd from his scrip, some provisions, wherewith the wretched wanderer satisfied his hunger: eating what they gave him like a distracted person, so ravenously that he made no interval between one mouthful and another, for he rather devoured than ate; and during his repast neither he nor the by-standers spoke a word. When he had finished, he made signs to them to follow him, which they did; and having conducted them a short distance to a little green plot, he there laid himself down, and the rest did the same. When the "Tattered Knight" had composed himself, he said:

"My name is Cardenio; the place of my birth, one of the best cities of Andalusia; my family noble; my parents wealthy; my wretchedness so great, that it must have been deplored by my parents, and felt by my relations, although not to be alleviated by all their wealth. In that city there existed Lucinda, a damsel as well-born and as rich as myself, though more fortunate, and less constant than my honourable intentions deserved. This Lucinda I loved and adored from my childhood; and she on her part loved me with that innocent affection proper to her age. Our parents were not unacquainted with our attachment, nor was it displeasing to them—foreseeing that it could only end in a union sanctioned, as it were, by the equality of our birth and circumstances. At last when she was of marriageable years I determined to demand her of her father for my lawful wife; which I immediately did. In reply, he thanked me for the desire I expressed to honour him by an alliance with his family; but that, as my father was living, it belonged more properly to him to make this demand; for without his entire concurrence the act would appear secret, and unworthy of his Lucinda. I returned him thanks for the kindness of his reception; his scruples I thought were reasonable, and I made sure of my father's ready acquiescence. I went therefore directly to him, and upon entering his apartment found him with a letter open in his hand, which he gave me before I spoke a word, saying, 'By this letter, you will see, Cardenio, the inclination Duke Ricardo has to do you service.' Duke Ricardo, gentlemen, as you cannot but know, is a grandee of Spain, whose estate lies in the best part of Andalusia. I read the letter, which was so extremely kind, that I thought, even myself, it would be wrong in my father not to comply with its request, which was that I should be sent immediately to the duke, who was desirous of placing me, not as a man-servant, but as a companion to his eldest son; which honour should be accompanied by such preferment as should correspond with the estimation in which he held me. I was nevertheless much perplexed by the letter, and quite confounded when I heard my father say, 'Two days hence, Cardenio, you shall depart, in compliance with the duke's desire; and give thanks to God for opening you a way to that fortune I know you deserve;' to which he added other paternal admonitions.

"The time fixed for my departure came. I conversed the night before with Lucinda, and told her all that had passed; and also entreated her father to wait a few days, and not to dispose of her until I knew what Duke Ricardo's pleasure was with me. He promised me all I desired, and she confirmed it with a thousand vows and a thousand faintings. I arrived, in short, at the residence of Duke Ricardo, who received and treated me with so much kindness that envy soon became active, by possessing his old servants with an opinion that every favour the duke conferred upon me was prejudicial to their interests. But the person most pleased at my arrival was a second son of the duke, called Fernando, a sprightly young gentleman, of a gallant, liberal, and amorous disposition ; who in a short time contracted so intimate a friendship with me, that it became the subject of general conversation ; and though I was treated with much favour by his elder brother, it was not equal to the kindness and affection of Don Fernando.

" Now, as unbounded confidence is always the effect of such intimacy, and my friendship for Don Fernando being most sincere, he revealed to me all his thoughts, and particularly an amour which gave him some disquiet. He loved a country girl, the daughter of one of his father's vassals. Her parents were rich, and she herself was so beautiful, discreet, and modest, that no one could determine in which of these qualities she most excelled. Don Fernando's passion for this lovely maiden was so excessive that, in order to overcome the difficulties opposed by her virtue, he resolved to promise her marriage : knowing that she was to be conquered by no other means. Prompted by friendship, I employed the best arguments I could suggest, to divert him from such a purpose ; but, finding it was all in vain, I resolved to acquaint his father the duke with the affair.

" Don Fernando, being artful and shrewd, suspected and feared no less ; knowing that I could not, as a faithful servant, conceal from my lord and master a concern so prejudicial to his honour : and therefore, to amuse and deceive me, he said, that he knew no better remedy for effacing the remembrance of the beauty that had so captivated him than to absent himself for some months : this, he said, might be effected by our going together to my father's house, under pretence, as he would tell the duke, of purchasing horses in our town, which is remarkable for producing the best in the world. No sooner had he made this proposal than, prompted by my own love, I expressed my approbation of it, as the best that possibly could be devised ; and should have done so, even had it been less plausible, since it afforded me so good an opportunity of seeing my dear Lucinda. Thus influenced, I seconded his design, and desired him to put it in execution without delay ; since absence, I assured him, would certainly have its effect in spite of the strongest inclination. At the very time he made this proposal to me he had already, as appeared afterwards, married the maiden, and only waited for a convenient season to divulge it with safety to himself, being afraid of what the duke his father might do, when he should hear of his folly.

" Now, as love in young men is, for the most part, nothing but fancy, and pleasure its ultimate end, it expires with the attainment of its object ; and what seems to be love vanishes, because it has nothing of the durable nature of true affection. In short, Don Fernando having obtained his desire, his fondness abated ; and that absence which he proposed as a remedy for his passion, he only chose to avoid what was now no longer agreeable to him. The duke consented to his proposal, and ordered me to bear him company. We reached our city, and my father received him according to his quality. I immediately visited Lucinda : my passion revived (though, in truth, it had been neither dead nor asleep), and, unfortunately for me, I revealed it to Don Fernando ; thinking that, by the laws of friendship, nothing should be concealed from him. I expatiated so much on the beauty, grace, and discretion of Lucinda, that my praises excited in him a desire of seeing a damsel endowed with such accomplishments.

" Unhappily, I consented to gratify him, and showed her to him one night by the light of a taper at a window where we were accustomed to converse together. He beheld her, and every beauty he had hitherto seen was cast in oblivion. He was struck dumb ; he lost all sense : he was entranced—in short, he became deeply enamoured of her. From that time I began to fear and suspect him ; for he was every moment talking of Lucinda, and would begin the subject himself, however abruptly, which awakened in me I know not what jealousy ; and though I feared no change in the goodness and fidelity of Lucinda, yet I could not but dread the very thing against which they seemed to secure me. He also constantly importuned me to show him the letters I wrote to Lucinda, as well as her answers, pretending to be extremely delighted with both.

" Now it happened that Lucinda, having desired me to lend her a book of chivalry, of which she was very fond, entitled Amadis de Gaul——" Scarcely had Don Quixote heard him mention a book of chivalry, than he said, " Had you told me, sir, at the beginning of your history, that the Lady Lucinda was fond of reading books of chivalry, no more would have been necessary to convince me of the sublimity of her understanding. Pardon me, sir, for having broken my promise by this interruption ; but when I hear of matters appertaining to knights-errant and chivalry, I can as well forbear talking of them as the beams of the sun can cease to give heat, or those of the moon to moisten. Pray, therefore, excuse me, and proceed ; for that is of most importance to us at present."

While Don Quixote was saying all this, Cardenio hung down his head upon his breast, apparently in profound thought ; and although Don Quixote twice desired him to continue his story, he neither lifted up his head nor answered a word. After a time, however, catching at a stone that lay close by him, he threw it with such violence at Don Quixote's breast that it threw him on his back. Sancho Panza, seeing his master treated in this manner, attacked the madman with his clenched fist ; and the Ragged Knight received him in such sort, that with one blow he laid him at his feet, and then trampled him to his heart's content. The goatherd, who endeavoured to defend him, fared little better ; and when the madman had sufficiently vented his fury upon them all, he left them, and quietly retired to his rocky haunts among the mountains.

Sancho got up in a rage to find himself so roughly handled, and so undeservedly withal, and was proceeding to take revenge on the goatherd, telling him the fault was his, for not having given them warning that this man was subject to these mad fits ; for had they known it they might have been upon their guard. The goatherd answered that he had given them notice of it, and that, if they had not attended to it, the fault was not his. Sancho Panza replied, the goatherd rejoined ; and the replies and rejoinders ended in taking each other by the beard, and coming to such blows, that, if Don Quixote had not interposed, they would have demolished each other. But Sancho still kept fast hold of the goatherd, and said, " Let me alone, Sir Knight of the Sorrowful Figure, for this fellow being a bumpkin like myself, and not a knight, I may very safely revenge myself by fighting with him hand to hand, like a man of honour."

" True," said Don Quixote, " but I know that he is not to

blame for what has happened." Hereupon they were pacified; and Don Quixote again inquired of the goatherd whether it were possible to find out Cardenio; for he had a vehement desire to learn the end of his story. The goatherd told him, as before, that he did not exactly know his haunts, but that, if he waited some time about that part, he would not fail to meet him, either in or out of his senses.

CHAPTER XIX

THE STRANGE THINGS THAT BEFEL THE KNIGHT OF LA MANCHA IN SIERRA MORENA, AND HOW HE IMITATED THE PENANCE OF BELTENEBROS

Don Quixote took his leave of the goatherd, and, mounting Rozinante, commanded Sancho to follow him; which he did very unwillingly. They proceeded slowly on, making their way in the most difficult recesses of the mountain; in the mean time Sancho was dying to converse with his master, but would fain have had him begin the discourse, that he might not disobey his orders. Being, however, unable to hold out any longer, he said to him:

"Señor Don Quixote, be pleased to give me your worship's blessing, and my dismission; for I will get home to my wife and children, with whom I shall at least have the privilege of talking and speaking my mind; for, to desire me to bear your worship company through these solitudes night and day, without suffering me to talk when I list, is to bury me alive."

"I understand thee, Sancho," answered Don Quixote; "thou art impatient until I take off the embargo I have laid on thy tongue. Suppose it, then, removed, and thou art permitted to say what thou wilt, upon condition that this revocation is to last no longer than whilst we are wandering amongst these rocks."

"Be it so," said Sancho; "let me talk now, for God knows what will be hereafter. And now, taking the benefit of this licence, I ask, What is it your worship really intends to do in so remote a place as this?"

" Have I not told thee ? " answered Don Quixote, "that I design to imitate Amadis, acting here the desperate, raving, and furious lover; at the same time following the example of the valiant Don Orlando, when he found by the side of a fountain some indications that Angelica the fair loved his rival Medoro; at grief whereof he ran mad, tore up trees by the roots, disturbed the waters of the crystal springs, slew shepherds, destroyed flocks, fired cottages, demolished houses, dragged mares along the ground, and committed a hundred thousand other extravagances, worthy of eternal record. I may, perhaps, be content to imitate only Amadis, who, without committing any mischievous excesses, by tears and lamentations alone attained as much fame as all of them."

" It seems to me," quoth Sancho, "that the knights who acted in such manner were provoked to it, and had a reason for these follies and penances; but pray what cause has your worship to run mad ? What lady has disdained you ? or what tokens have you discovered to convince you that the lady Dulcinea del Toboso has committed folly either with Moor or Christian ? "

" There lies the point," answered Don Quixote, "and in this consists the refinement of my plan. A knight-errant who runs mad with just cause deserves no thanks; but to do so without reason is the point; giving my lady to understand what I should perform in the wet if I do this in the dry. Besides, I have cause enough given me by so long an absence from my ever-honoured lady Dulcinea del Toboso; for as thou hast often heard the shepherds say, ' The absent feel and fear every ill.' Therefore, friend Sancho, counsel me not to refrain from so rare, so happy, and so unparalleled an imitation. Mad I am, and mad I must be until thy return with an answer to a letter I intend to send by thee to my lady Dulcinea; and if it proves such as my fidelity deserves, my madness and my penance will terminate. " But, tell me, Sancho, hast thou taken care of Mambrino's helmet ? for I saw thee take it from the ground, when that ungrateful wretch proved the excellence of its quality, by vainly endeavouring to break it to pieces."

To which Sancho answered, "As God liveth, Sir Knight of the Sorrowful Figure, I cannot bear with patience some things your worship says : they are enough to make me think that all you tell me of chivalry, and of winning kingdoms and empires, of bestowing islands, and doing other favours and mighty things, according to the custom of knights-errant, must be matter of mere smoke, and all friction or fiction, or how do you call it? For, to hear you say that a barber's basin is Mambrino's helmet, and to persist in that error for near about four days, what can one think, but that he who says and affirms such a thing, must be crack-brained?"

"Take care of the helmet, friend Sancho," said the knight, "since I must strip off all my armour, and remain as naked as I was born, save for it, if I should determine upon imitating Orlando, in my penance, instead of Amadis." While they were thus discoursing, they arrived at the foot of a high mountain, which stood separated from several others that surrounded it, as if it had been hewn out from them. Near its base ran a gentle stream, that watered a verdant and luxuriant vale, adorned with many wide-spreading trees, plants, and wild flowers of various hues. This was the spot in which the Knight of the Sorrowful Figure chose to perform his penance; and, while contemplating the scene, he thus broke forth in a loud voice, "This is the place, O ye heavens! which I select and appoint for bewailing the misfortune in which ye have involved me. This is the spot where my flowing tears shall increase the waters of this crystal stream, and my sighs, continual and deep, shall incessantly move the foliage of these lofty trees, in testimony and token of the pain my persecuted heart endures. O my Dulcinea del Toboso, light of my darkness, glory of my pain, the north-star of my travels, and over-ruling planet of my fortune (so may Heaven listen to all thy petitions), consider, I beseech thee, to what a condition thy absence hath reduced me, and reward me as my fidelity deserves! And then, O squire, agreeable companion in my prosperous and adverse fortunes, carefully imprint on thy memory what thou shalt see me here perform, that thou mayest recount and recite it to her who is the sole cause of all!" Thus saying, he alighted from Rozinante, and in an instant took off his bridle and saddle, and, clapping him on the hinder parts, said to him, "O steed, as excellent for thy performance as unfortunate in thy fate! he gives thee liberty who is himself deprived of it. Go whither thou wilt; for thou hast it written on thy forehead that neither

Astolpho's Hippogriff, nor the famous Frontino, which cost Bradamante so dear, could match thee in speed."

Sancho, observing all this, said, "Heaven's peace be with him who saved us the trouble of unharnessing Dapple; for in faith he should have wanted neither slaps nor speeches in his praise. Yet if he were here, I would not consent to his being unpannelled, there being no occasion for it, for he had nothing to do with love or despair, any more than I, who was once his master, when it so pleased God. And truly, sir Knight of the Sorrowful Figure, if it be so, that my departure and your madness take place in earnest, it will be well to saddle Rozinante again, that he may supply the loss of my Dapple, and save me time in going and coming; for if I walk, I know not how I shall be able either to go or return, being in truth but a sorry traveller on foot."

"Be that as thou wilt," answered Don Quixote, "for I do not disapprove thy proposal; and I say thou shalt depart within three days, during which time I intend thee to bear witness of what I do say for her, that thou mayest report it accordingly."

"What have I more to see," quoth Sancho, "than what I have already seen?"

"So far, thou art well prepared," answered Don Quixote; "but I have now to rend my garments, scatter my arms about, and dash my head against these rocks; with other things of the like sort, which will strike thee with admiration."

"For the love of Heaven," said Sancho, "beware how you give yourself those blows, for you may chance to touch upon some unlucky point of a rock, that may at once put an end to this new project of penance; and I should think, since your worship is of opinion that knocks of the head are necessary, and that this work cannot be done without them, you might content yourself, since all is a fiction, a counterfeit, and a sham,—I say, you might content yourself with running your head against water, or some soft thing, such as cotton; and leave it to me to tell my lady that you dashed your head against the point of a rock, harder than a diamond."

"I thank thee for thy good intentions, friend Sancho," answered Don Quixote; "but I would have thee to know, that all these actions of mine are no mockery, but done very much in earnest; for to act otherwise would be an infraction of the rules of chivalry, which enjoin us to utter no falsehood, on pain of being punished as apostates; and the doing one thing for another is the same as lying: therefore, blows must be real and substantial, without artifice or evasion. However, it will be necessary to leave me some lint for my wounds, since it was the will of fortune that we should lose the balsam."

"It was worse to lose the ass," answered Sancho; "for with him we lost lint and everything else. And I beseech your worship not to put me in mind of that cursed drench; for at barely hearing it mentioned, my very soul, as well as my stomach, is turned inside out. As for the three days allowed me for seeing your mad pranks, I beseech you to reckon them as already passed, for I take all for granted, and will tell wonders to my lady. Do you write the letter and dispatch me quickly, for I long to come back and release your worship from this purgatory, in which I leave you. Let me but once get to Toboso, and into the presence of my Lady Dulcinea, and I will tell her such a story of the foolish, mad things (for they are all no better) which your worship has done and is still doing, that I shall bring her to be as supple as a glove, though I find her harder than a cork-tree; and with her answer, all sweetness and honey, will I return through the air, like a witch, and fetch your worship out of this purgatory, which, though it seems so, is no hell, because, as I said, your worship may hope to get out of it."

"That is true," answered the Knight of the Sorrowful Figure—"but how shall we contrive to write the letter?"

"And the ass-colt bill?" added Sancho.

"Nothing shall be omitted," said Don Quixote; "and since we have no paper, we shall do well to write it as the ancients did, on the leaves of trees, or on tablets of wax; though it will be as difficult at present to meet with these as with paper. But, now I recollect, it may be as well, or indeed better, to write it in Cardenio's pocket-book, and you will take care to get it fairly transcribed upon paper in the first town you reach where there is a schoolmaster; or, if there be none, any parish-clerk will transcribe it for you: but be sure you give it to no hackney-writer of the law; for the devil himself will never be able to read their confounded law-hand."

"But what must we do about the signing it with your own hand?" said Sancho.

"The letters of Amadis were never subscribed," answered Don Quixote.

"Very well," replied Sancho: "but the order for the colts must needs be signed by yourself; for if that be copied they will say it is a false signature, and I shall be forced to go without the colts."

"The order shall be signed in the same pocket-book; and at sight of it my niece will make no difficulty in complying with it. As to the love-letter, let it be subscribed thus, 'Yours, until death, the Knight of the Sorrowful Figure.' And it is of little importance whether it be written in another hand; for I remember Dulcinea can neither write nor read, nor has she ever seen a letter or writing of mine in her whole life; for our loves have always been of the Platonic kind, extending no farther than to modest glances at each other; and even those so very rarely that I can truly swear that, during the twelve years that I have loved her more than the light of these eyes, which the earth must one day consume, I have not seen her four times; and perhaps of these four times she may not have once perceived that I looked upon her—such is the reserve and seclusion in which she is brought up by her father, Lorenzo Corchuelo, and her mother, Aldonza Nogales!"

"Hey day!" quoth Sancho, "what, the daughter of Lorenzo Corchuelo! Is she the lady Dulcinea del Toboso, otherwise called Aldonza Lorenzo?"

"It is even she," said Don Quixote, "and she deserves to be mistress of the universe."

"I know her well," quoth Sancho; "and I can assure you she will pitch the bar with the lustiest swain in the parish. Long live the giver! why, she is a lass of mettle, tall, straight, and vigorous, and I warrant can make her part good with any knight-errant that shall have her for a mistress. O, the jade, what a pair of lungs and a voice she has! I remember she got out one day upon the bell-tower of the church, to call some young ploughmen who were in a field of her father's; and though they were half a league off, they heard her as plainly as if they had stood at the foot of the tower; I would fain be gone, if it is only to see her ; for I have not seen her this many a day, and by this time she must needs be altered ; for it mightily spoils women's faces to be always abroad in the field, exposed to the sun and weather. I confess to your worship, Señor Don Quixote, that hitherto I have been hugely mistaken, for I thought for certain that the lady Dulcinea was some great princess, with whom you were in love. But, all things considered, what good can it do the lady Aldonza Lorenza—I mean the lady Dulcinea del Toboso—to have the vanquished whom your worship sends or may send, falling upon their knees before her ? For perhaps at the time they arrive she may be carding flax, or threshing in the barn, and they may be confounded at the sight of her, and she may laugh and care little for the present."

"I have often told thee, Sancho," said Don Quixote, "that thou art an eternal babbler, and, though void of wit, thy bluntness often stings."

"Your worship," replied Sancho, "is always in the right, and I am an ass—why do I mention an ass ?—one should not talk of halters in the house of the hanged. But I am off—give me the letter, sir, and God be with you."

Don Quixote took out the pocket-book, and, stepping aside, began with much composure to write the letter ; and having finished, he called Sancho, and said he would read it to him, that he might have it by heart, lest he might perchance lose it by the way : for everything was to be feared from his evil destiny. To which Sancho answered, "Write it, sir, two or three times in the book, and give it me, and I will take good care of it : but to suppose that I can carry it in my memory, is a folly : for mine is so bad that I often forget my own name. Your worship, however, may read it to me ; I shall be glad to hear it, for it must needs be very much to the purpose." "Listen, then," said Don Quixote, "this is what I have written :—

"*Don Quixote's letter to Dulcinea del Toboso.*

"High and sovereign lady,

"He who is stabbed by the point of absence, and pierced by the arrows of love, O sweetest Dulcinea del Toboso, greets thee with wishes for that health which he enjoys not himself. If thy beauty despise me, if thy worth favour me not, and if thy disdain still pursue me, although inured to suffering I shall ill support an affliction which is not only severe but lasting. My good squire Sancho will tell thee, O ungrateful fair, and most beloved foe, to what a state I am reduced on thy account. If it be thy pleasure to relieve me, I am thine ; if not, do what seemeth good to thee : for by my death I shall at once appease thy cruelty and my own passion.—Until death thine,

"THE KNIGHT OF THE SORROWFUL FIGURE."

"By the life of my father," quoth Sancho, after hearing the letter, "it is the finest thing I ever heard. Odds boddikins ! how choicely your worship expresses whatever you please ! and how well you close all with ' the knight of the sorrowful figure !' Verily, your worship is the devil himself—there is nothing but what you know."

"The profession which I have embraced," answered Don Quixote, "requires a knowledge of everything."

"Well, then," said Sancho, "pray clap on the other side of the leaf, the order for the three ass-colts, and sign it very plain, that people may know your hand at first sight."

"With all my heart," said the knight ; and having written it, he read as follows :—

"DEAR NIECE,—At sight of this my first bill of ass-colts, give order that three out of the five I left at home in your custody, be delivered to Sancho Panza, my squire : which three colts I order to be delivered and paid for the like number received of him here in tale ; and this, with his acquittance, shall be your discharge. Done in the heart of the Sierra Morena, the twenty-second of August, this present year——"

"It is mighty well," said Sancho ; "now you have only to sign it."

"It wants no signing," said Don Quixote ; "I need only put my cypher to it, which is the same thing, and is sufficient not only for three but for three hundred asses."

"I rely upon your worship," answered Sancho ; "let me go and saddle Rozinante, and prepare to give me your blessing, for I intend to depart immediately, without staying to see the mad frolics you are about to commit; and I will tell quite enough to satisfy her."

"At least, Sancho," said Don Quixote, "I wish, nay, it is necessary, and I will have thee see me naked, and perform a dozen or two frantic actions, for I shall dispatch them in less than half an hour."

"Now I think of it, sir," said Sancho, "how shall I be able to find my way back again to this bye-place?"

"Observe and mark well the spot, and I will endeavour to remain near it," said Don Quixote; "and will, moreover, ascend some of the highest ridges to discover thee upon thy return. But the surest way not to miss me, or lose thyself, will be to cut down some of the broom that abounds here, and scatter it here and there, on the way to the plain, to serve as marks and tokens to guide thee on thy return, in imitation of Theseus' clue to the labyrinth."

Sancho Panza followed this counsel; and having provided himself with branches, he begged his master's blessing, and, not without many tears on both sides, took his leave of him; and mounting upon Rozinante, with especial charge from Don Quixote to regard him as he would his own proper person, he rode towards the plain, strewing the boughs at intervals, as his master directed him. Thus he departed, although Don Quixote still importuned him to stay and see him perform if it were but a couple of his gambols. He had not gone above a hundred paces when he turned back and said, "Your worship, sir, said right that, to enable me to swear with a safe conscience, it would be proper I should at least see one of your mad tricks; though, in plain truth, I have seen enough in seeing you stay here."

"Did I not tell thee so?" quoth Don Quixote: "stay but a moment, Sancho—I will dispatch them as quickly as you can say a Credo." Then stripping off his clothes in all haste, without more ado he cut a couple of capers in the air, and as many tumbles heels over head. Sancho turned Rozinante about, fully satisfied that he might swear his master was stark mad: we will therefore leave him pursuing his journey until his return, which was speedy.

DON QUIXOTE.

CHAPTER XX

DON QUIXOTE'S PENANCE, AS A LOVER IN THE SIERRA MORENA

THE Knight of the Sorrowful Figure when he found himself alone, having finished his gambols, and perceiving that Sancho was gone, without caring to be witness of any more of his pranks, he mounted the top of a high rock, and there began to deliberate on a subject that he had often considered before, without coming to any resolution ; and that was which of the two was the best and most proper model for his imitation, Orlando in his furious fits, or Amadis in his melancholy moods : and having long argued with himself, he at length said, "All honour to the memory of Amadis ! and let him be the model of Don Quixote de la Mancha, of whom shall be said, what was said of another, that, if he did not achieve great things, he at least died in attempting them ; and though neither rejected nor disdained by my Dulcinea, it is sufficient that I am absent from her. Now then to the work. Come to my memory, ye deeds of Amadis, and instruct me where to begin the task of imitation ! It now occurs to me that he prayed much—that will I also do." Whereupon he strung some large galls of a cork-tree, which served him for a rosary ; but he regretted exceedingly that there was no hermit to hear his confession, and administer consolation to him. He thus passed the time, walking about and writing, and graving on the barks of trees, or tracing in the fine sand, many verses of a plaintive kind, in praise of his Dulcinea.

In such tender and melancholy occupations, sighing, or invoking the sylvan deities, the nymphs of the mountain streams, and the mournful echo, to listen and answer to his moan, he passed the time ; and sometimes in gathering herbs to sustain himself until Sancho's return ; who, if he had tarried three weeks instead of three days, "the Knight of the Sorrowful Figure" would have been so disfigured that he would not have been recognised by his own mother. Here, however, it would be proper to leave him, wrapped up in poetry and grief, to relate what happened to the squire during his embassy.

As soon as Sancho had gained the high-road, he directed his course immediately to Toboso, and the next day he came within sight of the inn where the misfortune of the blanket had befallen him, and, fancying himself again flying in the air, he felt no disposition to enter it, although it was then the hour of dinner, and he longed for something warm—all having been cold-treat with him for many days past. This inclination, nevertheless, drew him forcibly towards the inn ; and, as he stood doubtful whether or not to enter, two persons came out, who immediately recognised him.

"Pray, Señor Licentiate," said one to the other, "is not that Sancho Panza yonder on horseback, who, as our friend's house-keeper told us, accompanied her master as his squire ?"

"Truly it is," said the licentiate ; "and that is our Don Quixote's horse." No wonder they knew him so well, for they were the priest or curate and barber of his village, and the very persons who had tried and passed sentence of execution on the mischievous books. Being now certain it was Sancho Panza and Rozinante, and hoping to hear some tidings of Don Quixote, the curate went up to him, and, calling him by his name,

"Friend Sancho Panza," said he, "where have you left your master ?" Sancho immediately knew them, and resolved to conceal the circumstances and place of Don Quixote's retreat ; he therefore told them that his master was very busy in a certain place, about a certain affair of the greatest importance to himself, which he durst not discover for the eyes in his head.

"No, no, Sancho," quoth the barber, "that story will not pass. If you do not tell us where he is, we shall conclude, as we suspect already, that you have murdered and robbed him, since you come thus upon his horse. See, then, that you produce the owner of that horse, or woe be to you !"

"There is no reason why you should threaten me," quoth Sancho ; "for I am not a man to rob or murder anybody. Let every man's fate kill him, or God who made him. My master is doing a certain penance much to his liking in the midst of yon mountains."

He then, very freely and without hesitation, related to them in what state he had left him, the adventures that had befallen them, and how he was then carrying a letter to the lady Dulcinea del Toboso—the daughter of Lorenzo Corchuelo, with whom his master was up to the ears in love.

They were both astonished at Sancho's report; and, though they already knew the nature of Don Quixote's derangement, yet every fresh instance of it was to them a new source of wonder. They begged Sancho Panza to show them the letter he was carrying to the lady Dulcinea del Toboso. He said it was written in a pocket-book, and that his master had ordered him to get it copied out upon paper at the first town he should arrive at. The curate said, if he would show it to him, he would transcribe it in a very fair character. Sancho Panza put his hand into his bosom to take out the book, but found it not; nor could he have found it had he searched until this time; for it remained with Don Quixote, who had forgotten to give it to him. When Sancho found he had no book, he turned as pale as death; and, having felt again all over his body in great perturbation, without success; he laid hold of his beard with both hands, and tore away half of it, and then gave himself sundry cuffs on the nose and mouth, bathing them all in blood. The curate and barber seeing this, asked him wherefore he treated himself so roughly.

"Wherefore?" answered Sancho, "but that I have let slip through my fingers three ass-colts, each of them a castle!"

"How so?" replied the barber.

"I have lost the pocket-book," answered Sancho, "that contained the letter to Dulcinea, and a bill signed by my master, in which he ordered his niece to deliver to me three colts out of four or five he had at home." This led him to mention his loss of Dapple; but the priest bid him be of good cheer, telling him that, when he saw his master, he would engage him to renew the order upon paper in a regular way; for one written in a pocket-book would not be accepted. Sancho was comforted by this assurance, and said that he did not care for the loss of the letter to Dulcinea, as he could almost say it by heart; so that they might write it down, where and when they pleased.

"Repeat it, then, Sancho," quoth the barber, "and we will write it afterwards." Sancho then began to scratch his head, in order to fetch the letter to his remembrance; now he stood upon one foot, and then upon the other; sometimes he looked down upon the ground, and sometimes up to the sky : then, after biting off half a nail of one finger, and keeping his hearers long in expectation, he said :

"The devil take all I remember of the letter; though at the beginning I believe it said, 'High and subterrane lady.'"

"No," said the barber, "not subterrane, but superhumane, or sovereign lady."

"Aye, so it was," said Sancho. "Then, if I do not mistake, it went on, 'the stabbed, and the waking, and the pierced, kisses your honour's hands, ungrateful and most regardless fair;' and then it said I know not what of 'health and sickness that he sent;' and so he went on, until at last he ended with 'thine till death, the Knight of the Sorrowful Figure.'"

They were both not a little diverted at Sancho's excellent memory, and commended it much, desiring him to repeat the letter twice more, that they also might get it by heart, in order to write it down in due time. Thrice Sancho repeated it, and thrice he added three thousand other extravagancies : relating to them also many other things concerning his master, but not a word of the blanket. He informed them likewise how his lord, upon his return with a kind despatch from his lady Dulcinea del Toboso, was to set about endeavouring to become an emperor, or at least a king (for so it was concerted between them)—a thing that would be very easily done, considering the valour and strength of his arm ; and when this was accomplished, his master was to marry him (as by that time he should, no doubt, be a widower), and give him to wife one of the empress's maids of honour, heiress to a large and rich territory on the mainland ; for, as to islands, he was quite out of conceit with them. Sancho said all this with so much gravity, ever and anon wiping his nose, that they were amazed at the potency of Don Quixote's malady, which had borne along with it the senses also of this poor fellow. They would not give themselves the trouble to convince him of his folly, as it was of a harmless nature, and afforded them amusement ; they therefore told him he should pray for his lord's health, since it was very possible and very practicable for him in process of time to become an emperor, as he said, or at least an archbishop, or something else of equal dignity.

"We must now contrive to relieve your master from this

unprofitable penance," said the curate, " and, therefore let us go in to concert proper measures, and also to get our dinner, which by this time is ready." Sancho said they might go in, but that he should choose to stay without—he would tell them why another time; he begged them, however, to bring him out something warm to eat, and also some barley for Rozinante. Accordingly they left him and entered the inn, and soon after the barber returned to him with some food.

The curate and barber having deliberated together on the best means of accomplishing their purpose, a device occurred to the priest, exactly fitted to Don Quixote's humour, and likely to effect what they desired : which was, that he should perform himself the part of a damsel-errant, and the barber equip himself as her squire; in which disguise they should repair to Don Quixote : and the curate presenting himself as an afflicted and distressed lady, should beg a boon of him, which he, as a valorous knight-errant, could not do otherwise than grant; and this should be a request that he would accompany her whither she should lead him, to redress an injury done her by a discourteous knight ; entreating him, at the same time, not to desire her to remove her mask, nor make any farther inquiries concerning her, until he had done her justice on that wicked knight. He made no doubt but that Don Quixote would consent to any such terms, and they might thus get him away from that place, and carry him home, where they would endeavour to find some remedy for his extraordinary malady.

CHAPTER XXI

THE PLOT OF THE PRIEST AND THE BARBER

THE barber liked the curate's contrivance so well that they immediately began to carry it into execution. They borrowed a petticoat and head-dress from the landlady, leaving in pawn for them a new cassock belonging to the priest ; and the barber made himself a huge beard of the tail of a pied ox, in which the innkeeper used to hang his comb. The hostess having asked them for what purpose they wanted those things, the priest gave her a brief account of Don Quixote's insanity, and the necessity of that disguise to draw him from his present retreat. The host and hostess immediately conjectured that this was the same person who had once been their guest, the maker of the balsam, and the master of the blanketed squire; and they related to the priest what had passed between them, without omitting what Sancho had been so careful to conceal.

In the mean time, the landlady equipped the curate to admiration: she put him on a cloth petticoat, laid thick with stripes of black velvet, each the breadth of a span, all pinked and slashed; and a corset of green velvet, bordered with white satin, which, together with the petticoat, must have been made in the days of King Bamba. The curate would not consent to wear a woman's head-dress, but put on a little white quilted cap, which he used as a nightcap, and bound one of his garters of black taffeta about his head, and with the other made a kind of veil, which covered his face and beard very well. Over his face he then pulled his hat, which was so large that it served him for an umbrella, and wrapping his cloak around him, he got upon his mule sideways like a woman. The barber mounted also, with a beard that reached to his girdle, of a colour between sorrel and white, being, as before said, made of the tail of a pied ox. They took leave of all, not excepting the good Maritornes, who promised, though a sinner, to pray over an entire rosary that Heaven might give them good success in so arduous and Christian a business as that which they had undertaken.

But scarcely had they got out of the inn, when the curate began to think he had done amiss, and that it was indecent for a priest to be so accoutred, although for so good a purpose; and acquainting the barber with his scruples, he begged him to exchange apparel, as it would better become him to personate the distressed damsel, and he would himself act the squire, as being a less profanation of his dignity; and if he would not consent, he was determined to proceed no farther, though the devil should run away with Don Quixote.

They were now joined by Sancho, who was highly diverted at their appearance. The barber consented to the proposed exchange; upon which the priest began to instruct him how to act his part, and what expressions to use to Don Quixote, in order

E

to prevail unto him to accompany them, and leave the place of his penance. The barber assured him that, without his instructions, he would undertake to manage that point to a tittle. The dress, however, he would not put on, until they came near to the place of Don Quixote's retreat. The curate then adjusted his beard, and they proceeded forward, guided by Sancho Panza, who on the way related to them their adventure with the madman whom they had encountered in the mountain; but said not a word about the portmanteau and its contents: for with all his folly and simplicity, the rogue was somewhat covetous.

The next day they arrived at the place where Sancho had strewed the branches to ascertain the place where he had left his master; and, upon seeing them, he gave notice that they had entered the mountain pass, and would therefore do well to put on their disguise, if that had any concern with the delivery of his master. They had before told him that their disguise was of the utmost importance towards disengaging his master from the miserable life he had chosen; and that he must by no means tell him who they were: and if he should inquire, as no doubt he would, whether he had delivered the letter to Dulcinea, he should say he had; and that she, not being able to read or write, had answered by word of mouth, and commanded the knight, on pain of her displeasure, to repair to her immediately, upon an affair of much importance: for, with this, and what they intended to say themselves, they should certainly reconcile him to a better mode of life, and put him in the way of soon becoming an emperor, or a king; as to an archbishop, he had nothing to fear on that subject.

Sancho listened to all this, and imprinted it well on his memory, and gave them many thanks for promising to advise his lord to be an emperor, and not an archbishop; for he was persuaded that, in rewarding their squires, emperors could do more than archbishops-errant. He told them also it would be proper he should go before, to find him, and deliver his lady's answer: for, perhaps, that alone would be sufficient to bring him out of that place, without farther trouble. They agreed with Sancho, and determined to wait for his return with intelligence of his master. Sancho entered the mountain pass, and left them in a pleasant spot, refreshed by a streamlet of clear water, and shaded by rocks and overhanging foliage.

It was in the month of August, when in those parts the heats are violent, and about three o'clock in the afternoon ; on which account they found the situation very agreeable, and consented the more readily to wait there till Sancho's return. While they were reposing in the shade, a voice reached their ears, which, although unaccompanied by any instrument, sounded sweet and melodious. They were much surprised, since the verses they heard were not those of a rustic muse, but of refined and courtly invention.

The hour, the season, the solitude, the voice, and the skill of the singer, all conspired to impress the auditors with wonder and delight, and they remained for some time motionless, in expectation of hearing more.

The song ended with a deep sigh, and they again listened very attentively, in hopes of hearing more ; but the music being changed into sobs of lamentation, they went in search of the unhappy person whose voice was no less excellent than his complaints were mournful. They had not gone far, when, turning the point of a rock, they perceived a man of the same stature and appearance that Sancho had described Cardenio to them. The man expressed no surprise at the sight of them, but stood still, inclining his head upon his breast, in a pensive posture, without again raising his eyes from the ground. The priest, who was a well-spoken man, being already acquainted with his misfortune, went up to him, and in a few but very impressive words entreated him to forsake that miserable kind of life, and not hazard so great a misfortune as to lose it in that inhospitable place. Cardenio was then perfectly tranquil, and free from those outrageous fits with which he was so often seized ; he likewise appeared to be sensible that the persons who now accosted him were unlike the inhabitants of those mountains ; he was still more surprised to hear them speak of his concerns, and he replied, "It is very evident to me, gentlemen, whoever you are, that Heaven, which succours the good, and often even the wicked, unworthy as I am, sends to me in this solitude, so remote from the commerce of human kind, persons who, representing to me by various and forcible arguments how irrational is my mode of life, endeavour to divert me from it; but not knowing as I do that by flying from this misery I shall be plunged into worse, they doubtless take me for a fool or madman. Gentlemen, if you come with the same intention that others have done, before you proceed any farther in your prudent counsel, I beseech you to hear my sad story; for then you will probably spare yourselves the trouble of endeavouring to find consolation for an evil which has no remedy."

The two friends being desirous of hearing his own account of himself, entreated him to indulge them, assuring him they would do nothing but what was agreeable to him, either in the way of remedy or advice. The unhappy young man began his melancholy story almost in the same words in which he had related it to Don Quixote and the goatherd some few days before, when, on account of Don Quixote's zeal in defending the honour of knight-errantry, the tale was abruptly suspended; but Cardenio's sane interval now enabled him to conclude it quietly. On coming to the circumstance of the love-letter which Don Fernando found between the leaves of the book of Amadis de Gaul, he said he remembered it perfectly well, and that it was as follows :—

"'Each day I discover in you qualities which raise you in my esteem ; and, therefore, if you would put it in my power to discharge my obligations to you, without prejudice to my honour, you may easily do it. I have a father who knows you, and has an affection for me ; who will never force my inclinations, and will comply with whatever you can justly desire, if you really have that value for me which you profess, and which I trust you have.'

"This letter made me resolve to demand Lucinda in marriage, as I have already related, and was one of those which pleased Don Fernando so much. It was this letter, also, which made him determine upon my ruin before my design could be effected. I told Don Fernando that Lucinda's father expected that the proposal should come from mine, but that I durst not mention it to him, lest he should refuse his consent : not that he was ignorant of Lucinda's exalted merits, which might ennoble any family of

Spain, but because I had understood from him that he was desirous I should not marry until it should be seen what Duke Ricardo would do for me. In short, I told him that I had not courage to speak to my father about it, being full of vague apprehensions and sad forebodings. In reply to all this, Don Fernando engaged to induce my father to propose me to the father of Lucinda.

"Don Fernando, thinking my presence an obstacle to the execution of his treacherous design, resolved to send me to his elder brother for money to pay for six horses which he bought, merely for a pretence to get me out of the way. Could I foresee his treachery? Surely not: on the contrary, well satisfied with his purchase, I cheerfully consented to depart immediately. That night I had an interview with Lucinda, and told her what had been agreed upon between Don Fernando and myself, assuring her of my hopes of a successful result. She, equally unsuspicious of Don Fernando, desired me to return speedily, since she believed the completion of our wishes was only deferred until proposals should be made to her father by mine.

"I executed my commission to Don Fernando's brother, by whom I was well received, but not soon dismissed; for, to my grief, he ordered me to wait eight days, and to keep out of his father's sight; because his brother had desired that a certain sum of money might be sent to him without the duke's knowledge. All this was a contrivance of the false Fernando; and I felt disposed to resist the injunction, as it seemed to me impossible to support life so many days absent from Lucinda, especially having left her in such a state of dejection. Nevertheless, I did obey, like a good servant, although at the expense of my health. But four days after my arrival a man came in quest of me with a letter, which by the superscription I knew to be from Lucinda. I opened it with alarm, convinced it must be something extraordinary that had induced her to write. Before I read it, I made some inquiries of the messenger. He told me that passing accidentally through a street in the town, a very beautiful lady, with tears in her eyes, called to him from a window, and said to him, in great agitation, 'Friend, if you are a Christian, I beg of you, for the love of Heaven, to carry this letter with all expedition to the place and person to whom it is directed; in so doing you will perform an act of charity; and to supply you with the necessary expense take what is tied up in this handkerchief;' so saying, she threw the handkerchief out of the window; which contained a hundred reals, and this gold ring, with the letter I have given you. She saw me take up the letter and the hand-kerchief, and assure her by signs that I would do what she commanded, and she then quitted the window. Finding myself so well paid for the trouble, and knowing by the superscription it was for you, sir; induced moreover by the tears of that beautiful lady, I resolved to trust no other person, but deliver it with my own hands: and within sixteen hours I have performed the journey, which you know is eighteen leagues. While the grateful messenger thus spoke, I hung upon his words, my legs trembling so that I could scarcely stand. At length I opened the letter, which contained these words :—

"'The promise Don Fernando gave you to intercede with your father, he has fulfilled, more for his own gratification than your interest. Know, sir, that he has demanded me to wife: and my father, allured by the advantage he thinks Don Fernando possesses over you, has accepted this proposal so eagerly that the marriage is to be solemnized two days hence, and with so much privacy that, except Heaven, a few of our own family are alone to witness it. Conceive my situation! and think whether you ought not to return. Whether I love you or not, the event will prove. Heaven grant this may come to your hand before mine be compelled to join his who breaks his promised faith!'"

"I set out immediately, without waiting for any other answer, or the money: for now I plainly saw it was not the purchase of horses, but the indulgence of his pleasure, that had induced Don Fernando to send me to his brother. My rage against Don Fernando, and the fear of losing the rich reward of my long service and affection, gave wings to my speed; and the next day I reached our town, at the moment favourable for an interview with Lucinda. I went privately, having left my mule with the honest man who brought me the letter: and fortune was just then so propitious that I found Lucinda at the grate, the constant witness of our loves. We saw each other—but how! Who is there in the world that can boast of having fathomed, and thoroughly penetrated the intricate and ever-changing nature of a woman? Certainly none.

"As soon as Lucinda saw me she said, 'Cardenio, I am in my bridal habit; they are now waiting for me in the hall; the treacherous Don Fernando and my covetous father, with some others, who shall sooner be witnesses of my death than of my nuptials. Be not afflicted, my friend; but endeavour to be present at this sacrifice, which, if my arguments cannot avert, I carry a dagger about me, which can oppose a more effectual resistance, by putting an end to my life, and will give you a convincing proof of the affection I have ever borne you.' I answered with confusion and precipitation :

"'Let your actions, madam, prove the truth of your words. If you carry a dagger to secure your honour, I carry a sword to defend you, or kill myself, if fortune proves adverse.' I do not believe she heard all I said, being hastily called away : for the bridegroom waited for her.

"Being perfectly acquainted with all the avenues, and the whole household engaged, I escaped observation, and concealed myself in the recess of a window in the hall, behind the hangings, where two pieces of tapestry met; whence I could see all that passed. Who can describe the flutterings of my heart, and my various sensations, as I stood there? The bridegroom entered the hall, in his usual dress, accompanied by a cousin of Lucinda, and no other person was present, except the servants of the house. Soon after, from a dressing room, came forth Lucinda, accompanied by her mother and two of her own maids, adorned in the extreme of courtly splendour.

"All being all assembled in the hall," continued Cardenio, "the priest entered, and, having taken them both by the hand, in order to perform what is necessary on such occasions, when he came to these words, 'Will you, Señora Lucinda, take Señor Don Fernando, who is here present, for your lawful husband, as our holy mother the Church commands?' I thrust out my head and neck through the tapestry, and with attentive ears and distracted soul awaited Lucinda's reply, as the sentence of my death, or the confirmation of my life. O ! that I had then dared to venture forth, and to have cried aloud—'Ah, Lucinda, Lucinda ! beware what you do ; consider what you owe to me ! Remember that you are mine, and cannot belong to another.'

"The priest stood expecting Lucinda's answer, who paused

for a long time; and when I thought she would draw forth the
dagger in defence of her honour, or make some declaration which
might redound to my advantage, I heard her say in a low and
faint voice, ' I will.' Don Fernando said the same, and the ring
being put on, they remained tied in an indissoluble band. The
bridegroom approached to embrace his bride; and she, laying her
hand on her heart, fainted in the arms of her mother. I was totally
confounded—I thought myself abandoned by heaven and earth;
the air denying me breath for my sighs, and the water moisture
for my tears: fire alone supplied me with rage and jealousy. On
Lucinda's fainting, all were in confusion, and her mother unlacing
her bosom to give her air, discovered in it a folded paper, which
Don Fernando instantly seized, and read it by one of the flam-
beaux, after which, he sat himself down in a chair, apparently full
of thought, and without attending to the exertions made to
recover his bride.

"During this general consternation, I departed, indifferent
whether I was seen or not. In short, I quitted the house; and
returning to the place where I had left the mule, I mounted and
rode out of the town, not daring, like another Lot, to look
behind me; and when I found myself alone on the plain, concealed by the darkness of the night, the silence inviting my
lamentations, I gave vent to a thousand execrations on Lucinda
and Don Fernando, as if that, alas! would afford me satisfaction
for the wrongs I had sustained. I called her cruel, false, and ungrateful; and, above all, mercenary, since the wealth of my
enemy had seduced her affections from me.

"In the utmost perturbation of mind, I journeyed on the rest
of the night, and at daybreak reached these mountains, over
which I wandered three days more, without road or path, until I
came to a valley not far hence; and inquiring of some shepherds
for the most rude and solitary part, they directed me to this place,
where I instantly came, determined to pass here the remainder of
my life. Among these crags, my mule fell down dead through
weariness and hunger, or, what is more probable, to be relieved
of so useless a burden; and thus was I left, extended on the
ground, famished and exhausted, neither hoping nor caring for
relief. How long I continued in this state, I know not; but at
length I got up, without the sensation of hunger, and found near

Dorothea.

me some goatherds, who had undoubtedly relieved my wants. They told me of the condition in which they found me, and of many wild and extravagant things that I had uttered, clearly proving the derangement of my intellect. Thus I pass my miserable life, waiting until it shall please Heaven to bring it to a period, or erase from my memory the beauty and treachery of Lucinda, and the perfidy of Don Fernando; otherwise, Heaven have mercy on me! for I feel no power to change my mode of life."

Here Cardenio terminated the long recital of his story, no less full of misfortunes than of love; and just as the priest was preparing to say something to him, by way of consolation, he was prevented by a voice which in mournful accents uttered these complaints.

CHAPTER XXII

THE NEW AND AGREEABLE ADVENTURE THAT BEFEL THE PRIEST AND THE BARBER IN THE SIERRA MORENA

As narrated in the last chapter, the priest was preparing to say something consolatory to Cardenio, when he was prevented by a voice uttering these mournful accents :—

"O heavens! have I then at last found a place which may afford a secret grave for this wretched body? Yes—if the silence of this rocky desert deceive me not, here I may die in peace. Ah, woe is me! Here at least I may freely pour forth my lamentations to Heaven, and shall be less wretched than among men, from whom I should in vain seek counsel, redress, or consolation."

These words being distinctly heard by the curate and his companions, they rose up to seek the mourner, who they knew by the voice to be near them; and they had not gone many paces when they espied a youth dressed like a peasant sitting under an ash-tree at the foot of a rock. They could not at first see his face, as he was stooping to bathe his feet in a rivulet which ran by. They drew near so silently that he did not hear them : and while he continued thus employed they stood in admiration at the beauty and whiteness of his feet, which looked like pure crystal among the pebbles of the brook, and did not seem formed for breaking clods or following the plough, as might have been expected from the apparel of the youth. The curate, who went foremost, made a sign to the others to crouch down and conceal themselves behind some fragments of a rock, whence they might watch his motions. He was clad in a drab-coloured jerkin, girded closely round his body with a piece of white linen; his breeches, gaiters, and his cap, were all of the same colour. His gaiters being now pulled up, exposed his legs, which in colour resembled alabaster. After bathing his lovely feet he wiped them with a handkerchief, which he drew from under his cap; and in doing this he displayed a face of such exquisite beauty, that Cardenio said to the priest, in a low voice, "Since it is not Lucinda, this can be no human creature." The youth then took off his cap, and shaking his head, a profusion of hair, that Apollo himself might envy, fell over his shoulders—and betrayed the woman, and the most beautiful one that two of the party had ever beheld. Cardenio declared that Lucinda alone could be compared to her. Her long and golden tresses covered not only her shoulders but nearly her whole body; and her snowy fingers served her for a comb. Her beauty made the three spectators impatient to find out who she was, and they now determined to accost her. The lovely maiden looked up on hearing them approach, and with both her hands putting her hair from before her eyes, she saw the intruders; upon which she hastily rose, and snatched up a bundle, apparently of clothes, which lay near her, and without staying to put on her shoes or bind up her hair, she fled with precipitation and alarm; but had scarcely gone six paces when, her tender feet being unable to bear the sharp stones, she fell to the ground. The priest now addressed himself to her:

"Do not fly, madam, I entreat you; for we only desire to serve you; indeed there is no reason why you should attempt so inconvenient a flight." Surprised and confounded, she made no reply. The priest then, taking her hand, proceeded to say:

"Your hair reveals to us, madam, what your habit would conceal; and it is manifest that no slight cause has induced you to disguise your beauty in such unworthy attire, and brought you to a solitude like this, where it has been our good fortune to find you ; and I hope you will give us an opportunity of rendering you some assistance."

When the curate thus addressed her, the disguised maiden stood like one stupefied, her eyes fixed on them, without answering one word—like a country clown when he is suddenly surprised by some new sight. At length, after the priest had said more to the same purpose, she heaved a deep sigh, and breaking silence, said :

"Since even these retired mountains have failed to conceal me, and my hair has betrayed me, I can no longer attempt to disguise myself. Indeed, gentlemen, I feel very grateful for your kind offers to serve me, but such is my unfortunate situation that commiseration is all I can expect ; nevertheless, that I may not suffer in your opinion from the strange circumstances under which you have discovered me, I will tell you the cause without reserve, whatever pain it may give me." She spoke with so much grace, and in so sweet a voice, that they were still charmed with her, and repeated their kind offers and solicitations for her confidence. Having first modestly put on her shoes and stockings, and gathered up her hair, she seated herself upon a flat stone, her three auditors placing themselves around her ; and after some efforts to restrain her tears she began her story in this manner :

"There is a town in the province of Andalusia, from which a duke takes his title, that makes him a grandee of Spain. This duke has two sons ; the elder, heir to his estate, and apparently to his virtues : the younger, heir to I know not what, unless it be to the treachery of Vellido and the deceitfulness of Galalon. My parents are vassals to this nobleman, and are very rich, though of humble birth.

"But what they prized above rank or riches was their daughter, sole heiress of their fortune, and I was always treated by them with the utmost indulgence and affection. To me they intrusted the management of the household : through my hands passed the accounts of all that was sown and reaped : the oil-mills, the wine-presses, the numerous herds, flocks, and the bee-hives—everything, in short, was intrusted to my care. I was both steward and mistress, and always performed my duties to their satisfaction. The leisure hours that remained I passed in sewing, spinning, or making lace, and sometimes in reading good books, or, if my spirits required the relief of music, I had recourse to my gittern. Thus I passed my time, constantly occupied and in retirement, seen only, as I imagined, by our own servants; for when I went to mass it was early in the morning, accompanied by my mother, and so closely veiled that my eyes saw no more ground than the space which my foot covered. Yet the eyes of love, or rather of idleness, which are like those of a lynx, discovered me. Don Fernando, the younger son of the duke, whom I mentioned to you"—she had no sooner named Don Fernando, than Cardenio's colour changed, and he was so violently agitated that the priest and the barber were afraid that he would be seized with one of those paroxysms of frenzy to which he was subject. But he remained quiet, fixing his eyes attentively on the country-maid, well conjecturing who she was; while she, not observing the emotions of Cardenio, continued her story, saying, "No sooner had he seen me, than (as he afterwards declared) he conceived for me a violent affection—but, to shorten the account of my misfortunes, I pass over in silence the devices Don Fernando employed to make his passion known to me. He bribed all our servants; he offered presents to my relations; every day was a festival in our streets: and at night nobody could sleep for serenades. Infinite were the billets-doux that came, I knew not how, to my hands, filled with amorous declarations.

"Don Fernando, having discovered my parents' provisions for my security, was determined to defeat them; and one night, as I was in my chamber, the door fast locked, and only my maid present, he suddenly stood before me. Terrified at his unexpected appearance, I was deprived of the power of utterance, and, all my strength failing me, he caught me in his arms. The traitor then pleaded by sighs and tears, and with such an appearance of truth, that I, a poor simple creature, without experience, began to give some credit to him. At last I exerted myself, and said to him, 'If my life depended on the sacrifice of my honour, I would not preserve it on such terms. Had I been thus solicited by one who had obtained the sanction of my parents, and honourably demanded my hand, I might have listened to proposals—but to no others than those of a lawful husband.'

"'If that be all, beautiful Dorothea!' said the treacherous man, 'here I pledge to you my hand; and let all-seeing Heaven and that image of our Lady witness the agreement!'"

When Cardenio heard her call herself Dorothea, he was confirmed in his conjecture; but he would not interrupt the story, being desirous to hear the event of what in part he knew already; and he only said:

"What, madam! is your name Dorothea? I have heard of one of that name whose misfortunes much resemble yours. But proceed."

Dorothea proceeded:—"Don Fernando then took up the holy image and called upon it to witness our espousals: pledging himself by the most solemn vows, to become my husband, notwithstanding my entreaties that he would consider the displeasure of his family, and other disadvantages that might result from so unequal a union. I called my maid to bear testimony to his plighted faith—again he repeated the most solemn vows, attesting new saints to hear them, and thus he finally succeeded in becoming a perjured traitor.

"On the morning that followed that fatal night, Don Fernando quitted me without reluctance: he assured me indeed of his truth and honour, but not with the warmth and vehemence of the preceding night; and at parting he drew a valuable ring from his finger, and put it upon mine. That perfidious man visited me but once more, although access was free to him, as I had become his wife. Months passed away, and in vain I watched for his coming; yet he was in the town, and every day amusing himself with hunting. What melancholy days and hours were those to me! for I began to doubt his fidelity; but suddenly my forbearance was at an end, with all regard to delicacy and fame, upon the intelligence reaching me that Don Fernando was married, in a neighbouring village, to a beautiful young lady, of some rank and fortune, named Lucinda."— Cardenio heard the name of Lucinda, at first, only with signs of indignation, but soon after a flood of tears burst from his eyes. Dorothea, however, pursued her story, saying, "When this sad news reached my ears, my heart, instead of being chilled by it, was so incensed and inflamed with rage, that I could scarcely forbear rushing into the streets and proclaiming the baseness and treachery I had experienced. But I became more tranquil after forming a project, which I executed the same night. I borrowed this apparel of a shepherd swain in my father's service, whom I entrusted with my secret, and begged him to attend me in my pursuit of Don Fernando. He assured me it was a rash undertaking; but finding me resolute, he said he would go with me to the end of the world. Immediately I packed up some of my own clothes, with money and jewels, and at night secretly left the house, attended only by my servant and a thousand anxious thoughts; and travelled on foot to the town where I expected to find my husband; impatient to arrive, if not in time to prevent his perfidy, to reproach him for it.

"I inquired where the parents of Lucinda lived; and the first person to whom I addressed myself told me more than I desired to hear. He directed me to the house and gave me an account of all that had happened at the young lady's marriage. He told me also that on the night Don Fernando was married to Lucinda, after she had pronounced the fatal Yes, she fell into a swoon; and the bridegroom in unclasping her bosom to give her air, found a paper written by herself, in which she affirmed that she could not be wife to Don Fernando because she was already betrothed to Cardenio (who, as the man told me, was a gentleman of the same town), and that she had pronounced her assent to Don Fernando merely in obedience to her parents. The paper also revealed her intention to kill herself as soon as the ceremony was over, which was confirmed by a poniard they found concealed upon her. Don Fernando was so enraged to find himself thus mocked and slighted, that he seized hold of the same poniard, and would certainly have stabbed her, had he not been prevented by those present; whereupon he immediately quitted the place. When Lucinda revived, she confessed to her parents the engagement she had formed with Cardenio, who it was suspected, had witnessed the ceremony, and had hastened from the city in despair; for he left a paper expressing his sense of the wrong he had suffered, and declaring his resolution to fly from mankind for ever.

"In this situation, undecided what course to take, I heard myself proclaimed by the public crier, offering a great reward for discovering me, and describing my person and dress. It was also reported that I had eloped from my father's house with the lad that attended me. I was stung to the soul to find how very low I had fallen in public opinion; and, urged by the fear of discovery, I instantly left the city, and at night took refuge among these mountains. But it is truly said one evil produces another, and misfortunes never come singly; for my servant, hitherto so faithful, took advantage of this solitary place, and, dismissing all regard either to God or his mistress, began to make love to me; and, on my answering him as he deserved, he would have used force, but merciful Heaven favoured me, and endued me with strength to push him down a precipice, where I left him, whether dead or alive I know not, for, in spite of terror and fatigue, I fled from the spot with the utmost speed. After this I engaged myself in the service of a shepherd, and have lived for some months among these wilds, always endeavouring to be abroad, lest I should betray myself. Yet all my care was to no purpose, for my master at length discovered that I was not a man, and the same evil thoughts sprang up in his breast that had possessed my servant. Lest I might not find the same means at hand to free myself from violence, I sought for security in flight, and have endeavoured to hide myself amongst these rocks."

CHAPTER XXIII

THE ARRIVAL OF THE PRINCESS MICOMICONA

"This, gentlemen," added Dorothea, "is my tragical story; think whether the sighs and tears which you have witnessed have not been more than justified: for although I am certain of a kind reception from my parents, so overwhelmed am I with shame, that I choose rather to banish myself for ever from their sight than appear before them the object of such hateful suspicions."

Here she was silent, while her blushes and confusion sufficiently manifested the shame and agony of her soul. Her auditors were much affected by her tale, and the curate was just going to address her, when Cardenio interrupted him, saying:

"You, madam, then, are the beautiful Dorothea, only

" Heaven endued me with strength to push him down a precipice."

daughter of the rich Clenardo?" Dorothea stared at hearing her father named by such a miserable-looking object, and she asked him who he was, since he knew her father.

"I am that hapless Cardenio," he replied, "who suffers from the base author of your misfortunes, reduced, as you now behold, to nakedness and misery—deprived even of reason! Yes, Dorothea, I heard that fatal 'yes' pronounced by Lucinda, and, unable to bear my anguish, I fled precipitately from her house. Amidst these mountains I thought to have terminated my wretched existence; but the account you have just given has inspired me with hope that Heaven may still have happiness in store for us. Lucinda has avowed herself to be mine, and therefore cannot wed another; Don Fernando, being yours, cannot have Lucinda. Let us then, my dear lady, indulge the hope that we may both yet recover our own, since it is not absolutely lost. Indeed, I swear to you that, although I leave it to Heaven to avenge my own injuries, your claims will I assert; nor will I leave you until I have obliged Don Fernando, either by argument or my sword, to do you justice."

Dorothea would have thrown herself at the feet of Cardenio, to express her gratitude to him, had he not prevented her. The licentiate too commended his generous determination, and entreated them both to accompany him to his village, where they might consult on the most proper measures to be adopted in the present state of their affairs: a proposal to which they thankfully acceded. The barber, who had hitherto been silent, now joined in expressing his good wishes to them; he also briefly related the circumstances which had brought them to that place; and when he mentioned the extraordinary insanity of Don Quixote, Cardenio had an indistinct recollection of having had some altercation with the knight, but could not remember whence it arose.

They were now interrupted by the voice of Sancho Panza, who, not finding them where he left them, began to call out loudly: they went instantly to meet him, and were eager in their inquiries after Don Quixote. He told them that he had found the knight naked to his shirt, feeble, wan, and half-dead with hunger, sighing for his lady Dulcinea; and though Sancho had informed him that it was her express desire that he should leave that place, and repair to Toboso, where she expected him, his answer was that he positively would not appear before her beauty, until he had performed exploits that might render him worthy of her favour ; if his master, he added, persisted in that humour, he would run a risk of never becoming an emperor, as in honour bound ; nor even an archbishop, which was the least he could be : so they must consider what was to be done to get him away. The licentiate begged him not give himself any uneasiness on that account, for they should certainly contrive to get him out of his present retreat.

The curate then informed Cardenio and Dorothea of their plan for Don Quixote's cure, or at least for decoying him to his own house. Upon which Dorothea said she would undertake to act the distressed damsel better than the barber, especially as she had apparel with which she could perform it to the life ; and they might have reliance upon her, as she had read many works of chivalry, and was well acquainted with the style in which distressed damsels were wont to beg their boons of knights-errant

"Let us then hasten to put our design into execution," exclaimed the curate ; "since fortune seems to favour all our views."

Dorothea immediately took from her bundle a petticoat of very rich stuff, and a mantle of fine green silk ; and out of a casket a necklace and other jewels, with which she quickly adorned herself, in such a manner that she had all the appearance of a rich and noble lady. They were charmed with her beauty, grace, and elegance ; and agreed that Don Fernando must be a man of little taste, since he could slight so much excellence. But her greatest admirer was Sancho Panza, who thought that in all his life he had never seen so beautiful a creature ; and he earnestly desired the priest to tell him who this beautiful lady was, and what she was looking for in those parts ?

"This beautiful lady, friend Sancho," answered the priest, "is the Princess Micomicona, heiress, in the direct male line, of the great kingdom of Micomicon ; and she comes in quest of your master, to beg a boon of him, which is, to redress a wrong or injury done her by a wicked giant : for it is the fame of your master's prowess, which is spread over all Guinea, that has brought this princess to seek him."

"Now, a happy seeking, and a happy finding!" quoth Sancho Panza; "especially if my master is so fortunate as to redress that injury, and right that wrong, by killing the rascally giant you mention; and kill him he certainly will, if he encounters him, unless he be a goblin; for my master has no power at all over goblins. But one thing I must again beg of your worship, Señor Licentiate, and that is, to prevent my master from taking it into his head to be an archbishop. Advise him to marry this princess out of hand; for then, not being qualified to receive archiepiscopal orders, he will come with ease to his kingdom, and I to the end of my wishes."

"As to your master's marrying this princess," said the priest; "I will promote it to the utmost of my power." With which assurance Sancho was no less satisfied than the curate was amazed at his simplicity in thus entering into the extravagant fancies of his master.

Dorothea having now mounted the priest's mule, and the barber fitted on the ox-tail beard, they desired Sancho to conduct them to Don Quixote, cautioning him not to say that he knew the licentiate or the barber, since on that depended all his fortune. Neither the curate nor Cardenio would go with them; the latter, that he might not remind Don Quixote of the dispute which he had had with him; and the priest, because his presence was not then necessary: so the others, therefore, went on before, while they followed slowly on foot. The priest would have instructed Dorothea in her part; but she would not trouble him, assuring him that she would perform it precisely according to the rules and precepts of chivalry.

Having proceeded about three-quarters of a league, they discovered Don Quixote in a wild, rocky recess, at that time clothed, but not armed. Dorothea now whipped on her palfrey, attended by the well-bearded squire; and having approached the knight, the squire leaped from his mule to assist his lady, who, lightly dismounting, went and threw herself at Don Quixote's feet, where, in spite of his efforts to raise her, she remained kneeling, as she thus addressed him:

"I will never arise from this place, O valorous and redoubted knight, until your goodness and courtesy vouchsafe me a boon, which will redound to the honour and glory of your person, and to the lasting benefit of the most disconsolate and aggrieved damsel the sun has ever beheld."

"It is impossible for me to answer you, fair lady," said Don Quixote, "while you remain in that posture."

"I will not arise, Señor," answered the afflicted damsel, "until your courtesy shall vouchsafe the boon I ask."

"I do vouchsafe and grant it to you," answered Don Quixote, "provided my compliance be of no detriment to my king, my country, or to her who keeps the key of my heart and liberty."

"It will not be to the prejudice of either of these, dear sir," replied the afflicted damsel. Sancho, now approaching his master, whispered softly in his ear :

"Your worship may very safely grant the boon she asks : for it is a mere trifle—only to kill a great lubberly giant ; and she who begs it is the mighty Princess Micomicona, queen of the great kingdom of Micomicon, in Æthiopia."

"Whosoever the lady may be," answered Don Quixote, "I shall act as my duty and my conscience dictate, in conformity to the rules of my profession : " then addressing himself to the damsel, he said :

"Fairest lady, arise ; for I vouchsafe you whatever boon you ask."

"My request then is," said the damsel, "that your magnanimity will go whither I shall conduct you ; and that you will promise not to engage in any other adventure until you have avenged me on a giant Pandafilando, who, against all right, human and divine, has usurped my kingdom, bequeathed to me by my father, Trinacrio the Wise."

"I grant your request," answered Don Quixote ; "and therefore, lady, dispel that melancholy which oppresses you, and let your fainting hopes recover fresh life and strength ; for, by the help of Heaven, and my powerful arm, you shall soon be restored to your kingdom ; therefore we will instantly proceed to action, for there is always danger in delay." The distressed damsel would fain have kissed his hands ; but Don Quixote, who was in every respect a most gallant and courteous knight, would by no means consent to it, but, making her arise, embraced her with much politeness and respect, and ordered Sancho to look after Rozinante's girths, and to assist him to arm. Sancho took down the armour from a tree, where it hung like a trophy ; and having got Rozinante ready, quickly armed his master, who then cried, " In God's name, let us hasten to succour this great lady."

The barber was still upon his knees, and under much difficulty to forbear laughing, and keep his beard from falling—an accident which might have occasioned the miscarriage of their ingenious stratagem ; but seeing that the boon was already granted, and that Don Quixote prepared to fulfil his engagement, he got up and took his lady by the other hand ; when they both assisted to place her upon the mule, and then mounted themselves. Sancho alone remained on foot, which renewed his grief for the loss of his Dapple : but he bore it cheerfully ; reflecting that his master was now in the right road, and just upon the point of becoming an emperor ; for he made no doubt but that he was to marry that princess, and be at least king of Micomicon. One thing only troubled him, which was that, his kingdom being in the land of negroes, his subjects would all be blacks ; but presently recollecting a special remedy, he said to himself, " What care I, if my subjects be blacks ?—what have I to do but to ship them off to Spain, where I may sell them for ready money, with which money I may buy some title or office, on which I may live at ease all the days of my life ? "   After these reflections, he went on in such good spirits, that he forgot the fatigue of travelling on foot.

Cardenio and the curate, concealed among the bushes, had observed all that passed, and being now desirous to join them, the priest, who had a ready invention, soon hit upon an expedient ; for with a pair of scissors, which he carried in a case, he quickly cut off Cardenio's beard ; then put on him a grey capouch, and gave him his own black cloak (himself remaining in his breeches and doublet), which so changed Cardenio's appearance, that had he looked in a mirror he would not have known himself. Although the others had in the mean time been proceeding onward, they easily gained the high road first, because the narrow passes between the rocks were more difficult to horse than to foot travellers. They waited in the plain until Don Quixote and his party came up ; whereupon the curate, after gazing for some time earnestly at him, at last ran towards him with open arms, exclaiming aloud :

"Happy is this meeting, O thou mirror of chivalry, my noble countryman, Don Quixote de la Mancha! the flower and cream of gentility,—the protector of suffering mankind,—the quintessence of knight-errantry!" Having thus spoken, he embraced Don Quixote by the knee of his left leg.

The knight was surprised at this address; but after attentively surveying the features of the speaker, he recognised him, and would immediately have alighted; but the priest would not suffer it.

"You must permit me to alight, Señor Licentiate," answered Don Quixote; "for it would be very improper that I should remain on horseback while so reverend a person as you were travelling on foot."

"I will by no means consent to your dismounting," replied the priest, "since on horseback you have achieved the greatest exploits this age has witnessed. As for myself, an unworthy priest, I shall be satisfied if one of these gentleman of your company will allow me to mount behind him."

"I did not think of that, dear Señor Licentiate," said Don Quixote; "and I know her highness the princess will for my sake order her squire to accommodate you with the saddle of his mule; and he may ride behind, if the beast will carry double."

"I believe she will," answered the princess; "and I know it is unnecessary for me to lay my commands upon my squire; for he is too courteous and well-bred to suffer an ecclesiastic to go on foot, when he may ride."

"Most certainly," answered the barber; and, alighting in an instant, he complimented the priest with the saddle, which he accepted without much persuasion. But it unluckily happened that, as the barber was getting upon the crupper, the animal, which was a hackney, and consequently a vicious jade, threw up her hind legs twice or thrice into the air: and had they met with Master Nicholas's breast or head, he would have wished his rambling after Don Quixote at the devil. He was, however, thrown to the ground, and so suddenly, that he forgot to take due care of his beard, which fell of; and all he could do was to cover his face with both hands, and cry out that his jaw-bone was broken. Don Quixote seeing such a mass of beard without jaws and without blood, lying at a distance from the face of the fallen squire, exclaimed:

"Heavens! what a miracle! His beard has fallen as clean from his face as if he had been shaven!" The curate, seeing the danger they were in of discovery, instantly seized the beard, and ran to Master Nicholas, who was still on the ground moaning; and going up close to him, with one twitch replaced it, muttering over him some words which he said were a specific charm for fixing on beards, as they should soon see; and when it was adjusted, the squire remained as well bearded and as whole as before. They now agreed that the priest should mount first, and that all three should ride by turns until they came to the inn, which was distant about two leagues.

Don Quixote, the princess, and the priest, being thus mounted, attended by Cardenio, the barber, and Sancho Panza on foot, Don Quixote said to the damsel:

"Your highness will now be pleased to lead on, in whatever direction you choose." Before she could reply, the licentiate interposing said, "Whither would your ladyship go? To the kingdom of Micomicon, I presume, or I am much mistaken." She, being aware that she was to answer in the affirmative, said:

"Yes, señor, that kingdom is indeed the place of my destination."

"If so," said the curate, "we must pass through my native village; and thence you must go straight to Carthagena, where you may embark."

"Lead on, dear madam," said the knight; "all I can say is that my powers, such as they are, shall be employed in your service, even at the forfeit of my life; but waiving these matters for the present, I beg the Señor Licentiate to tell me what has brought him into these parts, alone, unattended, and so lightly apparelled."

"I can soon satisfy your worship," answered the curate; "our friend, Master Nicholas, and I were going to Seville, to receive a legacy left me by a relation in India, and no inconsiderable sum, being sixty thousand crowns; and on our road, yesterday, we were attacked by four highway robbers, who stripped us of all we had, to our very beards; and for this youth here (pointing to Cardenio), you see how they have treated him. It is publicly reported here that those who robbed us were galley-slaves, set at liberty near this very place by a man so valiant that in spite of the commissary and his guards he released them all ; but he must have been mad to do such a villainous deed."

Sancho had communicated the adventure of the galley-slaves, so gloriously achieved by his master ; and the curate laid it on thus heavily to see what effect it would have upon Don Quixote ; whose colour changed at every word.

" These," said the priest, " were the persons that robbed us ; and God of His mercy pardon him who prevented the punishment they so richly deserved."

CHAPTER XXIV

THE PRINCESS RECORDS HER STORY

LAUGHING in his sleeve, Sancho said, as soon as the curate had done speaking :

" By my troth, Señor Licentiate, it was my master who did that feat ; not but that I gave him fair warning."

" Blockhead ! " said Don Quixote, " knights-errant are not bound to inquire whether the afflicted, fettered, and oppressed whom they meet upon the road, are brought to that situation by their faults or their misfortunes. As for the rest, I care not ; and whoever takes it amiss, saving the holy dignity of Señor the Licentiate, and his reverend person, I say he knows but little of the principles of chivalry, and lies in his throat ; and this I will maintain with the edge of my sword ! " So saying, he fixed himself firmly in his stirrups and lowered his vizor ; for Mambrino's helmet, as he called it, hung useless at his saddle-bow, until it could be repaired of the damage it had received from the galley-slaves.

Dorothea was possessed of too much humour and sprightly wit not to join with the rest in their diversion at Don Quixote's expense : but perceiving his wrath, she made peace between them, and amity was restored.

Presently Don Quixote said, " Madam, I beseech you to inform me of the particulars of your grievance, as well as the number and quality of the persons on whom I must take due, satisfactory, and complete revenge."

"That I will do most willingly," answered Dorothea, "if a detail of my afflictions will not be wearisome to you."

"Not in the least, my dear madam," replied the knight.

"Well, then," said Dorothea, "you have only to favour me with your attention." Cardenio and the barber now walked by her side, curious to hear what kind of story she would invent. Sancho, who was as much deceived as his master, did the same; and after a hem or two, and other preparatory airs, with much grace she told the story of the usurpation by the giant Pandafilando of the throne of Micomicona, concluding her account with the statement, "My good father, moreover, left an order, written either in Chaldean or Greek (for I cannot read them), that if the knight mentioned in his prophecy, after cutting off the giant's head, should desire to marry me, I must immediately submit to be his lawful wife, and with my person give him also possession of my kingdom."

"Now, what thinkest thou, friend Sancho?" quoth Don Quixote. "Dost thou hear that? Did not I tell thee so? See whether we have not now a kingdom to command, and a queen to marry!"

"Odds my life! so it is," cried Sancho; "and plague take him who will not marry as soon as Señor Pandafilando's wizen is cut. About it then; her majesty's a dainty lady: I wish I never had a worse." And, so saying, he cut a couple of capers, and exhibited other tokens of delight. Then laying hold of the reins of Dorothea's mule, and making her stop, he fell down upon his knees before her, beseeching her to give him her hand to kiss, in token that he acknowledged her for his queen and mistress. With difficulty could the rest of the party restrain their laughter at the madness of the master and the simplicity of the man. Dorothea held out her hand to him, and promised to make him a great lord in her kingdom, when Heaven should be so propitious as to put her again in possession of it. Sancho returned her thanks in expressions which served to increase their mirth.

"O most worthy and exalted lady!" cried Don Quixote, "whatever I may be called upon to endure in your service, I shall cheerfully bear it. And again I confirm my engagement, and swear to accompany you to the remotest regions of the earth until I shall meet and grapple with that fierce enemy of yours, whose proud head, by the help of Heaven and this my strong arm, I will cut off with the edge of this (I will not say good) sword; thanks be to Gines de Passamonte, who carried off my own." These last words he uttered in a lower tone; then, again raising his voice, he proceeded to say:

"Having severed it from his body, and replaced you in peaceable possession of your dominions, the disposal of your person will be at your own discretion, since, while my memory is engrossed, my heart enthralled, and my mind subjected to her who—I say no more—it is impossible I should prevail upon myself even to think of marrying, although it were a phœnix."

Don Quixote's last declaration was so displeasing to Sancho that, in a great fury, he exclaimed:

"I vow and swear, Señor Don Quixote, your worship cannot be in your right senses! How else is it possible you should scruple to marry so great a princess? Do you think that fortune is to offer you at every turn such good luck as this? Is my lady Dulcinea more beautiful? no, indeed, not by half! nay, I could almost say she is not worthy to tie this lady's shoe-string. I am like, indeed, to get the earldom if your worship stands fishing for mushrooms at the bottom of the sea! Marry, marry at once, in the devil's name, and take this kingdom that drops into your hand; and when you are a king, make me a marquis or a lord-lieutenant, and then the devil take the rest!"

Don Quixote, unable to endure such blasphemies against his lady Dulcinea, raised his lance, and, without word or warning, let it fall with such violence upon Sancho that he was laid flat on the ground; and had not Dorothea called out entreating him to forbear, the squire had doubtless been killed on the spot.

"Thinkest thou," said Don Quixote to him, after a short pause, "base varlet! that I am always to stand with my arms folded; and that there is to be nothing but transgression on thy side, and forgiveness on mine? Expect it not, excommunicated wretch! for so thou surely art, having presumed to speak ill or the peerless Dulcinea. Knowest thou not, rustic, slave, beggar! that were it not for the power she infuses into my arm, I should not have strength enough to kill a flea?"

Sancho was not so much hurt but that he heard all his master said to him; and getting up nimbly, he ran behind Dorothea's palfrey; and thus sheltered, he said to him:

"Pray, sir, tell me if you are resolved not to marry this princess, it is plain the kingdom will not be yours—what favours then will you be able to bestow on me? That is what I complain of. Marry this queen, sir, once for all, now we have her, as it were, rained down upon us from heaven, and afterwards you may turn to my lady Dulcinea: for there have been kings who have had mistresses. As to the matter of beauty, I have nothing to say to that; but if I must speak the truth, I really think them both very well to pass, though I never saw the lady Dulcinea."

"How! never saw her, blasphemous traitor!" said Don Quixote; "hast thou not just brought me a message from her?"

"I say I did not see her so leisurely," said Sancho, "as to take particular notice of her features piece by piece; but take her altogether, she looks well enough."

"Let there be no more of this," said Dorothea; "go, Sancho, and kiss your master's hand, and ask his pardon. Henceforward be more cautious in your praises and dispraises; and speak no ill of that lady Toboso, of whom I know no more than that I am her humble servant. Put your trust in Heaven: for you shall not want an estate to live upon like a prince." Sancho went with his head hanging down, and begged his master's hand, who presented it to him with much gravity; and when he had kissed it, Don Quixote gave him his blessing.

At this time they saw a man coming towards them mounted upon an ass, and as he drew near he had the appearance of a gipsy. But Sancho Panza, who, whenever he saw an ass followed it with eyes and heart, had no sooner got a glimpse of the man, than he recognised Gines de Passamonte, and, by the same clue, was directed to his lost ass; it being really Dapple himself on which Gines was mounted! for in order to escape discovery and sell the animal, he had disguised himself like a gipsy, as he could speak their language, among many others, as readily as his native tongue. Sancho immediately called out aloud to him:

"Ah, rogue Ginesillo! leave my darling, let go my life, rob me not of my comfort—fly!—get you gone, thief! and give up

"How hast thou done, my dearest Dapple?"

what is not your own." So much railing was not necessary; for at the first word Gines dismounted in a trice, and taking to his heels, was out of sight in an instant. Sancho ran to his Dapple, and embracing him, said, "How hast thou done, my dearest Dapple, delight of my eyes, my sweet companion?" Then he kissed and caressed him, as if he had been a human creature. The ass held his peace, and suffered himself to be thus kissed and caressed by Sancho without answering him one word. They all came up, and wished him joy on the restoration of his Dapple; especially Don Quixote, who at the same time assured him that he should not on that account revoke his order for three colts, for which he had Sancho's hearty thanks.

CHAPTER XXV

SANCHO'S REPORT OF HIS INTERVIEW WITH DULCINEA

THEY were thus pursuing their conversation while Don Quixote proceeded in his with Sancho.

"Let us forget, friend Panza, what is past; and tell me now, all rancour and animosity apart, where, how, and when didst thou find Dulcinea? What was she doing? What didst thou say to her? What answer did she return? How did she look when she read my letter? Who transcribed it for thee? Tell me all that is worth knowing, inquiring, or answering. Inform me of all, without adding or diminishing aught to deprive me of any satisfaction."

"Sir," answered Sancho, "to say the truth, nobody transcribed the letter for me; for I carried no letter at all."

"Thou sayest true," quoth Don Quixote, "for I found the pocket-book in which I wrote it two days after thy departure; which troubled me exceedingly; and I thought thou wouldst return for it."

"So I should have done," answered Sancho, "had I not got it by heart, when your worship read it to me; and so perfectly that I repeated it to a parish clerk, who wrote it down so exactly that he said, though he had read many letters of excommunication he had never in all his life seen or read so pretty a letter."

" And hast thou it still by heart, Sancho ? " said Don Quixote.

" No, sir," answered Sancho ; " for after I had delivered it, seeing it was to be of no further use, I forgot it on purpose. If I remember anything, it is 'subterrane,' I mean 'sovereign' lady, and the conclusion, ' thine until death, the Knight of the Sorrowful Figure ; ' and between these two things I put above three hundred souls, and lives, and dear eyes."

" This is very well—proceed," said Don Quixote. "On thy arrival, what was that queen of beauty doing ? I suppose thou foundest her stringing pearls, or embroidering some device with threads of gold for this her captive knight."

"No, faith !" answered Sancho ; " I found her winnowing two bushels of wheat in a back-yard of her house."

" Then be assured," said Don Quixote," that the grains of that wheat were so many grains of pearl, when touched by her hands. And didst thou observe, friend, whether the wheat was fine, or of the ordinary sort ?"

" It was neither," answered Sancho, " but of the reddish kind."

" Rely upon it, however," quoth Don Quixote, "that when winnowed by her hands it made the finest manchet bread—but go on. When thou gavest her my letter, did she kiss it ? Did she put it upon her head ? Did she use any ceremony worthy of such a letter ?—or what did she do ? "

"When I was going to give it to her," answered Sancho, "she was so busy winnowing a good sieveful of the wheat, that she said to me, ' Lay the letter, friend, upon that sack ; for I cannot read it until I have done what I am about.' "

" Discreet lady !" said Don Quixote ; "this was assuredly that she might read and enjoy it at leisure ! Proceed, Sancho ; while thus employed, what discourse had she with thee ?—what did she inquire concerning me ? And what didst thou answer ? Tell me all ; omit not the slightest circumstance."

" She asked me nothing," said Sancho ; " but I told her how your worship was doing penance for her service, among these rocks, naked from the waist upwards, just like a savage : sleeping on the ground, not eating bread on a napkin, nor combing your beard, weeping, and cursing your fortune."

"In saying that I cursed my fortune, thou saidst wrong," quoth Don Quixote : "I rather bless it, and shall bless it all the days of my life, for having made me worthy to love so high a lady as Dulcinea del Toboso. Well, then," continued Don Quixote, "she has now done winnowing, and the corn is sent to the mill. What did she do when she had read the letter?"

"The letter," quoth Sancho, "she did not read; for she said that she could neither read nor write; so she tore it to pieces, saying she would not give it to anybody to read, that her secrets might not be known all over the village; and that what I had told her by word of mouth concerning your worship's love, and all you were doing for her sake, was enough; and she bid me tell your worship that she kissed your hands, and that she would rather see you than write to you; so begged and commanded you, at sight hereof, to quit those brakes and bushes, and leave off these foolish pranks, and set out immediately for Toboso, if business of more consequence did not prevent you; for she wished mightily to see your worship. She laughed heartily when I told her how you called yourself the Knight of the Sorrowful Figure. I asked her whether the Biscayan had been there with her; she told me he had, and that he was a very good kind of fellow. I asked her also after the galley-slaves, but she had not yet seen any of them."

"All this is well," said Don Quixote; "but, tell me, what jewel did she present thee with at thy departure, in return for the tidings thou hadst brought her; for it is an ancient and universal custom among knights and ladies-errant to bestow some rich jewel on the squires, damsels, or dwarfs who bring them news of their mistresses or knights, as a reward or acknowledgment of their welcome intelligence."

"Very likely," quoth Sancho, "and a good custom it was; but it must have been in days of yore, for now-a-days the custom is to give only a piece of bread and cheese, for that was what my lady Dulcinea gave me, over the pales of the yard, when she dismissed me; and, by the way, the cheese was made of sheep's milk."

"She is extremely generous," said Don Quixote; "and if she did not give thee a jewel, it must have been because she had none about her; but gifts are good after Easter.* I shall see her, and all will then be rectified. Yet about going to her I am in a difficulty. I am bound to obey her commands, yet how is it

---

* A proverbial expression, signifying that a good thing is always seasonable.

F

possible, on account of the boon I have promised to the princess? The laws of chivalry oblige me to consider my honour rather than my pleasure. On the one hand, I am torn with impatience to see my lady—on the other, I am incited by glory to the accomplishment of this enterprise. My best plan, I believe, will be to travel with all possible expedition, cut off the giant's head, replace the princess on her throne, and then instantly return to that sun which illumines my senses, who will pardon a delay which was only to augment her fame and glory; since all my victories past, present, and to come, are but emanations from her favour."

"Alack!" cried Sancho, "your worship must needs be downright crazy! Tell me, pray, do you mean to take this journey for nothing? And will you let slip such a match as this, when the dowry is a kingdom, which, they say, is above twenty thousand leagues round?"

"Hear me, Sancho," replied Don Quixote, "if thou advisest me to marry, only that I may have it in my power to reward thee, be assured that I can gratify thy desire without taking such a measure; before the battle I will make an agreement to possess part of the kingdom without marrying the princess; and when I have it to whom dost thou think I shall give it but to thyself?"

"No doubt," answered Sancho; "but pray, sir, take care to choose it towards the sea, that, if I should not like living there, I may ship off my black subjects, and dispose of them, as I said before. I would not have your worship trouble yourself now about seeing my lady Dulcinea, but go and kill the giant, and let us make an end of this business; for, before Heaven, I verily believe it will bring us much honour and profit."

While they were thus talking, Master Nicholas called aloud to them to stop, as they wished to quench their thirst at a small spring near the road. Don Quixote halted, much to the satisfaction of Sancho, who began to be tired of telling so many lies, and was afraid his master should at last catch him tripping: for although he knew Dulcinea was a peasant-girl of Toboso, he had never seen her in his life. Meanwhile Cardenio had put on the clothes worn by Dorothea in her disguise, being better than his own. They alighted at the fountain, and with the provisions which the curate had brought from the inn, they all appeased their hunger.

CHAPTER XXVI

MORE ADVENTURES AT THE ENCHANTED INN

LEAVING the fountain, after having made a hearty repast, they forthwith mounted, and without encountering any adventure worth relating, arrived the next day at the inn so much the dread and terror of Sancho Panza, who now, much against his will, was obliged to enter it. The hostess, the host, their daughter, and Maritornes, seeing Don Quixote and his squire, went out to meet and welcome them. The knight received them with a grave but approving countenance, desiring them to prepare a better bed than they had given him before; to which the hostess answered, that provided he would pay better than he did before, she would get him a bed for a prince. Don Quixote having satisfied them by his promises, they provided him with a tolerable bed, in the same apartment which he had before occupied; and, being so much shattered both in body and brains, he immediately threw himself down upon it.

He was no sooner shut into his chamber, but the hostess fell upon the barber, and, taking him by the beard, said:

" By my faith, you shall use my tail no longer for a beard: give me my tail again, for my husband's comb is so thrown about that it is a shame." The barber would not part with it for all her tugging, until the licentiate told him that he might give it to her; for as there was no farther need of that artifice, he might now appear in his own shape, and tell Don Quixote that, being robbed by the galley-slaves, he had fled to this inn: and if he should ask for the princess's squire, they should say she had despatched him before, with intelligence to her subjects of her approach with their common deliverer. Upon which the barber willingly surrendered the tail to the hostess, together with the other articles she had lent them in order to effect Don Quixote's enlargement. All the people at the inn were struck with the beauty of Dorothea, and the comely person of Cardenio. The curate ordered them to get ready what the house afforded, and the host, hoping to be well paid, quickly served up a decent supper. Don Quixote still continued asleep, and they agreed not to awake him; for at that time he had more occasion for sleep than food.

During the supper, at which the host and his family were present, as well as the strangers who happened to be then at the inn, the discourse turned upon the extraordinary derangement of Don Quixote, and the state in which he had been found in the mountain. The hostess, seeing that Sancho was not present, related to them his adventure with the carrier, and also the whole story of the blanket, at which they were not a little diverted. The priest happening to remark that the books of chivalry which Don Quixote had read had turned his brain, the innkeeper said:

"I cannot conceive how that can be; for, really, in my opinion, there is no choicer reading in the world. I have three or four of them by me, with some manuscripts, which in good truth have kept me alive, and many others."

"Well, well," said the priest; "pray, landlord, let us see those books."

"With all my heart," answered the host: and going into his chamber, he brought out an old trunk, with a padlock and chain to it, and opening it he took out three large volumes, and some manuscript papers written in a very fair character. The first book which he opened he found to be Don Cirongilio of Thrace, the next, Felixmarte of Hyrcania, and the third the history of the Grand Captain Gonzalo Hernandez of Cordova, with the life of Diego Garcia de Paredes. When the curate had read the titles of the two first, he turned to the barber, and said, "We want here our friend's housekeeper and niece."

The innkeeper was carrying away the books after his guests had seen them, when the curate said to him:

"Pray, stop till I have looked at those papers which are written in so fair a character." The host took them out, and having given them to him, he found about eight sheets in manuscript, with a large title-page, on which was written, "The Novel of the Curious Impertinent." The priest having read three or four lines to himself, said:

"In truth, I do not dislike the title of this novel, and I feel disposed to read the whole."

"Your reverence will do well," answered the innkeeper; "some of my guests who have read it liked it mightily, and earnestly begged it of me; but I would not give it them, meaning to restore it to the person who left behind him the portmanteau with these books and papers. Perhaps their owner may come this way again some time or other; and though I shall feel the loss of the books, I will faithfully restore them; for though I am an innkeeper, thank Heaven I am a Christian."

"You are much in the right, friend," said the curate; "nevertheless, if the novel pleases me, you must give me leave to take a copy of it."

"With all my heart," answered the innkeeper. In the mean time Cardenio had taken up the novel, and being likewise pleased with what he saw, he requested the priest to read it aloud.

"I will," said the priest, "unless you think we had better spend our time in sleeping."

"I would rather listen to some tale," said Dorothea; "for my spirits are not so tranquil as to allow me to sleep." Master Nicholas and Sancho expressed the same inclination.

"Well, then," said the priest, "I will read it; for I myself feel a little curiosity, and possibly it may yield us some amusement." Accordingly the priest proceeded to read the novel, the rest of the company listening intently.

CHAPTER XXVII

THE BATTLE WITH THE GIANT PANDAFILANDO, WITH OTHER INCIDENTS

THE novel was nearly finished, when Sancho Panza, who had gone to see how his master was doing, came running full of dismay out of Don Quixote's chamber, crying aloud:

"Run, gentlemen, quickly, and succour my master, who is over head and ears in the toughest battle my eyes ever beheld.

As God shall save me, he has given the giant, that enemy of the Princess Micomicona, such a stroke that he has cut his head as clean off his shoulders as if it had been a turnip!"

"What say you, brother?" quoth the curate, laying aside the novel. "Are you in your senses, Sancho? How can this possibly be, since the giant is two thousand leagues off?" At that instant they heard a great noise in the room, and Don Quixote calling aloud:

"Stay, cowardly thief! robber! rogue! Here I have you, and your scimitar shall avail you nothing!" Then followed the sound of strokes and slashes against the walls.

"Do not stand listening," quoth Sancho, "but go in and end the fray, or help my master: though by this time there will be no occasion; as I dare say the giant is dead, and giving an account to God of his past wicked life: for I saw the blood run about the floor, and the head cut off, lying on one side, and as big as a wine-skin."

"I will be hanged," exclaimed the innkeeper, "if Don Quixote, or Don Devil, has not gashed some of the wine-skins that hung at his bed's-head; and the wine he has spilt this block-head takes for blood." So saying, he rushed into the room, followed by the whole company: and they found Don Quixote in the strangest situation imaginable. He was in his shirt, and on his head a little greasy red cap which belonged to the inn-keeper. About his left arm he had twisted a bed-blanket, and in his right hand he held his drawn sword, with which he was lay-ing about him on all sides, calling out as if in actual combat; his eyes were shut, being still asleep, and dreaming that he was engaged in battle with the giant: for his mind was so full of the adventure which he had undertaken that he dreamt that, having reached the kingdom of Micomicon and engaged in combat with his enemy, he was cleaving the giant down with a stroke that also proved fatal to the wine-skins, and set the whole room afloat with wine. The innkeeper seeing this, was in such a rage, that with his clenched fists he fell so furiously upon Don Quixote, that if Cardenio and the priest had not taken him off, he would have put an end to the war of the giant. The barber seeing that the poor gentleman was not awake, he brought a large bucket of cold water, with which he soused him all over; and even that

"Stay, cowardly thief! robber! rogue! Here I have you."

ablution did not restore him so entirely as to make him sensible of his situation. Dorothea, perceiving how scantily he was arrayed, would not stay to see the fight between her champion and his adversary. Sancho searched about the floor for the head of the giant, and not finding it, he said :

"Well, I see plainly that everything about this house is enchantment : for the last time I was here I had thumps and blows given me in this very same place by an invisible hand ; and now the head is vanished, which I saw cut off with my own eyes, and the blood spouting from the body like any fountain."

"What blood, and what fountain ? thou enemy to God and His saints ! " said the innkeeper : " dost thou not see, fellow, that the blood and the fountain are nothing but these skins ripped open, and the red wine floating about the room ? Perdition catch his soul that pierced them ! "

"So much the worse for me," said Sancho ; "for want of this head, I shall see my earldom melt away like salt in water." Thus Sancho awake was as wise as Don Quixote asleep, his head being quite turned by his master's promises. The inn-keeper lost all patience at the indifference of the squire and the mischievous havoc of the knight ; and he swore they should not escape, as they did before, without paying ; and that the privileges of his chivalry should not exempt him this time from discharging both reckonings, even to the patching of the wine-skins.

Don Quixote (whose hands were held by the priest) now conceiving the adventure to be finished, and that he was in the presence of the Princess Micomicona, fell on his knees before the priest, and said :

"High and renowned lady, your highness may henceforward live secure of harm from that ill-born wretch. I have now dis-charged the promise I gave you, since, by the assistance of Heaven, and through the favour of her by whom I live and breathe, I have so happily accomplished the enterprise."

"Did not I tell you so ? " quoth Sancho, hearing this : " you see I was not drunk—look if my master has not already put the giant in pickle ! Here are the bulls ! * my earldom is cock-sure." Who could help laughing at the absurdities of both master and man ? They were all diverted except the innkeeper, who swore

---

* In allusion to the joy of the mob of Spain, when they see the bulls coming.

like a trooper. At length the barber, Cardenio, and the priest, with much difficulty, got Don Quixote upon his bed again, where, exhausted with his labour, he slept soundly. They left him to his repose, and went out to the inn-door, trying to comfort Sancho for his disappointment in not finding the giant's head; but they had most trouble in pacifying the innkeeper, who was in despair at the untimely death of his wine-skins The hostess grumbled too, muttering to herself:

"In an evil hour this knight-errant came into my house, for he has been a dear guest to me!"

The curate endeavoured to quiet all of them; promising to make the best reparation in his power for the skins as well as the wine; and especially for the damage done to the tail which they valued so much. Dorothea comforted Sancho Panza, telling him that if it should really appear that his master had cut off the giant's head, she would, when peaceably seated on her throne, bestow on him the best earldom in her dominions. With this promise Sancho was comforted, and he assured the princess that she might depend upon it he had seen the giant's head, and that it had a beard which reached down to the girdle; and if it could not be found it was owing to the witchcraft in that house, of which he had seen and felt enough the last time they lodged there. Dorothea agreed with him; but assured him that all would end well and to his heart's desire. Tranquillity being now restored, the curate was requested by Cardenio, Dorothea, and the rest, to read the remainder of the novel, which he did. While they were discussing it after the curate had stopped reading, the host suddenly called out:

"By our Lady! here comes a goodly company of guests! If they stop here we shall sing, O let us be joyful!"

"What are they?" said Cardenio.

"Four men," answered the host, "on horseback, à la Gineta,* with lances and targets, and black masks† on their faces; and there is a woman with them, on a side-saddle, dressed in white, and her face likewise covered: besides these, there are two lads on foot."

---

* A mode of riding with short stirrups, which the Spaniards took from the Arabs.

† A piece of thin black silk worn before the face in travelling, not for disguise, but to keep off the dust and sun.

" Are they near ? " said the priest.

" So near," replied the innkeeper, " that they are already at the door." Dorothea, hearing this, veiled her face, and Cardenio retired to Don Quixote's chamber. When the persons mentioned by the host entered the yard, the four horsemen (who appeared to be gentlemen), having alighted, went to assist the lady to dismount ; and one of them taking her in his arms, placed her in a chair near the door of the chamber to which Cardenio had retired. During all this time not one of the party had taken off their masks, or spoken a word. The lady when seated in a chair heaved a deep sigh, and her arms hung listlessly down, as if she were in a weak and fainting state. When the servants took the horses to the stable, the curate followed and questioned one of them, being curious to know who these people were.

" In truth, Señor," replied the servant, " I cannot tell you who they are ; but they must be people of quality, especially he who took the lady in his arms, because all the rest pay him such respect, and do nothing but what he orders and directs."

" And the lady, pray who is she ? " asked the priest.

" Neither can I tell that," replied the lacquey ; " for I have not once seen her face during the whole journey. I often, indeed, hear her sigh, and utter such groans that any one of them was enough to break her heart : but it is no wonder that we cannot tell you any more, as my comrade and I have been only two days in their service ; for having met us upon the road, they persuaded us to go with them as far as Andalusia, and promised to pay us well."

" Have you heard any of their names ? " said the curate.

" No, indeed," answered the lad, " for they all travel in so much silence we hear nothing but the sighs and the sobs of the poor lady, which move our pity ; and wheresoever she is going, we suspect it is against her will. From her habit she must be a nun, or perhaps going to be made one, and not from her own choice, which makes her so sorrowful."

" Very likely," quoth the priest ; and then leaving them, he returned to the room where he had left Dorothea, whose compassion being excited by the sighs of the masked lady, she approached her and said, " You seem in distress, dear madam ;

if it be in the power of woman to render you any service, most willingly I offer you mine." The afflicted lady returned no answer ; and although Dorothea renewed her offers, she persisted in her silence until the cavalier in the mask, who seemed to be superior of the party, came up and said to Dorothea :

"Trouble not yourself, madam, to offer anything to this woman ; for she is very ungrateful ; nor endeavour to get an answer from her, unless you wish to hear some falsehood."

"No," said the lady, who had hitherto been silent ; "on the contrary, it is from my aversion to falsehood that I am thus wretched ; for it is my truth alone which makes you act so false and treacherous a part."

These words were distinctly heard by Cardenio, who was very near to the speaker, being separated only by the door of Don Quixote's chamber ; and, on hearing them, he cried aloud :

"Good Heaven, what do I hear ? what voice is that which has reached my ears ?" The lady, in much surprise, turned her head at these exclamations ; and, not seeing who uttered them, she started up, and was going into the room, when the cavalier detained her, and would not suffer her to move a step. In this sudden commotion her mask fell off, and discovered a face of incomparable beauty, although pale and full of terror ; for she looked wildly around her, examining every place with so much eagerness that she seemed distracted, and excited the sympathy of Dorothea and others of the party, who could not conjecture the cause of her agitation. The cavalier held her fast by the shoulders, and his hands being thus engaged he could not keep on his mask, which at length fell to the ground, and Dorothea, who also had her arms round the lady, raising her eyes, discovered in the stranger—her husband, Don Fernando ! when instantly, with a long and dismal Oh ! she fell backward in a swoon ; and had not the barber, who stood close by, caught her in his arms, she would have fallen to the ground. The priest then hastily removed her veil to throw water on her face ; upon which Don Fernando recognised her, and seemed petrified at the sight. Nevertheless, he still kept his hold of Lucinda, who was the lady that was endeavouring to release herself from him ; for she knew Cardenio's voice, and he well recollected hers. The groan of Dorothea when she fainted was also heard by Cardenio, who believing it came from his Lucinda, rushed into the room, and the first object he saw was Don Fernando, holding Lucinda in his arms. They all gazed upon each other in silence ; for none seemed able to utter a word. Lucinda was the first who recovered the power of speech, and she thus addressed Don Fernando, " Let me go, my lord : I entreat you, as you are a gentleman, that you will suffer me to fly to the protection of him from whom in vain you have endeavoured to separate me. See how mysteriously Heaven has conducted me into the presence of my true husband ? You well know, by a thousand proofs, that nothing can shake the faith I have pledged to him."

Dorothea in the mean time had recovered her senses, and hearing what Lucinda said, she conjectured who she was. Seeing that Don Fernando still held her, she approached him, and threw herself at his feet, her lovely face bathed in tears.

" Ah, my lord !" said she, " were you not dazzled by that beauty in your arms, you would see the unhappy Dorothea, who is now prostrate at your feet. I am that humble country girl whom you vouchsafed to call yours ; she who lived a happy and modest life until, seduced by your importunities, and the apparent sincerity of your affection, she resigned her liberty to you. How you requited her is now too manifest ! But do not think that I have followed the path of dishonour : grief and misery alone have attended my steps since your cruel desertion. When I was persuaded to bind myself to you, it was with ties that, changed as your sentiments may be, can never be dissolved. I am still your wife."

The afflicted Dorothea urged these and other arguments in so affecting a manner that she excited the most lively interest in all present. Don Fernando listened in silence to her words, which were followed by such bursts of overwhelming grief, that no human heart could witness it without emotion. Lucinda longed to comfort her, and condole with her, but she was still detained. Don Fernando at length suddenly disengaged his arms from her, after having gazed awhile on Dorothea. " You have conquered, fair Dorothea !" he exclaimed,—" you have conquered. There is no resisting you ! "

Lucinda was so faint, when released from Don Fernando's embrace, that she was just falling to the ground ; but Cardenio hastened to her support : " These arms," said he, " shall protect thee, my beloved, my faithful mistress ! Heaven grant you may now find repose ! " Lucinda looked up, to be assured that it was indeed her Cardenio, and on seeing his beloved face, regardless of forms, she threw her arms around his neck, and embraced him with the utmost tenderness.

" Oh, Cardenio ! you are my true lord ! Whatever the fates may condemn me to suffer, I am for ever yours ! "

This was an affecting scene to'all present. Dorothea watched Don Fernando, and fearing that he meditated revenge on Cardenio, as he looked agitated, and put his hand to his sword, she clung around him, embracing his knees, and said to him :

" What means my love, my only refuge ? Behold your true wife at your feet ! Lucinda is in the arms of her husband, and even in your presence bedews his bosom with tears of love ; how then can you think of uniting yourself to her ! "

While Dorothea spoke, Cardenio kept his eyes fixed on Don Fernando, and was prepared to defend himself if assaulted by him. But that nobleman was now surrounded by the whole party, not excepting honest Sancho, who all interceded for Dorothea ; and the curate represented to him that so singular a meeting must not be ascribed to chance, but to the special providence of Heaven. He begged him also to consider how vain would be the attempt to separate Cardenio and Lucinda, who would be happy even to die proving each other's faith ; and how prudent as well as noble it would be in him to triumph over his passion, and freely leave the two lovers to enjoy the happiness of mutual affection. That he should turn to the lovely Dorothea, who had such strong claims upon him, not only on account of her extreme tenderness for him, but the promises he had made to her, which, as a Christian and a man of honour, he was bound to perform : adding to these arguments, that it would be no derogation to his rank to elevate beauty adorned with virtue.

These truths, so forcibly urged, were not lost upon the mind of Don Fernando, who embraced Dorothea, saying :

" Rise, my dear lady, for that is not a posture for the mistress of my soul ; and if I have offended against you, surely it has been by the will of Heaven, that I might know your true value, by such proofs of your constancy and affection. I only entreat that you will not reproach me for my involuntary offence, but look at the now happy Lucinda, and her eyes will plead my excuse. May she enjoy long years of happiness with her Cardenio, and Heaven grant me the same with my Dorothea!" Again he pressed her to his heart, and could scarcely forbear showing his emotions of tenderness and repentance by tears : indeed, all the company present were so much affected, that their tears of sympathy might have been mistaken for those of sorrow. Even Sancho Panza wept ; though he owned afterwards that it was only because Dorothea turned out not to be the Queen Micomicona who was to have made his fortune. Cardenio and Lucinda expressed their acknowledgments to Don Fernando for his present conduct, in so feeling a manner, that he was too much moved to find words to reply to them.

Dorothea being now questioned by Don Fernando as to the circumstances which had brought her to that place, she gave a brief detail of what she had before related to Cardenio ; and so interesting was her narrative to Don Fernando and his party, and so graceful her delivery, that they even regretted when the story of her misfortunes was ended. Don Fernando then related what he had done after finding in Lucinda's bosom the paper declaring herself the wife of Cardenio. He confessed that his first impulse was to take her life, and that he should actually have done so, had he not been prevented by her parents ; upon which he immediately quitted the house, full of shame and fury, determined to seize the first opportunity of revenge. On the following day he heard that she had left her father's house, concealing the place of her retreat ; but after some months he discovered that she had retired to a convent, whither he immediately pursued her, accompanied by the three gentlemen then present. He then watched an opportunity when the convent gate was open to make his entrance, leaving two of his companions to secure the gate ; and having found Lucinda walking in the cloisters, attended only by a nun, they seized her, and bore her away to a place where they had prepared every accommodation necessary for their project. Lucinda, he said, had fainted on seeing herself in his power, and when her senses returned, she wept and sighed, but never spoke a single word. Thus, in silence and sorrow, they had reached that inn, which, he trusted, was the goal of all their earthly misfortunes.

CHAPTER XXVIII

THE ARRIVAL OF THE CAPTIVE WITH THE MOORISH LADY

SANCHO experienced no small grief of mind on thus seeing all his hopes of preferment fast disappearing and vanishing into smoke, by the transformation of the fair Princess Micomicona into Dorothea, and the giant into Don Fernando; while his master, unconscious of what was passing, lay wrapped in profound sleep. Dorothea could not be certain whether the happiness she enjoyed was not a dream; and Cardenio and Lucinda entertained the same doubts. Don Fernando gave thanks to Heaven for having delivered him from a perilous situation, in which his honour as well as his soul were in imminent danger. In short, all were pleased at the happy conclusion of such intricate and hopeless affairs. The priest, like a man of sense, placed everything in its true light, and congratulated each upon their share of the good fortune that had befallen them. But the landlady was more delighted than all; as Cardenio and the priest had promised to pay her with interest for every loss she had sustained upon Don Quixote's account.

Sancho alone was afflicted, unhappy, and full of sorrow; and, with dismal looks, he went in to his master, just then awake, to whom he said:

"Your worship may sleep on, Señor Sorrowful Figure, without troubling yourself about killing any giant or restoring the princess to her kingdom, for that is already done and over."

"I verily believe it," answered Don Quixote, "for I have had the most monstrous and dreadful battle with the giant that ever I expect to have in the whole course of my life; with one back stroke I tumbled his head to the ground, and so great was the quantity of blood that gushed from it, that the stream ran along the ground like a torrent of water."

"Like red wine, your worship might better say," answered Sancho; "for I can tell you, if you do not know it already, that the dead giant is a pierced wine-skin, and the blood eighteen gallons of red wine contained in the belly; and may the devil take all for me!"

"What sayest thou, fool?" replied Don Quixote. "Art thou in thy senses?"

"Pray, get up, sir," quoth Sancho, "and you will see what a fine day's work you have made, and what a reckoning we have to pay; and you will see, too, the queen converted into a private lady called Dorothea, with other matters which, if you take them rightly, will astonish you."

"I shall wonder at nothing," replied Don Quixote: "for, thou mayest remember, the last time we were here, I told thee that all things in this place went by enchantment; and there can be nothing surprising in it if this were the case again."

"I should believe so too," answered Sancho, "if my being tossed in the blanket had been a matter of this nature: but it was downright real and true; and I saw the very same innkeeper hold a corner of the blanket, and cant me towards heaven with notable alacrity, laughing too all the time; and where it happens that we know persons, in my opinion (simple and a sinner as I am), there is no enchantment at all, but much misusage and much mishap."

"Well, Heaven will remedy it," quoth Don Quixote: "give me my clothes, that I may go and see the events and transformations thou hast mentioned."

Sancho reached him his apparel: and while he was dressing, the curate gave Don Fernando and his companions an account of Don Quixote's madness, and of the artifice they had used to get him from the barren mountain to which he imagined himself banished through his lady's disdain. He related also most of the adventures which Sancho had communicated to them, to their great diversion and astonishment; for they, like others, considered it as the most singular species of insanity that ever took possession of the imagination. The curate said further that, since the lady Dorothea's good fortune would not permit her to prosecute their design, it was necessary to contrive some other expedient to get him home. Cardenio offered his assistance, and proposed that Lucinda should personate Dorothea.

"No," said Don Fernando, "it must not be so; for I will have Dorothea herself proceed in her part; and as this good gentleman's village is not far distant, I shall be glad to contribute to his cure."

" It is not above two days' journey," said the curate. " If it were farther," said Don Fernando, " I would undertake it with pleasure for so good a purpose."

Don Quixote now came forth, clad in all his armour ; Mambrino's helmet, though bruised and battered, on his head ; his target braced, and resting on his sapling or lance. His strange appearance greatly surprised Don Fernando and his company, who failed not to observe his long and withered visage of sallow hue, his ill-matched armour, and measured pace. They paused in silent expectation of hearing him speak, when with much gravity and solemnity, fixing his eyes upon the fair Dorothea, he said :

" I am informed, fair lady, by this my squire, that your grandeur is annihilated, and your very being demolished ; and that from a queen you are metamorphosed into a private maiden. If this has been done by order of the necromantic king your father, fearing lest I should not afford you the necessary aid, I say he knew not one half of his art, and that he was but little versed in histories of knight-errantry ; for there is no danger upon earth through which my sword shall not force a way ; and by bringing down the head of your enemy to the ground, shortly place upon your own the crown of your kingdom."

Here Don Quixote ceased, and waited the answer of the princess, who, knowing it to be Don Fernando's desire that she should carry on the deception until Don Quixote's return home, with much dignity and grace replied :

" Whosoever told you, valorous Knight of the Sorrowful Figure, that I was changed and altered from what I was, spoke not the truth ; for I am the same to-day that I was yesterday. It is true, indeed, that certain events, fortunate beyond my hopes, have befallen me since then, yet I do not cease to be what I was before, and to entertain the same thoughts I have ever indulged of availing myself of the valour of your valiant and invincible arm. Let us then proceed on our journey to-morrow (for to-day it is too late) ; and to Heaven and your prowess I trust for a successful issue."

Thus spoke the discreet Dorothea ; whereupon Don Quixote, turning with marks of anger on his visage to Sancho, said to him :

"I tell thee, Sancho, thou art the greatest liar and rascal in Spain ; say, vagabond ! didst thou not tell me just now that this princess was transformed into a damsel called Dorothea ; with other absurdities, which were enough to confound me ? I vow " (and here he looked up to heaven, and gnashed his teeth) " I have a great inclination to make such an example of thee, as shall put sense into the brains of all the lying squires of future times ! "

"Pray, sir, be pacified," answered Sancho : "for I may have been mistaken as to the change of my lady the Princess Micomicona ; but as to the giant's head, or at least the piercing of the skins, and the blood being red wine, I am not deceived, as God liveth ; for there are the skins at your worship's bed's-head, cut and slashed, and the red wine has made a pond of the room : and you will find I speak true when our host demands damages. As for the rest, I rejoice in my heart that my lady-queen is as she was ; for I have my share in it, like every neighbour's child."

"I tell thee, Sancho," said Don Quixote, "thou art an ass. Excuse me, that's enough."

"It is enough," said Don Fernando, "and let no more be said on the subject : and since the princess hath declared that we are to set forward in the morning, it being too late to-day, let us pass this night in agreeable conversation ; and to-morrow we will all accompany Señor Don Quixote, for we desire to be eye-witnesses of the valorous and unheard-of deeds which he is to perform in the accomplishment of this great enterprise."

"It is my part to serve and attend you," answered Don Quixote ; "and much am I indebted to you for your good opinion ; which it shall be my endeavour not to disappoint, even at the expense of my life, or even more, if more were possible."

Many were the compliments, and polite offers of service passing between Don Quixote and Don Fernando, when they were interrupted by the arrival of two other persons at the inn. The one was a man, who by his garb seemed to be a Christian lately come from among the Moors ; for he had on a blue cloth coat, with short skirts, half-sleeves, and no collar. His breeches also were of blue cloth, and his cap of the same colour. He had on a pair of date-coloured buskins, and a Moorish scimitar hung in a shoulder-belt across his breast. He was accompanied by a female in a Moorish dress, mounted on an ass, her face veiled, a brocade turban on her head, and covered with a mantle from her shoulders to her feet. The man was of a robust and agreeable figure, rather above forty years of age, of a dark complexion, with large mustachios, and a well-set beard; in short, his deportment, had he been well-dressed, would have marked him for a gentleman. Upon his entrance he asked for a room, and seemed disconcerted on hearing that there was not one unoccupied; nevertheless, he assisted his female companion, who was evidently a Moor, to alight. The other ladies, as well as the landlady, her daughter, and maid, all surrounded the stranger, attracted by the novelty of her appearance; and Dorothea, who was always obliging and considerate, perceiving they were disappointed at not having an apartment, accosted her, saying:

"Do not be distressed, my dear madam, at an inconvenience which must be expected in places of this kind; but if you will please to share with us (pointing to Lucinda) such accommodation as we have, you may perhaps have found worse in the course of your journey." The veiled lady returned her no answer, but, rising from her seat, and laying her hands across her breast, bowed her head and body in token that she thanked her. By her silence they conjectured that she could not speak their language, and were confirmed in their opinion of her being a Moor.

Her companion, who had been engaged out of the room, now entered, and seeing that she was addressed by some of the company, he said:

"Ladies, this young person understands scarcely anything of the Spanish language, and is therefore unable to converse with you. We have just escaped from Algiers, where I have been in captivity, and where I was saved by the goodness of this lady, who enabled me to ransom myself, also to buy a vessel wherein we could escape, and who has given up wealth and high rank in her own country in order to marry me."

"We have only been requesting her to favour us with her company, and share our accommodation," said Lucinda; "and we will show her all the attention due to strangers, who need it, especially those of our own sex."

"My dear madam," he replied, "I return you a thousand thanks both for this lady and myself, and am fully sensible of the extent of the favour you offer us."

"Allow me to ask you, Señor, whether the lady is a Christian or a Moor?"

"By birth she is a Moor," replied the stranger; "but in heart she is a Christian, having an ardent wish to become one."

"She is not yet baptized, then?" inquired Lucinda.

"There has not yet been an opportunity," answered the stranger, "since she left Algiers, her native country; and she has not hitherto been in such imminent danger of death as to make it necessary to have her baptized before she be instructed in all the ceremonies enjoined by our Church; but, if it please Heaven, she will be soon baptized in a manner becoming her rank, which is beyond what either her appearance or mine indicates."

These strangers excited the curiosity of the whole party, who refrained, however, from importuning them with questions; conceiving they would be more inclined to take repose than to satisfy them. Dorothea now took the lady's hand, and, leading her to a seat, placed herself by her, and then requested her to unveil; upon which she gave an inquiring look at her companion; and he having interpreted what had been said to her in Arabic, she removed her veil, and discovered a face so exquisitely beautiful that Dorothea thought she exceeded Lucinda, who, on her part, thought her handsomer than Dorothea; while their admirers all seemed to confess that if either of them could have a rival in beauty it was in this Moorish lady; and, as it is the privilege of beauty to conciliate and attract good-will, they were all eager to show her attention. Don Fernando inquired her name of her companion; "Lela Zoraida," he replied; when she interposed in a sweet, earnest manner—"No, not Zoraida; Maria, Maria"—giving them to understand that her name was Maria, not Zoraida. These words were pronounced in so touching a voice that they were all affected, especially the ladies, who were naturally tender-hearted. Lucinda embraced her most affectionately, saying, "Yes, yes; Maria, Maria;" who answered, "Yes, Maria; Zoraida macange"—meaning not Zoraida.

It being now night, supper was served up (in providing which the landlord had, by Don Fernando's order, exerted himself to

"Thus they banqueted much to their satisfaction."

the utmost). They seated themselves at a long table, like those in halls; for there was no other, either round or square, in the house. They insisted on Don Quixote taking the head of the table, though he would have declined it; the Princess Micomicona he placed next to him, being her champion; Lucinda and Zoraida seated themselves beside her; opposite them sat Don Fernando and Cardenio; the curate and barber sat next to the ladies, and the rest of the gentlemen opposite to them; and thus they banqueted much to their satisfaction. Don Quixote added to their amusement, for being moved by the same spirit which had inspired him with eloquence at the goatherd's supper, instead of eating he again harangued the company on knight-errantry.

The knight, however, pursued his discourse so rationally, that his auditors could scarcely think him insane; on the contrary, most of them being gentlemen, to whom the exercise of arms properly appertains, they listened to him with particular pleasure and expressed themselves to that effect.

Don Quixote made this long harangue while the rest were eating, forgetting to raise a morsel to his mouth, though Sancho Panza ever and anon reminded him of his supper, telling him he would have time enough afterwards to talk as much as he pleased. His other auditors were concerned that a man who seemed to possess so good an understanding should, on a particular point, be so egregiously in want of it. The curate told him there was great reason in all that he had said in favour of arms, and although himself a scholar and a graduate, he acquiesced in his opinion.

The collation being over, the cloth was removed; and while the hostess and her damsels were preparing the chamber which Don Quixote had occupied for the ladies, Don Fernando requested the stranger to gratify them by relating his adventures. This the captive consented to do, recounting a very stirring series of adventures in which Zoraida played a prominent part. The narrative was not without its pathetic side, inasmuch as they had been obliged to kidnap and carry away with them Zoraida's father, Agi Morato, and to leave him with others on a desolate part of the coast of Africa. When the old Moor found that his daughter was running away with the Christian captive, and had made up her mind to become a Christian, he stood on the shore

watching the vanishing vessel and poured out a stream of maledictions and plaints against her, which affected her much. "But
I trust all our troubles are over now, thank Heaven."

While the company were congratulating the captive on his
escape, news was brought that another party had arrived at the
inn, and that accommodation must be found for his Worship the
Judge of the High Courts of Mexico. The host and hostess
agreed to give up their room and the strangers were introduced
to the company.

Don Quixote in their name welcomed the newcomers
in the following words, " Welcome to this castle, for room will
always be found for arms and letters ; especially when, like your
worship, they appear under the patronage of beauty : for to this
fair maiden not only castles should throw open wide their gates,
but rocks divide and separate, and mountains bow their lofty heads
in salutation." The judge marvelled greatly at this speech, and
he earnestly surveyed the knight, no less astonished by his appearance than his discourse, and was considering what to say in reply,
when the other ladies made their appearance, attracted by the
account the hostess had given of the beauty of the young lady.
Don Fernando, Cardenio, and the priest, paid their compliments
in a more intelligible manner than Don Quixote, and all the
ladies of the castle welcomed the fair stranger. In short, the
judge easily perceived that he was in the company of persons of
distinction ; but the mien, visage, and behaviour of Don Quixote
confounded him. After mutual courtesies and inquiries as to
what accommodation the inn afforded, the arrangements
previously made were adopted : namely, that all the women
should lodge in the large chamber, and the men remain without,
as their guard. The judge was content that the young lady, who
was his daughter, should accompany the other ladies, and she
herself readily consented : thus, with part of the innkeeper's
narrow bed, together with that which the judge had brought with
him, they accommodated themselves during the night better than
they had expected.

The captive, from the moment he saw the judge, felt
certain that the latter was one of his brothers, whom he had left
behind when he went to the wars. He therefore inquired his
name and country of one of the servants, who told him that he was

"Poured out a stream of maledictions against her."

the licentiate John Perez de Viedma, and he had heard that his native place was in Leon. This account confirmed him in the opinion that this was indeed a brother who, by the advice of his father, had applied himself to letters. Agitated and overjoyed, he called aside Don Fernando, Cardenio, and the curate, and communicated to them his discovery. The servant had also told him that he was going to the Indies, as judge of the courts of Mexico, and that the young lady was his daughter, whose mother had died in giving her birth, but had left her a rich inheritance. He asked them how they thought he had best make himself known, or how he could ascertain whether his brother, seeing him so poor, would not be ashamed to own him, or receive him to his bosom with affection.

"Leave me to make that experiment," said the priest; "not that I make any doubt, Señor captain, of your meeting with a kind reception; for there is an appearance of worth and good sense in your brother which neither implies arrogance nor inability to appreciate duly the accidents of fortune."

"Nevertheless," said the captain, "I would rather not discover myself abruptly to him."

"Leave all to me," answered the priest, "and I will manage the affair to your satisfaction," which he unquestionably did.

The meeting was indeed affecting beyond description. From time to time their mutual inquiries were suspended by demonstrations of fraternal love: often the judge embraced Zoraida, and as often returned her to the caresses of his daughter: and a most pleasing sight it was to see the mutual embraces of the fair Christian and lovely Moor.

Don Quixote was all this time a silent but attentive observer, satisfied at the correspondence of these singular events with the annals of chivalry. It was agreed that the captain and Zoraida should go with their brother to Seville, and acquaint their father of his return, so that the old man might be present at the baptism and nuptials of Zoraida, as it was impossible for the judge to defer his journey beyond a month. The night being now far advanced, they proposed retiring to repose during the remainder, Don Quixote offering his service to guard the castle, lest some giant, or rather miscreant errant, tempted by the treasure of beauty there enclosed, should presume to make an attack upon it. His friends thanked him, and took occasion to amuse the judge with an account of his strange frenzy. Sancho Panza alone was out of all patience at sitting up so late. However, he was better accommodated than any of them, upon the accoutrements of his ass, for which he dearly paid, as shall be hereafter related. The ladies having retired to their chamber, and the rest accommodated as well as they could be, Don Quixote, according to promise, sallied out of the inn to take his post at the castle gate.

CHAPTER XXIX

THE ADVENTURE OF THE YOUNG MULETEER; SUNDRY STRANGE ACCIDENTS THAT HAPPENED AT THE ENCHANTED INN

JUST before daybreak a voice reached the ears of the ladies, so sweet and melodious that it forcibly arrested their attention, especially that of Dorothea, by whose side slept Donna Clara de Viedma, the daughter of the judge. The voice was unaccompanied by any instrument, and they were surprised at the skill of the singer. Sometimes they fancied that the sound proceeded from the yard, and at other times from the stable. While they were in this uncertainty, Cardenio came to the chamber-door, and said:

"If you are not asleep, pray listen; and you will hear one of the muleteers singing enchantingly." Dorothea told him that they had heard him; upon which Cardenio retired.

Dorothea thought it was a great loss to Donna Clara not to hear such excellent singing, she therefore gave her a gentle shake and awoke her.

"Excuse me, my dear, for disturbing you," she said, "since it is only that you may have the pleasure of hearing the sweetest voice which perhaps you ever heard in your life!" Clara, half awake, was obliged to ask Dorothea to repeat what she had said to her: after which she endeavoured to command her attention, but had no sooner heard a few words of the song than she was seized with a fit of trembling as violent as the attack of a quartan ague: and, clinging round Dorothea, she cried:

"Ah, my dear lady! why did you wake me? The greatest service that could be done me would be for ever to close both my

" Don Quixote sallied out of the inn to take his post at the castle gate."

eyes and ears, that I might neither see nor hear that unhappy musician."

"What did you say, my dear?" answered Dorothea: "is it not a muleteer who is singing?"

"Oh no," replied Clara; "he is Don Louis, a young gentleman of large possessions, and so much master of my heart that, if he reject me not, it shall be his eternally. I wish, however, this young man would go back, and leave me: absence, perhaps, may lessen the pain I now feel; though I fear it will not have much effect. What a strange sorcery this love is! I know not how it came to possess me, so young as I am—in truth, I believe he and I are both of the same age, and I am not yet sixteen, nor shall I be, as my father says, until next Michaelmas." Dorothea could not forbear smiling at Donna Clara's childish simplicity; however, she entreated her again to sleep the remainder of the night, and to hope for everything in the morning.

Profound silence now reigned over the whole house; all being asleep except the innkeeper's daughter and her maid Maritornes, who, knowing Don Quixote's weak points, determined to amuse themselves by playing him some trick while he was keeping guard without doors. There was no window on that side of the house which overlooked the field, except a small opening in the straw-loft, whence the straw was thrown out. At this hole the pair of damsels planted themselves, whence they commanded a view of the knight on horseback, leaning on his lance, and could hear him ever and anon heaving such deep and mournful sighs that they seemed torn from the very bottom of his soul. They could also distinguish words, uttered in a soft, soothing, amorous tone; such as:

"O my Lady Dulcinea del Toboso! perfection of all beauty, quintessence of discretion, treasury of wit, and pledge of modesty! what may now be thy sweet employment? Art thou, peradventure, thinking of thy captive knight, who voluntarily exposes himself to so many perils for thy sake! O thou triformed luminary, bring me swift tidings of her! Perhaps thou art now gazing at her, envious of her beauty, as she walks through some gallery of her sumptuous palace."

Thus far Don Quixote had proceeded in his soliloquy, when the innkeeper's daughter softly called to him, saying:

"Pray, sir, come a little this way." Don Quixote turned his head, and perceiving by the light of the moon, which then shone bright, that some person beckoned him towards the spike-hole, which to his fancy was a window with gilded bars, suitable to the rich castle he conceived the inn to be, and his former visions again recurring, he concluded that the fair damsel of the castle, irresistibly enamoured of him, had now come to repeat her visit. Unwilling, therefore, to appear discourteous or ungrateful, he approached the aperture, and replied :

"I lament, fair lady, that you should have placed your affections where it is impossible for you to meet with that return which your great merit and beauty deserve : yet ought you not to blame an unfortunate knight whom love has already enthralled. Pardon me, dear lady ; retire, and do not by any farther disclosure of your sentiments make me appear yet more ungrateful ; but if I can repay you by any other way than a return of passion, I entreat that you will command me, and I swear, by that sweet absent enemy of mine, to gratify you immediately, though you should require a lock of Medusa's hair, which was composed of snakes, or the sunbeams enclosed in a vial."

"Sir," quoth Maritornes, "my lady wants none of these."

"What then doth your lady require, discreet duenna?" answered Don Quixote.

"Only one of your beautiful hands," quoth Maritornes, "whereby partly to satisfy that longing which brought her to this window, so much to the peril of her honour, that if her lord and father should know of it he would whip off at least one of her ears."

"Let him dare to do it !" cried Don Quixote ; "fatal should be his punishment for presuming to lay violent hands on the delicate members of an enamoured daughter." Maritornes, not doubting but that he would grant the request, hastened down into the stable, and brought back the halter belonging to Sancho's dapple, just as Don Quixote had got upon Rozinante's saddle to reach the gilded window at which the enamoured damsel stood ; and giving her his hand, he said :

"Accept, madam, this hand, or rather this scourge of the wicked : accept, I say, this hand, which that of woman never before touched, not even hers who has the entire right of my whole person.

"We shall soon see that," quoth Maritornes. Then, making a running-knot in the halter, she fixed it on his wrist, and tied the other end of it fast to the staple of the hay-loft door. Don Quixote, feeling the harsh rope about his wrist, said:

"You seem rather to rasp than grasp my hand — pray do not treat it so roughly, since it is not to blame for my adverse inclination." But his expostulations were unheard; for as soon as Maritornes had tied the knot, they both went laughing away, having fastened it in such a manner that it was impossible for him to get loose.

Thus he remained standing upright on Rozinante, his hand close to the hole, and tied by the wrist to the bolt of the door; and in the utmost alarm lest Rozinante should move on either side, and leave him suspended. He durst not, therefore, make the least motion; though indeed he might well have expected, from the sobriety and patience of Rozinante, that he would remain in that position an entire century. In short, Don Quixote, finding himself thus situated and the ladies gone, concluded that it was an affair of enchantment, like others which had formerly happened to him in the same castle. He then cursed his own indiscretion for having entered it a second time: since he might have learnt from his chivalry, that when a knight was unsuccessful in an adventure, it was a sign that its accomplishment was reserved for another, and that second trials were always fruitless.

He made many attempts to release himself, though he was afraid of making any great exertion lest Rozinante should stir; but his efforts were all in vain, and he was compelled either to remain standing on the saddle or to tear off his hand. He verily thought himself and his horse must remain in the same posture, without eating, drinking, or sleeping, until the evil influence of the stars had passed over, or some more powerful sage should disenchant him.

But he was mistaken; for it was scarcely daylight, when four men on horseback stopped at the inn, well appointed and accoutred, with carbines hanging on their saddle-bows. Not finding the inn-door open, they called aloud and knocked very hard; upon which Don Quixote called out from the place where he stood sentinel, in an arrogant and loud voice, "Knights, or squires, or whoever you are, desist from knocking at the gate of this castle; for at this early hour its inmates are doubtless sleeping; at least they are not accustomed to open the gates of their fortress until the sun has spread his beams over the whole horizon: retire, therefore from the portcullis until brighter daylight shall inform us whether it be proper to admit you or not."

"What the devil of a fortress or castle is this," quoth one of them, "that we are obliged to observe all this ceremony? If you are the innkeeper, make somebody open the door, for we are travellers, and only want to bait our horses, and go on, as we are in haste."

"What say ye, sirs—do I look like an innkeeper?" said Don Quixote.

"I know not what you look like," answered the other; "but I am sure you talk preposterously to call this inn a castle."

"A castle it is," replied Don Quixote, "and one of the best in the whole province; and at this moment contains within its walls persons who have had crowns on their heads and sceptres in their hands."

"You had better have said the reverse," quoth the traveller; "the sceptre on the head and the crown in the hand: but perhaps some company of strolling players are here, who frequently wear such things; this is not a place for any other sort of crowned heads."

"Your ignorance must be great," replied Don Quixote, "if you know not that such events are very common in chivalry." The other horseman, impatient at the dialogue, repeated his knocks with so much violence that he roused not only the host but all the company in the house.

Just at that time it happened that the horse of one of the travellers was seized with an inclination to smell at Rozinante, who, sad and spiritless, was then supporting his distended lord; but being in fact a horse of flesh, although he seemed to be one of stone, he could not be insensible to the compliment, nor refuse to return it with equal kindness. But scarcely had he stirred a step, when Don Quixote's feet slipped from the saddle, and he remained suspended by the arm, in so much torture that he fancied his wrist or his arm was being torn from his body.

G

He hung so near the ground that he could just reach it with the tips of his toes, which only made his situation the worse; for feeling how near he was to *terra firma*, he stretched and strained with all his might to reach it; like those who are tortured by the strappado, and who, being placed in the same dilemma, aggravate their sufferings by their fruitless efforts to stretch themselves.

CHAPTER XXX

THE EXTRAORDINARY ADVENTURES THAT HAPPENED IN THE ENCHANTED INN

EXERTING his lungs to the utmost, Don Quixote roared so loudly that the host opened the inn-door, in great alarm, to discover the cause of the outcry. Maritornes, being awakened by the noise, and guessing the cause, went to the straw-loft and privately untied the halter which held up Don Quixote, who immediately came to the ground. Without answering a word to the many inquiries that were made to him by the innkeeper and travellers who ran up to help him, he slipped the rope from off his wrist, and springing from the earth, mounted Rozinante, braced his target, couched his lance, and taking a good compass about the field, came up at a half gallop, saying, "Whoever shall dare to affirm that I was fairly enchanted, I say he lies; and provided my sovereign lady, the Princess Micomicona, gives me leave, I challenge him to single combat." The new comers were amazed at Don Quixote's words, till the innkeeper explained the wonder, by telling them that he was disordered in his senses. They then inquired of the host whether there was not in the house a youth about fifteen years old, habited like a muleteer—in short, describing Donna Clara's lover. The host said that there were so many people in the inn, that he had not observed such a person as they described. But one of them just then seeing the judge's coach, said:

"He must certainly be here, for there is the coach which he is said to have followed. Let one of us remain here, and the rest go in search for him ; and it would not be amiss for one of us to ride round the house, in case he should attempt to escape over the pales of the yard." All this they immediately did, much to the innkeeper's surprise, who could not guess the meaning of so much activity.

It was now full daylight, and most of the company in the house were rising ; among the first, were Donna Clara and Dorothea, who had slept but indifferently ; the one from concern at being so near her lover, and the other from a desire of seeing him. Don Quixote, finding that the four travellers regarded neither him nor his challenge, was furious with rage ; and, could he have found a precedent among the ordinances of chivalry for engaging in a new adventure after he had pledged his word to forbear until the first had been accomplished, he would now have fiercely attacked them all, and compelled them to reply : but reflecting that he was bound in honour first to reinstate the princess on her throne, he endeavoured to tranquillise himself. In the mean time the men pursued their search after the youth, and at last found him peaceably sleeping by the side of a muleteer. One of them pulling him by the arm, said, " Upon my word, Señor Don Louis, your dress is very becoming a gentleman like you, and the bed you lie on is very suitable to the tenderness with which your mother brought you up !" The youth was roused from his sleep, and looking earnestly at the man who held him, he soon recollected him to be one of his father's servants, and was so confounded that he could not say a word.

" Señor Don Louis," continued the servant, "you must instantly return home, unless you would cause the death of my lord your father, he is in such grief at your absence."

"Why, how did my father know," said Don Louis, " that I came this road, and in this dress ?"

"He was informed by a student, to whom you mentioned your project, and who was induced to disclose it from compassion at your father's distress. There are four of us here at your service, and we shall be rejoiced to restore you to your family."

"That will be as I shall please, or as Heaven may ordain," answered Don Louis.

"What, Señor, should you please to do, but return home?" rejoined the servant: "indeed you cannot do otherwise."

The muleteer who had been Don Louis's companion hearing this contest, went to acquaint Don Fernando and the rest of the company with what was passing: telling them that the man had called the young lad Don, and wanted him to return to his father's house, but that he refused to go. They all recollected his fine voice, and being eager to know who he was, and to assist him if any violence were offered to him, they repaired to the place where he was contending with his servant. Dorothea now came out of her chamber, with Donna Clara: and, calling Cardenio aside, she related to him in a few words the history of the musician and Donna Clara. He then told her of the search that had been made after the young man by the servants, and although he whispered, he was overheard by Donna Clara, who was thrown into such an agony by the intelligence, that she would have fallen to the ground if Dorothea had not supported her. Cardenio advised her to retire with Donna Clara, while he endeavoured to make some arrangements on their behalf. Don Louis was now surrounded by all the four servants, entreating that he would immediately return to comfort his father. He answered that he could not possibly do so until he had accomplished that on which his life, his honour, and his soul depended. The servants still urged him, saying that they would certainly not go back without him, and that they must compel him to return if he refused.

"That you shall not do," replied Don Louis; "at least you shall not take me living." This contest had now drawn together most of the people in the house, Don Fernando, Cardenio, the judge, the priest, the barber; and even Don Quixote had quitted his post of castle-guard. Cardenio, already knowing the young man's story, asked the men why they would take away the youth against his will?

"To save his father's life," replied one of them; "which is in danger from distress of mind."

"There is no occasion to give an account of my affairs here," said Don Louis; "I am free, and will go back if I please; otherwise, none of you shall force me."

"But reason will prevail with you," answered the servant; "and if not, we must do our duty."

"Hold!" said the judge; "let us know the whole of this affair." The man (who recollected him) answered:

"Does not your worship know this gentleman? He is your neighbour's son, and has absented himself from his father's house, in a garb very unbecoming his quality, as your worship may see." The judge, after looking at him with attention, recognised him, and accosted him in a friendly manner:

"What childish frolic is this, Señor Don Louis," said he, "or what powerful motive has induced you to disguise yourself in a manner so unbecoming your rank?" The eyes of the youth were filled with tears, and he could not say a word. The judge desired the servants to be quiet, promising that all should be well; and, taking Don Louis by the hand, he led him aside and questioned him, why he had left home in such a garb.

The youth clasping his hands, as if some great affliction wrung his heart, and shedding tears in abundance, said in answer:

"I can only say, dear sir, that from the moment Heaven was pleased by means of our vicinity to give me a sight of Donna Clara, your daughter, she became sovereign mistress of my affections; and if you, my true lord and father, do not oppose it, this very day she shall be my wife. You know, my lord, the wealth and rank of my family, of whom I am the sole heir; if these circumstances can plead in my favour, receive me immediately for your son: for though my father, influenced by other views of his own, should not approve my choice, time may reconcile him to it." Here the enamoured youth was silent, and the judge remained in suspense: no less surprised by the ingenuous confession of Don Louis than perplexed how to act in the affair; in reply, therefore, he only desired him to be calm for the present, and not let his servants return that day, that there might be time to consider what was most expedient to be done. Don Louis kissed his hands with vehemence, bathing them with tears, that might have softened a heart of marble, much more that of the judge, who, being a man of sense, was aware how advantageous this match would be for his daughter. Nevertheless, he would rather, if possible, that it should take place with the consent of Don Louis's father, who he knew had pretensions to a title for his son.

And now the devil, who never sleeps, so ordered it that at this time, the very barber entered the inn who had been deprived of Mambrino's helmet by Don Quixote, and of the trappings of his ass by Sancho Panza ; and as he was leading his beast to the stable he espied Sancho Panza, who at that moment was repairing something about the self-same pannel. He instantly fell upon him with fury :

"Ah, thief !" said he, "have I got you at last !—give me my basin and my pannel, with all the furniture you stole from me !" Sancho finding himself thus suddenly attacked and abused, secured the pannel with one hand, and with the other made the barber such a return that his mouth was bathed in blood. Nevertheless, the barber would not let go his hold ; but raised his voice so high that he drew everybody around him, while he called out :

"Justice, in the king's name ! This rogue and highway-robber here would murder me for endeavouring to recover my own goods."

"You lie !" answered Sancho, "I am no highway-robber ; my master, Don Quixote, won these spoils in fair war." Don Quixote was now present and not a little pleased to see how well his squire acted both on the offensive and defensive ; and regard-ing him thenceforward as a man of mettle, he resolved in his mind to dub him a knight the first opportunity that offered, thinking the order of chivalry would be well bestowed upon him.

During this contest the barber made many protestations.

"Gentlemen," said he, "this pannel is as certainly mine as the death I owe to God ; I know it as well as if it were made by myself; and yonder stands my ass in the stable, who will not suffer me to lie—pray do but try it, and if it does not fit him to a hair, let me be infamous : and moreover, the very day they took this from me, they robbed me likewise of a new brass basin, never hanselled, that cost me a crown." Here Don Quixote could no longer contain himself from speaking ; and separating the two combatants, he made them lay down the pannel on the ground to public view, until the truth should be decided.

"Here Don Quixote could no longer
contain himself from speaking;"

"The error of this honest squire," said he, "is manifest, in calling that a basin which was, is, and ever shall be, Mambrino's helmet—that helmet which I won in fair war, and am therefore its right and lawful possessor. With regard to the pannel, I decline any interference ; all I can say is, that my squire, Sancho, asked my permission to take the trappings belonging to the horse of this conquered coward, to adorn his own withal. I gave him leave—he took them, and if from horse-trappings they are metamorphosed into an ass's pannel, I have no other reasons to give than that these transformations are frequent in affairs of chivalry. In confirmation of what I say, go, Sancho, and bring hither the helmet which this honest man terms a basin."

"In faith, sir," quoth Sancho, "if we have no better proof than that your worship speaks of, Mambrino's helmet will prove as errant a basin as the honest man's trappings are a pack-saddle."

"Do what I command," replied Don Quixote ; "for surely all things in this castle cannot be governed by enchantment." Sancho went for the basin, and returning with it, he gave it to Don Quixote.

"Only behold, gentlemen !" said he ; "how can this squire have the face to declare that this is a basin, and not the helmet which I have described to you ? By the order of knighthood which I profess, I swear that this very helmet is the same which I took from him, without addition or diminution."

"There is no doubt of that," quoth Sancho, "for from the time my master won it, until now, he has fought but one battle in it, which was when he freed those unlucky galley-slaves ; and had it not been for that same basin-helmet, he would not have got off so well from the showers of stones which rained upon him in that skirmish.

CHAPTER XXXI

THE DISPUTE CONCERNING MAMBRINO'S HELMET AND THE PANNEL; AND OTHER ADVENTURES

"Good sirs," quoth the barber, "hear what these gentlefolks say! They will have it that this is no basin, but a helmet!"

"Aye," said Don Quixote, "and whoever shall affirm the contrary, I will convince him, if he be a knight, that he lies; and if a squire, that he lies and lies again, a thousand times." Our barber, Master Nicholas, who was present, wishing to carry on the jest for the amusement of the company, addressed himself to the other barber, and said:

"Señor barber, or whoever you are, know that I also am of your profession, and have had my certificate of examination above these twenty years, and am well acquainted with all the instruments of barber-surgery, without exception. I have likewise been a soldier in my youth, and therefore know what a helmet is, and what a morion or cap of steel is, as well as a casque with its beaver, and other matters relating to soldiery—I mean to the arms commonly used by soldiers. And I say, with submission always to better judgments, that the piece before us, which that gentleman holds in his hand, not only is not a barber's basin, but is as far from being so as white is from black, and truth from falsehood. At the same time I say, that although it be a helmet, it is not a complete helmet."

"Certainly not," said Don Quixote; "for one-half of it is wanting, namely the beaver."

"Undoubtedly," said the curate, who perceived his friend the barber's design; and Cardenio, Don Fernando, and his companions, all confirmed the same: even the judge, had not his thoughts been engrossed by the affair of Don Louis, would have taken some share in the jest; but in the perplexed state of his mind he could attend but little to these pleasantries.

"Mercy on me!" quoth the astonished barber, "how is it possible that so many honourable gentlemen should maintain that this is not a basin, but a helmet! Well, if the basin be a helmet, then the pannel must needs be a horse's furniture, as the gentleman has said."

"To me, indeed, it seems to be a pannel," said Don Quixote; "but I have already told you I will not interfere on that subject."

"Whether it be the pannel of an ass, or the caparison of a horse," said the priest, "must be left to the decision of Señor Don Quixote: for in matters of chivalry, all these gentlemen and myself submit to his judgment."

"By all that is holy, gentlemen," said Don Quixote, "such extraordinary things have befallen me in this castle, that I dare not vouch for the certainty of anything that it may contain; for I verily believe that all is conducted by the powers of enchantment. During my first visit, I was tormented by an enchanted Moor, while Sancho fared no better among some of his followers: and this night I have been suspended for nearly two hours by my arm, without knowing either the means or the cause of my persecution: it would be rash in me, therefore, to give my opinion in an affair of so much perplexity. Perhaps, as you are not knights-errant, the enchantments of this place may not have the same power over you; and, your understandings remaining free, you may judge of things as they really are, and not as they appear to me."

"There is no doubt," answered Don Fernando, "that Señor Don Quixote is right in leaving the decision of this case to us; and that we may proceed in it upon solid grounds, I will take the votes of these gentlemen in secret, and then give you a clear and full account of the result."

To those acquainted with Don Quixote, all this was choice entertainment; while to others it seemed the height of folly, among whom were Don Louis, his servants, and three other guests, troopers of the Holy Brotherhood, who just then arrived at the inn. As for the barber, he was beside himself to see his basin converted into Mambrino's helmet before his eyes, and he made no doubt but his pannel would undergo a like transformation. It was diverting to see Don Fernando walking round and taking the opinion of each person at his ear, whether that precious object of contention was a pannel or comparison; and after he had taken the votes of all those who knew Don Quixote, he said aloud to the barber:

"In truth, honest friend, I am weary of collecting votes; for I propose the question to nobody who does not say in reply, that it is quite ridiculous to assert that this is an ass's pannel, and not the caparison of a horse, and even of a well-bred horse; and as you have given us no proofs to the contrary, you must have patience and submit, for in spite of both you and your ass, this is no pannel."

"Let me never enjoy a place in heaven!" exclaimed the barber, "if your worships are not all mistaken; and so may my soul appear in heaven as this appears to me a pannel, and not a caparison: but so go the laws:—I say no more."

The barber's simplicity caused no less merriment than the vagaries of the knight, who now said, "As sentence is passed, let each take his own; and him to whom God giveth may St. Peter bless." One of Don Louis's four servants now interposed.

"How is it possible," said he, "that men of common understanding should say that this is not a basin nor that a pannel? But since you do actually affirm it, I suspect that there must be some mystery in obstinately maintaining a thing so contrary to the plain truth: for by—(and out he rapped a round oath) all the votes in the world shall never persuade me that this is not a barber's basin and that a jackass's pannel."

"May it not be that of a she-ass?" quoth the priest.

"That is all one," said the servant; "the question is only whether it be or be not a pannel." One of the officers of the Holy Brotherhood, who had overheard the dispute, cried out, full of indignation:

"It is as surely a pannel as my father is my father; and whoever says, or shall say, to the contrary must be drunk."

"You lie, like a pitiful scoundrel!" answered Don Quixote; and lifting up his lance, which was still in his hand, he aimed such a blow at the trooper, that, had he not slipped aside, he would have been levelled to the ground. The lance came down with such fury that it was shivered to pieces.

"Help! help the Holy Brotherhood!" cried out the other officers. The innkeeper, being himself one of that body, ran instantly for his wand and sword, to support his comrades. Don Louis's servants surrounded their master, lest he should escape during the confusion. The barber perceiving the house turned topsy-turvy, laid hold again of his pannel, and Sancho did the same. Don Quixote drew his sword, and fell upon the troopers : and Don Louis called out to his servants to leave him, that they might assist Don Quixote, Cardenio, the captive and Don Fernando, who both took part with the knight. The priest cried out, the hostess shrieked, her daughter wept, Maritornes roared, Dorothea was alarmed, Lucinda stood amazed, and Donna Clara fainted away. The barber cuffed Sancho, and Sancho pummelled the barber. Don Louis gave one of his servants, who had presumed to hold him by the arm lest he should escape, such a blow with his fist that his mouth was bathed in blood, which caused the judge to interpose in his defence. Don Fernando got one of the troopers down, and laid on his blows most unmercifully ; while the innkeeper bawled aloud for help to the Holy Brotherhood ; thus was the whole inn filled with cries, wailings, and shrieks, dismay, confusion and terror, kicks, cudgellings, and effusion of blood. In the midst of this chaos and hurly-burly Don Quixote suddenly conceived that he was involved over head and ears in the discord of King Agramante's camp, and he called out in a voice which made the whole inn shake :

"Hold, all of you ! Put up your swords ; be pacified, and listen all to me, if ye would live ! " His vehemence made them desist, and he went on saying :

"Let, my lord judge and his reverence the priest come forward, and restore us to peace ; for by the powers divine it were most disgraceful and iniquitous that so many gentlemen of our rank should slay each other for such trivial matters." The troopers not understanding Don Quixote's language, and finding themselves still roughly handled by Don Fernando, Cardenio, and their companions, would not be pacified ; but the barber submitted : for both his beard and his pannel were demolished in the scuffle ; and Sancho, like a dutiful servant, obeyed the least word of his master. Don Louis's four servants were also quiet, seeing how unprofitable it was to interfere. The innkeeper, still refractory, insisted that the insolence of that madman ought to be chastised, who was continually turning his house upside down. At length the tumult subsided ; the pannel was to remain a caparison, and the basin a helmet, and the inn a castle, at least in Don Quixote's imagination, until the day of judgment.

Amity and peace being now restored by the interposition of the judge and the priest, the servants of Don Louis renewed their solicitations for his return. The judge having in the meantime informed Don Fernando, Cardenio, and the priest, of what had passed between himself and the young man, he consulted with them on the affair, and it was finally agreed that Don Fernando should make himself known to Don Louis's servants, and inform them that it was his desire that the young gentleman should accompany him to Andalusia, where he would be treated by the marquis his brother in a manner suitable to his quality; for his determination was at all events not to return just at that time into his father's presence. The servants being apprised of Don Fernando's rank, and finding Don Louis resolute, agreed among themselves that three of them should return to give his father account of what had passed, and that the other should stay to attend Don Louis, and not leave him until he knew his lord's pleasure. Thus was this complicated tumult appeased.

But the enemy of peace and concord finding himself foiled and disappointed in the scanty produce of so promising a field, resolved to try his fortune once more, by contriving new frays and disturbances. The officers of the Holy Brotherhood, on hearing the rank of their opponents, retreated from the fray, thinking that whatever might be the issue they were likely to be losers. But one of this body, who had been severely handled by Don Fernando, happened to recollect that among other warrants in his possession he had one against Don Quixote, whom his superiors had ordered to be taken into custody for releasing galley-slaves: thus confirming Sancho's just apprehensions. In order to examine whether the person of Don Quixote answered the description, he drew forth a parchment scroll from his doublet, and began to read it slowly (for he was not much of a scholar), ever and anon as he proceeded fixing his eyes on Don Quixote, comparing the marks in the warrant with the lines of the knight's physiognomy. Finding them exactly to correspond, and being convinced that he was the very person therein described, he held out the warrant in his left hand, while with his right he seized Don Quixote by the collar with so powerful a grasp as almost to strangle him, at the same time crying aloud, "Help the Holy Brotherhood! and that you may see I require it in earnest, read this warrant, wherein it is expressly ordered that this highway robber should be apprehended."

The priest took the warrant, and found what the trooper said was true ; the description exactly corresponding with the person of Don Quixote. The knight, finding himself so rudely handled by this scoundrel, was exasperated to the highest pitch, and trembling with rage caught the trooper by the throat with both hands ; and had he not been immediately rescued by his comrades, he would certainly have been strangled before Don Quixote had loosed his hold. The innkeeper, who was bound to aid his brother in office, ran instantly to help him. The hostess, seeing her husband again engaged in battle, again exalted her voice ; her daughter and Maritornes added their pipes to the same tune, calling upon Heaven and all around them for assistance.

"As God shall save me!" exclaimed Sancho, "what my master says is true about the enchantments of this castle ; for it is impossible to live an hour quietly in it." Don Fernando at length parted the officer and Don Quixote ; and, to the satisfaction of both, unlocked their hands from the doublet-collar of the one and from the wind-pipe of the other. Nevertheless, the troopers persisted in claiming their prisoner, declaring that the king's service and that of the Holy Brotherhood required it, in whose name they again demanded help and assistance in apprehending that common robber and highway thief. Don Quixote smiled at these expressions, and with great calmness said, "Come hither, base and ill-born crew : call ye it robbing on the highway to loosen the chains of the captive, to set the prisoner free, to succour the oppressed, to raise the fallen, and relieve the needy and wretched ? Ah, scoundrel race ! undeserving, by the meanness and baseness of your understand-ings, that Heaven should reveal to you the worth inherent in knight-errantry, or make you sensible of your own sin and ignorance in not revering the shadow much more the presence of any knight-errant ! "

Thus eloquently did Don Quixote harangue the officers, while at the same time the priest endeavoured to persuade them that since the knight, as they might easily perceive, was deranged in his mind, it was useless for them to proceed further in the affair : for if they were to apprehend him, he would soon be released as insane. But the trooper only said in answer that it was not his business to judge of the state of Don Quixote's intellect, but to obey the order of his superior ; and that when he had once secured him, they might set him free as often as they pleased.

"Indeed," said the priest, "you must forbear this once ; nor do I think that he will suffer himself to be taken."

In fact, the priest said so much, and Don Quixote acted so extravagantly, that the officers would have been more crazy than himself had they not desisted after such evidence of his infirmity. They judged it best, therefore, to be quiet, and endeavour to make peace between the barber and Sancho Panza, who still continued their scuffle with great rancour. As officers of justice, therefore, they compounded the matter, and pronounced such a decision that, if both parties were not perfectly contented, at least they were in some degree satisfied ; it being settled that they should exchange pannels, but neither girths nor halters. As for Mambrino's helmet, the priest, unknown to Don Quixote, paid the barber eight reals, for which he received a discharge in full, acquitting him of all fraud thenceforth and for evermore.

CHAPTER XXXII

THE ENCHANTMENT OF THE KNIGHT

THUS were these important contests decided : and fortune seemed to smile on all the heroes and heroines of the inn ; even the face of Donna Clara betrayed the joy of her heart, as the servants of Don Louis had acquiesced in his wishes. Zoraida, although she could not understand everything, looked sad or gay in conformity to the expressions she observed in their several countenances, especially that of her Spaniard, on whom not only her eyes but her soul rested. The innkeeper, observing the recompense the curate had made the barber, claimed also the payment of his demands upon Don Quixote, with ample satisfaction for the damage done to his skins, and the loss of his wine; and swore that neither Rozinante nor the ass should stir out of the inn until he had been paid the uttermost farthing. The curate, however, endeavoured to soothe him; and, what was more, Don Fernando settled the knight's account, although the judge would fain have taken the debt upon himself. Peace was, therefore, entirely restored; and the inn no longer displayed the confusion of Agramante's camp, as Don Quixote had called it; but rather the tranquillity of the days of Octavius Cæsar. Thanks to the mediation and eloquence of the curate, and the liberality of Don Fernando.

Don Quixote now finding himself disengaged, thought it was time to pursue his journey, and accomplish the grand enterprise for which he had been elected. Accordingly, he approached the princess, and threw himself upon his knees before her urging her to make a start. The pseudo-princess, with an air of majesty, and in a style corresponding to that of her knight, thus replied:

"I am obliged to you, Sir Knight, for the zeal you testify in my cause, so worthy of a true knight. As to my departure, let it be instantly; for I have no other will but yours. Dispose of me entirely at your pleasure."

"By Heaven!" exclaimed Don Quixote, "I will not lose the opportunity of exalting a lady who thus humbleth herself. I will replace her on the throne of her ancestors."

Sancho, who had been present all the time, shook his head mysteriously, saying:

"Ah, master of mine! there are more tricks in the town than are dreamt of by you; with all respect be it spoken."

"What tricks can there be to my prejudice in any town or city in the world, thou bumpkin?" said Don Quixote.

"If your worship puts yourself into a passion," answered Sancho, "I will hold my tongue, and not say what I am bound to say as a faithful squire and a dutiful servant."

"Say what thou wilt," replied Don Quixote; "but think not to intimidate me: for it is thy nature to be faint-hearted—mine to be proof against all fear."

"As I am a sinner to Heaven," answered Sancho, "I mean nothing of all this; I mean only that I am sure and positively certain this lady who calls herself queen of the great kingdom of Micomicon is no more a queen than my mother; for if she were so she would not be nuzzling at every turn and in every corner with a certain person in the company." Dorothea's colour rose at Sancho's remark; for it was indeed true that her spouse, Don Fernando, now and then by stealth had snatched with his lips an earnest of that reward which his affections deserved; and Sancho, having observed it, thought this freedom very unbecoming the queen of so vast a kingdom. As Dorothea could not contradict Sancho, she remained silent, and suffered him to continue his remarks.

"I say this, sir, because supposing after we have travelled through thick and thin, and passed many bad nights and worse days, one who is now enjoying himself in this inn should chance to reap the fruit of our labours, there would be no use in my hastening to saddle Rozinante, or get ready the ass and the palfrey; therefore we had better be quiet. Let every drab mind her spinning, and let us to dinner." Good Heaven! how great was the indignation of Don Quixote on hearing his squire speak in terms so disrespectful! It was so great that, with a faltering voice and stammering tongue, while living fire darted from his eyes, he cried:

"Scoundrel! unmannerly, ignorant, ill-spoken, foul-mouthed, impudent, murmuring and back-biting villain! How darest thou utter such words in my presence, and in the presence of these illustrious ladies! How darest thou to entertain such rude and insolent thoughts in thy confused imagination! Avoid my presence, monster of nature, treasury of lies, magazine of deceits, storehouse of rogueries, inventor of mischiefs, publisher of absurdities, and foe to all the honour due to royalty! Begone!— appear not before me again on pain of my severest indignation!"

And as he spoke he arched his eyebrows, swelled his cheeks, stared around him, and gave a violent stamp with his right foot on the ground; plainly indicating the fury that raged in his breast. Poor Sancho was so terrified by the storm of passion, that he would have been glad if the earth had opened that instant and swallowed him up. He knew not what to say or do; so he turned his back and hastened out of the presence of his furious master.

But the discreet Dorothea, perfectly understanding Don Quixote, in order to pacify his wrath, said :

" Be not offended, Sir Knight of the Sorrowful Figure, at the impertinence of your good squire, for perhaps he has not spoken without some foundation ; nor can it be suspected, considering his good sense and Christian conscience, that he would bear false witness against anybody ; is it not possible that since, as you affirm yourself, Sir Knight, the powers of enchantment prevail in this castle, Sancho may, by the same diabolical illusion, have seen what he has affirmed so much to the prejudice of my honour ? "

" By the Omnipotent, I swear," quoth Don Quixote, " your highness has hit the mark !—some evil apparition must have appeared to this sinner, and represented to him what it was impossible for him to see any other way ; for I am perfectly assured of the simplicity and innocence of the unhappy wretch, and that he is incapable of slandering any person living."

" So it is, and so it shall be," said Don Fernando : " therefore, Señor Don Quixote, you ought to pardon him and restore him to your favour, *sicut erat in principio* before these illusions turned his brain." Don Quixote having promised his forgiveness, the priest went for Sancho, who came in with much humility, and on his knees begged his master's hand, which was given to him ; and after he had allowed him to kiss it, he gave him his blessing, adding :

" Thou wilt now, son Sancho, be thoroughly convinced of what I have often told thee, that all things in this castle are conducted by enchantment."

" I believe so, too," quoth Sancho, " except the business of the blanket, which really fell out in the ordinary way."

This illustrious company had now passed two whole days in the inn ; and thinking it time to depart, they considered how the curate and barber might convey the knight to his home without troubling Dorothea and Don Fernando to accompany them ; and for that purpose, having first engaged a waggoner who happened to pass by with his team of oxen, they proceeded in the following manner. They formed a kind of cage, with poles grate-wise, large enough to contain Don Quixote at his ease ; then, by the direction of the priest, Don Fernando and his companions, with

Don Louis's servants, the officers of the Holy Brotherhood, and the innkeeper, covered their faces, and disguised themselves so as not to be recognised by Don Quixote. This done, they silently entered the room where the knight lay fast asleep, reposing after his late exertions, and secured him with cords; so that when he awoke, he stared about in amazement at the strange visages that surrounded him, but found himself totally unable to move. His disordered imagination operating as usual, immediately suggested to him that these were goblins of the enchanted castle, and that he was entangled in their charms, since he felt himself unable to stir in his own defence, a surmise which the curate, who projected the stratagem, had anticipated.

Sancho alone was in his own proper figure: and though he wanted but little of being infected with his master's infirmity, yet he was not ignorant who all these counterfeit goblins were; but he thought it best to be quiet until he saw what was intended by this seizure and imprisonment of his master. Neither did the knight utter a word, but submissively waited the issue of his misfortune. Having brought the cage into the chamber, they placed him within it, and secured it so that it was impossible he could make his escape. In this situation he was conveyed out of the house; and on leaving the chamber a voice was heard, as dreadful as barber Nicholas could form it, saying:

"O Knight of the Sorrowful Figure! let not thy present confinement afflict thee, since it is essential to the speedy accomplishment of the adventure in which thy great valour hath engaged thee, which shall be finished when the furious Manchegan lion shall be coupled with the white Tobosian dove, after having submitted their stately necks to the soft matrimonial yoke; from which wonderful conjunction shall spring into the light of the world brave whelps who shall emulate the ravaging claws of their valorous sire. And this shall come to pass before the pursuer of the fugitive nymph shall have made two circuits to visit the bright constellations, in his rapid and natural course. And thou, O most noble and obedient squire that ever had sword in belt, beard on face, and smell in nostrils, be not dismayed nor afflicted to see the flower of knight-errantry carried thus away before thine eyes; for ere long, if it so please the great Artificer of the World, thou shalt see thyself so exalted and sublimated as not to know thyself; and thus will the promises of thy valorous lord be fulfilled." As he delivered this solemn prediction, the prophet first raised his voice high, then gradually lowered it to so pathetic a tone, that even those who were in the plot were not unmoved.

Don Quixote was much comforted by this prophecy, quickly comprehending the whole signification thereof; for he saw that it promised him the felicity of being joined in holy wedlock with his beloved Dulcinea del Toboso, from whom should issue the whelps, his sons, to the everlasting honour of La Mancha. The goblins then took the cage on their shoulders, and placed it on the waggon.

CHAPTER XXXIII

SANCHO HAS SUSPICIONS ABOUT THE ENCHANTMENT

"Learned and very grave historians of knights-errant have I read," said Don Quixote, on finding himself thus cooped up and carted; "but I never read, saw, nor heard of enchanted knights being transported in this manner, and so slowly as these lazy, heavy animals seem to proceed; for they were usually conveyed through the air with wonderful speed, enveloped in some thick and dark cloud, or on some fiery chariot, or mounted upon a hippogriff, or some such animal. But to be carried upon a team drawn by oxen—before Heaven, it overwhelms me with confusion! Perhaps, however, the enchantments of these our times may differ from those of the ancients; and it is also possible that as I am a new knight in the world, and the first who revived the long-forgotten exercise of knight-errantry, new modes may have been invented. What thinkest thou of this, son Sancho?"

"I do not know what to think," answered Sancho, "not being so well read as your worship in scriptures-errant; yet I dare affirm and swear that these hobgoblins here about us are not altogether catholic."

"Catholic, my father!" answered Don Quixote: "how can they be catholic, being devils who have assumed fantastic shapes to effect their purpose, and throw me into this state? To convince thyself of this, try to touch and feel them, and thou wilt find their bodies have no substance, but are of air, existing only to the sight."

"'Fore Heaven, sir!" replied Sancho, "I have already touched them; and this devil, who is so very busy here about us, is as plump as a partridge, and has another property very different from what your devils are wont to have—for it is said, they all smell of brimstone, and other bad scents; but this spark smells of amber, at half a league's distance." Sancho spoke of Don Fernando, who, being a cavalier of rank, must have been perfumed as Sancho described.

"Wonder not at this, friend Sancho," answered Don Quixote, "for thou must know that devils are cunning; and although they may carry perfumes about them, they have no scent themselves, being spirits; or, if they do smell, it can be of nothing but what is foul and offensive, since wherever they are they carry hell about them, and have no respite from their torments."

Thus were the knight and squire discoursing together, when Don Fernando and Cardenio, fearing lest Sancho should see into the whole of their plot, being already not far from it, resolved to hasten their departure; and, calling the innkeeper aside, they ordered him to saddle Rozinante, and pannel the ass, which he did with great expedition. In the meanwhile the curate engaged to pay the troopers of the Holy Brotherhood to accompany Don Quixote home to his village. Cardenio fastened the buckler on one side of the pommel of Rozinante's saddle, and the basin on the other; then, after placing the two troopers with their carbines on each side of the waggon, he made signs to Sancho to mount his ass, and lead Rozinante by the bridle. But before the car moved forward, the hostess, her daughter, and Maritornes, came out to take their leave of Don Quixote, pretending to shed tears for grief at his misfortune.

While this passed between the ladies of the castle and Don Quixote, the curate and the barber took their leave of Don Fernando and his companions, the captain, and of all the ladies, now supremely happy. Don Fernando requested the priest to give him intelligence of Don Quixote, assuring him that nothing would afford him more satisfaction than to hear of his future proceedings; and he promised, on his part, to inform him of whatever might amuse or please him respecting his own marriage, the baptism of Zoraida, and the return of Lucinda to her parents, and also the issue of Don Louis's amour. The priest engaged to perform all that was desired of him with the utmost punctuality; after which they separated, with many expressions of mutual cordiality and good-will.

He and the barber then joined the cavalcade, which was arranged in the following order:—In the front was the car, guided by the owner, and on each side the troopers with their matchlocks; then came Sancho upon his ass, leading Rozinante by the bridle; and in the rear the priest and his friend Nicholas, mounted on their stately mules; and thus the whole moved on with great solemnity, regulated by the slow pace of the oxen. Don Quixote sat in the cage, with his hands tied and his legs stretched out, leaning against the bars as silently and patiently as if he had been not a man of flesh and blood, but a statue of stone. In this manner they travelled about two leagues, when they came to a valley which the waggoner thought a convenient place for resting and baiting his cattle; but on his proposing it, the barber recommended that they should travel a little farther, as beyond the next rising ground there was another vale that afforded much better pasture; and this advice was followed.

The curate, happening about this time to look back, perceived behind them six or seven horsemen, well mounted and accoutred, who soon came up with them; for they were not travelling with the phlegmatic pace of the oxen, but like persons mounted on good ecclesiastical mules, and eager to reach a place of shelter against the midday sun. The speedy overtook the slow, and each party courteously saluted the other. One of the travellers, who was a canon of Toledo, and master to those who accompanied him, observing the orderly procession of the waggon, the troopers, Sancho, Rozinante, the curate, and the barber, and especially Don Quixote caged up and imprisoned, after making some inquiries, proposed to proceed in their company, which was agreed to.

The canon and his servants then rode on before with the priest, who entertained him with a circumstantial account of Don Quixote, from the first symptoms of his derangement to his present situation in the cage. The canon was profoundly surprised at what he heard. Therefore, induced by the beauty of the place and the pleasure he found in the priest's conversation as well as by the curiosity he felt to see and hear more of Don Quixote, he ordered some of his attendants to go to the nearest inn and bring provisions for the whole party. He was told by one of them that their sumpter-mule, which had gone forward, carried abundance of refreshment, and that they should want nothing from the inn but barley; upon which he despatched them in haste for the mule.

CHAPTER XXXIV

THE KNIGHT AND THE CANON

THE knight-errant and his faithful squire were deeply engaged in conversation, until they came to the place where the priest, the canon, and the barber were already alighted and waiting for them. The waggoner then unyoked the oxen from his team, and turned them loose upon that green and delicious spot, the freshness of which was inviting, not only to those who were enchanted, like Don Quixote, but to discreet and enlightened persons like his squire, who besought the priest to permit his master to come out of the cage for a short time; otherwise that prison would not be quite so clean as decency required in the accommodation of such a knight as his master. The priest understood him, and said that he would readily consent to his request; but he feared lest his master, finding himself at liberty, should play his old pranks, and be gone where he might never be seen more. "I will be security for his not running away," replied Sancho.

"And I also," said the canon, "if he will give his parole of honour."

"I give it," said Don Quixote. And upon his faith and word they released him.

The servants who went to the inn for the sumpter-mule had now returned; and, having spread a carpet over the green grass, the party seated themselves under the shade of some trees, and there enjoyed their repast, while the cattle luxuriated on the fresh pasture. As they were thus employed, they suddenly heard a noise and the sound of a little bell from a thicket near them; at the same instant a beautiful she-goat, speckled with black, white, and grey, ran out of the thicket, followed by a goatherd, calling to her aloud, in the usual language, to stop and come back to the fold. The fugitive animal, trembling and affrighted, ran to the company, claiming, as it were, their protection; but the goatherd pursued her, and seizing her by the horns, addressed her as a rational creature:

"Ah, wanton, spotted thing! how hast thou strayed of late! What wolves have frightened thee, child? Wilt thou tell me, pretty one, what this means? But what else can it mean, but that thou art a female, and therefore canst not be quiet! A plague on thy humours, and all theirs whom thou resemblest! Turn back, my love, turn back; for though not content, at least thou wilt be more safe in thine own fold, and among thy companions; for if thou, who shouldst protect and guide them, go astray, what must become of them?"

The party were very much amused by the goatherd's remonstrances, and the canon said, "I entreat you, brother, not to be in such haste to force back this goat to her fold; for, since she is a female, she will follow her natural inclination in spite of all your opposition. Come, do not be angry, but eat and drink with us, and let the wayward creature rest herself." At the same time he offered him the hinder quarter of a cold rabbit on the point of a fork. The goatherd thanked him, and accepted his offer, and being then in a better temper, he said:

"Do not think me a fool, gentlemen, for talking so seriously to this animal: for, in truth, my words were not without a meaning; and though I am a rustic, I know the difference between conversing with men and beasts."

"I doubt it not," said the priest; "indeed, it is well known that the mountains breed learned men, and the huts of shepherds contain philosophers."

"At least, sir," replied the goatherd, "they contain men who have some knowledge gained from experience; and if I shall not be intruding, I will tell a circumstance which confirms it."

"Somewhat of a dandy."

"Since this affair," said Don Quixote, "bears somewhat the semblance of an adventure, for my own part, friend, I shall listen to you most willingly: I can answer also for these gentlemen, who are persons of sense, and will relish the curious, the entertaining, and the marvellous, which, I doubt not, your story contains: I entreat you, friend, to begin it immediately."

"I shall take myself away to the side of yonder brook," said Sancho, "with this pasty, of which I mean to lay in enough to last three days at least: for I have heard my master, Don Quixote, say that the squire of a knight-errant should eat when he can, and as long as he can, because he may lose his way for six days together in a wood; and then, if a man has not his belly well lined or his wallet well provided, there he may stay till he is turned into a mummy."

"Thou art in the right, Sancho," said Don Quixote; "go where thou wilt, and eat what thou canst; my appetite is already satisfied, and my mind only needs refreshment."

The goatherd then related his story, which was to the effect that the grief visible in his countenance proceeded from the fact that his sweetheart had been placed in a nunnery for indulging in an indiscreet flirtation with a rival. The latter, whose name was Vincent de la Rosa, had returned from the wars, and by his moving tales, in which he always played a hero's part, had captivated the heart of the silly Leandra. Perhaps the smooth tongue of the warrior might not have effected this triumph had he not been somewhat of a dandy. His soldier's garb was bedizened with a variety of trinkets and glittering chains, but all of little value. To-day he put on one piece, to-morrow another, and although he had in reality only three complete suits of different colours, he used so many disguisements and interchanged them so skilfully that one would have sworn he had ten suits and twenty plumes of feathers. After inducing Leandra to elope with him, and obtaining possession of her money and jewellery he deserted her, and for this the wayward maiden had been placed out of harm's way in a nunnery, much to her goatherd-admirer's chagrin.

CHAPTER XXXV

THE RARE ADVENTURE OF THE DISCIPLINANTS, WHICH HE HAPPILY ACCOMPLISHED WITH THE SWEAT OF HIS BROW

EUGENIO's tale amused his auditors. They all offered their services to Eugenio : but the most liberal in his offers was Don Quixote, who said to him :

"In truth, brother goatherd, were I in a situation to undertake any new adventure, I would immediately engage myself in your service, and release your lady from the nunnery in spite of the abbess and all opposers, then deliver her into your hands, to be disposed of at your pleasure, so far as is consistent with the laws of chivalry, which enjoin that no kind of outrage be offered to damsels. I trust, however, in Heaven, that the power of one malicious enchanter shall not be so prevalent over another but that a better disposed one may triumph ; and then I promise you my aid and protection, according to the duty of my profession, which is no other than to favour the weak and necessitous."

The goatherd stared at Don Quixote, and observing his sad plight and scurvy appearance, he whispered to the barber, who sat next to him :

"Pray, sir, who is that man that looks and talks so strangely ? "

"Who should he be," answered the barber, "but the famous Don Quixote de la Mancha, the redresser of injuries, the righter of wrongs, the protector of maidens, the dread of giants, and the conqueror of battles ? "

"Why, this is like what we hear in the stories of knights-errant," said the goatherd ; "but I take it either your worship is in jest, or the apartments in this gentleman's skull are unfurnished."

"You are a very great rascal," exclaimed the knight ; "it is yourself who are empty-skulled and shallow-brained ; for mine is fuller than was ever the head of any of your vile generation ! " and as he spoke, he snatched up a loaf and threw it at the goatherd's face with so much fury that he laid his nose flat.

The goatherd did not much relish the jest ; so without any

respect to the table-cloth or to the company present, he leaped upon Don Quixote, and seizing him by the throat with both hands, would doubtless have strangled him, had not Sancho Panza, who came up at that moment, taken him by the shoulders and thrown him back on the table-cloth, demolishing dishes and platters, and spilling and overturning all that was upon it. Don Quixote finding himself free, turned upon the goatherd, who, being kicked and trampled upon by Sancho, was feeling about, upon all-fours, for some knife or weapon to take a bloody revenge withal : but the canon and the priest prevented him. The barber, however, maliciously contrived that the goatherd should get Don Quixote under him, whom he buffeted so unmercifully that he had ample retaliation for his own sufferings.

This ludicrous encounter overcame the gravity of both the churchmen, while the troopers of the Holy Brotherhood, enjoying the conflict, stood urging on the combatants, as if it had been a dog-fight. Sancho struggled in vain to release himself from one of the canon's servants, who prevented him from going to assist his master. In the midst of this sport a trumpet was suddenly heard sounding so dismally that every face was instantly turned in the direction whence the sound proceeded. Don Quixote's attention was particularly excited, though he still lay under the goatherd in a bruised and battered condition.

"Thou devil," he said to him, "for a devil thou must be to have such power over me, I beg that thou wilt grant a truce for one hour, as the solemn sound of that trumpet seems to call me to some new adventure." The goatherd, whose revenge was by this time sated, immediately let him go, and Don Quixote, having got upon his legs again, presently saw several people descending from a rising ground, arrayed in white, after the manner of disciplinants.*

That year the heavens having failed to refresh the earth with seasonable showers, throughout all the villages of that district processions, disciplines, and public prayers were ordered, beseeching Heaven to show its mercy by sending them rain. For this purpose the people of a neighbouring village were coming in procession to a holy hermitage built upon the side of a

---

* Persons, either volunteers or hirelings, who march in processions, whipping themselves by way of public penance.

hill not far from that spot.   The strange attire of the disciplinants struck Don Quixote, who, not recollecting what he must often have seen before, imagined it to be some adventure which, as a knight-errant, was reserved for him alone ; and he was confirmed in his opinion on seeing an image clothed in black, that they carried with them, and which he doubted not was some illustrious lady forcibly borne away by ruffians and miscreants.   With all the expedition in his power, he therefore went up to Rozinante, and taking the bridle and buckler from the pommel of the saddle, he bridled him in a trice, and calling to Sancho for his sword, he mounted, braced his target, and in a loud voice said to all that were present :

"Now, my worthy companions, ye shall see how important to the world is the profession of chivalry ! now shall ye see, in the restoration of that captive lady to liberty, whether knights-errant are to be valued or not !"

So saying, he clapped heels to Rozinante (for spurs he had none), and on a hand-gallop (for we nowhere read, in all this faithful history, that Rozinante ever went full speed), he advanced to encounter the disciplinants.   The curate, the canon, and the barber, fruitlessly endeavoured to stop him ; and in vain did Sancho cry out :

"Whither go you, Señor Don Quixote ?   What devils drive you to assault the Catholic faith ?   Evil befal me : do but look— it is a procession of disciplinants, and the lady carried upon the bier is the blessed image of our Holy Virgin : take heed, for this once I am sure you know not what you are about."   Sancho wearied himself to no purpose ; for his master was so bent upon an encounter, that he heard not a word : nor would he have turned back though the king himself had commanded him.

Having reached the procession, he checked Rozinante, who already wanted to rest a little, and in a hoarse and agitated voice cried out, "Stop there, ye who cover your faces for an evil purpose, I doubt not—stop and listen to me."   The bearers of the image stood still, and one of the four ecclesiastics, who sung the litanies, observing the strange figure of Don Quixote, the leanness of Rozinante, and other ludicrous circumstances attending the knight, replied :

"Friend, if you have anything to say to us, say it quickly ;

for these our brethren are scourging their flesh, and we cannot stay to hear anything that cannot be said in two words."

"I will say it in one," replied Don Quixote: "you must immediately release that fair lady, whose tears and sorrowful countenance clearly prove that she is carried away against her will, and that you have done her some atrocious injury. I, who was born to redress such wrongs, command you, therefore, not to proceed one step farther until you have given her the liberty she desires and deserves." By these expressions they concluded that Don Quixote must be some whimsical madman, and only laughed at him, which enraged him to such a degree that, without saying another word, he drew his sword and attacked the bearers ; one of whom leaving the burden to his comrades, stepped forward, brandishing the pole on which the bier had been supported ; but it was quickly broken in two by a powerful stroke, aimed by the knight, who, however, received instantly such a blow on the shoulder of his sword-arm, that, his buckler being of no avail against rustic strength, he was felled to the ground. Sancho, who had followed him, now called out to the man not to strike again, for he was a poor enchanted knight, who had never done anybody harm in all his life. The peasant forebore, it is true, though not on account of Sancho's appeal, but because he saw his opponent without motion ; and, thinking he had killed him, he hastily tucked up his vest under his girdle, and fled like a deer over the field.

By this time all Don Quixote's party had come up ; and those in the procession, seeing among them troopers of the Holy Brotherhood, armed with their cross-bows, began to be alarmed, and drew up in a circle round the image ; then lifting up their hoods, * and grasping their whips, and the ecclesiastics their tapers, they waited the assault, determined to defend themselves, or, if possible, offend their aggressors, while Sancho threw himself upon the body of his master, and believing him to be really dead, poured forth the most dolorous lamentation. The alarm of both squadrons was speedily dissipated, as our curate was recognised by one of the ecclesiastics in the procession : and, on hearing from him who Don Quixote was, they all hastened to see whether the

---

* The disciplinants wear hoods that they may not be known, but which they can see through.

poor knight had really suffered a mortal injury or not; when they heard Sancho Panza with streaming eyes exclaim:

"O flower of chivalry, who at last hast finished the career of thy well-spent life! O glory of thy race, credit and renown of La Mancha, yea, of the whole world, which, by wanting thee, will be overrun with evildoers, who will no longer fear chastisement for their iniquities! O liberal above all Alexanders, since for eight months' service only thou hast given me the best island that sea doth compass or surround! O thou that wert humble with the haughty, and arrogant with the humble, undertaker of dangers, sufferer of affronts, in love without cause, imitator of the good, scourge of the wicked, enemy of the base; in a word, knight-errant—which is all in all." Sancho's cries roused Don Quixote, who faintly said:

"He who lives absent from thee, sweetest Dulcinea, endures far greater miseries than this!—Help, friend Sancho, to place me upon the enchanted car: I am no longer in a condition to press the saddle of Rozinante, for this shoulder is broken to pieces."

"That I will do with all my heart, dear sir," answered Sancho; "and let us return to our homes with these gentlemen, who wish you well; and there we can prepare for another sally, that may turn out more profitable."

"Thou sayest well, Sancho," answered Don Quixote, "and it will be highly prudent in us to wait until the evil influence of the star which now reigns is passed over." The canon, the curate; and the barber, told him they approved his resolution: and the knight being now placed in the waggon, as before, they prepared to depart.

The goatherd took his leave; and the troopers, not being disposed to attend them farther, were discharged. The canon also separated from them, having first obtained a promise from the priest that he would acquaint him with the future fate of Don Quixote. Thus the party now consisted only of the priest, the barber, Don Quixote, and Sancho, with good Rozinante, who bore all accidents as patiently as his master. The waggoner yoked his oxen, and, having accommodated Don Quixote with a truss of hay, they jogged on in the way the curate directed; and at the end of six days reached Don Quixote's village. It was about noon when they made their entrance; and, it being

Sunday, all the people were standing about the market-place, through which the waggon passed. Everybody ran to see who was in it, and were not a little surprised when they recognised their townsman; and a boy ran off at full speed with tidings to the housekeeper, that he was coming home, lean and pale, stretched out at length in a waggon drawn by oxen. On hearing this, the two good women made the most pathetic lamentations, and renewed their curses against books of chivalry; especially when they saw the poor knight entering the gate.

Upon the news of Don Quixote's arrival, Sancho Panza's wife repaired thither, and on meeting him, her first inquiry was whither the ass had come home well. Sancho told her that he was in a better condition than his master.

" The Lord be praised," replied she, " for so great a mercy to me! But tell me, husband, what good have you got by your squireship? Have you brought a petticoat home for me, and shoes for your children?"

" I have brought you nothing of that sort, dear wife," quoth Sancho; " but I have got other things of greater consequence."

" I am very glad of that," answered the wife, " pray show me your things of greater consequence, friend; for I would fain see them, to gladden my heart, which has been so sad, all the long time you have been away."

" You shall see them at home, wife," quoth Sancho, " and be satisfied at present; for if it please God that we make another sally in quest of adventures, you will soon see me an earl or governor of an island, and no common one either, but one of the best that is to be had."

" Grant Heaven it may be so, husband," quoth the wife, " for we have need enough of it. But pray tell me what you mean by islands; for I do not understand you."

" Honey is not for the mouth of an ass," answered Sancho: " in good time, wife, you shall see, yea, and admire to hear yourself styled ladyship by all your vassals."

" What do you mean, Sancho, by ladyship, islands, and vassals?" answered Teresa Panza, for that was the name of Sancho's wife, though they were not of kin, but because it was the custom of La Mancha for the wife to take the husband's name.

H

"Do not be in so much haste, Teresa," said Sancho; "it is enough that I tell you what is true, so lock up your mouth;— only take this by the way, that there is nothing in the world so pleasant as to be an honourable esquire to a knight-errant and seeker of adventures. To be sure most of them are not so much to a man's mind as he could wish; for, as I know by experience, ninety-nine out of an hundred fall out cross and unlucky; especially when one happens to be tossed in a blanket, or well cudgelled: yet, for all that, it is a fine thing to go about in ex- pectation of accidents, traversing mountains, searching woods, marching over rocks, visiting castles, lodging in inns, all at pleasure, and the devil a farthing to pay."

While this discourse was passing between Sancho Panza and his wife Teresa, the housekeeper and the niece received Don Quixote, and, after undressing him, they laid him in his old bed, whence he looked at them with eyes askance, not knowing per- fectly where he was. Often did the women raise their voices in abuse of all books of chivalry, overwhelming their authors with the bitterest maledictions. His niece was charged by the curate to take great care of him, and to keep a watchful eye that he did not again make his escape, after taking so much pains to get him home. Yet they were full of apprehensions lest they should lose him again as soon as he found himself a little better; and indeed the event proved that their fears were not groundless.

CHAPTER XXXVI

CONVERSATION BETWEEN THE CURATE, THE BARBER, AND DON QUIXOTE, CONCERNING HIS INDISPOSITION

THE curate and the barber refrained during a whole month from seeing Don Quixote, lest they should revive in his mind the remembrance of things past. However, they paid frequent visits to the niece and housekeeper, charging them to take great care of him, and to give him good nourishing diet, as that would be salutary to his heart and his brain, whence all the mischief proceeded. The good women assured them of their continual

"Not knowing perfectly where he was."

care of the patient, and said they occasionally observed in him symptoms of returning reason. The curate and the barber were greatly pleased to hear this, and congratulated themselves on the success of the scheme they had adopted of bringing him home enchanted in the ox-waggon, as it is related in the last chapter of the first part of this no less great than accurate history. They resolved, therefore, to visit him, and make trial of his amendment: at the same time, thinking it scarcely possible that his cure could be complete, they agreed not to touch upon the subject of knight-errantry, lest they might open a wound which must yet be so tender.

They found him sitting on his bed, clad in a waistcoat of green baize, with a red Toleda cap on his head, and so lean and shrivelled that he looked like a mummy. He received them with much politeness, and when they inquired after his health, he answered them in a very sensible manner, and with much elegance of expression, so that he seemed in full possession of his senses. The niece and the housekeeper were present at the conversation, and, hearing from their master such proofs of a sound mind, thought they could never sufficiently thank Heaven. The priest, changing his former purpose of not touching upon matters of chivalry, was now resolved to put the question of his amendment fairly to the test: he therefore mentioned, among other things, some intelligence lately brought from court, that the Turk was advancing with a powerful fleet, and that, his object being unknown, it was impossible to say where the storm would burst; that all Christendom was in great alarm, and that the king had already provided for the security of Naples, Sicily, and the island of Malta. To this Don Quixote replied:

"His Majesty has acted with great prudence in providing in time for the defence of his dominions, but, if my counsel might be taken, I would advise him to a measure which probably never yet entered into His Majesty's mind."

"Indeed, what is that," said the curate.

"His Majesty," cried Don Quixote, "has only to issue a proclamation ordering all the knights-errant now wandering about Spain to repair, on an appointed day, to court? If not more than half-a-dozen came, there might be one of that number able, with his single arm, to destroy the whole power

The Curate.

of the Turk. Pray, gentlemen, be attentive, and listen to me. Is it anything new for a single knight-errant to defeat an army of two hundred thousand men, as if they had all but one throat, or were made of pastry? How many examples of such prowess does history supply! If, in an evil hour for me (I will not say for any other), the famous Don Belianis, or some one of the numerous race of Amadis de Gaul, were in being at this day to confront the Turk, in good faith I would not farm his winnings! But God will protect His people, and provide some one, if not as strong as the knights-errant of old, at least not inferior to them in courage. Heaven knows my meaning; I say no more!"

"Alas!" exclaimed the niece at this instant: "may I perish if my uncle has not a mind to turn knight-errant again?" Whereupon Don Quixote said:

"A knight-errant I will live and die; and let the Turk come, down or up, when he pleases, and with all the forces he can raise—once more, I say, Heaven knows my meaning."

"Well," said the curate, "though I have yet scarcely spoken, I should be very glad to relieve my conscience of a scruple which has been started by what Señor Don Quixote just now said, and which certainly occasions me very great anxiety and uneasiness of mind. Will he have the goodness to resolve my difficulty?"

"You may command me, Señor Curate, in such matters," answered Don Quixote; "out then with your scruple: for there can be no peace with a scrupulous conscience."

"With this license, then," said the curate, "I must tell you that I can by no means persuade myself that the multitude of knights-errant your worship has mentioned were really and truly persons of flesh and blood existing in the world; on the contrary, I imagine that the accounts given of them are all fictions and dreams, invented by men awake, or to speak more properly, half asleep."

"This is a common mistake," answered Don Quixote, "which I have, upon sundry occasions, and in many companies, endeavoured to correct. But Scripture itself is not more authentic. We believe in the prophets, why not in knights-errant?"

"Engaged in defending the door against Sancho Panza."

At this moment, they were interrupted by a noise in the court-yard; and hearing the niece and housekeeper vociferating aloud, they hastened to learn the cause.

Looking out of the window, Don Quixote, the priest, and the barber, saw the niece and housekeeper engaged in defending the door against Sancho Panza, who came to pay his master a visit.

"Fellow, get home!" said one of them, "what have you to do here? It is by you our master is led astray and carried rambling about the country, like a vagabond."

"Thou devilish housekeeper!" retorted Sancho, "it is I that am led astray, and carried rambling up and down the highways: and it was your master that led me this dance:—so there you are quite mistaken. He tempted me from home with promises of an island, which I still hope for."

"May the cursed islands choke thee, wretch!" answered the niece; "and pray, what are islands? Are they anything eat-able?—glutton, cormorant as thou art!"

"They are not to be eaten," replied Sancho, "but governed, and are better things than any four cities, or four justiceships at court."

"For all that," said the housekeeper, "you shall not come in here, you bag of mischief, and bundle of roguery! Get you home and govern there; go, plough and cart, and do not trouble your silly pate about islands." The priest and the barber were highly diverted at this dialogue; but Don Quixote, fearing lest Sancho should blunder out something unseasonably, and touch upon certain points not advantageous to his reputation, ordered the women to hold their peace, and let him in. Sancho entered, and the priest and the barber took their leave of Don Quixote, now quite despairing of his cure: seeing that he was more intoxicated than ever with knight-errantry.

"You will see, neighbour," said the curate, as they walked away, "our friend will soon take another flight."

"No doubt of it," said the barber, "yet I think the credulity of the squire still more extraordinary:—it seems impossible to drive that same island out of his head."

Don Quixote having shut himself up in his chamber with Sancho, he said to him:

"It concerns me much, Sancho, that thou wilt persist in saying that I enticed thee from thy home. How? Did we not both leave our homes together, journey together, and were both exposed to the same fortune! If thou wert once tossed in a blanket, I have only had the advantage of thee, in being a hundred times exposed to hard blows."

"This is but reasonable," answered Sancho; "for, as your worship says, misfortunes belong more properly to knights-errant than to their squires."

"Thou art mistakén, Sancho," said Don Quixote; "for, according to the saying, *Quando caput dolet*, &c."

"I understand no other language than my own," replied Sancho.

"I mean," said Don Quixote, "that when the head aches, all the members ache also; and therefore I, being thy lord and master, am thy head, and thou, being my servant, art a portion of me; and, therefore, whatever evil I suffer must be felt by thee, as thy sufferings likewise affect me."

"And so it should be," quoth Sancho; "but when I as a member, suffered in the blanket, my head stood on t'other side of the pales, seeing me tossed in the air, without taking the smallest share in my pain, though, as the members are bound to grieve at the ills of the head, the head should have done the like for them."

"Wouldst thou then insinuate, Sancho," replied Don Quixote, "that I was not grieved when I saw thee tossed in the air? If that be thy meaning, be assured thou art deceived. But let us dismiss this subject at present; for a time will come when we may set this matter to rights. And now tell me, friend Sancho, what do they say of me in the village? What opinion do the common people entertain of me? What think the gentlemen and the cavaliers? What is said of my prowess, of my exploits, and of my courteous demeanour? Tell me all."

"That I will, with all my heart, sir," answered Sancho, "on condition that your worship be not angry at what I say, since you desire to have the truth, just as it came to me."

"I will in no wise be angry," replied Don Quixote; "speak then freely, Sancho, and without any circumlocution."

"First and foremost, then," said Sancho, "the common people take your worship for a downright madman, and me for no less than a fool. The gentry say that, not content to keep to your own proper rank of a gentleman, you call yourself Don, and set up for a knight, with no more than a paltry vineyard and a couple of acres of land. The cavaliers say they do not choose to be vied with by those country squires who clout their shoes, and take up the fallen stitches of their black stockings with green silk."

"That," said Don Quixote, "is no reflection upon me ; for I always go well clad, and my apparel is never patched ; a little torn it may be, but more by the fretting of my armour than by time."

"As to your valour, courtesy, achievements, and undertakings," continued Sancho, "there are many different opinions. Some say you are mad, but humorous ; others, valiant, but unfortunate ; others, courteous, but absurd ; and thus they pull us to pieces, till they leave neither your worship nor me a single feather upon our backs."

"Take notice, Sancho," said Don Quixote, "that, wherever virtue exists in any eminent degree, it is always persecuted. Few, or none, of the famous men of antiquity escaped the calumny of their malicious contemporaries."

"Ah, but all the things I have told you are tarts and cheesecakes to what remains behind," replied Sancho. "If your worship would have all, to the very dregs, I will bring one hither presently who can tell you everything, without missing a tittle ; for last night the son of Bartholomew Carrasco returned from his studies at Salamanca, where he has taken his bachelor's degree ; and when I went to bid him welcome home, he told me that the history of your worship was already printed in books, under the title of ' Don Quixote de la Mancha ' ; and he says it mentions me too by my very name of Sancho Panza, and also the lady Dulcinea del Toboso, and several other private matters which passed between us two only ; insomuch that I crossed myself out of pure amazement, to think how the historian who wrote it should come to know them."

"Depend upon it, Sancho," said Don Quixote, "that the author of this our history must be some sage enchanter : for nothing is concealed from them."

"A sage and an enchanter ?" quoth Sancho : "why, the

bachelor Sampson Carrasco says the author of this story is called Cid Hamet Berengena." *

"That is a Moorish name," answered Don Quixote.

"It may be so," replied Sancho; "for I have heard that your Moors, for the most part, are lovers of Berengenas."

"Sancho," said Don Quixote, "thou must be mistaken in the surname of that same 'Cid,' which, in Arabic, signifies 'a lord.'"

"That may be," answered Sancho, "but if your worship would like to see him, I will run and fetch him."

"Thou wilt give me singular pleasure, friend," said Don Quixote; "for I am surprised at what thou hast told me, and shall be impatient till I am informed of every particular."

"I will go for him directly," said Sancho; then, leaving his master, he went to seek the bachelor, with whom he soon returned, and a most delectable conversation passed between them, which is recorded in the next chapter.

CHAPTER XXXVII

OF THE PLEASANT CONVERSATION WHICH PASSED BETWEEN DON QUIXOTE, SANCHO PANZA, AND THE BACHELOR SAMPSON CARRASCO

Don Quixote, full of thought, was impatient for the return of Sancho and the bachelor Carrasco, anxious to hear about the printed accounts of himself, yet scarcely believing that such a history could really be published, since the blood of the enemies he had slain was still reeking on his sword-blade—indeed, he did not see how it was possible that his high feats of arms should be already in print. However, he finally concluded that some sage, either friend or enemy, by art-magic, had sent them to the press: if a friend, to proclaim and extol them above the most signal achievements of knights-errant—if an enemy, to annihilate and sink them below the meanest that ever were written even of a squire: though again he recollected that the feats of squires were

* Sancho mistakes Berengena, a species of fruit, for Benengeli.

Sampson Carrasco

never recorded.　At any rate he was certain, if it should prove
the fact that such a history was really extant, being that of a
knight-errant, it could not be otherwise than lofty, illustrious,
magnificent, and true.　While he was agitated by these and a
thousand other fancies, Sancho returned, accompanied by the
bachelor, who was received with all possible courtesy.

This bachelor, though Sampson by name, was no giant in
person, but a little mirth-loving man, with a good understanding ;
about twenty-four years of age, of a pale complexion, round-faced,
flat-nosed, and wide-mouthed : all indicating humour and native
relish for jocularity, which, indeed showed itself when, on approaching Don Quixote, he threw himself upon his knees, and
said to him :

"Señor Don Quixote de la Mancha, allow me the honour of
kissing your illustrious hand, for by the habit of St. Peter, which
I wear—though I have yet taken only the four first degrees
towards holy orders—your worship is one of the most famous
knights-errant that hath ever been or shall be, upon the whole
circumference of the earth !　A blessing light on Cid Hamet
Benengeli, who has recorded the history of your mighty deeds ;
and blessings upon blessings light on that ingenious scribe whose
laudable curiosity was the cause of its being translated out of
Arabic into our vulgar Castilian, for the profit and amusement of
all mankind ! "　Don Quixote having raised him from the
ground, said to him :

"It is true, then, that my history is really published to the
world, and that it was written by a Moor and a sage ? "

"So true it is, sir," said Sampson, "that I verily believe there
are, at this very day, above twelve thousand copies published of
that history :—witness Portugal, Barcelona, and Valencia, where
they were printed ; and it is said to be now printing at Antwerp
—indeed, I prophesy that no nation or language will be without
a translation of it."

"There cannot be a more legitimate source of gratification to
a virtuous and distinguished man," said Don Quixote, "than to
have his good name celebrated during his lifetime, and circulated
over different nations :—I say his good name, for if it were otherwise than good, death in any shape would be preferable."

"As to high reputation and a good name," said the bachelor,

" your worship bears the palm over all past knights-errant : for the Moor in the Arabian language, and the Castilian in his translation, have both taken care to paint to the life that gallant deportment which distinguishes you, that greatness of soul in confronting dangers, that patience in adversity, that fortitude in suffering, that modesty and continence in love, so truly Platonic, as that subsisting between you and my lady Donna Dulcinea del Toboso."

Sancho here interposed, saying :

" I never heard my lady Dulcinea called Donna before, but only plain Dulcinea del Toboso ; so that here the history is already mistaken."

" That objection is of no importance," answered Carrasco.

" No, certainly," replied Don Quixote ; "but pray tell me, Señor bachelor, on which of my exploits do they lay the greatest stress in that same history ? "

" As to that matter," said the bachelor, "opinions vary according to the difference of tastes. Some are for the adventure of the wind-mills, which your worship took for so many Briareuses and giants ; others prefer that of the fulling-mills; one cries up for the two armies, which turned out to be flocks of sheep ; another for the dead body being carried for interment to Segovia. Some maintain that the affair of the galley-slaves is the flower of all ; while others will have it that none can be compared to that of the two Benedictine giants, and the combat with the valorous Biscayan."

" Pray tell me, Señor bachelor," quoth Sancho, " has it got, among the rest, the affair of the Yanguesian carriers, when our good Rozinante was tempted to go astray ? "

" The sage," answered Sampson, " has omitted nothing—he minutely details everything, even to the capers Sancho cut in the blanket."

" I cut no capers in the blanket," answered Sancho ; " in the air I own I did, and not much to my liking."

" There is no history of human affairs, I conceive," said Don Quixote, "which is not full of reverses, and none more than those of chivalry."

" Nevertheless," replied the bachelor, "some who have read the history say they should have been better pleased if the authors of it had forborne to enumerate all the buffetings endured by Señor Don Quixote in his different encounters."

"Therein consists the truth of the history," quoth Sancho, "and I hear that I am one of the principal parsons in it."

"Persons, not parsons, friend Sancho," quoth Sampson.

"What, have we another corrector of words?" quoth Sancho: "if we are to go on at this rate, we shall make slow work of it."

"As sure as I live, Sancho," answered the bachelor, "you are the second person of the history:—nay, there are those who had rather hear you talk than the finest fellow of them all: though there are also some who charge you with being too credulous in expecting the government of that island promised you by Señor Don Quixote, here present."

"There is still sunshine on the wall," quoth Don Quixote; "and when Sancho is more advanced in age, with the experience that years bestow, he will be better qualified to be a governor than he is at present."

"'Fore Gad! sir," quoth Sancho, "if I am not fit to govern an island at these years, I shall be no better able at the age of Methusalem. The mischief of it is, that the said island sticks somewhere else, and not in my want of a headpiece to govern it."

"Recommend the matter to God, Sancho," said Don Quixote, "and all will be well—perhaps better than thou mayest think: for not a leaf stirs on the tree without His permission."

"That is very true," quoth Sampson; "and if it please God, Sancho will not want a thousand islands to govern, much less one."

"I have seen governors ere now," quoth Sancho, "who, in my opinion, do not come up to the sole of my shoe: and yet they are called 'your lordship,' and eat their victuals upon plate."

"Those are not governors of islands," replied Sampson, "but of other governments more manageable; for those who govern islands must at least understand grammar."

"Faith it is all Greek to me," said Sancho.

"Some people," continued the bachelor, "have taxed the author with having a treacherous memory, since he never explained who it was that stole Sancho's Dapple : it only appears that he was stolen, yet soon after we find him mounted upon the same beast, without being told how it was recovered. They complain also, that he has omitted to inform us, what Sancho did with the hundred crowns which he found in the portmanteau in the Sierra Morena : for he never mentions them again, to the great disappointment of many curious persons, who reckon it one of the most material defects in the work."

"Well, Master Sampson Carrasco, you want to know when and how my Dapple was stolen, and who was the thief ? You must know, then, that on the very night then we marched off, to avoid the officers of the holy brotherhood, after the unlucky affair of the galley-slaves, having made our way into the Sierra Morena, my master and I got into a thicket, where he, leaning upon his lance, and I, sitting upon Dapple, mauled and tired by our late skirmishes, we both fell as fast asleep as if we had been stretched upon four feather-beds. For my own part, I slept so soundly that the thief, whoever he was, had leisure enough to prop me up on four stakes, which he planted under the four corners of the pannel, and then drawing Dapple from under me, he left me fairly mounted, without ever dreaming of my loss."

"That is an easy matter, and no new device," said Don Quixote ; " for it is recorded, that at the siege of Albraca the famous robber Brunelo, by the very same stratagem, stole the horse of Sacripante from between his legs."

"At daybreak," continued Sancho, "when I awoke and began to stretch myself, the stakes gave way, and down I came, with a confounded squelch, to the ground. I looked about me, but could see no Dapple ; tears came into my eyes, and I made such a lamentation that if the author of our history has not set it down, he has surely omitted an excellent thing. After some days—I cannot exactly say how many—as I was following the princess Micomicona, I saw my ass again, and who should be mounted on him but that cunning rogue and notorious malefactor Gines de Passamonte, whom my master and I freed from the galley-chain ! "

" The mistake does not lie there," said Sampson, " but in the author making Sancho ride upon the same beast before he is said to have recovered him."

" All this," said Sancho, " I know nothing about; it might be a mistake of the historian, or perhaps, a blunder of his printer."

" No doubt it was so," quoth Sampson : " but what became of the hundred crowns ?—for there we are in the dark."

" I laid them out," replied Sancho, " for the benefit of my own person and that of my wife and children ; and they have been the cause of her bearing quietly my rambles from home in the service of my master Don Quixote : for had I returned after so long a time, ass-less and penny-less, I must have looked for a scurvy greeting : and if you want to know anything more of me, here I am, ready to answer the king himself in person ; though it is nothing to anybody whether I bought or bought not, whether I spent or spent not : for if the cuffs and blows that have been given me in our travels were to be paid for in ready money, and rated only at four maravedis a-piece, another hundred crowns would not pay for half of them : so let every man lay his hand upon his heart, and not take white for black, nor black for white ; for we are all as God made us, and often-times a great deal worse."

" I will take care," said Carrasco, " to warn the author of the history not to forget, in his next edition, what honest Sancho has told us, which will make the book as good again."

" Are there any other explanations wanting in the work, Señor Bachelor ? " quoth Don Quixote.

" There may be others," answered Carrasco, " but none of equal importance with those already mentioned."

" Peradventure," said Don Quixote, " the author promises a second part ? "

" He does," answered Sampson, " but says he has not yet been able to find out the possessor of it ; and therefore we are in doubt whether or not it will ever make its appearance. Besides, some people say that second parts are never good for anything ; and others that there is enough of Don Quixote already."

At this moment, while Sancho was yet speaking, the neigh-ing of Rozinante reached their ears ; which Don Quixote took for a most happy omen, and resolved, without delay, to resume his functions, and again sally forth into the world. He therefore consulted the bachelor as to what course he should take, and was advised by him to go staight to the kingdom of Arragon and the city of Saragossa, where, in a few days, a most solemn tournament was to be held in honour of the festival of Saint George; and there, by vanquishing the Arragonian knights, he would acquire the ascendency over all the knights in the world. The bachelor commended his resolution as most honourable and brave: at the same time cautioning him to be more wary in encountering great and needless perils, because his life was not his own, but belonged to those who stood in need of his aid and protection.

The knight now requested Sampson Carrasco, if he were a poet, to do him the favour to compose some verses for him, as a farewell to his lady, and to place a letter of her name at the beginning of each verse, so that the initials joined together might make *Dulcinea del Toboso.* The bachelor said that, though he was not one of the great poets of Spain, who were said to be three-and-a-half in number, he would endeavour to comply with his request; at the same time, he foresaw that it would be no easy task, as the name consisted of seventeen letters; for if he made four stanzas of four verses each, there would be a letter too much, and if he made them of five, which are called Decimas or Redondillas, there would be three letters wanting: however, he said that he would endeavour to sink a letter as well as he could, so that the name of Dulcinea del Toboso should be included in the four stanzas. "Let it be so by all means," said Don Quixote; for, when the name is not plain and manifest, the lady is always doubtful whether the verses be really composed for her." On this point they agreed, and also that they should set out within eight days from that time. Don Quixote enjoined the bachelor to keep his intention secret of setting out again, especially from the priest and master Nicholas, as well as his niece and housekeeper, lest they might endeavour to obstruct his honourable purpose. Carrasco promised to attend to his caution, and took his leave, after obtaining a promise on his part to send him tidings of his progress whenever an opportunity offered. Sancho also went home to prepare for the intended expedition.

CHAPTER XXXVIII

OF THE DISCREET AND PLEASANT CONVERSATION WHICH PASSED BETWEEN SANCHO PANZA AND HIS WIFE TERESA

SANCHO went home in such high spirits that his wife observed his gaiety a bow-shot off, insomuch that she could not help saying :

"What makes you look so blithe, friend Sancho?" To which he answered :

"Would to Heaven, dear wife, I were not so well pleased as I seem to be!"

"I know not what you mean, husband," replied she, "by saying you wish you were not so much pleased; now, silly as I am, I cannot guess how any one can desire not to be pleased."

"Look you, Teresa," answered Sancho, "I am thus merry because I am about to return to the service of my master Don Quixote, who is going again in search after adventures, and I am to accompany him : for so my fate wills it. Besides, I am merry with the hopes of finding another hundred crowns like those we have spent; though it grieves me to part from you and my children ; and if Heaven would be pleased to give me bread, dryshod and at home, without dragging me over crags and cross-paths, it is plain that my joy would be better grounded, since it is now mingled with sorrow for leaving you : so that I was right in saying that I should be glad if it pleased Heaven I were not so well pleased."

"Look you, Sancho," replied Teresa, "ever since you have been a knight-errant man, you talk in such a roundabout manner that nobody can understand you."

"It is enough, wife," said Sancho, "that God understands me. For He is the understander of all things; and so much for that. And do you hear, wife, it behoves you to take special care of Dapple for these three or four days to come, that he may be in a condition to bear arms ; so double his allowance, and get the pack-saddle in order, and the rest of his tackling : for we are not going to a wedding, but to roam about the world, and to give and take with giants, fiery dragons, and goblins, and to hear hissings, roarings, bellowings, and bleatings, all which would be but flowers of lavender, if we had not to do with Yangueses and enchanted Moors."

"I believe, indeed, husband," replied Teresa, "that your squires-errant do not eat their bread for nothing, and therefore I shall not fail to beseech Heaven to deliver you speedily from so much evil hap."

"I tell you, wife," answered Sancho, "that did I not expect, ere long, to see myself governor of an island, I vow I should drop down dead upon the spot."

"Not so, good husband," quoth Teresa : "let the hen live though it be with the pip. Do you live, and the devil take all the governments in the world."

The niece and housekeeper of Don Quixote, during the conversation of Sancho Panza and his wife Teresa Cascajo, were not idle ; for they were led to suspect, from a thousand symptoms, that he was inclined to break loose a third time, and return to the exercise of his unlucky knight-errantry ; and therefore they endeavoured, by all possible means, to divert him from his unhappy purpose : but it was all like preaching in the desert, and hammering on cold iron.

As soon as the housekeeper saw that Sancho and her master were so frequently shut up together, she suspected the drift of their conference ; and doubting not that another unfortunate expedition would be the result, she put on her veil and set off, full of trouble and anxiety, to seek the bachelor Sampson Carrasco : thinking that as he was a well-spoken person, and a new acquaintance of her master, he might be able to dissuade him from so extravagant a project. She found him walking to and fro in the courtyard of his house, and she immediately opened her mind to him. He listened to her patiently then said :

"Go, get you home, and leave the matter with me, while I consult with the curate." Away went the housekeeper home, while the bachelor repaired to the priest, with whom he held a consultation, the issue of which will come out in due time.

Meantime Sancho returned after his consultation with his his wife. The squire looked grave and perplexed. "Well now, Sancho, what's amiss? What would you be at?"

"What I would be at," quoth Sancho, "is that your worship would be pleased to allow me wages—so much a month, as long as I shall serve you, and that, in case of need, the same may be paid out of your estate : for I have no mind to trust to rewards, which may come late or never."

"Yes," returned Don Quixote. "I plainly see the mark at which thou art levelling thy proverbs ; but hear me, Sancho : I should have no objection to appoint thee wages had I ever met with any example among the histories of knights-errant that showed the least glimmering of any such monthly or yearly stipend. I have read all, or most of those histories, and do not remember ever to have read that any knight-errant allowed his squire fixed wages ; on the contrary, they all served upon courtesy : and when least expecting it, if their masters were fortunate, they were rewarded with an island, or something equal to it ; at all events, they were certain of title and rank. If, Sancho, upon the strength of these expectations, thou art willing to return to my service, in Heaven's name do so ; but thou art mistaken if thou hast any hope that I shall act in opposition to the ancient usages of chivalry. Return home, therefore, Sancho, and inform thy wife of my determination ; and if she is willing and thou art disposed to stay with me upon the terms I mentioned —bene quidem; if not, we will at least part friends and I shall easily get another squire."

On hearing this fixed resolution, the hopes of Sancho were overclouded, and his heart sunk within him : for hitherto he had never supposed it possible that his master would go without him for the world's worth ; and, as he was standing thoughtful and dejected, Sampson Carrasco entered the chamber, followed by the niece and housekeeper, who were curious to hear what arguments he would use to dissuade the knight from his threatened expedition. The waggish bachelor approached him with great respect, and after embracing him, said, in an elevated tone :

"O flower of knight-errantry! O resplendent light of arms! O mirror and glory of the Spanish nation! May it please Heaven that all those who shall seek to prevent or impede your third sally be lost in the labyrinth of their own wiles, nor ever accomplish their evil desire!" Then turning to the housekeeper, he said, "Now, mistress housekeeper, you may save yourself the trouble of saying the prayer of St. Appollonia as I directed; for I know that it is the positive determination of the stars that Señor Don Quixote shall resume his glorious career, and I should greatly burthen my conscience did I not give intimation thereof, and persuade this knight no longer to restrain the force of his valorous arm, nor check the virtuous ardour of his soul. Go on then, dear Señor Don Quixote, my brave and gallant knight! Lose no time; if your excellency stand in need of a squire, I shall esteem myself singularly fortunate in having the honour to serve you in that capacity."

"Did I not tell thee," said Don Quixote, turning to Sancho, "that I should be in no want of squires? Behold who now offers himself! The renowned bachelor Sampson Carrasco, the darling and delight of the Salamancan schools! But Heaven forbid that, to gratify my own private inclination, I should endanger this pillar of literature, and lop off so flourishing a branch of the noble and liberal arts. No, let our new Sampson abide in his country, and do honour to the grey hairs of his venerable parents, by becoming its ornament. I will be content without a squire, since Sancho deigns not to accompany me."

"I do deign," said Sancho, with eyes swimming in tears; "it shall never be said of me, dear master, 'the bread eaten, the company broke up.' I am not come of an ungrateful stock: for all the world knows, especially our village, who the Panzas were, that have gone before me. Besides, I know, by many good works and better words, your worship's inclination to do me a kindness: and if I have said too much upon the article of wages, it was to please my wife, who, when once she sets about persuading one to a thing, no mallet drives the hoops of a tub as she does to get her will: but a man must be a man, and a woman a woman, and I will follow your worship to the world's end."

The bachelor listened in admiration to Sancho, for though he had read the first part of the history, he had hardly conceived it possible that he should really be so pleasant a fellow as he is therein described; but now he could believe all that had been said of him : in short, he set down both the master and man as the most extraordinary couple the world had ever yet produced. Don Quixote and Sancho being now perfectly reconciled, they agreed, with the approbation of the great Carrasco, their oracle, to depart within three days, in which time they might have leisure to provide what was necessary for the expedition, and especially a complete helmet, which Don Quixote declared to be indispensable. Sampson engaged to procure one from a friend, who he was sure would not refuse it; though he confessed the brightness of the steel was not a little obscured by tarnish and rust.

The niece and housekeeper, on hearing this determination, made a woeful outcry, inveighing bitterly against Carrasco, who had been acting agreeably to a plan previously concerted with the priest and barber. They tore their hair, scratched and disfigured their faces, like the funeral mourners * of former times, and lamented the approaching departure of their master as if it were his death.

Three days were now employed in preparation, at the end of which time, Sancho having appeased his wife, and Don Quixote his niece and housekeeper, they issued forth in the evening, unobserved by any except the bachelor, who insisted on bearing them company half a league from the village. The knight was mounted on his good Rozinante, and the squire on his trusty Dapple, his wallets stored with food, and his purse with money, providentially supplied by his master in case of need. When Sampson took his leave, he expressed an earnest desire to have advice of his good or ill fortune, that he might rejoice or condole with him, as the laws of friendship required. Don Quixote having promised to comply with this request, the bachelor returned to the village, and the knight and squire pursued their way towards the great city of Toboso.

* It was formerly the custom to hire these mourners or bewailers, to lament over the body of the deceased.

CHAPTER XXXIX

WHAT BEFEL DON QUIXOTE AS HE WAS GOING TO VISIT HIS LADY DULCINEA DEL TOBOSO

DON QUIXOTE and Sancho were now left together, and scarcely had Sampson quitted them when Rozinante began to neigh, and Dapple to bray, which both knight and squire regarded as a good omen. It must be confessed that the snorting and braying of Dapple exceeded the neighings of the steed; whence Sancho gathered that his good luck was to rise above and exceed that of his master.

"Friend Sancho," said Don Quixote to his squire, "the night comes on apace, and it will be dark before we reach Toboso, whither I am resolved to go before I undertake any other adventure. There will I receive the farewell benediction of the peerless Dulcinea, by which I shall secure the happy accomplishment of every perilous enterprise: for nothing in this life inspires a knight-errant with so much valour as the favour of his mistress."

"I believe it," answered Sancho; "but I am of opinion it will be difficult for your worship to speak with her alone—at least, in any place where you may receive her benediction; unless she tosses it over the pales of the yard where I saw her last, when I carried her the letter that gave an account of the pranks your worship was playing on the mountain."

"Didst thou conceive those to be pales, Sancho," quoth Don Quixote, "over which thou didst behold that paragon of gentility and beauty? Impossible! Thou must mean galleries, arcades, or cloisters, of some rich and royal palace."

"All that may be," answered Sancho; "but if I do not forget, to me they seemed pales, or I have a very shallow memory."

"However, let us go thither, Sancho," said Don Quixote; "for, so I but gaze on her, be it through pales, the chinks of a hut, or lattice window, the smallest ray from the bright sun of her beauty will soon enlighten my understanding, and fortify my heart, that I shall remain without a rival either in prudence or valour." "In truth, sir," answered Sancho, "when I saw this sun of the lady Dulcinea del Toboso, it was not bright enough to cast forth any beams, owing, I take it, to the dust from the grain which, I told you, her ladyship was winnowing, and which overcast her face like a cloud."

In this and the like conversation they passed that night and the following day, without having encountered anything worth relating, to the no little mortification of Don Quixote: but the next day they came in view of the great city of Toboso, at the sight of which Don Quixote's spirits were much elevated, and those of Sancho as much dejected; because he knew not the abode of Dulcinea, nor had he ever seen her in his life, any more than his master. Thus both were in a state of suffering, the one anxious to see her, and the other anxious because he had not seen her; for Sancho knew not what he should do in case his master should despatch him to the city. Don Quixote having determined not to enter it until nightfall, he waited in the mean time under the shade of some oak-trees; and then proceeded towards the city, where things befel them that were things indeed!

It was late at night when Don Quixote and Sancho left their retreat and entered Toboso. All the town was hushed in silence: for its inhabitants were sound asleep, stretched out at their ease. The night was clear, though Sancho wished it were otherwise, having occasion for its darkness to conceal his prevarications. No noise was heard in any part save the barking of dogs, which annoyed the ears of Don Quixote, and disquieted Sancho's heart. Now and then, it is true, asses brayed, swine grunted, and cats mewed—sounds which seemed to be augumented by the absence of every other noise. All these circumstances the enamoured knight regarded as boding ill. Nevertheless, he said to his squire:

"Son Sancho, lead on to Dulcinea's palace; for it is possible we may find her awake."

"To what palace? Body of the sun!" answered Sancho, "that in which I saw her highness was but a little mean house."

"It was, I suppose, some small apartment of her castle

which she had retired to," said the knight, "to amuse herself with her damsels, as is usual with great ladies and princesses."

"Since your worship," quoth Sancho, "will needs have my lady Dulcinea's house to be a castle, is this an hour to find the gates open? and is it fit that we should stand thundering at them till they open and let us in, putting the whole house in an uproar?"

"First, however, let us find this castle," replied Don Quixote, "and then I will tell thee how it is proper to act; but look, Sancho—either my eyes deceive me or that huge dark pile we see yonder must be Dulcinea's palace."

"Then, lead on yourself, sir," answered Sancho; "perhaps it may be so; though, if I were to see it with my eyes, and touch it with my hands, I will believe it just as much as that it is now day."

Don Quixote led the way, and having gone about two hundred paces, he came up to the edifice which cast the dark shade, and, perceiving a large tower, he soon found that the building was no palace, but the principal church of the place: whereupon he said:

"We are come to the church, Sancho."

"I see we are," answered Sancho; "and pray Heaven we be not come to our graves; for it is no very good sign to be rambling about churchyards at such hours, and especially since I have already told your worship, if I remember right, that this same lady's house stands in a blind alley."

"God's curse light on thee, blockhead!" said the knight; "where hast thou ever found castles and royal palaces built in blind alleys?"

"Sir," replied Sancho, "each country has its customs; so perhaps it is the fashion, here in Toboso, to build your palaces and great edifices in alleys: and, therefore, I beseech your worship to let me look about among these lanes and alleys just before me; and perhaps in one nook or other I may pop upon this same palace."

Sancho seeing his master perplexed and dissatisfied, said to him:

"Sir, the day comes on apace, and we shall soon have the sun upon us, which will not be very pleasant in the streets: so I think we had better get out of this place, and, while your worship takes shelter in some wood hereabouts, I will return and leave not a corner in all the town unsearched, for this house, castle, or palace of my lady ; and it shall go hard with me but I find it ; and as soon as I have done so, I will speak to her ladyship, and tell her where your worship is waiting for her orders and directions how you may see her without damage to her honour and reputation."

"Sancho," quoth Don Quixote, "thou hast uttered a thousand sentences in the compass of a few words. Thy counsel I relish much, and shall most willingly follow it. Come on, son, and let us seek for some shelter : then shalt thou return and seek out my lady, from whose discretion and courtesy I expect more than miraculous favours." Sancho was impatient till he got his master out of the town, lest his lies should be detected : he therefore hastened on as fast as possible, and when they had got about the distance of two miles, the knight retired into a shady grove, while the squire returned in quest of the lady Dulcinea.

CHAPTER XL

THE CUNNING USED BY SANCHO, IN ENCHANTING THE LADY DULCINEA ; WITH OTHER EVENTS NO LESS LUDICROUS THAN TRUE

DON QUIXOTE having retired into a grove near the city of Toboso, despatched Sancho, with orders not to return into his presence till he had spoken to his lady, beseeching her that she would be pleased to grant her captive knight permission to wait upon her, and that she would deign to bestow on him her benediction, whereby he might secure complete success in all his encounters and arduous enterprises. Sancho promised to execute his commands, and to return with an answer no less favourable than that which he had formerly brought him.

"Go, then, son," replied Don Quixote, "and be not in confusion when thou standest in the blaze of that sun of beauty. Go, and may better fortune than mine conduct thee : be thou more successful than my anxious heart will bode during the painful period of thy absence."

"I will go, and return quickly," quoth Sancho. "Meantime, good sir, cheer up, and remember the saying, that a good heart breaks bad luck; and if there is no hook, there is no bacon, and where we least expect it, the hare starts; this I say because, though we could not find the castle nor palace of my lady Dulcinea in the dark, now that it is daylight I reckon I shall soon find it, and then—let me alone to deal with her."

"Verily, Sancho," quoth Don Quixote, "thou dost apply thy proverbs most happily : yet Heaven grant me better luck in the attainment of my hopes !"

Sancho now switched his Dapple, and set off, leaving Don Quixote on horseback, resting on his stirrups and leaning on his lance, full of melancholy and confused fancies, where we will leave him, and attend Sancho Panza, who departed no less perplexed and thoughtful : insomuch that, after he had got out of the grove and looked behind him to ascertain that his master was out of sight, he alighted, and sitting down at the foot of a tree he began to hold a parley with himself.

"Tell me now, brother Sancho," quoth he, "whither is your worship going ? Are you going to seek some ass that is lost ?" "No, verily." "Then what are you going to seek ?" "Why, I go to look for a thing of nothing—a princess, the sun of beauty, and all heaven together !" "Well, Sancho, and where think you to find all this ?"

"Where ? In the great city of Toboso." "Very well ; and pray who sent you on this errand ?" "Why, the renowned knight Don Quixote de la Mancha, who redresses wrongs, and gives drink to the hungry and meat to the thirsty."

"All this is mighty well; and do you know her house, Sancho ?" "My master says it must be some royal palace or stately castle." "And have you ever seen her ?" "Neither I nor my master have ever seen her ?" "And do you think it would be right or advisable that the people of Toboso should know you are coming to kidnap their princesses and lead their ladies astray ! What if, for this offence, they should come and grind your ribs to powder with true dry basting, and not leave you a whole bone in your skin ?" "Truly they would be much in the right of it, unless they please to consider, that I, being only a messenger, am not in fault." "Trust not to that, Sancho; for the Manchegans are very choleric, and their honour so ticklish that it will not bear touching." "God's my life! If we should be scented, woe be to us. But why do I go looking for a cat with three legs for another man's pleasure? Besides, to look for Dulcinea up and down Toboso, is just as if one should look for little Mary in Rabena, or a bachelor in Salamanca: the devil, and nobody else, has put me upon such a business! This being the case, I say, it will not be very difficult to make him believe that a country wench (the first I light upon) is the lady Dulcinea; and, should he not believe it, I will swear to it; and if he swears, I will outswear him; and if he persists, I will persist the more, so that mine shall still be uppermost, come what will of it. By this plan I may, perhaps, tire him of sending me on such errands; or he may take it into his head that some wicked enchanter has changed his lady's form, out of pure spite."

This project set Sancho's spirit at rest, and he reckoned his business as good as half done; so he stayed where he was till towards evening, that Don Quixote might suppose him travelling on his mission. Fortunately for him, just as he was going to mount his Dapple, he espied three country wenches coming from Toboso, each mounted on a young ass. Sancho no sooner got sight of them than he rode back at a good pace to seek his master Don Quixote, whom he found breathing a thousand sighs and amorous lamentations. When Don Quixote saw him, he said, "Well, friend Sancho, am I to mark this day with a white or a black stone?"

"Your worship," answered Sancho, "had better mark it with red ochre, as they do the inscriptions on the professors' chairs, to be the more easily read by the lookers-on."

"Thou bringest me good news, then?" cried Don Quixote.

"So good," answered Sancho, "that your worship has only to clap spurs to Rozinante, and get out upon the plain, to see the lady Dulcinea del Toboso, who, with a couple of her damsels, is coming to pay your worship a visit."

"Gracious Heaven!" exclaimed Don Quixote, "what dost thou say? Take care that thou beguilest not my real sorrow by a counterfeit joy."

"What should I get," answered Sancho, "by deceiving your worship, only to be found out the next moment? Come, sir, put on, and you will see the princess our mistress all arrayed and adorned—in short, like herself. She and her damsels are one blaze of flaming gold; all strings of pearls, all diamonds, all rubies, all cloth of tissue above ten hands deep; their hair loose about their shoulders, like so many sunbeams blowing about in the wind; and what is more, they come mounted upon three flea-bitten gambling belfreys, the finest you ever laid eyes on."

"Ambling palfreys, thou wouldst say, Sancho," quoth Don Quixote.

"Well, well," answered Sancho, "belfreys and palfreys are much the same thing; but let them be mounted how they will, they are the finest creatures one would wish to see; especially the princess Dulcinea, who dazzles one's senses."

"Let us go, son Sancho," answered Don Quixote; "and as a reward for this welcome news, I bequeath to thee the choicest spoils I shall gain in my next adventure; and, if that will not satisfy thee, I bequeath thee the colts which my three mares will foal this year upon our village common."

"I stick to the colts," answered Sancho: "for we cannot yet reckon up the worth of the spoils."

They were now got out of the wood, and saw the three wenches very near. Don Quixote looked eagerly along the road towards Toboso, and, seeing nobody but the three wenches, he asked Sancho, in much agitation, whether they were out of the city when he left them.

"Out of the city!" answered Sancho; "are your worship's eyes in the nape of your neck, that you do not see them now before you, shining like the sun at noonday?"

"I see only three country girls," answered Don Quixote, "on three asses."

"Now, Heaven keep me from the devil," answered Sancho; "is it possible that three palfreys, or how do you call them, white as the driven snow, should look to you like asses? As the Lord liveth, you shall pluck off this beard of mine if it be so."

"I tell thee, friend Sancho," answered Don Quixote, "that it is as certain they are asses, as that I am Don Quixote and thou Sancho Panza;—at least, so they seem to me."

"Sir," quoth Sancho, "say not such a thing ; but snuff those eyes of yours, and come and pay reverence to the mistress of your soul." So saying, he advanced forward to meet the peasant girls, and, alighting from Dapple, he laid hold of one of their asses by the halter, and, bending both knees to the ground, said to the girl :

"Queen, princess, and duchess of beauty, let your haughtiness and greatness be pleased to receive into grace and good-liking your captive knight, who stands turned there into stone, all disorder and without any pulse, to find himself before your magnificent presence. I am Sancho Panza, his squire, and he is that wayworn knight Don Quixote de la Mancha, otherwise called the Knight of the Sorrowful Figure."

Don Quixote had now placed himself on his knees by Sancho, and, with wild and staring eyes, surveyed her whom Sancho called his queen ; and, seeing nothing but a peasant girl, with a broad face, flat nose, coarse and homely, he was so confounded that he could not open his lips. The wenches were also surprised to find themselves stopped by two men so different in aspect, and both on their knees ; but the lady who was stopped, breaking silence, said in an angry tone :

"Get out of the road, plague on ye ! and let us pass by, for we are in haste."

"O princess, and universal lady of Toboso !" cried Sancho, "is not your magnificent heart melting to see on his knees before your sublimated presence, the pillar and prop of knight-errantry ?"

"Hey day ! what's here to do ?" cried another of the girls ; "look how your small gentry come to jeer us poor country girls, as if we could not give them as good as they bring : go ! get off about your business, and let us mind ours, and so speed you well."

"Rise, Sancho," said Don Quixote, on hearing this : "for I now perceive that fortune, not yet satisfied with persecuting me, has barred every avenue whereby relief might come to this wretched soul I bear about me in the flesh. And thou, O extreme of all that is valuable, summit of human perfection, thou sole balm to this disconsolate heart that adores thee, though now some wicked enchanter spreads clouds and cataracts over my

eyes, changing, and to them only, thy peerless beauty into that
of a poor rustic ; if he has not converted mine also into that
of some goblin, to render it horrible to thy view, bestow on me
one kind and amorous look, and let this submissive posture,
these bended knees, before thy disguised beauty, declare the
humility with which my soul adores thee ! "

"Marry come up," quoth the wench, "with your idle
gibberish ; get on with you, and let us go, and we shall take it
kindly."

Sancho now let go the halter, delighted that he had come off
so well with his contrivance. The imaginary Dulcinea was no
sooner set at liberty than, pricking her beast with a sharp-pointed
stick, which she held in her hand, she scourged along the field ;
but the ass, smarting more than usual under the goad, began to
kick and wince in such a manner that down came the lady
Dulcinea to the ground. Don Quixote instantly ran to her
assistance, and Sancho to replace the pannel that had got
under the ass's belly. Don Quixote was then proceeding to
raise his enchanted mistress, but the lady saved him that trouble :
for, immediately upon getting up from the ground, she retired
three or four steps back, took a little run, then, clapping both
hands upon the ass's crupper, jumped into the saddle lighter than
a falcon, and seated herself astride like a man.

"By Saint Roque !" cried Sancho, "our lady mistress is
lighter than a bird, and could teach the nimblest Cordovan or
Mexican how to mount : she springs into a saddle at a jump,
and without the help of spurs, makes her palfrey run like a wild
ass ; and her damsels are not a whit short of her, for they all fly
like the wind ! " And this was the truth : for, Dulcinea being
remounted, the other two made after her, full speed, without
looking behind them for above half a league.

Don Quixote followed them with his eyes as far as he was
able, and when they were out of sight, turning to Sancho, he
said :

"What dost thou think now, Sancho ? See how I am persecuted by enchanters ! Mark how far their malice extends,
even to depriving me of the pleasure of seeing my mistress in
her own proper form ! Surely I was born to be an example of
wretchedness, and the butt and mark at which all the arrows

I

of ill fortune are aimed!" The sly rogue Sancho had much difficulty to forbear laughing, to think how exquisitely his master was gulled. After more dialogue of the same kind, they mounted their beasts again, and followed the road to Saragossa, still intending to be present at a solemn festival annually held in that city.

CHAPTER XLI

THE STRANGE ADVENTURE OF THE CART, OR WAIN OF DEATH *

The further converse of Don Quixote and Sancho was prevented by the passing of a cart across the road, full of the strangest-looking people imaginable; it was without any awning above, or covering to the sides, and the carter who drove the mules had the appearance of a frightful demon. The first figure that caught Don Quixote's attention, was that of Death, with a human visage; close to him sat an angel, with large painted wings: on the other side stood an emperor, with a crown, seemingly of gold, on his head. At Death's feet sat the god Cupid, not blindfold, but with his bow, quiver, and arrows; a knight also appeared among them, in complete armour; only instead of a morion, or casque, he wore a hat with a large plume of feathers of divers colours; and there were several other persons of equal diversity in appearance. Such a sight coming thus abruptly upon them, somewhat startled Don Quixote, and the heart of Sancho was struck with dismay. But with the knight, surprise soon gave place to joy; for he anticipated some new and perilous adventure; and under this impression, with a resolution prepared for any danger, he planted himself just before the cart, and cried out in a loud menacing voice, "Carter, coachman, or devil, or whatever be thy denomination, tell me instantly what thou art, whither going, and who are the persons thou conveyest in that

---

* These Autos are dramatic allegories, symbolical of religious Mysteries: they were represented on the festival of the Corpus Christi, and the Octave, not only at the theatres, but before the councils of state, and even the tribune of the Holy Inquisition. These allegorical shows are now wisely prohibited.

vehicle, which, by its freight, looks like Charon's ferry-boat?"
To which the devil calmly replied:

"Sir, we are travelling players, belonging to Angulo el Malo's company. To-day, being the Octave of Corpus Christi, we have been performing a piece representing the 'Cortes of Death'; this evening we are to play it again in the village just before us; and, not having far to go, we travel in the dresses of our parts, to save trouble. This young man represents Death; he an angel: that woman, who is our author's wife, plays a queen; the other a soldier; this one is an emperor, and I am the devil, one of the principal personages of the drama: for in this company I have all the chief parts. If your worship desires any further information, I am ready to answer your questions: for, being a devil, I know everything."

"Upon the faith of a knight-errant," answered Don Quixote, "when I first espied this cart, I imagined some great adventure offered itself; but appearances are not always to be trusted. Heaven be with you, good people; go and perform your play, and if there be anything in which I may be of service to you, command me, for I will do it most readily, having been, from my youth, a great admirer of masques and theatrical representations."

While they were speaking, one of the motley crew came up capering towards them, in an antic dress, frisking about with his morris-bells, and three full-blown ox-bladders tied to the end of a stick. Approaching the knight, he flourished his bladders in the air, and bounced them against the ground close under the nose of Rozinante, who was so startled by the noise that Don Quixote lost all command over him, and having got the curb between his teeth, away he scampered over the plain, with more speed than might have been expected from such an assemblage of dry bones. Sancho, seeing his master's danger, leaped from Dapple and ran to his assistance; but, before his squire could reach him, he was upon the ground, and close by him Rozinante, who fell with his master, the usual termination of Rozinante's frolics. Sancho had no sooner dismounted, to assist Don Quixote, than the bladder-dancing devil jumped upon Dapple, and thumping him with the bladders, fear at the noise, more than the smart, set him also flying over the field towards the village where they were going to act. Thus Sancho, beholding at one and the same moment

Dapple's flight and his master's fall, was at a loss to which of the two duties he should first attend : but, like a good squire and faithful servant, the love he bore to his master prevailed over his affection for his ass ; though as often as he saw the bladders hoisted in the air, and fall upon the body of his Dapple, he felt the pangs and tortures of death, and he would rather those blows had fallen on the apple of his own eyes than on the least hair of his ass's tail.

In this tribulation he came up to Don Quixote, who was in a much worse plight than he could have wished ; and, as he helped him to get upon Rozinante, he said :

"Sir, the devil has run away with Dapple."

"What devil ? " demanded Don Quixote.

"He with the bladders," answered Sancho.

"I will recover him," replied Don Quixote, "though he should hide himself in the deepest and darkest dungeon of the earth. Follow me, Sancho ; for the cart moves but slowly, and the mules shall make compensation for the loss of Dapple."

"Stay, sir," cried Sancho, "you may cool your anger, for I see the devil has left Dapple, and gone his way." And so it was ; for Dapple and the devil having tumbled, as well as Rozinante and his master, the merry imp left him and made off on foot to the village, while Dapple turned back to his rightful owner.

"Nevertheless," said Don Quixote, "it will not be amiss to chastise the insolence of this devil on some of his company, even upon the emperor himself."

"Good your worship," quoth Sancho : "do not think of such a thing, but take my advice and never meddle with players ; for they are a people mightily beloved. I have seen a player taken up for two murders, and get off scot-free. As they are merry folks and give pleasure, everybody favours them, and is ready to stand their friend ; particularly if they are of the king's or some nobleman's company, who look and dress like any princes."

"That capering buffoon shall not escape with impunity, though he were favoured by the whole human race ! " cried Don Quixote, as he rode off in pursuit of the cart, which was now very near the town, and he called aloud :

"Halt a little, merry sirs ; stay, and let me teach you how to treat cattle belonging to the squires of knights-errant." Don Quixote's words were loud enough to be heard by the players, who, perceiving his adverse designs upon them, instantly jumped out of the cart, Death first, and after him the emperor, the carter-devil, and the angel; nor did the queen or the god Cupid stay behind; and, all armed with stones, waited in battle-array, ready to receive Don Quixote at the points of their pebbles. Don Quixote, seeing the gallant squadron, with arms uplifted, ready to discharge such a fearful volley, checked Rozinante with the bridle, and after considering the situation, prudently thought discretion the better part of valour and retired, following in this Sancho's sage advice.

CHAPTER XLII

THE MEETING BETWEEN DON QUIXOTE AND THE KNIGHT OF THE MIRRORS

DON QUIXOTE and his squire passed the night following their encounter with Death under some tall, umbrageous trees; and after refreshing themselves, by Sancho's advice, from the store of provisions carried by Dapple, Sancho fell asleep at the foot of a cork tree while Don Quixote slumbered beneath a branching oak. But it was not long before he was disturbed by a noise near him; he started up, and looking in the direction whence the sounds proceeded, could discern two men on horseback, one of whom dismounting, said to the other:

"Alight, friend, and unbridle the horses; for this place will afford them pasture, and offers to me that silence and solitude which my amorous thoughts require." As he spoke, he threw himself on the ground, and in this motion a rattling of armour was heard, which convinced Don Quixote that this was a knight-errant; and going to Sancho, who was fast asleep, he pulled him by the arm, and having with some difficulty aroused him, he said in a low voice:

"Friend Sancho, we have got an adventure here."

"Heaven send it be a good one," answered Sancho; "and pray, sir, where may this same adventure be?"

"Where, sayest thou, Sancho?" replied Don Quixote : "turn thine eyes that way, and thou wilt see a knight-errant lying extended, who seems to me not over happy in his mind; for I just now saw him dismount and throw himself upon the ground, as if much oppressed with grief, and his armour rattled as he fell."

"But how do you know," quoth Sancho, "that this is an adventure?"

"Though I cannot yet positively call it an adventure, it has the usual signs of one—but listen, he is tuning an instrument, and seems to be preparing to sing."

"By my troth, so he is," cried Sancho, "and he must be some knight or other in love."

"As all knights-errant must be," quoth Don Quixote; "but hearken, and we shall discover his thoughts by his song, for out of the abundance of the heart the mouth speaketh." Sancho would have replied, but the Knight of the Wood, whose voice was only moderately good, began to sing a lyric in praise of his mistress.

With a deep sigh that seemed to be drawn from the very bottom of his heart, the Knight of the Wood ended his song; and after some pause, in a plaintive and dolorous voice, he exclaimed :

"O thou most beautiful and most ungrateful of woman-kind ! O divine Casildea de Vandalia ! Wilt thou then suffer this thy captive knight to consume and pine away in continual peregrinations, and in severest toils ? Is it not enough that I have caused thee to be acknowledged the most consummate beauty in the world, by all the knights of Navarre, of Leon, of Tartesia, of Castile, and in fine, by all the knights of La Mancha?"

"Not so," said Don Quixote, "for I am of La Mancha, and never have made such an acknowledgment, nor ever will admit an assertion so prejudicial to the beauty of my mistress. Thou seest, Sancho, how this knight raves—but let us listen; perhaps he will make some farther declaration."

"Ay, marry will he," replied Sancho, "for he seems to be in a humour to complain for a month to come." But they were mistaken; for the knight hearing voices near them, proceeded no farther in his lamentations, but, rising up, said aloud in a courteous voice, "Who goes there? What are ye? Of the number of the happy, or of the afflicted?"

"Of the afflicted," answered Don Quixote.

"Come to me, then," answered the Knight of the Wood, "and you will find sorrow and misery itself!" These expressions were uttered in so moving a tone that Don Quixote, followed by Sancho, went up to the mournful knight, who, taking his hand, said to him, "Sit down here, sir knight, for to be assured that you profess the order of chivalry, it is sufficient that I find you here, encompassed by solitude and the cold dews of night: the proper station for knights-errant."

"A knight I am," replied Don Quixote, "and of the order you name; and, although my heart is the mansion of misery and woe, yet can I sympathise in the sorrows of others; from the strain I just now heard from you, I conclude that yours are of the amorous kind—arising, I mean, from a passion for some ungrateful fair."

Whilst thus discoursing, they were seated together on the ground, peaceably and sociably, not as if, at daybreak, they were to fall upon each other with mortal fury. Perchance you, too, are in love, sir knight," said he of the Wood to Don Quixote.

"Such is my cruel destiny," answered Don Quixote; "though the sorrows that may arise from well-placed affections ought rather to be accounted blessings than calamities."

"That is true," replied the Knight of the Wood, "provided our reason and understanding be not affected by disdain, which when carried to excess is more like vengeance." "I never was disdained by my mistress," answered Don Quixote. "No, verily," quoth Sancho, who stood close by, "for my lady is as gentle as a lamb, and as soft as butter." "Is this your squire?" demanded the Knight of the Wood. "He is," replied Don Quixote. "I never in my life saw a squire," said the Knight of the Wood, "who durst presume to speak where his lord was conversing: at least there stands mine, as tall as his father, and it cannot be proved that he ever opened his lips when I was speaking." "I' faith!" quoth Sancho, "I have talked, and can talk before one as good as—and perhaps,— but let that rest: perhaps the less said the better." The Knight of the Wood's squire now took Sancho by the arm, and said,

"Let us two go where we may chat squire-like together, and leave these masters of ours to talk over their loves to each other: for I warrant they will not have done before to-morrow morning." "With all my heart," quoth Sancho, "and I will tell you who I am, that you may judge whether I am not fit to make one among the talking squires." The squires then withdrew, and a dialogue passed between them as lively as that of their masters was grave.

Squires and knights being thus separated, the latter were engaged on the subject of their loves, while the former gave an account to each other of their lives. The history first relates the conversation between the servants, and afterwards proceeds to that of the masters. Having retired a little apart, the Squire of the Wood said to Sancho:

"This is a toilsome life we squires to knights-errant lead; in good truth, we eat our bread by the sweat of our brows, which is one of the curses laid upon our first parents."

"You may say, too, that we eat it by the frost of our bodies," added Sancho; "for who has to bear more cold, as well as heat, than your miserable squires to knights-errant? It would not be quite so bad if we could always get something to eat; for good fare lessens care; but how often we must pass whole days without breaking our fast—unless it be upon air!"

"All this may be endured," quoth he of the Wood, "with the hopes of reward: for that knight-errant must be unlucky indeed who does not speedily recompense his squire with, at least, a handsome government, or some pretty earldom."

"I," replied Sancho, "have already told my master that I should be satisfied with the government of an island; and he is so noble and generous that he has promised it me a thousand times."

"And I," said he of the Wood, "should think myself amply rewarded for all my services with a canonry, and I have my master's word for it too."

"Why then," quoth Sancho, "belike your master is some knight of the church, and so can bestow rewards of that kind on his squires; mine is only a layman. Some of his wise friends advised him once to be an archbishop, but he would be nothing but an emperor."

"The good squires went on talking and drinking."

"Let me tell you, friend," quoth he of the Wood, "you are quite in the wrong; for these island governments are often more plague than profit. Some are crabbed, some beggarly,—in short the best of them are sure to bring more care than they are worth. I suspect it would be wiser in us to quit this thankless drudgery and stay at home, where we may find easier work and better pastime; for he must be a sorry squire who has not his nag, his brace of greyhounds, and an angling-rod to enjoy himself with at home."

"I am not without these things," answered Sancho; "it is true I have no horse, but then I have an ass which is worth twice as much as my master's steed. Greyhound I cannot be in want of for our town is overstocked with them; besides the rarest sporting is that we find at other people's cost."

Here the Squire of the Wood observing Sancho to spit very often, as if very thirsty:

"Methinks," said he, "we have talked till our tongues cleave to the roofs of our mouths: but I have got, hanging at my saddle-bow, that which will loosen them;" when, rising up, he quickly produced a large bottle of wine, and a pasty half a yard long, without any exaggeration; for it was made of so large a rabbit that Sancho thought verily it must contain a whole goat, or at least a kid; and, after due examination:

"How," said he, "do you carry such things about with you?"

"Why, what did you think?" answered the other; "did you take me for some starveling squire? No, no, I have a better cupboard behind me on my horse than a general carries with him upon a march." Sancho fell to, without waiting for entreaties, and swallowed down huge mouthfuls in the dark. "Your worship," said he, "is indeed a squire, trusty and loyal, round and sound, magnificent and great withal, as this banquet proves (if it did not come by enchantment); and not a poor wretch like myself, with nothing in my wallet but a piece of cheese, and that so hard that you may knock out a giant's brains with it: and four dozens of carobes * to bear it company, with as many filberts—thanks to my master's stinginess, and

* A pod so called in La Mancha, with a flat pulse in it, which green or ripe is harsh, but sweet and pleasant after it is dried.

to the fancy he has taken, that knights-errant ought to feed, like cattle, upon roots and wild herbs."

"Troth, brother," replied he of the Wood, "I have no stomach for your wild pears, nor sweet thistles, nor your mountain roots; let our masters have them, with their fancies and their laws of chivalry, and let them eat what they commend. I carry cold meats and this bottle at the pommel of my saddle, happen what will; and such is my love and reverence for it, that I kiss and hug it every moment;" and as he spoke he put it into Sancho's hand, who grasped it, and, applying it straightway to his mouth, continued gazing at the stars for a quarter of an hour; then, having finished his draught, he let his head fall on one side, and, fetching a deep sigh, said:

"O the rascal! How catholic it is!"

Thus the good squires went on talking, and eating and drinking, until it was full time that sleep should give their tongues a respite, and allay their thirst, for to quench it seemed impossible; and both of them, still keeping hold of the almost empty bottle, fell fast asleep; in which situation we will leave them at present.

CHAPTER XLIII

THE JOUSTING BETWEEN DON QUIXOTE AND THE KNIGHT OF THE MIRRORS

PEACEABLY and amicably the two knights continued to converse; and among other things the history informs us that he of the wood said to Don Quixote, "In fact, sir knight, I must confess that, by destiny, or rather by choice, I became enamoured of the peerless Casildea de Vandalia:—peerless I call her because she is without her peer, either in rank, beauty, or form. Casildea repaid my honourable and virtuous passion by employing me as Hercules was employed by his step-mother, in many and various perils: promising me, at the end of each of them, that the next should crown my hopes: but, alas! she still goes on, adding link after link to the chain of my labours, insomuch that they are now countless; nor can I tell when they are to cease, and my tender wishes be gratified. One time she commanded me to go and challenge Giralda,* the famous giantess of Seville, who is as stout and strong as if she were made of brass, and, though never stirring from one spot, is the most changeable and unsteady woman in the world. I came, I saw, I conquered—I made her stand still, and fixed her to a point: for, during a whole week, no wind blew but from the north. Another time she commanded me to weigh those ancient statues, the fierce bulls of Guisando,† an enterprise better suited to a porter than a knight. Another time she commanded me to plunge headlong into Cabra's cave, (direful mandate!) and bring her a particular detail of all the lies enclosed within its dark abyss. I stopped the motion of Giralda, I weighed the bulls of Guisanda, I plunged headlong into the cavern of Cabra, and brought to light its hidden secrets; yet still my hopes are dead—O how dead! And her commands and disdains alive—O how alive! In short, she has now commanded me to travel over all the provinces of Spain, and compel every knight whom I meet to confess that, in beauty, she excels all others now in existence; and that I am the most valiant and the most enamoured knight in the universe. In obedience to this command I have already traversed the greatest part of Spain, and have vanquished divers knights who have had the presumption to contradict me. But what I value myself most upon is having vanquished, in single combat, that renowned knight Don Quixote de la Mancha, and made him confess that my Casildea is more beautiful than his Dulcinea; and I reckon that, in this conquest alone, I have vanquished all the knights in the world; for this Don Quixote has conquered them all, and I, having overcome him, his glory, his fame, and his honour, are consequently transferred to me. All the innumerable exploits of the said Don Quixote I therefore consider as already mine, and placed to my account."

Don Quixote was amazed at the assertions of the Knight of the Wood, and had been every moment on the point of giving him the lie; but he restrained himself that he might convict him

---

* A brass statue on a steeple at Seville, which serves for a weathercock.
† Two large statues in that town, supposed to have been placed there by Metellus, in the time of the Romans.

of falsehood from his own mouth; and therefore he' said, very calmly:

"That you may have vanquished, sir knight, most of the knights-errant of Spain, or even of the whole world, I will not dispute ; but that you have conquered Don Quixote de la Mancha I have much reason to doubt. Some one resembling him, I allow, it might have been, though, in truth, I believe there are not many like him."

"How say you ? " cried he of the Wood : " by the canopy of heaven, I fought with Don Quixote, vanquished him, and made him surrender to me ! He is a man of an erect figure, withered face, long and meagre limbs, grizzle-haired, hawk-nosed, with large black moustaches, and styles himself the 'Knight of the Sorrowful Figure.' The name of his squire is Sancho Panza ; he presses the back, and governs the reins, of a famous steed called Rozinante—in a word, the mistress of his thoughts is one Dulcinea del Toboso, formerly called Aldonza Lorenzo, as my Casildea, being of Andalusia, is now distinguished by the name of Casildea de Vandalia. And now, if I have not sufficiently proved what I have said, here is my sword, which shall make incredulity itself believe ! "

"Softly, sir knight," said Don Quixote, "and hear what I have to say. You must know that this Don Quixote you speak of is the dearest friend I have in the world, insomuch that he is, as it were, another self; and, notwithstanding the very accurate description you have given of him, I am convinced, by the evidence of my senses, that you have never subdued him. It is, indeed, possible that, as he is continually persecuted by enchanters, some one of these may have assumed his shape, and suffered himself to be vanquished, in order to defraud him of the fame which his exalted feats of chivalry have acquired him over the whole face of the earth. A proof of their malice occurred but a few days since, when they transformed the figure and face of the beautiful Dulcinea del Toboso into the form of a mean rustic wench. And now if, after all, you doubt the truth of what I say, behold the true Don Quixote himself before you, ready to convince you of your error, by force of arms, on foot, or on horseback, or in whatever manner you please." He then rose up, and, grasping his sword, awaited the determination of the Knight of the Wood, who, very calmly, said in reply :

" A good paymaster wants no pledge : he who could vanquish Señor Don Quixote, under transformation, may well hope to make him yield in his proper person. But as knights-errant should by no means perform their feats in the dark, like robbers and ruffians, let us wait for daylight, that the sun may witness our exploits ; and let the condition of our combat be, that the conquered shall remain entirely at the mercy and disposal of the conqueror ; provided that he require nothing of him but what a knight may with honour submit to." Don Quixote having expressed himself entirely satisfied with these conditions, they went to seek their squires, whom they found snoring, in the very same posture as that in which sleep had first surprised them. They were soon awakened by their masters, and ordered to prepare the steeds, so that they might be ready, at sunrise, for a bloody single combat. At this intelligence Sancho was thunder-struck, and ready to swoon away with fear for his master, from what he had been told, by the Squire of the Wood, of his knight's prowess. Both the squires, however, without saying a word, went to seek their cattle ; and the three horses and Dapple, having smelt each other out, were found all very sociably together.

" You must understand, brother," said the Squire of the Wood to Sancho, " that it is not the custom in Andalusia for the seconds to stand idle, with their arms folded, while their godsons * are engaged in combat. So this is to give you notice that, while our masters are at it, we must fight too, and make splinters of one another."

" This custom, Señor Squire," answered Sancho, " may pass among ruffians ; but among the squires of knights-errant no such practice is thought of—at least I have not heard my master talk of any such custom ; and he knows by heart all the laws of knight-errantry. But, supposing there is any such law, I shall not obey it. I would rather pay the penalty laid upon such peaceable squires, which, I dare say, cannot be above a couple of pounds of wax ; † and that will cost me less money than plasters to cure a

---

* In tilts and tournaments the seconds were a kind of godfathers to the principals, and certain ceremonies were performed on those occasions.

† Small offences, in Spain, are fined at a pound or two of white wax, for the tapers in churches, &c., and confessors frequently enjoin it as a penance.

broken head. Besides, how can I fight when I have got no sword, and never had one in my life?"

"I know a remedy for that," said he of the Wood; "here are a couple of linen bags of the same size; you shall take one, and I the other, and so, with equal weapons, we will have a bout at bag-blows."

"With all my heart," answered Sancho; "for such a battle will only dust our jackets."

"It must not be quite so, either," replied the other; "for, lest the wind should blow them aside, we must put in them half-a-dozen clean and smooth pebbles, of equal weight; and thus we may brush one another without much harm or damage."

But scarcely had hill and dale received the welcome light of day, and objects become visible, when the first thing that presented itself to the eyes of Sancho Panza was the Squire of the Wood's nose, which was so large that it almost overshadowed his whole body. Its magnitude was indeed extraordinary; it was moreover a hawk-nose, full of warts and carbuncles, of the colour of a mulberry, and hanging two fingers' breadth below his mouth. The size, the colour, the carbuncles, and the crookedness, produced such a countenance of horror, that Sancho, at the sight thereof, began to tremble from head to foot, and he resolved within himself to take two hundred cuffs before he would be provoked to attack such a hobgoblin.

Don Quixote also surveyed his antagonist, but, the beaver of his helmet being down, his face was concealed; it was evident, however, that he was a strong-made man, not very tall, and that over his armour he wore a kind of surtout or loose coat, apparently of the finest gold cloth, besprinkled with little moons of polished glass, which made a very gay and shining appearance; a large plume of feathers, green, yellow, and white, waved about his helmet. His lance, which was leaning against a tree, was very large and thick, and headed with pointed steel, above a span long. All these circumstances Don Quixote attentively marked, and inferred, from appearances, that he was a very potent knight, but he was not therefore daunted, like Sancho Panza; on the contrary, with a gallant spirit, he said to the Knight of the Mirrors, as his antagonist called himself.

"Sir knight, if your eagerness for combat has not exhausted

your courtesy, I entreat you to lift up your beaver a little, that I may see whether your countenance corresponds with your gallant demeanour."

"Whether vanquished or victorious in this enterprise, sir knight," answered he of the Mirrors, "you will have time and leisure enough for seeing me; and if I comply not now with your request, it is because I think it would be an indignity to the beauteous Casildea de Vandalia to lose any time in forcing you to make the confession required."

"However, while we are mounting our horses," said Don Quixote, "you can tell me whether I resemble that Don Quixote whom you said you had vanquished."

"As like as one egg is to another," replied he of the Mirrors; "though, as you say you are persecuted by enchanters, I dare not affirm that you are actually the same person."

"I am satisfied that you acknowledge you may be deceived," said Don Quixote; "however, to remove all doubt, let us to horse, and in less time than you would have spent in raising your beaver, if God, my mistress, and my arm avail me, I will see your face, and you shall be convinced I am not the vanquished Don Quixote."

They now mounted without more words, and Don Quixote wheeled Rozinante about, to take sufficient ground for the encounter, while the other knight did the same; but before Don Quixote had gone twenty paces, he heard himself called by his opponent, who, meeting him half-way, said:

"Remember, sir knight, our agreement, which is, that the conquered shall remain at the discretion of the conqueror."

"I know it," answered Don Quixote; "provided that which is imposed shall not transgress the laws of chivalry."

"Certainly," answered he of the Mirrors. At this juncture the squire's strange nose presented itself to Don Quixote's sight, who was no less struck than Sancho, insomuch that he looked upon him as a monster, or some creature of a new species. Sancho, seeing his master set forth to take his career, would not stay alone with Long-nose, lest, perchance, he should get a filip from that dreadful snout, which would level him to the ground, either by force or fright. So he ran after his master, holding by the stirrup-leather, and when he thought it was nearly time for him to face about. "I beseech your worship," he cried, "before you turn, to help me into yon cork-tree, where I can see better and more to my liking the brave battle you are going to have with that knight."

"I rather believe, Sancho," quoth Don Quixote, "that thou art for mounting a scaffold to see the bull-sports without danger."

"To tell you the truth, sir," answered Sancho, "that squire's monstrous nose fills me with dread, and I dare not stand near him."

"It is indeed a fearful sight," said Don Quixote, "to any other but myself; come, therefore, and I will help thee up."

While Don Quixote was engaged in helping Sancho up into the cork-tree, the Knight of the Mirrors took as large a compass as he thought necessary, and, believing that Don Quixote had done the same, without waiting for sound of trumpet, or any other signal, he turned about his horse, who was not a whit more active nor more sightly than Rozinante, and at his best speed, though not exceeding a middling trot, he advanced to encounter the enemy; but, seeing him employed with Sancho, he reined in his steed and stopped in the midst of his career; for which his horse was most thankful, being unable to stir any farther. Don Quixote, thinking his enemy was coming full speed against him, clapped spurs to Rozinante's lean flanks, and made him so bestir himself that, as the history relates, this was the only time in his life that he approached to something like a gallop; and with this unprecedented fury he soon came up to where his adversary stood, striking his spurs rowel-deep into the sides of his charger, without being able to make him stir a finger's length from the place where he had been checked in his career. At this fortunate juncture Don Quixote met his adversary, embarrassed not only with his horse but his lance, which he either knew not how, or had not time, to fix in its rest, and therefore our knight, who saw not these perplexities, assailed him with perfect security, and with such force that he soon brought him to the ground, over his horse's crupper, leaving him motionless and without any signs of life. Sancho, on seeing this, immediately slid down from the cork-tree, and in all haste ran to his master, who alighted from Rozinante and went up to the vanquished knight, when, unlacing his helmet to see whether he was dead, or if yet alive, to give him air, he beheld—but who can relate what he beheld—without causing amazement, wonder, and terror, in all that hear it? He saw, says the history, the very face, the very figure, the very aspect, the very physiognomy, the very effigy and semblance of the bachelor Sampson Carrasco!

"Come hither, Sancho," cried he aloud, "and see, but believe not; make haste, son, and mark what wizards and enchanters can do!" Sancho approached, and seeing the face of the bachelor Sampson Carrasco, he began to cross and bless himself a thousand times over. All this time the overthrown cavalier showed no signs of life.

"My advice is," said Sancho, "that, at all events, your worship should thrust your sword down the throat of this man, who is so like the bachelor Sampson Carrasco: for in despatching him you may destroy one of those enchanters, your enemies."

"Thou sayest not amiss," quoth Don Quixote, "for the fewer enemies the better." He then drew his sword to put Sancho's advice into execution, when the Squire of the Mirrors came running up, but without the frightful nose and cried aloud:

"Have a care, Señor Don Quixote, what you do; for he is the bachelor Sampson Carrasco, your friend, and I am his squire." Sancho seeing his face now shorn of its deformity, exclaimed, "The nose! where is the nose?" "Here it is," said the other; taking from his right-hand pocket a pasteboard nose, formed and painted in the manner already described; and Sancho, now looking earnestly at him, made another exclamation, "Blessed Virgin defend me!" cried he, "is not this Tom Cecial, my neighbour?" "Indeed am I," answered the unnosed squire; "Tom Cecial I am, friend Sancho Panza, and I will tell you presently what tricks brought me hither; but now, good Sancho, entreat, in the mean time, your master not to hurt the Knight of the Mirrors at his feet; for he is truly no other than the rash and ill-advised bachelor Sampson Carrasco, our townsman."

By this time the Knight of the Mirrors began to recover his senses, which Don Quixote perceiving, he clapped the point of his naked sword to his throat and said, "You are a dead man, sir knight, if you confess not that the peerless Dulcinea del Toboso excels in beauty your Casildea de Vandalia; you must promise also, on my sparing your life, to go to the city of Toboso, and present yourself before her from me, that she may dispose of you as she shall think fit; and, if she leaves you at liberty, then shall you return to me without delay—the fame of my exploits being your guide—to relate to me the circumstances of your interview; these conditions being strictly conformable to the terms agreed on before our encounter, and also to the rules of knight-errantry."

"I confess," said the fallen knight, "that the lady Dulcinea del Toboso's torn and dirty shoe is preferable to the ill-combed, though clean locks of Casildea; and I promise to go and return from her presence to yours, and give you the exact and particular account which you require of me."

"You must likewise confess and believe," added Don Quixote, "that the knight you vanquished was not Don Quixote de la Mancha, but some one resembling him; as I do confess and believe that, though resembling the bachelor Sampson Carrasco, you are not he, but some other whom my enemies have purposely transformed into his likeness to restrain the impetuosity of my rage, and make me use with moderation the glory of my conquest."

"I confess, judge, and believe everything, precisely as you do yourself," answered the disjointed knight; "and now suffer me to rise, I beseech you, if my bruises do not prevent me." Don Quixote raised him with the assistance of his squire, on whom Sancho still kept his eyes fixed; and though from some conversation that passed between them he had much reason to believe it was really his old friend Tom Cecial, he was so prepossessed by all that his master had said about enchanters, that he would not trust his own eyes. In short, both master and man persisted in their error; and the Knight of the Mirrors, with his squire, much out of humour and in ill-plight, went in search of some convenient place where he might searcloth himself and splinter his ribs. Don Quixote and Sancho continued their journey to Saragossa, where the history leaves them to give some account of the Knight of the Mirrors and his squire.

When the bachelor Sampson Carrasco advised Don Quixote to resume his functions of knight-errantry, he had previously consulted with the priest and the barber upon the best means of inducing Don Quixote to stay peaceably and quietly at home ; and it was agreed by general vote, as well as by the particular advice of Carrasco, that they should let Don Quixote make another sally (since it seemed impossible to detain him), and that the bachelor should then also sally forth like a knight-errant, and take an opportunity of engaging him to fight ; and after vanquishing him, which they held to be an easy matter, he should remain, according to a previous agreement, at the disposal of the conqueror, who should command him to return home, and not quit it for the space of two years, or till he had received further orders from him.   They doubted not but that he would readily comply, rather than infringe the laws of chivalry ; and they hoped that, during this interval, he might forget his follies, or that some means might be discovered of curing his malady. Carrasco engaged in the enterprise, and Tom Cecial, Sancho Panza's neighbour, a merry shallow-brained fellow, proffered his service as squire.   Sampson armed himself in the manner already described, and Tom Cecial fitted the counterfeit nose to his face for the purpose of disguising himself ; and, following the same road that Don Quixote had taken, they were not far off when the adventure of Death's car took place ; but it was in the wood they overtook him, which was the scene of the late action, and where, had it not been for Don Quixote's extraordinary conceit that the bachelor was not the bachelor, that gentleman, not meeting even so much as nests, where he thought to find birds, would have been incapacitated for ever from taking the degree of licentiate.

Tom Cecial, after the unlucky issue of their expedition, said to the bachelor, " Most certainly, Señor Carrasco, we have been rightly served.   It is easy to plan a thing, but very often difficult to get through with it.   Don Quixote is mad, and we are in our senses ; he gets off sound and laughing, and your worship remains sore and sorrowful : now, pray, which is the greater madman, he who is so because he cannot help it, or he who is so on purpose ? "

" The difference between these two sorts of madmen is," replied Sampson, " that he who cannot help it will remain so, and he who deliberately plays the fool may leave off when he thinks fit."

"That being the case," said Tom Cecial, "I was mad when I desired to be your worship's squire, and now I desire to be so no longer, but shall hasten home again."

"That you may do," answered Sampson, "but, for myself, I cannot think of returning to mine, till I have soundly banged this same Don Quixote. It is not now with the hope of curing him of his madness, that I shall seek him, but a desire for revenge; the pain of my ribs will not allow me to entertain a more charitable purpose." In this humour they went on talking till they came to a village, where they luckily met with a bone-setter, who undertook to cure the unfortunate Sampson. Tom Cecial now returned home, leaving his master meditating schemes of revenge; and though the history will have occasion to mention him again hereafter, it must now attend the motions of our triumphant knight.

CHAPTER XLI

OF WHAT BEFEL DON QUIXOTE WITH A WORTHY GENTLEMAN OF LA MANCHA

DON QUIXOTE pursued his journey with pleasure, satisfaction, and self-complacency, as already described: imagining, because of his late victory, that he was the most valiant knight the world could then boast of. He cared neither for enchantments nor enchanters, and looked upon all the adventures which should henceforth befal him as already achieved and brought to a happy conclusion. He no longer remembered his innumerable sufferings during the progress of his chivalries; the stoning that demolished half his grinders, the ingratitude of the galley-slaves, nor the audacity of the Yanguesian carriers and their shower of pack-staves:—in short, he inwardly exclaimed that, could he devise any means of disenchanting his lady Dulcinea, he should not envy the highest fortune that ever was, or could be, attained by the most prosperous knight-errant of past ages.

While thus discoursing, they were overtaken by a gentleman, mounted on a very fine flea-bitten mare, and dressed in a green cloth riding-coat, faced with murry-coloured velvet, and a hunter's cap of the same ; the mare's furniture corresponded in colour with the rider's dress, and was adapted to field sports ; a Moorish scimitar hung at his shoulder-belt, which was green and gold ; his buskins were wrought like the belt, and his spurs were not gilt, but green, and polished so neatly that, as they suited his clothes, they looked better than if they had been of pure gold. He saluted them courteously, and, spurring his mare, was passing on, when Don Quixote said to him, "If you are travelling our road, Señor, and are not in haste, will you favour us with your company ? "

"Indeed, Señor," replied he, "I should not have passed on, but I was afraid your horse might prove unruly in the company of my mare."

"Sir," answered Sancho, "if that be all, you may safely trust your mare ; for ours is the noblest and best-behaved horse in the world ; and, at such a time, was never guilty of a roguish trick in his life, but once, and then my master and I paid for it seven-fold. I say, again, your worship need not fear ; for if she were served up betwixt two dishes, I assure you, he would not so much as look her in the face." The traveller checked his mare, his curiosity being excited by the appearance of Don Quixote, who rode without his helmet, which Sancho carried like a cloak-bag, at the pommel of his ass's pannel ; but if he stared at Don Quixote, he was himself surveyed with no less attention by the knight, who conceived him to be some person of consequence. His age seemed to be about fifty, though he had but few grey hairs ; his face was of the aquiline form, of a countenance neither too gay, nor too grave, and by his whole exterior it was evident that he was no ordinary person. It was not less manifest that the traveller, as he contemplated Don Quixote, thought he had never seen any one like him before. With wonder he gazed upon his tall person, his meagre, shallow visage, his lank horse, his armour, and stately deportment ; altogether presenting a figure, like which nothing, for many centuries past, had been seen in that country.

Don Quixote perceived that he had attracted the attention of the traveller, and, being always desirous of pleasing, he antici-pated his questions, by saying, after he had told him his name, "You are probably surprised, Señor, at my appearance, which is certainly uncommon in the present age ; but this will be explained when I tell you that I am a knight in search of adventures. I left my country, mortgaged my estate, quitted ease and pleasures, and threw myself into the arms of fortune. I wished to revive chivalry, so long deceased; and for some time past, exposed to many vicissitudes, stumbling in one place, and rising again in another, I have prosecuted my design; succouring widows and protecting damsels."

After an interval of silence, the traveller in green said, in reply:

"You are indeed right, Señor, in conceiving me to be struck by your appearance: but you have rather increased than lessened my wonder by the account you give of yourself. How! Is it possible that there are knights-errant now in the world, and that there are histories printed of real chivalries? I had no idea that there was anybody now upon earth who relieved widows, succoured damsels, aided wives, or protected orphans: nor should yet have believed it, had I not been now convinced with my own eyes."

"There is much to be said," answered Don Quixote, "upon the question of the truth or fiction of the histories of knights-errant."

"Why, is there any one," answered he in green, "who doubts the falsehood of those histories?" "I doubt it," replied Don Quixote—"but no more of that at present; for, if we travel together much farther, I hope to convince you, sir, that you have been wrong in suffering yourself to be carried in the stream with those who cavil at their truth." The traveller now first began to suspect the state of his companion's intellect, and watched for a further confirmation of his suspicion: but, before they entered into any other discourse, Don Quixote said that, since he had so freely described himself, he hoped he might be permitted to ask who he was. To which the traveller answered, "I, Sir Knight of the Sorrowful Figure, am a gentleman, and native of a village where, if it please Heaven, we shall dine to-day. My fortune is affluent, and my name is Don Diego de Miranda. I spend my time with my wife, my children, and my friends: my diversions are hunting and fishing; but I keep neither hawks nor greyhounds, only some decoy partridges, and a stout ferret. I have about six dozen of books, Spanish and Latin, some of history, and some of devotion : those of chivalry have not come over my threshold. I am more inclined to the reading of profane than devout authors, provided they are well written, ingenious, and harmless in their tendency, though, in truth, there are very few books of this kind in Spain. Sometimes I eat with my neighbours and friends, and frequently I invite them ; my table is neat and clean, and not parsimoniously furnished. I slander no one, nor do I listen to slander from others. I pry not into other men's lives, nor scrutinize their actions. I hear mass every day ; I share my substance with the poor, making no parade of my good works, lest hypocrisy and vain-glory, those insidious enemies of the human breast, should find access to mine. It is always my endeavour to make peace between those who are at variance. I am devoted to our blessed Lady, and ever trust in the infinite mercy of God our Lord."

Sancho was very attentive to the account of this gentleman's life, which appeared to him to be good and holy ; and, thinking that one of such a character must needs work miracles, he flung himself off his Dapple, and, running up to him, he laid hold of his right stirrup ; then, devoutly, and almost with tears, he kissed his feet more than once.

"What mean you by this, brother ? " said the gentleman ; " why these embraces ? "

" Pray let me kiss on," answered Sancho ; " for your worship is the first saint on horseback I ever saw in all my life."

" I am not a saint," answered the gentleman, " but a great sinner : you, my friend, must indeed be good, as your simplicity proves." Sancho retired, and mounted his ass again ; having forced a smile from the profound gravity of his master, and caused fresh astonishment in Don Diego.

Don Quixote then asked him how many children he had, at the same time observing that the ancient philosophers, being without the true knowledge of God, held supreme happiness to consist in the gifts of nature and fortune, in having many friends and many good children. "I have one son," answered the gentleman ; " and if I had him not, perhaps I should think my-self happier : not that he is bad, but because he is not all that I would have him. He is eighteen years old : six of which he has spent at Salamanca, learning the Latin and Greek languages, and, when I wished him to proceed to other studies, I found him infatuated with poetry, and could not prevail upon him to look into the law, which it was my desire he should study ; nor into theology, the queen of all sciences. I was desirous that he should be an honour to his family, since we live in an age in which useful and virtuous literature is rewarded by the sovereign—I say virtuous, for letters without virtue are pearls on a dunghill. He passes whole days in examining whether Homer expressed himself well in such a verse of the Iliad ; whether Martial, in such an epigram, be obscene or not ; whether such a line in Virgil should be understood this or that way." Don Quixote after commending the young man's studies, went into an elaborate defence of the latter's devotion to poetry and the classics. To this Don Diego replied that his son did not neglect Spanish literature, and that he was at that time engrossed by a paraphrase on four verses sent him from Salamanca, and which was intended for a scholastic prize.

"Children, my good sir," replied Don Quixote, "are the flesh and blood of their parents, and, whether good or bad, must be loved and cherished as part of themselves. It is the duty of parents to train them up from their infancy, in the paths of virtue and good manners, and in Christian discipline, so that they may become the staff of their age and an honour to their posterity. As to forcing them to this or that pursuit, I do not hold it to be right, though I think there is a propriety in advising them."

Don Quixote by his rational discourse made his companion waver in the opinion he had formed of his insanity. Sancho, in the mean time, not finding the conversation to his taste, had gone a short distance out of the road to beg a little milk of some shepherds whom he saw milking their ewes : and just as the traveller, highly satisfied with Don Quixote's ingenuity and good sense, was about to resume the conversation, Don Quixote perceived a cart with royal banners advancing on the same road, and, believing it to be something that fell under his jurisdiction, he called aloud to Sancho to bring him his helmet.

CHAPTER XLV

THE ADVENTURE OF THE CAGE OF LIONS

LITTLE expecting a fresh adventure, Sancho, as the history carefully relates, was leisurely buying some curds of the shepherds; and, being summoned in such haste to his master, he knew not what to do with them, nor how to carry them; so that, to prevent their being wasted, he poured them into the helmet; and, satisfied with this excellent device, he hurried away to receive the commands of his lord.

"Sancho," said the knight, " give me my helmet: for either I know little of adventures, or that which I descry yonder is one that will oblige me to have recourse to arms." He of the green riding-coat, hearing this, looked on all sides, and could see nothing but a cart coming towards them, with two or three small flags, by which he thought it probable that it was conveying some of the king's money. The knight then took his helmet from Sancho's hand before he had discharged the curds, and, without observing its contents, clapped it hastily upon his head. The curds being squeezed and pressed, the whey began to run down the face and beard of the knight, to his great consternation.

"What can this mean, Sancho?" said he; " methinks my skull is softening, or my brains melting, or I sweat from head to foot! If so, it is certainly not through fear, though I verily believe that this will prove a terrible adventure. Give me something to wipe myself, Sancho; for this copious sweat blinds me." Sancho said nothing, but gave him a cloth; at the same time, thanking Heaven that his master had not found out the truth. Don Quixote wiped himself, and took off his helmet to see what it was, so cool to his head: and, observing some white lumps in it, he put them to his nose, and smelling them, " By the lady of my soul," he exclaimed, "these are curds which thou hast put here, thou base unmannerly squire!" Sancho replied with much coolness and cunning:

"If they are curds, sir, give them to me and I will eat them

—no, now I think of it, the devil may eat them for me, for he only could have put them there. What! I offer to foul your worship's helmet! Egad! it seems as if I had my enchanters too, who persecute me as a creature and member of your worship and have put that filthiness there to provoke your wrath against me. But, truly this time they have missed their aim ; for I trust to my master's good judgment, who will consider that I have neither curds, nor cream, nor anything like it ; and that if I had, I should sooner have put them into my stomach than into your worship's helmet."

"Well," said Don Quixote, "there may be something in that." The gentleman, who had been observing all that had passed, was astonished ; and still more so at what followed ; for Don Quixote, after having wiped his head, face, beard, and helmet, again put it on, and fixing himself firm in his stirrups, adjusting his sword, and grasping his lance, he exclaimed :

"Now, come what may, I am prepared to encounter Satan himself!"

They were soon overtaken by the cart with flags, which was attended only by the driver, who rode upon one of the mules, and a man sitting upon the fore part of it. Don Quixote planted himself just before them, and said :

"Whither go ye, brethren ? What carriage is this ? What does it contain, and what are those banners ?"

"The cart is mine," answered the carter, "and in it are two fierce lions, which the general of Oran is sending to court as a present to his majesty ; the flags belong to our liege the king, to show that what is in the cart belongs to him."

"And are the lions large ?" demanded Don Quixote.

"Larger never came from Africa to Spain," said the man on the front of the cart ; "I am their keeper, and in my time have had charge of many lions, but never of any so large as these. They are a male and a female ; the male is in the first cage, and the female is in that behind. Not having eaten to-day, they are now hungry ; and therefore, sir, stand aside, for we must make haste to the place where they are to be fed."

"What!" said Don Quixote, with a scornful smile, "Lion-whelps against me! Against me, your puny monsters! and at this time of day! By yon blessed sun! those who sent them hither shall see whether I am a man to be scared by lions. Alight, honest friend! and, since you are their keeper, open the cages and turn out your savages of the desert: for in the midst of this field will I make them know who Don Quixote de la Mancha is, in spite of the enchanters that sent them hither to me."

"So, so," quoth the gentleman to himself, "our good knight has now given us a specimen of what he is; doubtless the curds have softened his skull, and made his brains mellow." Sancho now coming up to him:

"For Heaven's sake, sir," cried he, "hinder my master from meddling with these lions; for if he does, they will tear us all to pieces."

"What then, is your master so mad," answered the gentleman, "that you really fear he will attack such fierce animals?"

"He is not mad," answered Sancho, "but daring."

"I will make him desist," replied the gentleman; and, going up to Don Quixote, who was importuning the keeper to open the cages:

"Sir," said he, "knights-errant should engage in adventures that, at least, afford some prospect of success, and not such as are altogether desperate; for the valour which borders on temerity has in it more of madness than courage. Besides, sir knight, these lions do not come to assail you: they are going to be presented to his majesty; and it is, therefore, improper to detain them or retard their journey."

"Sweet sir," answered Don Quixote, "go hence, and mind your decoy partridge and your stout ferret, and leave every one to his functions. This is mine, and I shall see whether these gentlemen lions will come against me or not." Then, turning to the keeper, he said:

"I vow to Heaven, Don Rascal, if thou dost not instantly open the cages, with this lance I will pin thee to the cart." The carter seeing that the armed lunatic was resolute:

"Good sir," said he, "for charity's sake, be pleased to let me take off my mules and get with them out of danger, before the lions are let loose: for should my cattle be killed, I am undone for ever, as I have no other means of living than by this cart and these mules."

"Incredulous wretch!" cried Don Quixote, "unyoke and

do as thou wilt ; but thou shalt soon see that thy trouble might have been spared."

The carter alighted and unyoked in great haste. The keeper then said aloud :

" Bear witness, all here present, that against my will, and by compulsion, I open the cages and let the lions loose. I protest against what this gentleman is doing, and declare all the mischief done by these beasts shall be placed to his account, with my salary and perquisites over and above. Pray, gentlemen, take care of yourselves before I open the door ; for, as to myself, I am sure they will do me no hurt." Again the gentleman pressed Don Quixote to desist from so mad an action ; declaring to him that he was thereby provoking God's wrath. Don Quixote replied that he knew what he was doing. The gentleman rejoined, and entreated him to consider well of it, for he was certainly deceived.

" Nay, sir," replied Don Quixote, " if you will not be a spectator of what you think will prove a tragedy, spur your flea-bitten, and save yourself." Sancho too besought him, with tears in his eyes, to desist from an enterprise compared with which that of the windmills, the dreadful one of the fulling-mills, and, in short, all the exploits he had performed in the whole course of his life, were mere tarts and cheesecakes.

" Consider, sir," added Sancho, " here is no enchantment, nor anything like it ; for I saw, through the grates and chinks of the cage, the paw of a true lion ; and I guess, by the size of its claw, that it is bigger than a mountain."

" Thy fears," answered Don Quixote, " would make it appear to thee larger than half the world. Retire, Sancho, and leave me ; and if I perish here, thou knowest our old agreement : repair to Dulcinea—I say no more." To these he added other expressions, which showed the firmness of his purpose, and that all arguments would be fruitless. The gentleman therefore spurred his mare, Sancho his Dapple, and the carter his mules, and all endeavoured to get as far off as possible from the cart, before the lions were let loose. Sancho bewailed the death of his master ; verily believing it would now overtake him between the paws of the lions ; he cursed his hard fortune, and the unlucky hour when he again entered into his service. But, notwithstand-

ing his tears and lamentations, he kept urging on his Dapple to
get far enough from the cart. The keeper seeing that the
fugitives were at a good distance, repeated his arguments and entreaties, but to no purpose: Don Quixote answered that he
heard him, and desired he would trouble himself no more, but
immediately obey his commands, and open the door.

Whilst the keeper was unbarring the first gate, Don Quixote
deliberated within himself whether it would be best to engage
on horseback or not; and finally determined it should be on foot,
as Rozinante might be terrified at the sight of the lions. He
therefore leaped from his horse, flung aside his lance, braced on
his shield, and drew his sword; then slowly advancing, with
marvellous intrepidity and an undaunted heart, he planted himself
before the lion's cage, devoutly commending himself first to God,
and then to his mistress Dulcinea.

The keeper seeing Don Quixote fixed in his posture, and that
he could not avoid letting loose the lion without incurring the
resentment of the angry and daring knight, set wide open the
door of the first cage, where the monster lay, which appeared to
be of an extraordinary size, and of a hideous and frightful aspect.
The first thing the creature did was to turn himself round in the
cage, reach out a paw, and stretch himself at full length. Then
he opened his mouth and yawned very leisurely; after which he
threw out some half-yard of tongue, wherewith he licked and
washed his face. This done, he thrust his head out of the cage,
and stared round on all sides with eyes like red-hot coals: a sight
to have struck temerity itself with terror! Don Quixote observed him with fixed attention, impatient for him to leap out
of his den, that he might grapple with him and tear him to
pieces; to such a height of extravagance was he transported by
his unheard-of frenzy! But the generous lion, more gentle than
arrogant, taking no notice of his vapouring and bravadoes, after
having stared about him, turned himself round, and, showing his
posteriors to Don Quixote, calmly and quietly laid himself down
again in the cage. Upon which Don Quixote ordered the
keeper to give him some blows, and provoke him to come
forth.

"That I will not do," answered the keeper; "for, should I
provoke him, I shall be the first whom he will tear to pieces. Be

satisfied, Señor cavalier, with what is done, which is everything in point of courage, and do not tempt fortune a second time. The lion has the door open to him and the liberty to come forth; and since he has not yet done so, he will not come out to-day. The greatness of your worship's courage is already sufficiently shown: no brave combatant, as I take it, is bound to do more than to challenge his foe, and wait his coming in the field; and if the antagonist does not meet him, the disgrace falls on him, while the challenger is entitled to the crown of victory."

"That is true," answered Don Quixote; "shut the door, and give me a certificate, in the best form you can, of what you have here seen me perform. It should be known that you opened the door to the lion; that I waited for him; that he came not out; again I waited for him; again he came not out; and again he laid himself down. I am bound to no more—enchantments, avaunt! So Heaven prosper right and justice, and true chivalry! Shut the door, as I told thee, while I make a signal to the fugitive and absent, that from your own mouth they may have an account of this exploit."

The keeper closed the door, and Don Quixote, having fixed the linen cloth with which he had wiped the curds from his face upon the point of his lance, began to hail the troop in the distance, who, with the gentleman in green at their head, were still retiring, but looking round at every step, when, suddenly, Sancho observed the signal of the white cloth.

"May I be hanged," cried he, "if my master has not vanquished the wild beasts, for he is calling to us!" They all stopped, and saw that it was Don Quixote that had made the sign; and, their fear in some degree abating, they ventured to return slowly, till they could distinctly hear the words of Don Quixote, who continued calling to them. When they had reached the cart again, Don Quixote said to the driver:

"Now, friend, put on your mules again, and in Heaven's name proceed; and, Sancho, give two crowns to him and the keeper, to make them amends for this delay."

"That I will, with all my heart," answered Sancho; "but what is become of the lions? are they dead or alive?" The keeper then very minutely, and with due pauses, gave an account of the conflict, enlarging, to the best of his skill, on the valour of

Don Quixote, at sight of whom the daunted lion would not, or durst not, stir out of the cage, though he had held open the door a good while; and, upon his representing to the knight that it was tempting God to provoke the lion, and to force him out, he had at length, very reluctantly, permitted him to close it again.

"What sayest thou to this, Sancho?" said Don Quixote; "can any enchantment prevail against true courage? Enchanters may, indeed, deprive me of good fortune; but of courage and resolution they never can." Sancho gave the gold crowns; the carter yoked his mules; the keeper thanked Don Quixote for his present, and promised to relate this valorous exploit to the king himself, when he arrived at court.

"If, perchance, his majesty," said Don Quixote, "should inquire who performed it, tell him the Knight of the Lions: for henceforward I resolve that the title I have hitherto borne, of the Knight of the Sorrowful Figure, shall be thus changed, converted, and altered: and herein I follow the ancient practice of knights-errant, who changed their names at pleasure."

The cart now went forward, and Don Quixote, Sancho, and Don Diego de Miranda pursued their way in friendly companionship, Don Quixote enlarging on the uses of knight-errantry. Don Diego did not say a word for some time, his attention having been totally engrossed by the singular conduct and language of Don Quixote, whom he accounted a sensible madman, or one whose madness was mingled with good sense. He had never seen the first part of our knight's history, or he would have felt less astonishment at what he had witnessed.

"All that you have just now said, Señor Don Quixote," remarked Don Diego, "is levelled by the line of right reason; and I think if the laws and ordinances of knight-errantry should be lost, they might be found in your worship's breast, as their proper depository and register. But, as it grows late, let us quicken our pace, and we shall soon reach my habitation, where you may repose yourself after your late toil, which, if not of the body, must have been a labour of the mind." "I accept your kind offer with thanks," said the knight; then, proceeding a little faster than before, they reached, about two o'clock in the afternoon, the mansion of Don Diego, whom Don Quixote called the Knight of the Green Riding-coat.

CHAPTER XLVI

OF WHAT BEFEL DON QUIXOTE IN THE CASTLE, OR HOUSE, OF
THE KNIGHT OF THE GREEN RIDING-COAT; WITH OTHER
EXTRAORDINARY MATTERS

DON QUIXOTE, on approaching Don Diego's house, observed it
to be a spacious mansion, having, after the country fashion, the
arms of the family roughly carved in stone over the great gates,
the buttery in the court-yard, the cellar under the porch, and
likewise on several earthen wine-jars placed around it, which, being
of the ware of Toboso, recalled to his memory his enchanted and
metamorphosed Dulcinea. Don Diego's son, with his mother,
came out to receive him; and both mother and son were not a
little astonished at the appearance of their guest, who, alighting
from Rozinante, very courteously desired leave to kiss the lady's
hands. "Madam," said Don Diego, "this gentleman is Don
Quixote de la Mancha, the wisest and most valiant knight-errant
in the world; receive him, I pray, with your accustomed hospitality." The lady, whose name was Donna Christina, welcomed
the knight with much kindness and courtesy, which Don Quixote
returned in expressions of the utmost politeness. The same kind
of compliments passed between him and the student, with whom
Don Quixote was much pleased, judging him, by his conversation, to be a young man of wit and good sense.

Don Quixote was led into a hall, and Sancho having unarmed
him, he remained in his wide Walloon breeches, and in a chamois
doublet, stained all over with the rust of his armour; his band
was of the college cut, unstarched, and without lace: his buskins
were date-coloured, and his shoes waxed. He girt on his trusty
sword, which was hung at a belt made of a sea-wolf's skin, on
account of a weakness he was said to have been troubled with in
his loins; and over the whole he wore a cloak of good grey cloth.
But, first of all, he washed his head and face. The water still
continued of a whey colour—thanks to Sancho's gluttony, and
his foul curds, that had so defiled his master's visage. Thus
accoutred, with a graceful and gallant air Don Quixote walked

K

into another hall, where the student was waiting to entertain him till the table was prepared ; for the lady Donna Christina wished to show her noble guest that she knew how to regale such visitors.

While the knight was unarming, Don Lorenzo (for that was the name of Don Diego's son) had taken an opportunity to question his father concerning him.

" Pray, sir," said he, " who is this gentleman ? for my mother and I are completely puzzled both by his strange figure and the title you give him."

"I scarcely know how to answer you, son," replied Don Diego ; " and can only say that, from what I have witnessed, his tongue belies his actions ; for he converses like a man of sense, and acts like an outrageous madman. Talk you to him, and feel the pulse of his understanding, and exercise all the discernment you possess, to ascertain the real state of his intellects ; for my part I suspect them to be rather in a distracted condition."

Don Lorenzo accordingly addressed himself to Don Quixote ; and they had much pleasant discourse on poetry and knight-errantry.

Their conversation was interrupted, as they were summoned to the dining-hall ; but Don Diego took an opportunity of asking his son what opinion he had formed of his guest.

" His madness, sir, is beyond the reach of all the doctors in the world," replied Don Lorenzo ; " yet it is full of lucid intervals." They now sat down to the repast, which was such as Don Diego had said he usually gave to his visitors : neat, plentiful, and savoury. Don Quixote was, morever, particularly pleased with the marvellous silence that prevailed throughout the whole house, as if it had been a convent of Carthusians.

The cloth being taken away, grace said, and their hands washed, Don Quixote earnestly entreated Don Lorenzo to repeat the verses which he intended for the prize.

" I will do as you desire," replied he, " that I may not seem like those poets who, when entreated, refuse to produce their verses ; but, if unasked, often enforce them upon unwilling hearers : mine, however, were not written with any view to obtain a prize, but simply as an exercise."

" It is the opinion of an ingenious friend of mine," said Don

Quixote, "that these kinds of composition are not worth the trouble they require ; because the paraphrase can never equal the text ; they seldom exactly agree in sense, and often deviate widely. He says that the rules for this species of poetry are much too strict : suffering no interrogations, nor such expressions as ' said he,' ' I shall say,' and the like ; nor changing verbs into nouns, nor altering the sense ; with other restrictions which, you well know, confine the writer."

"Truly, Señor Don Quixote," said Don Lorenzo, "I would fain catch your worship tripping in some false Latin, but I cannot : for you slide through my fingers like an eel."

"I do not comprehend your meaning," said Don Quixote.

"I will explain myself another time," replied Don Lorenzo, "and will now recite the text and its comment."

As soon as Don Lorenzo had recited his verses, Don Quixote started up, and, grasping him by the hand, exclaimed in a loud voice :

"By Heaven, noble youth, there is not a better poet in the universe, and you deserve to wear the laurel, not of Cyprus, nor of Gaëta, as a certain poet said, whom Heaven forgive, but of the universities of Athens, did they now exist, and those of Paris, Bologna, and Salamanca ! If the judges deprive you of the first prize, may they be transfixed by the arrows of Apollo, and may the Muses never cross the threshold of their doors ! Be pleased, sir, to repeat some other of your lofty verses ; for I would fain have a further taste of your admirable genius."

How diverting that the young poet should be gratified by the praises of one whom he believed to be a madman ! O flattery, how potent is thy sway ! how wide are the bounds of thy pleasing jurisdiction ! This was verified in Don Lorenzo, who, yielding to the request of Don Quixote, repeated a sonnet on the story of Pyramus and Thisbe.

"Now, Heaven be thanked," exclaimed Don Quixote, "that, among the infinite number of rhymers now in being, I have at last met with one who is truly a poet, which you, sir, have proved yourself by the composition of that sonnet."

Four days was Don Quixote nobly regaled in Don Diego's house ; at the end of which he begged leave to depart, express-ing his thanks for the generous hospitality he had experienced ;

but as inactivity and repose, he said, were unbecoming knights-errant, the duties of his function required him to proceed in quest of adventures, which he was told might be expected in abundance in those parts, and sufficient to occupy him until the time fixed for the tournament of Saragossa, where it was his intention to be present. Previously, however, he meant to visit the cave of Montesinos, concerning which so many extraordinary things were reported, and at the same time to discover, if possible, the true source of the seven lakes, commonly called the lakes of Ruydera. Don Diego and his son applauded his honourable resolution, desiring him to furnish himself with whatever their house afforded for his accommodation : since his personal merit and noble profession justly claimed their services.

At length the day of his departure came—a day of joy to Don Quixote, but of sorrow to Sancho Panza, who was too sensible of the comforts and abundance that reigned in Don Diego's house not to feel great unwillingness to return to the hunger of forests and wildernesses, and to the misery of ill-provided wallets. However, these he filled and stuffed with what he thought most necessary ; and Don Quixote, on taking leave of Don Lorenzo, said, " I know not whether I have mentioned it to you before, but if I have, I repeat it, that whenever you may feel disposed to shorten your way up the rugged steep that leads to the temple of fame, you have only to turn aside from the narrow path of poetry, and follow the still narrower one of knight-errantry, which may, nevertheless, raise you in a trice to imperial dignity." With these expressions Don Quixote completed, as it were, the evidence of his madness. The father and son again wondered at the medley of extravagance and good sense which they observed in Don Quixote, and the unfortunate obstinacy with which he persevered in the disastrous pursuit that seemed to occupy his whole soul. After repeating compliments and offers of service, and taking formal leave of the lady of the mansion, the knight and the squire—the one mounted upon Rozinante, the other upon Dapple—quitted their friends and departed.

CHAPTER XLVII

WHEREIN ARE RELATED THE ADVENTURES OF THE ENAMOURED
SHEPHERD, WITH OTHER TRULY PLEASING INCIDENTS

Don Quixote had not travelled far, when he overtook two
persons like ecclesiastics or scholars, accompanied by two country
fellows, all of whom were mounted upon asses. One of the
students carried behind him a small bundle of linen and two pairs
of thread stockings, wrapped up in green buckram like a portmanteau ; the other appeared to have nothing but a pair of new
black fencing foils, with their points guarded. The countymen
carried other things, which showed that they had been making
purchases in some large town, and were returning with them to
their own village. But the scholars and the countrymen were
astonished, as all others had been, on first seeing Don Quixote,
and were curious to know what man this was so different in
appearance from other men. Don Quixote saluted them, and
hearing they were travelling the same road, he offered to bear
them company, begging them to slacken their pace, as their asses
went faster than his horse : and, to oblige them, he briefly told
them who he was, and that his employment and profession was
that of a knight-errant, seeking adventures over the world. He
told them his proper name was Don Quixote de la Mancha, and his
appellative "the Knight of the Lions."

All this to the countrymen was Greek or gibberish : but not
so to the scholars, who soon discovered the soft part of Don
Quixote's skull : they nevertheless viewed him with respectful
attention, and one of them said :

"If, sir knight, you are not fixed to one particular road, as
those in search of adventures seldom are, come with us, and you
will see one of the greatest and richest weddings that has ever
been celebrated in La Mancha, or for many leagues round."

"The nuptials of some prince, I presume?" said Don
Quixote.

"No," replied the scholar, "only that of a farmer and a
country maid : he the wealthiest in this part of the country,

and she the most beautiful that eyes ever beheld. The preparations are very uncommon : for the wedding is to be celebrated in a meadow near the village where the bride lives, who is called Quiteria the Fair, and the bridegroom Camacho the Rich ; she is about the age of eighteen, and he twenty-two, both equally matched : though some nice folks, who have all the pedigrees in the world in their heads, pretend that the family of Quiteria the Fair has the advantage over that of Camacho ; but that is now little regarded, for riches are able to solder up abundance of flaws. In short, this same Camacho is as liberal as a prince ; and, intending to be at some cost in this wedding, has taken it into his head to convert a whole meadow into a kind of arbour, shading it so that the sun itself will find some difficulty to visit the green grass beneath. He will also have morris-dances, both with swords and bells ; for there are people in the village who jingle and clatter them with great dexterity. As to the number of shoe-clappers * invited, it is impossible to count them ; but what will give the greatest interest to this wedding is the effect it is expected to have on the slighted Basilius.

"This Basilius is a swain of the same village as Quiteria ; his house is next to that of her parents, and separated only by a wall, whence Cupid took occasion to revive the ancient loves of Pyramus and Thisbe ; for Basilius was in love with Quiteria from his childhood, and she returned his affection with a thousand modest favours, insomuch that the loves of the two children Basilius and Quiteria became the common talk of the village. When they were grown up, the father of Quiteria resolved to forbid Basilius the usual access to his family ; and to relieve himself of all fears on his account, he determined to marry his daughter to the rich Camacho : not choosing to bestow her on Basilius, whose endowments are less the gifts of fortune than of nature.

"From the moment Basilius heard of the intended marriage of Quiteria to Camacho the Rich, he has never been seen to smile, nor speak coherently ; he is always pensive and sad, and talking to himself—a certain and clear proof that he is

---

* "Zapateadores." Dancers that strike the soles of their shoes with the palms of their hands, in time and measure.

distracted. He eats nothing but a little fruit; and if he sleeps, it is in the fields, like cattle upon the hard earth. Sometimes he casts his eyes up to heaven; and then fixes them on the ground, remaining motionless like a statue. In short, he gives such indications of a love-stricken heart, that we all expect that Quiteria's fatal 'Yes' will be the sentence of his death."

It now began to grow dark, and as they approached the village, there appeared before them a new heaven, blazing with innumerable stars. At the same time they heard the sweet and mingled sounds of various instruments — such as flutes, tambourines, psalters, cymbals, drums, and bells; and, drawing still nearer, they perceived a spacious arbour, formed near the entrance into the town, hung round with lights, that shone undisturbed by the breeze; for it was so calm, that not a leaf was seen to move. The musicians, who are the life and joy of such festivals, paraded in bands up and down this delightful place, some dancing, others singing, and others playing upon different instruments; in short, nothing was there to be seen but mirth and pleasure. Several were employed in raising scaffolds, from which they might commodiously behold the shows and entertainments of the following day, that were to be dedicated to the nuptial ceremony of the rich Camacho, and the obsequies of poor Basilius. Don Quixote refused to enter the town, though pressed by the countrymen and the bachelor; pleading what appeared to him a sufficient excuse, the practice of knights-errant to sleep in fields and forests, rather than in towns, though under gilded roofs: he therefore turned a little out of the road, much against Sancho's will, who had not yet forgotten the good lodging he had met with in the hospitable mansion of Don Diego.

CHAPTER XLVIII

GIVING AN ACCOUNT OF THE MARRIAGE OF CAMACHO THE
RICH, AND ALSO THE ADVENTURE OF BASILIUS THE POOR

SCARCELY had the beautiful Aurora appeared, and given bright
Phœbus time, by the warmth of his early rays, to exhale the
liquid pearls that hung glittering on his golden hair, when
Don Quixote, shaking off sloth from his drowsy members,
rose up, and proceeded to call his squire Sancho Panza.

Sancho obeyed his master's commands; and saddling and
pannelling their steeds, they both mounted, and at a slow pace
entered the artificial shade. The first thing that presented itself
to Sancho's sight, was a whole bullock, spitted upon a large elm.
The fire by which it was roasted was composed of a mountain of
wood, and round it were placed six huge pots—not cast in
common moulds, but each large enough to contain a whole
shamble of flesh. Entire sheep were swallowed up in them, and
floated like so many pigeons. The hares ready flayed, and the
fowls plucked, that hung about the branches, in order to be
buried in these cauldrons, were without number. Infinite was
the wild-fowl and venison hanging about the trees to receive the
cool air. Sancho counted above three-score skins, each holding
above twenty-four quarts, and all, as appeared afterwards, full of
generous wines. Hillocks, too, he saw, of the whitest bread,
ranged like heaps of wheat on the threshing-floor, and cheeses,
piled up in the manner of bricks, formed a kind of wall. Two
cauldrons of oil, larger than dyer's vats, stood ready for frying all
sorts of batter-ware; and, with a couple of stout peels, they
shovelled them up, when fried, and forthwith immersed them in a
kettle of prepared honey that stood near. The men and women
cooks were about fifty in number, all clean, all active, and all in
good humour. In the bullock's distended belly were sewed up a
dozen sucking-pigs, to make it savoury and tender. The spices
of various kinds, which seemed to have been bought, not by the
pound, but by the hundred weight, were deposited in a great
chest, and open to every hand. In short the preparation for the

" At a slow pace entered the artificial shade."

wedding was all rustic, but in sufficient abundance to have feasted
an army.

Sancho beheld all with wonder and delight. The first that
captivated and subdued his inclinations were the flesh-pots, out of
which he would have been glad to have filled a moderate pipkin ;
next the wine-skins drew his affections ; and, lastly, the products
of the frying-pans—if such capacious vessels might be so called ;
and, being unable any longer to abstain, he ventured to approach
one of the busy cooks, and, in persuasive and hungry terms,
begged leave to sop a luncheon of bread in one of the pots. To
which the cook answered :

"This, friend, is not a day for hunger to be abroad—
thanks to rich Camacho. Alight, and look about you for a
ladle to skim out a fowl or two, and much good may they do
you."

"I see no ladle," answered Sancho.

"Stay," quoth the cook : "Heaven save me, what a helpless
varlet !" So saying, he laid hold of a kettle, and, sowsing it
into one of the half jars, he fished out three pullets, and a
couple of geese, and said to Sancho, "Eat, friend, and make
a breakfast of this scum, to stay your stomach till dinner-
time."

"I have nothing to put it in," answered Sancho.

"Then take ladle and all," quoth the cook ; "for Camacho's
riches and joy supply everything."

While Sancho was thus employed, Don Quixote stood
observing the entrance of a dozen peasants at one side of the
spacious arbour, each mounted upon a beautiful mare, in rich and
gay caparisons, hung round with little bells. They were clad in
holiday apparel, and, in a regular troop, made sundry careers
about the meadow, with a joyful Moorish cry of "Long live
Camacho and Quiteria ! he as rich as she is fair, and she the
fairest of the world !" Don Quixote hearing this, said to himself, "These people, it is plain, have never seen my Dulcinea del
Toboso ; otherwise they would have been less extravagant in the
praise of their Quiteria." Soon after there entered, on different
sides of the arbour, various sets of dancers, among which was one
consisting of four-and-twenty sword-dancers ; handsome, sprightly
swains, all arrayed in fine white linen, and handkerchiefs wrought

with several colours of fine silk, also pantomimic dances led respectively by "Cupid" and "Interest."

" Don Quixote asked one of the nymphs, Who had composed and arranged the show ? She told him that it was a clergyman of that village, who had a notable head-piece for such kind of inventions.

"I would venture a wager," said Don Quixote, "that this bachelor, or clergyman, is more a friend to Camacho than to Basilius, and understands satire better than vespers; for in his dance he has ingeniously opposed the talents of Basilius to the riches of Camacho."

"I hold with Camacho," quoth Sancho, who stood listening ; "the king is my cock."

"It is plain," said Don Quixote, "that thou art an arrant bumpkin, and one of those who always cry, long live the conqueror ! "

" I know not who I am one of," answered Sancho ; "but this I know, I shall never get such elegant scum from Basilius's pots as I have done from Camacho's." And showing his kettle-ful of geese and hens, he laid hold of one and began to eat with notable good-will and appetite ; "A fig for the talents of Basilius ! " said he, " for so much thou art worth as thou hast, and so much thou hast as thou art worth. There are but two lineages in the world, as my grandmother used to say : 'the Have's and the Have-not's,' and she stuck to the Have's. Now-a-days, Master Don Quixote, people are more inclined to feel the pulse of Have than of Know. An ass with golden furniture makes a better figure than a horse with a pack-saddle : so that I tell you again, I hold with Camacho, for the plentiful scum of his kettles are geese and hens, hares and coneys ; while that of Basilius, if he has any, must be mere dishwater."

As Don Quixote and Sancho were engaged in conversation, they suddenly heard a great outcry and noise raised by those mounted on the mares, shouting as they galloped to meet the bride and bridegroom, who were entering the bower, saluted by a thousand musical instruments of all kinds and inventions, accompanied by the parish priest and kindred on both sides, and by a number of the better class of people from the neighbouring towns, all in their holiday apparel. When Sancho espied the bride he said, "In good faith, she is not clad like a country-girl, but like any court lady! By the mass! her breast-piece seems to me at this distance to be of rich coral, and her gown, instead of green stuff of Cuenza, is no less than a thirty-piled velvet! Besides, the trimming, I vow, is of satin! Do but observe her hands—instead of rings of jet, let me never thrive but they are of gold, ay, and of real gold, with pearls as white as a curd, every one of them worth an eye of one's head."

Don Quixote smiled at Sancho's homely praises; at the same time he thought that, excepting the mistress of his soul, he had never seen a more beautiful woman. The fair Quiteria looked a little pale, occasioned, perhaps, by a want of rest the preceding night, which brides usually employ in preparing their wedding finery.

The bridal pair proceeded towards a theatre on one side of the arbour, decorated with tapestry and garlands, where the nuptial ceremony was to be performed, and whence they were to view the dances and shows prepared for the occasion. Immediately on their arrival at that place, a loud noise was heard at a distance, amidst which a voice was distinguished calling aloud, "Hold a little, rash and thoughtless people!" On turning their heads they saw that these words were uttered by a man who was advancing towards them, clad in a black doublet, welted with flaming crimson. He was crowned with a garland of mournful cypress, and held in his hand a large truncheon; and, as he drew near, all recognised the gallant Basilius, and waited in fearful expectation of some disastrous result from this unseasonable visit. At length he came up, tired and out of breath, and placed himself just before the betrothed couple; then, pressing his staff, which was pointed with steel, into the ground, he fixed his eyes on Quiteria, and, in a broken and tremulous voice, thus addressed her, "Ah, false and forgetful Quiteria, well thou knowest that, by the laws of our holy religion, thou canst not marry another man whilst I am living; neither art thou ignorant that, while waiting till time and mine own industry should improve my fortune, I have never failed in the respect due to thy honour. But thou hast cast aside every obligation due to my lawful love, and art going to make another man master of what is mine: a man who is not only enriched, but rendered eminently happy by his wealth; and, in obedience to the will of Heaven, the only impediment to his supreme felicity I will remove, by withdrawing this wretched being. Long live the rich Camacho with the ungrateful Quiteria! Long and happily may they live, and let poor Basilius die, who would have risen to good fortune had not poverty clipped his wings and laid him in an early grave!"

So saying, he plucked his staff from the ground, and, drawing out a short tuck, to which it had served as a scabbard, he fixed what might be called the hilt into the ground, and, with a nimble spring and resolute air, he threw himself on the point, which, instantly appearing at his back, the poor wretch lay stretched on the ground, pierced through and through, and weltering in his blood.

His friends, struck with horror and grief, rushed forward to help him, and Don Quixote, dismounting, hastened also to lend his aid, and, taking the dying man in his arms, found that he was still alive. They would have drawn out the tuck, but the priest who was present thought that it should not be done till he had made his confession; as, the moment it was taken out of his body, he would certainly expire. But Basilius, not having quite lost the power of utterance, in a faint and doleful voice said:

"If, cruel Quiteria, in this my last and fatal agony, thou wouldst give me thy hand, as my spouse, I should hope my rashness might find pardon in heaven, since it procured me the blessing of being thine." Upon which the priest advised him to attend rather to the salvation of his soul than to his bodily appetites, and seriously implore pardon of God for his sins, especially for this last desperate action. Basilius replied that he could not make any confession till Quiteria had given him her hand in marriage, as that would be a solace to his mind, and enable him to confess his sins.

Don Quixote, hearing the wounded man's request, said, in a loud voice, that Basilius had made a very just and reasonable request, and that it would be equally honourable for Signor Camacho to take Quiteria, a widow of the brave Basilius, as if he received her at her father's hand; nothing being required but the simple word, "Yes," which could be of no consequence, since, in these espousals, the nuptial bed must be the grave. Camacho heard all this, and was perplexed and undecided what to do or say; but so much was he importuned by the friends of Basilius to permit Quiteria to give him her hand, and thereby save his soul from perdition, that they at length moved, nay forced, him to say that, if it pleased Quiteria to give it to him, he should not object, since it was only delaying for a moment the accomplishment of his wishes. They all immediately applied to Quiteria, and, with entreaties, tears, and persuasive arguments, pressed and importuned her to give her hand to Basilius; but she, harder than marble, and more immovable than a statue, returned no answer, until the priest told her that she must decide promptly as the soul of Basilius was already between his teeth, and there was no time for hesitation.

Then the beautiful Quiteria, in silence, and to all appearance troubled and sad, approached Basilius, whose eyes were already turned in his head, and he breathed short and quick, muttering the name of Quiteria, and giving tokens of dying more like a heathen than a Christian. At last, Quiteria, kneeling down by him, made signs to him for his hand. Basilius unclosed his eyes, and fixing them steadfastly upon her, said, "O Quiteria, thou relentest at a time when thy pity is a sword to put a final period to this wretched life: I cannot accept thee unless thou bestowest thy hand upon me as thy lawful husband, without any compulsion on thy will—for it would be cruel in this extremity to deal falsely or impose on him who has been so true to thee."

Here he fainted, and the bystanders thought his soul was just departing. Quiteria, all modesty and bashfulness, taking Basilius's right hand in hers, said:

"No force would be sufficient to bias my will; and, therefore, with all the freedom I have, I give thee my hand to be thy lawful wife, and receive thine, if it be as freely given, and if the anguish caused by thy rash act doth not trouble and prevent thee."

"Yes, I give it thee," answered Basilius, "neither discomposed nor confused, but with the clearest understanding that Heaven was ever pleased to bestow on me; and so I give and engage myself to be thy husband."

" And I to be thy wife," answered Quiteria, " whether thou livest many years, or art carried from my arms to the grave."

" For one so much wounded," observed Sancho, " this young man talks a great deal. Advise him to leave off his courtship, and mind the business of his soul : though to my thinking he has it more on his tongue than between his teeth."

Basilius and Quiteria being thus, with hands joined, the tender-hearted priest, with tears in his eyes, pronounced the benediction upon them, and prayed to Heaven for the repose of the bridegroom's soul ; who, as soon as he had received the benediction, suddenly started up, and nimbly drew out the tuck which was sheathed in his body. All the spectators were astonished, and some more simple than the rest cried out, " A miracle, a miracle !" But Basilius replied, " No miracle, no miracle, but a stratagem, a stratagem !" The priest, astonished and confounded, ran to feel, with both his hands, the wound, and found that the sword had passed, not through Basilius's flesh and ribs, but through a hollow iron pipe, cunningly fitted to the place, and filled with blood, so prepared as not to congeal. In short, the priest, Camacho, and the rest of the spectators, found they were imposed upon, and completely duped. The bride showed no signs of regret at the artifice : on the contrary, hearing it said the marriage, as being fraudulent, was not valid, she said that she confirmed it anew ; it was, therefore, generally supposed that the matter had been concerted with the privity and concurrence of both parties ; which so enraged Camacho and his friends that they immediately had recourse to vengeance, and unsheathing abundance of swords, they fell upon Basilius, in whose behalf as many more were instantly drawn, and Don Quixote, leading the van on horseback, his lance couched, and well covered with his shield, made them all give way. Sancho, who took no pleasure in such kind of frays, retired to the jars out of which he had gotten his charming skimmings ; regarding that place as a sanctuary which none would dare to violate.

Quiteria's disdain made such an impression upon Camacho, that he instantly banished her from his heart. The persuasions, therefore, of the priest, who was a prudent, well-meaning man, had their effect ; Camacho and his party sheathed their weapons, and remained satisfied ; blaming rather the fickleness of Quiteria than the cunning of Basilius. With much reason Camacho thought within himself that, if Quiteria loved Basilius when a virgin, she would love him also when married; and that he had more cause to thank Heaven for so fortunate an escape than to repine at the loss he had sustained. The disappointed bridegroom and his followers, being thus consoled and appeased, those of Basilius were so likewise; and the rich Camacho, to show that his mind was free from resentment, would have the diversions and entertainments go on as if they had been really married. The happy pair, however, not choosing to share in them, retired to their own dwelling, accompanied by their joyful adherents: for if the rich man can draw after him his attendants and flatterers, the poor man who is virtuous and deserving is followed by friends who honour and support him. Don Quixote joined the party of Basilius, having been invited by them as a person of worth and bravery; while Sancho, finding it impossible to remain and share the relishing delights of Camacho's festival, which continued till night, with a heavy heart accompanied his master, leaving behind the flesh-pots of Egypt, the skimmings of which, though now almost consumed, still reminded him of the glorious abundance he had lost; pensive and sorrowful, therefore, though not hungry, without alighting from Dapple, he followed the track of Rozinante.

CHAPTER XLIX

WHEREIN IS RELATED THE ADVENTURE OF THE CAVE OF MON-TESINOS, SITUATED IN THE HEART OF LA MANCHA, WHICH DON QUIXOTE HAPPILY ACCOMPLISHED

LOOKING upon themselves as greatly obliged for the valour he had shown in defending their cause, the newly-married couple made much of Don Quixote; and judging of his wisdom by his valour, they accounted him a Cid in arms and a Cicero in eloquence; and during three days honest Sancho solaced himself at their expense. The bridegroom explained to them his stratagem of the feigned wound, and told them it was a device of his own, and had been concerted with the fair Quiteria. He confessed, too, that he had let some of his friends into the secret, that they might support his deception.

"That ought not to be called deception which aims at a virtuous end," said Don Quixote : " and no end is more excellent than the marriage of true lovers ; though love," added he, " has its enemies, and none greater than hunger and poverty, for love is all gaiety, joy, and content."

Three days they remained with the new-married couple, where they were served and treated like kings ; at the end of which time, Don Quixote requested the student, to procure him a guide to the cave of Montesinos ; for he had a great desire to descend into it, in order to see with his own eyes if the wonders reported of it were really true. The student told him he would introduce him to a young relation of his, a good scholar, and much given to reading books of chivalry, who would very gladly accompany him to the very mouth of the cave, and also show him the lakes of Ruydera, so famous in La Mancha, and even all over Spain ; adding that he would find him a very entertaining companion, as he knew how to write books and dedicate them to princes. In short, the cousin appeared, mounted on an ass with foal, whose pack-saddle was covered with a double piece of an old carpet or sacking ; Sancho saddled Rozinante, pannelled Dapple, and replenished his wallets : those of the scholar being also well provided ; and thus, after taking leave of their friends, and commending themselves to Heaven, they set out, bending their course directly towards the famous cave of Montesinos.

Upon the road, Don Quixote asked the scholar what were his exercises, his profession, and his studies. The latter replied that his studies and profession were literary, and his employment, composing books for the press, on useful and entertaining subjects.

In much pleasant conversation they passed that day, and at night took up their lodging in a small village, which the scholar told Don Quixote was distant but two leagues from the cave of Montesinos, and that if he persevered in his resolution to enter into it, it was necessary to be provided with rope, by which he might let himself down. Don Quixote declared that, if it reached to the abyss, he would see the bottom. They procured, therefore, near a hundred fathoms of cord ; and about two in the afternoon of the following day arrived at the mouth of the cave, which they found to be wide and spacious, but so much over-grown with briars, thorns, and wild fig-trees, to be almost con-cealed. On perceiving the cave, they alighted, and the scholar and Sancho proceeded to bind the cord fast round Don Quixote, and, while they were thus employed, Sancho said, "Have a care, sir, dear sir, what you are about ; do not bury yourself alive, nor hang yourself dangling like a flask of wine let down to cool in a well : for it is no business of your worship to pry into that hole, which must needs be worse than any dungeon."

"Tie on," replied Don Quixote, "and hold thy peace ; for such an enterprise as this, friend Sancho, was reserved for me alone." The guide then said :

"I beseech your worship, Señor Don Quixote, to be observant and with a hundred eyes see, explore, and examine what is below ; perhaps many things may there be discovered worthy of being in-serted in my book of Metamorphoses."

"The drum," quoth Sancho, "is in a hand that knows full well how to rattle it."

The knight being well bound—not over his armour, but his doublet—he said :

"We have been careless in neglecting to provide a bell, to be tied to me with this rope, by the tinkling of which you might have heard me still descending, and thereby have known that I was alive : but since that is now impossible, be Heaven my guide !" Kneeling down, he first supplicated Heaven for protection and success in an adventure so new, and seemingly so perilous ; then raising his voice, he said, "O mistress of every act and movement of my life, most illustrious and peerless Dulcinea del Toboso ! if the prayers and requests of thy adven-turous lover reach thy ears, by the power of thy unparalleled beauty I conjure thee to listen to them, and grant me thy favour and protection in this moment of fearful necessity, when I am on the point of plunging, ingulfing, and precipitating myself into the profound abyss before me, solely to prove to the world that, if thou favourest me, there is no impossibility I will not attempt and overcome."

So saying he drew near to the cavity, and observing that the entrance was so choked with vegetation as to be almost im-penetrable, he drew his sword, and began to cut and hew down

"They stayed some half an hour."

the brambles and bushes with which it was covered; whereupon, disturbed at the noise and rustling which he made, presently out rushed such a flight of huge daws and ravens, as well as bats and other night birds, that he was thrown down, and had he been as superstitious as he was catholic, he would have taken it for an ill omen, and relinquished the enterprise. Rising again upon his legs, and seeing no more creatures fly out, the scholar and Sancho let him down into the fearful cavern; and, as he entered, Sancho gave him his blessing, and making a thousand crosses over him, said:

"God, and the rock of France, together with the Trinity of Gaeta,* speed thee, thou flower, and cream, and skimming of knights-errant! There thou goest, Hector of the world, heart of steel and arm of brass! Once more, Heaven guide thee, and send thee back safe and sound to the light of this world which thou art now forsaking for that horrible den of darkness." The scholar also added his prayers to those of Sancho for the knight's success and happy return.

Don Quixote went down, still calling as he descended for more rope, which they gave him by little and little; and when the voice, owing to the windings of the cave, could be heard no longer, and the hundred fathom of cordage was all let down, they thought that they should pull him up again, since they could give him no more rope. For all that, they stayed some half an hour, then began to gather up the rope, which they did so easily that it appeared to have no weight attached to it, whence they conjectured that Don Quixote remained in the cave; Sancho, in this belief, wept bitterly, and pulled up the rope in great haste, to know the truth; but having drawn it to a little above eight fathoms, they had the satisfaction again to feel the weight. In short, after raising it up to about the tenth fathom, they could see the knight very distinctly; upon which Sancho immediately called to him, saying:

"Welcome back again to us, dear sir, for we began to fear you meant to stay below!" But Don Quixote answered not a word; and being now drawn entirely out, they perceived that

---

* The Rock of France is a lofty mountain in the district of Alberca. The Trinity of Gaeta is a chapel and convent, founded by King Ferdinand V. of Arragon, on the summit of a promontory before the port of Gaeta and dedicated to the Holy Trinity.

his eyes were shut, as if he were asleep. They then laid him along the ground, and unbound him; but as he still did not awake, they turned, pulled, and shook him so much, that at last he came to himself, stretching and yawning just as if he had awaked out of a deep and heavy sleep; and looking wildly about him, he said:

"Heaven forgive ye, my friends, for having brought me away from the most delicious and charming state that ever mortal enjoyed! In truth, I am now thoroughly satisfied that all the pleasures of this life pass away like a shadow or dream, or fade like a flower of the field. O unhappy Montesinos! O desperately wounded Durandarte! O unhappy Belerma! O weeping Guadiana! And ye unfortunate daughters Ruydera, whose waters show what floods of tears have streamed from your fair eyes!"

The scholar and Sancho listened to Don Quixote's words, which he uttered as if drawn with excessive pain from his entrails. They entreated him to explain, and to tell them what he had seen in that bottomless pit. "Pit, do you call it?" said Don Quixote; "call it so no more, for it deserves not that name, as you shall presently hear." He then told them that he wanted food extremely, and desired they would give him something to eat. The scholar's carpet was accordingly spread upon the grass, and they immediately applied to the pantry of his wallets, and being all three seated in loving and social fellowship, they made their dinner and supper at one meal. When all were satisfied, and the carpet removed, Don Quixote de la Mancha said, "Remain where you are, my sons, and listen to me with attention."

It was about four o'clock in the afternoon, when the sun being covered by clouds, its temperate rays gave Don Quixote an opportunity, without heat or fatigue, of relating to his two illustrious hearers what he had seen in the cave of Montesinos; and he began in the following manner:

"About twelve or fourteen fathoms deep, in this dungeon, there is on the right hand a hollow space, wide enough to contain a large waggon, together with its mules, and faintly lighted by some distant apertures above. This cavity I happened to see, as I journeyed on through the dark, without knowing whither I was going : and, as I was just then beginning to be weary of hanging by the rope, I determined to enter, in order to rest a little. I called out to you aloud, and desired you not to let down more rope till I bid you ; but it seems you heard me not. I then collected the cord you had let down, and coiling it up in a heap, or bundle, I sat down upon it, full of thought, meditating how I might descend to the bottom, having nothing to support my weight. In this situation, pensive and embarrassed, a deep sleep suddenly came over me, from which, I know not how, I as suddenly awoke, and found that I had been transported into a verdant lawn, the most delightful that Nature could create, or the liveliest fancy imagine. I rubbed my eyes, wiped them, and perceived that I was not asleep, but really awake. Nevertheless I felt my head and breast, to be assured that it was I myself, and not some empty and counterfeit illusion ; but sensation, feeling, and the coherent discourse I held with myself, convinced me that I was the identical person which I am at this moment. I soon discovered a royal and splendid palace or castle, whereof the walls and battlements seemed to be composed of bright and transparent crystal ; and as I gazed upon it, the great gates of the portal opened, and a venerable old man issued forth and advanced towards me. He was clad in a long mourning cloak of purple bays, which trailed upon the ground ; over his shoulders and breast he wore a kind of collegiate tippet of green satin ; he had a black Milan cap on his head, and his hoary beard reached below his girdle. He carried no weapons, but held a rosary of beads in his hand as large as walnuts, and every tenth bead the size of an ordinary ostrich egg. His mien, his gait, his gravity, and his goodly presence, each singly and conjointly, filled me with surprise and admiration. On coming up, he embraced me, and said, ' The day is at length arrived, most renowned and valiant Don Quixote de la Mancha, that we who are enclosed in this enchanted solitude have long hoped would bring thee hither, that thou mayest proclaim to the world the things prodigious and incredible that lie concealed in this subterranean place, commonly called the cave of Montesinos—an exploit reserved for your invincible heart and stupendous courage ; come with me, illustrious sir, that I may show you the wonders contained in this transparent castle, of which I am warder and perpetual guard :

for I am Montesinos himself, from whom the cave derives its name.' He had no sooner told me that he was Montesinos than I asked him whether it was true what was reported in the world above, that with a little dagger he had taken out the heart of his great friend Durandarte, and conveyed it to the lady Belerma, agreeable to his dying request. He replied that the whole was true, excepting as to the dagger ; for it was not a small dagger, but a bright poniard, sharper than an awl."

" That poniard," interrupted Sancho, " must have been made by Raymond de Hozes, of Seville."

" I know not who was the maker," said Don Quixote : " but on reflection, it could not have been Raymond de Hozes, who lived but the other day, whereas the battle of Roncesvalles, where this misfortune happened, was fought some ages ago. But that question is of no importance, and does not affect the truth and connection of the story."

" True," anwered the scholar ; pray go on, Señor Don Quixote, for I listen to your account with the greatest pleasure imaginable."

" And I relate it with no less," answered Don Quixote : " and so to proceed—the venerable Montesinos conducted me to the crystalline palace, where, in a lower hall, formed of alabaster and extremely cool, there stood a marble tomb of exquisite work-manship, whereon I saw extended a knight, not of brass, or marble, or jasper, as is usual with other monuments, but of pure flesh and bones. His right hand, which seemed to me somewhat hairy and nervous (a token of great strength), was laid on the region of his heart ; and before I could ask any question, Montesinos, perceiving my attention fixed on the sepulchre, said, ' This is my friend Durandarte, the flower and model of all the enamoured and valiant knights-errant of his time. He is kept here enchanted, as well as myself and many others of both sexes, by that French enchanter Merlin, said to be the devil's son, which, however, I do not credit : though indeed I believe he knows one point more than the devil himself. How, or why, we are thus enchanted no one can tell ; but time will explain it, and that, too, I imagine, at no distant period. What astonishes me is, that I am as certain as that it is now day, that Durandarte expired in my arms, and that, after he was dead, with these hands

I pulled out his heart, which could not have weighed less than two pounds: confirming the opinion of naturalists that a man's valour is in proportion to the size of his heart. Yet, certain as it is that this cavalier is really dead, how comes it to pass that, ever and anon, he sighs and moans as if he were alive?'—Scarcely were these words uttered, than the wretched Durandarte, crying out aloud, said, 'O my cousin Montesinos! at the moment my soul was departing, my last request of you was, that after ripping my heart out of my breast with either a poniard or a dagger, you should carry it to Belerma.' The venerable Montesinos, hearing this, threw himself on his knees before the complaining knight, and with tears in his eyes, said to him, 'Long, long since, O Durandarte, dearest cousin! long since did I fulfil what you enjoined on that sad day when you expired. I took out your heart with all imaginable care, not leaving the smallest particle of it within your breast; I then wiped it with a lace handkerchief, and set off at full speed with it for France, having first laid your dear remains in the earth, shedding as many tears as sufficed to wash my hands and clean away the blood with which they were smeared by raking into your entrails; and furthermore, dear cousin of my soul, at the first place I stopped, after leaving Roncesvalles, I sprinkled a little salt over your heart, and thereby kept it, if not fresh, at least from emitting any unpleasant odour, until it was presented to the lady Belerma; who, together with you and myself, and your Squire Guadiana, and the duenna Ruydera, with her seven daughters, and two nieces, as well as several others of your friends and acquaintance, have been long confined here, enchanted by the sage Merlin; and though it is now above five hundred years since, we are still alive. It is true Ruydera and her daughters and nieces have left us, having so far moved the compassion of Merlin, by their incessant weeping, that he turned them into as many lakes, which at this time, in the world of the living, in the province of La Mancha, are called the lakes of Ruydera. The seven sisters belong to the kings of Spain, and the two nieces to the most holy order of Saint John. Guadiana also, your squire, bewailing your misfortune, was in like manner changed into a river, still retaining his name: but when he reached the surface of the earth, and saw the sun of another sky, he was so grieved at the thought of forsaking you that he plunged again into the bowels of the earth : nevertheless he was compelled by the laws of nature to rise again, and occasionally show himself to the eyes of men and the light of heaven. The lakes which I have mentioned supply him with their waters, and with them, joined by several others, he makes his majestic entrance into the kingdom of Portugal. Yet, wherever he flows, his grief and melancholy still continue, breeding only coarse and unsavoury fish, very different from those of the golden Tagus. All this, O my dearest cousin ! I have often told you before, and since you make me no answer, I fancy you either do not believe, or do not hear me, which, Heaven knows, afflicts me very much. But now I have other tidings to communicate, which if they do not alleviate, will in no wise increase, your sorrow. Open your eyes and behold here, in your presence, that great knight, of whom the sage Merlin has foretold so many wonders—that same Don Quixote de la Mancha, I say, who has revived with new splendour the long-neglected order of knight-errantry, and by whose prowess and favour, it may, perhaps, be our good fortune to be released from the spells by which we are here held in confinement : for great exploits are reserved for great men.' 'And though it should not be so,' answered the wretched Durandarte in a faint and low voice— 'though it should prove otherwise, O cousin ! I can only say, patience and shuffle the cards.' Then turning himself on one side, he relapsed into his accustomed silence.

"At that moment, hearing loud cries and lamentations, with other sounds of distress, I turned my head, and saw, through the crystal walls of the palace, a procession in two lines, of beautiful damsels, all attired in mourning, and with white turbans, in the Turkish fashion. These were followed by a lady—for so she seemed by the gravity of her air—clad also in black, with a white veil, so long that it reached the ground. Her turban was twice the size of the largest of the others ; she was beetle-browed, her nose somewhat flattish, her mouth wide, but her lips red ; her teeth, which she sometimes displayed, were thin-set and uneven, though as white as blanched almonds. She carried in her hand a fine linen handkerchief, in which I could discern a human heart, withered and dry, like that of a mummy. Montesinos told me that the damsels whom I saw were the attendants of Duran-

darte and Belerma—all enchanted like their master and mistress
—and that the female who closed the procession was the lady
Belerma herself, who four days in the week walked in that
manner with her damsels, singing, or rather weeping, dirges over
the body and piteous heart of his cousin ; and that if she appeared
to me less beautiful than fame reported, it was occasioned by the
bad nights and worse days she passed in that state of enchantment : as might be seen by her sallow complexion, and the deep
furrows in her face. 'Nor is the hollowness of her eyes and
pallid skin to be attributed to any disorders incident to women,
since with these she has not for months and years been tried,
but merely to that deep affliction which incessantly preys on her
heart for the untimely death of her lover, still renewed and kept
alive by what she continually carries in her hands : indeed, had it
not been for this, the great Dulcinea del Toboso herself, so much
celebrated here and over the whole world, would scarcely have
equalled her in beauty of person or sweetness of manner.'

"'Softly,' said I, ' good Señor Montesinos ; comparisons you
know are odious, and therefore let them be spared, I beseech you.
The peerless Dulcinea is what she is, and the lady Donna
Belerma is what she is, and what she has been, and there let it
rest.'

"'Pardon me, Señor Don Quixote,' said Montesinos, 'I
might have guessed that your worship was the lady Dulcinea's
knight, and ought to have bit my tongue off rather than it
should have compared her to anything less than heaven itself.'
This satisfaction being given me by the great Montesinos, my
heart recovered from the shock it had sustained on hearing my
mistress compared with Belerma."

"I wonder," quoth Sancho, "that your worship did not give
the old fellow a hearty kicking, and pluck his beard for him till
you had not left a single hair on his chin."

"No, friend Sancho," answered Don Quixote, "it did not
become me to do so ; for we are all bound to respect the aged,
although not of the order of knighthood ; still more those who
are so, and who besides are enchanted ; but trust me, Sancho,
in other discourse which we held together, I fairly matched
him."

Here the scholar said, "I cannot imagine, Señor Don

Quixote, how it was possible, having been so short a space of time below, that your worship should have seen so many things, and have heard and said so much."

" How long, then, may it be since I descended ? " quoth Don Quixote.

" A little above an hour," answered Sancho.

" That cannot be," replied Don Quixote, " for night came on, and was followed by morning three times successively ; so that I must have sojourned three days in these remote and hidden parts."

" My master," said Sancho, " must needs be in the right ; for, as everything has happened to him in the way of enchantment, what seems to us but an hour may there seem full three days and three nights."

" Doubtless it must be so," answered Don Quixote.

" I hope," said the scholar, " your worship was not without food all this time ? "

" Not one mouthful did I taste," said the knight, " nor was I sensible of hunger."

" What, then, do not the enchanted eat ? " said the scholar.

" No," answered Don Quixote, " although some think that their nails and beards still continue to grow."

" And pray, sir," said Sancho, " do they never sleep ? "

" Certainly never," said Don Quixote ; " at least, during the three days that I have been amongst them, not one of them has closed an eye, nor have I slept myself."

" Here," said Sancho, " the proverb is right : ' tell me thy company, and I will tell thee what thou art.' If your worship keeps company with those who fast and watch, no wonder that you neither eat nor sleep yourself. But pardon me, good master of mine, if I tell your worship that, of all you have been saying, Heaven—I was going to say the devil—take me if I believe one word."

" How ! " said the scholar, " do you think that Señor Don Quixote would lie ? But were he so disposed, he has not had time to invent and fabricate such a tale."

" I do not think my master lies," answered Sancho.

" What, then, dost thou think ? " said Don Quixote.

" I think," answered Sancho, " that the necromancers, or that same Merlin who enchanted all those whom your worship says you saw and talked with there below, have crammed into your head all the stuff you have told us, and all that you have yet to say."

"All that is possible," said Don Quixote, "only that it happens not to be so : for what I have related I saw with my own eyes and touched with my own hands. But what wilt thou say when I tell thee that, among an infinite number of wonderful and surprising things shown to me by Montesinos, whereof I will give an account hereafter (for this is not the time or place to speak of them), he pointed out to me three country wenches, dancing and capering like kids about those charming fields, and no sooner did I behold them than I recognised in one of the three the peerless Dulcinea herself, and in the other two the very same wenches that attended her, and with whom we held some parley, on the road from Toboso ! Upon my asking Montesinos whether he knew them, he said they were strangers to him, though he believed them to be some ladies of quality lately enchanted ; having made their appearance there but a few days before. Nor should that excite my wonder, he said, for many distinguished ladies, both of the past and present times, were enchanted there under different forms ; among whom he had discovered Queen Ginebra, and her duenna Quintannona, cupbearer to Lancelot when he came from Britain."

When Sancho heard his master say all this, he was ready to run distracted, or to die with laughter ; for, knowing that he was himself Dulcinea's enchanter, he now made no doubt that his master had lost his senses, and was raving mad. "In an evil hour and a woeful day, dear master of mine," said he, "did you go down to the other world ; and in a luckless moment did you meet with Signor Montesinos, who has sent you back to us in this plight. Your worship left us in your right senses, such as Heaven had given you, speaking sentences, and giving advice at every turn ;—but now—Lord bless us, how you talk !"

"As I know thee, Sancho," answered Don Quixote, "I heed not thy words."

"Now Heaven defend us !" cried Sancho ; "is it possible there should be anything like this in the world, and that enchanters and enchantment should so bewitch and change my master's good understanding! O sir! sir! for Heaven's sake, look to yourself, take care of your good name, and give no credit to these vanities which have robbed you of your senses."

"Thou lovest me, Sancho, I know," said Don Quixote, "and therefore I am induced to pardon thy prattle. To thy inexperienced mind whatever is uncommon, appears impossible; but, as I have said before, a time may come when I will tell thee of some things which I have seen below, whereof the truth cannot be doubted, and that will make thee give credit to what I have already related."

CHAPTER L

IN WHICH ARE RECOUNTED A THOUSAND TRIFLING MATTERS, EQUALLY PERTINENT AND NECESSARY TO THE RIGHT UNDERSTANDING OF THIS HISTORY

THE scholar was astonished no less at the boldness of Sancho Panza than at the patience of his master, but attributed his present mildness to the satisfaction he had just received in beholding his mistress Dulcinea del Toboso, though enchanted; for, had it not been so, he conceived that Sancho's freedom of speech would have had what it richly deserved—a manual chastisement. In truth he thought him much too presuming with the knight, to whom now addressing himself, he said, "For my own part, Señor Don Quixote, I account myself most fortunate in having undertaken this journey, as I have thereby made four important acquisitions. The first is the honour of your worship's acquaintance, which I esteem a great happiness; the second is a knowledge of the secrets enclosed in this wonderful cave, the metamorphoses of Guadiana, and the lakes of Ruydera, which will be of notable use in my Spanish Ovid now in hand; my third advantage is the discovery of the antiquity of cards, which, it now appears, were in use at least in the days of the Emperor Charlemagne, as may be gathered from the words that fell from Durandarte, when, after that long speech of Montesinos, he awaked, and said, 'Patience, and shuffle the cards.' And finally, it has, in the fourth place, been my good fortune thus to come at the knowledge of the true source of the river Guadiana, which has hitherto remained unknown."

"There is much reason in what you say," quoth the knight ; " but if, by Heaven's will, you should obtain a license for printing your books, which I much doubt, to whom would you inscribe them ?"

"O, sir," said the scholar, "we have lords and grandees in abundance, and are therefore in no want of patrons."

"Not so many as you may imagine," said Don Quixote ; " for all those who are worthy of such a token of respect are not equally disposed to make that generous return which seems due to the labour, as well as the politeness of the author."

While they were thus discoursing they perceived a man coming towards them, walking very fast, and switching on a mule laden with lances and halberds. When he came up to them he saluted them, and passed on. "Hold, honest friend," said Don Quixote to him, "methinks you go faster than is convenient for that mule." "I cannot stay," answered the man ; " as the weapons which I am carrying are to be made use of to-morrow ; I have no time to lose, and so adieu. But, if you would know for what use they are intended, I shall lodge to-night at the inn beyond the hermitage, and should you be travelling on the same road, you will find me there, where I will tell you wonders ; and, once more, Heaven be with you." He then pricked on his mule at such a rate that Don Quixote had no time to inquire after the wonders which he had to tell ; but, as he was not a little curious, and eager for anything new, he determined immediately to hasten forwards to the inn, and pass the night there, without touching at the hermitage.

Accordingly they quickened their pace. Sancho, who had been pondering over the incidents of the cave, followed, now muttering to himself, "The Lord bless thee for a master !" Said he : "who would believe that one who can say so many good things, should tell us such nonsense and riddles about that cave ! Well, we shall see what will come of it."

They reached the inn just at the close of day, and Sancho was pleased that his master did not, as usual, mistake it for a castle. Don Quixote immediately inquired for the man with the lances and halberds, and was told by the landlord that he was in the stable attending his mule. There also the scholar and Sancho disposed of their beasts, failing not to honour Rozinante with the best manger and best stall in the stable. Don Quixote being all impatience to hear the wonders which had been promised him by the arms-carrier, immediately went in search of him, and having found him in the stable, he begged him to relate without delay what he had promised on the road.

"My wonders," said the man, "must be told at leisure, and not on the wing. Wait, good sir, till I have done with my mule, and then I will tell you things that will amaze you."

"It shall not be delayed on that account," answered Don Quixote; "for I will help you." And so in truth he did, winnowing the barley and cleaning the manger; which condescension induced the man the more willingly to tell his tale. Seating himself, therefore, on a stone bench at the outside of the door, and having Don Quixote (who sat next to him), the scholar, Sancho Panza, the innkeeper, and a page who was on his way to the wars for auditors, he began in the following manner:

"You must know, gentlemen, that in a town four leagues and a half from this place, a certain alderman happened to lose his ass, all through the artful contrivance (too long to be told) of a wench, his maid-servant; and though he tried every means to recover his beast, it was to no purpose. Fifteen days passed, as public fame reports, after the ass was missing, and while the unlucky alderman was standing in the market-place, another alderman of the same town came up to him and said, 'Pay me for my good news, gossip, for your ass has made its appearance.' 'Most willingly, neighbour,' answered the other; 'but tell me—where has he been seen?' 'On the mountain,' answered the other; 'I saw him there this morning, with no pannel or furniture upon him of any kind, and so lank that it was grievous to behold him. I would have driven him before me, but he is already become so shy that when I went near him he took to his heels. Now, if you like it, we will both go seek him; but first let me put up this of mine at home, and I will return instantly.' 'You will do me a great favour,' said the owner of the lost ass, 'and I shall be happy at any time to do as much for you.'

"With all these particulars and in these very words is the story told by all who are thoroughly acquainted with the truth of

"Both began braying at the same instant."

the affair. In short, the two aldermen, hand in hand and side by side, trudged together up the hill; and on coming to the place where they expected to find the ass, they found him not, nor was he anywhere to be seen, though they made diligent search. Being thus disappointed, the alderman who had seen him said to the other, 'Hark you, friend, I have thought of a stratagem by which we shall certainly discover this animal, even though he had crept into the bowels of the earth, instead of the mountain; and it is this: I can bray marvellously well, and if you can do a little in that way the business is done.' 'A little, say you, neighbour?' quoth the other, 'before Heaven, in braying, I yield to none—no, not to asses themselves.' 'We shall soon see that,' answered the second alderman; 'go you on one side of the mountain, while I take the other, and let us walk round it, and every now and then you shall bray, and I will bray, and the ass will certainly hear and answer us, if he still remains in these parts.' 'Verily, neighbour, your device is excellent, and worthy your good parts,' said the owner of the ass. They then separated, according to agreement, and both began braying at the same instant, with such marvellous truth of imitation that, mutually deceived, each ran towards the other, not doubting but that the ass was found; and, on meeting, the loser said, 'Is it possible, friend, that it was not my ass that brayed?' 'No, it was I,' answered the other. 'I declare, then,' said the owner, 'that, as far as regards braying, there is not the least difference between you and an ass; for in my life I never heard anything more natural.' 'These praises and compliments,' answered the author of the stratagem, 'belong rather to you than to me, friend; for, by Him that made me, you could give the odds of two brays to the greatest and most skilful brayer in the world; for your tones are rich, your time correct, your notes well sustained, and cadences abrupt and beautiful; in short, I own myself vanquished, and yield to you the palm in this rare talent.' 'Truly,' answered the ass owner, 'I shall value and esteem myself the more henceforth, since I am not without some endowment. It is true, I fancy that I brayed indifferently well, yet never flattered myself that I excelled so much as you are pleased to say.' 'I tell you,' answered the second, 'there are rare abilities often lost to the world, and they are ill-bestowed on those who know not how to employ them to advantage.' 'Right, brother,' quoth the owner, 'though, except in cases like the present, ours may not turn to much account; and even in this business, Heaven grant it may prove of service.'

"This said, they separated again, to resume their braying; and each time were deceived as before, and met again, till they at length agreed, as a signal, to distinguish their own voices from that of the ass, that they should bray twice together, one immediately after the other. Thus, doubling their brayings, they made the tour of the whole mountain, without having any answer from the stray ass, not even by signs. How, indeed, could the poor creature answer, whom at last they found in a thicket, half devoured by wolves? On which the owner said, "Neighbour, though I have found him dead, my trouble in the search has been well repaid in listening to your exquisite braying.'

"'It is in good hands, friend,' answered the other; 'for, if the abbot sings well, the novice comes not far behind him.'

"Hereupon they returned home hoarse and disconsolate, and told their friends and neighbours all that had happened to them in their search after the ass; each of them extolling the other for his excellence in braying. The story spread all over the adjacent villages, and the devil, who sleeps not, as he loves to sow discord wherever he can, raising a bustle in the wind, and mischief out of nothing, so ordered it that all the neighbouring villagers, at the sight of any of our townspeople, would immediately begin to bray, as it were, hitting us in the teeth with the notable talent of our aldermen. The boys fell to it, which was the same as falling into the hands and mouths of a legion of devils; and thus braying spread far and wide, insomuch that the natives of the town of Bray are as well known and distinguished as the negroes are from white men. And this unhappy jest has been carried so far that our people have often sallied out in arms against their scoffers, and given them battle: neither king nor rook, nor fear nor shame, being able to restrain them. To-morrow, I believe, or next day, those of our town will take the field against the people of another village about two leagues from us, being one of those which persecute us most: and I have brought the lances and halberds which you saw, that we may be well prepared for them."

At this juncture a man entered the inn, clad from head to foot in chamois-skin, hose, doublet, and breeches, and calling with a loud voice :

"Master Host, have you any lodging? for here come the divining ape and the puppet-show of 'Melisendra's deliverance.'"

"What, Master Peter!" quoth the innkeeper, "Body of me! then we shall have a rare night of it." This same Master Peter, it should be observed, had his left eye, and almost half his cheek, covered with a patch of green taffeta, a sign that something was wrong on that side of his face.

"Welcome, Master Peter," continued the landlord: "where is the ape and the puppet-show? I do not see them."

"They are hard by," answered the man in leather; "I came before, to see if we could find lodging here."

"I would turn out the duke of Alva himself to make room for Master Peter," answered the innkeeper—"let the ape and the puppets come; for there are guests this evening in the inn who will be good customers to you, I warrant."

"Be it so, in God's name," answered he of the patch; "and I will lower the price, and reckon myself well paid with only bearing my charges. I shall now go back and bring on the cart with my ape and puppets;" for which purpose he immediately hastened away.

Don Quixote now inquired of the landlord concerning this Master Peter.

"He is," said the landlord, "a famous puppet-player, who has been some time past travelling about these parts with a show of the deliverance of Melisendra by the famous Don Gayferos: one of the best stories and the best performance that has been seen for many a day. He has also an ape whose talents go beyond all other apes, and even those of men; for if a question be put to him he listens attentively, then leaps upon his master's shoulders, and putting his mouth to his ear, whispers the answer to the question he has been asked, which Master Peter repeats aloud. He can tell both what is to come and what is past, and though in foretelling things to come he does not always hit the mark exactly, yet for the most part he is not so much out; so that we are inclined to believe the devil must be in him. His fee is two reals for every question the ape answers, or his master

Master Peter.

answers for him, which is all the same : so that Master Peter is thought to be rich. He is a rare fellow, too, and lives the merriest life in the world ; talks more than six, and drinks more than a dozen, and all by the help of his tongue, his ape, and his puppets."

By this time Master Peter had returned with his cart, in which he carried his puppets, and also his ape, which was large and without a tail, with posteriors as bare as felt, and a countenance most ugly. Don Quixote immediately began to question him, saying :

"Señor diviner, pray tell me what fish do we catch, and what will be our fortune ? See, here are my two reals," bidding Sancho to give them to Master Peter, who, answering for the ape, said, "My ape, signor, gives no reply nor information regarding the future : he knows something of the past, and a little of the present."

"Bodikins," quoth Sancho, "I would not give a brass farthing to be told what has happened to me : for who can tell that better than myself ? and I am not such a fool as to pay for hearing what I already know. But since he knows what is now passing, here are my two reals—and now, good master ape, tell me what my wife Teresa is doing at this moment—I say, what is she busied about ?" Master Peter would not take the money, saying, "I will not be paid beforehand, nor take your reward before the service is performed." Then giving with his right hand two or three claps upon his left shoulder, at one spring the ape jumped upon it, and laying its mouth to his ear, chattered and grated his teeth. Having made these grimaces for the space of a credo, at another skip down it jumped on the ground, and straightway Master Peter ran and threw himself on his knees before Don Quixote, and embracing his legs, said :

"These legs I embrace, just as I would embrace the two pillars of Hercules, O illustrious reviver of the long-forgotten order of chivalry ! O, never-sufficiently extolled knight, Don Quixote de la Mancha ! Thou reviver of drooping hearts, the prop and stay of the falling, the raiser of the fallen, the staff and comfort to all who are unfortunate !"

Don Quixote was thunderstruck, Sancho confounded, the scholar surprised,—in short, the page, the braying-man, the innkeeper, and every one present, were astonished at this harangue of the puppet-player, who proceeded, saying :

"And thou, O good Sancho Panza, the best squire to the best knight in the world, rejoice, for thy good wife Teresa is well, and at this instant is dressing a pound of flax. Moreover, by her left side stands a broken-mouthed pitcher, which holds a very pretty scantling of wine, with which ever and anon she cheers her spirits at her work."

"Egad, I verily believe it !" answered Sancho, "for she is a blessed one ; and, were she not a little jealous, I would not swap her for the giantess Andandona, who, in my master's opinion, was a brave lady, and a special housewife ; though my Teresa, I warrant, is one of those who take care of themselves, though others whistle for it."

"Well," quoth Don Quixote, "he who reads and travels much, sees and learns much. What testimony but that of my own eyes could have persuaded me that there are apes in the world which have the power of divination ? Yes, I am indeed Don Quixote de la Mancha, as this good animal has declared, though he has rather exaggerated in regard to my merits ; but, whatever I may be, I thank Heaven for endowing me with a tender and compassionate heart, inclined to do good to all, and harm to none."

"If I had money," said the page, "I would ask master ape what is to befal me in my intended expedition." To which Master Peter, who had now risen from Don Quixote's feet, answered :

"I have already told you that this little beast gives no answer concerning things to come ; otherwise, your being without money should have been no hindrance : for to serve Señor Don Quixote here present I willingly give up all views of profit. And now, as in duty bound to give pleasure, I intend to put my puppet-show in order, and entertain all the company in the inn gratis." The innkeeper rejoiced at hearing this, and pointed out a convenient place for setting up the show—which was done in an instant.

Don Quixote was not entirely satisfied with the ape's divinations, thinking it very improbable that such a creature should, of itself, know anything either of future or past : therefore, whilst Master Peter was preparing his show, he drew Sancho aside to a corner of the stable, where, in a low voice, he revealed to him his suspicion.

Here they were interrupted by Master Peter, who came to inform Don Quixote that the show was ready, and to request he would come to see it, assuring him that he would find it worthy of his attention. The knight told him that he had a question to put to the ape first, as he desired to be informed by it whether the things which happened to him in the cave of Montesinos were realities, or only sleeping fancies; though he had a suspicion himself that they were a mixture of both. Master Peter immediately brought his ape, and placing him before Don Quixote and Sancho, said, "Look you, master ape, this worthy knight would know whether certain things which befel him in the cave of Montesinos were real or visionary." Then making the usual signal, the ape leaped upon his left shoulder, and, after seeming to whisper in his ear, Master Peter said, "The ape tells me that some of the things your worship saw, or which befel you in the said cave, are not true, and some probable; which is all he now knows concerning this matter—for his virtue has just left him; but if your worship desires to hear more, on Friday next, when his faculty will return, he will answer to your heart's content."

"There now," quoth Sancho, "did I not say you would never make me believe all you told us about that same cave?—no, nor half of it."

"That will hereafter appear," answered Don Quixote; "for time brings all things to light, though hidden within the bowels of the earth; and now we will drop the subject for the present, and see the puppet-play, for I am of opinion there must be some novelty in it."

"Some!" exclaimed Master Peter; "sixty thousand novelties shall you see in this play of mine! I assure you, Señor Don Quixote, it is one of the rarest sights that the world affords this day; *Operibus credite et non verbis;* so let us to work, for it grows late, and we have a great deal to do, to say, and to show."

Don Quixote and Sancho complied with his request, and repaired to the place where the show was set out, filled in every part with small wax candles, so that it made a gay and brilliant appearance. Master Peter, who was to manage the figures, placed himself behind the show, and in front of the scene stood his boy, whose office it was to relate the story and expound the mystery of the piece; holding a wand in his hand to point to the several figures as they entered.

All the people of the inn being fixed, some standing opposite to the show, and Don Quixote, Sancho, the page, and the scholar, seated in the best places.

CHAPTER LI

ON QUIXOTE SUCCOURS THE FAIR MELISENDRA

THE young interpreter then began his harangue just as the audience had their ears saluted with the sound of drums and trumpets, and discharges of artillery. These flourishes being over, the boy raised his voice and said, "Gentlemen, we here present you with a true story, which tells you how Don Gayferos delivers his spouse Melisendra, who was imprisoned by the Moors, in the city of Sansuenna, now called Saragossa; and there you may see how Don Gayferos is playing at tables, according to the ballad,—

> Gayferos now at tables plays,
> Forgetful of his lady dear.

That personage whom you see with a crown on his head and a sceptre in his hand is the Emperor Charlemagne, the fair Melisendra's reputed father, who, vexed at the idleness and negligence of his son-in-law, comes forth and chides him. Pray, observe, gentlemen, how the Emperor turns his back, and leaves Don Gayferos in a fret.

"See him now in a rage, tossing the table-board one way, and pieces another! Now calling hastily for his armour, and now asking Don Orlando, his cousin, to lend him his sword Durindana, which Don Orlando refuses, though he offers to bear him company in his perilous undertaking; but the furious knight will not accept of his help, saying that he is able alone to deliver his spouse. Hereupon he goes out to arm himself, in order to set forward immediately. Now, gentlemen, turn your eyes towards that tower which appears yonder, which you are to suppose to be one of the Moorish towers of Saragossa, now called the Aljaferia ; and that lady in a Moorish habit, who appears in the balcony, is the peerless Melisendra, who from that window has cast many a wistful look towards the road that leads to France, and soothed her captivity by thinking of the city of Paris and her dear husband. Now behold a strange incident, the like perhaps you never heard of before. Do you not see that Moor stealing along softly, and how, step by step, with his finger on his mouth, he comes behind Melisendra ? Hear what a smack he gives on her sweet lips, and see how she spits and wipes her mouth with her white smock-sleeves, and tears her beauteous hair from pure vexation ! Observe, also, the grave Moor who stands in that open gallery—he is Marsilius, king of Sansuenna, who, seeing the insolence of the Moor, though he is a kinsman, and a great favourite, orders him to be seized immediately, and two hundred stripes given him, and to be led through the principal streets of the city, with criers before, to proclaim his crime, followed by the public whippers with their rods.

"The figure you see there on horseback, muffled up in a Gascoigne cloak, is Don Gayferos himself, whom his lady (after being revenged on the impertinence of the Moor) sees from the battlements of the tower, and, taking him for a stranger, holds that discourse with him which is recorded in the ballad :—

> If towards France your course you bend,
> Let me entreat you, gentle friend,
> Make diligent inquiry there
> For Gayferos, my husband dear.

It is sufficient that Don Gayferos makes himself known to her, as you may perceive by the signs of joy she discovers, and especially now that you see how nimbly she lets herself down from the balcony, to get on horseback behind her loving spouse. But alas, poor lady ! the border of her under-petticoat has caught one of the iron rails of the balcony, and there she hangs dangling in the air, without being able to reach the ground.

But see how Heaven is merciful, and sends relief in the greatest distress! For now comes Don Gayferos, and, without caring for the richness of her petticoat, see how he lays hold of her, and, tearing her from the hooks, brings her at once to the ground, and then, at a spring, sets her behind him on the crupper, astride like a man, bidding her hold very fast, and clasp her arms about him till they cross and meet over his breast, that she may not fall; because the lady Melisendra was not accustomed to that way of riding. See how they now wheel about, and, turning their backs upon the city, scamper away merrily and joyfully to Paris.

"Now, sirs," continued the boy, "quickly as this was done, idle and evil eyes, are not wanting to mark the descent and mounting of the fair Melisendra, and to give notice to King Marsilius, who immediately ordered an alarm to be sounded; and now observe the hurry and tumult which follow! See how the whole city shakes with the ringing of bells in the steeples of the mosques——

"See, gentlemen, the squadrons of glittering cavalry that now rush out of the city, in pursuit of the two Catholic lovers! How many trumpets sound, how many dulcimers play, and how many drums and kettle-drums rattle! Alack, I fear the fugitives will be overtaken and brought back tied to their own horse's tail, which would be a lamentable spectacle."

Don Quixote, roused at the din and seeing such a number of Moors, thought it incumbent on him to succour the flying pair; and, rising up, said in a loud voice:

"It shall never be said while I live that I suffered such a wrong to be committed against so famous a knight and so daring a lover as Don Gayferos. Hold, base-born rabble!—follow him not, or expect to feel the fury of my resentment!"

'Twas no sooner said than done; he unsheathed his sword, and, at one spring, he planted himself close to the show, and with the utmost fury began to rain hacks and slashes on the Moorish puppets, overthrowing some, and beheading others, laming this, and demolishing that; and among other mighty strokes, one fell with mortal force in such a direction that, had not Master Peter dexterously slipped aside, he would have taken off his head as clean as if it had been made of sugar-paste.

"Hold, Señor Don Quixote!" cried out the showman, "hold, for pity's sake!—these are not real Moors that you are cutting and destroying, but puppets of pasteboard. Think of what you are doing: sinner that I am! you will ruin me for ever." These remonstrances were lost upon the exasperated knight, who still laid about him, showering down and redoubling his blows, fore-stroke and back-stroke, with such fury, that in less than the saying of two credos he demolished the whole machine, hacking to pieces all the tackling and figures. King Marsilius was in a grievous condition, and the Emperor Charlemagne's head, as well as crown, cleft in twain! The whole audience was in a consternation; the ape flew to the top of the house, the scholar and the page were panic-struck, and Sancho trembled exceedingly; for, as he afterwards declared when the storm was over, he had never seen his master in such a rage before.

After this chastisement of the Moors, and the general destruction which accompanied it, Don Quixote's fury began to abate, and he calmly said:

"I wish all those were at this moment present who obstinately refuse to be convinced of the infinite benefit that knights-errant are to the world: for, had I not been fortunately at hand, what would have become of good Don Gayferos and the fair Melisendra? No doubt these infidel dogs would have overtaken them by this time, and treated them with their wonted cruelty.—Long live knight-errantry, above all things in the world!"

"In Heaven's name let it live, and let me die!" replied Master Peter, in a dolorous tone, "for such is my wretched fate that I can say with King Roderigo, 'Yesterday I was a sovereign of Spain, and to-day I have not a foot of land to call my own.' It is not half an hour ago, nor scarcely half a minute, since I was master of kings and emperors, my stalls full of horses, and my trunks and sacks full of fine things; now I am destitute and wretched, poor and a beggar."

Sancho Panza was moved to compassion by Master Peter's lamentations, and said to him, "Come, do not weep, Master Peter; for it breaks my heart to see you grieve and take on so. I can assure you my master Don Quixote is too catholic and scrupulous a Christian to let any poor man come to loss by him."

" Here," said Don Quixote, " is a fresh confirmation of what I have often thought, and can now no longer doubt, that those enchanters who persecute me are continually leading me into error by first allowing me to see things as they really are, and then transforming them to my eyes into whatever shape they please. I protest to you, gentlemen, that the spectacle we have just beheld seemed to me a real occurrence, and I doubted not the identity of Melisendra, Don Gayferos, Marsilius, and Charlemagne. I was therefore moved with indignation at what I conceived to be injustice, and, in compliance with the duty of my profession as a knight-errant, I wished to assist and succour the fugitives : and with this good intention I did what you have witnessed. If I have been deceived and things have fallen out unhappily, it is not I who am to blame, but my wicked persecutors, the enchanters. Nevertheless, though this error of mine proceeded not from malice, yet I will condemn myself in costs—consider, Master Peter, your demand for the damaged figures, and I will pay it you down in current and lawful money of Castile."

Master Peter made him a low bow, saying :

" I expected no less from the unexampled Christianity of the valorous Don Quixote de la Mancha, the true protector of all needy and distressed wanderers, and let Master Innkeeper and the great Sancho be umpires and appraisers between your worship and me, of what the demolished figures are, or might be, worth."

The innkeeper and Sancho consented, whereupon Master Peter set his price upon the dead and wounded, which the arbitrators moderated to the satisfaction of both parties ; and the whole amounted to forty reals and three quartillos, which Sancho having paid down, Master Peter demanded two reals more for the trouble he should have in catching his ape.

" Give him the two reals, Sancho," said Don Quixote ; " and now would I give two hundred more to be assured that the lady Melisendra and Señor Don Gayferos are at this time in France and among their friends."

" Nobody can tell us that better than my ape," said Master Peter ; " but the devil himself cannot catch him now ; though, perhaps, either his love for me, or hunger, will force him to return at night. However, to-morrow is a new day, and we shall then see each other again."

The bustle of the puppet-show being quite over, they all supped together in peace and good fellowship, at the expense of Don Quixote, whose liberality was boundless. The man who carried the lances and halberds left the inn before daybreak, and after the sun had risen the scholar and the page came to take leave of Don Quixote; the former to return home, and the latter to pursue his intended journey : Don Quixote having given him a dozen reals to assist in defraying his expenses. Master Peter had no mind for any further intercourse with Don Quixote, whom he knew perfectly well, and therefore he also arose before the sun, and, collecting the fragments of his show, he set off with his ape in quest of adventures of his own. Master Peter was no other than the escaped convict Gines de Passamonte who to disguise himself had set up as a showman. The innkeeper, who was not so well acquainted with Don Quixote, was equally surprised at his madness and liberality. In short, Sancho, by order of his master, paid him well, and about eight in the morning, having taken leave of him, they left the inn and proceeded on their journey, where we will leave them, to relate other things necessary to the elucidation of this famous history.

CHAPTER LII

ADVENTURE WITH THE "BRAYERS"

LET us now return to our illustrious knight of La Mancha, who, after quitting the inn, determined to visit the banks of the river Ebro and the neighbouring country : finding that he would have time sufficient for that purpose before the tournaments at Saragossa began. With this intention he pursued his journey, and travelled two days without encountering anything worth recording, till, on the third day, as he was ascending a hill, he heard a distant sound of drums, trumpets, and other martial instruments, which at first he imagined to proceed from a body of military on the march ; and, spurring Rozinante, he ascended a rising ground, whence he perceived, as he thought, in the valley beneath, above two hundred men, armed with various

"Surrounded by the motley band."

weapons, as spears, cross-bows, partisans, halberds, and spikes, with some fire-arms. He then descended, and advanced near the troop.

They soon ascertained that it was the town that had been derided sallying forth to attack another, which had ridiculed them more than was reasonable or becoming in good neighbours. Don Quixote advanced towards them, to the no small concern of Sancho, who never had any liking to meddle in such matters, and he was presently surrounded by the motley band, who supposed him to be some friend to their cause. Don Quixote then, raising his vizor with an easy and graceful deportment, approached the ass-banner, and all the chiefs of the army collected around him, being struck with the same astonishment which the first sight of him usually excited. Don Quixote, seeing them gaze so earnestly at him, without being spoken to by any of the party, took advantage of the silence, and addressed them.

"The devil fetch me," quoth Sancho to himself, "if this master of mine be not a perfect priest ; or, if not, he is as like one as one egg is like another." Don Quixote took breath a little, and perceiving his auditors were still attentive, he would have continued his harangue, had he not been prevented by the zeal of his squire, who seized the opportunity offered him by a pause, to make a speech in his turn.

"Gentlemen," said he, "my master, Don Quixote de la Mancha, once called the 'Knight of the Sorrowful Figure,' and now the 'Knight of the Lions,' is a choice scholar, and understands Latin, and talks the vulgar tongue like any bachelor of arts ; and in all he meddles and advises, proceeds like an old soldier ; having all the laws and statutes of what is called duelling at his fingers' ends ; and so you have nothing to do but to follow his advice, and while you abide by that, let the blame be mine if ever you make a false step. And, indeed, as you have already been told, it is mighty foolish in you to be offended at hearing any one bray ; when I was a boy, I well remember nobody ever hindered me from braying as often as I pleased ; and I could do it so rarely that all the asses in the town answered me ; yet for all that was I still the son of my parents, who were very honest people : and though I must say a few of the proudest of my neighbours envied me the gift, yet I cared not a rush ; and, to convince you that I speak the truth, do but listen to me ; for this art, like that of swimming, once learned, is never forgotten."

Then, putting his hands to his nostrils, he began to bray so strenuously that the adjacent valleys resounded again ; whereupon a man who stood near him, supposing that he was mocking them, raised his pole, and gave him such a blow that it brought the unlucky squire to the ground. Don Quixote, seeing him so ill-treated, made at the striker with his lance, but was instantly opposed by so many of his comrades, that he saw it was impossible for him to be revenged : on the contrary, feeling a shower of stones come thick upon him, and seeing a thousand cross-bows presented, and as many guns levelled at him, he turned Rozinante about, and, as fast as he could gallop, got out from among them, heartily recommending himself to Heaven, and praying, as he fled, to be delivered from so imminent a danger : at the same time expecting, at every step, to be pierced through and through with bullets, he went on drawing his breath at every moment, to try whether or not it failed him. The rustic battalion, however, seeing him fly, were contented to save their ammunition. As for Sancho, they set him again upon his ass, though scarcely recovered from the blow, and suffered him to follow his master. The army kept the field till nightfall, when no enemy coming forth to battle, they joyfully returned home : and had they known the practice of the ancient Greeks, they would have erected a trophy in that place.

Don Quixote, not choosing to expose himself to the fury of an incensed and evil-disposed multitude, prudently retired out of their reach, without once recollecting his faithful squire, or the perilous situation in which he left him ; nor did he stop till he got as far off as he deemed sufficient for his safety. Sancho followed the track of his master, hanging, as before described, athwart his ass, and, having recovered his senses, at length came up to him ; when, unable to support himself, he dropped from his pack-saddle at Rozinante's feet, overcome with the pain of the bruises and blows he had received.

Don Quixote dismounted to examine the state of Sancho's body : but, finding no bones broken, and the skin whole from head to foot, he said angrily :

" In an evil hour, Sancho, must thou needs show thy skill in braying : where didst thou learn that it was proper to name a halter in the house of a man that was hanged ? To thy braying music what counterpoint couldst thou expect but that of a cudgel ? Return thanks to Heaven, Sancho, that, instead of crossing thy back with a cudgel, they did not make the sign of the cross on thee with a scimitar."

"I am not now in a condition to answer," replied Sancho, "for methinks I speak through my shoulders. Let us mount, and be gone from this place. As for braying, I will have done with it for ever ; —but not with telling that knights-errant can fly, and leave their faithful squires to be beaten to powder in the midst of their enemies."

"To retire is not to fly," answered Don Quixote ; " for thou must know, Sancho, that the valour which has not prudence for its basis is termed rashness, and the successful exploits of the rash are rather to be ascribed to good fortune than to courage. I confess I did retire, but not fly."

By this time Sancho had mounted again, with the assistance of his master, who likewise got upon Rozinante, and they proceeded slowly towards a grove of poplars which they discovered about a quarter of a league off, Sancho every now and then heaving most profound sighs, accompanied by dolorous groans : and, when asked the cause of his distress, he said that, from the nape of his neck to the lowest point of his back-bone, he was so bruised and sore that the pain made him mad.

"Doubtless," said Don Quixote, " this pain must have been caused by the pole with which they struck thee, and which, being long, extended over the whole of thy back, including all the parts which now grieve thee so much ; and, had the weapon been still larger, thy pain would have been increased."

"Before Heaven," quoth Sancho, " your worship has relieved me from a mighty doubt, and explained it, forsooth, in notable terms ! Body o' me ! was the cause of my pain so hidden that it was necessary to tell me that I felt pain in all those parts which the pole reached ? If my ankles had ached, then might you have tried to unriddle the cause ; but to find out that I am pained because I was beaten is, truly, no great matter. In faith, master of mine, other men's harms are easily borne ; I descry land more and more every day, and see plainly how little I am to expect from following your worship."

"I would lay a good wager with thee, Sancho," quoth Don Quixote, "that now thou art talking, and without interruption, thou feelest no pain in thy body. Go on, my son, and say all that comes into thy head, or to thy tongue; for, so thou art relieved from pain, I shall take pleasure even in the vexation thy impertinence occasions me—nay more, if thou hast really so great a desire to return home to thy wife and children, God forbid I should hinder thee. Thou hast money of mine in thy hands; see how long it is since we made this third sally from our town, and how much thou couldst have earned monthly, and pay thyself."

"When I served Thomas Carrasco," replied Sancho, "father of the bachelor Sampson Carrasco, whom your worship knows full well, I got two ducats a month, besides my victuals; with your worship I cannot tell what I may get; but I am sure it is greater drudgery to be squire to a knight-errant than servant to a farmer; for, if we work for husbandmen, though we labour hard in the day, at night we are sure of supper from the pot, and a bed to sleep on."

"I confess, Sancho," said Don Quixote, "that all thou sayest is true—how much dost thou think I ought to pay thee more than what thou hadst from Thomas Carrasco?"

"I think," quoth Sancho, "if your worship adds two reals a month, I should reckon myself well paid. This is for the wages due for my labour; but as to the promise your worship made of the government of an island, it would be fair that you add six reals more, making thirty in all."

"Very well," replied Don Quixote, "it is five-and-twenty days since we sallied from our village, and, according to the wages thou hast allotted thyself, calculate the proportion and see what I owe thee, and pay thyself, as I said before, with thine own hand."

"Body o' me," quoth Sancho, "your worship is clean out of the reckoning, for, as to the promised island, we must reckon from the day you promised me to the present hour."

"How long then is it since I promised it to thee?" said Don Quixote.

"If I remember right," answered Sancho, "it is about twenty years and three days, more or less."

Here Don Quixote, clapping his forehead with the palm of his hand, began to laugh heartily, and said, " Why, all my sallies, including the time I sojourned in the Sierra Morena, have scarcely taken up more than two months, and dost thou say, Sancho, it is twenty years since I promised thee an island ? I perceive that thou art determined to lay claim to all the money thou hast of mine ; if such be thy wish, take it, and much good may it do thee : for to rid myself of so worthless a squire I will gladly be left poor and penniless. But tell me, thou perverter of the squirely ordinances of knight-errantry ! where hast thou seen or read that any squire to knight-errant ever presumed to bargain with his master, and say, so much per month you must give me to serve you ? Turn about the bridle, or halter, of Dapple, and get home ! for not one single step farther shalt thou go with me. O bread ill-bestowed ! O promises ill-placed ! O man, thou hast more of the beast than of the human creature ! Now, when I thought of establishing thee, and in such a way that, in spite of thy wife, thou shouldst have been styled 'your lordship,' now dost thou leave me ? now, when I had just taken a firm and effectual resolution to make thee lord of the best island in the world ? But, as thou thyself hast often said, ' honey is not for the mouth of an ass.' An ass thou art, an ass thou wilt continue to be, and an ass thou wilt die ; for I verily believe thou wilt never acquire even sense enough to know that thou art a beast ! "

Sancho looked at his master with a sad and sorrowful countenance, all the time he thus reproached and rated him ; and when the storm was past, with tears in his eyes and in a faint and doleful voice, he said :

" I confess, dear sir, that to be a complete ass I want nothing but a tail, and if your worship will be pleased to put me on one I shall deem it well placed, and will then serve you as your faithful ass all the days I have yet to live. Pardon me, sir, I entreat you ; have pity on my ignorance, and consider that, if my tongue runs too fast, it is more from folly than evil-meaning : ' he who errs and mends, himself to Heaven commends.'"

" I should have wondered much, Sancho," quoth Don Quixote, " if thy proverbs had been wanting on such an occasion. Well, I forgive thee, on the promise of thy amendment, and in the hope that henceforth thou mayest prove less craving and selfish. I would hope also to see thy mind prepared to wait with becoming patience the due accomplishment of my promises, which, though deferred, are not on that account the less certain." Sancho promised compliance, though, to do it, he should have to draw strength out of weakness.

They now entered the poplar-grove, and Don Quixote seated himself at the foot of an elm, and Sancho under a beech. In that situation they passed the night: Sancho suffering from the pain of his bruises, and his master indulging his wonted meditations; nevertheless they both slept, and in the morning pursued their way towards the banks of the famous Ebro, where that befel them which shall be related in the ensuing chapter.

CHAPTER LIII

OF THE ADVENTURE OF THE ENCHANTED BARK

AFTER travelling leisurely for two days, Don Quixote and his squire reached the banks of the river Ebro, and the knight experienced much pleasure while he contemplated the verdure of its margin, the smoothness of its current, and the abundance of its crystal waters. Cheered and delighted with the scene, a thousand tender recollections rushed upon his mind, and particularly what he had witnessed in the cave of Montesinos; for although Master Peter's ape had pronounced a part only of those wonders to be true, he rather inclined to believe the whole than allow any part to be doubtful: quite the reverse of Sancho, who held them all to be false.

Thus musing and sauntering along, they observed a small vessel without oars or any kind of tackle, fastened by a rope to the shore. Don Quixote looked round him on all sides, and, seeing nobody, he alighted, and ordered Sancho to do the same, and make fast both their beasts to the trunk of a poplar or willow that grew by the side of the river. On Sancho's requesting to know why he was to do so, "Thou must know," said Don Quixote, "that this vessel is placed here expressly for my reception, and in order that I might proceed therein to the succour of some knight or other person of high degree who is in extreme distress: for such is the practice of enchanters, as we learn in the books of chivalry, when some knight happens to be involved in a situation of extraordinary peril, from which he can only be delivered by the hand of another knight. Then, although distant from each other two or three thousand leagues, and even more, they either snatch him up in a cloud, or, as thus, provide him with a boat, and in less than the twinkling of an eye convey him through the air, or over the surface of the ocean, wherever they list."

"Since it must be so," said Sancho, "and that your worship is determined to be always running into these vagaries, there is nothing left for me but to obey: following the proverb, ' do your master's bidding, and sit down with him at his table.' But for all that, to discharge my conscience, I am bound to tell your worship that, to my mind, this same boat belongs to no enchanter, but to some fisherman on this part of the river : for here, it is said, they catch the best shads in the world."

This caution Sancho ventured to give, while, with much grief of soul, he was tying the cattle, where they were to be left under the protection of enchanters. Don Quixote told him to be under no concern about forsaking those animals ; for he, by whom they were themselves to be transported to far distant longitudes, would take care that they should not want food.

"I do not understand your longitudes," said Sancho, " nor have I ever heard of such a word in all my life."

"Longitudes," replied Don Quixote, "means length ;— but no wonder thou dost not understand it, for thou art not bound to know Latin : though some there are who pretend to know it, and are as ignorant as thyself."

"Now they are tied," quoth Sancho, "what is next to be done ?"

"What ?" answered Don Quixote ; "why, cross ourselves and weigh anchor—I mean embark, and cut the rope with which the vessel is now tied." Then, leaping into it, followed by Sancho, he cut the cord, and the boat floated gently from the shore ; and when Sancho saw himself a few yards from the bank, he began to quake with fear ; but on hearing his friend Dapple

"He began to weep so bitterly."

bray, and seeing Rozinante struggle to get loose, he was quite overcome.

"The poor ass," said he, "brays for pure grief at being deserted, and Rozinante is endeavouring to get loose, that he may plunge into the river and follow us. O, dearest friends! abide where you are in peace, and may the mad freak which is the cause of our doleful parting, be quickly followed by a repentance that will bring us back again to your sweet company!"

Here he began to weep so bitterly that Don Quixote lost all patience.

"Of what art thou afraid? cowardly wretch!" cried he, "heart of butter! Why weepest thou?"

The boat was gently gliding along the surface of the river—not moved by the secret influence of enchantment, but by the current, which was then gentle, and the whole surface smooth and calm.

After a time several corn-mills appeared before them in the midst of the stream, which Don Quixote no sooner espied than he exclaimed in a loud voice:

"Behold, O Sancho! seest thou yon city, castle, or fortress?—there lies some knight under oppression, or some queen, infanta, or princess, confined in evil plight; to whose relief I am brought hither."

"What the devil of a city, fortress, or castle do you talk of, sir?" quoth Sancho; "do you not see that they are mills standing in the river for the grinding of corn?"

"Peace, Sancho," quoth Don Quixote; "for though they seem to be mills, they are not so. How often must I tell thee that enchanters have the power to transform whatever they please? I do not say that things are totally changed by them, but to our eyes they are made to appear so; whereof we have had a woeful proof in the transformation of Dulcinea, the sole refuge of my hopes."

The boat having now got into the current of the river, was carried on with more celerity than before; and, as it approached the mill, the labourers within, seeing it drifting towards them, and just entering the mill-stream, several of them ran out in haste with long poles to stop it; and, their faces and clothes being all covered with meal-dust, they had a ghostly appearance. "Devils of men !" said they, bawling aloud, "what do you there? Are you mad, or do you intend to drown yourselves, or be torn to pieces by the wheels?"

"Did I not tell thee, Sancho," said Don Quixote, "that we should certainly arrive where it would be necessary for me to display the valour of my arm? Look, what assassins and hob-goblins come out to oppose us! See their horrid visages with which they think to scare us! Now, rascals, have at you!" Then standing up in the boat, he began to threaten the millers aloud. "Ill-advised scoundrels!" said he, "set at liberty the person ye keep under oppression in that castle or fortress of yours, whether he be of high or low degree; for I am Don Quixote de la Mancha, otherwise called the Knight of the Lions, for whom, by Heaven's high destiny, the happy accomplishment of this adventure is reserved." So saying, he drew his sword and began to flourish with it in the air, as if he would smite the millers, who, not understanding his menaces, endeavoured to stop the boat, now on the point of entering into the swift current that rushed under the wheels. Sancho fell upon his knees and prayed devoutly to Heaven for his deliverance, which was accomplished by the agility and adroitness of the millers with their poles,—but not without oversetting the boat, whereby the knight and squire were plunged into the water. Although Don Quixote could swim like a goose, the weight of his armour now carried him twice to the bottom; and, had it not been for the millers who leaped into the river, and hauled them both out, they must have inevitably perished.

After having been dragged on shore, much more wet than thirsty, Sancho again fell on his knees, and long and devoutly prayed that Heaven would thenceforward protect him from the dangers to which he was likely to be exposed through the rash enterprises of his master. Now came the fishermen, owners of the boat, which had been entirely destroyed by the mill-wheels, and loudly demanded reparation for the loss they had sustained, and for that purpose began to strip Sancho, when Don Quixote, with as much unconcern as if nothing had happened, gravely told the millers and fishermen that he would willingly pay for the boat on condition of their delivering up, free and without ransom, the person, or persons, whom they unjustly detained in their castle.

"What persons, or what castles, madman ! do you mean ? " said one of the millers ; " would you carry off those who come to have their corn ground at our mills ? "

" There let it rest," thought Don Quixote to himself : " it is only preaching to the desert to endeavour, either by argument or entreaty, to incite these dregs of human kind to a generous action ! In this adventure it is manifest that two powerful enchanters must have engaged, the one frustrating what the other attempts ; the one providing me a bark and the other over-setting it. Heaven help me ! in this world there is nothing but plots and counter-plots, mines and counter-mines !—I can do no more." Then, casting a look of melancholy towards the mills :

" Friends," he said, " whoever ye are that live immured in that prison, pardon me, I beseech you, for not having delivered you from affliction ; by your ill fate and mine it is ordained that this adventure should be reserved for some more fortunate knight ! " He then compounded with the fishermen, and agreed to give them fifty reals for the boat, which sum Sancho, with much reluctance, paid down, saying :

" A couple more of such embarkations as this will sink our whole capital."

The fishermen and millers stood gazing with astonishment at two figures so far out of the fashion and semblance of other men, and were quite at a loss to find out the meaning of Don Quixote's speeches ; but, conceiving their intellects to be disordered, they left them ; the millers retiring to their mills, and the fishermen to their cabins ; whereupon Don Quixote and Sancho, like a pair of senseless animals themselves, returned to the animals they had left ; and thus ended the adventure of the enchanted bark.

CHAPTER LIV

DON QUIXOTE'S ADVENTURE WITH A FAIR HUNTRESS

LOW-SPIRITED, wet, and out of humour, the knight and squire reached their cattle ; Sancho more especially was grieved to the very soul to have encroached so much upon their stock of money : all that was taken thence seeming to him as so much taken from the apples of his eyes. In short, they mounted, without exchanging a word, and silently quitted the banks of that famous river : Don Quixote buried in amorous meditations, and Sancho in those of his preferment, which seemed at that moment to be very dim and remote ; for, dull as he was, he saw clearly enough that his master's actions were for the most part little better than crazy, and he only waited for an opportunity, without coming to accounts and reckonings, to steal off and march home. But fortune was kinder to him than he expected.

It happened on the following day, near sunset, as they were issuing from a forest, that Don Quixote espied sundry persons at a distance, who, it appeared, as he drew nearer to them, were taking the diversion of hawking ; and among them he remarked a gay lady mounted on a palfrey, or milk-white pad, with green furniture and a side-saddle of cloth of silver. Her own attire was also green, and so rich and beautiful that she was elegance itself. On her left hand she carried a hawk ; whence Don Quixote conjectured that she must be a lady of high rank, and mistress of the hunting-party (as in truth she was), and therefore he said to his squire :

"Hasten, Sancho, and make known to the lady of the palfrey and the hawk, that I, 'the Knight of the Lions,' humbly salute her highness, and, with her gracious leave, would be proud to kiss her fair hands, and serve her to the utmost of my power and her highness's commands ; but take especial care, Sancho, how thou deliverest my message, and be mindful not to interlard thy embassy with any of thy proverbs."

"So, then," quoth Sancho, "you must twit the interlarder !—

but why this to me ? as if this, forsooth, were the first time I had
carried messages to high and mighty ladies !"

"Excepting that to the lady Dulcinea," replied Don Quixote,
"I know of none thou hast carried — at least, none from
me."

"That is true," answered Sancho ; "but a good paymaster
needs no surety : and where there is plenty, dinner is soon
dressed : I mean, there is no need of schooling me; for I am
prepared for all, and know something of everything."

"I believe it, Sancho," quoth Don Quixote ; "go, then, and
Heaven direct thee."

Sancho set off at a good rate, forcing Dapple out of his usual
pace, and went up to the fair huntress ; then alighting, and
kneeling before her, he said :

"Beauteous lady, that knight yonder, called 'the Knight of
the Lions,' is my master, and I am his squire, Sancho Panza by
name. That same Knight of the Lions, lately called the Knight
of the Sorrowful Figure, sends me to beg your grandeur would be
pleased to give leave that, with your liking and goodwill, he may
approach and accomplish his wishes, which, as he says, and I
believe, are no other than to serve your exalted beauty, which if
your ladyship grant, you will do a thing that will redound to the
great benefit of your highness ; and to him it will be a mighty
favour and satisfaction."

"Truly, good squire," answered the lady, "you have delivered your message with all the circumstances which such
embassies require ; rise up, I pray ; for it is not fit the squire
of so renowned a knight as he of the Sorrowful Figure, of whom
we have already heard much in these parts, should remain upon
his knees—rise, friend, and desire your master, by all means, to
honour us with his company, that my lord duke and I may pay
our respects at a rural mansion we have here, hard by." Sancho
rose up, no less amazed at the lady's beauty than at her affability
and courteous deportment, and yet more that her ladyship should
have any knowledge of his master, the Knight of the Sorrowful
Figure ! And if she did not give him his true title, he concluded
it was because he had assumed it so lately.

"Pray," said the duchess (whose title is yet unknown), "is
not your master the person of whom there is a history in print,

called, 'The ingenious gentleman Don Quixote de la Mancha,' and who has for the mistress of his affections a certain lady named Dulcinea del Toboso?"

"The very same," answered Sancho; "and that squire of his, called Sancho Panza, who is, or ought to be, spoken of in the same history, am I, unless I was changed in the cradle—I mean in the printing."

"I am much delighted by what you tell me," quoth the duchess; "go to your master, good Panza, and give him my invitation and hearty welcome to my house; and tell him that nothing could happen to me which would afford me greater pleasure."

Sancho, overjoyed at this gracious answer, hastened back to his master, and repeated to him all that the great lady had said to him; extolling to the skies, in his rustic phrase, her extraordinary beauty and courteous behaviour. Don Quixote seated himself handsomely in his saddle, adjusted his visor, enlivened Rozinante's mettle, and assuming a polite and stately deportment, advanced to kiss the hand of the duchess. Her grace in the meantime having called the duke her husband, had already given him an account of the embassy she had just received; and, as they had read the first part of this history, and were, therefore, aware of the extravagant humour of Don Quixote, they waited for him with infinite pleasure and the most eager desire to be acquainted with him: determined to indulge his humour to the utmost, and, while he remained with them, treat him as a knight-errant, with all the ceremonies described in books of chivalry, which they took pleasure in reading.

Don Quixote now arrived, with his beaver up; and signifying his intention to alight, Sancho was hastening to hold his stirrup, but unfortunately in dismounting from Dapple, his foot caught in one of the rope-stirrups, in such a manner that it was impossible for him to disentangle himself: and he hung by it, with his face and breast on the ground. Don Quixote, who was not accustomed to alight without having his stirrup held, thinking that Sancho was already there to do his office, threw his body off with a swing of his right leg, that brought down Rozinante's saddle; and the girth giving way, both he and the saddle, to his great shame and mortification, came to the ground, where he lay, muttering between his teeth many a heavy execration against the unfortunate Sancho, who was still hanging by the leg. The duke having commanded some of his attendants to relieve the knight and squire, they raised Don Quixote, who, though much discomposed by his fall, and limping, made an effort to approach and kneel before the lord and lady. The duke, however, would by no means suffer it ; on the contrary, alighting from his horse, he immediately went up and embraced him, saying :

"I am very sorry, Sir Knight, that such a mischance should happen to you on your first arrival on my domains ; but the negligence of squires is often the occasion of even greater disasters."

"The moment cannot be unfortunate that introduces me to your highness," replied Don Quixote, "and, had my fall been to the centre of the deep abyss, the glory of seeing your highness would have raised me thence. My squire, whom Heaven confound, is better at letting loose his tongue to utter impertinence than at securing a saddle : but whether down or up, on horseback or on foot, I shall always be at the service of your highness, and that of my lady duchess your worthy consort—the sovereign lady of beauty, and universal princess of all courtesy."

"Softly, dear Señor Don Quixote de la Mancha," quoth the duke, "for, while the peerless Dulcinea del Toboso exists, no other beauty can be named."

Sancho Panza had now got freed from the noose, and being near, before his master could answer, he said :

"It cannot be denied—nay, it must be declared, that my lady Dulcinea del Toboso is a rare beauty ; but, 'where we are least aware, there starts the hare.' I have heard say that what they call nature is like a potter who makes earthen vessels, and he who makes one handsome vessel may also make two, and three, and a hundred. This I say because, by my faith, her highness there comes not a whit behind my mistress the lady Dulcinea del Toboso."

Don Quixote here turned to the Duchess, and said :

"I assure your grace, never any knight-errant in the world had a more conceited and troublesome prater for his squire than I have ; of this he will give ample proof, if it please your highness to accept of my service for some days."

"I am glad to hear that my friend Sancho is conceited," replied the duchess, "it is a sign he has good sense; for wit and gay conceits, as you well know, Señor Don Quixote, proceed not from dull heads; and since you acknowledge that Sancho has wit and pleasantry, I shall henceforth pronounce him to be wise "—

"And a prater," added Don Quixote.

"So much the better," said the duke, "for many good things cannot be expressed in a few words; and, that we may not throw away all our time upon them, come on, Sir Knight of the Sorrowful Figure."

"Of the Lions, your highness should say," quoth Sancho; "the Sorrowful Figure is no more."

"Of the Lions then let it be," continued the duke; "I say come on, Sir Knight of the Lions, to a castle of mine hard by, where you shall be received in a manner suitable to a person of your distinction, and as the duchess and I are accustomed to receive all knights-errant who honour us with their society."

By this time, Sancho having adjusted and well-girthed Rozinante's saddle, Don Quixote remounted, and thus he and the duke, who rode a stately courser, with the duchess between them, proceeded towards the castle. The duchess requested Sancho to be near her, being mightily pleased with his arch observations; nor did Sancho require much entreaty, but, joining the other three, made a fourth in the conversation, to the great satisfaction of the duke and duchess, who looked upon themselves as highly fortunate in having to introduce such guests to their castle, and the prospect of enjoying the company of such a knight-errant, and such an errant-squire.

Sancho's joy was excessive on seeing himself, as he thought, a favourite with the duchess: not doubting but that he should find in her castle the same abundance that prevailed in the mansion of Don Diego and Basilius; for good cheer was the delight of his heart, and therefore he always took care to seize by the forelock every opportunity to indulge that passion. Now the history relates that, before they came to the rural mansion, or castle, of the duke, his highness rode on before and gave directions to his servants in what manner they were to behave to Don Quixote; therefore, when he arrived with the duchess at the castle-gate, there immediately issued out two lacqueys or grooms, clad in a kind of robe or gown of fine crimson satin reaching to their feet; and, taking Don Quixote in their arms, they privately said to him, "Go, great sir, and assist our lady the duchess to alight."

The knight accordingly hastened to offer his services, which, after much ceremony and many compliments, her grace positively declined, saying that she would not alight from her palfrey, but into the duke's arms, as she did not think herself worthy to charge so great a knight with so unprofitable a burthen. At length the duke came out and lifted her from her horse; and on their entering into a large inner-court of the castle, two beautiful damsels advanced and threw over Don Quixote's shoulders a large mantle of the finest scarlet, and in an instant all the galleries of the courtyard were crowded with men and women—the domestic household of his grace, crying aloud:

"Welcome, the flower and cream of knights-errant!" Then they sprinkled whole bottles of sweet-scented waters upon the knight, and also on the duke and duchess; all which Don Quixote observed with surprise and pleasure: being now, for the first time, thoroughly convinced that he was a true knight, and no imaginary one, since he was treated just like the knights-errant of former times.

Sancho attached himself closely to the duchess and entered with her into the castle. Presently they ascended the great stairs, and conducted the knight into a spacious hall, sumptuously hung with cloth of gold and rich brocade. Six damsels attended to take off his armour and serve as pages, all tutored by the duke and duchess in their behaviour towards him, in order to confirm his delusion. Don Quixote, being now unarmed, remained in his straight breeches and chamois doublet, lean, tall, and stiff, with his cheeks shrunk into his head; making such a figure that the damsels who waited on him had much difficulty to restrain their mirth, and observe in his presence that decorum which had been strictly enjoined by their lord and lady. They begged he would suffer himself to be undressed, for the purpose of changing his linen; but he would by no means consent, saying that modesty was as becoming a knight-errant as courage. However, he bade them give the shirt to Sancho; and, retiring with him to an apartment where there was a rich bed, he pulled off his clothes, and there put it on.

Don Quixote then dressed himself, girt on his sword, threw the scarlet mantle over his shoulders, put on a green satin cap which the damsels had given him, and thus equipped marched out into the great saloon, where he found the damsels drawn up on each side in two equal ranks, and all of them provided with an equipage for washing his hands, which they administered with many reverences and much ceremony. Then came twelve pages, with the major-domo, to conduct him to dinner, the lord and lady being now waiting for him ; and, having placed him in the midst of them with great pomp and ceremony, they proceeded to another hall, where a rich table was spread with four covers only. The duke and duchess came to the door to receive him, accompanied by a grave ecclesiastic—one of those who govern great men's houses : one of those who, not being nobly born themselves, are unable to direct the conduct of those who are so ; who would have the liberality of the great measured by the narrowness of their own souls : making those whom they govern penurious, under the pretence of teaching them to be prudent. One of this species was the grave ecclesiastic who came out with the duke to receive Don Quixote. After a thousand courtly compliments mutually interchanged, Don Quixote advanced towards the table, between the duke and duchess, and, on preparing to seat themselves, they offered the upper end to Don Quixote, who would have declined it but for the pressing importunities of the duke. The ecclesiastic seated himself opposite to the knight, and the duke and duchess on each side.

Sancho was present all the while, in amazement to see the honour paid by those great people to his master, and at the numerous entreaties and ceremonies that were passing between the duke and Don Quixote, before he would sit down at the head of the table. This led him to adduce a string of proverbs, all of which were more plain than appropriate.

The natural brown of Don Quixote's face was flushed with anger and shame at Sancho's witticisms, so that the duke and duchess, seeing his distress, endeavoured to restrain their laughter ; and, to prevent further impertinence from Sancho, the duchess

M

asked Don Quixote what news he had last received of the lady
Dulcinea, and whether he had lately sent her any presents of
giants or caitiffs, since he must certainly have vanquished
many.

"Alas, madam!" answered he, "my misfortunes have had a
beginning, but they will never have an end. Giants I have conquered, and robbers, and wicked caitiffs; and many have I sent
to the mistress of my soul; but where should they find her,
transformed as she now is into the homeliest rustic wench that
the imagination ever conceived?"

"I know not, sir, how that can be," quoth Sancho, "for to
me she appeared the most beautiful creature in the world: at
least for nimbleness, or in a kind of a spring she has with her, I
am sure no stage tumbler can go beyond her. In good faith, my
lady duchess, she springs from the ground upon an ass as if she
were a cat."

"Have you seen her enchanted, Sancho?" quoth the duke.

"Seen her!" answered Sancho; "who the devil was it but
I that first hit upon the business of her enchantment? Yes, she
is as much enchanted as my father."

The ecclesiastic, when he heard talk of giants, caitiffs, and
enchantments, began to suspect that this must be the Don
Quixote de la Mancha whose history the duke was often reading; and he had as frequently reproved him for so doing; telling
him it was idle to read such fooleries. Being assured of the truth
of his suspicion, with much indignation he said to the duke:

"Your excellency will be accountable to Heaven for the
actions of this poor man—this Don Quixote, or Don Coxcomb,
or whatever you are pleased to call him, cannot be quite so mad
as your excellency would make him by thus encouraging his
extravagant fancies." Then turning to Don Quixote, he said—
"And you, Señor Addle-pate, who has thrust it into your brain
that you are a knight-errant, and that you vanquish giants and
robbers? Go, get you home in a good hour, and in such are you
now admonished; return to your family, and look to your
children, if you have any: mind your affairs, and cease to be a
vagabond about the world, sucking the wind, and drawing on
yourself the derision of all that know you, or know you not.
Where are there giants in Spain, or caitiffs in La Mancha, or

enchanted Dulcineas, or all the rabble rout of follies that are told of you?" Don Quixote was very attentive to the words of the reverend gentleman, and, finding that he was now silent, regardless of the respect due to the duke and duchess, up he started, with indignation and fury in his looks.

Don Quixote, trembling like quicksilver from head to foot, in an agitated voice said, "The place where I am, and the presence of the noble personages before whom I stand, as well as the respect which I have ever entertained for your profession, restrain my just indignation; for these reasons, and because I know, as all the world knows, that the weapons of gownsmen, like those of women, are their tongues, with the same weapon, in equal combat, I will engage your reverence, from whom good counsel might have been expected, rather than scurrility. Charitable and wholesome reproof requires a different language; at least it must be owned that reproach so public, as well as rude, exceeds the bounds of decent reprehension. Mildness, sir, would have been better than asperity; but was it either just or decent, at once, and without knowledge of the fault, plainly to proclaim the offender madman and idiot? Tell me, I beseech your reverence, for which of the follies you have observed in me do you thus condemn and revile me, desiring me to go home and take care of my house, and of my wife and children, without knowing whether I have either? I have redressed grievances, righted wrongs, chastised insolence, vanquished giants, and trampled upon hobgoblins: I am enamoured—for knights-errant must be so; but I am conscious of no licentious passion—my love is of the chaste Platonic kind. My intentions are always directed to virtuous ends—to do good to all, and injury to none. Whether he who thus means, thus acts, and thus lives, deserves to be called fool, let your highnesses judge, most excellent duke and duchess."

"Well said, i' faith!" quoth Sancho. "Say no more for yourself, good lord and master: for there is nothing more in the world to be said, thought, or done. And, besides, as regards this gentleman denying, as he has denied, that there either are, or ever were, knights-errant, it is no wonder, for he knows nothing of what he has been talking about."

"So then," said the ecclesiastic, "you, I suppose, are the

same Sancho Panza they talk of, to whom it is said your master has promised an island ?' "

"I am that Sancho," replied the squire, "and deserve it too, as well as any other he whatever. Of such as me, it is said, 'Keep company with the good, and thou wilt be one of them;' and, 'Not with whom thou wert bred, but with whom thou hast fed;' and, 'He that leaneth against a good tree, a good shelter findeth he.' I have leaned and stuck to a good master these many months, and shall be such another as he, if it be God's good pleasure; and, if he lives, and I live, neither shall he want kingdoms to rule, nor I islands to govern."

"That you shall not, friend Sancho," said the duke, "for in the name of Señor Don Quixote, I promise you the government of one of mine now vacant, and of no inconsiderable value."

"Kneel, Sancho," said Don Quixote, "and kiss his excellency's feet for the favour he has done thee." Sancho did so.

Upon this the ecclesiastic got up from the table in great wrath, saying, "By the habit I wear, I could find it in my heart to say that your excellency is as simple as these sinners; no wonder they are mad, since wise men authorize their follies! Your excellency may stay with them, if you please; but while they are in this house I will remain in my own, and save myself the trouble of reproving where I cannot amend." Then, without saying another word, and leaving his meal unfinished, away he went, in spite of the entreaties of the duke and duchess : though, indeed, the duke could not say much, through laughter at his foolish petulance.

As soon as his laughter would allow him, the duke said to Don Quixote :

"Sir Knight of the Lions, you have answered so well for yourself and your profession, that you can require no further satisfaction of the angry clergyman; especially if you consider that, whatever he might say, it was impossible for him, as you well know, to affront a person of your character."

"It is true, my lord," answered Don Quixote, "whoever cannot receive an affront cannot give one. Women, children, and churchmen, as they cannot defend themselves if attacked, so they cannot be affronted, because, as your excellency better knows, there is this difference between an injury and an affront : an affront must come from a person, who not only gives it, but who can maintain it when it is given : an injury may come from any hand."

Sancho's remarks interspersed during the discussion were so humorous that the duchess thought him more diverting and mad than his master.

At length, Don Quixote being pacified and calm, and the dinner ended, the cloth was removed ; whereupon four damsels entered, one with a silver ewer, another with a basin, also of silver, a third with two fine clean towels over her shoulder, and the fourth with her sleeves tucked up to her elbows, and in her white hands (for doubtless they were white) a wash-ball of Naples soap. The damsel who held the basin now respectfully approached the knight, and placed it under his beard, while he, wondering at the ceremony, yet believing it to be the custom of that country to wash beards instead of hands, obediently thrust out his chin as far as he could ; whereupon the ewer began to rain upon his face, while the damsel of the wash-ball lathered his beard with great dexterity, covering with a snow-white froth, not only the beard, but the whole face of the submissive knight, even over his eyes, which he was compelled to close. The duke and duchess, who were not in the secret, were eager to know the issue of this extraordinary ablution. The barber-damsel having raised a lather a span high, pretended that the water was all used, and ordered the girl with the ewer to fetch more, telling her that Señor Don Quixote would stay till she came back. Thus he was left, the strangest and most ridiculous figure imaginable, to the gaze of all that were present ; and, seeing him with his neck half an ell long, more than moderately swarthy, his eyes half-shut, and his whole visage under a covering of white foam, it was marvellous, and a sign of great discretion, that they were able to preserve their gravity.

The damsels concerned in the jest hung down their eyes, not daring to look at their lord or lady, who were divided between anger and mirth, not knowing whether to chastise the girls for their boldness, or reward them for the amusement their device had afforded. The water-nymph returned, and the beard-washing was finished, when she who was charged with the towels performed the office of wiping and drying with much deliberation ; and thus the ceremony being concluded, the four damsels at once, making him a profound reverence, were retiring when the duke, to prevent Don Quixote from suspecting the jest, called the damsel with the basin, and said, " Come and do your duty, and take care that you have water enough." The girl, who was shrewd and active, went up, and applied the basin to the duke's chin in the same manner she had done to that of Don Quixote ; and with equal adroitness, but more celerity, repeated the ceremony of lathering, washing, and wiping ; and the whole being done, they made their curtsies, and retired. The duke, however, had declared, as it afterwards appeared, that he would have chastised them for their pertness, if they had refused to serve him in the same manner.

Sancho was very attentive to this washing ceremony.

" Heaven guide me !" said he, muttering to himself, " is it the custom, I wonder, of this place to wash the beards of squires, as well as of knights ?   On my conscience and soul, I need it much ; and if they would give me a stroke of a razor, I should take it for a still greater favour."

" What are you saying to yourself, Sancho ?" quoth the duchess.

" I say, madam," answered Sancho, " that in other houses ot the great, I have always heard that, when the cloth is taken away, the custom is to bring water to wash hands, but not suds to scour beards ; and therefore one must live long to see much. It is also said he who lives long must suffer much ; though if I am not mistaken, to be so scoured must be rather a pleasure than a pain !"

" Be under no concern, friend Sancho," quoth the duchess ; " for I will order my damsels to see to your washing, and to lay you a bucking too, if needful."

" For the present, if my beard get a scouring I shall be content," said Sancho ; " for the rest, Heaven will provide hereafter."

" Here, steward," said the duchess, " attend to the wishes of good Sancho, and do precisely as he would have you." He answered that Señor Sancho should in all things be punctually obeyed ; and then he went to dinner, and took Sancho along with him.

Meantime, Don Quixote remained with the duke and duchess, discoursing on divers matters relating to arms and knight-errantry. The duchess entreated Don Quixote, since he seemed to have so happy a memory, that he would delineate and describe the beauty and accomplishments of the lady Dulcinea del Toboso: for, if fame spoke the truth, she must needs be the fairest creature in the world, and, consequently, in La Mancha.

"Madam," said Don Quixote, heaving a deep sigh, "if I could pluck out my heart and place it before you on this table, your highness would there behold her painted to the life, and I might save my tongue the fruitless labour of describing that which can scarcely be conceived: for how am I to delineate or describe the perfections of that paragon of excellence? My shoulders are unequal to so mighty a burthen."

"Nevertheless, Señor Don Quixote would give us great pleasure by endeavouring to paint her to us," said the duke, "for, though it be only a rough sketch, doubtless she will appear such as the most beautiful may envy."

"Ah! my lord, so she certainly would," answered Don Quixote, "had not the misfortune which lately befel her, blurred and defaced the lovely idea, and razed it from my memory:—such a misfortune, that I ought rather to bewail what she suffers than describe what she is; for your excellencies must know that, going, not many days since, to kiss her hands, and receive her benediction, with her commands and licence for this third sally, I found her quite another person than her I sought for. I found her enchanted and transformed from a princess into a country wench, from beautiful to ugly, from an angel to a fiend, from fragrant to pestiferous, from courtly to rustic, from light to darkness, from a dignified lady to a jumping Joan—in fine, from Dulcinea del Toboso to an unsightly bumpkin of Sayago."

"Heaven defend me!" exclaimed the duke, elevating his voice, "what villain can have done the world so much injury?"

"Who?" answered Don Quixote, "who could it be but some malicious enchanter, of the many that persecute me." Whereupon he gave a full account of all that had passed since he left his home on his first sally, of the adventures he had undergone in Montesinos' Cave and how Dulcinea's enchantment had affected him.

In this manner were the duke, the duchess, and Don Quixote conversing, when suddenly a great noise of many voices was heard in another part of the palace, and presently Sancho rushed into the saloon, with a terrified countenance, and a dishclout under his chin, followed by a number of kitchen-helpers, and other inferior servants; one of whom carried a trough full of something that seemed to be dish-water, with which he followed close upon Sancho, and made many efforts to place it under his chin, while another scullion seemed equally eager to wash his beard with it.

"What is the matter, fellows?" quoth the duchess; "what would you do with this good man? do you not know that he is a governor-elect?"

"This gentleman," said the roguish beard-washer, "will not suffer himself to be washed, according to custom, as our lord the duke and his master have been."

"Yes, I will," answered Sancho, in great wrath, "but I would have cleaner towels and cleaner suds, and not such filthy hands; for there is no such difference between me and my master, that he should be washed with angel water and I with devil's ley. The customs of countries or of great men's houses are good as far as they are agreeable; but this of beard-scouring here is worse than the friar's scourge. My beard is clean, and I have no need of such refreshings; and he who offers to scour me, or touch a hair of my head—my beard I should say—with due reverence be it spoken, shall feel the full weight of my fist upon his skull; for such ceremonies and soapings to my thinking look more like jokes and jibes than a civil welcome."

The duchess was convulsed with laughter at Sancho's remonstrances and rage, but Don Quixote could not endure to behold his squire so accoutred with a filthy towel, and baited by a kitchen rabble. Making, therefore, a low bow to the duke and duchess, as if requesting their permission to speak, he said to the greasy tribe, in a solemn voice:

"Hark ye, good people, be pleased to let the young man alone, and return whence ye came, or whither ye list; for my squire is as clean as another man, and these troughs are as odious to him as a narrow-necked jug. Take my advice, and leave him; for neither he nor I understand this kind of jesting."

"No, no," quoth Sancho (interrupting his master), " let them go on with their sport, and see whether I will bear it or no! Let them bring hither a comb, or what else they please, and curry this beard, and if they find anything there that should not be there, I will give them leave to shear me cross-wise."

"Sancho Panza is perfectly right," said the duchess, "and will be so in whatever he shall say: he is clean, and, as he truly says, needs no washing; and, if he be not pleased with our custom, he is master of his own will. Besides, unmannerly scourers, you who are so forward to purify others, are yourselves shamefully idle— in truth, I should say impudent, to bring your troughs and greasy dishclouts to such a personage and such a beard, instead of ewers and basins of pure gold, and towels of Dutch diaper. Out of my sight, barbarians! low-born wretches, who cannot help showing the spite and envy you bear to the squires of knights-errant!"

The roguish crew, and even the major-domo, who accompanied them, thought the duchess was in earnest, and, hastily removing the foul cloth from Sancho's neck, they slunk away in confusion. The squire, on being thus delivered from what he thought imminent danger, threw himself on his knees before the duchess.

"Heaven bless your highness," quoth he; "great persons are able to do great kindnesses. For my part I know not how to repay your ladyship for that you have just done me, and can only wish myself dubbed a knight-errant, that I may employ all the days of my life in the service of so high a lady."

"It plainly appears, Sancho," said the duchess, "that you have learned to be courteous in the school of courtesy itself— I mean under the wing of Señor Don Quixote, who is the cream of courtesy."

CHAPTER LV

OF THE CONVERSATION WHICH PASSED BETWEEN THE
DUCHESS, HER DAMSELS, AND SANCHO PANZA

Don Quixote having gone to take his rest, Sancho Panza did not take his afternoon sleep, but went immediately after his dinner to see the duchess, who, being delighted to hear him talk, desired him to sit down by her on a stool, although Sancho, out of pure good manners, would have declined it; but the duchess told him that he must be seated as a governor, and talk as a squire, since in both those capacities he deserved the very seat of the famous champion Cid Ruy Dias. Sancho therefore submitted, and placed himself close by the duchess, while all her damsels and duennas drew near and stood in silent attention to hear the conversation. " Now that we are alone," said the duchess, " where nobody can overhear us, I wish Señor Governor would satisfy me as to certain doubts that have arisen from the printed history of the great Don Quixote; one of which is that, as honest Sancho never saw Dulcinea— I mean the lady Dulcinea del Toboso—nor delivered to her the letter of Don Quixote, which was left in the pocket-book in the Sierra Morena, I would be glad to know how he could presume to feign an answer to that letter, or assert that he found her winnowing wheat, which he must have known to be altogether false, and much to the prejudice of the peerless Dulcinea's character, as well as inconsistent with the duty and fidelity of a trusty squire."

At these words, without making any reply, Sancho got up from his stool, and with his body bent, and the tip of his fore-finger on his lips, he stepped softly round the room, lifting up the hangings: and this done, he sat himself down again and said:

" Now, madam, that I am sure that nobody but the company present can hear us, I will answer, without fear, to all you ask of me: and the first thing I tell you is that I take my master Don Quixote for a downright madman; and though sometimes he will talk in a way which, to my thinking, and in the opinion of all who hear him, is so much to the purpose that Satan himself could not speak better, yet for all that, I believe him to be really and truly mad. Now this being so, as in my mind it is, nothing is more easy than to make him believe anything, though it has neither head nor tail : like that affair of the answer to the letter, and another matter of some six or eight days' standing, which is not yet in print—I mean the enchantment of my mistress Donna Dulcinea ; for you must know I made him believe she was enchanted, though it was no more true than that the moon is a horn lantern."

The duchess desired him to tell her the particulars of that enchantment or jest ; and Sancho recounted the whole, exactly as it had passed, very much to the entertainment of his hearers.

"From what honest Sancho has told me," said the duchess, "a certain scruple troubles me, and something whispers in my ear, saying, 'Since Don Quixote de la Mancha is such a lunatic and simpleton, surely Sancho Panza, his squire, who knows it, and yet follows and serves him, relying on his vain promises, must be more mad than his master ! Now this being the case, it will surely turn to bad account, lady duchess, if to such a Sancho Panza thou givest an island to govern ; for how should he who rules himself so ill, be able to govern others ?' "

"Faith, madam," quoth Sancho, "that same scruple is an honest scruple, and need not speak in a whisper, but plain out, or as it lists ; for I know it says true, and had I been wise, I should long since have left my master ;—but such is my lot, or such my evil-errantry. I cannot help it—follow him I must : we are both of the same town, I have eaten his bread, I love him, and he returns my love ; he gave me his ass-colts :—above all, I am faithful, so that nothing in the world can part us but the sexton's spade and shovel ; and if your highness does not choose to give me the government you promised, God made me without it, and perhaps it may be all the better for my conscience if I do not get it ; and perhaps it may be easier for Sancho the squire to get to heaven than for Sancho the governor. They make as good bread here as in France ; and by night all cats are grey ; unhappy is he who has not breakfasted at three ; and no stomach is a span bigger than another, and may be filled, as they say, with straw or with hay. Of the little birds in the air, God himself takes the care ; and four yards of coarse cloth of Cuenza are warmer than as many of fine Segovia serge ; and in travelling from this world to the next, the road is no wider for the prince than the peasant."

The duchess was highly amused with Sancho's proverbs and philosophy.

" My good Sancho knows full well," said she, " that the promise of a knight is held so sacred by him that he will perform it even at the expense of life. The duke, my lord and husband, though he is not of the errant order, is nevertheless a knight, and therefore will infallibly keep his word as to the promised government. Let Sancho, then, be of good cheer ; for in spite of the envy and malice of the world, before he is aware of it, he may find himself seated in the state chair of his island and territory, and in full possession of a government for which he would refuse one of brocade three storeys high. What I charge him is, to take heed how he governs his vassals, and forget not that they are well-born, and of approved loyalty."

" As to the matter of governing," answered Sancho, " let me alone for that. I am naturally charitable and good to the poor, and ' None shall dare the loaf to steal from him that sifts and kneads the meal : '—by my beads ! they shall put no false dice upon me. An old dog is not to be coaxed with a crust, and I know how to snuff my eyes and keep the cobwebs from them. And, as to governing well, the main point, in my mind, is to make a good beginning ; and, that being done, who knows but that by the time I have been fifteen days a governor, my fingers may get so nimble in the office that they will tickle it off better than the drudgery I was bred to in the field ! "

" You are in the right, Sancho," quoth the duchess, " for everything wants time : men are not scholars at their birth, and bishops are made of men, not of stones. But, to return to the subject we were just now upon, concerning the transformation of the lady Dulcinea ; I have reason to think that Sancho's artifice to deceive his master, and make him believe the peasant-girl to be Dulcinea enchanted, was, in fact, all a contrivance of some one of the magicians who persecute Don Quixote ; for really, and in truth, I know from very good authority that the country wench who so lightly sprang upon her ass was verily Dulcinea del

Toboso herself; and that my good Sancho, in thinking he had deceived his master, was himself much more deceived; and there is no more doubt of this than of any other things that we never saw. For Señor Sancho Panza must know that here also we have our enchanters, who favour us and tell us faithfully all that passes in the world; and believe me, Sancho, the jumping wench was really Dulcinea, and is as certainly charmed as the mother that bore her; and, when we least expect it, we shall see her again in her own true shape: then will Sancho discover that it was he who has been imposed upon, and not his master."

"All that might well be," quoth Sancho; "and now I begin to believe what my master told of Montesinos' cave, where he saw my lady Dulcinea del Toboso in exactly the same figure and dress as when it came into my head to enchant her, with my own will, as I fancied, though, as your ladyship says, it must have been quite otherwise. Lord bless us! How can it be supposed that my poor head-piece could, in an instant, have contrived so cunning a device, or who could think my master such a goose as to believe so unlikely a matter, upon no better voucher than myself! But, madam, your goodness will know better than to think the worse of me for all that. Lack-a-day! it cannot be expected that an ignorant lout, as I am, should be able to smell out the tricks and wiles of wicked magicians. I contrived the thing with no intention to offend my master, but only to escape his chiding; and, if it has happened otherwise, God is in heaven, and He is the judge of hearts."

"That is honestly spoken," quoth the duchess; "but, Sancho, did you not mention something of Montesinos' cave? I should be glad to know what you meant."

Sancho then gave her highness an account of that adventure, with it circumstances, and when he had done:

"See now," quoth the duchess, "if this does not confirm what I have just said! for, since the great Don Quixote affirms that he saw the very same country wench whom Sancho met coming from Toboso, she certainly must be Dulcinea, and it shows that the enchanters hereabouts are very busy and excessively officious."

Sancho again kissed the duchess's hand, and begged of her, as a favour, that good care might be taken of his Dapple, for he was the light of his eyes.

"What mean you by Dapple?" quoth the duchess.

"I mean my ass, please your highness," replied Sancho; "for not to give him that name, I commonly call him Dapple."

"Enough," quoth the duchess, "leave the care of making much of your Dapple to me; for, being a jewel of Sancho's, I will lay him upon the apple of my eye."

"Let him lie in the stable, my good lady," answered Sancho, "for upon the apple of your grandeur's eye neither he nor I are worthy to lie one single moment,—'s life! they should stick me like a sheep sooner than I would consent to such a thing."

"Carry him, Sancho," quoth the duchess, "to your government, and there you may regale him as you please, and set him free from further labour."

"Think not, my lady duchess," quoth Sancho, "that you have said much; for I have seen more asses than one go to governments, and therefore, if I should carry mine, it would be nothing new." The relish of Sancho's conversation was not lost upon the duchess, who, after dismissing him to his repose, went to give the duke an account of all that had passed between them. They afterwards consulted together how they should practise some jest upon Don Quixote, to humour his knight-errantry; and indeed they devised many of that kind, so ingenious and appropriate as to be accounted among the prime adventures that occur in this great history.

The duke and duchess were extremely diverted with the humours of their two guests; and resolving to improve their sport by practising some pleasantries that should have the appearance of a romantic adventure, they contrived to dress up a very choice entertainment from Don Quixote's account of the cave of Montesinos: taking that subject, because the duchess had observed, with astonishment, that Sancho now believed his lady Dulcinea was really enchanted, although he himself had been her sole enchanter! Accordingly, after the servants had been well instructed as to their deportment towards Don Quixote, a boar-hunt was proposed, and it was determined to set out in five or six days with a princely train of huntsmen. The knight was presented with a hunting suit proper for the occasion, which, however, he declined, saying that he must soon return to the severe duties of his profession, when, having no sumpters nor wardrobes, such things would be superfluous. But Sancho readily accepted a suit of fine green cloth which was offered to him, intending to sell it the first opportunity.

The appointed day being come, Don Quixote armed himself, and Sancho in his new suit mounted Dapple (which he preferred to a horse which was offered him) and joined the troop of hunters. The duchess issued forth magnificently attired, and Don Quixote, out of pure politeness, would hold the reins of the palfrey, though the duke was unwilling to allow it. Having arrived at the proposed scene of their diversion, which was in a wood between two lofty mountains, they posted themselves in places where the toils were to be pitched; and all the party having taken their different stations, the sport began with prodigious noise and clamour, insomuch that, between the shouts of the huntsmen, the cry of the hounds, and the sound of the horns, they could not hear each other. The duchess alighted, and with a boar-spear in her hand, took her stand in a place where she expected the boars would pass. The duke and Don Quixote dismounted also, and placed themselves by her side: while Sancho took his station behind them all, with his Dapple, whom he would not quit, lest some mischance should befall him. Scarcely had they ranged themselves in order, when a hideous boar of monstrous size rushed out of cover, pursued by the dogs and hunters, and made directly towards them, gnashing his teeth and tossing foam with his mouth. Don Quixote, on seeing him approach, braced his shield, and drawing his sword, stepped before the rest to meet him. The duke joined him with his boar-spear; and the duchess would have been the foremost, had not the duke prevented her. Sancho alone stood aghast, and, at the sight of the fierce animal, leaving even his Dapple, ran in terror towards a lofty oak, in which he hoped to be secure; but his hopes were in vain, for, as he was struggling to reach the top, and had got half-way up, unfortunately a branch to which he clung gave way, and, falling with it, he was caught by the stump of another, and here left suspended in the air, so that he could neither get up nor down. Finding himself in this situation, with his new green coat tearing, and almost in reach of the terrible creature should it chance to come that way, he began to bawl so loud and to call for help so vehemently, that all who heard him and did not see him thought verily he was between the teeth of some wild beast. The tusked boar, however, was soon laid· at length by the numerous spears that were levelled at him from all sides ; at which time Sancho's cries and lamentations reached the ears of Don Quixote, who, turning round, beheld him hanging from the oak with his head downwards, and close by him stood Dapple, who never forsook him in adversity ;—indeed, it was remarked by Cid Hamet, that he seldom saw Sancho Panza without Dapple, or Dapple without Sancho Panza : such was the amity and cordial love that subsisted between them !

Don Quixote hastened to the assistance of his squire, who was no sooner released than he began to examine the rent in his hunting suit, which grieved him to the soul : for he looked upon that suit as a rich inheritance.

The huge animal they had slain was laid across a sumpter-mule, and after covering it with branches of rosemary and myrtle, they carried it, as the spoils of victory, to a large field-tent, erected in the midst of the wood, where a sumptuous entertainment was prepared, worthy of the magnificence of the donor. Sancho, showing the wounds of the torn garments to the duchess, said :

" Had hares or birds been our game, I should not have had this misfortune. For my part I cannot think what pleasure there can be in beating about for a monster that, if it reaches you with a tusk, may be the death of you. There is an old ballad which says,—

> May fate of Fabila be thine,
> And make thee food for bears or swine."

" That Fabila," said Don Quixote, " was a king of the Goths, who, going to the chase, was devoured by a bear."

" What I mean," quoth Sancho, " is, that I would not have kings and other great folks run into such dangers merely for pleasure ; and indeed, methinks it ought to be none to kill poor beasts that never meant any harm."

" You are mistaken, Sancho," said the duke ; " hunting wild beasts is the most proper exercise for knights and princes. The chase is an image of war. Besides, it is the peculiar sport of the great. Therefore, Sancho, change your opinion before you become a governor; for then you will find your account in these diversions."

"Not so, i' faith," replied Sancho; "the good governor and the broken leg should keep at home. It would be fine indeed for people to come after him about business, and find him gadding in the mountains for his pleasure. The good paymaster wants no pawn; and God's help is better than early rising: and the belly carries the legs, and not the legs the belly:—I mean that, with the help of Heaven and a good intention, I warrant I shall govern better than a goss-hawk. Ay, ay, let them put their fingers in my mouth and try whether or not I can bite."

"A curse upon thy proverbs," said Don Quixote, "when will the day come that I shall hear thee utter one coherent sentence without that base intermixture? Let this blockhead alone, I beseech your excellencies; he will grind your souls to death, not between two, but two thousand proverbs—all timed as well, and as much to the purpose, as I wish God may grant him health, or me, if I desire to hear them."

"Sancho Panza's proverbs," said the duchess, "though more numerous than those of the Greek commentator, are equally admirable for their sententious brevity. For my own part, I must confess, they give me more pleasure than many others, more aptly suited and better timed."

After this and such-like pleasant conversation, they left the tent, and retired into the wood to examine their nets and snares. The day passed and night came on, not clear and calm, like the usual evening in summer, but in a kind of murky twilight, extremely favourable to the projects of the duke and duchess. Soon after the close of day the wood suddenly seemed to be in flames on all sides, and from every quarter was heard the sounds of numerous trumpets, and other martial instruments, as if great bodies of cavalry were passing through the wood. All present seemed petrified with astonishment at what they heard and saw. To these noises others succeeded, like the Moorish yells at the onset of battle. Trumpets, clarions, drums, and fifes, were heard, all at once, so loud and incessant, that he must have been without sense who did not lose it in the midst of so discordant and horrible a din. The duke and duchess were alarmed, Don Quixote in amazement, and Sancho Panza trembled :—in short, even those who were in the secret were terrified, and consternation held them all in silence. A post-boy, habited like a fiend, now made his appearance, blowing, as he passed onward, a monstrous horn, which produced a hoarse and frightful sound.

"Ho, courier!" cried the duke, "who are you? Whither go you? And what soldiers are those who seem to be crossing this wood?" To which the courier answered in a terrific voice :

"I am the devil, and am going in quest of Don Quixote de la Mancha. Those you inquire about are six troops of enchanters, conducting the peerless Dulcinea del Toboso, accompanied by the gallant Frenchman Montesinos, who comes to inform her knight by what means she is to be released from the power of enchantment."

"If you were the devil, as you say, and, indeed, appear to be," quoth the knight, "you would have known that I who stand before you am that same Don Quixote de la Mancha."

"Before Heaven, and on my conscience," replied the devil, "in my hurry and distraction I did not see him."

"This devil," quoth Sancho, "must needs be an honest fellow, and a good Christian, else he would not have sworn by Heaven and his conscience ; for my part, I verily believe there are some good people even in hell." The devil now, without alighting, directed his eyes to Don Quixote, and said :

"To thee, Knight of the Lions—and may I see thee between their paws! — I am sent by the valiant but unfortunate Montesinos, by whom I am directed to command thee to wait his arrival on the very spot wherever I should find thee. With him comes the lady Dulcinea del Toboso, in order to inform thee by what means thou mayst deliver her from the thraldom of enchantment. Thou hast heard my message ; I now return ;—devils like myself have thee in their keeping! and good angels that noble pair!" All were in perplexity, but especially the knight and squire : Sancho to see how Dulcinea must be enchanted in spite of plain truth, and Don Quixote from certain qualms respecting the truth of his adventures in the cave of Montesinos. While he stood musing on his subject, the duke said to him :

"Do you mean to wait, Señor Don Quixote?"

"Why not?" answered he; "here will I wait, intrepid and firm, though all hell should come to assault me."

"By my faith!" quoth Sancho, "if I should see another devil, and hear another such horn, I will no more stay here than in Flanders."

The night now grew darker, and numerous lights were seen glancing through the wood, like those exhalations which in the air appear like shooting stars. A dreadful noise was likewise heard, like that caused by the ponderous wheels of an ox-waggon, from whose harsh and continued creaking, it is said, wolves and bears fly away in terror. The turmoil, however, still increased, for at the four quarters of the wood, hostile armies seemed to be engaged: here was heard the dreadful thunder of artillery; there volleys of innumerable musqueteers; the clashing of arms, and shouts of nearer combatants, joined with the Moorish war-whoop at a distance;—in short, the horns, clarions, trumpets, drums, cannon, muskets, and above all, the frightful creaking of the waggons, formed altogether so tremendous a din, that Don Quixote had need of all his courage to stand firm, and wait the issue. But Sancho's heart quite failed him, and he fell down in a swoon at the duchess's feet. Cold water being brought at her grace's command, it was sprinkled upon his face, and his senses returned just in time to witness the arrival of one of the creaking waggons. It was drawn by four heavy oxen all covered with black palls, having also a large flaming torch fastened to each horn. On the floor of the waggon was placed a seat, much elevated, on which sat a venerable old man, with a beard whiter than snow, that reached below his girdle. His vestment was a long gown of black buckram (for the carriage was so illuminated that everything might be easily distinguished), and the drivers were two demons clothed also in black, and of such hideous aspect that Sancho, having once seen them, shut his eyes, and would not venture upon a second look.

When the waggon had arrived opposite the party, the venerable person within it arose from his seat, and, standing erect, with a solemn voice, he said:

"I am the sage Lirgandeo." He then sat down, and the waggon went forward. After that another waggon passed in the same manner, with another old man enthroned, who, when the carriage stopped, arose, and, in a voice no less solemn, said :

"I am the sage Alquife, the great friend of Urganda the Unknown." He passed on, and a third waggon advanced at the same pace ; but the person seated on the throne was not an old man, like the two former, but a man of robust form and ill-favoured countenance, who, when he came near, stood up as the others had done, and said, with a voice hoarse and diabolical :

"I am Arcalaus, the enchanter, mortal enemy of Amadis de Gaul, and all his race," and immediately proceeded onward. The three waggons halting at a little distance, the painful noise of their wheels ceased, and it was followed by the sweet and harmonious sounds of music, delightful to Sancho's ears, who, taking it for a favourable omen, said to the duchess (from whose side he had not stirred an inch) :

"Where there is music, madam, there can be no mischief."

CHAPTER LVI

THE METHOD WHEREBY DULCINEA WAS TO BE DISENCHANTED ; WITH OTHER WONDERFUL EVENTS

As the agreeable music approached, they observed that it attended a stately triumphal car, drawn by six grey mules, covered with white linen ; and upon each of them rode a penitent of light, * clothed also in white, and holding a lighted torch in his hand. The car was more than double the size of the others which had passed, and twelve penitents were ranged in order within it, all carrying lighted torches ; a sight which at once caused surprise and terror. Upon an elevated throne sat a nymph, covered with a thousand veils of silver tissue, bespangled with innumerable flowers of gold, so that her dress, if not rich, was gay and glittering. Over her head was thrown a transparent gauze, so thin that through its folds might be seen a most beautiful face ; and from

---

* In England also to be clothed in a white sheet, and bear a candle or torch in the hand, is penance ; and in the same manner the "amende honorable" is performed in France.

the multitude of lights, it was easy to discern that she was young as well as beautiful ; for she was evidently under twenty years of age, though not less than seventeen. Close by her sat a figure, clad in a magnificent robe, reaching to the feet, having his head covered with a black veil. The moment this vast machine arrived opposite to where the duke and duchess and Don Quixote stood, the attending music ceased, as well as the harps and lutes within the car. The figure in the gown then stood up, and throwing open the robe and uncovering his face, displayed the ghastly countenance of death, looking so terrific that Don Quixote started, Sancho was struck with terror, and even the duke and duchess seemed to betray some symptoms of fear. This living death, standing erect, in a dull and drowsy tone, and with a sleepy articulation, spoke as follows :

> " Merlin I am, miscalled the devil's son
> In lying annals, authorised by time :
> Monarch supreme, and great depositary
> Of magic art and Zoroastric skill ;
> Rival of envious ages, that would hide
> The glorious deeds of errant cavaliers,
> Favour'd by me and my peculiar charge,
> Though vile enchanters, still on mischief bent,
> To plague mankind their baleful art employ,
> Merlin's soft nature, ever prone to good,
> His power inclines to bless the human race.

> In Hades' chambers, where my busied ghost
> Was forming spells and mystic characters,
> Dulcinea's voice, peerless Tobosan maid,
> With mournful accents reach'd my pitying ears,
> I knew her woe, her metamorphos'd form,
> From high-born beauty in a palace graced,
> To the loathed features of a cottage wench
> With sympathising grief I straight revolved
> The numerous tomes of my detested art,
> And in the hollow of this skeleton
> My soul inclosing, hither am I come,
> To tell the cure of such uncommon ills.

O glory thou of all that case their limbs
In polished steel and fenceful adamant !
Light, beacon, polar star, and glorious guide
Of all who, starting from the lazy down,
Banish ignoble sleep for the rude toil
And hardy exercise of errant arms !
Spain's boasted pride, La Mancha's matchless knight,
Whose valiant deeds outstrip pursuing fame !
Would'st thou to beauty's pristine state restore
Th' enchanted dame, Sancho, thy faithful squire,
Must to his brawny back to the air expos'd,
Three thousand and three hundred stripes apply,
Such as may sting and give him smarting pain :
The authors of her change have thus decreed,
And this is Merlin's errand from the shades."

"What !" quoth Sancho, "three thousand lashes ! Odd's-flesh ! I will as soon give myself three stabs as three single lashes—much less three thousand ! The devil take this way of disenchanting ! I cannot see what my back has to do with enchantments. Before Heaven ! if Señor Merlin can find out no other way to disenchant the lady Dulcinea del Toboso, enchanted she may go to her grave for me !"

"Not lash thyself ! thou garlic-eating wretch !" quoth Don Quixote ; "I shall take thee to a tree, and tie thee naked as thou wert born, and there, not three thousand and three hundred, but six thousand six hundred lashes will I give thee !"

"It must not be so," said Merlin ; "the lashes that honest Sancho is to receive must not be applied by force, but with his good will, and at whatever time he pleases, for no term is fixed : and furthermore, he is allowed, if he please, to save himself half the trouble of applying so many lashes, by having half the number laid on by another hand, provided that hand be somewhat heavier than his own."

"Neither another hand nor my own," quoth Sancho, "no hand, either heavy or light, shall touch my flesh. Was the lady Dulcinea brought forth by me, that my back must pay for the transgressions of her eyes ? My master, indeed, who is part of her, since at every step he is calling her his life, his soul, his support, and stay—he it is who ought to lash himself for her, and do all that is needful for her delivery : but for me to whip myself—no, I pronounce it !"

No sooner had Sancho thus declared himself, than the spangled nymph who sat by the side of Merlin arose, and throwing aside her veil, discovered a face of extraordinary beauty : and with a masculine air, and no very amiable voice, addressed herself to Sancho : "O wretched squire—with no more soul than a pitcher ! thou heart of cork and bowels of flint ! hadst thou been required, nose-slitting thief ! to throw thyself from some high tower ; hadst thou been desired, enemy of human kind ! to eat a dozen of toads, two dozen of lizards, and three dozen of snakes ; hadst thou been requested to kill thy wife and children with some bloody and sharp scimitar—no wonder if thou hadst betrayed some squeamishness ; but to hesitate about three thousand three hundred lashes, which there is not a wretched school-boy but receives every month, it amazes, stupefies, and affrights the tender heart of all who hear it. Cast, thou marble-hearted wretch !—cast, I say, those huge goggle eyes upon these lovely orbs of mine, that shine like glittering stars, and thou wilt see them weep, drop by drop, and stream after stream, making furrows, tracks, and paths down these beautiful cheeks ! Relent, malicious and evil-minded monster ! be moved by my blooming youth, which, though yet in its teens, is pining and withering beneath the vile bark of a peasant-wench ; and if at this moment I appear otherwise, it is by the special favour of Señor Merlin, hoping that these charms may soften that iron heart ; for the tears of afflicted beauty turn rocks into cotton, and tigers into lambs. Let the anguish of that miserable knight thy master, whose soul I see sticking crosswise in his throat, not ten inches from his lips, waiting only thy cruel or kind answer either to fly out of his mouth, or return joyfully into his bosom, stir thee to compassion."

Don Quixote here putting his finger to his throat, "Before Heaven !" said he, "Dulcinea is right, for I here feel my soul sticking in my throat, like the stopper of a cross-bow !"

"What say you to that, Sancho ? " quoth the duchess.

"I say, madam," answered Sancho, "what I have already said, that, as to the lashes, I pronounce them."

"Renounce, you should say, Sancho," quoth the duke, "and not 'pronounce.'"

"Please your grandeur to let me alone," replied Sancho, "for I cannot stand now to a letter more or less: these lashes so torment me that I know not what I say or do. But I would fain know one thing from the lady Dulcinea del Toboso, and that is, where she learnt her manner of asking a favour? She comes to desire me to tear my flesh with stripes, and at the same time lays upon me such a bead-roll of ill names that the devil may bear them for me. What! does she think my flesh is made of brass? or that I care a rush whether she is enchanted or not!"

"In truth, friend Sancho," said the duke, "if you do not relent and become softer than a ripe fig, you finger no government of mine. It would be a fine thing, indeed, were I to send my good islanders a cruel, flinty-hearted tyrant. Really, Sancho, I am compelled to say—no stripes, no government."

"May I not be allowed two days, my lord," quoth Sancho, "to consider what is best for me to do?"

"In no wise can that be," cried Merlin; "on this spot and at this instant you must determine; for Dulcinea must either return to Montesinos' cave and to her rustic shape, or in her present form be carried to the Elysian fields, there to wait until the penance be completed."

"Come, friend Sancho," said the duchess, "be of good cheer, and show yourself grateful to your master, whose bread you have eaten, and to whose generous nature and noble feats of chivalry we are all so much beholden. Come, my son, give your consent, and let the devil go to the devil; leave fear to the cowardly; a good heart breaks bad fortune, as you well know."

"Well, since everybody tells me so, though the thing is out of all reason," said Sancho, "I promise to give myself the three thousand three hundred lashes, upon condition that I may lay them on whenever I please, without being tied to days or times; and I will endeavour to get out of debt as soon as I possibly can, that the beauty of my lady Dulcinea del Toboso may shine forth to all the world; as it seems she is really beautiful, which I much doubted. Another condition is, that I will not be bound to draw blood, and if some lashes happen only to fly-flap, they shall all go into the account. Moreover, if I should mistake in the reckoning, Señor Merlin here, who knows everything, shall give me notice how many I want or have exceeded."

"As for the exceedings, there is no need of keeping account of them," answered Merlin; "for when the number is completed, that instant will the lady Dulcinea del Toboso be disenchanted, and come full of gratitude in search of good Sancho, to thank and even reward him for the generous deed. So that no scruples are necessary about surplus and deficiency; and Heaven forbid that I should allow anybody to be cheated of a single hair of their head."

"Go to, then, in God's name," quoth Sancho, "I must submit to my ill fortune: I say I consent to the penance upon the conditions I have mentioned."

No sooner had Sancho pronounced his consent than the innumerable instruments poured forth their music, the volleys of musquetry were discharged, while Don Quixote clung about Sancho's neck, giving him, on his forehead and brawny cheeks, a thousand kisses; the duke and duchess, and all who were present, likewise testified their satisfaction. The car now moved on, and in departing the fair Dulcinea bowed her head to the duke and duchess, and made a low curtesy to Sancho. The party now returned home highly delighted with the evening's amusement.

CHAPTER LVII

THE STRANGE ADVENTURE OF THE ILL-USED DUENNA, OR THE COUNTESS OF TRIFALDI; AND LIKEWISE SANCHO PANZA'S LETTER TO HIS WIFE TERESA PANZA

THE whole contrivance of the last adventure was the work of the duke's steward; a man of a humorous and facetious turn of mind. He it was who composed the verses, instructed a page to perform the part of Dulcinea, and personated himself the shade of

Merlin. Assisted by the duke and duchess, he now prepared another scene still more entertaining than the former.

The next day the duchess inquired of Sancho if he had begun his penance for the relief of his unhappy lady.

"By my faith, I have," said he, "for last night I gave myself five lashes." The duchess desired to know how he had given them.

"With the palm of my hand," said he.

"That," replied the duchess, "is rather clapping than whipping, and I am of opinion that Señor Merlin will not be so easily satisfied. My good Sancho must get a rod of briars or of whipcord, that the strokes may be followed by sufficient smarting : for letters written in blood cannot be disputed, and the deliverance of a great lady like Dulcinea is not to be purchased with a song."

"Give me, then, madam, some rod or bough," quoth Sancho, "and I will use it, if it does not smart too much ; for I would have your ladyship know that, though I am a clown, my flesh has more of the cotton than of the rush, and there is no reason why I should flay myself for other folk's gain."

"Fear not," answered the duchess, "it shall be my care to provide you with a whip that shall suit you exactly, and agree with the tenderness of your flesh as if it were its own brother."

"But now, my dear lady," quoth Sancho, "you must know that I have written a letter to my wife Teresa Panza, giving her an account of all that has befallen me since I parted from her :— here it is in my bosom, and it wants nothing but the name on the outside. I wish your discretion would read it, for methinks it is written like a governor—I mean in the manner that governors ought to write."

"And who indited it ?" demanded the duchess.

"Who should indite it but I myself, sinner as I am ?" replied Sancho.

"And did you write it too ?" said the duchess.

"No, indeed," answered Sancho, "for I can neither read nor write, though I can set my mark."

"Let us see it," said the duchess, "for I dare say it shows the quality and extent of your genius." Sancho took the letter out of his bosom, unsealed it, and the duchess having taken it, read as follows :

SANCHO PANZA'S LETTER TO HIS WIFE TERESA PANZA

"If I have been finely lashed, I have been finely mounted up ; if I have got a good government, it has cost me many good lashes. This, my dear Teresa, thou canst not understand at present ; another time thou wilt. Thou must know, Teresa, that I am determined that thou shalt ride in thy coach, which is somewhat to the purpose ; for all other ways of going are no better than creeping upon all fours, like a cat. Thou shalt be a governor's wife : see then whether anybody will dare to tread on thy heels. I here send thee a green hunting-suit, which my lady duchess gave me : fit it up so that it may serve our daughter for a jacket and petticoat. They say in this country that my master Don Quixote is a sensible madman and a pleasant fool, and that I am not a whit behind him. We have been in Montesinos' cave, and the sage Merlin, the wizard, has pitched upon me to disenchant the lady Dulcinea del Toboso, who among you is called Aldonza Lorenzo. When I have given myself three thousand and three hundred lashes, lacking five, she will be as free from enchantment as the mother that bore her. Say nothing of this to anybody ; for, bring your affairs into council, and one will cry it is white, another, it is black. A few days hence I shall go to the government, whither I go with a huge desire to get money ; and I am told it is the same with all new governors. I will first see how matters stand, and send thee word whether or not thou shalt come to me. Dapple is well, and sends thee his hearty service ; part with him I will not, though I were to be made the great Turk. The duchess, my mistress, kisses thy hands a thousand times over ; return her two thousand ; for, as my master says, nothing is cheaper than civil words. God has not been pleased to throw in my way another portmanteau, and another hundred crowns, as once before : but take no heed, my dear Teresa, for he that has the game in his hand need not mind the loss of a trick—the government will make up for all. One thing only troubles me : I am told if I once try it, I shall eat my very fingers after it ; and if so, it will not be much of a bargain, though, indeed, the crippled and maimed enjoy a petty-canonry in the alms they receive ; so that, one way or another, thou art sure to be rich and happy.   God send it may be so—as He easily can, and keep me for thy sake.—Thy husband, the governor,

"SANCHO PANZA.

" From this Castle, the 20th of July, 1614."

The duchess having read the letter, said to Sancho, " In two things the good governor is a little out of the way : the one is saying, or insinuating, that this government is conferred on him on account of the lashes he is to give himself ; whereas he cannot deny, for he knows it well, that, when my lord duke promised it to him, nobody dreamt of lashes : the other is, that he appears to be covetous, and I hope no harm may come of it ; for avarice bursts the bag, and the covetous governor doeth ungoverned justice."

" Truly, madam, that is not my meaning," replied Sancho ; " and, if your highness does not like this letter, it is but tearing it, and writing a new one, which, mayhap, may prove worse, if left to thy mending."

" No, no," replied the duchess, " this is a very good one, and the duke shall see it."

They then repaired to a garden, where they were to dine that day ; and there Sancho's letter was shown to the duke, who read it with great pleasure.   After dinner, as Sancho was entertaining the company with some of his relishing conversation, they suddenly heard the dismal sound of an unbraced drum, accompanied by a fife.   All were surprised at this martial and doleful harmony, especially Don Quixote, who was so agitated that he could scarcely keep his seat.   As for Sancho, it is enough to say that fear carried him to his usual refuge, which was the duchess's side or the skirts of her petticoat ; for the sounds which they heard were truly dismal and melancholy.   While they were thus held in suspense, two young men, clad in mourning robes trailing upon the ground, entered the garden, each of them beating a great drum, covered also with black ; and with these a third, playing on the fife, in mourning like the rest.   These were followed by a person of gigantic stature, not dressed, but rather enveloped, in a robe of the blackest dye, the train whereof was of immoderate length, and over it he wore a broad black belt, in which was slung a mighty scimitar, enclosed within a sable scabbard. His face was covered by a thin black veil, through which might be discovered a long beard, white as snow. He marched forward, regulating his steps to the sound of the drums, with much gravity and stateliness. In short, his dark robe, his enormous bulk, his solemn deportment, and the funeral gloom of his figure, together with his attendants, might well produce the surprise that appeared on every countenance.

With all imaginable respect and formality he approached and knelt down before the duke, who received him standing, and would in no wise suffer him to speak till he rose up. The monstrous apparition, then rising, lifted up his veil, and exposed to view his fearful length of beard—the longest, whitest, and most luxuriant that ever human eyes beheld ; when, fixing his eyes on the duke, in a voice grave and sonorous, he said :

"Most high and potent lord, my name is Trifaldin of the White Beard, and I am squire to the Countess Trifaldi, otherwise called the Afflicted Duenna, from whom I bear a message to your highness, requesting that you will be pleased to give her ladyship permission to approach, and relate to your magnificence the unhappy and wonderful circumstances of her misfortune. But, first, she desires to know whether the valorous and invincible knight, Don Quixote de la Mancha, resides at this time in your castle ; for in quest of him she has travelled on foot, and fasting, from the kingdom of Candaya to this your territory ; an exertion miraculous and incredible, were it not wrought by enchantment. She is now at the outward gate of this castle, and only waits your highness's invitation to enter."

Having said this, he hemmed, stroked his beard from top to bottom, and with much gravity and composure stood expecting the duke's answer, which was to this effect :

"Worthy Trifaldin of the White Beard, long since have we been apprised of the afflictions of my lady the Countess Trifaldi, who, through the malice of enchanters, is too truly called the Dolorous Duenna : tell her, therefore, stupendous squire, that she may enter, and that the valiant knight Don Quixote de la Mancha is here present, from whose generous assistance she may safely promise herself all the redress she requires. Tell her also that, if my aid be necessary, she may command my services, since, as a knight, I am bound to protect all women, more especially injured and afflicted matrons like her ladyship." Trifaldin, on receiving the duke's answer, bent one knee to the ground, then giving a signal to his musical attendants, he retired with the same solemnity as he entered, leaving all in astonishment at the majesty of his figure and deportment.

The duke then turning to Don Quixote, said :

"It is evident, Sir Knight, that neither the clouds of malice nor of ignorance can obscure the light of your valour and virtue : six days have scarcely elapsed since you have honoured this castle with your presence, and, behold, the afflicted and oppressed flock hither in quest of you from far distant countries ; not in coaches, or upon dromedaries, but on foot, and fasting !—such is their confidence in the strength of that arm the fame whereof spreads over the whole face of the earth !"

"I wish, my lord duke," answered Don Quixote, "that holy person, who but a few days since expressed himself with so much acrimony against knights-errant, were now here, that he might have ascertained, with his own eyes, whether or not such knights were necessary in the world."

The sound of the drum and fife now announced the approach of the afflicted lady. The duchess asked the duke whether it would not be proper for him to go and met her, since she was a countess, and a person of quality.

"Look you," quoth Sancho before the duke could answer, "in regard to her being a countess, it is fitting your highness should go to receive her ; but, inasmuch as she is a duenna, I am of opinion you should not stir a step."

"Who desires thee to intermeddle in this matter, Sancho?" said Don Quixote.

"Who, sir," answered Sancho, "but I myself? have I not a right to intermeddle, being a squire, who has learned the rules of good manners in the school of your worship? Have I not had the flower of courtesy for my master, who has often told me that one may as well lose the game by a card too much as a card too little ; and a word is enough to the wise."

"Sancho is right," quoth the duke ; "but let us see what kind of a countess this is, and then we shall judge what courtesy is due to her." The drums and fife now advanced as before, and

"Then came the Countess Trifaldi herself, led by her squire
Trifaldin of the White Beard."

the doleful musicians were followed by twelve duennas, in two ranks, clad in large mourning robes, seemingly of milled serge, and covered with white veils of thin muslin that almost reached to their feet. Then came the Countess Trifaldi herself, led by her squire Trifaldin of the White Beard. She was clad in a robe of the finest serge, which, had it been napped, each grain would have been of the size of a good ronceval pea. This great countess, however, was induced, from the singular form of her garments, to exchange her original title of Lobuna for that of Trifaldi. The twelve duennas, with the lady, advanced slowly in procession, having their faces covered with black veils—not transparent, like that of the squire Trifaldin, but so thick that nothing could be seen through them.

On the approach of this battalion of duennas, the duke, duchess, Don Quixote, and all the other spectators, rose from their seats; and now the attendant duennas halted, and separating, opened a passage through which their afflicted lady, still led by the squire Trifaldin, advanced towards the noble party, who stepped some dozen paces forward to receive her. She then cast herself on her knees, and, with a voice rather harsh and coarse than clear and delicate, said:

"I entreat your graces will not condescend to so much courtesy to this your valet—I mean your handmaid; for my mind, already bewildered with affliction, will only be still more confounded. Alas! my unparalleled misfortune has seized and carried off my understanding, I know not whither; but surely it must be to a great distance, for the more I seek it the further it seems from me."

"He must be wholly destitute of understanding, lady countess," quoth the duke, "who could not discern your merit by your person, which alone claims all the cream of courtesy and all the flower of well-bred ceremony." Then raising her by the hand, he led her to a chair close by the duchess, who also received her with much politeness.

During the ceremony Don Quixote was silent, and Sancho dying with impatience to see the face of the Trifaldi, or of some one of her many duennas: but it was impossible, till they chose to unveil themselves. All was expectation, and not a whisper was heard, till at length the afflicted lady began in these words:

"Confident I am, most potent lord, most beautiful lady, and most discreet spectators, that my most unfortunate miserableness will find, in your generous and compassionate bowels, a most merciful sanctuary; for so doleful and dolorous is my wretched state that it is sufficient to mollify marble, to soften adamant, and melt down the steel of the hardest hearts. But, before the rehearsal of my misfortunes is commenced on the public stage of your hearing faculties, I earnestly desire to be informed whether this noble circle be adorned by that renownedissimo knight, Don Quixote de la Manchissima, and his squirissimo Panza."

"That same Panza," said Sancho, before any other could answer, "stands here before you, and also Don Quixotissimo; and therefore, most dolorous duennissima, say what you willissima; for we are all ready to be your most humble servantissimos."

Upon this Don Quixote stood up, and, addressing himself to the doleful countess, he said: "If your misfortunes, afflicted lady, can admit of remedy from the valour or fortitude of a knight-errant, the little all that I possess shall be employed in your service. I am Don Quixote de la Mancha, whose function it is to relieve every species of distress; you need not, therefore, madam, implore benevolence, nor have recourse to preambles, but plainly, and without circumlocution, declare your grievances, for you have auditors who will bestow commiseration if not redress." On hearing this the afflicted duenna attempted to throw herself at Don Quixote's feet—in truth, she did so, and, struggling to kiss them, said:

"I prostrate myself, O invincible knight, before these feet, and legs, which are the bases and pillars of knight-errantry, and will kiss these feet, whose steps lead to the end and termination of my misfortunes!"

Then, leaving Don Quixote, she turned to Sancho Panza, and taking him by the hand, said: "O thou, the most trusty squire that ever served knight-errant in present or past ages, whose goodness is of greater extent than that beard of my usher Trifaldin; I adjure thee, by thy inviolable fidelity, to intercede with thy lord on my behalf, that the light of his favour may forthwith shine upon the humblest and unhappiest of countesses."

To which Sancho answered: "Whether my goodness, madam countess, be, or be not, as long and as broad as your squire's

N

beard, is no concern of mine ; I care little or nothing for beards here below : but, without all this coaxing and beseeching, I will put in a word for you to my master, who I know has a kindness for me ; besides, just now he stands in need of me about a certain business—so, take my word for it, he shall do what he can for you. Now pray unload your griefs, madam ; let us hear all you have to say, and leave us to manage the matter."

The duke and duchess could scarcely preserve their gravity on seeing this adventure take so pleasant a turn, and were highly pleased with the ingenuity and good management of the Countess Trifaldi, who, returning to her seat, thus began her tale of sorrow : " The famous kingdom of Candaya, which lies between the great Taprobana and the South Sea, two leagues beyond Cape Comorin, had for its queen the lady Donna Maguncia, widow of King Archipiela, who died leaving the Infanta Antonomasia, their only child, heiress to the crown. This princess was brought up and educated under my care and instruction ; I being the eldest and chief of the duennas in the household of her royal mother. Now, in process of time the young Antonomasia arrived at the age of fourteen, with such perfection of beauty that nature could not raise it a pitch higher ; and, what is more, discretion itself was but a child to her ; for she was as discreet as fair, and she was the fairest creature living ; and so she still remains, if the envious fates and hard-hearted destinies have not cut short her thread of life. Her beauty attracted many suitors. Among the rest a private cavalier of the court had the audacity to aspire to that earthly heaven ; confiding in his youth, his gallantry, his sprightly and happy wit, with numerous other graces and qualifications. Indeed, I must confess to your highnesses—though with reverence be it spoken—he could touch the guitar to a miracle. He was, besides, a poet and a fine dancer, and had so rare a talent for making bird-cages that he might have gained his living by it, in case of need. So many parts and elegant endowments were sufficient to have moved a mountain, much more the tender heart of a virgin. But all his graces and accomplishments would have proved ineffectual against the virtue of my beautiful charge, had not the robber and ruffian first artfully contrived to make a conquest of me. The assassin and barbarous vagabond began with endeavouring to obtain my good will and suborn my inclination, that I might betray my trust. In short, he so plied me with toys and trinkets, and so insinuated himself into my soul, that I was bewitched. But that which chiefly brought me down, and levelled me with the ground, was a copy of verses which I heard him sing one night under my window ; and if I remember right the words were these :

> The tyrant fair whose beauty sent
>   The throbbing mischief to my heart,
> The more my anguish to augment,
>   Forbids me to reveal the smart.

"Woe is me again, miserable creature ! No, it was not his verses that vanquished me, but my own weakness ; music did not subdue me ; no, it was my own levity, my ignorance and lack of caution that melted me down, that opened the way and smoothed the passage for Don Clavijo ;—for that is the name of the treacherous cavalier. Thus being made the go-between, the wicked man was often in the chamber of the—not by him, but by me, betrayed Antonomasia, as her lawful spouse ; for, sinner as I am, never would I have consented unless he had been her true husband that he should have come within the shadow of her shoe-string ! the only mischief in the affair was that they were ill-sorted, Don Clavijo being but a private gentleman, and the Infanta Antonomasia, as I have already said, heiress of the kingdom.

"For some time this intercourse, enveloped in the sagacity of my circumspection, was concealed from every eye. At length we laid our three heads together and determined that Don Clavijo should demand Antonomasia in marriage before the vicar, in virtue of a contract signed and given him by the Infanta herself to be his wife, and so worded by my wit, that the force of Samson could not have broken through it. Our plan was immediately carried into execution ; the vicar examined the contract, took the lady's confession, and she was placed in the custody of an honest alguazil."

"Bless me !" said Sancho, "alguazils too, and poets, and songs, and roundelays, in Candaya ! I swear the world is the same everywhere ! But pray get on, good Madam Trifaldi, for it grows late, and I am on thorns till I know the end of this long story."

"I shall be brief," answered the countess.

Every word uttered by Sancho was the cause of much delight to the duchess, and disgust to Don Quixote, who having commanded him to hold his peace, the afflicted lady went on. "After many questions and answers," said she, "the Infanta stood firm to her engagement, without varying a tittle from her first declaration ; the vicar, therefore, confirmed their union as lawful man and wife, which so affected the queen Donna Maguncia, mother to the Infanta Antonomasia, that three days after we buried her.

"Scarcely, however, had we covered her with earth and pronounced the last farewell, when, ' *Quis talia fando temperet a lacrymis ?* '—lo, upon the queen's sepulchre who should appear, mounted on a wooden horse, but her cousin-german the giant Malambruno ! Yes, that cruel necromancer came expressly to revenge the death of his cousin, and to chastise the presumptuous Don Clavijo and the foolish Antonomasia, both of whom, by his cursed art, he instantly transformed—her into a monkey of brass, and him into a frightful crocodile of some strange metal ; fixing upon them, at the same time, a plate of metal, engraven with Syriac characters ; which being first rendered into the Candayan, and now into the Castilian language, have this meaning : ' These two presumptuous lovers shall not regain their pristine form till the valorous Manchegan engages with me in single combat ; since for his mighty arm alone have the destinies reserved the achievement of that stupendous adventure.' No sooner was the wicked deed performed, than out he drew from its scabbard a dreadful scimitar, and taking me by the hair of my head, he seemed prepared to cut my throat, or whip off my head at a blow ! Though struck with horror and almost speechless, trembling and weeping, I begged for mercy in such moving tones and melting words that I at last prevailed on him to stop the cruel execution which he meditated. In short, he ordered into his presence all the duennas of the palace, being those you see here present—and, after having expatiated on our fault, inveighed against duennas, their wicked plots, and worse intrigues, and reviled all for the crime of which I alone was guilty, he said, though he would vouchsafe to spare our lives, he would inflict on us a punishment that should be a lasting shame. At the same instant, we all felt the pores of our faces open, and a sharp pain all over them, like the pricking of needle-points; upon which we clapped our hands to our faces, and found them in the condition you shall now behold."

Hereupon the afflicted lady and the rest of the duennas lifted up the veils which had hitherto concealed them, and discovered their faces planted with beards of all colours, black, brown, white, and pie-bald! The duke and duchess viewed the spectacle with surprise, and Don Quixote, Sancho, and the rest were all lost in amazement.

"Thus," continued the Trifaldi, "hath that wicked and evil-minded felon Malambruno punished us!—covering our soft and delicate faces with these rugged bristles—would to heaven he had struck off our heads with his huge scimitar, rather than have obscured the light of our countenances with such an odious cloud! Alas in an evil hour were we begotten! in an evil hour were we brought into the world! Oh!"—here, being overcome with the strong sense of her calamity, she fell in a swoon.

CHAPTER LVIII

THE ADVENTURE OF THE COUNTESS TRIFALDI

WHEN Sancho saw the afflicted lady faint away, he said, "Upon the word of an honest man, and by the blood of all my ancestors, the Panzas, I swear, I never heard or saw, nor has my master ever told me, nor did such an adventure as this ever enter into his thoughts! A thousand devils take thee, Malambruno, for an enchanter and giant! Couldst thou, beast! hit upon no other punishment for those poor sinners than clapping beards upon them?"

"I would pluck off my own in the land of the Moors," said Don Quixote, "if I failed to deliver you from yours."

"Ah, valorous knight!" cried the Trifaldi, at that moment recovering from her fainting fit, "the sweet tinkling of that promise reached my hearing faculty and restored me to life. Once again, then, illustrious knight-errant and invincible hero ! let me beseech that your gracious promises may be converted into deeds."

"The business shall not sleep with me," answered Don Quixote; "therefore say, madam, what I am to do, and you shall soon be convinced of my readiness to serve you."

"Be it known then to you, sir," replied the afflicted dame, "that from this place to the kingdom of Candaya by land is computed to be about five thousand leagues, one or two more or less ; but, through the air in a direct line, it is three thousand two hundred and twenty-seven. You are likewise to understand that Malambruno told me that, whenever fortune should direct me to the knight who was to be our deliverer, he would send him a steed—not like the vicious jades let out for hire, for it should be that very wooden horse upon which Peter of Provence carried off the fair Magalona. This horse is governed by a peg in his forehead, which serves instead of a bridle, and he flies as swiftly through the air, as if the devil himself was switching him. This famous steed, tradition reports to have been formed by the cunning hand of Merlin the enchanter, who sometimes allowed him to be used by his particular friends, or those who paid him handsomely ; and he it was who lent him to his friend the valiant Peter, when, as I said before, he stole the fair Magalona : whisking her through the air behind him on the crupper, and leaving all that beheld him from the earth gaping with astonishment. Since the time of Peter, to the present moment, we know of none that mounted him ; but this we know, that Malambruno, by his art, has now got possession of him, and by this means posts about to every part of the world. To-day he is here, to-morrow in France, and the next day in Potosi ; and the best of it is, that this same horse neither eats nor sleeps, nor wants shoeing ; and, without wings, he ambles so smoothly that, in his most rapid flight the rider may carry in his hand a cup full of water without spilling a drop ! No wonder, then, that the fair Magalona took such a delight in riding him."

"As for easy going," quoth Sancho, "commend me to my Dapple, though he is no highflyer ; but by land I will match him against all the amblers in the world." The gravity of the company was disturbed for a moment by Sancho's observation; but the unhappy lady proceeded:

"Now this horse," said she, "if it be Malambruno's intention that our misfortune should have an end, will be here this very evening: for he told me that the sign by which I should be assured of my having arrived in the presence of my deliverer, would be his sending me the horse thither with all convenient despatch."

"And pray," quoth Sancho, "how many will that same horse carry?"

"Two persons," answered the lady, "one in the saddle and the other on the crupper; and generally these two persons are the knight and his squire, when there is no stolen damsel in the case."

"I would fain know," quoth Sancho, "by what name he is called."

"The name he bears is correct and significant," said the lady, "for he is called Clavileno el Aligero; * whereby his miraculous peg, his wooden frame, and extraordinary speed, are all curiously expressed: so that, in respect of his name, he may vie with the renowned Rozinante."

"I dislike not his name," replied Sancho; "but with what bridle or what halter is he guided?"

"I have already told you," answered the Trifaldi, "that he is guided by a peg, which the rider turning this way and that, makes him go either aloft in the air, or else sweeping, and, as it were, brushing the earth; or in the middle region:—a course which the discreet and wise generally endeavour to keep."

"I have a mighty desire to see him," quoth Sancho; "but to think I will get upon him, either in the saddle or behind upon the crupper, is to look for pears upon an elm-tree. It were a jest, indeed, for me, who can hardly sit my own Dapple, though upon a pannel softer than silk, to think of bestriding a wooden crupper, without either pillow or cushion! In faith, I do not intend to flay myself to unbeard the best lady in the land. Let every one shave or shear as he likes best; I have no mind for so long a journey: my master may travel by himself. Besides, I have

* Wooden-peg the Winged; compounded of "Clave," a nail, "Leno," wood.

nothing to do with it—I am not wanted for the taking off these beards, as well as the business of my lady Dulcinea."

"Indeed, my friend, you are," said the Trifaldi; "and so much need is there of your kind help, that without it nothing can be done."

"In the name of all the saints in heaven!" quoth Sancho, "what have squires to do with their masters' adventures? Are we always to share the trouble, and they to reap all the glory? Body o' me! it might be something if the writers who recount their adventures would but set down in their books, 'such a knight achieved such an adventure, with the help of such a one, his squire, without whom the devil a bit could he have done it.' I say it would be something if we had our due; but, instead of this, they coolly tell us that, 'Don Paralipomenon of the Three Stars finished the notable adventure of the six goblins,' and the like, without once mentioning his squire any more than if he had been a thousand miles off: though mayhap he, poor devil, was in the thick of it all the while! In truth, my good lord and lady, I say again, my master may manage this adventure by himself; and much good may it do him. I will stay with my lady duchess here, and perhaps when he comes back he may find Madam Dulcinea's business pretty forward: for I intend at my leisure whiles to lay it on to some purpose, so that I shall not have a hair to shelter me."

"Nevertheless, honest Sancho," quoth the duchess, "if your company be really necessary, you will not refuse to go; indeed all good people will make it their business to entreat you: for piteous, truly, would it be that, through your groundless fears, these poor ladies should remain in this unseemly plight."

"Odds my life!" exclaimed Sancho, "were this piece of charity undertaken for modest maidens, or poor charity-girls, a man might engage to undergo something: but to take all this trouble to rid duennas of their beards!—plague take them! I had rather see the whole finical and squeamish tribe bearded, from the highest to the lowest of them!"

"You seem to be upon bad terms with duennas, friend Sancho," said the duchess, "and are of the same mind as the Toledan apothecary; but in truth, you are in the wrong: for I have duennas in my family who might serve as models to all duennas;

and here is my Donna Rodriguez, who will not allow me to say otherwise."

"Your excellency may say what you please," said Rodriguez; "but Heaven knows the truth of everything, and, good or bad, bearded or smooth, such as we are, our mothers brought us forth like other women; and, since God has cast us into the world, He knows why and wherefore; and upon His mercy I rely, and not upon anybody's beard whatever."

"Enough, Signora Rodriguez," quoth Don Quixote; "as for you, Lady Trifaldi and your persecuted friends, I trust that Heaven will speedily look with a pitying eye upon your sorrows, and that Sancho will do his duty, in obedience to my wishes. Would that Clavileno were here, and on his back Malambruno himself! for I am confident no razor would more easily shave your ladyships' beards than my sword shall shave off Malambruno's head from his shoulders. If Heaven in its wisdom permits the wicked to prosper, it is but for a time."

"Ah, valorous knight!" exclaimed the afflicted lady, "may all the stars of the celestial regions regard your excellency with eyes of benignity, and impart strength to your arm and courage to your heart, to be the shield and refuge of the reviled and oppressed duennian order, abominated by apothecaries, calumniated by squires, and scoffed at by pages! O giant Malambruno! who, though enchanter, art punctual in thy promises, send us the incomparable Clavileno, that our misfortune may cease; for if the heats come on, and these beards of ours remain, woe be to us!" The Trifaldi uttered this with so much pathos that she drew tears from the eyes of all present; and so much was the heart of Sancho moved, that he secretly resolved to accompany his master to the farthest part of the world, if that would contribute to remove the bristles which deformed those venerable faces.

CHAPTER LIX

OF THE ARRIVAL OF CLAVILENO, WITH THE CONCLUSION OF THE ADVENTURE OF THE COUNTESS TRIFALDI

EVENING now came on, which was the time when the famous horse Clavileno was expected to arrive, whose delay troubled Don Quixote much, being apprehensive that, by its not arriving, either he was not the knight for whom this adventure was reserved, or that Malambruno had not the courage to meet him in single combat. But lo, on a sudden, four savages entered the garden, all clad in green ivy, and bearing on their shoulders a large wooden horse ! They set him upon his legs on the ground, and one of the savages said :

" Let the knight mount who has the courage to bestride this wondrous machine."

" Not I," quoth Sancho ; " for neither have I courage, nor am I knight."

" And let the squire, if he has one," continued the savage, " mount the crupper, and trust to valorous Malambruno ; for no other shall do him harm. Turn but the pin on his forehead and he will rush through the air to the spot where Malambruno waits ; and to shun the danger of a lofty flight, let the eyes of the riders be covered till the neighing of the horse shall give the signal of his completed journey. Having thus spoken, he left Clavileno, and with courteous demeanour departed with his companions.

The afflicted lady no sooner perceived the horse, than, almost with tears, addressing herself to Don Quixote :

"Valorous knight," said she, "Malambruno has kept his word ; here is the horse ; our beards are increasing and every one of us, with every hair of them, entreat and conjure you to shave and shear us. Mount, therefore, with your squire behind you, and give a happy beginning to your journey."

"Madam," said Don Quixote, "I will do it with all my heart, without waiting for either cushions or spurs : so great is my desire to see your ladyship and these your unfortunate friends shaven and clean."

"That will not I," quoth Sancho, "either with a bad or good will, or anywise ; and, if this shaving cannot be done without my mounting that crupper, let my master seek some other squire, or these madams some other barber : for, being no wizard, I have no stomach for these journeys. What will my islanders say when they hear that their governor goes riding upon the wind? Besides, it is three thousand leagues from here to Candaya,— what if the horse should tire upon the road, or the giant be fickle and change his mind? Seven years, at least, it would take us to travel home, and by that time I should have neither island nor islanders that would own me ! No, no, I know better things ; I know, too, that delay breeds danger ; and when they bring you a heifer, be ready with a rope. These gentlewomen's beards must excuse me ;—faith ! St. Peter is well at Rome ; and so am I too, in this house, where I am made much of ; and through the noble master thereof, hope to see myself a governor."

"Friend Sancho," said the duke, "your island neither floats nor stirs, and therefore it will keep till your return ; indeed, so fast is it rooted in the earth, that three good pulls would not tear it from its place ; and, as your know that all offices of any value are obtained by some service or other consideration, what I expect in return for this government I have conferred upon you, is only that you attend your master on this memorable occasion ; and, whether you return upon Clavileno with the expedition his speed promises, or be it your fortune to return on foot, like a pilgrim from house to house, and from inn to inn,—however it may be, you will find your island where you left it, and your islanders with the same desire to receive you for their governor. My goodwill is equally unchangeable ; and to doubt that truth, Señor Sancho, would be a notorious injury to the inclination I have to serve you."

"Good, your worship, say no more," quoth Sancho ; "I am a poor squire, and my shoulders cannot bear the weight of so much kindness. Let my master mount, let my eyes be covered, and good luck go with us. But tell me, when we are aloft, may I not say my prayers and entreat the saints and angels to help me ?"

"Yes, surely," answered the Trifaldi, "you may invoke whomsoever you please : for Malambruno is a Christian, and performs his enchantments with great discretion and much precaution."

"Well, let us away," quoth Sancho, "and Heaven prosper us ! "

"Since the memorable business of the fulling-mill," said Don Quixote, "I have never seen thee, Sancho, in such trepidation ; and were I superstitious, as some people, this extraordinary fear of thine would a little discourage me. But come hither, friend ; for, with the leave of these nobles, I would speak a word or two with thee in private."

Don Quixote then drew aside Sancho among some trees out of hearing, and taking hold of both his hands said to him, " Thou seest, my good Sancho, the long journey we are about to undertake ; the period of our return is uncertain, and Heaven alone knows what leisure or convenience our affairs may admit during our absence ; I earnestly beg, therefore, now that opportunity serves, thou wilt retire to thy chamber, as if to fetch something necessary for the journey, and there, in a trice, give thyself, if it be but five hundred lashes, in part of the three thousand and three hundred for which thou art pledged : for work well begun is half ended."

"By my soul," quoth Sancho, " your worship is stark mad ! I am just going to gallop a thousand leagues upon a bare board, and you would have me first flay myself !—verily, verily, your worship is out of all reason. Let us go and shave these duennas, and on my return I promise to make such despatch in getting out of debt, that your worship shall be contented,—can I say more ? "

"With that promise," said Don Quixote, "I feel somewhat comforted, and believe thou wilt perform it ; for, though thou art not over wise, thou art true blue in thy integrity."

"I am not blue but brown," quoth Sancho ; "but though I were a mixture of both, I would make good my promise."

The knight and squire now returned to the company ; and as they were preparing to mount Clavileno, Don Quixote said :

"Hoodwink thyself, Sancho, and get up : he that sends for us from countries so remote cannot surely intend to betray us, for he would gain little glory by deceiving those who confide in him. And supposing the success of the adventure should not be equal to our hopes, yet of the glory of so brave an attempt no malice can deprive us."

"Let us begone, sir," quoth Sancho, "for the beards and tears of these ladies have pierced my heart, and I shall not eat to do me good till I see them smooth again. Mount, sir, and hoodwink first, for if I am to have the crupper, your worship, who sits in the saddle, must get up first."

"That is true," replied Don Quixote; and, pulling a hand-kerchief out of his pocket, he requested the afflicted lady to place the bandage over his eyes; but it was no sooner done than he uncovered them saying, "I remember to have read in the Æneid of Virgil, that the fatal wooden horse dedicated by the Greeks to their tutelary goddess Minerva, was filled with armed knights, who by that stratagem got admittance into Troy, and wrought its downfall. Will it not, therefore, be prudent, before I trust myself upon Clavileno, to examine what may be in his belly?"

"There is no need of that," said the Trifaldi; "for I am confident Malambruno has nothing in him of the traitor; your worship may mount him without fear, and should any harm ensue, let the blame fall on me alone."

Don Quixote, now considering that to betray any further doubts would be a reflection on his courage, vaulted at once into his saddle. He then tried the pin, which he found would turn very easily: stirrups he had none, so that, with his legs dangling, he looked like a figure in some Roman trumph woven in Flemish tapestry.

Very slowly, and much against his will, Sancho then got up oehind, fixing himself as well as he could upon the crupper; and finding it very deficient in softness, he humbly begged the duke to accommodate him, if possible, with some pillow or cushion, though it were from the duchess's state sofa, or from one of the page's beds, as the horse's crupper seemed rather to be of marble than of wood: but the Trifaldi, interfering, assured him that Clavileno would not endure any more furniture upon him; but that, by sitting sideways, as women ride, he would find himself greatly relieved. Sancho followed her advice; and, after taking leave of the company, he suffered his eyes to be covered. But soon after he raised the bandage, and, looking sorrowfully at his friends, begged them, with a countenance of woe, to assist him at that perilous crisis with a few Pater-nosters and Ave-marias, as they hoped for the same charity from others when in the like extremity.

"What, then !" said Don Quixote, "art thou a thief in the hands of the executioner, and at the point of death, that thou hast recourse to such prayers ?   Dastardly wretch, without a soul ! dost thou not know that the fair Magalona sat in the same place, and, if there be truth in history, alighted from it, not into the grave, but into the throne of France ?   And do not I sit by thee —I that may vie with the valorous Peter, who pressed this very seat that I now press ?   Cover, cover thine eyes, heartless animal, and publish not thy shame—at least in my presence."

"Hoodwink me, then," answered Sancho ; "but, since I must neither pray myself, nor beg others to do it for me, no wonder if I am afraid that we may be followed by a legion of devils, who may watch their opportunity to fly away with us."

They were now blindfolded, and Don Quixote, feeling himself firmly seated, put his hand to the peg, upon which all the duennas, and the whole company, raised their voices at once, calling out, "Speed you well, valorous knight ! Heaven guide thee, undaunted squire ! now you fly aloft !—see how they cut the air more swiftly than an arrow ! now they mount and soar, and astonish the world below !   Steady, steady, valorous Sancho ! you seem to reel and totter in your seat—beware of falling : for, should you drop from that tremendous height, your fall would be more terrible than that of Phaeton !"   Sancho, hearing all this, pressed closer to his master, and, grasping him fast, he said, "How can they say, sir, that we are got so high, when we hear them as plain as if they were close by us ?"

"Take no heed of that, Sancho," said Don Quixote, "for in these extraordinary flights, to see or hear a thousand leagues is nothing—but squeeze me not quite so hard, good Sancho, or thou wilt unhorse me.   In truth, I see not why thou shouldst be so alarmed, for I can safely swear, an easier-paced steed I never rode in all my life—faith, it goes as glibly as if it did not move at all ! Banish fear, my friend ; the business goes on swimmingly, with a gale fresh and fair behind us."

"Speed you well, valorous knight."

"Gad, I think so too!" quoth Sancho, "for I feel the wind here, upon my hinder quarter, as if a thousand pairs of bellows were puffing at my tail." And, indeed, this was the fact, as sundry large bellows were just then pouring upon them an artificial storm; in truth, so well was this adventure managed and contrived, that nothing was wanting to make it complete.

Don Quixote now feeling the wind, "Without doubt," said he, "we have now reached the second region of the air, where the hail and snow are formed: thunder and lightning are engendered in the third region: and, if we go on mounting at this rate, we shall soon be in the region of fire; and how to manage this peg I know not, so as to avoid mounting to where we shall be burnt alive."

Just at that time some flax, set on fire, at the end of a long cane, was held near their faces: the warmth of which being felt.

"May I be hanged," said Sancho, "if we are not already there, or very near it, for half my beard is singed off—I have a huge mind, sir, to peep out and see whereabouts we are."

"Heaven forbid such rashness!" said Don Quixote: "remember the true story of the licentiate Torralvo, who was carried by devils, hoodwinked, riding on a cane, with his eyes shut, and in twelve hours reached Rome, where, lighting on the tower of Nona, he saw the tumult, witnessed the assault and death of the constable of Bourbon, and the next morning returned to Madrid, where he gave an account of all that he had seen. During his passage through the air, he said that a devil told him to open his eyes, which he did, and found himself, as he thought so near the body of the moon that he could have laid hold of it with his hand; but that he durst not look downwards to the earth, lest his brain should turn. Therefore, Sancho, let us not run the risk of uncovering in such a place, but rather trust to him who has taken charge of us, as he will be responsible: perhaps we are just now soaring aloft to a certain height, in order to come souse down upon the kingdom of Candaya, like a hawk upon a heron; and though it seems not more than half an hour since we left the garden, doubtless we have travelled through an amazing space."

"As to that I can say nothing," quoth Sancho Panza; "I can only say, that if Madam Magalona was content to ride upon this crupper without a cushion, her flesh could not have been the tenderest in the world."

This conversation between the two heroes was overheard by the duke and duchess, and all who were in the garden, to their great diversion; and, being now disposed to finish the adventure, they applied some lighted flax to Clavileno's tail; upon which, his body being full of combustibles, he instantly blew up with a prodigious report, and threw his riders to the ground. The Trifaldi, with the whole bearded squadron of duennas, vanished, and all that remained in the garden were laid stretched on the ground as if in a trance. Don Quixote and Sancho got upon their legs in but an indifferent plight, and looking round, were amazed to find themselves in the same garden with such a number of people strewed about them on all sides; but their wonder was increased, when, on a huge lance sticking in the earth, they beheld a sheet of white parchment attached to it by silken strings, whereon was written, in letters of gold, the following words:

"The renowned knight Don Quixote de la Mancha has achieved the stupendous adventure of Trifaldi the afflicted, and her companions in grief, only by attempting it. Malambruno is satisfied, his wrath is appeased, the beards of the unhappy have vanished, and Don Clavijo and Antonomasia have recovered their pristine state. When the squirely penance shall be completed, then shall the white dove, delivered from the cruel talons of the pursuing hawks, be enfolded in the arms of her beloved turtle:— such is the will of Merlin, prince of enchanters."

Don Quixote having read the prophetic decree, and perceiving at once that it referred to the disenchantment of Dulcinea, he expressed his gratitude to Heaven for having, with so much ease, performed so great an exploit, whereby many venerable females had been happily rescued from disgrace. He then went to the spot where the duke and duchess lay on the ground, and, taking the duke by the arm, he said, "Courage, courage, my good lord; the adventure is over without damage to the bars, as you will find by that record." The duke gradually, as if awaking from a sound sleep, seemed to recover his senses, as did the duchess and the rest of the party; expressing, at the same time, so much wonder and affright that what they feigned so well seemed almost reality to themselves.

Though scarcely awake, the duke eagerly looked for the scroll, and, having read it, with open arms embraced Don Quixote, declaring him to be the bravest of knights. Sancho looked all about for the afflicted dame, to see what kind of face she had when beardless, and whether she was now as goodly to the sight as her stately presence seemed to promise; but he was told that, when Clavileno came tumbling down in the flames through the air, the Trifaldi, with her whole train, vanished, with not a beard to be seen among them—every hair was gone, root and branch!

The duchess inquired of Sancho how he had fared during that long voyage?

"Why truly, madam," answered he, "I have seen wonders; for, as we were passing through the region of fire, as my master called it, I had, you must know, a mighty mind to take a peep; and though my master would not consent to it, I, who have an itch to know everything, and a hankering after whatever is forbidden, could not help, softly and unperceived, shoving the cloth a little aside, when through a crevice I looked down and there I saw (Heaven bless us!) the earth so far off that it looked to me no bigger than a grain of mustard-seed, and the men that walked upon it little bigger than hazel-nuts!—only think, then, what a height we must have been!" "Take care what you say, friend," said the duchess; "had it been so, you could not have seen the earth nor the people upon it;—a hazel-nut, good man, would have covered the whole earth." "Like enough," said Sancho, "but for all that, I had a side-view of it, and saw it all." "Take heed, Sancho," said the duchess; "for one cannot see the whole of anything by a side-view." "I know nothing about views," replied Sancho; "I only know that your ladyship should remember that, since we flew by enchantment, by enchantment I might see the whole earth, and all the men upon it, in whatever way I looked; and, if your ladyship will not credit that, neither will you believe me when I tell you that, thrusting up the kerchief close to my eyebrows, I found myself so near to heaven that it was not above a span and a half from me (bless us all! what a place it is for bigness!) and it so fell out that we passed close by the place where the seven little she-goats* are kept; and, by my faith, having been a goatherd in my youth, I no sooner saw them

---

* The Pleiades are vulgarly called in Spain, "the seven little she-goats."

but I longed to play with them awhile; and had I not done it, I verily think I should have died; so what did I but, without saying a word, softly slide down from Clavileno, and play with the sweet little creatures, which are like so many violets, for almost three-quarters of an hour; and all the while Clavileno seemed not to move from the place, nor stir a jot."

"And while honest Sancho was diverting himself with the goats," quoth the duke, "how did Señor Don Quixote amuse himself?" To which the knight answered:

"As these and such-like concerns are out of the order of nature, I do not wonder at Sancho's assertions; for my own part, I can truly say I neither looked up nor down, and saw neither heaven nor earth, nor sea nor sands. It is nevertheless certain, that I was sensible of our passing through the region of the air, and even touched upon that of fire; but that we passed beyond it, I cannot believe; for, the fiery region lying between the sphere of the moon and the uppermost region of the air, we could not reach that heaven where the seven goats are which Sancho speaks of, without being burnt; and, since we were not burnt, either Sancho lies, or Sancho dreams."

"I neither lie nor dream," answered Sancho: "only ask me the marks of these same goats, and by them you may guess whether I speak the truth or not."

"Tell us what they were, Sancho," quoth the duchess.

"Two of them," replied Sancho, "are green, two carnation, two blue, and one motley-coloured."

"A new kind of goats are those," said the duke: "in our region of the earth we have none of such colours."

"The reason is plain," quoth Sancho; "your highness will allow that there must be some difference between the goats of heaven and those of earth."

"Pr'ythee, Sancho," said the duke, "was there a he-goat * among them?"

"Not one, sir," answered Sancho; "and I was told that none are suffered to pass beyond the horns of the moon."

They did not choose to question Sancho any more concerning his journey, perceiving him to be in the humour to ramble all

---

* "Cabron."—A jest on the double meaning of that word, which signifies both he-goat and cuckold.

over the heavens, and tell them of all that was passing there without having stirred a foot from the place where he mounted.

Thus concluded the adventure of the afflicted duenna, which furnished the duke and duchess with a subject of mirth, not only at the time, but for the rest of their lives, and Sancho something to relate had he lived for ages.

"Sancho," said Don Quixote (whispering him in the ear), "if thou wouldst have us credit all thou hast told us of heaven, I expect thee to believe what I saw in Montesinos' cave—I say no more."

CHAPTER LX

THE INSTRUCTIONS DON QUIXOTE GAVE TO SANCHO PANZA BEFORE HE WENT TO HIS GOVERNMENT

THE duke and duchess being so well pleased with the afflicted duenna, were encouraged to proceed with other projects, seeing that there was nothing too extravagant for the credulity of the knight and squire. The necessary orders were accordingly issued to their servants and vassals with regard to their behaviour towards Sancho in his government of the promised island. The day after the flight of Clavileno, the duke bid Sancho prepare and get himself in readiness to assume his office, for his islanders were already wishing for him as for rain in May. Sancho made a low bow, and said:

"Ever since my journey to heaven, when I looked down and saw the earth so very small, my desire to be a governor has partly cooled: for what mighty matter is it to command on a spot no bigger than a grain of mustard-seed: where is the majesty and pomp of governing half a dozen creatures no bigger than hazel-nuts? If your lordship will be pleased to offer me some small portion of heaven, though it be but half a league, I would jump at it sooner than for the largest island in the world."

At this time Don Quixote came up to them, and hearing how soon Sancho was to depart to his government, he took him by the hand, and, with the duke's leave, led him to his chamber, in

"Sancho listened to his master with great attention."

order to give him some advice respecting his conduct in office : and, having entered, he shut the door, and, almost by force, made Sancho sit down by him, and with much solemnity proceeded to give him advice as to his conduct, mode of life, manner of bearing himself towards his fellowmen, etc. The rules of life he laid down for his squire were in the highest degree excellent, both morally and socially.

During the whole of this private conference, Sancho listened to his master with great attention, and endeavoured so to register his counsel in his mind, that he might thereby be enabled to bear the burden of government and acquit himself honourably. But so pointed did the knight at last become in his injunctions that the honest squire began to get uneasy.

"Look you, sir," replied Sancho, "if your worship thinks I am not fit for this government, I renounce it from this time ; for I have more regard for a single nail's-breadth of my soul, than for my whole body ; and plain Sancho can live as well upon bread and onions, as governor Sancho upon capon and partridge. Besides, sleep makes us all alike, great and small, rich and poor. Call to mind, too, who first put this whim of governor into my head— who was it but yourself ? for, alack, I know no more about governing islands than a bustard ; and if you fancy that in case I should be a governor, the devil will have me—in God's name, let me rather go to heaven plain Sancho, than a governor to the other place."

"Before Heaven, Sancho," quoth Don Quixote, "for those last words of thine I think that thou deservest to be governor of a thousand islands. Thou hast a good disposition, without which knowledge is of no value. Pray to God, and endeavour not to err in thy intention ; I mean, let it ever be thy unshaken purpose and design to do right in whatever business occurs ; for Heaven constantly favours a good intention. And now let us go to dinner, for I believe their highnesses wait for us."

CHAPTER LXI

HOW SANCHO PANZA WAS CONDUCTED TO HIS GOVERNMENT, AND OF THE STRANGE ADVENTURE WHICH BEFEL DON QUIXOTE IN THE CASTLE

DON QUIXOTE, in the evening of the day in which Sancho had received his admonitions, gave him a copy of them in writing, that he might get them read to him occasionally ; but they were no sooner delivered to Sancho than he dropped them, and they fell into the duke's hands, who communicated them to the duchess, and both were again surprised at the good sense and madness of Don Quixote. That very evening, in prosecution of their merry project, they despatched Sancho, with a large retinue, to the place which, to him, was to be an island. The person who had the management of the business was steward to the duke, a man of much humour, and who had, besides, a good understanding—indeed, without that there can be no true pleasantry. He it was who had already personated the Countess Trifaldi in the manner before related ; and being so well qualified, and likewise so well tutored by his lord and lady as to his behaviour towards Sancho, no wonder he performed his part to admiration.

At length Sancho set out with a numerous train. He was dressed like one of the long robe, wearing a loose gown of sad-coloured camlet, and a cap of the same. He was mounted upon a mule, which he rode gineta fashion, and behind him, by the duke's order, was led his Dapple, adorned with shining trappings of silk ; which so delighted Sancho that every now and then he turned his head to look upon him, and thought himself so happy that he would not have changed conditions with the Emperor of Germany. On taking leave of the duke and duchess, he kissed their hands : at the same time he received his master's blessing, not without tears on both sides.

It is related, then, that immediately after Sancho's departure, Don Quixote began to feel the solitary state in which he was now left, and had it been possible for him to have revoked the commission, and deprived Sancho of his government, he would certainly have done it. The duchess, perceiving this change, inquired the cause of this sadness; adding that, if it was on account of Sancho's absence, her home contained abundance of squires, duennas and damsels, all ready to serve him to his heart's desire.

"It is true, madam," answered Don Quixote, "that Sancho's absence somewhat weighs upon my heart, but that is not the principal cause of my apparent sadness; and of all your excellency's kind offers I accept only of the good-will with which they are tendered: saving that I humbly entreat that your excellency will be pleased to permit me to wait upon myself in my own apartment."

"By my faith, Señor Don Quixote," quoth the duchess, "that must not be; you shall be served by four of my damsels, all beautiful as roses."

"To me," answered Don Quixote, "they will not be roses, but even as thorns pricking me to the soul;—they must in nowise enter my chamber. If your grace would continue your favours to me, unmerited as they are, suffer me to be alone, and leave me without attendants in my chamber, that I may still keep a wall betwixt my passions and my modesty: a practice I would not forego for all your highness's liberality towards me; in truth I would rather sleep in my garments than consent that others should undress me."

"Enough, enough, Señor Don Quixote," replied the duchess: "I will surely give orders that not so much as a fly shall enter your chamber, much less a damsel. I would by no means be accessory to the violation of Señor Don Quixote's delicacy; for, by what I can perceive, the most conspicuous of his virtues is modesty."

Don Quixote repeated his thanks to the duchess; and after supper he retired to his chamber, where, comformably to his determination, he remained alone; suffering no attendants to approach him, lest he should be moved to transgress those bounds of virtuous decorum which he had ever observed towards his lady Dulcinea, and always bearing in mind the chastity of Amadis, that flower and mirror of knights-errant. He closed his door after him, and undressed himself by the light of two wax candles:

but on pulling off his stockings forth bursts some two dozen stitches in one of his stockings, giving it the resmblance of a lattice-window ! The good knight was extremely afflicted, and would have given an ounce of silver to have had just then a drachm of green silk—I say green, because his stockings were of that colour.

These melancholy reflections passed through Don Quixote's mind as he surveyed the fracture in his stocking ; nevertheless he was much comforted on finding that Sancho had left him a pair of travelling-boots, in which he immediately resolved to make his appearance the next day. He now laid himself down, pensive and heavy-hearted, not more for lack of Sancho than for the misfortune of his stocking, which he would gladly have darned, even with silk of another colour :—that more expressive token of gentlemanly poverty ! His lights were now extinguished, but the weather was sultry, and he could not compose himself to sleep ; he therefore got out of bed, and opened a casement which looked into the garden, which he had no sooner done than he heard the voices of some persons walking on the terrace below. He listened and could distinctly hear these words :

" Press me not to sing, dear Emerencia, for you know that ever since this stranger entered our castle and my eyes beheld him, I cannot sing, I can only weep. Besides, my lady does not sleep sound, and I would not for the world she should find us here. But though she should not awake, what will my singing avail, if this new Æneas, who comes hither only to leave me forlorn, awakes not to hear it ? "

" Do not fancy so, dear Altisidora," answered the other, " for I doubt not but the duchess is asleep, and everybody else in the house except the master of your heart, and disturber of your repose : he, I am sure, is awake, for even now I heard his casement open. Sing, my unhappy friend, in a low and sweet voice to the sound of your lute, and if my lady should hear us, we will plead in excuse the excessive heat of the weather."

" My fears are not on that account, my Emerencia," answered Altisidora, " but I fear lest my song should betray my heart, and that, by those who know not the mighty force of love, I might be taken for a light and wanton damsel ; but come what may, I will venture : better a blush in the face than a blot in the heart." And presently she began to touch a lute so sweetly that Don Quixote was delighted and surprised ; at the same time an infinite number of similar adventures rushed into his mind, of casements, grates, and gardens, serenades, courtships, and swoonings, with which his memory was well stored, and he forthwith imagined that some damsel belonging to the duchess had become enamoured of him : though somewhat fearful of the beautiful foe, he resolved to fortify his heart, and on no account to yield ; so, commending himself with fervent devotion to his mistress Dulcinea del Toboso, he determined to listen to the music ; and, to let the damsel know he was there, he gave a feigned sneeze, at which they were not a little pleased, as they desired above all things that he should hear them. The harp being now tuned, Altisidora sung the lyric—beginning, "Wake, Sir Knight, now love's invading."

The song of the amorous Altisidora ended, and now began the alarm of the courted Don Quixote ; who, fetching a deep sigh, said within himself : "Why am I so unhappy a knight-errant that no damsel can see but she must presently fall in love with me ? Why is the peerless Dulcinea so unlucky that she must not be suffered singly to enjoy this my incomparable constancy ? Queens, what would ye have with her ? Empresses, why do ye persecute her ? Damsels from fourteen to fifteen, why do ye plague her ? Leave, leave the poor creature ; let her triumph and glory in the lot which love bestowed upon her in the conquest of my heart, and the surrender of my soul."

Having so said, he clapped-to the casement, and, in despite and sorrow, as if some great misfortune had befallen him, threw himself upon his bed, where we will leave him for the present, to attend the great Sancho Panza, who is desirous of beginning his famous government.

CHAPTER LXII

HOW SANCHO PANZA TOOK POSSESSION OF HIS ISLAND, AND
OF THE MANNER OF HIS BEGINNING TO GOVERN IT

SANCHO, then, with all his attendants, arrived at a town containing about a thousand inhabitants, which was one of the largest and best the duke had. They gave him to understand that it was called the island of Barataria, either because Barataria was really the name of the place, or because he obtained the government of it at so cheap a rate. On his arrival near the gates of the town, which was walled about, the municipal officers came out to receive him. The bells rung, and, with all the demonstrations of a general joy and a great deal of pomp, the people conducted him to the great church to give thanks to God. Presently after, with certain ridiculous ceremonies, they presented to him the keys of the town, and constituted him perpetual governor of the island of Barataria. The garb, the beard, the thickness, and shortness of the new governor, surprised all that were not in the secret, and, indeed, those that were, who were not a few. In fine, as soon as they had brought him out of the church, they carried him to the tribunal of justice, and placed him in the chair. The duke's steward then said to him:—"It is an ancient custom here, my lord governor, that he who comes to take possession of this famous island is obliged to answer a question put to him, which is to be somewhat intricate and difficult. By his answer, the people are enabled to feel the pulse of their new governor's understanding, and, accordingly, are either glad or sorry for his coming."

While the steward was saying this, Sancho was staring at some capital letters written on the wall opposite to his chair, and, being unable to read, he asked what that writing was on the wall. He was answered: "Sir, it is there written on what day your honour took possession of this island. The inscription runs thus: 'This day, such a day of the month and year, Señor Don Sancho Panza took possession of this island. Long may he enjoy it.'"

" Pray who is it they call Don Sancho Panza ? " demanded Sancho.

" Your lordship," answered the steward ; " for no other **Panza**, besides him now in the chair, ever came into this island."

" Take notice, then, brother," returned Sancho, " that the *Don* does not belong to me, nor ever did to any of my family. I am called plain Sancho Panza ; my father was a Sancho, and my grandfather was a Sancho, and they were all Panzas, without any addition of *Dons*, or any other title whatever. I fancy there are more *Dons* than stones in this island. But enough, God knows my meaning ; and, perhaps, if my government lasts four days, I may weed out these *Dons* that overrun the country, and, by their numbers, are as troublesome as musquitoes and cousins.* On with your question, master steward, and I will answer the best I can, let the people be sorry or rejoice."

About this time two men came into court, the one clad like a country-fellow, and the other like a tailor, with a pair of shears in his hand ; and the tailor said :

" My lord governor, I and this countryman come before your worship by reason this honest man came yesterday to my shop (saving your presence, I am a tailor, and have passed my examination, God be thanked), and putting a piece of cloth into my hands, asked me : ' Sir, is there enough of this to make me a cap ? ' I, measuring the piece, answered yes. Now he, thinking that doubtless I had a mind to cabbage some of the cloth, grounding his conceit upon his own knavery, and upon the common ill opinion of tailors, bade me view it again, and see if there was not enough for two. I guessed his drift, and told him there was. Persisting in his knavish intentions, my customer went on increasing the number of caps, and I still saying yes, till we came to five caps. A little time ago he came to claim them. I offered them to him, but he refuses to pay me for the making, and insists I shall either return him his cloth, or pay him for it."

" Is all this so, brother ? " demanded Sancho.

" Yes," answered the man ; " but pray, my lord, make him produce the five caps he has made me."

* Many plebeians in Cervantes' time already arrogated to themselves the title of *Don*, which was until then reserved exclusively for the nobility.

"With all my heart," answered the tailor ; and pulling his hand from under his cloak, he showed the five caps on the ends of his fingers and thumb, saying, " Here are the five caps this honest man would have me make, and on my soul and conscience, not a shred of the cloth is left, and I submit the work to be viewed by any inspectors of the trade."

All present laughed at the number of the caps and the novelty of the suit. Sancho reflected a moment, and then said :

"I am of opinion there needs no great delay in this suit, and it may be decided very equitably off hand. Therefore I pronounce, that the tailor lose the making, and the countryman the stuff, and that the caps be confiscated to the use of the poor ; and there is an end of that."

If the sentence Sancho afterwards passed on the purse of the herdsman caused the admiration of all the bystanders, this excited their laughter. However, what the governor commanded was executed, and two old men next presented themselves before him. One of them carried a cane in his hand for a staff ; the other, who had no staff, said to Sancho :

" My lord, some time ago I lent this man ten crowns of gold to oblige and serve him, upon condition that he should return them on demand. I let some time pass without asking for them, being loth to put him to a greater strait to pay me than he was in when I lent them. But at length, thinking it full time to be repaid, I asked him for my money more than once, but to no purpose : he not only refuses payment, but denies the debt, and says I never lent him any such sum, or, if I did, that he had already paid me. I have no witnesses to the loan, nor has he of the payment which he pretends to have made, but which I deny ; yet if he will swear before your worship that he has returned the money, I from this minute acquit him before God and the world."

"What say you to this, old gentleman ? " quoth Sancho.

" I confess, my lord," replied the old fellow, "that he did lend me the money, and if your worship pleases to hold down your wand of justice, since he leaves it to my oath, I will swear I have really and truly returned it to him." The governor accordingly held down his wand, and the old fellow, seeming encumbered with his staff, gave it to his creditor to hold while he was swearing ; and then taking hold of the cross of the wand, he said it was true indeed the other had lent him ten crowns, but that he had restored them to him into his own hand : but having, he supposed, forgotten it, he was continually dunning him for them. Upon which his lordship the governor demanded of the creditor what he had to say in reply to the solemn declaration he had heard. He said that he submitted, and could not doubt but that his debtor had sworn the truth ; for he believed him to be an honest man and a good Christian ; and that, as the fault must have been in his own memory, he would thenceforward ask him no more for his money. The debtor now took his staff again, and bowing to the governor, went out of court.

Sancho having observed the defendant take his staff and walk away, and noticing also the resignation of the plaintiff, he began to meditate, and laying the fore-finger of his right hand upon his forehead, he continued a short time apparently full of thought ; and then raising his head, he ordered the old man with the staff to be called back ; and when he had returned :

"Honest friend," said the governor, "give me that staff, for I have occasion for it."

"With all my heart," answered the old fellow ; and delivered it into his hand. Sancho took it, and immediately giving it to the other old man, he said :

"There, take that, and go about your business in God's name, for you are now paid."

"I paid, my lord !" answered the old man, "what ! is this cane worth ten golden crowns ?" "Yes," quoth the governor, "or I am the greatest dunce in the world : and it shall now appear whether or not I have a head to govern a whole kingdom." He then ordered the cane to be broken in court ; which being done, ten crowns of gold were found within it. All the spectators were struck with admiration, and began to look upon their new governor as a second Solomon. They asked him how he had discovered that the ten crowns were in the cane. He told them that, having observed the defendant give it to the plaintiff to hold, while he took his oath that he had truly restored the money into his own hands, and that being done he took his staff again, it came into his head that the money in dispute must be inclosed within it.

This cause was no sooner ended, than there came into court

a woman keeping fast hold of a man clad like a rich herdsman. She came, crying aloud, "Justice, my lord governor, justice! If I cannot find it on earth, I will seek it in heaven! Lord governor of my soul, this wicked man surprised me in the middle of a field, and assaulted me." "That remains to be inquired into," said Sancho; "let us now proceed to see whether this gallant's hands are clean or not;" and, turning to the man, he asked him what he had to say in answer to this woman's complaint. The man, all in confusion, replied:

"Sir, I am a poor herdsman, and deal in swine; and this morning I went out of this town, after having sold, under correction be it spoken, four hogs; and, what between dues and exactions, the officers took from me little less than they were worth. As I was returning home, by the way I lighted upon this good dame, and the devil, the author of all mischief, led me to address her, whereupon she laid hold of me, and has never let me go till she has dragged me to this place. This is the whole truth."

Then the governor asked him if he had any silver money about him. The man answered that he had about twenty ducats in a leathern purse in his bosom. Sancho ordered him to produce it, and deliver it just as it was to the plaintiff. He did so, trembling; the woman took the purse, and making a thousand curtsies, and praying to God for the life and health of the lord governor, who took such care of poor orphans and maidens, out of the court she went, holding the purse with both hands, taking care first to see if the money that was in it was silver.

She had no sooner left the room, than Sancho said to the herdsman, who was in tears, and whose eyes and heart were gone after his purse:

"Honest man, follow that woman, and take away the purse from her, whether she will or not, and come back hither with it." This was not said to one deaf or stupid, for the man instantly flew after her like lightning, and went about doing what he was bidden.

All present were in great suspense, expecting the issue of this suit. In a few minutes came in the man and the woman, clinging together closer than the first time, she with her petticoat tucked up and the purse lapped up in it, and the man struggling to take it from her, but in vain, she defended it so stoutly. "Justice from God and the world!" cried she at the top of her lungs, "See, my lord governor, the impudence and want of fear of this varlet, who, in the midst of the town and of the street, would take from me the purse your worship commanded to be given to me."

"And has he got it?" demanded the governor.

"Got it!" answered the woman; "I would sooner let him take away my life than my purse. A pretty baby I should be, indeed! Other-guise cats must claw my beard, and not such pitiful, sneaking tools as this. Pincers and hammers, crows and chisels, shall not get it out of my clutches, nor even the paws of a lion. My soul and body shall sooner part."

"She is in the right," added the man; "I yield myself worsted and spent, and confess I have not strength enough to take it from her." That said, he left her.

Then said the governor to the womans, "Give me that purse, valiant heroine." She presently delivered it, and the governor returned it to the man, and said to the damsel, "Sister of mine, had you shown the same, or but half as much, courage and resolution in defending yourself, as you have done in defending your purse, the strength of Hercules could not have prevailed against you. Begone, in God's name, and in an ill hour, and be not found in all this island, nor in six leagues round about it, upon pain of two hundred stripes. Begone instantly, I say, thou prating, shameless, cheating hussey!" The woman was confounded and went away hanging down her head and not very well pleased. "Now, friend," said the governor to the man, "in Heaven's name get you home with your money, and hence-foward, if you would avoid worse luck, yoke not with such cattle." The countryman thanked him in the best manner he could, and went his way, leaving all the court in admiration at the acuteness and wisdom of their new governor: all of whose sentences and decrees, being noted down by the appointed historiographer, were immediately transmitted to the duke, who waited for these accounts with the utmost impatience. Here let us leave honest Sancho and return to his master, who earnestly requires our attendance—Altisidora's serenade having strangely discomposed his mind.

CHAPTER LXIII

OF THE DREADFUL ADVENTURE OF THE CATS WHICH HAPPENED TO DON QUIXOTE

WE left the great Don Quixote in bed, harassed with reflections on the conduct of the love-stricken Altisidora; not to mention others, which arose from the disaster of his stocking. He carried them with him to his couch, and had they been fleas, they could not more effectually have disturbed his rest. But Time is ever moving, and on he came leading up, at a brisk pace, the welcome morn; which was no sooner perceived by Don Quixote than, forsaking his pillow, he hastily put on his chamois doublet, and also his travelling-boots, to conceal the misfortune of his stocking. He then threw over his shoulders his scarlet mantle, and put on his head a green velvet cap trimmed with silver lace; his sharp and trusty blade he next slung over his shoulder by its belt, and now, taking up a large rosary, which he always carried about him, he marched with great state and solemnity towards the ante-chamber, where the duke and duchess expected him; and, as he passed through the gallery, he encountered Altisidora and her damsel friend, who had placed themselves in his way.

The moment Altisidora caught sight of him, she pretended to fall into a swoon, and dropped into the arms of her companion, who in haste began to unclasp her bosom. Don Quixote, observing this, approached them, and turning to the damsel:

"I well know the meaning of this," said he, "and whence these faintings proceed."

"It is more than I do," replied her friend, "for this I am sure of, that no damsel in all this family had better health than Altisidora; I have never heard so much as a sigh from her since I have known her:—ill betide all the knights-errant in the world, say I, if they are all so ungrateful. Pray, my lord Don Quixote, for pity's sake leave this place: for this poor young creature will not come to herself while you are near."

O

" Madam," said the knight, " be pleased to order a lute to be left in my chamber to-night, and I will comfort this poor damsel as far as I am able; for love in the beginning is most easily cured."

He then retreated, to avoid observation; and Altisidora, immediately recovering from her swoon, said to her companion, " By all means let him have the lute; for doubtless he intends to give us some music, which being his, cannot but be precious." When they gave the duchess an account of their jest, and of Don Quixote's desire to have a lute in his apartment, she was exceedingly diverted, and seized the occasion, in concert with the duke and her women, to plot new schemes of harmless merriment; with great glee, therefore, they waited for night, which, notwithstanding their impatience, did not seem tardy in its approach, since the day was spent in relishing conversation with Don Quixote. On the same day the duchess had also despatched a page of hers (one who had personated Dulcinea in the wood) to Teresa Panza, with her husband's letter and the bundle he had left to be sent; charging him to bring back an exact account of all that should pass.

At the hour of eleven Don Quixote retired to his chamber, where he found a lute, as he had desired. After touching the instrument lightly, he opened his casement, and, on listening, heard footsteps in the garden; whereupon he again ran over the strings of his instrument, and, after tuning it as nicely as he could, he hemmed, cleared his throat, and then with a hoarse, though not unmusical voice, sung the following song, which he had himself composed that day :

> Love, with idleness is friend,
> O'er a maiden gains its end :
> But let business and employment
> Fill up ev'ry careful moment;
> These an antidote will prove
> 'Gainst the pois'nous arts of love.
> Fair Dulcinea, queen of beauty,
> Rules my heart, and claims its duty,
> Nothing there can take her place,
> Nought her image can erase.

Whether fortune smile or frown,
Constancy's the lover's crown ;
And, its force divine to prove,
Miracles performs in love.

Thus far had Don Quixote proceeded in his song, which was heard by the duke and duchess, Altisidora, and almost all the inmates of the castle ; when suddenly from an open gallery directly over Don Quixote's window, a rope was let down, to which above a hundred little tinkling bells were fastened ; and immediately after, a huge sackful of cats, each furnished with similar bells, tied to their tails, was also let down to the window. The noise made by these cats and bells was so great and strange that the duke and duchess, though the inventors of the jest, were alarmed, and Don Quixote himself was panic-struck. Two or three of the cats made their way into his room, where, scouring about from side to side, it seemed as if a legion of devils had broken loose, and were flying about the room. They soon extinguished the lights in the chamber, and endeavoured to make their escape ; in the mean time the rope to which the bells were fastened was playing its part, and added to the discord, insomuch that all those who were not in the secret of the plot were amazed and confounded.

Don Quixote seized his sword, and made thrusts at the casement, crying out aloud :

"Avaunt, ye malicious enchanters ! avaunt, ye wizard tribe ! for I am Don Quixote de la Mancha, against whom your wicked arts avail not." Then, assailing the cats in the room, they fled to the window, where they all escaped except one, which, being hard pressed by the knight, sprung at his face, and, fixing his claws in his nose, made him roar so loud that the duke and duchess, hearing and guessing the cause, ran up in haste to his chamber, which they opened with a master-key, and there they found the poor gentleman endeavouring to disengage the creature from his face. On observing the unequal combat, the duke hastened to relieve Don Quixote ; but he cried out :

"Let no one take him off ! leave me to battle with this demon, this wizard, this enchanter ! I will teach him what it is to deal with Don Quixote de la Mancha !" The cat, however, not regarding these menaces, kept his hold till the duke happily disengaged the furious animal, and put him out of the window.

Don Quixote's face was hideously scratched all over, not excepting his nose, which had fared but ill ; nevertheless, he was much dissatisfied by the interference which had prevented him from chastising that villainous enchanter. Oil of Aparicio was brought for him, and Altisidora herself, with her lily-white hands, bound up his wounds : and while she was so employed, she said to him in a low voice :

" All these misadventures befal thee, hard-hearted knight ! as a punishment for your stubborn disdain."

To all this Don Quixote answered only with a profound sigh, and then stretched himself at full length upon his bed, thanking the duke and duchess, not for their assistance against that catish, bell-ringing crew of rascally enchanters, which he despised, but for their kind intention in coming to his succour. His noble friends then left him to repose, not a little concerned at the event of their jest, on which they had not calculated : for it was far from their intention that it should prove so severe to the worthy knight as to cost him five days' confinement to his chamber. During that period, however, an adventure befel him more relishing than the former, but which cannot, in this place, be recorded, as the historian must now turn to Sancho Panza, who had, hitherto, proceeded very smoothly in his government.

CHAPTER LXIV

GIVING A FURTHER ACCOUNT OF SANCHO'S BEHAVIOUR IN HIS GOVERNMENT

THE history relates that Sancho Panza was conducted from the court of justice to a sumptuous palace, where in a great hall he found a magnificent entertainment prepared. He had no sooner entered than his ears were saluted by the sound of many instruments, and four pages served him with water to wash his hands, which the governor received with becoming gravity. The music having ceased. Sancho now sat down to dinner in a chair of state placed at the upper end of the table; for there was but one seat, and only one plate and napkin. A personage who, as it afterwards appeared, was a physician, took his stand at one side of his chair with a whalebone rod in his hand. They then removed the beautiful white cloth which covered a variety of fruits and other eatables. Grace was said by one in a student's dress, and a laced bib was placed by a page under Sancho's chin. Another, who performed the office of sewer, now set a plate of fruit before him; but he had scarcely tasted it, when, on being touched by the wand-bearer, it was snatched away, and another containing meat instantly supplied its place. Yet, before Sancho could make a beginning, it vanished, like the former, on a signal of the wand.

The governor was surprised at this proceeding, and, looking around him, asked if this dinner was only to show off their sleight of hand.

"My lord," said the wand-bearer, "your lordship's food must here be watched with the same care as is customary with the governors of other islands. I am a doctor of physic, sir, and my duty, for which I receive a salary, is to watch over the governor's health, whereof I am more careful than of my own. I study his constitution night and day, that I may know how to restore him when sick; and therefore think it incumbent on me to pay especial regard to his meals, at which I constantly preside, to see that he eats what is good and salutary, and prevent his touching whatever I imagine may be prejudicial to his health, or offensive to his stomach. It was for that reason, my lord," continued he, "I ordered the dish of fruit to be taken away, as being too watery, and that other dish as being too hot, and over-seasoned with spices, which are apt to provoke thirst; and he that drinks much destroys and consumes the radical moisture, which is the fuel of life."

"Well, then," quoth Sancho, "that plate of roasted partridges, which seem to me to be very well seasoned, I suppose will do me no manner of harm?"

"Hold," said the doctor; "my lord governor shall not eat them while I live to prevent it."

"Pray, why not?" quoth Sancho.

"Because," answered the doctor, "our great master Hippocrates, says, 'All repletion is bad, but that from partridges the worst.'"

"If it be so," quoth Sancho, "pray cast your eye, signor doctor, over all these dishes here on the table, and see which will do me the most good, or the least harm, and let me eat of it, without whisking it away with your conjuring-stick : for, by my soul, and as Heaven shall give me life to enjoy this government, I am dying with hunger."

"Your worship is in the right, my lord governor," answered the physician. "And therefore I am of opinion you should not eat of these stewed rabbits, as being a food that is tough and acute ; of that veal, indeed, you might have taken a little, had it been neither roasted nor stewed ; but as it is, not a morsel."

"What think you, then," said Sancho, "of that huge dish there, smoking hot, which I take to be an olla-podrida ?—for, among the many things contained in it, I surely may light upon something both wholesome and toothsome."

"Absit !" quoth the doctor ; "far be such a thought from us. Olla-podrida ! there is no worse dish in the world ;—leave them to prebends and rectors of colleges, or lusty feeders at country weddings ; but let them not be seen on the tables of governors, where nothing contrary to health and delicacy should be tolerated. Simple medicines are always more estimable and safe, for in them there can be no mistake ; whereas, in such as are compounded, all is hazard and uncertainty. Therefore, what I would at present advise my lord governor to eat, in order to corroborate and preserve his health, is about a hundred small rolled-up wafers, with some thin slices of marmalade, that may sit upon the stomach, and help digestion."

Sancho, hearing this, threw himself backward in his chair, and, looking at the doctor from head to foot very seriously, asked him his name, and where he had studied. To which he answered :

"My lord governor, my name is Doctor Pedro Rezio de Aguero, I am a native of a place called Tirteafuera, lying between Caraquel and Almoddobar del Campo, on the right hand, and I have taken my doctor's degrees in the university of Ossuna."

"Then hark you," said Sancho, in a rage, "Señor Doctor

Pedro Rezio de Aguero, native of Tirteafuera, lying on the right hand as we go from Caraquel to Almoddobar del Campo, graduate in Ossuna, get out of my sight this instant!—or, by the light of heaven, I will take a cudgel, and, beginning with your carcase, will so belabour all the physic-mongers in the island, that not one of the tribe shall be left!"

On seeing the governor in such a fury, the doctor would have fled out in the hall, had not the sound of a courier's horn at that instant been heard in the street.

"A courier from my lord duke," said the sewer (who had looked out of the window), "and he must certainly have brought despatches of importance." The courier entered hastily, foaming with sweat, and in great agitation, and, pulling a packet out of his bosom, he delivered it into the governor's hands, and by him it was given to the steward, telling him to read the superscription, which was this: "To Don Sancho Panza, governor of the island of Barataria, to be delivered only to himself, or to his secretary."

"Who is my secretary?" said Sancho.

"It is I, my lord," answered one who was present, "for I can read and write, and am, besides, a Biscayan."

"With that addition," quoth Sancho, "you may well be secretary to the emperor himself;—open the packet, and see what it holds." The new secretary did so, and having run his eye over the contents, he said it was a business which required privacy. Accordingly Sancho commanded all to retire excepting the steward and sewer; and when the hall was cleared, the secretary read the following letter:

"It has just come to my knowledge, Señor Don Sancho Panza, that certain enemies of mine intend very soon to make a desperate attack, by night, upon the island under your command; it is necessary, therefore, to be vigilant and alert, that you may not be taken by surprise. I have also received intelligence, from trusty spies, that four persons in disguise are now in your town, sent thither by the enemy, who, fearful of your great talents, have a design upon your life. Keep a strict watch; be careful who are admitted to you, and eat nothing sent you as a present. I will not fail to send you assistance if you are in want of it. Whatever may be attempted, I have full reliance on your activity and judgment.—Your friend, the Duke.

"From this place, the 16th of August, at four in the morning."

Sancho was astonished at this information, and the others appeared to be no less so. At length, turning to the steward :
"I will tell you," said he, "the first thing to be done, which is, to clap Doctor Rezio into a dungeon ; for if anybody had a design to kill me, it is he, and that by the most lingering and the worst of all deaths—starvation."
"Be that as it may," said the steward, "it is my opinion your honour would do well to eat none of the meat here upon the table, for it was presented by some nuns, and it is a saying, ' The devil lurks behind the cross.' "
"You are in the right," quoth Sancho, "and for the present, give me only a piece of bread and some four pounds of grapes :— there can be no poison in them : for, in truth, I cannot live without food, and if we must keep in readiness for these battles that threaten us, it is fit that we should be well fed ; for the stomach upholds the heart, and the heart the man. Do you, Mr Secretary, answer the letter of my lord duke, and tell him his commands shall be obeyed throughout most faithfully ; and present my dutiful respects to my lady duchess, and beg her not to forget to send a special messenger with my letter and bundle to my wife Teresa Panza, which I shall take as a particular favour, and will be her humble servant to the utmost of my power. And, by the way, you may put in my hearty service to my master Don Quixote de la Mancha, that he may see that I am neither forgetful nor ungrateful ; and as to the rest, I leave it to you, as a good secretary and a true Biscayan, to add whatever you please, or that may turn to the best account. Now away with this cloth, and bring me something that may be eaten, and then let these spies, murderers, and enchanters see how they meddle with me or my island."
A page now entered, saying, "Here is a countryman who would speak with your lordship on business, as he says, of great importance."

"It is very strange," quoth Sancho, "that these men of business should be so silly as not to see that this is not a time for such matters. What! we who govern and are judges, belike, are not made of flesh and bone like other men? We are made of marblestone, forsooth, and have no need of rest or refreshment! Before Heaven, and upon my conscience, if my government lasts, as I have a glimmering it will not, I shall hamper more than one of these men of business! Well, for this once, tell the fellow to come in; but first see that he is no spy, nor one of my murderers."

"He looks, my lord," answered the page, "like a simple fellow: and I am much mistaken if he be not as harmless as a crust of bread."

The countryman, who was of goodly presence, then came in, and it might be seen a thousand leagues off that he was an honest, good soul.

"Which among you here is the lord governor?" said he.

"Who should it be," answered the secretary, "but he who is seated in the chair?"

"I humble myself in his presence," quoth the countryman; and kneeling down, he begged for his hand to kiss. Sancho refused it, and commanded him to rise and tell his business. The countryman did so, and said:

"My lord, I am a husbandman, a native of Miguel Terra, two leagues from Ciudad Real."

"What! another Tirteafuera?" quoth Sancho—"say on, brother; for let me tell you, I know Miguel Terra very well: it is not very far from my own village."

"The business is this, sir," continued the peasant: "by the mercy of Heaven, I was married in peace and in the face of the holy Roman Catholic Church. I have two sons, bred scholars; the younger studies for bachelor, and the elder for licentiate. I am a widower—for my wife died, or rather a wicked physician killed her by improper medicines; and if it had been God's will that I had had another son I would have put him to study for doctor, that he might not envy his two brothers, the bachelor and the licentiate."

"So that, if your wife," quoth Sancho, "had not died, or had not been killed, you would not now be a widower!"

" No, certainly, my lord," answered the peasant.

" We are much the nearer," replied Sancho—" go on, friend : for this is an hour rather for bed than business."

" I say, then," quoth the countryman, "that my son who is to be the bachelor, fell in love with a damsel in the same village, called Clara Perlerino, daughter of Andres Perlerino, a very rich farmer ; which name of Perlerino came to them not by lineal or any other descent, but because all of that race are paralytic ; and to mend the name, they call them Perlerinos :—indeed, to say the truth, the damsel is like any oriental pearl, and looked at on the right side, seems a very flower of the field. Pardon me if I paint her so minutely."

" Paint what you will," quoth Sancho, " for I am mightily taken with the picture : and had I but dined, I would have desired no better dessert."   " So far, so good," continued Sancho ; "and now, brother, that you have painted her from head to foot, what is it you would be at ? come to the point, without so many windings and turnings."

" What I desire, my lord," answered the countryman, " is that your lordship would do me the favour to give me a letter of recommendation to her father, begging his consent to the match, since we are pretty equal in the gifts of fortune and of nature : for, to say the truth, my lord governor, my son is possessed, and scarcely a day passes in which the evil spirits do not torment him three or four times ; and having thereby once fallen into the fire, his face is as shrivelled as a piece of scorched parchment, and his eyes are somewhat bleared and running ; but, bless him ! he has the temper of an angel ; and did he not buffet and belabour himself, he would be a very saint for gentleness."

" Would you have anything else, honest friend ? " said Sancho.

" One thing more I would ask," quoth the peasant, " but that I dare not ;—yet out it shall :—come what may, it shall not rot my breast. I say then, my lord, I could wish your worship to give me three or six hundred ducats towards mending the fortune of my bachelor—I mean, to assist in furnishing his house ; for it is agreed they shall live by themselves, without being subject to the impertinences of their fathers-in-law."

"Well," quoth Sancho, "see if there is anything else you would have, and be not squeamish in asking."

"No, nothing more," answered the peasant. The governor then rising, and seizing the chair on which he had been seated, exclaimed:

"I vow to Heaven, Don lubberly, saucy bumpkin, if you do not instantly get out of my sight, I will break your head with this chair! Son of a rascal, and the devil's own painter! At this time of day to come and ask me for six hundred ducats! Where should I have them, villain! And if I had them, idiot! why should I give them to thee? What care I for Miguel Terra, or for the whole race of the Perlerinos? Begone, I say! or by the life of my lord duke, I will be as good as my word!" The sewer made signs to the countryman to go out of the hall, which he did, hanging down his head, and seemingly much afraid lest the governor should put his threat into execution; for the knave knew very well how to play his part.

CHAPTER LXV

OF THE ADVENTURE THAT BEFEL DON QUIXOTE WITH DONNA RODRIGUEZ, THE DUCHESS'S DUENNA

THE sore-wounded Don Quixote was exceedingly discontented and melancholy, with his face bound up and marked, not by the hand of God, but by the claws of a cat: such are the misfortunes incident to knight-errantry! During six days he appeared not in public. One night, in the course of that time, lying stretched on his bed, awake and meditating on his misfortunes, and the persecution he had suffered from Altisidora, he heard a key applied to his chamber-door, and immediately concluded that the enamoured damsel herself was coming, with a determination to assault his chastity and overcome by temptation the fidelity he owed to his Lady Dulcinea del Toboso. "No," said he, not doubting the truth of what he fancied, and speaking so loud as to be overheard, "no, not the greatest beauty upon earth shall prevail upon me to cease adoring her whose image is engraven and stamped in the bottom of my soul, and in the inmost recesses of my heart!"

As he concluded these words, the door opened, and he rose up in the bed, wrapped from top to toe in a quilt of yellow satin, a woollen cap on his head, and his face and his mustachios bound up : his face, on account of its scratches, and his mustachios to keep them from flagging : in which guise a more extraordinary phantom imagination never conceived. He riveted his eyes on the door, and when he expected to see the captivated and sorrowful Altisidora enter, he perceived something that resembled a most reverend duenna gliding in, covered with a long white veil that reached from head to foot. Between the fore-finger and the thumb of her left hand she carried half a lighted candle, and held her right over it to keep the glare from her eyes, which were hidden behind a huge pair of spectacles. She advanced very slowly and with cautious tread, and as Don Quixote gazed at her form and face from his watch-tower, he was convinced that some witch or sorceress was come in that disguise to do him secret mischief, and therefore began to cross himself with much diligence.

The apparition kept moving forward, and having reached the middle of the room, it paused and raised its eyes, as if remarking how devoutly the knight was crossing himself : and if he was alarmed at seeing such a figure, she was no less dismayed at the sight of him—so lank, so yellow! enveloped in the quilt, and disfigured with bandages!

"Jesu! what do I see?" she exclaimed—and in the fright the candle fell out of her hand. Finding herself in the dark, she endeavoured to regain the door, but her feet becoming entangled in the skirts of her garment, she stumbled and fell. Don Quixote was in the utmost consternation.

"Phantom!" he cried, "or whatever thou art, say, I conjure thee : what art thou and what requirest thou of me? If thou art a soul in torment, tell me, and I will do all I can to help thee, for I am a Catholic Christian, and love to do good to all mankind. It was for that purpose I took upon me the profession of knight-errantry, which engages me to relieve even the souls in purgatory."

The fallen duenna hearing herself thus exorcised, guessed at Don Quixote's fear by her own, and in a low and doleful voice answered, " Señor Don Quixote (if peradventure your worship be Don Quixote), I am no phantom, nor apparition, nor soul in purgatory, as your worship seems to think, but Donna Rodriguez, duenna of honour to my lady duchess, and am to come to your worship with one of those cases of distress which your worship is wont to remedy."

" Tell me, then, Señora Donna Rodriguez," quoth Don Quixote, " if it happens that your ladyship comes in quality of love-messenger ? because, if so, I would have you understand that your labour will be fruitless :—thanks to the peerless beauty of my mistress, Dulcinea del Toboso."

"I bring messages, good sir !" answered the duenna ; "your worship mistakes me much : it is not so late in life with me yet as to be compelled to take such base employment. But wait, sir, till I have lighted my candle, when I will return and communicate my griefs to your worship, who are the redresser of all the grievances in the world." Thereupon she quitted the room without waiting for a reply from the knight, whom she left in a state of great suspense.

A thousand thoughts now crowded into his mind touching this new adventure, and he was of opinion that he had judged and acted improperly, to expose himself to the hazard of breaking his plighted troth to this lady, and he said to himself :

" Who knows but the devil, that father of mischief, means to deceive me now with a duenna, though he could not effect it with empresses, queens, duchesses, and ladies of high degree ? For I have often heard wise men say, ' the devil finds a better bait in a flat-nosed than a hawk-nosed woman.' "

So saying, he jumped off the bed, intending to lock the door so as to prevent the duenna's return ; but before he could effect his purpose, Señora Rodriguez entered with a lighted taper of white wax : and coming at once upon Don Quixote, wrapped up in his quilt, with bandages and nightcap, she was again alarmed, and, retreating two or three steps, she said :

" Sir Knight, am I safe ? for I take it to be no sign of modesty that your worship has got out of bed."

" I should rather ask you that question, madam," answered

Don Quixote, "and therefore tell me if I am secure from assault and ravishment."

"Of whom, or from whom, Sir Knight, do you demand that security ?" answered the duenna.

"From you, madam," replied Don Quixote : "for I am not made of marble, nor are you, I suppose, of brass ; nor is it noonday, but midnight, and even later, if I am not mistaken. But give me your hand ; for I desire no greater security than my own continence and reserve, and what that most reverend veil inspires." So saying, he kissed his right hand, and took hold of hers, which she gave him with the same ceremony.

To have seen the knight and matron walking from the chamber-door to the bedside, would have been a sight for the gods. Don Quixote resumed his situation in bed, and Donna Rodriguez sat down in a chair at some little distance from it, without taking off her spectacles or setting down her candle. Don Quixote covered himself up close, all but his face ; and after a short pause, the first who broke silence was the knight. "Now, Señora Donna Rodriguez," said he, "you may unbosom all that is in your oppressed and afflicted heart ; for you shall be listened to by me with chaste ears, and assisted with compassionate deeds." "That I verily believe," said the duenna; "and no other than so Christian an answer could be expected from a person of your worship's courtly and seemly presence." She then related that her daughter had been jilted after promise of marriage by one, of the duke's men, and that the duke himself refused to interfere.

"Be pleased, sir, I entreat you, to take pity on a fatherless daughter, and let her youth, her beauty, and all her other good parts, move you to compassion : for, on my conscience, among all my lady's damsels, there is not one that comes up to the sole of her shoe—no, not she who is cried up as the liveliest and finest of them all, whom they call Altisidora—she is not to be named with my daughter ; for, let me tell you, dear sir, that all is not gold that glitters, and that that same little Altisidora, after all, has more self-conceit than beauty ; besides, she is none of the soundest, for her breath is so foul that nobody can stand near her for a moment. Nay, indeed, as for that, even my lady duchess—but, mum, for they say walls have ears "

"Donna Rodriguez sat down in a chair without taking off her
spectacles or setting down her candle."

"What of my lady duchess?" quoth Don Quixote; "tell me, Madam Rodriguez, I conjure you."

"Your entreaties," said the duenna, "cannot be resisted; and I must tell you the truth. Has not your worship observed the beauty of my lady duchess?—that softness, that clearness of complexion, smooth and shining like any polished sword? Let me tell you, sir, she may thank God for it, in the first place, and in the next, two issues, one in each leg, that carry off all the bad humours in which, the physicians say, her ladyship abounds."

"Holy Virgin!" quoth Don Quixote, "is it possible that my lady duchess should have such drains! I should never have credited such a thing, though barefooted friars themselves had sworn it; but, since Madam Donna Rodriguez says it, so it must needs be. Yet, assuredly, from such perfection no ill humours can flow, but rather liquid amber. Well, I am now convinced that such conduits may be of importance to health."

Scarcely had Don Quixote said this, when the chamber-door suddenly burst open, which so startled Donna Rodriguez that the candle fell out of her hand, leaving the room as dark as a wolf's mouth; when instantly the poor duenna felt her throat gripped by two hands, and so hard that she had not power to cry out, while other two hands so unmercifully beslapped with a slipper, as it seemed, her scantily-protected nethermost parts, that she was presently in a woeful plight. Yet, notwithstanding the compassion which Don Quixote felt for her, he remained quietly in bed : being at a great loss what to think of the matter, and doubtful whether the same calamity might not fall on himself. Nor were his apprehensions groundless, for, after having well curried the duenna, who durst not cry out, the silent executioners then came to Don Quixote, and, turning up the bedclothes, they so pinched and tweaked him all over, that he could not forbear laying about him with his fists, in his own defence; till at last, after a scuffle of almost half an hour, the silent and invisible phantoms vanished. Donna Rodriguez then adjusted her disordered garments, and, bewailing her misfortune, hastened out of the chamber without speaking a word to the knight; who, vexed with the pinching he had received, remained in deep thought, utterly at a loss to conceive who the malicious enchanter could be that had treated him so rudely.

CHAPTER LXVI

OF WHAT BEFEL SANCHO PANZA IN GOING THE ROUND OF HIS ISLAND

NEVER was the great governor more out of humour than when we left him, from the provocation he had received from the knave of a peasant, who was one of the steward's instruments for executing the duke's projects upon Sancho. Nevertheless, simple, rough, and round as he was, he held out toughly against them all; and, addressing himself to those about him, among others the doctor Pedro Rezio (who had returned after the private despatch had been read), "I now plainly perceive," said he, "that judges and governors must or ought to be made of brass, to endure the importunities of your men of business."

At length the soul of Doctor Pedro Rezio de Tirteafuera relented, and he promised the governor he should sup that night, although it were in direct opposition to all the aphorisms of Hippocrates. With this promise his excellency was satisfied, and looked forward with great impatience to the hour of supper; and though time, as he thought, stood stock still, yet the wished-for moment came at last, when messes of cow-beef, hashed with onions, and boiled calves' feet, somewhat of the stalest, were set before him. Nevertheless, he laid about him with more relish than if they had given him Milan godwits, Roman pheasants, veal of Sorento, partridges of Moron, or geese of Lavajos; and, in the midst of supper, turning to the doctor:

"Look you, master doctor," said he, "never trouble yourself again to provide me your delicacies, or your tit-bits; for they will only unhinge my stomach, which is accustomed to goats'-flesh, cow-beef, and bacon with turnips and onions; and if you ply me with court kickshaws, it will only make my stomach queasy and loathing."

"Indeed, my lord governor," quoth the sewer, "your lordship is much in the right in all you have said, and I dare engage, in the name of all the inhabitants of this island, that they will serve your worship with all punctuality, love, and good-will; for your gentle way of governing, from the very first, leaves us no room to do, or think, anything to the disadvantage of your worship."

"I believe as much," replied Sancho, "and they would be little better than fools if they did, or thought, otherwise ; therefore I tell you once again, it is my pleasure that you look well to me and my Dapple in the article of food ; for that is the main point : and when the hour comes, we will go the round, as my intention is to clear this island of all manner of filth and rubbish ; especially vagabonds, idlers, and sharpers : for I would have you know, friends, that your idle and lazy people in a commonwealth are like drones in a beehive, which devour the honey that the labouring bees gather."

"My lord governor speaks so well," replied the steward, "that I am all admiration to hear one devoid of learning, like your worship, utter so many notable things, so far beyond the expectation of your subjects, or those who appointed you. But every day produces something new in the world ; jests turn into earnest, and the biters are bit."

The governor having supped by license of Señor Doctor Rezio, they prepared for going the round, and he set out with the secretary, the steward, the sewer, and the historiographer, who had the charge of recording his actions, together with serjeants and notaries ; altogether forming a little battalion. Sancho, with his rod of office, marched in the midst of them, making a goodly show. After traversing a few streets, they heard the clashing of swords, and, hastening to the place, they found two men fighting. On seeing the officers coming they desisted, and one of them said, "Help, in the name of Heaven and the king ! Are people to be attacked here, and robbed in the open streets ? "

"Hold, honest man," quoth Sancho, "and tell me what is the occasion of this fray ; for I am the governor."

His antagonist, interposing, said, "My lord governor, I will briefly relate the matter :—Your honour must know that this gentleman is just come from the gaming-house over the way, where he has been winning above a thousand reals, and Heaven knows how, except that I, happening to be present, was induced, even against my conscience, to give judgment in his favour in many a doubtful point; and when I expected he would have given me something, though it were but the small matter of a crown, by way of present, as it is usual with gentlemen of character like myself, who stand by, ready to back unreasonable demands, and to prevent quarrels, up he got, with his pockets filled, and marched out of the house. Surprised and vexed at such conduct, I followed him, civilly reminded him that he could not refuse me the small sum of eight reals, as he knew me to be a man of honour, without either office or pension."

"What say you to this, friend?" quoth Sancho to the other. He acknowledged that what his adversary had said was true : "he meant to give him no more than four reals, for he was continually giving him something; and they who expect snacks should be modest, and take cheerfully whatever is given them, and not haggle with the winners; unless they know them to be sharpers, and their gains unfairly gotten; and that he was no such person, was evident from his resisting an unreasonable demand : for cheats are always at the mercy of their accomplices."

"That is true," quoth the steward : "be pleased, my lord governor, to say what shall be done with these men."

"What shall be done," replied Sancho, "is this : you, master winner, whether by fair play or foul, instantly give your huckster here a hundred reals, and pay down thirty more for the poor prisoners; and you, sir, who have neither office nor pension, nor honest employment, take the hundred reals, and, some time to-morrow, be sure you get out of this island, nor set foot in it again these ten years, unless you would finish your banishment in the next life; for if I find you here, I will make you swing on a gibbet—at least the hangman shall do it for me : so let no man reply, or he shall repent it." The decree was immediately executed : the one disbursed, the other received; the one quitted the island, the other went home; and the governor said, "Either my power is small, or I will demolish these gaming-houses; for I strongly suspect that much harm comes of them."

"The house here before us," said one of the officers, "I fear your honour cannot put down; being kept by a person of quality, whose losses far exceed his gains. Your worship may exert your authority against petty gaming-houses, which do more harm and shelter more abuses than those of the gentry, where notorious cheats dare not show their faces; and since the vice of play is become so common, it is better that it should be permitted in the houses of the great than in those of low condition, where night after night unfortunate gulls are taken in, and stripped of their very skins."

"Well, master notary," quoth Sancho, "I know there is much to be said on the subject."

Soon after two serjeants came up, saying, "We have brought you, my lord governor, one in disguise who seems to be a man, but is, in fact, a woman, and no ugly one either." Two or three lanterns were immediately held up to her face, by the light of which they indeed perceived it to be that of a female, seemingly about sixteen years of age; she was beautiful as a thousand pearls, with her hair enclosed under a net of gold and green silk. They viewed her from head to foot, and observed that her stockings were flesh-coloured, her garters of white taffeta, with tassels of gold and seed pearl; her breeches were of green and gold tissue, her cloak of the same, under which she wore a very fine waistcoat of white and gold stuff, and her shoes were white like those worn by men. She had no sword, but a very rich dagger; and on her fingers were many valuable rings. All were struck with admiration of the maiden, but nobody knew her, not even the inhabitants of the town. Indeed, those who were in the secret of these jests were as much interested as the rest, for this circumstance was not of their contriving, and being, therefore, unexpected, their surprise and curiosity were more strongly excited.

The governor admired the young lady's beauty, and asked her who she was, whither she was going, and what had induced her to dress herself in that habit. With downcast eyes, she modestly answered:

"I hope, sir, you will excuse my answering so publicly what I wish so much to be kept secret:—of one thing be assured, gentlemen, I am no thief, nor a criminal, but an unhappy maiden, who, from a jealous and rigorous confinement, has been tempted to transgress the rules of decorum." The steward, on hearing this, said:

"Be pleased, my lord governor, to order your attendants to retire, that this lady may speak more freely."

The governor did so, and they all removed to a distance, excepting the steward, the sewer, and the secretary ; upon which the damsel proceeded thus :

"I am the daughter, gentlemen, of Pedro Perez Mazorca, who farms the wool of this town, and often comes to my father's house."

"This will not pass, madam," said the steward ; "for I know Pedro Perez very well, and I am sure he has neither sons nor daughters ; besides, after telling us he is your father, you immediately say that he comes often to your father's house."

"I took notice of that," quoth Sancho.

"Indeed, gentlemen," said she, "I am in such confusion that I know not what I say ; but the truth is, I am daughter to Diego de la Llana, whom you all must know."

"That may be true," answered the steward, "for I know Diego de la Llana : he is a gentleman of birth and fortune, and has a son and a daughter ; and, since he has been a widower, nobody in this town can say they have seen the face of his daughter, for he keeps her so confined that he hardly suffers the sun to look upon her ; the common report, too, is, that she is extremely handsome."

"What you say is true, sir," said the damsel, "and whether fame lies or not ; as to my beauty, you, gentlemen, who have seen me may judge." She then began to weep most bitterly ; upon which the secretary whispered the sewer :

"Something of importance, surely, must have caused a person of so much consequence as this young lady to leave her own house in such a dress, and at this unseasonable hour."

"No doubt of that," replied the sewer : "besides, this suspicion is confirmed by her tears." Sancho comforted her as well as he could, and desired her to tell the whole matter without fear, for they would be her friends, and serve her in the best manner they were able.

"The truth is, gentlemen," replied she, "that since my mother died, which is now ten years ago, my father has kept me close confined. We have a chapel in the house, where we hear mass ; and in all that time I have seen nothing but the sun in the heavens by day, and the moon and stars by night, nor do I know what streets, squares, and churches are ; nor even men, excepting my father and brother, and Pedro Perez the wool-farmer, whose constant visits to our house led me to say he was my father, to conceal the truth.   This close confinement, and being forbidden to set my foot out of doors, though it were but to church, has for many days and months past disquieted me very much, and gave me a constant longing to see the world, or at least the town where I was born ; and I persuaded myself that this desire was neither unlawful nor unbecoming.   When I heard talk of bull-fights, running at the ring, and theatrical shows, I asked my brother, who is a year younger than myself, to tell me what those things were, and several others that I have never seen. He described them as well as he could, but it only inflamed my curiosity to see them myself.   In a word, to shorten the story of my ruin, I prayed and entreated my brother—O that I had never so prayed nor entreated ! "—and here a flood of tears interrupted her narrative.

"Pray, madam," said the steward, "be comforted, and proceed ; for your words and tears keep us all in anxious suspense."

"I have but few more words," answered the damsel, "though many tears to shed : for misplaced desires like mine can be atoned for no other way."

The beauty of the damsel had made an impression on the soul of the sewer, and again he held up his lantern to have another view of her, when he verily thought her tears were orient pearls and dew-drops of the morning, and he heartily wished her misfortune might not be so great as her tears and sighs seemed to indicate.   But the governor was out of all patience at the length of her story, and therefore bid her make an end and keep them no longer, as it grew late, and they had much ground yet to pass over.   As well as the frequent interruption of sobs and sighs would let her, she continued, saying :

"My misfortune and misery is no other than this, that I desired my brother to let me put on his clothes, and take me out some night when my father was asleep, to see the town.   Yielding to my frequent entreaties, he at length gave me this habit, and dressed himself in a suit of mine, which fits him exactly, and he looks like a beautiful girl—for he has yet no beard ; and this night, about an hour ago, we contrived to get out of the house,

and with no other guide than a footboy and our own unruly
fancies, we have walked through the whole town; and as we
were returning home, we saw a great company of people before
us, which my brother said was the round, and that we must run,
or rather fly, for if we should be discovered it would be worse for
us. Upon which he set off at full speed, leaving me to follow
him; but I had not got many paces before I stumbled and fell,
and that instant a man seized me and brought me hither, where
my indiscreet longing has covered me with shame."

"Has nothing, then," quoth Sancho, "befallen you but this?
—you mentioned at first something of jealousy, I think, which
had brought you from home."

"Nothing," said she, "has befallen me but what I have said,
nor has anything brought me out but a desire to see the world,
which went no farther than seeing the streets of this town."

The truth of the damsel's story was now confirmed by the
arrival of two other serjeants, who had overtaken and seized the
brother as he fled from the sister. The female dress of the youth
was only a rich petticoat and a blue damask mantle bordered
with gold; on his head he had no other ornament or cover than
his own hair, which appeared like so many waves of gold. The
governor, the steward, and the sewer, examined him apart, and,
out of the hearing of his sister, asked why he had disguised himself in that manner. With no less bashfulness and distress, he
repeated the same story they had heard from his sister, to the
great satisfaction of the enamoured sewer.

"Really, young gentlefolks," said the governor, "this seems
only a piece of childish folly, and all these sobs and tears might
well have been spared in giving an account of your frolic. Had
you but told us your names, and said you had got out of your
father's house only to satisfy your curiosity, there would have
been an end of the story."

"That is true," answered the damsel; "but my confusion
was so great, that I knew not what I said, or how to behave
myself."

"Well, madam," said Sancho, "there is no harm done; we
will see you safe to your father's house, who, perhaps, has not
missed you; and henceforward be not so childish nor so eager to
get abroad; for 'the modest maiden and the broken leg should

keep at home'; 'the woman and the hen are lost by gadding'; and 'she who wishes to see, wishes no less to be seen'—I say no more."

The young man thanked the governor for the favour he intended them, in seeing them safe home, whither they all went; and, having reached the house, the youth threw a pebble up at a grated window, which immediately brought down one of the domestics, who opened the door, and they went in, leaving every one in admiration of their beauty and graceful demeanour, and much entertained by their desire of seeing the world by night. The sewer finding that his heart was pierced through and through, secretly resolved to demand the young lady in marriage of her father the next day, and he flattered himself that, being a servant of the duke, he should not be refused. Sancho, too, had some thoughts of matching the young man with his daughter Sanchica, and determined to bring it about the first opportunity; feeling assured that no man's son would think himself too good for a governor's daughter. Thus ended the night's round of the great Sancho: two days after also ended his government, which put an end to all his great designs and expectations, as shall hereafter be shown.

Cid Hamet, the most laborious and careful investigator into the minutest particles of this true history, says that, when Donna Rodriguez went out of her chamber to go to that of Don Quixote, another duenna, who had slept with her, observed her, and as all duennas are addicted to listening, prying into, and smelling out everything, she followed her, and with so light a foot that the good Rodriguez did not hear it; and no sooner had she entered Don Quixote's chamber, than the other, that she might not be deficient in the laudable practice of tale-bearing, in which duennas usually excel, hastened to acquaint the duchess that Donna Rodriguez was then actually in Don Quixote's chamber. The duchess immediately told the duke, and having gained his permission to go with Altisidora to satisfy her curiosity respecting this night-visit of her duenna, they silently posted themselves at the door of the knight's apartment, where they stood listening to all that was said within: but when the duchess heard her secret imperfections exposed, neither she nor Altisidora could bear it, and so, brimful of rage and eager for revenge, they bounced into

Teresa Panza.

the chamber, and seizing the offenders, inflicted the whipping and pinching before mentioned, and in the manner already related—for nothing awakens the wrath of women and inflames them with a desire of vengeance more effectually than affronts levelled at their beauty or other objects of their vanity.

The duke was much diverted with his lady's account of this night-adventure; and the duchess being still merrily disposed, now despatched a messenger extraordinary to Teresa Panza to announce her husband's promotion and also with Sancho's own letter to her (for he, having his head so full of the great concerns of his government, had quite forgotten it), and with another letter from the duchess's self, to which she added as a present a large string of rich coral beads.

Now the history tells us that the messenger employed on this occasion was a shrewd fellow, and the same page who personated Dulcinea in the wood, and, being desirous to please his lord and lady, he set off with much glee to Sancho's village, and discharged his errand admirably. Both Teresa Panza, Sancho's wife, and Sanchica, his daughter, were much impressed at what the page told them. So were their neighbours and especially the curate and the bachelor Carrasco, who came in to see and talk with the page.

The bachelor offered Teresa to write answers to her letters; but, as she looked upon him to be somewhat of a wag, she would not let him meddle in her concerns; so she gave a couple of eggs and a modicum of bread to a noviciate friar who was a penman, and he wrote two letters for her, one to her husband and the other to the duchess, both of her own inditing; and they are none of the worst things recorded in this great history, as will be seen hereafter.

CHAPTER LXVII

OF THE PROGRESS OF SANCHO PANZA'S GOVERNMENT, WITH OTHER ENTERTAINING MATTERS

Now the morning dawned that succeeded the night of the governor's round ; the remainder of which the sewer passed, not in sleep, but in pleasing thoughts of the lovely face and charming air of the disguised damsel ; and the steward in writing an account to his lord and lady of the words and actions of the new governor, who appeared to him a marvellous mixture of ignorance and sagacity. His lordship being risen, they gave him, by order of Dr Pedro Rezio, a little conserve, and four draughts of clear spring water, which, however, he would gladly have exchanged for a luncheon of bread and a few grapes. But, seeing it was rather a matter of compulsion than choice, he submitted, although with much grief of heart, and mortification of appetite : being assured by his doctor that spare and delicate food sharpened that acute judgment which was so necessary for persons in authority and high employment, where a brawny strength of body is much less needful than a vigorous understanding. By this sophistry Sancho was induced to struggle with hunger, while he inwardly cursed the government, and even him that gave it.

Nevertheless, on this fasting fare did the worthy magistrate attend to the administration of justice, and win golden opinions.

" For my part," said the steward on the conclusion of the morning sitting, "I think Lycurgus himself, who gave laws to the Lacedæmonians, could not have decided more wisely than the great Panza has done. And now let the business of the court cease for this morning, and I will give orders that my lord governor shall dine to-day much to his satisfaction."

"That," quoth Sancho, "is what I desire ; give us fair play, feed us well, and then let cases and questions rain upon me ever so thick I will despatch them in a trice."

The steward was as good as his word, for it would have gone much against his conscience to starve so excellent a governor ;

besides, he intended to come to a conclusion with him that very night, and to play off the last trick he had in commission.

Now Sancho, having dined to his heart's content, though against all the rules and aphorisms of Doctor Tirteafuera, when the cloth was removed, a courier arrived with a letter from Don Quixote to the governor. Sancho desired the secretary to read it first to himself, and then, if it contained nothing that required secrecy, to read it aloud. The secretary having done as he was commanded, "My lord," said he, "well may it be read aloud, for what Señor Don Quixote writes to your lordship deserves to be engraven in letters of gold. Pray listen to me.

"DON QUIXOTE DE LA MANCHA TO SANCHO PANZA, GOVERNOR
OF THE ISLAND OF BARATARIA.

"When I expected, friend Sancho, to have heard only of thy carelessness and blunders, I have had accounts of thy vigilance and discretion ; for which I return particular thanks to Heaven, that can raise up the lowest from their poverty, and convert the fool into a wise man. I am told, that as a governor thou art a man ; yet, as a man thou art scarcely above the brute creature—such is the humility of thy demeanour. But I would observe to thee, Sancho, that it is often expedient and necessary, for the due support of authority, to act in contradiction to the humility of the heart. The personal adornments of one that is raised to a high situation must correspond with his present greatness, and not with his former lowliness : let thy apparel, therefore, be good and becoming ; for the hedgestake, when decorated no longer, appears what it really is.

"My lady duchess has despatched a messenger to thy wife Teresa with thy hunting-suit, and also a present from herself. We expect an answer every moment. I have been a little out of order with a certain cat-clawing which befel me, not much to the advantage of my nose ; but it was nothing ; for, if there are enchanters who persecute me, there are others who defend me. Let me know if the steward who is with thee had any hand in the actions of the Trifaldi, as thou hast suspected : and give me advice, from time to time, of all that happens to thee, since the distance between us is so short. I think of quitting this idle life very soon, for I was not born for luxury and ease. A circumstance has occurred which may, I believe, tend to deprive me of the favour of the duke and duchess ; but, though it afflicts me much, it affects not my determination, for I must comply with the duties of my profession in preference to any other claim ; as it is often said, *Amicus Plato, sed magis amica Veritas.* I write this in Latin, being persuaded that thou hast learned that language since thy promotion. Farewell, and God have thee in His keeping ; so mayest thou escape the pity of the world.—Thy friend,

"DON QUIXOTE DE LA MANCHA."

Sancho listened with great attention to the letter, which was praised for its wisdom by all who heard it ; and, rising from table, he took his secretary with him into his private chamber, being desirous to send an immediate answer to his master ; and he ordered him to write, without adding or diminishing a tittle, what he should dictate to him. He was obeyed, and the answer was as follow :

"SANCHO PANZA TO DON QUIXOTE DE LA MANCHA.

"I am so taken up with business, that I have scarcely time either to scratch my head or even to pare my nails, and therefore, Heaven help me ! I wear them very long. I tell your worship this, that you may not wonder why I have given you no account before of my well or ill being in this government, where I suffer more hunger than when we both wandered about through woods and deserts.

"My lord duke wrote to me the other day, to tell me of certain spies that were come into this island to take away my life ; but, as yet, I have been able to find none, except a certain doctor, hired by the islanders to kill their governors. He calls himself Doctor Pedro Rezio, and is a native of Tirteafuera ; so your worship may see by his name that one is in danger of dying under his hands. The same doctor owns that he does not cure distempers, but prevents them, for which he prescribes nothing but fasting and fasting, till he reduces his patient to bare bones ; as if a consumption was not worse than a fever. In short, by this man's help I am in a fair way to perish by hunger and vexation ; and, instead of coming hither, as I expected, to eat hot, and drink cool, and lay my body at night between holland sheets, upon soft beds of down, I am come to do penance, like a hermit; and this goes so much against me, that I do believe the devil will have me at last.

"Hitherto, I have neither touched fee nor bribe; and how I am to fare hereafter, I know not; but I have been told that it was the custom with the governors of this island, on taking possession, to receive a good round sum by way of gift or loan from the townspeople, and furthermore, that it is the same in all other governments.

"I should be grieved to hear that you have had any disagreement with my lord and lady, for if you quarrel with them, I must come to the ground. It would ill become your worship, however, to be ungrateful towards those who have done you so many kindnesses, and entertained you so nobly in their castle.

"The cat business I don't understand—one of the tricks, mayhap, of your worship's old enemies, the enchanters; but I shall know more about it when we meet.

"I would fain send your worship a token, but I cannot tell what; but, if I continue in office I shall get fees and other pickings worth sending you. If my wife, Teresa Panza, writes to me, be so kind as to pay the postage and send me the letter; for I have a mighty desire to know how fares it with her, and my house and children. So Heaven protect your worship from evil-minded enchanters, and bring me safe and sound out of this government; which I very much doubt, seeing how I am treated by Doctor Pedro Rezio.—Your worship's servant,

"SANCHO PANZA, the Governor."

The secretary sealed the letter, and it was forthwith despatched by the courier; and, as it was now judged expedient to release the governor from the troubles of office, measures were concerted by those who had the management of these jests. Sancho passed that afternoon in making divers regulations for the benefit of his people. Among others, he strictly prohibited the monopoly and forestalling of provisions; wines he allowed to be imported from all parts, requiring only the merchant to declare of what growth it was, that a just price might be set upon it;

and whoever adulterated it, or gave it a false name, should be punished with death.　He moderated the prices of all sorts of hose and shoes, especially the latter, the current price of which he thought exorbitant.　He limited the wages of servants, which were mounting fast to an extravagant height.　He laid several penalties upon all those who should sing lewd and immoral songs, either by day or by night ; and prohibited the vagrant blind from going about singing their miracles in rhyme, unless they could produce unquestionable evidence of their truth ; being persuaded that such counterfeit tales brought discredit upon those which were genuine.　He appointed an overseer of the poor,—not to persecute them, but to examine their true claims : for under the disguise of pretended lameness and counterfeit sores are often found sturdy thieves and hale drunkards.　In short, he made many good and wholesome ordinances, which are still observed in that town ; and, bearing his name, are called, "The Regulations of the great Governor, Sancho Panza."

CHAPTER LXVIII

THE ADVENTURE OF THE SECOND AFFLICTED MATRON, OTHERWISE CALLED DONNA RODRIGUEZ

Don Quixote, being now properly healed of his wounds, began to think the life he led in that castle was against all the rules of his profession, and therefore he determined to request his noble host and hostess to grant him their permission to depart for Saragossa, as the approaching tournament drew near, wherein he proposed to win the suit of armour which was the prize at that festival.

But as he was dining one day with their highnesses, and preparing to unfold his purpose, lo ! two women, clad in deep mourning, entered the great hall, and one of them, advancing towards the table, threw herself at Don Quixote's feet, which she embraced, at the same time pouring forth so many groans that all present were astonished, and the duke and duchess suspected it to be some jest of their domestics ; yet the groans and sobs of the female appeared so much like real distress that they were in doubt, until the compassionate Don Quixote raised her from the ground, and prevailed with her to remove the veil from her weeping visage, when, to their surprise, they beheld the duenna Donna Rodriguez, accompanied by her unfortunate daughter, who had been deluded by the rich farmer's son. This discovery was a fresh cause of amazement, especially to the duke and duchess, for, though they knew the good woman's simplicity and folly, they had not thought her quite so absurd. At length Donna Rodriguez, turning to her lord and lady :

"May it please your excellencies," said she, "to permit me to speak with this gentleman, by whom I hope to be relieved from a perplexity in which we are involved by a cruel, impudent villain." The duke told her that she had his permission to say what she pleased to Don Quixote. Whereupon, addressing herself to the knight, she said, "It is not long, valorous knight, since I gave you an account how basely and treacherously a wicked peasant had used my poor dear child, this unfortunate girl here present, and you promised me to stand up in her defence and see her righted ; and now I understand that you are about to leave this castle in search of good adventures—which Heaven send you—my desire is that, before you go forth into the wide world, you would challenge that graceless villain, and force him to wed my daughter, as he promised before he over-came her maiden scruples ; for to expect justice in this affair from my lord duke would, for the reasons I mentioned to you, be to look for pears on an elm-tree ; so Heaven preserve your worship, and still be our defence."

"Worthy madam," replied Don Quixote, with much gravity and stateliness, "moderate your tears—or rather dry them up, and spare your sighs ; for I take upon me the charge of seeing your daughter's wrongs redressed : though it had been better if she had not been so ready to believe the promises of lovers, who, for the most part, are forward to make promises, and very slow to perform them. However, I will, with my lord duke's leave, depart immediately in search of this ungracious youth, and will challenge and slay him if he refuse to perform his contract : for the chief end and purpose of my profession is, to spare the humble, and chastise the proud ;—I mean to succour the wretched, and destroy the oppressor."

P

"Sir Knight," said the duke, "you need not trouble yourself to seek the rustic of whom this good duenna complains; nor need you ask my permission to challenge him: regard him as already challenged, and leave it to me to oblige him to answer it, and meet you in person here in this castle, within the lists, where all the usual ceremonies shall be observed, and impartial justice distributed; conformable to the practice of all princes, who grant the lists to combatants within the bounds of their territories."

"Upon that assurance," said Don Quixote, "with your grace's leave, I waive on this occasion the punctilios of my gentility, and degrade myself to the level of the offender, that he may be qualified to meet me in equal combat. Thus, then, though absent, I challenge and defy him, upon account of the injury he has done in deceiving this poor girl, who through his fault is no longer a maiden; and he shall either perform his promise of becoming her lawful husband, or die in the contest." Thereupon pulling off his glove, he cast it into the middle of the hall, and the duke immediately took it up, declaring, as he had done before, that he accepted the challenge in the name of his vassal, and that the combat should take place six days after, in the inner court of his castle: the arms to be those customary among knights—namely, a lance, shield, and laced suit of armour, and all the other pieces, without deceit, fraud, or any superstition whatever, to be first viewed and examined by the judges of the field.

"But first it will be necessary," he further said, "that this good duenna here, and this naughty damsel, should commit the justice of their cause to the hand of their champion Don Quixote: for otherwise the challenge would become void, and nothing be done."

"I do commit it," answered the duenna.

"And I too," added the daughter, all in tears, ashamed and confused.

The day being fixed, and the duke determined within himself what should be done, the mourning supplicants retired; at the same time the duchess gave orders that they should not be regarded as domestics, but as ladies-errant, who came to seek justice in her castle. A separate apartment was therefore allotted to them, and they were served as strangers—to the amusement of the rest of the household, who could not imagine what was to be the end of the folly and presumption on the part of the duenna and her forsaken daughter.

A choice dessert to their entertainment now succeeded, and to give it a happy completion, in came the page who had carried the letters and presents to Governor Sancho's wife, Teresa. The duke and duchess were much pleased at his return, and eager to learn the particulars of his journey. He said, in reply to their inquiries, that he could not give his report so publicly, nor in few words, and therefore entreated their graces would be pleased to hear it in private, and in the mean time accept of what amusement the letters he had brought might afford. He thereupon delivered his packet, when one of the letters was found to be addressed "To my lady duchess, of I know not where," and the other, "To my husband, Sancho Panza, governor of the island of Barataria, whom God prosper more years than me." The duchess's cake was dough, as it is said, till she had perused her letter, which she eagerly opened, and, after hastily running her eye over it, finding nothing that required secrecy, she read it aloud to the duke and the rest of the company, and the following were its contents :

TERESA PANZA'S LETTER TO THE DUCHESS.

" My lady,

" The letter your greatness sent to me made me right glad, and, in faith, I longed for it mightily. The string of corals is very good, and my husband's hunting-suit comes not short of it. All the people in our town talk of your ladyship's goodness in making my husband a governor, though nobody believes it ;— especially the priest and Master Nicholas the barber, and the bachelor Sampson Carrasco. But what care I ? for so long as the thing is so as it is, they may say what they list ; though, to own the truth, I should not have believed it myself but for the coral and the habit ; for in this village everybody takes my husband for a dolt, and cannot think what government he can be good for, but over a herd of goats. Heaven be his guide, and speed him in what is best for his children. As for me, dear honey-sweet madam, I am bent upon making hay while the sun shines, and hie me to court, to loll in my coach, though it makes a thousand that I could name stare their eyes out to see me. So pray bid my husband to send me a little money—and let it be enough : for I reckon it is dear living at court, where bread sells for sixpence, and meat for thirty maravedis the pound, which is a judgment ; and if he is not for my going, let him send me word in time, for my feet tingle to be on the tramp ; and besides, my neighbours all tell me that if I and my daughter go stately and fine at court, my husband will be better known by me than I by him ; and to be sure, many will ask, what ladies are those in that coach ? and will be told by a footman of ours that 'tis the wife and daughter of Sancho Panza, governor of the island of Barataria ; and so shall my husband be known, and I much looked upon—to Rome for everything !

"I am as sorry as sorry can be, that hereabouts there has been no gathering of acorns this year of any account ; but, for all that, I send your highness about half a peck, which I went to the hills for, and with my own hands picked them one by one, and could find no better—I wish they had been as big as ostrich eggs.

"Pray let not your mightiness forget to write to me, and I will take care to answer, and send you tidings of my health, and all the news of the village where I now remain, praying our Lord to preserve your greatness, and not to forget me. My daughter Sanchica and my son kiss your ladyship's hands.—She who is more minded to see than to write to your ladyship.—Your servant,   TERESA PANZA."

Teresa's letter gave great pleasure to all who heard it, especially the duke and duchess, insomuch that her grace asked Don Quixote if he thought her letter to the governor might with propriety be opened, as it must needs be admirable : to which he replied that, to satisfy her highness's curiosity, he would open it. Accordingly he did so, and found it to contain what follows :

TERESA PANZA'S LETTER TO HER HUSBAND SANCHO PANZA.

"I received thy letter, dear husband of my soul, and I vow and swear to thee, as I am a Catholic Christian, that I was within

two fingers' breadth of running mad with joy. Yes, indeed, when
I came to hear that thou wast a governor, methought I should
have dropped down dead for mere gladness; for 'tis said, thou
know'st, that sudden joy kills as soon as great sorrow. And as
for our daughter Sanchica, verily she could not contain herself,
for pure pleasure. There I had before my eyes thy suit, and the
corals sent by my lady duchess about my neck, and the letters in
my hands, and the young man that brought them standing by;
yet, for all that, I thought it could be nothing but a dream: for
who could think that a goatherd should ever come to be a governor
of islands! My mother used to say that 'he who would see
much must live long.' I say this because, if I live longer, I hope
to see more;—no, faith, I shall not rest till I see thee a tax-
farmer, or a collector of the customs: for, though they be offices
that send many to the devil, there is much money to be touched
and turned. My lady duchess will tell thee how I have a huge
longing to go to court—think of it, and let me know thy mind:
for I would fain do thee credit there by riding in a
coach.

" Neither the priest, the barber, the bachelor, nor even the
sexton, can yet believe thou art a governor, and will have it that
it is all a cheat, or a matter of enchantment, like the rest of thy
master Don Quixote's affairs; and Sampson says he will find
thee out, and drive this government out of thy pate, and scour
thy master's brains. Sanchica makes bone-lace, and gets eight
maravedis a day, which she drops into a saving-box, to help her
towards household stuff; but now that she is a governor's
daughter she has no need to work, for thou wilt give her a
portion without it. The fountain in our market-place is dried
up. A thunderbolt fell upon the pillory, and there may they all
light! I expect an answer to this, and about my going to court.
And so God grant thee more years than myself, or as many,
for I would not willingly leave thee behind me.—Thy wife,
"TERESA PANZA."

This letter caused much merriment, applause, and admiration;
and to complete all, the courier now arrived, who brought the
letter sent by Sancho to his master, which was also read aloud,
and occasioned the governor's folly to be much questioned. The

duchess retired to hear from the page the particulars of his journey to Sancho's village, all of which he related very minutely, without omitting a single circumstance. He delivered the acorns, also a cheese, which Teresa presented as an excellent one, and better than those of Tronchon. These the duchess received with great satisfaction ; and here we will leave them, to record how the government ended of the great Sancho Panza, the flower and mirror of all island governors.

CHAPTER LXIX

OF THE TOILSOME END AND CONCLUSION OF SANCHO PANZA'S GOVERNMENT

THE governor being in bed on the seventh night of his administration, not sated with bread or wine, but with sitting in judgment, deciding causes, and making statutes and proclamations ; and just at the moment when sleep, in despite of hunger, was closing his eyelids, he heard such a noise of bells and voices that he verily thought the whole island had been sinking. He started up in his bed, and listened with great attention, to find out, if possible, the cause of so alarming an uproar : but far from discovering it, his confusion and terror were only augmented by the din of an infinite number of trumpets and drums being added to the former noises. Quitting his bed, he put on his slippers, on account of the damp floor ; but, without night-gown, or other apparel, he opened his chamber-door, and saw more than twenty persons coming along a gallery with lighted torches in their hands, and their swords drawn, all crying aloud, "Arm, arm, my lord governor, arm !—a world of enemies are got into the island, and we are undone for ever, if your conduct and valour do not save us." Thus advancing, with noise and disorder, they came up to where Sancho stood, astonished and stupefied with what he heard and saw. "Arm yourself quickly, my lord," said one of them, "unless you would be ruined, and the whole island with you." "What have I to do with arming," replied Sancho, "who know nothing of arms or fighting ? It

were better to leave these matters to my master Don Quixote,
who will despatch them and secure us in a trice: for as I am a
sinner to Heaven, I understand nothing at all of these hurly-
burlys." "How! Señor Governor?" said another; "what
faint-heartedness is this? Here we bring you arms and weapons
—harness yourself, my lord, and come forth to the market-place,
and be our leader and our captain, which, as governor, you ought
to be." "Why then arm me, in God's name," replied Sancho:
and instantly they brought two large old targets, which they had
provided for the occasion, and, without allowing him to put on
other garments, clapped them over his shirt, the one before and
the other behind. They thrust his arms through holes they had
made in them, and bound them so fast together with cords that
the poor commander remained cased and boarded up as stiff and
straight as a spindle, without power to bend his knees, or stir a
single step. They then put a lance into his hand, upon which he
leaned to keep himself up; and thus accoutred, they desired him
to lead on and animate his people; for he being their north-pole,
their lanthorn, and their morning star, their affairs could not fail
to have a prosperous issue.

"How should I march—wretch that I am!" said the
governor, "when I cannot stir a joint between these boards, that
press into my flesh? Your only way is to carry me in your arms,
and lay me athwart, or set me upright, at some gate, which I
will maintain either with my lance or my body."

"Fie, Señor Governor!" said another, "it is more fear than
the targets that hinders your marching. Hasten and exert yourself, for time advances, the enemy pours in upon us, and every
moment increases our danger."

The unfortunate governor, thus urged and upbraided, made
efforts to move, and down he fell, with such violence that he
thought every bone had been broken; and there he lay, like a
tortoise in his shell, or like a flitch of bacon packed between two
boards, or like a boat on the sands keel upwards. Though they
saw his disaster, those jesting rogues had no compassion; on the
contrary, putting out their torches, they renewed the alarm, and,
with terrible noise and precipitation, trampled over his body; and
bestowed numerous blows upon the targets, insomuch that, if he
had not contrived to shelter his head between the bucklers, it had

gone hard with the poor governor, who, pent up within his narrow lodging, and sweating with fear, prayed, from the bottom of his heart, for deliverance from that horrible situation. Some kicked him, others stumbled, and fell over him, and one among them jumped upon his body, and there stood as on a watch-tower, issuing his orders to the troops. " There, boys, there ! that way the enemy charges thickest ; defend that breach ; secure yon gate : down with those scaling ladders ; this way with your kettles of melted pitch, resin, and flaming oil ; quick ! fly !—get woolpacks and barricade the streets ! " In short, he called for all the instruments of death, and everything employed in the defence of a city besieged and stormed. All this while Sancho, pressed and battered, lay and heard what was passing, and often said to himself, " O that it would please the Lord that this island were but taken, and I could see myself either dead or delivered out of this devil's den ! " Heaven at last heard his prayers, and, when least expecting it, he was cheered with shouts of triumph.

"Victory ! victory ! " they cried, " the enemy is routed. Rise, Señor Governor, enjoy the conquest, and divide the spoils taken from the foe by the valour of that invincible arm ! "

" Raise me up," quoth Sancho, in a woeful tone ; and when they had placed him upon his legs, he said, " All the enemies I have routed may be nailed to my forehead. I will divide no spoils ; but I beg and entreat some friend, if I have any, to give me a draught of wine to keep me from choking with thirst, and help me to dry up the sweat ; for I am almost turned into water." They untied the targets, wiped him, and brought him, wine ; and, when seated upon his bed, such had been his fatigue, agony, and terror, that he fainted away. Those concerned in the joke were now sorry they had laid it on so heavily ; but were consoled on seeing him recover. He asked them what time it was and they told him it was daybreak. He said no more, but proceeded, in silence, to put on his clothes ; while the rest looked on, curious to know what were his intentions.

At length, having put on his clothes, which he did slowly and with much difficulty, from his bruises, he bent his way to the stable, followed by all present, and going straight to Dapple he embraced him, and gave him a kiss of peace on his forehead.

" Come hither," said he, with tears in his eyes, " my friend, and the partner of my fatigues and miseries. When I consorted with thee, and had no other care but mending thy furniture, and feeding that little carcase of thine, happy were my hours, my days, and my years: but since I forsook thee, and mounted the towers of ambition and pride, a thousand toils, a thousand torments, and ten thousand tribulations, have seized and worried my soul." While he thus spoke, he fixed the panel upon his ass without interruption from anybody, and when he had done, with great difficulty and pain he got upon him, and said to the steward, the secretary, the doctor, Pedro Rezio, and many others who were present:

"Make way, gentlemen, make way, and let me return to my ancient liberty; let me seek the life I have left, that I may rise again from this grave. I was not born to be a governor, nor to defend islands nor cities from enemies that break in upon them. I understand better how to plough and dig, to plant and prune vines, than to make laws, and take care of provinces or kingdoms. Saint Peter is well at Rome:—I mean to say, that nothing becomes a man so well as the employment he was born for. In my hand a sickle is better than a sceptre. I had rather have my bellyful of my own poor porridge, than to be mocked with dainties by an officious doctor, who would kill me with hunger; I had rather lie under the shade of an oak in summer, and wrap myself in a jerkin of double sheep's-skin in winter, at my liberty, than lay me down, under the slavery of a government, between holland sheets, and be robed in fine sables. Heaven be with you gentlefolks; tell my lord duke that naked was I born, and naked I am; I neither win nor lose; for without a penny came I to this government, and without a penny do I leave it—all governors cannot say the like. Make way, gentlemen, I beseech you, that I may go and plaister myself, for I verily believe all my ribs are broken—thanks to the enemies who have been trampling over me all night long."

"It must not be so, Señor Governor," said the doctor, "for I will give your lordship a balsamic draught, good against all kinds of bruises, that shall presently restore you to your former health and vigour; and as to your food, my lord, I promise to amend that, and let you eat abundantly of whatever you desire."

"Your promises come too late, Mr Doctor," quoth Sancho;

"I will as soon turn Turk as remain here. These tricks are not to be played twice;—'fore Heaven, I will no more hold this not any other government, though it were served up to me in a covered dish, than I will fly to heaven without wings. I am of the race of the Panzas, who are made of stubborn stuff; and if they once cry, Odd!—odds it shall be, come of it what will. Every sheep with its like; stretch not your feet beyond your sheet; so let me be gone, for it grows late."

"Señor Governor," said the steward, "we would not presume to hinder your departure, although we are grieved to lose you, because of your wise and Christian conduct: but your lordship knows that every governor before he lays down his authority is bound to render an account of his administration. Be pleased, my lord, to do so for the time which you have been among us; then peace be with you."

"Nobody can require that of me," replied Sancho, "but my lord duke; to him I go, and to him I shall give a fair and square account; though, in going away naked, as I do, there needs nothing more to show that I have governed like an angel."

"Before Heaven," said Doctor Pedro Rezio, "the great Sancho is in the right, and I am of opinion we should let him go; for without doubt his highness will be glad to see him." They all agreed, therefore, that he should be allowed to depart, and also offered to attend him and provide him with whatever was necessary, or convenient, for his journey. Sancho told them he wanted only a little barley for Dapple, and half a cheese and half a loaf for himself; that having so short a distance to travel, nothing more would be needful. Hereupon they all embraced him, which kindness he returned with tears in his eyes, and he left them in admiration both of his good sense and unalterable firmness.

The duke and duchess resolved that Don Quixote's challenge of their vassal should not be neglected: and though the young man had fled into Flanders to avoid having Donna Rodriguez for his mother-in-law, they made choice of a Gascon lacquey, named Tosilos, to supply his place, and for that purpose gave him instructions how to perform his part; and the duke informed Don Quixote that his opponent would in four days present himself in the lists, armed as a knight, and prepared to maintain

" He saw on the road six pilgrims."

that the damsel lied by half his beard, and even by the whole beard, in saying that he had given her a promise of marriage. The information was highly delightful to Don Quixote, who flattered himself that the occasion would offer him an opportunity of performing wonders, and thought himself singularly fortunate that he should be able in the presence of such noble spectators to give proofs of the valour of his heart and the strength of his arm ; and so with infinite content he waited the four days, which his eager impatience made him think were so many ages.

Now letting them pass, as we have done many other matters, we will turn to our friend Sancho, who, partly glad and partly sorrowful, was hastening as fast as his Dapple would carry him to his master, whose society he loved better than being governor of all the islands in the world. He had not, however, proceeded far from this island, city, or town (for which of these it was, he had never given himself the trouble to determine), when he saw on the road six pilgrims with their staves, being foreigners of that class who were wont to sing their supplications for alms. As they drew near, they placed themselves in order, and began their song in the language of their country ; but Sancho understood nothing except the word signifying alms : whence he concluded that alms was the object of their chanting ; and he being, as Cid Hamet says, extremely charitable, he took the half loaf and half cheese out of his wallet and gave it them, making signs, at the same time, that he had nothing else to give.

They received his donation eagerly, saying, " Guelte, guelte." *   " I do not understand you," answered Sancho ; " what is it you would have, good people ? " One of them then drew out of his bosom a purse, and, showing it to Sancho, intimated that it was money they wanted, upon which Sancho placing his thumb to his throat, and extending his hand upward, gave them to understand he had not a penny in the world. Then clapping heels to Dapple, he made way through them ; but as he passed by, one of them, looking at him with particular attention, caught hold of him, and throwing his arms about his waist :

" God be my aid ! " said he, in good Castilian, " what is it I see ? Is it possible I hold in my arms my dear friend and good neighbour, Sancho Panza ? Yes, truly, it must be so, for I am

* A Dutch word, signifying " money."

neither drunk nor sleeping." Sancho, much surprised to hear himself called by his name, and to be embraced by the stranger pilgrim, stared at him for some time, without speaking a word, but though he viewed him earnestly, he could not recollect him.

"How!" said the pilgrim, observing his amazement, "have you forgotten your neighbour Ricote, the Morisco shopkeeper of your town?" Sancho at length, after a fresh examination, recognised the face of an old acquaintance who had been obliged to leave Spain in consequence of the proclamation that all the Moors should leave it, and, without alighting from his beast, he embraced him, and said:

"Who, in the devil's name, Ricote, would know you in this covering? Tell me how you came to be thus Frenchified, and how you dare venture to come again into Spain, where, if you are found out, egad, that coat of yours will not save you?"

"If you do not discover me, Sancho," answered the pilgrim, "I am safe enough: for in this habit nobody can know me. But go with us to yonder poplar-grove, where my comrades mean to dine and rest themselves, and you shall eat with us. They are honest souls, I can assure you; there I shall have an opportunity to tell you what has befallen me since I was obliged to leave the town by the king's edict, which, as you know, caused so much misery to our people."

Sancho consented, and after Ricote had conferred with his comrades, they all retired together to the poplar-grove, which was far enough out of the high-road. There they flung down their staves, and putting off their pilgrim's attire, every man appeared in his doublet, excepting Ricote, who was somewhat advanced in years. They were all good-looking young fellows; each had his wallet, which, as it soon appeared, was well stored, at least with relishing incentives to thirst, and such as provoke it at two leagues' distance. They laid themselves along on the ground, and, making the grass their table-cloth, there was presently a comfortable display of bread, salt, nuts, and cheese, with some bacon-bones, which, though they would not bear picking, were to be sucked with advantage. Caviére too was produced, a kind of black eatable, made of the roes of fish:—a notable awakener of thirst. Even olives were not wanting, and though somewhat dry, they were savoury and in good keeping. But the glory of the feast was six bottles of wine : each wallet being charged with one, even honest Ricote, who from a Moor had become a German, or Hollander, and like the rest, drew forth his bottle, which in size might vie with the other five. They now began their feast, dwelling upon each morsel with great relish and satisfaction, and as if they were determined to make the most of them ; then pausing, they altogether raised their arms and bottles aloft into the air, mouth to mouth, and with eyes fixed upwards, as if taking aim at the heavens ; and, in this posture, waving their heads from side to side in token of the pleasure they received, they continued a long time, transfusing the precious fluid into their stomachs. Sancho beheld all this, and, nothing grieved thereat, but rather in compliance with a proverb he well knew, "When in Rome, do as Rome does," he asked Ricote for his bottle, and took his aim as the others had done, and with equal delight. Four times the bottles were tilted with effect, but the fifth was to no purpose, for alas ! they were now all empty, and as dry as a rush, which struck a damp on the spirits of the party. In short, the finishing of the wine was the beginning of a sound sleep, which seized them all, upon their very board and table-cloth,—Ricote and Sancho excepted :—they having drunk less and eaten more, remained awake, and leaving their companions in a deep sleep, went a little aside and sat down under the shade of a beech tree, where Ricote, in pure Castilian, without once stumbling into his Morisco jargon, had a long chat with Sancho.

At length, after they had given each other all the news, Ricote said :

"God be with you, brother Sancho. My comrades are stirring, and it is time for us also to be on our way." They then embraced each other ; Sancho mounted his Dapple, and Ricote leaned on his pilgrim's staff, and so they parted.

creature was within hearing, and after many trials he gave himself up as dead and buried. Seeing that his dear Dapple was yet lying upon his back, with his mouth upwards, he endeavoured to get him upon his legs, which, with much ado, he accomplished, though the poor animal could scarcely stand; he then took a luncheon of bread out of his wallet (which had shared in the disaster) and gave it to his beast, saying to him, "Bread is relief for all kind of grief:" all of which the ass appeared to take very kindly. At last, however, Sancho perceived a crevice on one side of the pit large enough to admit the body of a man. He immediately thrust himself into the hole, and creeping upon all-fours, he found it to enlarge as he proceeded, and that it led into another cavity, which, by a ray of light that glanced through some cranny above, he saw was large and spacious. He saw also that it led into another vault equally capacious; and having made this discovery he returned for his ass, and by removing the earth about the hole, he soon made it large enough for Dapple to pass. Then laying hold of his halter, he led him along through the several cavities, to try if he could not find a way out on the other side. Thus he went on, sometimes in the dusk, sometimes in the dark, but always in fear and trembling. Thus he went on, lamenting and despairing; and when he had gone, as he supposed, somewhat more than half-a-league, he perceived a kind of glimmering light, like that of day, breaking through some aperture above, that seemed to him an entrance to the other world; in which situation Cid Hamet leaves him for a while, and returns to Don Quixote, who, with great pleasure, looked forward to the day appointed for the combat, by which he hoped to revenge the injury done to the honour of Donna Rodriguez's daughter.

One morning as the knight was riding out to exercise and prepare himself for the approaching conflict, now urging, now checking the mettle of his steed, it happened that Rozinante, in one of his curvetings, pitched his feet so near the brink of a deep cave, that had not Don Quixote used his reins with all his skill, he must inevitably have fallen into it. But, having escaped that danger, he was curious to examine the chasm, and as he was earnestly surveying it, still sitting on his horse, he thought he heard a noise issuing from below, like a human voice; and listening more attentively, he distinctly heard these words:

"Ho! above there! is there any Christian that hears me, or any charitable gentleman to take pity on a sinner buried alive; a poor governor without a government?" Don Quixote thought it was the voice of Sancho Panza; at which he was greatly amazed, and, raising his voice as high as he could, he cried:

"Who are you below there? Who is it that complains?"

"Who should be here, and who complain," answered the voice, "but the most wretched soul alive, Sancho Panza, governor, for his sins and evil-errantry, of the island of Barataria, and late squire to the famous knight Don Quixote de la Mancha."

On hearing this Don Quixote's wonder and alarm increased; for he conceived that Sancho Panza was dead, and that his soul was there doing penance; and in this persuasion, he said:

"I conjure thee, as far as a Catholic Christian may, to tell me who thou art; and if thou art a soul in purgatory, let me know what I can do for thee; for since my profession obliges me to aid and succour all that are afflicted in this world, I shall also be ready to aid and assist the distressed in the world below, where they cannot help themselves."

"Surely," answered the voice from below, "it is my master, Don Quixote de la Mancha, who speaks to me—by the sound of the voice it can be no other!"

"Don Quixote I am," replied the knight, "he whose profession and duty it is to relieve and succour the living and the dead in their necessities. Tell me, then, who thou art, for I am amazed at what I hear. If thou art really my squire Sancho Panza, and art dead, since the devils have not got thee, and through God's mercy thou art still in purgatory, our holy mother the Roman Catholic church has power by her supplications to deliver thee from the pains which afflict thee; and I will myself solicit her in thy behalf, as far as my estate and purse will go: speak, therefore, and tell me quickly who thou art!"

"Why then, I vow to Heaven," said the voice, "and will swear by whatever your worship pleases, Señor Don Quixote de la Mancha, that I am your squire Sancho Panza, and that I never died in the whole course of my life; but that, having left my government for reasons and causes that require more leisure to be told, I fell last night into this cavern, where I now am, and Dapple with me, who will not let me lie ; and, as a further proof, here the good creature stands by me."

Now it would seem the ass understood what Sancho said, and willing to add his testimony, at that instant began to bray so lustily that the whole cave resounded.

"A credible witness !" quoth Don Quixote ; "that bray I know as well as if I myself had brought it forth : and thy voice, too, I know, my dear Sancho—wait a little, and I will go to the duke's castle and bring some people to get thee out of this pit, into which thou hast certainly been cast for thy sins."

"Pray go, for the Lord's sake," quoth Sancho, "and return speedily ; for I cannot bear any longer to be buried alive, and am dying with fear." Don Quixote left him, and hastened to the castle to tell the duke and duchess what had happened to Sancho Panza ; at which they were not a little surprised, though they readily accounted for his being there, and conceived that he might easily have fallen down the pit, which was well known, and had been there time out of mind ; but they could not imagine how he should have left his government without their having been apprised of it. Ropes and pullies were, however, immediately sent ; and, with much labour, and many hands, Dapple and his master were drawn out of that gloomy den, to the welcome light of the sun.

Amidst a rabblement of boys and other followers, they arrived at the castle, where the duke and duchess were already in a gallery waiting for them. Sancho would not go up to see the duke till he had first taken the necessary care of Dapple in the stable, because the poor creature, he said, had had but an indifferent night's lodging ; and, that done, he went up to the duke and duchess, and kneeling before them, he said :

"My lord and lady, you made me governor of your island of Barataria ; and not from any desert of mine, but because your grandeurs would have it so. Naked I entered it, and naked have I left it. I neither win nor lose ; whether I have governed well or ill, there are witnesses, who may say what they please. I have cleared up doubts, and pronounced sentences, and all the while famished with hunger : so far it was ordered by Pedro Rezio, native of Tirteafuera, doctor in ordinary to the island and its governor. Enemies attacked us by night ; and, though they put us in great danger, I heard many say that the island was delivered ; and according as they speak the truth, so help them Heaven. In short, I have by this time been able to reckon up the cares and burthens the trade of governing brings with it, and find them, by my account, too heavy for my shoulders or ribs to bear ; and so, before the government left me, I e'en resolved to leave the government ; and yesterday morning, turning my back on the island, I left it just as I found it, with the same streets, the same houses, with the selfsame roofs to them as they had when I first entered it. I have neither borrowed nor hoarded ; and though I intended to make some wholesome laws, I made none, fearing they would not be observed, which is the same as if they were not made. I came away, as I said, from the island without any company but my Dapple. In the dark, I fell head-long into a pit, and crept along under ground, till this morning by the light of the sun I discovered a way out, though not so easy a one but that if Heaven had not sent my master Don Quixote, there I might have stayed till the end of the world. So that, my lord duke and my lady duchess, behold here your governor Sancho Panza, who in the ten days that he held his office, found out by experience that he would not give a single farthing to be governor, not of an island only, but even of the whole world. This then being the case, kissing your honours' feet, and imitating the boys at play, who cry, leap and away, I give a leap out of the government, and pass over to the service of my master Don Quixote : for, after all, though with him I eat my bread in bodily fear, at least I have enough ; and, for my part, so I have but that well stuffed, it is all one to me whether it be with carrots or partridges."

Here Sancho ended his long speech, Don Quixote dreading all the while a thousand absurdities, and when he had ended with so few, he gave thanks to Heaven in his heart. The duke embraced Sancho, and said that it grieved him to the soul he had left the government so soon : but that he would take care he should have some other employment in his territories, of less trouble and more profit. The duchess was no less kind, and ordered that he should be taken good care of ; for he seemed to be much bruised and in wretched plight.

CHAPTER LXXI

OF THE BATTLE BETWEEN DON QUIXOTE DE LA MANCHA AND
TOSILOS, IN DEFENCE OF THE DUENNA DONNA RODRIGUEZ'
DAUGHTER

THE duke and duchess repented not of the jest they had practised
upon Sancho Panza, when the steward, on his return, gave them
a minute relation of almost every word and action of the
governor during that time ; and he failed not to enlarge upon
the assault of the island, with his terror and final abdication,
which gave them not a little entertainment. The appointed day
of combat arrived ; nor had the duke neglected to give his
lacquey Tosilos all the necessary instructions how to vanquish his
antagonist, and yet neither kill nor wound him ; for which
purpose he gave orders that the iron heads of their lances should
be taken off, because, as he told Don Quixote, that Christianity
upon which he valued himself forbade that in this battle their
lives should be exposed to danger ; and though contrary to the
decree of the holy council, which prohibits such encounters,
he should allow them free field-room in his territories ; but he
did not wish the affair pushed to the utmost extremity. Don
Quixote begged his excellency would arrange all things as he
deemed best ; and assured him that he would acquiesce in every
particular.

On the dreadful day, the duke having commanded a spacious
scaffold to be erected before the court of the castle for the
judges of the field, and the two duennas, mother and daughter,
appellants, an infinite number of people, from all the neighbouring towns and villages, flocked to see the novel spectacle, for, in
latter times, nothing like it had ever been seen or heard of in that
country either by the living or the dead.

The first who entered the lists was the master of the
ceremonies, who walked over the ground, and examined it in
every part, to guard against foul play and see that there was
nothing on the surface to occasion stumbling or falling. The
duennas now entered, and took seats, covered with veils even to

their breasts, and betraying much emotion. Don Quixote next presented himself in the lists, and soon after the sound of trumpets announced the entrance of the great Tosilos, mounted on a stately steed, making the earth shake beneath him ; with vizor down, and stiffly cased within a suit of strong and shining armour. The horse seemed to be a Frieslander, broad-built, and flea-bitten, with abundance of hair upon each fetlock. The courageous Tosilos came well instructed by the duke his lord how to behave towards the valorous Don Quixote de la Mancha, and cautioned in nowise to hurt him, and also to be careful to elude his adversary at the first onset, lest he should himself be slain, which would be inevitable if he met him in full career. He traversed the enclosure, and, advancing towards the duennas, he surveyed the lady who demanded him for her husband. The marshal of the field, attended by Don Quixote and Tosilos, now formally demanded of the duennas whether they consented that Don Quixote de la Mancha should maintain their right. They answered, that they did, and that whatever he should do in their behalf they should confirm, and hold to be right, firm, and valid.

The duke and duchess now took their seats, in a balcony over the barriers, which were crowded by an infinite number of people, all in full expectation of beholding this terrible and extra-ordinary conflict. It was stipulated, between Don Quixote and Tosilos, that if the former should conquer his adversary, the latter should be obliged to marry Donna Rodriguez' daughter ; and if he should be overcome, his adversary should be released from his engagement with the lady, and every other claim on her account. And now the master of the ceremonies divided the sun equally between them, and fixed each at his post. The drums beat ; the sound of trumpets filled the air, earth shook beneath the steeds of the combatants ; the hearts of the gazing multitude palpitated, some with fear, some with hope, for the issue of this affair ; finally, Don Quixote, recommending himself to Heaven, and to his lady Dulcinea del Toboso, stood waiting the signal for the onset. But our lacquey's thoughts were differently employed, for it so happened that, while he stood looking at his female enemy, she appeared to him the most beautiful woman he had ever seen in his life, and the little blind boy called Cupid seized the opportunity of adding a lacquey's heart to the list of his trophies. Softly, and unperceived, therefore, he approached his victim, and, taking aim at the left side of the devoted youth, with an arrow two yards long he pierced his heart through and through : and this the amorous archer could do with perfect safety, for he is invisible, and goes and comes when and where he pleases, and to none is he accountable. So that when the signal was given for the onset, our lacquey stood transported, contemplating the beauty of her who was now the mistress of his liberty, and therefore attended not to the trumpet's sound. It was not so with Don Quixote, who instantly spurring forward, advanced towards his enemy at Rozinante's best speed ; while his trusty squire Sancho cried aloud :

"God guide you, cream and flower of knights-errant! Heaven give you victory, for the right is on your side ! "

Though Tosilos saw Don Quixote making towards him, he stirred not a step from the place where he stood, but loudly calling the marshal of the field to him, he said :

"Is not this combat, sir, to decide whether I shall marry, or not marry, that young lady ? "

"It is," answered the marshal.

"Then," quoth the lacquey, " my conscience will not let me proceed any further ; and I declare that I yield myself vanquished, and am ready to marry that gentlewoman this moment." The marshal was surprised at what Tosilos said, and being privy to the contrivance, he was at a loss how to answer him. Don Quixote, perceiving that his adversary was not advancing, stopped short in the midst of his career. The duke could not conceive why the combat was retarded ; and, when the marshal explained the cause, he was angry at the disappointment. In the mean time, however, Tosilos approached Donna Rodriguez, and said aloud, " I am willing, good madam, to marry your daughter, and would not seek, by strife and bloodshed, what I may have peaceably, and without danger." "Since that is the case," said the valorous Don Quixote, " I am absolved from my promise ; let them be married, in God's name, and, as God has given her, Saint Peter bless her."

The duke now came down into the court of the castle, and, going up to Tosilos, he said :

"Is it true, knight, that you yield yourself vanquished, and that, instigated by your timorous conscience, you intend to marry this damsel?"

"Yes, an't please your grace," replied Tosilos.

"And, faith, 'tis the wisest course," quoth Sancho Panza. "What you would give to the mouse give to the cat, and you will save trouble." Tosilos, was, in the mean time, unlacing his helmet, to do which he begged for prompt assistance, as his spirits and breath were just failing him, unable to remain any longer pent up in so straight a lodging. They presently unarmed him, and the face of the lacquey being exposed to view, Donna Rodriguez and her daughter cried aloud:

"A cheat! a cheat! Tosilos, my lord duke's lackey, is put upon us instead of our true spouse! Justice from Heaven and the king against so much deceit, not to say villany!"

"Afflict not yourselves, ladies," quoth Don Quixote, "for this is neither deceit nor villany, or, if it be so, the duke is not to blame, but the wicked enchanters, my persecutors, who, envying me the glory I should have acquired by this conquest, have transformed the countenance of your husband into that of another, who, you say, is a lacquey belonging to my lord duke. Take my advice, and, in spite of the malice of my enemies, marry him; for, without doubt, he is the very man you desire for your husband."

The duke, hearing this, angry as he was, could not forbear laughing.

"Truly," said he, "so many extraordinary things happen every day to the great Don Quixote that I am inclined to believe this is not my lacquey; but, for our better satisfaction, and to detect the artifice, let us, if you please, defer the marriage for fifteen days, and, in the mean time, keep this doubtful youth in safe custody; by that time, perhaps, he may return to his own proper form; for doubtless the malice of those wicked magicians against the noble Don Quixote cannot last so long: especially when they find these tricks and transformations avail them so little."

"O, sir," quoth Sancho, "the wicked wretches are for ever at this work, changing from one shape to another, whatever my master has to do with. It was but lately they turned a famous knight he had beaten, called the Knight of the Mirrors, into the very shape of the bachelor Sampson Carrasco, a fellow-townsman and special friend of ours ; and more than that, they changed my lady Dulcinea del Toboso from a princess into a downright country bumpkin ; so that I verily believe this lacquey here will live and die a lacquey all the days of his life."

"Let him be who he will," said the duenna's daughter, "as he demands me to wife I take it kindly of him ; for I had rather be lawful wife to a lacquey than the cast mistress of a gentleman, though indeed he who deluded me is not one."

All these events, in short, ended in the imprisonment of Tosilos, where it was determined he should remain till it was seen in what his transformation would end ; and although the victory was adjudged to Don Quixote by general acclamation, the greater part of the spectators were disappointed and out of humour that the long-expected combatants had not hacked each other to pieces : as the rabble are wont to repine when the criminal is pardoned whom they expected to see hanged. The crowd now dispersed ; the duke and Don Quixote returned to the castle, after ordering the lacquey into close keeping ; Donna Rodriguez and her daughter were extremely well pleased to see that, one way or other, this business was likely to end in matrimony ; and Tosilos was consoled with the like expectation.

CHAPTER LXXII

WHICH RELATES HOW DON QUIXOTE TOOK HIS LEAVE OF THE
DUKE, AND OF WHAT BEFEL HIM WITH THE WITTY AND
WANTON ALTISIDORA, ONE OF THE DUCHESS'S DAMSELS

EVEN Don Quixote now thought it full time to quit so inactive a life as that which he had led in the castle, deeming himself culpable in living thus in indolence, amidst the luxuries prepared for him, as a knight-errant, by the duke and duchess ; and he believed he should have to account to Heaven for this neglect of the duties of his profession. He therefore requested permission of their graces to depart, which they granted him, but with every expression of regret. The duchess gave Sancho Panza his wife's letters, which he wept over, saying, " Who could have thought that all the mighty hopes which my wife puffed herself up with on the news of my government, should come at last to this, and that it should again be my lot to follow my master Don Quixote in search of hungry and toilsome adventures ! "

In this manner Sancho communed with himself while preparing for his departure. That same evening Don Quixote took leave of the duke and duchess, and early the next morning he sallied forth, completely armed, into the great court, the surrounding galleries of which were crowded with the inmates of the castle, all eager to behold the knight ; nor were the duke and duchess absent on that occasion. Sancho was mounted upon Dapple, his wallets well furnished, and himself much pleased ; for the duke's steward, who had played the part of the Trifaldi, had given him, unknown to Don Quixote, a little purse with two hundred crowns in gold, to supply the occasions of the journey. And now, whilst all were gazing at Don Quixote, the arch and witty Altisidora, who was with the duennas and damsels of the duchess, came forward, and, in a doleful tone, addressed herself to him :

> Stay, cruel knight,
> Take not thy flight,
> Nor spur thy batter'd jade.
> Thy haste restrain,
> Draw in the rein,
> Pity a love-sick maid.

Whilst Altisidora thus poured forth her tuneful complaints, Don Quixote stood looking at her attentively, and when she had done, he said to the duke, " This damsel talks (as she owns) like one in love, which is no fault of mine ; and, therefore, I have no reason to ask pardon either of her or of your excellency, whom I entreat to think better of me, and again desire your permission to depart."

" Farewell, Señor Don Quixote," said the duchess, "and Heaven send you so prosperous a journey that we may always hear happy tidings of your exploits. Go, and Heaven be with you ; for the longer you stay, the more you stir up the flames that scorch the hearts of these tender damsels while they gaze on you. As for this wanton, take my word, I will so deal with her that she shall not again offend either in word or deed." Don Quixote made his obeisance to the duke and duchess, and to all the spectators; then, turning Rozinante's head, he sallied out at the castle gate, and, followed by Sancho upon Dapple, took the road leading to Saragossa.

On finding himself in the open country, unrestrained and free from the troublesome fondness of Altisidora, Don Quixote felt all his chivalric ardour revive within him, and turning to his squire, he said, "Liberty, friend Sancho, is one of the choicest gifts that Heaven hath bestowed upon man, and exceeds in value all the treasures which the earth contains within its bosom, or the sea covers. Liberty, as well as honour, man ought to preserve at the hazard of his life; for without it life is insupportable." "For all that," quoth Sancho, "we ought to feel ourselves much bound to the duke's steward for the two hundred crowns in gold which he gave me in a purse I carry here, next my heart, as a cordial and comfort in case of need; for we are not likely to find many castles where we shall be made so much of, but more likely inns, where we shall be rib-roasted."

While the knight and squire were conversing, they entered a wood that was near the road side, but had not penetrated far when Don Quixote found himself entangled among some nets of green thread which were extended from tree to tree; and, surprised at the incident, he said, "These nets, Sancho, surely promise some new and extraordinary adventure—may I die this moment if it be not some new device of the enchanters, my enemies, to stop my way, out of revenge, for having slighted the wanton Altisidora! But I would have them know that, if these nets were chains of adamant, or stronger than that in which the jealous god of blacksmiths entangled Mars and Venus, to me they would be nets of rushes and yarn!" Just as he was about to break through the frail enclosure, two lovely shepherdesses, issuing from the covert, suddenly presented themselves before him; at least, their dress resembled that of shepherdesses, excepting that it was of fine brocade, and rich gold tabby. Their hair, bright as sunbeams, flowed over their shoulders; and chaplets composed of laurel and interwoven with the purple amaranth, adorned their heads; and they appeared to be from fifteen to eighteen years of age.

Sancho was dazzled, and Don Quixote amazed, at so un-expected a vision, which the sun himself must have stopped in his course to admire. "Hold! Señor Cavalier," said one of them, "pray do not break the nets we have placed here, not to offend you, but to divert ourselves; and as you may wish to know why we spread them, and who we are, I will, in a few words, tell you. About two leagues off, sir, there is a village where many persons of quality and wealth reside, several of whom lately made up a company, of friends, neighbours, and relations, to come and take their diversion at this place, which is accounted the most delightful in these parts. Here we have formed among ourselves a new Arcadia; the young men have put on the dress of shepherds, and the maidens that of shepherdesses. We have learnt by heart two eclogues, one by our admired Garcilaso, and the other by the excellent Camoëns, in his own Portuguese tongue; which, however, we have not yet recited, as it was only yesterday that we came hither. Our tents are pitched among the trees, near the side of a beautiful stream. Last night we spread these nets to catch such simple birds as our calls could allure into the snare: and now, sir, if you please to be our guest, you shall be entertained liberally and courteously: for we allow neither care nor sorrow to be of our party."

"Truly, fair lady," answered Don Quixote, "Actæon was not more lost in admiration and surprise when unawares he saw Diana bathing, than I am in beholding your beauty. I approve and admire your project, and return thanks for your kind invitation, and, if I can do you any service, lay your commands upon me, in full assurance of being obeyed; for by my profession I am enjoined to be grateful and useful to all. And, that you may afford some credit to a declaration which may seen extravagant, know, ladies, that he who makes it is no other than Don Quixote de la Mancha—if, perchance, that name has ever reached your ears."

"Bless me!" exclaimed the other shepherdess, addressing her companion, "what good fortune, my dear friend, has befallen us! See you this gentleman here before us? Believe me, he is the most valiant, the most enamoured, and the most courteous knight in the whole world, if the history of his exploits, which is in print, does not deceive us. I have read it, my dear, through and through ; and I will lay a wager that the good man who attends him is that very Sancho Panza, his squire, whose pleasantries none can equal."

" I' faith, madam, it is very true," quoth Sancho, " I am, indeed, that same jocular person, and squire, and this gentleman is my master, the very Don Quixote de la Mancha you have read of in print."

" Pray, my dear," said the other, " let us entreat him to stay, for our fathers and brothers will be infinitely pleased to have him here. I also have heard what you say of his valour and great merit, and, above all, that he is the most true and constant or lovers, and that his mistress, who is called Dulcinea del Toboso, bears away the palm from all the beauties in Spain."

" And with great justice," quoth Don Quixote, " unless your wondrous charms should make it questionable. But do not, I beseech you, ladies, endeavour to detain me : for the indispensable duties of my profession allow me no intermission of labour."

At this moment a brother of one of the fair damsels came up to them, dressed as a shepherd, and with the same richness and gaiety. They instantly told him that the persons he saw were the valorous Don Quixote de la Mancha and his squire Sancho Panza, whom he also knew by their history. The gay shepherd saluted the knight, and so urgently importuned him to honour their party with his presence, that, unable to refuse, he at length accepted their invitation. Just at that time the nets were drawn, and a great number of small birds, deceived by their artifices, were taken. The gallant party assembled on that occasion, being not less than thirty in number, all in pastoral habits, received Don Quixote and his squire in a manner very much to their satisfaction : for none were strangers to the knight's history. They all now repaired together to the tents, where they found the table spread with elegance and plenty. The place of honour was given to Don Quixote, and all gazed on him with admiration.

When the cloth was removed, the knight, with much gravity, and in an audible voice, thus addressed the company : " Of all the sins that men commit, though some say pride, in my opinion, ingratitude is the worst ; it is truly said that hell is full of the ungrateful. From that foul crime I have endeavoured to abstain ever since I enjoyed the use of reason ; I can only show my gratitude by doing that little which is in my power. I therefore engage to maintain, for two whole days, in the middle of the king's highway, leading to Saragossa, that these lady - shepherdesses in disguise are the most beautiful and the most courteous damsels in the world : excepting only the peerless Dulcinea del Toboso, the sole mistress of my thoughts—without offence to any present be it spoken."

The company nevertheless endeavoured to dissuade him from his challenge, telling him that they were sufficiently assured of his grateful nature as well as his valour, by the true history of his exploits. Resolute, however, in his purpose, the knight was not to be moved ; and, being now mounted upon Rozinante, bracing his shield, and grasping his lance, he planted himself in the middle of the highway, not far from the Arcadian tents. Sancho followed upon his Dapple, with all the pastoral company, who were curious to see the event of so arrogant and extraordinary a defiance.

Don Quixote, being thus posted, he made the air resound with such words as these, "O ye passengers, whoever ye are, knights, squires, travellers on foot and on horseback, who now pass this way, or shall pass, in the course of these two successive days ! know that Don Quixote de la Mancha, knight-errant, is posted here, ready to maintain that the nymphs who inhabit these meadows and groves excel in beauty and courtesy all the rest of the world, excepting only the mistress of my soul, Dulcinea del Toboso ! Let him, therefore, who dares to uphold the contrary, forthwith show himself, for here I stand ready to receive him."

Twice he repeated the same words, and twice they were repeated in vain. But better fortune soon followed, for it so happened that a number of horsemen appeared, several of them armed with lances, hastily advancing in a body. Those who had accompanied Don Quixote no sooner saw them than they retired to a distance, thinking it might be dangerous to remain. Don Quixote alone, with an intrepid heart, stood firm, and Sancho Panza sheltered himself close under Rozinante's crupper. When

"Stop! scoundrels! a single knight defies ye all."

the troop of horsemen came up, one of the foremost called aloud
to Don Quixote :

"Get out of the way, devil of a man ! or these bulls will
trample you to dust."

"Caitiffs !" replied Don Quixote, "I fear not your bulls,
though they were the fiercest that ever bellowed on the banks
of Xarama.   Confess, ye scoundrels ! unsight, unseen, that what
I here proclaimed is true ; if not, I challenge ye to battle."

The herdsmen had no time to answer, nor Don Quixote to
get out of the way, had he been willing : and now a herd of fierce
bulls, together with some tame kine, hurried past with a multitude
of herdsmen and others, driving them to a neighbouring town
where they were to be baited.   Don Quixote, Sancho, Rozinante,
and Dapple, were in a moment overturned, and, after being
trampled upon without mercy, were left sprawling on the ground.
After the whole had passed, here lay Sancho mauled, there Don
Quixote stunned, Dapple bruised, and Rozinante in no enviable
plight !   Nevertheless, they all contrived to recover the use of
their legs, and the knight, in great haste, stumbling and reeling,
began to pursue the herd, crying aloud :

"Hold ! stop ! scoundrels ! a single knight defies ye all, who
scorns the coward maxim, ' Make a bridge of silver for a flying
enemy.'"   But the drovers had no time to attend to him, and
made no more account of his threats than of last year's clouds.
Fatigue obliged Don Quixote to desist from the pursuit ; and,
more enraged than revenged, he sat down in the road, to wait
for Sancho, Rozinante, and Dapple.   On their coming up, the
knight and squire mounted again, and, with more shame than
satisfaction, pursued their journey, without taking leave of the
shepherds of new Arcadia.

DON QUIXOTE

"The knight, from pure chagrin, refused to eat."

CHAPTER LXXIII

WHEREIN IS RELATED AN EXTRAORDINARY ACCIDENT WHICH
BEFEL DON QUIXOTE, AND WHICH MAY PASS
FOR AN ADVENTURE

Don Quixote and Sancho removed, by immersion in the waters of a clear fountain, which they found in a cool and shady grove, the fatigue, the dust, and other effects caused by the rude encounter of the bulls. Here the way-worn pair seated themselves: and after giving liberty to Rozinante and Dapple, Sancho had recourse to the store of his wallet, and speedily drew out what he was wont to call his sauce. He rinsed his mouth, and Don Quixote washed his face, by which they were in some degree refreshed: but the knight, from pure chagrin, refused to eat, and Sancho abstained from pure good manners; though waiting and wishing for his master to begin. At length, seeing his master so wrapped in thought as to forget to convey a morsel to his mouth, he opened his own, and banishing all kind of ceremony, made a fierce attack upon the bread and cheese before him.

"Let me tell you, sir," said Sancho, "that there is no greater folly than to give way to despair. Believe what I say, and when you have eaten, try to sleep a little upon this green mattress, and I warrant on waking you will find yourself another man."

"Ah, Sancho, my sorrow is too great to permit me to eat. I feel Dulcinea is doomed to remain enchanted. But if thou desirest to raise my spirits, do thou step aside a little and with Rozinante's bridle give thyself some three hundred or four hundred lashes on account of the three thousand odd thou are bound to give thyself for the disenchantment of Dulcinea."

"Let my Lady Dulcinea have a little patience, and mayhap when she least thinks it, she shall see my body a perfect sieve by dint of lashing. Until death all is life: I am still alive, and with a full intention to make good my promise." Don Quixote thanked him, ate a little, and Sancho much; and both of them laid themselves down to sleep, leaving Rozinante and Dapple, those inseparable companions and friends, at their own discretion, either to repose or feed upon the tender grass, of which they here had abundance.

They awoke somewhat late in the day, mounted again, and pursued their journey; hastening to reach what seemed to be an inn, about a league before them. An inn it is here called, because Don Quixote himself gave it that name; not happening, as usual, to mistake it for a castle. Having arrived there, they inquired of the host if he could provide them with lodging, and he promised as good accommodation and entertainment as could be found in Saragossa. On alighting, Sancho's first care was to deposit his travelling larder in a chamber of which the landlord gave him the key. He then led Rozinante and Dapple to the stable, and, after seeing them well provided for, he went to receive the further commands of his master, whom he found seated on a stone bench; the squire blessing himself that the knight had not taken the inn for a castle.

Supper-time approaching, Don Quixote retired to his apartment, and Sancho inquired of the host what they could have to eat. The landlord told him that his palate should be suited—for whatever the air, earth, and sea produced, of birds, beasts or fish, that inn was abundantly provided with.

"There is no need of all that," quoth Sancho, "roast us but a couple of chickens, and we shall be satisfied; for my master has a delicate stomach, and I am no glutton."

"As for chickens," said the innkeeper, "truly we have none, for the kites have devoured them."

"Then let a pullet be roasted," said Sancho; "only see that it be tender."

"A pullet? my father!" answered the host; "faith and troth, I sent above fifty yesterday to the city to be sold; but, excepting pullets, ask for whatever you will."

"Why then," quoth Sancho, "e'en give us a good joint of veal or kid, for they cannot be wanting."

"Veal or kid?" replied the host, "ah, now I remember we have none in the house at present, for it is all eaten; but next week there will be enough, and to spare."

"We are much the better for that," answered Sancho; "but I dare say all these deficiencies will be made up with plenty of eggs and bacon."

"'Fore Heaven," answered the host, "my customer is a choice guesser! I told him I had neither pullets nor hens, and he expects me to have eggs; talk of other delicacies, but ask no more for hens."

"Body of me!" quoth Sancho, "let us come to something— tell me, in short, what you have, master host, and let us have done with your flourishes."

"Then," quoth the innkeeper, "what I really and truly have is a pair of cow-heels, that may be taken for calves' feet; or a pair of calves' feet, that are like cow-heels. They are stewed with peas, onions, and bacon, and at this very minute are crying out, ' Come eat me, come eat me.'"

"From this moment, I mark them for my own," quoth Sancho; "and let nobody lay finger on them. I will pay you well, for there is nothing like them—give me but cow-heel, and I care not a fig for calves' feet."

"They are yours," said the host, "nobody shall touch them; for my other guests, merely for gentility sake, bring their cook, their sewer, and provisions along with them."

Supper being prepared, and Don Quixote in his chamber, the host carried in his dish of cow-heel, and, without ceremony, sat himself down to supper. The adjoining room being separated from that occupied by Don Quixote only by a thin partition, he could distinctly hear the voices of persons within. " Don Jeronimo," said one of them, "I entreat you, till supper is brought in, to let us have another chapter of Don Quixote de la Mancha." The knight hearing himself named, got up, and, listening attentively, he heard another person answer, "Why, Señor Don John, would you have us read such absurdities? Whoever has read the first part of the history of Don Quixote de la Mancha cannot be pleased with the second."

"But for all that," said Don John, "let us read it; for there is no book so bad as not to have something good in it. What displeases me the most in this second part is, that the author describes Don Quixote as no longer enamoured of Dulcinea del Toboso."

On hearing this, Don Quixote, full of wrath and indignation, raised his voice, and said, "Whoever shall say that Don Quixote de la Mancha has forgotten, or ever can forget, Dulcinea del

Toboso, I will make him know, with equal arms, that he asserts what is not true ; for neither can the peerless Dulcinea be forgotten, nor Don Quixote ever cease to remember her. His motto is Constancy ; and to maintain it his pleasure and his duty."

"Who speaks to us ? " replied one in the other room.

"Who should it be," quoth Sancho, "but Don Quixote de la Mancha himself?—who will make good all he says and all he shall say : for a good paymaster is in no want of a pawn."

At these words two gentlemen rushed into the room, and one of them throwing his arms about Don Quixote's neck, said, "Your person belies not your name, nor can your name do otherwise than give credit to your person. I cannot doubt, Señor, of your being the true Don Quixote de la Mancha, the north and morning-star of knight-errantry, in despite of him who would usurp your name, and annihilate your exploits, as the author of this book has vainly attempted." Don Quixote, without making any reply, took up the book ; and, after turning over some of the leaves, he laid it down again, saying, "In the little I have seen of this volume, three things I have noticed for which the author deserves reprehension. The first is some expressions in the preface ; the next that his language is Arragonian, for he sometimes omits the articles ; and the third is a much more serious objection, inasmuch as he shows his ignorance and disregard of truth in a material point of the history : for he says that the wife of my squire Sancho Panza is called Mary Gutierrez, whereas her name is Teresa Panza ; and he who errs in a circumstance of such importance may well be suspected of inaccuracy in the rest of the history."

Here Sancho put in his word :

"Pretty work, indeed, of that same history-maker ! Sure he knows much of our concerns to call my wife, Teresa Panza, Mary Gutierrez ! Pray, your worship, look into it again, and see whether I am there, and if my name be changed too."

"By what you say, friend," quoth Don Jeronimo, "I presume you are Sancho Panza, squire to Señor Don Quixote ? "

"That I am," replied Sancho, "and value myself upon it."

"In faith, then," said the gentleman, "this last author treats you but scurvily, and not as you seem to deserve. He describes you as a dull fool, and a glutton, without pleasantry—in short, quite a different Sancho from him represented in the first part of your master's history."

The two gentlemen entreated Don Quixote to go to their chamber and sup with them, as they well knew the inn had nothing fit for his entertainment. Don Quixote, who was always courteous, consented to their request, and Sancho remained with the flesh-pot, *cum mero mixto imperio :* ∗ placing himself at the head of the table, with the innkeeper for his messmate, whose love for cow-heel was equal to that of the squire.

In friendly conversation they passed the greater part of the night ; and though Don John would fain have had Don Quixote read more of the book, he declined it, saying he deemed it read ; and, by the sample he had seen, he pronounced it foolish throughout. He was unwilling, also, to indulge the scribbler's vanity so far as to let him think he had read his book, should he happen to learn that it had been put into his hands ; "and, besides, it is proper," he added, "that the eyes, as well as the thoughts, should be turned from everything filthy and obscene."

They then asked him which way he was travelling, and he told them that he should go to Saragossa, to be present at the jousts of that city for the annual prize of a suit of armour. Don John told him that, in the new history, Don Quixote is said to have been there, running at the ring, of which the author gives a wretched account ; dull in the contrivance, mean in style, miserably poor in devices, and rich only in absurdity.

"For that very reason," answered Don Quixote, "I will not set foot in Saragossa, but will go to Barcelona, and thus I shall expose the falsity of this new historian, and all the world will be convinced that I am not the Don Quixote of whom he speaks."

Don Quixote and Sancho then retired to their chamber, leaving the two strangers surprised at the medley of sense and madness they had witnessed, and with a full conviction that these were the genuine Don Quixote and Sancho, and those of

∗ That is, with a deputed or subordinate power.

"Sancho . . . trembling with fear."

the Arragonese author certainly spurious. Don Quixote arose early, and, tapping at the partition of the other room, he again bid his new friends adieu. Sancho paid the innkeeper most magnificently, and at the same time advised him either to boast less of the provision of his inn, or to supply it better.

CHAPTER LXXIV

OF WHAT BEFEL DON QUIXOTE ON HIS WAY TO BARCELONA

In the morning, which was cool, and promised a temperate day, Don Quixote left the inn, having first informed himself which was the most direct road to Barcelona, avoiding Saragossa ; for he was determined to prove the falsehood of the new history, which he understood had so grossly misrepresented him. Six days he pursued his course without meeting with any adventure worth recording ; at the end of which time, leaving the high road, night overtook them among some shady trees, but whether of cork or oak, it does not appear ; Cid Hamet, in this instance, not observing his wonted minuteness of description. Master and man having alighted, they laid themselves down at the foot of these trees.

Sancho was going to lay himself under one of the trees, when he thought something touched his head ; and reaching up his hands, he felt a couple of dangling feet, with hose and shoes. Trembling with fear, he moved on a little further, but was incommoded by other legs ; upon which he called to his master for help. Don Quixote went up to him, and asked him what was the matter : when Sancho told him that all the trees were full of men's feet and legs. Don Quixote felt them, and immediately guessing the cause, he said, " Be not afraid, Sancho ; doubtless these are the legs of robbers and banditti, who have been punished for their crimes : for here the officers of justice hang them by scores at a time, when they can lay hold of them, and from this circumstance I conclude we are not far from Barcelona." In truth Don Quixote was right in his conjecture, for when day began to dawn, they plainly saw that the legs they had felt in the dark belonged to the bodies of thieves.

But if they were alarmed at these dead banditti, how much more were they disturbed at being suddenly surrounded by more than forty of their living comrades, who commanded them to stand, and not to move till their captain came up. Don Quixote was on foot, his horse unbridled, his lance leaning against a tree at some distance; in short, being defenceless, he thought it best to cross his hands, hang down his head, and reserve himself for better occasions. The robbers, however, were not idle, but immediately fell to work upon Dapple, and in a trice emptied both wallet and cloak-bag. Fortunately for Sancho, he had secured the crowns given him by the duke, with his other money, in a belt which he wore about his waist; nevertheless, they would not have escaped the searching eyes of these good people, who spare not even what is hid between the flesh and the skin, had they not been checked by the arrival of their captain. His age seemed to be about four-and-thirty, his body was robust, his stature tall, his visage austere, and his complexion swarthy; he was mounted upon a powerful steed, clad in a coat of steel, and his belt was stuck round with pistols. Observing that his squires (for so they call men of their vocation) were about to rifle Sancho, he commanded them to forbear, and was instantly obeyed, and thus the girdle escaped. He wondered to see a lance standing against a tree, a target on the ground, and Don Quixote in armour, and pensive, with the most sad and melancholy countenance that sadness itself could frame.

Going up to the knight, he said:

"Be not so dejected, good sir, for you are not fallen into the hands of a cruel Osiris, but into those of Roque Guinart, who has more of compassion in his nature than cruelty."

"My dejection," answered Don Quixote, "is not on account of having fallen into your hands, O valorous Roque, whose fame extends over the whole earth, but for my negligence in having suffered myself to be surprised by your soldiers, contrary to the bounden duty of a knight-errant, which requires that I should be continually on the alert, and, at all hours, my own sentinel: for, let me tell you, illustrious Roque, had they met me on horseback with my lance and my target, they would have found it no very easy task to make me yield. Know, sir, I am Don Quixote de la Mancha, he with whose exploits the whole globe resounds."

Roque Guinart presently perceived Don Quixote's infirmity, and that it had in it more of madness than valour ; and, though he had sometimes heard his name mentioned, he always thought that what had been said of him was a fiction, conceiving that such a character could not exist : he was therefore delighted with this meeting, as he might now know, from his own observations, what degree of credit was really due to the reports in circulation.

"Be not concerned," said Roque, addressing himself to Don Quixote, "nor tax Fortune with unkindness ; by thus stumbling, you may chance to stand more firmly than ever : for Heaven, by strange and circuitous ways, incomprehensible to men, is wont to raise the fallen, and enrich the needy."

Roque Guinart requiring to be absent for a short time found his band of desperadoes in the place he had appointed to meet them, and Don Quixote in the midst of them, endeavouring, in a formal speech, to persuade them to quit that kind of life, so prejudicial both to soul and body. But his auditors were chiefly Gascons, a wild and ungovernable race, and therefore this harangue made but little impression upon them. Roque having asked Sancho Panza whether they had restored to him all the property which had been taken from Dapple, he said they had returned all but three nightcaps, which were worth three cities.

"What does the fellow say ?" quoth one of the party : "I have got them, and they are not worth three reals."

"That is true," quoth Don Quixote ; "but my squire justly values the gift for the sake of the giver." Roque Guinart insisted upon their being immediately restored ; then, after commanding his men to draw up in a line before him, he caused all the clothes, jewels, and money, and, in short, all they had plundered since the last division, to be brought out and spread before them ; which being done, he made a short appraisement, reducing into money what could not be divided, and shared the whole among his company with the utmost exactness and impartiality.

After sharing the booty in this manner, by which all were satisfied, Roque said to Don Quixote:

"If I were not thus exact in dealing with these fellows, there would be no living with them."

"Well," quoth Sancho, "justice must needs be a good thing, for it is necessary, I see, even among thieves." On hearing this, one of the squires raised the butt-end of his piece, and would surely have split poor Sancho's head, if Roque had not called out to him to forbear. Terrified at his narrow escape, Sancho resolved to seal up his lips while he remained in such company.

Just at this time intelligence was brought by the scouts that, not far distant, on the Barcelona road, a large body of people were seen coming that way.

"Can you discover," said Roque, "whether they are such as we look for, or such as look for us?"

"Such as we look for, sir."

"Away, then," said Roque, "and bring them hither straight —and see that none escape." The command was instantly obeyed; the band sallied forth, while Don Quixote and Sancho remained with the chief, anxious to see what would follow. In the mean time Roque conversed with the knight on his own way of living.

The party which had been despatched by Roque soon returned with their captives, who consisted of two gentlemen on horseback, two pilgrims on foot, and a coach full of women, attended by six servants, some on foot, and some on horseback, and also two muleteers belonging to the gentlemen. They were surrounded by the victors, who, as well as the vanquished, waited in profound silence till the great Roque should declare his will. He first asked the gentlemen who they were, whither they were going, and what money they had?

"We are captains of infantry, sir," said one of them, "and are going to join our companies, which are at Naples, and, for that purpose, intend to embark at Barcelona, where, it is said, four galleys are about to sail for Sicily. Two or three hundred crowns is somewhere about the amount of our cash, and with that sum we accounted ourselves rich, considering that we are soldiers, whose purses are seldom overladen." The pilgrims being questioned in the same manner, said their intention was to embark for Rome, and that they had about them some threescore reals. The coach now came under examination, and Roque was informed, by one of the attendants, that the persons within were the lady Donna Guiomar de Quinones, wife of the Regent of the vicarship of Naples, her younger daughter, a waiting-maid, and a duenna; that six servants accompanied them, and their money amounted to six hundred crowns. "It appears, then," said Roque Guinart, "that we have here nine hundred crowns, and sixty reals: my soldiers are sixty in number; see how much falls to the share of each; for I am myself but an indifferent accomptant."

His armed ruffians, on hearing this, cried out, "Long live Roque Guinart! in spite of the dogs that seek his ruin." But the officers looked chapfallen, the lady-regent much dejected, and the pilgrims nothing pleased at witnessing this confiscation of their effects. Roque held them awhile in suspense, but would not long protract their suffering, which was visible a bow-shot off, and therefore, turning to the captains, he said, "Pray, gentlemen, do me the favour to lend me sixty crowns; and you, lady-regent, fourscore, as a slight perquisite which these honest gentlemen of mine expect: for 'the abbot must eat that sings for his meat;' and you may then depart, and prosecute your journey without molestation; being secured by a pass which I will give you, in case of your meeting with any other of my people, who are dispersed about this part of the country: for it is not a practice with me to molest soldiers, and I should be loath, madam, to be found wanting in respect to the fair sex—especially to ladies of your quality."

The captains were liberal in their acknowledgments to Roque for his courtesy and moderation in having generously left them a part of their money; and Donna Guiomar de Quinones would have thrown herself out of the coach to kiss the feet and hands of the great Roque, but he would not suffer it, and entreated her pardon for the injury he was forced to do them, in compliance with the duties of an office which his evil fortune had imposed upon him. The lady then ordered the fourscore crowns to be immediately paid to him, as her share of the assessment; the captains had already disbursed their quota, and the pilgrims were

proceeding to offer their little all, when Roque told them to wait ;
then, turning to his men, he said :

"Of these crowns two fall to each man's share, and twenty
remain : let ten be given to these pilgrims, and the other ten to
this honest squire, that, in relating his travels, he may have cause
to speak well of us." Then, producing his writing-implements,
with which he was always provided, he gave them a pass, directed
to the chiefs of his several parties ; and, taking his leave, he dismissed them, all admiring his generosity, his gallantry, and extraordinary conduct, and looking upon him rather as an Alexander
the Great, than a notorious robber.*

Roque then withdrew a little, and wrote a letter to a friend
at Barcelona, to inform him that he had with him the famous
Don Quixote de la Mancha, of whom so much had been reported,
and that, being on his way to Barcelona, he might be sure to see
him there on the approaching festival of St John the Baptist,
parading the strand, armed at all points, mounted on his steed
Rozinante, and attended by his squire Sancho Panza, upon an
ass ; adding, that he had found him wonderfully sagacious and
entertaining. He also desired him to give notice of this to his
friends the Niarra, that they might be diverted with the knight,
and enjoy a pleasure, which he thought too good for his enemies
the Cadells, though he feared it was impossible to prevent their
coming in for a share of what all the world must know and be
delighted with. He despatched this epistle by one of his troop,
who, changing the habit of his vocation for that of a peasant,
entered the city, and delivered it as directed.

* Pellicer proves that this robber Guinart, properly named Pedro Rocha Guinarda,
was a person actually existing in the time of Cervantes, and the captain of a band of
freebooters. About the same period there were, likewise, other Andalusian robbers in
Sierra Cabrilla, who were no less equitable, and even more scrupulous, than the great
Roque himself. Their garb was that of good reformed people, and they took from
travellers but half their property.

CHAPTER LXXV

OF WHAT BEFEL DON QUIXOTE AT HIS ENTRANCE INTO BARCELONA

THREE days and three nights Don Quixote sojourned with the great Roque; and, had he remained with him three hundred years, in such a mode of life he might still have found new matter for observation and wonder. At last they had to part.

Roque, Don Quixote, and Sancho, attended by six squires, set out for Barcelona, and, taking the most secret and unfrequented ways, at night reached the strand on the Eve of St John. Roque now embraced the knight and squire, giving to Sancho the promised ten crowns; and thus they parted, with many friendly expressions and a thousand offers of service on both sides.

Roque returned back, and Don Quixote remained there on horseback waiting for daybreak. Aurora now retired, and the glorious sun gradually rising, at length appeared broad as an ample shield on the verge of the horizon. Don Quixote and Sancho now beheld the sea, which to them was a wondrous novelty, and seemed so boundless and so vast, that the lakes of Ruydera, which they had seen in La Mancha, could not be compared to it. They saw the galleys too, lying at anchor near the shore, which, on removing their awnings, appeared covered with flags and pennants all flickering in the wind, and kissing the surface of the water. Within them was heard the sound of trumpets, hautboys, and other martial instruments, that filled the air with sweet and cheering harmony. Presently the vessels were put in motion, and on the calm sea began a counterfeit engagement; at the same time a numerous body of cavaliers, in gorgeous liveries and nobly mounted, issued from the city, and performed corresponding movements on shore. Cannon were discharged on board the galleys, which were answered by those on the ramparts; and thus the air was rent by mimic thunder. The cheerful sea, the serene sky, only now and then obscured by the smoke of the artillery, seemed to exhilarate and gladden every heart.

Sancho wondered that the bulky monsters which he saw moving on the water should have so many legs : and while his master stood in silent astonishment at the marvellous scene before him, the body of gay cavaliers came galloping up towards him, shouting in the Moorish manner ; and one of them—the person to whom Roque had written—came forward, and said, " Welcome to our city, thou mirror and beacon, and polar-star of knight-errantry ! Welcome, I say, O valorous Don Quixote de la Mancha, not the spurious, the fictitious, the apocryphal one, lately sent amongst us in lying histories, but the true, the legitimate, the genuine Quixote of Cid Hamet Benengeli, the flower of historians !" Don Quixote answered not a word, nor did the cavaliers wait for any answer, but, wheeling round with all their followers, they began to curvet in a circle about Don Quixote, who, turning to Sancho, said, " These people seem to know us well, Sancho ; I dare engage they have read our history, and even that of the Arragonese, lately printed."

The gentleman who spoke to Don Quixote again addressed him, saying :

" Be pleased, Señor Don Quixote, to accompany us, for we are all the intimate and devoted friends of Roque Guinart." To which Don Quixote replied :

" If courtesy beget courtesy, yours, good sir, springs from that of the great Roque ; conduct me whither you please, for I am wholly at your disposal." The gentlemen answered in expressions no less polite, and, enclosing him in the midst of them, they all proceeded, to the sound of martial music, towards the city ; at the entrance of which the father of mischief so ordered it that, among the boys, all of whom are his willing instruments, two, more audacious than the rest, contrived to insinuate themselves within the crowd of horsemen, and one lifting Dapple's tail, and the other that of Rozinante, they lodged under each a handful of briers, the stings whereof being soon felt by the poor animals, they clapped their tails only the closer, which so augmented their suffering that, plunging and kicking from excess of pain, they quickly brought their riders to the ground. Don Quixote, abashed and indignant at the affront, hastened to relieve his tormented steed, while Sancho performed the same kind office for Dapple. Their cavalier escort would have chastised the offenders, but the young rogues presently found shelter in the rabble that followed. The knight and the squire then mounted again, and, accompanied by the same music and acclamations, proceeded until they reached the conductor's house, which was large and handsome, declaring the owner to be a man of wealth and consideration; and there we will leave them; for such is the will and pleasure of the author of this history, Cid Hamet Benengeli.

Learned, rich, sensible, and good-humoured, was Don Antonio Moreno, the present host of Don Quixote; and, being cheerfully disposed, with such an inmate, he soon began to consider how he might extract amusement from his whimsical infirmity; but without offence to his guest—for the jest that gives pain is no jest, nor is that lawful pastime which inflicts an injury. Having prevailed upon the knight to take off his armour, he led him to a balcony at the front of his house, and there, in his strait chamois doublet (which has already been mentioned), exposed him to the populace, who stood gazing at him as if he had been some strange baboon. The gay cavaliers again appeared, and paraded before him as in compliment to him alone, and not in honour of that day's festival. Sancho was highly delighted to find unexpectedly what he fancied to be another Camacho's wedding; another house like that of Don Diego de Miranda, and another duke's castle.

On that day several of Don Antonio's friends dined with him, all paying homage and respect to Don Quixote as a knight-errant; with which his vanity was so flattered that he could scarcely conceal the delight which it gave him. And such was the power of Sancho's wit, that every servant of the house, and indeed all who heard him, hung, as it were, upon his lips. While sitting at table, Don Antonio said to him, "We are told here, honest Sancho, that you are so great a lover of capons and sausages, that, when you have crammed your belly, you stuff your pockets with the fragments for another day." "'Tis not true, an't please your worship; I am not so filthy, nor am I a glutton, as my master Don Quixote here present can bear witness."

"In truth, gentlemen," said Don Quixote, "the frugality of my squire and his cleanliness in eating deserve to be recorded on plates of brass, to remain an eternal memorial for ages to come.

When he was a governor, such was his nicety in eating, that he would take up grapes, and even the grains of a pomegranate, with the point of a fork." "How!" quoth Don Antonio, "has Sancho been a governor?" "Yes, i'faith, I have," replied Sancho, "and of an island called Barataria. Ten days I governed it at my own will and pleasure; but I paid for it in sleepless nights, and learned to hate with all my heart the trade of governing."

Hereupon Don Quixote related minutely all the circumstances of Sancho's government, to the great entertainment of the hearers.

The dinner being ended, Don Quixote was led by his host into a distant apartment, in which there was no other furniture than a small table, apparently of jasper, supported by a pillar of the same: and upon it was placed a bust, seemingly of bronze, the effigy of some high personage. After taking a turn or two in the room, Don Antonio said, "Señor Don Quixote, now that we are alone, I will make known to you one of the most extraordinary circumstances, or rather, I should say, one of the greatest wonders, imaginable, upon condition that what I shall communicate be deposited in the inmost recesses of secrecy."

"It shall be there buried," answered Don Quixote; "and, to be more secure, I will cover it with a tombstone."

"I am satisfied," said Don Antonio, "and, confiding in your promise, I will at once raise your astonishment, and disburthen my own breast of a secret which I have long borne with pain, from the want of some person worthy to be made a confidant in matters which are not to be revealed to everybody."

Thus having, by his long preamble, strongly excited Don Quixote's curiosity, Don Antonio made him examine carefully the brazen head, the table, and the jasper pedestal upon which it stood; he then said:

"Know, Señor Don Quixote, that this extraordinary bust is the production of one of the greatest enchanters or wizards that ever existed. He was, I believe, a Polander, and a disciple of the famous Escotillo,* of whom so many wonders are related. He was here in my house, and, for the reward of a thousand crowns, fabricated this head for me, which has the virtue and property of answering to every question that is put to it. After much study

* Michael Scot.

and labour, drawing figures, erecting schemes, and frequent observation of the stars, he completed his work. To-day being Friday, it is mute, but to-morrow, Señor, you shall surely witness its marvellous powers. In the mean time you may prepare your questions, for you may rely on hearing the truth."

Don Quixote was much astonished at what he heard, and could scarcely credit Don Antonio's relation; but, considering how soon he should be satisfied, he was content to suspend his opinion, and express his acknowledgments to Don Antonio for so great a proof of his favour. Then leaving the chamber, and carefully locking the door, they both returned to the saloon, where the rest of the company were diverting themselves with Sancho's account of his master's adventures.

The same evening they carried Don Quixote abroad, to take the air, mounted on a large easy-paced mule, with handsome furniture, himself unarmed, and with a long wrapping-coat of tawny-coloured cloth, so warm that it would have put even frost into a sweat. They had given private orders to the servants to find amusement for Sancho, so as to prevent his leaving the house, as they had secretly fixed on the back of Don Quixote's coat a parchment, on which was written in capital letters:— "This is Don Quixote de la Mancha."

They had no sooner set out, than the parchment attracted the eyes of the passengers, and the inscription being read aloud, Don Quixote heard his name so frequently repeated that, turning to Don Antonio with much complacency, he said :

"How great the prerogative of knight-errantry, since its professors are known and renowned over the whole earth !"

On the approach of night the calvacade returned home, where preparations were made for a ball by the wife of Don Antonio, an accomplished and beautiful lady, who had invited other friends, both to do honour to her guest, and to entertain them with his singular humour. The ball, which was preceded by a splendid repast, began about ten o'clock at night. Among the ladies, there were two of an arch and jocose disposition, who, though they were modest, behaved with more freedom than usual ; and, to divert themselves and the rest, so plied Don Quixote with dancing that they worried both his soul and body. A sight it was indeed to behold his figure, long, lank, lean, and swarthy, straitened in his clothes, so awkward, and with so little agility.

These roguish ladies took occasion privately to pay their court to him, and he as often repelled them; till, at last, finding himself so pressed by their amorous attentions:

"*Fugite, partes adversæ!*" cried he aloud: "avaunt, ladies! your desires are poison to my soul! Leave me to repose, ye unwelcome thoughts, for the peerless Dulcinea del Toboso is the sole queen of my heart!"

He then threw himself on the floor, where he lay quite shattered by the violence of his exertions. Don Antonio ordered that the wearied knight should be taken up and carried to bed. Sancho was among the first to lend a helping hand; and as he raised him up:

"What, in Heaven's name, sir," said he, "put you upon this business? Think you that all who are valiant must be caperers, or all knights-errant dancing-masters? If so, you are much mistaken, I can tell you. Body of me! some that I know would rather cut a giant's weasand than a caper. Had you been for the shoe-jig,* I could have done your business for you, for I can frisk it away like any jer-falcon: but as for your fine dancing, I cannot work a stitch at it." The company were much diverted by Sancho's remarks, who now led his master to bed, where he left him well covered up, to sweat away the ill effects of his dancing.

The next day, Don Antonio determined to make experiment of the enchanted head: and for that purpose the knight and squire, the two mischievous ladies (who had been invited by Don Antonio's lady to sleep there that night), and two other friends, were conducted to the chamber in which the head was placed. After locking the door, Don Antonio proceeded to explain to them the properties of the miraculous bust, of which, he said, he should now for the first time make trial, but laid them all under an injunction of secrecy. The artifice was known only to the two gentlemen, who, had they not been apprised of it, would have been no less astonished than the rest at so ingenious a contrivance. The first who approached the head was Don Antonio himself, who whispered in its ear, not so low but he was overheard

---

* "Zapatera;" when the dancers slap the sole of their shoe with the palm of their hand, in time and measure.

by all, " Tell me, said he, "thou wondrous head, by the virtue inherent in thee, what are my present thoughts ? " In a clear and distinct voice, without any perceptible motion of its lips, the head replied, "I have no knowledge of thoughts."

All were astonished to hear articulate sounds proceed from the head, being convinced that no human creature present had uttered them. "Then tell me," said Don Antonio, "how many persons are here assembled ? " " Thou and thy wife, with two of thy friends, and two of hers ; and also a famous knight, called Don Quixote de la Mancha, with his squire, Sancho Panza."

At these words, the hair on every head stood erect with amazement and fear.

" Miraculous head ! " exclaimed Don Antonio (retiring a little from the bust), "I am now convinced he was no impostor from whose hands I received thee, O wise oracular, and eloquent head ! Let the experiment be now repeated by some other."

As women are commonly impatient and inquisitive, one of the two ladies next approached the oracle.

" Tell me, head," said she, "what means shall I take to improve my beauty ? "

" Be modest," replied the head.

" I have done," said the lady.

Her companion then went up and said, "I would be glad to know, wondrous head, whether I am beloved by my husband."

" That thou mayst discover by his conduct towards thee," said the oracle.

" That is true," said the married lady, " and the question was needless ; for surely by a man's actions may be seen the true disposition of his mind."

One of the gentlemen now approached the bust, and said, " Who am I ? "

" Thou knowest," was the answer.

" That is not an answer to my question—tell me, head, knowest thou who I am ? "

" Don Pedro Noriz," replied the head.

" 'Tis enough—amazing bust ! " exclaimed the gentleman, " thou knowest everything."

The other gentleman then put his question.

"Tell me, thou oracle of truth."

" Tell me, head, I beseech thee," said he, " what are the chief wishes of my son and heir ? "

" Thou hast already heard that I speak not of thoughts," answered the head, " yet be assured thy son wishes to see thee entombed."

" Truly, I believe it," said the gentleman : " it is but too plain. I have done."

Then came the lady of Don Antonio, and said :

" I know not what to ask thee, yet I would fain know if I shall enjoy my dear husband many years." Then listening, she heard these words :

" Yes, surely, from temperance and a sound body thou mayst expect no less."

Now came the flower of chivalry : " Tell me, thou oracle of truth," said the knight, " was it a reality or only an illusion that I beheld in the cave of Montesinos ? Will the penance imposed on my squire, Sancho Panza, ever be performed ? Will Dulcinea ever be disenchanted ? "

" What thou sawest in the cave," replied the bust, " partakes both of truth and falsehood : Sancho's penance will be slow in performance : and in due time the disenchantment of Dulcinea will be accomplished."

" I am satisfied," said Don Quixote ; " when I shall see the lady of my soul released from her present thraldom, fortune will have nothing more to give me."

The last querist was Sancho. " Shall I," quoth he, " have another government ? Shall I quit this hungry life of squireship ? Shall I see again my wife and children ? "

" If thou returnest home," said the oracle, " there shalt thou be a governor, and see again thy wife and children ; and shouldst thou quit service, thou wilt cease to be a squire."

" Odds my life ! " quoth Sancho Panza, " I could have told as much myself, and the prophet Perogrullo * could have told me no more."

" Beast ! " quoth Don Quixote, " what answer wouldst thou have ? Is it not enough that the answers given thee should correspond with the questions ? "

* The Spanish saying, " The prophecies of Perogrullo," is of similar satirical meaning as the " Vérités de M. de la Palaisse " of the French.

"Yes, truly, sir, quite enough; only I wish it had not been so sparing of its knowledge."

Thus ended the examination of the enchanted head, which left the whole company in amazement, excepting Don Antonio's two friends. Cid Hamet Benengeli, however, was determined to divulge the secret of this mysterious head, that the world might not ascribe its extraordinary properties to witchcraft or necromancy. He declares, therefore, that Don Antonio caused it to be made in imitation of one which he had seen at Madrid, intending it for his own amusement, and to surprise the ignorant; and he thus describes the machine : The table, including its legs and four eagle-claws, was made of wood, and coloured in imitation of jasper. The head, being a resemblance of one of the Cæsars, and painted like bronze, was hollow, with an opening below corresponding with another in the middle of the table, which passed through the leg, and was continued, by means of a metal tube, through the floor of the chamber into another beneath, where a person stood ready to receive the questions, and return answers to the same : the voice ascending and descending as clear and articulate as through a speaking trumpet; and, as no marks of the passage of communication were visible, it was impossible to detect the cheat. A shrewd, sensible youth, nephew to Don Antonio, was on this occasion the respondent, having been previously instructed by his uncle in what concerned the several persons with whom he was to communicate. The first question he readily answered, and to the rest he replied as his judgment directed.

CHAPTER LXXVI

OF SANCHO PANZA'S MISFORTUNE ON BOARD THE GALLEYS;
AND THE EXTRAORDINARY ADVENTURE OF THE
BEAUTIFUL MOOR.

IN the afternoon, Don Antonio Moreno and his two friends, with Don Quixote and Sancho, sallied forth, with an intention to go on board the galleys; and the commodore, who was already apprised of their coming, no sooner perceived them approach the shore than he ordered all the galleys to strike their awnings, and the musicians to play : at the same time he sent out the pinnace, spread with rich carpets and crimson velvet cushions, to convey them on board. The moment Don Quixote entered the boat, he was saluted by a discharge of artillery from the forecastle guns of the captain-galley, which was repeated by the rest ; and as he ascended the side of the vessel, the crew gave him three cheers, agreeable to the custom of receiving persons of rank and distinction. When on deck, the commander, who was a nobleman of Valencia,* gave him his hand, and embracing him, said, " This day, Sir Knight, will I mark with white, as one of the most fortunate of my life, in having been introduced to Señor Don Quixote de la Mancha, in whom is combined and centred all that is valuable in knight-errantry."

Don Quixote replied to him in terms no less courteous ; exceedingly elated to find himself so honoured. The visitors were then conducted to the quarter-deck, which was richly adorned, and there seated themselves. Presently the signal was given for the rowers to strip, when instantly a vast range of naked bodies were exposed to view, that filled Sancho with terror ; and when, in a moment after, the whole deck was covered with its awning, he thought all the devils were let loose. But this prelude was sugar-cake and honey compared with what followed.

Sancho had seated himself on the right side of the deck, and close to the sternmost rower, who, being instructed what he was to do, seized upon the squire, and, lifting him up, tossed him to the next man, and he to a third, and so on, passing from bank to bank through the whole range of slaves, with such astonishing celerity that he lost his sight with the motion, and fancied that the devils themselves were carrying him away ; nor did he stop till he had made the circuit of the vessel and was again replaced on the quarter-deck, where they left the poor man, bruised, breathless, and in a cold sweat, scarcely knowing what had befallen him.

Don Quixote, who beheld Sancho's flight without wings, asked the general if that was a ceremony commonly practised upon persons first coming aboard the galleys : for if so, added

* Don Pedro Coloma, Count d'Elda, commanded the squadron of Barcelona in 1014, when the Moors were expelled from Spain.

he, he must claim an exemption, having no inclination to perform the like exercise; then, rising up, and grasping his sword, he vowed to God that if any one presumed to lay hold of him to toss him in that manner, he would hew their souls out.

At that instant they struck the awning, and, with a great noise, lowered the main-yard from the top of the mast to the bottom. Sancho thought the sky was falling off its hinges and tumbling upon his head; and stooping down, he clapped it in terror between his legs. Nor was Don Quixote without alarm, as plainly appeared by his countenance and manner. With the same swiftness and noise, the yard was again hoisted, and during all these operations not a word was heard. The boatswain now made the signal for weighing anchor, and, at the same time, with his whip, he laid about him on the shoulders of the slaves, while the vessel gradually moved from the shore. Sancho, seeing so many red feet (for such the oars appeared to him) in motion all at once, said to himself, " Ay, these indeed are real enchantments! and not the things we have seen before!—I wonder what these unhappy wretches have done to be flogged at this rate. And how does that whistling fellow dare to whip so many? Surely, this must be purgatory at least."

Don Quixote seeing with what attention Sancho observed all that passed, " Ah, friend Sancho," said he, " if thou wouldst now but strip to the waist, and place thyself among these gentlemen, how easily and expeditiously mightest thou put an end to the enchantment of Dulcinea! For, having so many companions in pain, thou wouldst feel but little of thine own; besides, the sage Merlin would perhaps reckon every lash of theirs, coming from so good a hand, for ten of those which, sooner or later, thou must give thyself."

The commander would have asked what lashes he spoke of, and what he meant by the disenchantment of Dulcinea, but was prevented by information that a signal was perceived on the fort of Montjuich, of a vessel with oars being in sight to the westward. On hearing this, he leaped upon the middle gangway and cheered the rowers, saying, " Pull away, my lads, let her not escape us; she must be some Moorish thief!" The other galley now coming up to the commodore for orders, two were commanded to push out to sea immediately, while he attacked them on the land side, and thus they would be more certain of their prey. The crews of the different galleys plied their oars with such diligence that they seemed to fly. A vessel was soon descried about two miles off, which they judged to be one of fourteen or fifteen banks of oars; but on discovering the galleys in chase, she immediately made off, in the hope of escaping by her swiftness. Unfortunately, however, for her, the captain-galley was a remarkably fast sailer, and gained upon her so quickly that the corsairs, seeing they could not escape a superior force, dropped their oars, in order to yield themselves prisoners, and not exasperate the commander of the galley by their obstinacy. But fortune ordained otherwise, for, just as the captain galley had nearly closed with her, and she was summoned to surrender, two drunken Turks, who with twelve others were on board, discharged their muskets, with which they killed two of our soldiers upon the prow; whereupon the commander swore he would not leave a man of them alive; and, coming up with all fury to board her, she slipped away under the oars of the galley. The galley ran ahead some distance: in the mean time the corsairs, as their case was desperate, endeavoured to make off: but their presumption only aggravated their misfortune: for the captain-galley presently overtook them again, when, clapping her oars on the vessel, she was instantly taken possession of, without more bloodshed.

By this time the two other galleys had come up, and all four returned, with the captured vessel, to their former station near the shore, where a multitude of people had assembled to see what had been taken. On coming to anchor, the commander sent the pinnace on shore for the viceroy, whom he saw waiting to be conveyed on board, and at the same time ordered the main-yard to be lowered, intending, without delay, to hang the master of the vessel and the rest of the Turks he had taken in her, about six-and-thirty in number, all stout fellows, and most of them musketeers. The commander inquired which was their master, when one of the captives (who was afterwards discovered to be a Spanish renegado), answering him in Castilian :

"That young man, sir, is our captain," said he, pointing to a youth of singular grace and beauty, seemingly under twenty years of age.

"Tell me, ill-advised dog," said the commodore, "what moved

you to kill my soldiers, when you saw it was impossible to escape?
Is this the respect due to captain-galleys? Know you not that
temerity is not valour, and that doubtful hopes should make men
bold, but not rash?"

The viceroy, who at that moment came on board, was much
struck with his youth, his handsome person, and resigned behaviour,
and felt a great desire to save him.

"Tell me, corsair," said he, "what art thou? a Turk, Moor, or
renegado?"

"I am neither Turk, Moor, nor renegado," replied the youth, in
the Castilian tongue.

"What, then, art thou?" demanded the viceroy.

"A Christian woman, sir," answered the youth.

"A woman and a Christian, in this garb, and in such a post!"
said the viceroy: "this is indeed more wonderful than credible."

"Gentlemen," said the youth, "allow me to tell you the
brief story of my life: it will not long delay your revenge."
The request was urged so piteously, that it was impossible to deny
it, and the commodore told him to proceed, but not to expect
pardon for his offence. The youth then said she had been
hurried into Barbary by her parents, who, being Moors though
Christianised, had been expelled from Spain. Thither she had
been followed by Don Gregorio, a Christian youth (son of a
gentleman of wealth and rank) who had disguised himself as a
woman. The lad loved her and they would have been
married only Don Gregorio had been retained by the king as
one of his female attendants.

Here she ceased, and the tears that filled her lovely eyes drew
many from those of her auditors. The viceroy himself was much
affected, being a humane and compassionate man, and he went up
to her to untie the cord with which her beautiful hands were
fastened.

While the Christian Moor was relating her story, an old
pilgrim, who came aboard the galley with the viceroy's attendants,
fixed his eyes on her, and scarcely had she finished when, rushing
towards her, he cried:

"O, Anna Felix! my dear, unfortunate daughter! I am
thy father Ricote, and was returning to seek thee, being unable
to live without thee, who art my very soul."

At these words Sancho raised his head, which he had hitherto held down, ruminating on what he had lately suffered, and, staring at the pilgrim, recognised the same Ricote whom he had met with upon the day he had quitted his government; he was also satisfied that the damsel was indeed his daughter, who, being now unbound, was embracing her father, mingling her tears with his.

" This, gentlemen," said he, " is my daughter, happy in her name alone; Anna Felix she is called, with the surname of Ricote, as famous for her own beauty as for her father's riches. I left my native country to seek in foreign kingdoms a safe retreat; and having found one in Germany, I returned in this pilgrim's habit to seek my daughter, and take away the property I had left. My daughter was gone, but the treasure I have in my possession; and now, by a strange turn of fortune, I have found her, who is my greatest treasure. If our innocence and our united tears, through the uprightness of your justice, can open the gates of mercy, let it be extended to us, who never in thought offended you, nor in anywise conspired with those of our nation who have been justly banished."

Sancho, now putting in his word, said:

"I know Ricote well, and answer for the truth of what he says of Anna Felix being his daughter; but as for the story of going and coming, and of his good or bad intentions, I meddle not with them."

An incident so remarkable could not fail to make a strong impression upon all who were present; so that the commodore, sharing in the common feeling, said to the fair captive:

" My oath, madam, is washed away with your tears; live, fair Anna Felix, all the years Heaven has allotted you."

They now consulted on the means of Don Gregorio's deliverance. Ricote offered jewels, then in his possession, to the amount of more than two thousand ducats, towards effecting it; but the expedient most approved was the proposal of the renegado, who offered to return to Algiers in a small bark of six banks manned with Christians, for he knew when and where he might land, and was, moreover, acquainted with the house in which Don Gregorio was kept. Some doubts were expressed whether the Christian sailors could be safely trusted with the renegado; but they were removed by the confidence in him expressed by Anna

Felix, and the promise of her father to ransom them in case they should be taken.

The viceroy then returned on shore, charging Don Antonio Moreno with the care of Ricote and his daughter; desiring him at the same time to demand anything that, in his own house, might conduce to their entertainment; such was the kindness and good-will inspired by beauty and misfortune.

CHAPTER LXXVII

DEFEAT OF DON QUIXOTE

It is related in this history that the wife of Don Antonio Moreno received Anna Felix with extreme pleasure, and was equally delighted with her beauty and good sense: for the young lady excelled in both; and from all parts of the city people came in crowds to see her, as if they had been brought together by the sound of bell. Two days after that, the renegado sailed in a small bark of twelve oars, with a crew of stout and resolute fellows, and in two days after that, the galleys departed for the Levant, the viceroy having promised the commodore an account of the fortunes of Don Gregorio and Anna Felix.

One morning, Don Quixote having sallied forth to take the air on the strand, armed at all points—his favourite costume, for arms, he said, were his ornament, and fighting his recreation—he observed a knight advancing towards him, armed also like himself, and bearing a shield, on which was portrayed a resplendent moon; and when near enough to be heard, in an elevated voice he addressed himself to Don Quixote, saying:

" Illustrious knight, and never-enough-renowned Don Quixote de la Mancha, I am the Knight of the White Moon, of whose incredible achievements, peradventure, you have heard. I come to engage in combat with you, and to try the strength of your arm, in order to make you confess that my mistress, whoever she may be, is beyond comparison more beautiful than your Dulcinea del Toboso :—a truth which, if you fairly confess, you will spare your own life, and me the trouble of taking it. The terms of

the combat I require are, that if the victory be mine, you relinquish arms and the search of adventures for the space of
one year, and that, returning forthwith to your own dwelling,
you there live during that period in a state of profound quiet,
which will tend both to your temporal and spiritual welfare;
but if, on the contrary, my head should lie at your mercy, then
shall the spoils of my horse and arms be yours, and the fame of
my exploits transferred to you.   Consider which is best for you,
and determine quickly, for this very day must decide our
fate."

Don Quixote was no less surprised at the arrogance of the
Knight of the White Moon than the reason he gave for challeng-
ing him; and, with much gravity and composure, he answered,
" Knight of the White Moon, whose achievements have not as
yet reached my ears, I dare swear you have never seen the
illustrious Dulcinea; for, if so, I am confident you would have
taken care not to engage in this trial, since the sight of her must
have convinced you that there never was, nor ever can be,
beauty comparable to hers; and, therefore, without giving you
the lie, I only affirm that you are mistaken, and accept your
challenge; and that too upon the spot, even now, this very day,
as you desire. Of your conditions, I accept all but the transfer
of your exploits, which being unknown to me, I shall remain contented with my own, such as they are. Choose then your
ground, and expect to meet me; and he whom Heaven favours
may St. Peter bless ! "

In the mean time, the viceroy, who had been informed of the
appearance of the stranger knight, and that he was holding parley
with Don Quixote, hastened to the scene of action, accompanied
by Don Antonio and several others: not doubting but that it
was some new device of theirs to amuse themselves with the
knight. He arrived just as Don Quixote had wheeled Rozinante
about to take the necessary ground for his career, and perceiving
that they were ready for the onset, he went up and inquired the
cause of so sudden an encounter. The Knight of the White
Moon told him it was a question of pre-eminence in beauty,
and then briefly repeated what he had said to Don Quixote,
mentioning the conditions of the combat. The viceroy, in a
whisper to Don Antonio, asked him if he knew the stranger

knight, and whether it was some jest upon Don Quixote. Don Antonio assured him, in reply, that he neither knew who he was, nor whether this challenge was in jest or earnest. Puzzled with this answer, the viceroy was in doubt whether or not he should interpose, and prevent the encounter; but being assured it could only be some pleasantry, he withdrew, saying:

"Valorous knights, if there be no choice between confession and death; if Señor Don Quixote persists in denying, and you, Sir Knight of the White Moon, in affirming, to it, gentlemen, in Heaven's name!"

The knights made their acknowledgments to the viceroy for his gracious permission; and now Don Quixote, recommending himself to Heaven, and (as usual on such occasions) to his lady Dulcinea, retired again to take a larger compass, seeing his adversary do the like; and without sound of trumpet or other warlike instrument, to give signal for the onset, they both turned their horses about at the same instant; but he of the White Moon being mounted on the fleetest steed, met Don Quixote before he had run half his career, and then, without touching him with his lance, which he seemed purposely to raise, he encountered him with such impetuosity that both horse and rider came to the ground; he then sprang upon him, and, clapping his lance to his vizor, he said:

"Knight, you are vanquished and a dead man, if you confess not, according to the conditions of our challenge."

Don Quixote, bruised and stunned, without lifting up his vizor, and as if speaking from a tomb, said in a feeble and low voice:

"Dulcinea del Toboso is the most beautiful woman in the world, and I am the most unfortunate knight on earth, nor is it just that my weakness should discredit this truth; knight, push on your lance, and take away my life, since you have despoiled me of my honour."

"Not so, by my life!" quoth he of the White Moon: "long may the beauty and fame of the lady Dulcinea del Toboso flourish! All I demand of the great Don Quixote is, that he submit to one year's domestic repose and respite from the exercise of arms."

The viceroy, Don Antonio, with many others, were witnesses

to all that passed, and now heard Don Quixote promise that, since he required nothing of him to the prejudice of his lady Dulcinea, he should fulfil the terms of their engagement with the punctuality of a true knight.

This declaration bring made, he of the White Moon turned about his horse, and bowing to the viceroy, at a half-gallop entered the city, whither the viceroy ordered Don Antonio to follow him, and by all means to learn who he was. They now raised Don Quixote from the ground, and, uncovering his face, found him pale, and bedewed with cold sweat, and Rozinante in such a plight that he was unable to stir.

Sancho, quite sorrowful and cast down, knew not what to do or say; sometimes he fancied he was dreaming; at others, that the whole was an affair of witchcraft and enchantment. He saw his master discomfited, and bound, by his oath, to lay aside arms for a whole year! His glory, therefore, he thought was for ever extinguished, and his hopes of greatness scattered, like smoke, to the wind. Indeed he was afraid that both horse and rider were crippled, and hoped that it would prove no worse.

Finally, the vanquished knight was conveyed to the city in a chair, which had been ordered by the viceroy, who returned thither himself, impatient for some information concerning the knight who had left Don Quixote in such evil plight.

Don Antonio Moreno rode into the city after the Knight of the White Moon, who was also pursued to his inn by a swarm of boys; and he had no sooner entered the chamber where his squire waited to disarm him, than he was greeted by the inquisitive Don Antonio. Conjecturing the object of his visit, he said, "I doubt not, Señor, but that your design is to learn who I am; and as there is no cause for concealment, while my servant is unarming me, I will inform you without reserve. My name, Señor, is the bachelor Sampson Carrasco, and I am of the same town with Don Quixote de la Mancha, whose madness and folly have excited the pity of all who knew him. I have felt, for my own part, particularly concerned, and, believing his recovery to depend upon his remaining quietly at home, my projects have been solely directed to that end. About three months ago I sallied forth on the highway like a knight-errant, styling myself Knight of the Mirrors, intending to fight and conquer my friend, without doing him harm, and making his submission to my will the condition of our combat. Never doubting of success, I expected to send him home for twelve months, and hoped that, during that time, he might be restored to his senses. But fortune ordained it otherwise, for he was the victor; he tumbled me from my horse, and thereby defeated my design. He pursued his journey, and I returned home vanquished, abashed, and hurt by my fall. However, I did not relinquish my project, as you have seen this day; and, as he is so exact and punctual in observing the laws of knight-errantry, he will doubtless observe my injunctions. And now, sir, I have only to beg that you will not discover me to Don Quixote, that my good intentions may take effect, and his understanding be restored to him, which, when freed from the follies of chivalry, is excellent."

"O, sir!" exclaimed Don Antonio, "what have you to answer for in robbing the world of so diverting a madman? Is it not plain, sir, that no benefit to be derived from his recovery can be set against the pleasure which his extravagances afford? But I fancy, sir, his case is beyond the reach of your art; and, Heaven forgive me! for by his cure we should lose not only the pleasantries of the knight, but those of his squire, which are enough to transform Melancholy herself into mirth. Nevertheless, I will be silent, and wait in the full expectation that Señor Carrasco will lose his labour."

"Yet, all things considered," said the bachelor, "the business is in a promising way—I have no doubt of success."

Don Antonio then politely took his leave; and that same day the bachelor, after having his armour tied upon the back of a mule, mounted his charger, and quitted the city, directing his course homewards, where he arrived without meeting with any adventure on the road worthy of a place in this faithful history. Don Antonio reported his conversation with the bachelor Carrasco to the viceroy, who regretted that such conditions should have been imposed upon Don Quixote, as they might put an end to that diversion which he had so liberally supplied to all who were acquainted with his whimsical turn of mind.

During six days Don Quixote kept his bed, melancholy,

R

thoughtful, and out of humour, still dwelling upon his unfortunate overthrow. Sancho strove hard to comfort him:

"Cheer up, my dear master," said he, "pluck up a good
heart, sir, and be thankful you have come off without a broken
rib. Remember, sir, 'they that give must take;' and 'every
hook has not its flitch.' Come, come, sir—a fig for the doctor!
you have no need of him. Let us pack up, and be jogging homeward, and leave this rambling up and down to seek adventures the
Lord knows where—odds bodikins! after all, I am the greatest
loser, though mayhap your worship suffers the most; for though,
after a taste of governing, I now loathe it, I have never lost my
longing for an earldom or countship, which I may whistle for
if your worship refuses to be a king, by giving up knight-
errantry."

"Peace, friend Sancho," quoth Don Quixote, "and remember
that my retirement is not to exceed a year, and then I will resume
my honourable profession, and shall not want a kingdom for
myself, nor an earldom for thee."

"Heaven grant it, and sin be deaf!" quoth Sancho; "for I
have always been told that good expectation is better than bad
possession."

Here their conversation was interrupted by Don Antonio,
who entered the chamber with signs of great joy.

"Reward me, Señor Don Quixote," said he, "for my good
news—Don Gregorio and the renegado are safe in the harbour—
in the harbour, said I?—by this time they are at the viceroy's
palace, and will be here presently." Don Quixote seemed to
revive by this intelligence.

"Truly," said he, "I am almost sorry at what you tell me,
for, had it happened otherwise, I should have gone over to
Barbary, where, by the force of my arm, I should have given
liberty not only to Don Gregorio, but to all the Christian captives
in that land of slavery. But what do I say? wretch that I am!
Am I not vanquished? Am I not overthrown? Am I not forbidden to unsheath my sword for twelve whole months? Why,
then, do I promise and vaunt? A distaff better becomes my hand
than a sword!"

"No more, sir," quoth Sancho: "let the hen live, though she
have the pip; to-day for you, and to-morrow for me; and, as for

these matters of encounters and bangs, never trouble your head about them; he that falls to-day may rise to-morrow; unless he chooses to lie in bed and groan, instead of getting into heart and spirits, ready for fresh encounters. Rise, dear sir, and welcome Don Gregorio; for, by the bustle in the house, I reckon he is come."

And this was the fact. Don Gregorio, after giving the viceroy an account of the expedition, impatient to see his Anna Felix, hastened with his deliverer, the renegado, to Don Antonio's house. The female dress, in which he had escaped, he had exchanged for that of a captive who had come off with them; yet even in that disguise his handsome exterior commanded respect and admiration. He was young, too, for he seemed to be not more than seventeen or eighteen years of age. Ricote and his daughter went out to meet him—the father with tears, and the daughter with modest joy. The young couple did not embrace; for true and ardent love shrinks from public freedom of behaviour. Their beauty was universally admired, and, though they spoke not to each other, their eyes modestly revealed their joyful and pure emotions. The renegado gave a short account of his voyage, and the means he had employed to accomplish the purpose of the expedition; and Don Gregorio told the story of his difficulties and embarrassments, during his confinement, with good sense and discretion above his years. Ricote fully satisfied the boatmen, as well as the renegado, who was forthwith restored to the bosom of the church, and from a rotten member became, through penance and true repentance, clean and sound.

Two days afterwards, Don Quixote, who had hitherto been unable to travel, on account of his bruises, set forward on his journey home, Sancho trudging after him on foot — because Dapple was now employed in bearing his master's armour.

CHAPTER LXXVIII

THE VANQUISHED KNIGHT BEGINS THE JOURNEY HOMEWARD

As Don Quixote was leaving the city of Barcelona, he cast his eyes to the spot whereon he had been defeated; and pausing, he cried:—"There stood Troy! There my evil destiny, not cowardice, despoiled me of my glory; there I experienced the fickleness of fortune: there the lustre of my exploits was obscured; and, lastly, there fell my happiness, never more to rise!" Upon which Sancho said to him:

"Great hearts, dear sir, should be patient under misfortunes, as well as joyful when all goes well; and in that I judge by myself; for when I was made a governor, I was blithe and merry, and now that I am a poor squire on foot, I am not sad. I have heard say, that she they call Fortune is a drunken freakish dame, and withal so blind that she does not see what she is about; neither whom she raises, nor whom she pulls down."

That night the master and man took up their lodging in the middle of a field, under the spangled roof of heaven; and the next day, while pursuing their jouney, they saw a man coming towards them on foot, with a wallet about his neck, and a javelin, or half-pike, in his hand—the proper equipment of a foot-post; who, when he had got near them, quickened his pace, and, running up to Don Quixote, embraced his right thigh—for he could reach no higher,—and, testifying great joy, he said, "Oh! Señor Don Quixote de la Mancha! how rejoiced will my lord duke be when he hears that your worship is returning to his castle, where he still remains with my lady duchess!"

"I know you not, friend," answered Don Quixote; "nor can I conceive who you are unless you tell me."

"Señor Don Quixote," answered the courier, "I am Tosilos, the duke's lacquey; the same who would not fight with your worship about Donna Rodriguez' daughter."

"Heaven defend me!" exclaimed Don Quixote, "are you

he whom the enchanters, my enemies, transformed into the lacquey, to defraud me of the glory of that combat?"

"Softly, good sir," replied the messenger; "there was neither enchantment nor change in the case. Tosilos the lacquey I entered the lists, and the same I came out. I refused fighting, because I had a mind to marry the girl; but it turned out quite otherwise; for your worship had no sooner left the castle than, instead of a wife, I got a sound banging, by my lord duke's order, for not doing as he would have had me in that affair; and the end of it all is, that the girl is turned nun, and Donna Rodriguez packed off to Castile; and I am now going to Barcelona with a packet of letters from my lord to the viceroy; and if your worship will please to take a little of the dear creature, I have here a calabash full at your service, with a slice of good cheese that will awaken thirst, if it be sleeping."

"I take you at your word," quoth Sancho; "and, without more ado, let us be at it, good Tosilos, in spite of all the enchanters in the Indies."

"In truth, Sancho," quoth Don Quixote, "thou art a very glutton, and, moreover, the greatest simpleton on earth, to doubt that this courier is enchanted, and a counterfeit Tosilos. But, if thou art bent upon it, stay, in Heaven's name, and eat thy fill, while I go on slowly, and wait thy coming." The lacquey laughed, unsheathed his calabash, and unwalleted his cheese; and taking out a little loaf, he and Sancho sat down upon the grass, and in peace and good-fellowship quickly despatched the contents, and got to the bottom of the provision-bag, with so good an appetite that they licked the very packet of letters because it smelt of cheese.

While they were thus employed:

"Hang me, friend Sancho," said Tosilos, "if I know what to make of that master of yours—he must needs be a madman."

"Need!" quoth Sancho; "faith, he has no need! for, if madness pass current, he has plenty to pay every man his own. That I can see full well, and full often I tell him of it; but what boots it!—especially now that it is all over with him; for he has been worsted by the Knight of the White Moon."

Tosilos begged him to relate what had happened to him; but Sancho excused himself, saying it would be unmannerly to keep his master waiting ; but that, another time, if they should meet again, he would tell him the whole affair. He then rose up, shook the crumbs from his beard and apparel, and took leave of Tosilos ; then driving Dapple before him, he set off to overtake his master, whom he found waiting for him under the shade of a tree.

Don Quixote and his squire travelled on till they arrived at the very spot where they had been trampled upon by the bulls. Don Quixote recollecting it, "There, Sancho," said he, "is the meadow where we met the gay shepherdesses and gallant shepherds who proposed to revive, in this place, another pastoral Arcadia. The project was equally new and ingenious, and if thou thinkest well of it, Sancho, we will follow their example, and turn shepherds : at least for the term of my retirement. I will buy sheep, and whatever is necessary for a pastoral life ; and I, assuming the name of the shepherd Quixotiz, and thou that of the shepherd Panzino, we will range the woods, the hills, and the valleys, singing here and sighing there ; drinking from the clear springs, or limpid brooks, or the mighty rivers ; while the oaks, with liberal hand, shall give us their sweetest fruit—the hollow cork-trees, lodging—willows, their shade, and the roses, their delightful perfume. The spacious meads shall be our carpets of a thousand colours ; and, ever breathing the clear, pure air, the moon and stars shall be our tapers of the night, and light our evening walk ; and thus while singing will be our pleasure and complaining our delight, the god of song will provide harmonious verse, and love an ever-failing theme — so shall our fame be eternal as our song !"

"'Fore gad !" quoth Sancho, "that kind of life squares and corners with me exactly ; and I warrant if once the bachelor Sampson Carrasco, and Master Nicholas the barber, catch a glimpse of it, they will follow us, and turn shepherds too : and Heaven grant that the priest have not an inclination to make one in the fold—he is so gay and merrily inclined."

"Thou sayest well," quoth Don Quixote : "and if the bachelor Sampson Carrasco will make one amongst us, as I doubt not he will, he may call himself the shepherd Sampsonino, or Carrascon. Master Nicholas the barber may be called Niculoso, as old Boscan called himself Nomoroso."

"Alas ! sir," quoth Sancho, "I am so unlucky that I shall

never see those blessed days! O what neat wooden spoons shall I make when I am a shepherd! What curds and cream! what garlands! what pretty nick-nacks! An old dog I am at these trinkums, which though they may not set me up for one of the seven wise men, will get me the name of a clever fellow. My daughter Sanchica shall bring our dinner to us in the field—but hold there: she's a sightly wench, and shepherds are sometimes roguishly given."

They retired, and made a late and scanty supper, much against Sancho's inclination, for it brought the hardships of knight-errantry fresh upon his thoughts, and he grieved to think how seldom he encountered the plenty that reigned in the house of Don Diego de Miranda, at the wedding of the rich Camacho, and at Don Antonio Moreno's; but again reflecting that it could not be always day, nor always night, he betook himself to sleep, leaving his master thoughtful and awake.

CHAPTER LXXIX

OF THE BRISTLY ADVENTURE WHICH BEFEL DON QUIXOTE

DON QUIXOTE being satisfied with his first sleep, did not solicit more. As for Sancho, he never wanted a second, for the first lasted him from night to morning: indicating a sound body and mind free from care.

Thus were they engaged, when they heard a strange, dull kind of noise, with harsh sounds, issuing from every part of the valley. Don Quixote started up, and laid his hand to his sword; and Sancho squatted down under Dapple, and fortified himself with the bundle of armour on one side of him, and the ass's pannel on the other, trembling no less with fear than Don Quixote with surprise. Every moment the noise increased as the cause of it approached, to the great terror of one at least—for the courage of the other is too well known to be suspected. Now the cause of this fearful din was this:—some hog-dealers, eager to reach the market, happened at that early hour to be driving above six hundred of these creatures along the road to a fair, where they were to be sold ; which filthy herd, with their grunting and squeaking made such a horrible noise that both the knight and squire were stunned and confounded, and utterly at a loss how to account for it.

On they came without showing the smallest degree of respect for the lofty character of Don Quixote or of Sancho his squire, threw down both master and man, demolishing Sancho's entrench-ment, and laying even Rozinante in the dust ! On they went, and bore all before them, overthrowing pack-saddle, armour, knight, squire, horse, and all ; treading and trampling over every-thing without remorse. Sancho with some difficulty recovered his legs, and desired his master to lend him his sword, that he might slay half-a-dozen at least of those unmannerly swine—for he had now discovered what they were ; but Don Quixote admonished him not to hurt them.

" Heaven," said he, " has inflicted this disgrace upon my guilty head : it is no more than a just punishment that dogs should devour, hornets sting, and hogs trample on a vanquished knight-errant."

" And Heaven, I suppose," quoth Sancho, " has sent fleas to sting and bite, and hunger to famish us poor squires, for keeping such knights company. If we squires were the sons of the knights we serve, or their kinsmen, it would be no wonder that we should share in their punishments, even to the third and fourth generation : but what have the Panzas to do with the Quixotes ? Well, let us to our litter again, and try to sleep out the little that is left of the night, and God will send daylight, and mayhap better luck."

Daylight at length appeared, and the sun darting his beams full on Sancho's face, at last awoke him ; whereupon rubbing his eyes, yawning, and stretching his limbs, he perceived the swinish havoc made in his cupboard, and heartily wished the drove at the devil, and even went further than that in his wishes.

The knight and squire now started again, and journeyed on through the whole of that day, when towards evening they saw about half a score of men on horseback, and four or five on foot, making directly towards them. Don Quixote was much agitated by the sight of these men, and Sancho trembled with fear : for they were armed with lances and shields, and other warlike implements.

"Ah, Sancho," said Don Quixote, "had I my hands at liberty, I would make no more of that hostile squadron than if it were composed of gingerbread. However, matters may not turn out so bad as they promise." The horsemen soon came up, and instantly surrounded the knight and the squire, and in a threatening manner presented the points of their lances at their prisoners. One of those on foot putting his finger to his lips, as if commanding Don Quixote to be mute, seized on Rozinante's bridle, and drew him out of the road ; while the others, in like manner, took possession of Dapple and his rider, and the whole then moved on in silence. Don Quixote several times would have inquired whither they meant to take him, but scarcely had he moved his lips to speak, when they were ready to close them with the points of their spears. And so it was with Sancho : no sooner did he show an inclination to speak than one of those on foot pricked him with a goad, driving Dapple in the same manner, as if he also wished to speak.

Night advancing, they quickened their pace, and the fear of the prisoners likewise increased ; especially when they heard the fellows ever and anon say to them, "On, on, ye Troglodytes ! Peace, ye barbarian slaves ! Pay, ye Anthropophagi ! Complain not, ye Scythians ! Open not your eyes, ye murderous Polyphemuses—ye butcherly lions !" With these and other such names they tormented the ears of the unhappy master and man. Sancho went along muttering to himself—What ! call us ortolans ! barbers ! slaves ! Andrew popinjays ! and Polly famouses !—I dont like the sound of such names—a bad wind this to winnow our corn ; mischief has been lowering upon us of late, and now it falls thick, like kicks to a cur. It looks ill, God send it may not end worse !" Don Quixote proceeded onwards, quite confounded at the reproachful names that were given to him, and he could only conclude that no good was to be expected, and much harm to be feared. In this perplexing situation, about an hour after nightfall, they arrived at a castle, which Don Quixote presently recollected to be that belonging to the duke, where he had lately been. "Heaven defend me !" said he, as soon as he knew the place, "what can this mean ? In this house all is courtesy and kindness !—but, to the vanquished, good is converted into bad, bad into worse." On entering the principal court, they saw it decorated and set out in a manner that added still more to their fears, as well as their astonishment, as will be seen in the following chapter.

No sooner had the horsemen alighted, than assisted by those on foot, they seized Don Quixote and Sancho in their arms, and placed them in the midst of the court ; where a hundred torches, and above five hundred other lights, dispersed in the galleries around, set the whole in a blaze ; insomuch that, in spite of the darkness of the night, it appeared like day. In the middle of the court was erected a tomb, six feet from the ground, and over it was spread a large canopy of black velvet ; round which, upon its steps, were burning above a hundred wax tapers in silver candlesticks. On the tomb was visible the corpse of a damsel, so beautiful as to make death itself appear lovely. Her head was laid upon a cushion of gold brocade, crowned with a garland of fragrant flowers, and in her hands, which were laid crosswise upon her breast, was placed a green branch of victorious palm. On one side of the court was erected a theatre, where two personages were seated, whose crowns on their heads and sceptres in their hands denoted them to be kings, either real or feigned. On the side of the theatre, which was ascended by steps, were two other seats, upon which Don Quixote and Sancho were placed. This was performed in profound silence, and by signs they were both given to understand they were to hold their peace : though the caution was needless, for astonishment had tied up their tongues.

Two great persons now ascended the theatre with a numerous retinue, and seated themselves in two chairs of state, close to those who seemed to be monarchs. These Don Quixote immediately knew to be the duke and duchess who had so nobly entertained him. Everything he saw filled him with wonder, and nothing more than his discovery that the corpse lying extended on the tomb was that of the fair Altisidora ! When the duke and duchess had taken their places, Don Quixote and Sancho rose up, and made them a profound reverence, which their highnesses returned by a slight inclination of the head. Immediately after, an officer crossed the area, and, going up to Sancho, threw over him a robe of black buckram, painted over with flames, and, taking off his cap, he put on his head a pasteboard mitre, three feet high, like those used by the penitents of the Inquisition ; bidding him, in a whisper, not to open his lips, otherwise he would be either gagged or slain. Sancho viewed himself from top to toe, and saw his body covered with flames : but, finding they did not burn him, he cared not two straws. He took off his mitre, and saw it painted all over with devils : but he replaced it again on his head, saying within himself, "All is well enough yet ; these flames do not burn, nor do these imps fly away with me." Don Quixote also surveyed him, and in spite of his perturbation he could not forbear smiling at his strange appearance.

And now, in the midst of that profound silence (for not a breath was heard), a soft and pleasing sound of flutes stole upon the ear, seeming to proceed from the tomb. Then, on a sudden, near the couch of the dead body, appeared a beautiful youth, in a Roman habit, who, in a sweet and clear voice, to the sound of the harp, which he touched himself, sang a moving lay beginning :

> Till Heav'n in pity to the weeping world,
> Shall give Altisidora back to day,
> By Quixote's scorn to realms of Pluto hurl'd,
> Her every charm to cruel death a prey ;
> I'll sing the praises of this hapless maid,
> In sweeter notes than Thracian Orpheus ever play'd.

"Enough," said one of the kings, "enough, divine musician ! it were an endless task to describe the graces of the peerless Altisidora—dead, as the ignorant world believes, but still living in the breath of fame, and through the penance which Sancho Panza, here present, must undergo, in order to restore her to life : and therefore, O Rhadamanthus ! who, with me, judgest in the dark caverns of Pluto, since thou knowest all that destiny has decreed touching the restoration of this damsel, speak— declare it immediately ; nor delay the promised felicity of her return to the world."

Scarcely had Minos ceased, when Rhadamanthus, starting up,

cried, "Ho, there ! ye ministers and officers of the household, high and low, great and small ! Proceed ye, one after another, and mark me Sancho's face with four-and-twenty twitches, and let his arms and sides have twelve, and thrust therein six times the pin's sharp point : for on the due performance of this ceremony depends the restoration of that lifeless corse."

Sancho, hearing this, could hold out no longer.

"I vow to Heaven," cried he, "I will sooner turn Turk than let my flesh be so handled ! Body of me ! how is the mauling of my visage to give life to the dead ? 'The old woman has had a taste, and now her mouth waters.' Dulcinea is enchanted, and to unbewitch her I must be whipped ! and now here Altisidora dies of some disease that God has sent her, and, to bring her to life again, my flesh must be tweaked and pinched, and corking-pins thrust into my body ! No, put these tricks upon a brother-in-law : I am an old dog, and am not to be coaxed with a crust."

"Relent !" said Rhadamanthus, in a loud voice, "relent, tiger, or thou diest ! Submit, proud Nimrod ! suffer, and be silent, monster ! Impossibilities are not required of thee ; then talk not of difficulties. Twitched thou shalt be ; pricked thou shalt feel thyself, and pinched even to groaning. Ho, there ! officers do your duty—or, on the word of an honest man, thy destiny shall be fulfilled ! "

Immediately six duennas were seen advancing in procession along the court, four of them with spectacles, and all of them with their right hands raised, and four fingers' breadth of their wrist bared, to make their hands seem the longer, according to the fashion. No sooner had Sancho got a glimpse of his executioners than, bellowing aloud, he cried, "Do with me whatever you please : pour over me a sackful of mad cats to bite and claw me, as my master was served in this castle ; pierce and drill me through with sharp daggers ; tear off my flesh with red-hot pincers, and I will bear it all with patience to oblige your worships : but the devil may fly away with me at once before a duenna shall put a finger upon my flesh ! "

Don Quixote could no longer keep silence.

"Have patience, my son," said he ; "yield to the command of these noble persons, and give thanks to Heaven for having imparted to thy body a virtue so wonderful that, by a little torture, thou shouldst be able to break the spells of enchanters, and restore the dead to life."

By this time Sancho was surrounded by the duennas, and, being softened and persuaded by his master's entreaties, he fixed himself firmly in his chair, and held out his face and beard to the executioners. The first gave him a dexterous twitch, and then made him a low curtsey. "Spare me your complaisance, good madam, and give less of your slabber-sauce; for, Heaven take me! your fingers stink of vinegar." In short, all the duennas successively performed their office, and after them divers other persons repeated the same ceremony of tweaking and pinching, to all of which he submitted: but when they came to pierce his flesh with pins, he could contain himself no longer, and starting up in a fury, he caught hold of a lighted torch and began to lay about him with such agility that all his tormentors were put to flight. "Away!" he cried; "scamper, ye imps of the devil! do you take me to be made of brass, and suppose I cannot feel your cursed torments?"

At this moment Altisidora (who must have been tired with lying so long upon her back), turned herself on one side; upon which the whole assembly cried out with one voice, "She lives! she lives! Altisidora lives!" Rhadamanthus then told Sancho to calm his rage, for the work was accomplished. The moment Don Quixote perceived Altisidora move, he went to Sancho, and, kneeling before him, said:

"Now is the time, dear son of my bowels, rather than my squire, to inflict on thyself some of those lashes for which thou art pledged in order to effect the disenchantment of Dulcinea; this, I say, is the time, now that thy virtue is seasoned, and of efficacy to operate the good expected from thee."

"Why, this," replied Sancho, "is tangle upon tangle, and not honey upon fritters! A good jest, indeed, that pinches and prickings must be followed by lashes! Do, sir, take at once a great stone and tie it about my neck, and tumble me into a well; better kill me outright than break my back with other men's burthens. Look ye, if ye meddle any more with me, as I have a living soul, all shall out!"

Altisidora had now raised herself, and sat upright on her

tomb, whereupon the music immediately struck up, and the court resounded with the cries of "Live, live, Altisidora ! Altisidora, live !" The duke and duchess arose, and with Minos, Rhadamanthus, Don Quixote, and Sancho, went to receive the restored damsel, and assist her to descend from the tomb. Apparently near fainting, she bowed to the duke and duchess and the two kings ; then casting a side-glance at Don Quixote, she said :

"Heaven forgive thee, unrelenting knight ! by whose cruelty I have been imprisoned in the other world above a thousand years, as it seems to me, and where I must have for ever remained had it not been for thee, O Sancho ! Thanks, thou kindest and best of squires, for the life I now enjoy !" Sancho, with his mitre in his hand, and his knee on the ground, kissed her hand. The duke ordered him to be disrobed and his own garments returned to him ; but Sancho begged his grace to allow him to keep the frock and the mitre, that he might carry them to his own village, in token and memory of this unheard-of adventure. Whereupon the duchess assured him of her regard, and promised him that the frock and mitre should certainly be his. The court was now cleared by the duke's command ; all the company retired, and Don Quixote and Sancho were conducted to the apartments which they had before occupied.

The bachelor Sampson Carrasco had called at the castle before and after his encounter with Don Quixote, and the duke had arranged the disenchantment of Altisidora as being the last time in all probability he would see the knight and his diverting squire.

CHAPTER LXXX

THE DISENCHANTMENT OF DULCINEA

DON QUIXOTE took leave of the duke and duchess the next day. The vanquished knight pursued his journey homeward, sometimes overcome with grief, and sometimes joyful : for if his spirits were depressed by the recollection of his overthrow, they were again raised by the singular virtue that seemed to be lodged in the body of his squire, still giving him fresh hopes of his lady's

" The vanquished knight pursued his journey."

restoration ; at the same time, he was not without some qualms respecting Altisidora's resurrection.

"Sancho, my son," said Don Quixote at length, "I can say, if thou wouldst be paid for disenchanting Dulcinea, I should readily satisfy thee. Yet I know not whether payment be allowed in the conditions of the cure, and I should be grieved to cause any obstruction to the effects of the medicine. However, I think there can be no risk in making a trial ; therefore, Sancho, consider of it, and fix thy demand, so that no time may be lost. Set about the work immediately, and pay thyself in ready money, since thou hast cash of mine in thy hands."

At these offers Sancho opened his eyes and ears a span wider, resolving to strike the bargain without delay.

"Sir," said he, "I am ready and willing to give you satisfaction, since your worship speaks so much to the purpose. You know, sir, I have a wife and children to maintain, and the love I bear them makes me look to the main chance : how much, then, will your worship pay for each lash ?"

"Were I to pay thee, Sancho," answered Don Quixote, "in proportion to the magnitude of the service, the treasure of Venice, and the mines of Potosi would be too small a recompense : but examine and feel the strength of my purse, and then set thine own price upon each lash."

"The lashes to be given," quoth Sancho, "are three thousand three hundred and odd ; five of that number I have already given myself—the rest remains. Setting the five against the odd ones, let us take the three thousand three hundred, and reckon them at a quartil* each—and, for the world, I would not take less—the whole amount would be three thousand three hundred quartils. Now the three thousand quartils make one thousand five hundred half-reals, which comes to seven hundred and fifty reals, and the three hundred quartils make a hundred and fifty half-reals, or seventy-five reals ; which, added to the seven hundred and fifty, make, in all, eight hundred and twenty-five reals. That sum, then, I will take from your worship's money in my hands, and with it I shall return home rich and contented, though soundly whipped : but trouts are not to be caught† with dry breeches."

* A small coin about the fourth of a real.
† The entire proverb is, "They do not catch trouts with dry breeches."

"O blessed Sancho! O amiable Sancho!" replied Don Quixote, "how much shall Dulcinea and I be bound to serve thee as long as Heaven shall be pleased to give us life! Should she be restored to her former state, as she certainly will, her misfortune will prove a blessing—my defeat a most happy triumph! and when, good Sancho, dost thou propose to begin the discipline? I will add another hundred reals for greater despatch."

"When?" replied Sancho; "even this very night, without fail: do you take care to give me room enough, and open field, and I will take care to lay my flesh open."

So impatient was Don Quixote for night, and so slowly it seemed to approach, that he concluded the wheels of Apollo's chariot had been broken, and the day thereby extended beyond its usual length; as it is with expecting lovers, who always fancy time to be stationary. At length, however, it grew dark; when, quitting the road, they seated themselves on the grass under some trees, and took their evening's repast on such provisions as the squire's wallet afforded. Supper being ended, Sancho made himself a powerful whip out of Dapple's halter, with which he retired about twenty paces from his master. Don Quixote, seeing him proceed to business with such resolution and spirit, said to him, "Be careful, friend, not to lash thyself to pieces; take time, and pause between each stroke; hurry not thyself so as to be overcome in the midst of thy task. I mean, I would not have thee lay it on so unmercifully as to deprive thyself of life before the required number be completed. And, that thou mayst not lose - by a card too much or too little, I will stand aloof, and keep reckoning upon my beads the lashes thou shalt give thyself: so Heaven prosper thy pious undertaking!"

"The good paymaster needs no pledge," quoth Sancho; "I mean to lay it on so that it may smart, without killing me: for therein, as I take it, lies the secret of the cure."

He then stripped himself naked from the waist upwards, and, snatching up the whip, began to lash it away with great fury, and Don Quixote to keep account of strokes. But Sancho had not given himself above six or eight, when, feeling the jest a little too heavy, he began to think his terms too low, and stopping his hand, he told his master that he had been deceived, and must appeal, for every lash was well worth half a real, instead of a quartil.

"Proceed, friend Sancho," quoth Don Quixote, "and be not faint-hearted : thy pay shall be doubled."

"If so," quoth Sancho, "away with it, in God's name, and let it rain lashes."   But the sly knave, instead of laying them on his back, laid them on the trees, fetching, ever and anon, such groans, that he seemed to be tearing up his very soul by the roots. Don Quixote, besides being naturally humane, was now fearful that Sancho would destroy himself, and thus, by his indiscreet zeal, the object would be lost : and therefore he cried out :

"Hold, friend Sancho—let the business rest there, I conjure thee ; for this medicine seems to me too violent, when so administered ; take it, friend, more at leisure : Zamora* was not gained in one hour.   Thou hast already given thyself, if I reckon right, above a thousand lashes : let that suffice at present—for the ass (to speak in homely phrase) will carry the load, but not a double load."

"No, no," answered Sancho, "it shall never be said of me, 'the money paid, the work delayed.'   Pray, sir, get a little farther off, and let me give myself another thousand lashes at least ; for a couple of such bouts will finish the job, and stuff to spare."

"Since thou art in so good a disposition," quoth Don Quixote, "go on, and Heaven assist thee ; I will retire a little."

Sancho returned to his task with the same fury as before, and with so much effect did he apply the lash, that the trees within his reach were already disbarked.   At length, exalting his voice, in accompaniment to a prodigious stroke on the body of a beech, he cried, "Down, down with thee, Sampson, and all that are with thee !"   The frightful exclamation and blow were too much for the knight's tenderness, and he ran immediately, and, seizing hold of the twisted halter, said :

"Heaven forbid, friend Sancho, that thy death, and the ruin of thy helpless family, should be laid at my door !—let Dulcinea wait for another opportunity, and I will myself restrain my eager-ness for her deliverance within reasonable bounds, and stay till thou hast recovered fresh strength, so as to be able to finish thy task with safety."

"Since it is your worship's pleasure that I should leave off, be

* This was a town in the kingdom of Leon, a long while disputed for by the Arabs and Christians.

it so, in Heaven's name: and pray fling your cloak over my shoulders, for I am all in a sweat, and am loth to catch cold, as new disciplinants are apt to do." Don Quixote took off his cloak, and did as Sancho desired, leaving himself in his doublet; and the crafty squire, being covered up warm, fell fast asleep, and never stirred until the sun waked him.

The knight and squire now pursued their journey, and having travelled about three leagues, they alighted at the door of an inn, which, it is to be remarked, Don Quixote did not take for a turreted castle, with its moat and drawbridge: indeed, since his defeat, he was observed at times to discourse with a more steady judgment than usual.

That day Don Quixote and Sancho remained at the inn, waiting for night; the one to finish his penance in the open air, and the other to witness an event which promised the full accomplishment· of all his wishes. While they were thus waiting, a traveller on horseback, attended by three or four servants, stopped at the inn.

"Here, Señor Don Alvaro Tarfe," said one of the attendants to his master, "you may pass the heat of the day; the lodging seems to be cool and cleanly."

"If I remember right, Sancho," said Don Quixote, on hearing the gentleman's name, "when I was turning over the book called the second part of my history, I noticed the name of Don Alvaro Tarfe."

"It may be so," answered Sancho: "let him alight, and then we will put the question to him."

The gentleman alighted, and the landlady showed him into a room on the ground-floor adjoining to that of Don Quixote, and, like his, also hung with painted serge. This newly-arrived cavalier undressed and equipped himself for coolness, and stepping out to the porch, which was airy and spacious, where Don Quixote was walking backwards and forwards, he said to him:

"Pray, sir, whither are you bound?"

"To my native village, sir," replied Don Quixote, "which is not far distant. Allow me, sir, to ask you the same question."

"I am going, sir," answered the gentleman, "to Grenada, the country where I was born."

"And a fine country it is," replied Don Quixote. "But

pray, sir, will you favour me with your name? for I believe it particularly imports me to know it."

"My name is Don Alvaro Tarfe," answered the new guest.

"Then, I presume," said Don Quixote, "you are that Don Alvaro Tarfe mentioned in the second part of the history of Don Quixote de la Mancha, lately printed and published?"

"The very same," answered the gentleman, "and that Don Quixote the hero of the said history, was an intimate acquaintance of mine : and it was I indeed who drew him from his home— I mean, I prevailed upon him to accompany me to Saragossa, to be present at the jousts and tournaments held in that place : and in truth, while we were there, I did him much service, in saving his back from being well stroked by the hangman for being too daring."

"But pray, sir," said Don Quixote, "am I anything like that Don Quixote you speak of?"

"No, truly," answered the other, "the farthest from it in the world."

"And had he," said the knight, "a squire named Sancho Panza?"

"Yes, truly," answered Don Alvaro, "one who had the reputation of being a witty comical fellow, but for my part I thought him a very dull blockhead."

"Gad! I thought so," quoth Sancho, abruptly, "for it is not everybody that can say good things, and the Sancho you speak of must be some pitiful ragamuffin, some idiot and knave, I'll warrant you ; for the true Sancho Panza am I ;—'tis I am the merry-conceited squire, that have always a budget full of wit and waggery. Do but try me, sir,—keep me company but for a twelvemonth, and you will bless yourself at the notable things that drop from me at every step ;—they are so many, and so good too, that I make every beard wag without meaning it, or knowing why or wherefore. And there, sir, you have the true Don Quixote de la Mancha, the staunch, the famous, the valiant, the wise, the loving Don Quixote de la Mancha ; the righter of wrongs, the defender of the weak, the father of the fatherless, the safeguard of widows, the murderer of damsels ; but whose sole sweetheart and mistress is the peerless Dulcinea del Toboso ; here he is, and here am I, his squire ; all other

Don Quixotes and all other Sancho Panzas are downright phantoms and cheats."

" Now, by St Jago ! honest friend, I believe it," said Don Alvaro, " for the little thou hast now said has more of the spice of humour than all I ever heard from the other, though it was much. The fellow seemed to carry his brains in his stomach, for his belly supplied all his wit, which was too dull and stupid to be diverting ! "

" I know not," said Don Quixote, " whether I ought to avow myself the good one, but I dare venture to assert that I am not the bad one ; and, as a proof of what I say, you must know, dear Señor Alvaro Tarfe, that I never in my life saw the city of Saragossa. I therefore hope, sir, that you, as a gentleman, will not refuse to make a deposition before the magistrate of this town, that you never saw me before in your life till this day ; and that I am not the Don Quixote mentioned in the second part which has been published, nor this Sancho Panza my squire the same you formerly knew."

" That I will with all my heart," answered Don Alvaro ; " though I own it perplexes me to see two Don Quixotes and two Sancho Panzas, as different in their nature as alike in name, insomuch that I am inclined to believe that I have not seen what I have seen, nor has that happened to me which I thought had happened."

" Past all doubt," quoth Sancho, " your worship is enchanted, like my lady Dulcinea del Toboso ; and would to Heaven your disenchantment depended upon my giving myself another such three thousand and odd lashes, as I do for her !—I would do your business, and lay them on, without fee or reward."

" I do not understand what you mean by lashes," quoth Don Alvaro. Sancho said it was a tale too long to tell at that time, but he should hear it if they happened to travel the same road.

Don Quixote and Don Alvaro dined together ; and as it chanced that a magistrate of the town called at the inn, accompanied by a notary, Don Quixote requested they would take the deposition of a gentleman there present, Don Alvaro Tarfe, who proposed to make oath that he did not know another gentleman then before them, namely, Don Quixote de la Mancha, and that he was not the man spoken of in a certain book called " The Second Part of Don Quixote de la Mancha, written by such an one De Avellaneda, a native of Tordesillas." In short, the magistrate complied, and a deposition was produced according to the regular form, and expressed in the strongest terms, to the great satisfaction of Don Quixote and Sancho— as if the difference between them and their spurious imitators had not been sufficiently manifest without any such attestation. Many compliments and offers of service passed between Don Alvaro and Don Quixote, in which the great Manchegan showed so much good sense, that Don Alvaro Tarfe was convinced he had been deceived, and also that there was certainly some enchantment in the case, since he had touched with his own hand two such opposite Don Quixotes.

In the evening they all quitted the inn, and after proceeding together about half a league, the road branched into two ; the one led to Don Quixote's village, and the other was taken by Don Alvaro. During the short distance they had travelled together, Don Quixote informed him of his unfortunate defeat, the enchantment of Dulcinea, and the remedy prescribed by Merlin, to the great amusement of Don Alvaro, who, after embracing Don Quixote and Sancho, took his leave, each pursuing his own way.

Don Quixote passed that night among trees, to give Sancho an opportunity to resume his penance, in the performance of which the cunning rogue took special care, as on the preceding night, that the beech-trees should be the sufferers ; for the lashes he gave his back would not have brushed off a fly from it. The cheated knight counted the strokes with great exactness, and reckoning those which had been given him before, he found the whole amount to three thousand and twenty-nine. The sun seemed to rise earlier than usual to witness the important sacrifice, and to enable them to continue their journey. They travelled onward, discoursing together on the mistake of Don Alvaro, and their prudence in having obtained his deposition before a magistrate, and in so full and authentic a form. All that day and the following night they proceeded without meeting with any occurrence worth recording, unless it be that when it was dark Sancho finished his task, to the great joy of Don Quixote, who when all was over, anxiously waited the return of day, in the hope of meeting his disenchanted lady; and for that purpose, as he pursued his journey, he looked narrowly at every woman he came near, to recognise Dulcinea del Toboso; fully relying on the promises of the sage Merlin.

Thus hoping and expecting, the knight and squire ascended a little eminence, whence they discovered their village; which Sancho no sooner beheld than, kneeling down, he said, "Open thine eyes, O my beloved country! and behold thy son, Sancho Panza, returning to thee again, if not rich, yet well whipped! Open thine arms, and receive thy son Don Quixote too! who, though worsted by another, has conquered himself, which, as I have heard say, is the best kind of victory! Money I have gotten, and though I have been soundly banged, I have come off like a gentleman."

"Leave these fooleries, Sancho," quoth Don Quixote, "and let us go directly to our homes, where we will give full scope to our imagination, and settle our intended scheme of a pastoral life." They now descended the hill, and went straight to the village.

CHAPTER LXXXI

DON QUIXOTE ARRIVES AT HOME—HIS DEATH

In a field adjoining the village, Don Quixote and Sancho met the curate and the bachelor Sampson Carrasco, repeating their breviary. It must here be mentioned that Sancho Panza, by way of sumpter-cloth, had thrown the buckram robe painted with flames, which he had worn on the night of the Altisidora's revival, upon his ass. He likewise clapped the mitre on Dapple's head,— in short, never was an ass so honoured and bedizened. The priest and bachelor, immediately recognising their friends, ran towards them with open arms. Don Quixote alighted, and embraced them cordially. In the mean time, the boys, whose keen eyes nothing can escape, came flocking from all parts. "Ho!" cries one, "here comes Sancho Panza's ass, as gay as a parrot, and Don Quixote's old horse, leaner than ever!"

Thus surrounded by the children, and accompanied by the curate and the bachelor, they proceeded through the village till they arrived at Don Quixote's house, where, at the door, they found the housekeeper and the niece, who had already heard of his arrival. It had likewise reached the ears of Sancho's wife Teresa, who, half-naked, with her hair about her ears, and dragging Sanchica after her, ran to meet her husband ; and seeing him not so well equipped as she thought a governor ought to be, she said: "What makes you come thus, dear husband ? methinks you come afoot, and foundered ! This, I trow, is not as a governor should look."

" Peace, wife," quoth Sancho, " for the bacon is not so easily found as the pin to hang it on. Let us go home, and there you shall hear wonders. I have got money, and honestly, too, without wronging anybody."

" Hast thou got money, good husband ?—nay, then, 'tis well, however it be gotten, for, well or ill, it will have brought up no new custom in the world."

Sanchica clung to her father, and asked him what he had brought her home, for she had been wishing for him as they do for showers in May. Teresa then taking him by the hand on one side, and Sanchica laying hold of his belt on the other, and at the same time pulling Dapple by the halter, they went home, leaving Don Quixote to the care of his niece and housekeeper, and in the company of the priest and the bachelor.

Don Quixote, without waiting for a more fit occasion, immediately took the priest and bachelor aside, and briefly told them of his having been vanquished, and the obligation he had consequently been laid under to abstain from the exercise of arms for the space of twelve months, and which he said it was his intention strictly to observe, as became a true knight-errant. He also told them of his determination to turn shepherd, and during the period of his recess to pass his time in the rural occupations appertaining to that mode of life : that while thus innocently and virtuously employed, he might give free scope to his amorous thoughts. He then besought them, if they were free from engagements of greater moment, to follow his example, and bear him company ; adding that it should be his care to provide them with sheep, and whatever was necessary to equip them as shepherds : and, moreover, that his project had been so far matured, that he had already chosen names that would suit them exactly.   The priest having inquired what they were, he informed them that the name he proposed to take himself was the shepherd Quixotiz ; the bachelor should be the shepherd Carrascon ; and he, the curate, the shepherd Curiambro : and Sancho Panza, the shepherd Panzino.

This new madness of Don Quixote astonished his friends ; but, to prevent his rambling as before, and hoping also that a cure might, in the mean time, be found for his malady, they entered into his new project, and expressed their entire approbation of it ; consenting also to be companions of his rural life.

" This is excellent ! " said the bachelor ; " it will suit me to a hair, for, as everybody knows, I am a choice poet, and shall be continually composing amorous ditties and pastorals, to divert us as we range the flowery fields.   But there is one important thing to be done, which is, that each of us should choose the name of the shepherdess he intends to celebrate in his verses, and inscribe it on the bark of every tree he comes near, according to the custom of enamoured swains."

" Certainly," said the knight, " that should be done :—not that I have occasion to look out for a name, having the peerless Dulcinea del Toboso, the glory of these banks, the ornament of these meads, the flower of beauty, the cream of gentleness, and, lastly, the worthy subject of all praise, however excessive ! "

" That is true," said the curate ; " but as for us, we must look out shepherdesses of an inferior stamp, and be content. When our invention fails us in the choice of names, we have only to apply to books, and there we may be accommodated with Phillises, Amarillises, Dianas, Floridas, Galateas, and Belisardas in abundance, which, as they are goods for any man's penny, we may pick and choose."

No sooner had his friends left him than the housekeeper and niece, who had been listening to their conversation, came to him. " Bless me, uncle ! " cried the niece, " what has now got into your head ?   When we thought you were coming to stay at home, and live a quiet and decent life, you are about to entangle your-self in new mazes, aud turn shepherd, forsooth !—in truth, uncle, ' the straw is too hard to make pipes of.' "   Here the housekeeper put in her word :

"Lord, sir! how is your worship to bear the summer's heat and winter's pinching cold, in the open fields? And the howling of the wolves—Heaven bless us! No, good sir, don't think of it; that is the business of stout men who are born and bred to it: —why, as I live, your worship would find it worse even than being a knight-errant. Look you, sir, take my advice—which is not given by one full of bread and wine, but fasting, and with fifty years over my head—stay at home, look after your estate, go often to confession, and relieve the poor; and, if any ill come of it, let it lie at my door."

"Peace, daughters," answered Don Quixote, "for I know my duty; only help me to bed, for methinks I am not very well: and assure yourselves that whether a knight-errant or a shepherd-errant, I will not fail to provide for you, as you shall find by experience." The two good creatures—for they really were so— then carried him to bed, where they brought him food, and attended upon him with all imaginable care.

As all human things, especially the lives of men, are transitory, ever advancing from their beginning to their decline and final termination, and as Don Quixote was favoured by no privilege of exemption from the common fate, the period of his dissolution came—and when he least thought of it. Whether that event was hastened by the melancholy occasioned by the recollection of his defeat, or that his destined hour was come, true it is that he was seized with a fever, which, after six days' confinement to his bed, terminated his mortal course. During that time he was often visited by his friends the priest, the bachelor, and the barber; and his trusty squire Sancho Panza never quitted his bedside.

Supposing that the mortification of being vanquished, and the disappointment of his hopes as to the restoration of Dulcinea, were the causes of his present malady, they endeavoured by all possible means to revive his spirits. The bachelor bid him be of good courage and to think soon of beginning their pastoral life; telling him that he had already composed an eclogue on the occasion, which would eclipse all that Sannazarius had written, and that he had also bought of a shepherd of Quintanar two excellent dogs, to guard the flock, the one called Barcino and the other Butron. Nevertheless, Don Quixote's dejection still continued: it was therefore thought necessary to send for a physician, who, perceiving some unfavourable symptoms in his pulse, advised his patient to look to his soul's health, for that of his body was in danger. Don Quixote heard this admonition with more tranquillity than those about him; for his housekeeper, his niece, and his squire, began to weep as bitterly as if he were already dead and laid out before their eyes. Grief and other troublesome cares, the doctor told them, had brought him to this pass.

Don Quixote now feeling an inclination to sleep, desired that he might be left alone. They complied, and he slept full six hours at a stretch (as it is termed), so that the niece and housekeeper thought he would never awake more. At the end of that time, however, he awaked, and immediately exclaimed in an audible voice:

"Praised be Almighty God, who has vouchsafed me so great a blessing!—Boundless are His mercies; nor can the sins of men either lessen or obstruct them!"

The niece listened attentively to her uncle's words; for she thought she had perceived in him, especially since his illness, more consistency than usual, and she said to him:

"What is it you say, sir? Has anything extraordinary happened? What mercies and what sins do you speak of?"

"My good niece," replied Don Quixote, "the mercies I mean are those which God hath, in this instance, been pleased to show me, though my sins are so many. My judgment is now clear, and freed from the dark clouds of ignorance with which the continual reading of those detestable books of chivalry had obscured it. I now see their extravagance and folly, and am only grieved that this discovery happens so late as to leave me no time to profit by such books as might improve and enlighten my soul. I feel myself, niece, at the point of death, and I would fain wash away the stain of madness from my character; for though in my life I have been deservedly accounted a lunatic, I earnestly desire that the truth thereof shall not be confirmed at my death. Go, therefore, dear child, and call hither my good friends the priest, the bachelor Sampson Carrasco, and Master Nicholas the barber; for I would fain make my confession and my will."

Fortunately, at that moment, his three friends entered.   As soon as Don Quixote saw them, he exclaimed :

"Give me joy, good gentlemen, that I am no longer Don Quixote de la Mancha, but Alonzo Quixano, the same whom the world, for his fair and honest life, was pleased to surname the Good.   I am now an utter enemy to Amadis de Gaul and all his generation.   Now the senseless and profane histories of knight-errantry are to me digusting and odious ; I now acknowledge my folly, and perceive the danger into which I was led by reading them ; and now, through the mercy of God, and my own dear-bought experience, I abhor them."

When his three friends heard him speak thus, they imagined that some new frenzy had seized him.   "What! Señor Don Quixote," said the bachelor, "now that we have news of the lady Dulcinea being disenchanted, do you talk at this rate ?   And now that we are just upon the point of becoming shepherds, to sing and live like princes, would you turn hermit ?   Think not of it—be yourself again, and leave these idle stories."

"Such, indeed," replied Don Quixote, "were the stories that to me have proved so baneful : but my death, with Heaven's assistance, shall convert them to my good.   I feel, good sirs, that death advances fast upon me ; let us then be serious, and bring me a confessor, and a notary to draw up my will : for a man in my state must not trifle with his soul.   Let the notary be sent for, I beseech you, while my friend here, the priest, is taking my confession."

They looked at each other in surprise at his expressions, and though still dubious, they were inclined to believe him, and could not but regard as a fatal symptom this sudden change from madness to sanity.   He then conversed again in so rational and Christian a manner, that no doubt remained of the perfect restoration of his intellects.   The priest desired all the rest to leave the room, and when alone, he received his confession.   The bachelor went for the notary, and presently returned with him, followed by Sancho Panza, who having learned from the bachelor of the hopeless situation of his master, and seeing the niece and housekeeper in tears, also began to weep like the rest.   The priest, having taken his dying friend's confession, came out of the room, and told them that the good Alonzo Quixano was near his end, and certainly in his right senses; he therefore advised them to go in, as it was full time that his will should be made. This sad intelligence opened still wider the sluices of grief, and torrents of tears issued from the swollen eyes of the housekeeper, his niece, and Sancho Panza his trusty squire, and from the bottom of their aggrieved hearts a thousand sighs and groans; for, in truth, as it hath been said before, both while he was plain Alonzo Quixano, and while he was Don Quixote de la Mancha, he was ever of an amiable disposition, and kind and affable in his behaviour : so that he was beloved, not only by those of his own family, but by all that knew him.

The notary now entered the room with the others, and after the preamble of the will had been written, and Don Quixote had disposed of his soul in the usual Christian forms, coming to the distribution of his worldly goods he directed the notary to write as follows : namely—"Item, it is my will that, in regard to certain monies which Sancho Panza, whom in the wildness of my folly I called my squire, has in his custody, there being between him and me some reckonings, receipts, and disbursements, he shall not be charged with them, nor called to any account for them ; but if, after he has paid himself, there should be any overplus, which will be but little, it shall be his own, and much good may it do him ; and if, as in my distracted state I procured him the government of an island, I could, now that I am in my senses, procure him that of a kingdom, I would readily to it : for the simplicity of his heart, and the fidelity of his dealings, well deserve it." Then turning to Sancho, he said, "Forgive me, friend, for perverting thy understanding, and persuading thee to believe that there were, and still are, knights-errant in the world."

"Alas ! good sir," replied Sancho, "do not die, I pray you ; but take my advice, and live many years : for the greatest folly a man can commit in this world, is to give himself up to death, without any good cause for it, but only from melancholy. Good your worship, be not idle, but rise and let us be going to the field, dressed like shepherds, as we agreed to do ; and who knows but behind some bush or other we may find the lady Dulcinea disenchanted as fine as heart can wish ? If you pine at being vanquished, lay the blame upon me, and say you were unhorsed because I had not duly girthed Rozinante's saddle; and your worship must have seen in your books of chivalry that nothing is more common than for one knight to unhorse another, and that he who is vanquished to-day may be the conqueror to-morrow."

"It is so, indeed," quoth the bachelor; "honest Sancho is very much in the right."

"Gentlemen," quoth Don Quixote, "let us proceed fair and softly; look not for this year's birds in last year's nests. I was mad; I am now sane: I was Don Quixote de la Mancha; I am now, as formerly, styled Alonzo Quixano the Good, and may my repentance and sincerity restore me to the esteem you once had for me!—now let the notary proceed."

"Item, I bequeath to Antonia Quixano, my niece, here present, all my estate, real and personal, after the payment of all my debts and legacies; and the first to be discharged shall be the wages due to my housekeeper for the time she has been in my service, and twenty ducats besides for a suit of mourning.

"I appoint for my executors Señor the priest and Señor bachelor Sampson Carrasco, here present. Item, it is also my will that, if Antonia Quixano, my niece, should be inclined to marry, it shall be only with a man who, upon the strictest inquiry, shall be found to know nothing of books of chivalry; and, in case it appear that he is acquainted with such books, and that my niece, notwithstanding, will and doth marry him, then shall she forfeit all I have bequeathed her, which my executors may dispose of in pious uses as they think proper. And finally, I beseech the said gentlemen, my executors, that if haply they should come to the knowledge of the author of a certain history, dispersed abroad, entitled, 'The Second Part of the Exploits of Don Quixote de la Mancha,' they will, in my name, most earnestly entreat him to pardon the occasion I have unwittingly given him of writing so many and such gross absurdities as are contained in that book; for I depart this life with a burden upon my conscience, for having caused the publication of so much folly."

The will was then closed; and being seized with a fainting-fit, he stretched himself out at length on the bed, at which all were alarmed and hastened to his assistance; yet he survived three days : often fainting during that time in the same manner, which never failed to cause great distress in the house : nevertheless, the niece ate, the housekeeper drank, and Sancho Panza consoled himself—for legacies tend much to moderate grief that nature claims for the deceased. At last, after receiving the sacrament, and making all such pious preparations, as well as ex· pressing his abhorrence, in strong and pathetic terms, of the wicked books by which he had been led astray, Don Quixote's last moment arrived. The notary was present, and protested he had never read in any book of chivalry of a knight-errant dying in his bed in so composed and Christian a manner as Don Quixote, who passed away amidst the plaints and tears of all present.

This was the end of that extraordinary gentleman of La Mancha, whose birthplace Cid Hamet was careful to conceal, that all the towns and villages of that province might contend for the honour of having produced him, as did the seven cities of Greece for the glory of giving birth to Homer.

THE END